JUNGLE Days —

PARIS Nights

Ramona Alexander

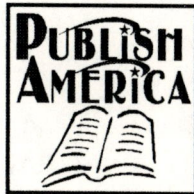

PublishAmerica

PublishAmerica
Baltimore

ISBN: 1-4137-3021-3
PUBLISHED BY PUBLISHAMERICA, LLLP
www.publishamerica.com
Baltimore

Printed in the United States of America

I would like to dedicate this book to the memory of my mother, Mara, and my father, Alexander, who inspired me to write this book, and to my sister, Ethel, who walked barefoot with me through the first part, and to my daughter, Tina Mara, who stood by me throughout the writing of the book.

Anthony Hansen, L.D

I asked myself "how can I thank him" and the words of Kahlil Gibran came to mind.

"It is well to give when asked but it is better to give unasked "LIKE YOU— through understanding— there are those who have little to give, and yet they give it all— It is when you give of yourself AND YOUR TALENT— That you truly give!

enjoy my book ♡

Ramona Alexander.

I thank all my friends, who stood by me during the writing of the book and contributed in many ways to make its writing possible. And for the readers whose honest criticisms gave me the courage to continue to tell my story.

Table of Contents

Jungle Days

Paris Nights

Jungle Days

1

Dad Delivers Me

The corrugated shack was stifling hot. The sun had been baking down on the iron roof the whole morning. Mara, my mother, lay on the crumpled bed, drenched in sweat, and had the first awareness of labor pains. My expected entry into the world. She was attended by a concerned three-year-old, Ethel, my future sister, who was mopping her brow with a moist washcloth.

The missionary nurse had come and gone, promising to return when the time was right, which she estimated wouldn't be till at least the first week in December. She told Mara she regretted having made a mistake in her calculations, but because I promised to be a big baby the expected date had moved up a week. Mara saw her stop on the hill where my father was clearing land for the town's extenuation to tell him to relax for another week. But her buckboard had no sooner disappeared over the hill when first contractions started. Fear came with it. With the news Alex received it meant he wouldn't be home till late that day. She certainly couldn't send Ethel to fetch him, and couldn't go herself for fear of having the baby on the way. She had seen indigenous women squat beside a field, deliver their baby, rest for a few minutes, and after burying the placenta, suckle the child, then continue on the interrupted journey. She wasn't on the road but the shack was almost as primitive. She would have to deliver the baby herself. Between contractions she started to set up the things she would need for the delivery.

On the newly scrubbed kitchen table she placed the sun bleached sheets and towels, also a flannel baby receiving gown she had embroidered with bunnies and flowers, and a blue baby blanket, should this little one turn out to be a boy. Then she carefully folded a stack of flannel diapers into triangles. The last one she held against her cheek, smelling the sunlight in its softness, before she pinned two safety pins carefully in the corner.

Early in the morning Alex had packed the fire in the wood burning stove, filled the twelve- gallon drum, and put it on the back burner for her to have a bath that night. It was needed now. She scooped enough into the basin that stood on a chair, giving herself a sponge bath with disinfectant soap. A strong contraction nearly doubled her over. She felt across the now familiar bump, soothing it as she rubbed.

"Hold on a little bit longer, little one, we're not quite ready for you yet!"

Stumbling over to the bed, she trailed a silver streak of water. Now there was no doubt, her time had come. Ethel had never seen her do a naughty thing like that, so she rushed over to the table and promptly brought her a diaper. Through her pain Mara couldn't help laughing. The gentle presence of her firstborn just gave her the needed assurance that she wasn't entirely alone, but what could a three-year-old do? She hurriedly changed into a light linen nightdress, lay down, and pulled her legs all the way up to ease the pain that was now coming more frequently.

Alex, my future father, was pulling the last of the stumps from the field he had cleared of brush the day before. He hated the job! But this was the only work he could find. The strangling fingers of depression had reached across continents, into the very heart of Southern Africa. His choice was the bread lines or pulling stumps, for a measly two shillings a day that provided only enough for the most basic of supplies. They were caught in the grip of poverty that was hard to break. The job promised compensations.

"Accommodations?" He found himself saying it aloud. "If you could truly call the one-room shack that. Oh yes, and free medical attention!" That was a laugh; so far they have had only two visits from the District nurse in the nine months of Mara's pregnancy. It was very little compensation for the back breaking work without heavy equipment, only mules and elbow grease. The land would soon be cleared, then what? Now there would be four of them. He certainly didn't regret it. Secretly he hoped that this one would be a little boy to carry on his name, but would be grateful if he or she would be born healthy and strong to weather these unsure, depression times.

He was lucky the earth here in Brits was brown, and rich and he had managed to plant a small garden, but the rains had stayed away. He was able to keep the little garden going by using the communal well water, but the well was drying up, too. He worried about the news the nurse had brought, because she could be wrong. Normally by now Mara had brought him some lunch, but it was way past noon and she had not yet turned up. He had been at it since an hour after dawn. It was time to take a break. His body ached all over, every muscle tense from overexertion. He unhitched the mule team, They, too, were tired. Their big eyes said nothing, but in them he read their despair. He pulled several buckets of water out of the canal and poured it into the cement trough. They didn't hesitate, sticking their noses deep in drinking thirstily. He didn't want to hobble them, but if he didn't, he would lose the whole day's work looking for them when he returned from checking up on what was happening back home. He hobbled them and led them into the feeding compound. The field there still had good grass and he had the assurance that they wouldn't wander off. The mules were dead tired. He would have to ride one of them should a medical emergency arise, and he had to search for the nurse, who could be anywhere in the district by now.

Even yards away from the shack, he could hear the groans and cries of birthing. The process had already started. There would be no time for getting help, he would have to assist on his own.

After kissing Mara and seeing to her comfort and reassuring her, he drew some water from the twelve-gallon drum on the stove, removed his shirt, and hastily scrubbed up. Trying to go through the steps he still remembered from the birth of his firstborn.

The nurse then told him to get a lot of water boiling, he thought it was just a polite way to keep husbands preoccupied and out of the way. But it was really a necessity for all the cleaning up after. The next thing she did really baffled him. She tied a sheet to the head board of the bed, explaining that it was something to hang onto for the birthing mother while she was doing the pushing.

Mara wasn't one to hide her emotions, and a scream that shook the very walls, woke him from his reverie. "This is it!"

The miracle of birth waits for no one. It was like a tidal wave. It came in sweeping waves so intense that nature contracts in its effort to expel the creature it had protected for nine long months. The woman gets the terrible urge to push. Tears ran over Alex's cheeks. He was witnessing the earth's greatest miracle. The head was crowning, but something did not look right. A thin sheet of membrane covered the head. He remembered overhearing something once. A group of women were discussing a child born with a caul. Part of the amniotic sack was over the head. This was a sign they said, that the child would have many talents and blessings, and also posses the talent of looking into the future. Well that was all well and good, but what was he to do at this very moment? He recognized it to be a deterrent for breathing properly. There was noone to tell him what to do, but he wasn't going to wait until it was too late. He pulled gently on the membrane but it refused to move. This time he gripped it firmly between thumb and forefinger and yanked, and the piece slipped easily off. The nurse said that the baby felt nothing at that stage. But how was that possible?

In the beginning the baby had lots of room but in the months that followed as the child grew, the space in which it existed became a prison. The space shrank smaller and smaller until one day near the ninth month, it had shrunk so much that it became impossible for the child to move. Its head pushed up against the top of the sack, its back arched in the confined space, and there was no more room to stretch or turn. It kicked and kicked but the small space kept it captive. Till then it was lulled only by the faint sound of the heartbeat and soothing voice of its mother. It had the compulsion to move freely again. Struggling in the small space it turned around, head down. Then something started to squeeze so hard that it had no option but to push itself in the direction of least resistance, till at last he or she was engulfed in the strange thing called light, struggling against the new freedom. But just when it was finished with the struggle through the narrow canal, something grabbed it harshly by the feet, swung the up till then weightless body up side down and gave it several stinging slaps that made it scream and pull in great gulps of air. Before it had time to do it on its own.

"NO! This baby was going to have a more gentle beginning."

I was not aware of my father's thoughts or actions that followed as my mother and I struggled toward my entrance and existence, nor of the prediction "that I would have many talents and blessings," but years later when I could fully understand, he would tell me over and over what transpired then.

My father instinctively turned the lamp down low, put one of his favorite records on the gramophone so that pleasant music could fill my ears and soul. When I finally made my grand entrance, he cradled me gently, turned me on my side, cleared my breathing passage without the accustomed slap. I took a deep breath on my own of the warm moist air. Freed from my amphibian water cradle, I gave a hearty cry that echoed over the fields and stones: "Here I am, world!" Next he filled a warm bath and swabbed me down, and then

16

swaddled me in soft flannel.

The mission nurse, who had second thoughts about her prediction of December and turned around, arrived at the moment my father placed me in my mothers arms. Perhaps I was aware of his gentle touch, and of my mother's tears of pride as she smiled on me for the first time, and of the shouts of joy of my *ousus* (older sister) about her new sister, because it stayed somewhere in the pleasure chambers of my subconscious, but I was not aware of the profound changes the nurse would bring to our family, nor the dramatic course the path of our future would take.

Embarrassed at her inability to do anything more, the nurse spread a week old newspaper on the kitchen table, pulled a baby scale out of her magic black bag, and weighed me. I weighed in at nine pounds even and measured twenty-two inches.

"I said she was going to be a big one, and a handful!"

A headline in the newspaper under the scale caught my father's eye.

WANTED: ADVENTUROUS MEN WITH POLICE EXPERIENCE TO TRAIN AS GAME WARDENS. Moving the scale aside, he read further. Foot and Mouth disease had broken out in the Northern Transvaal and was spreading into adjoining provinces. Poachers, killing the weakened animals by the thousands, were taking the contaminated trophies over the Limpopo river and shipping it out of the country, endangering animals world wide. The article continued about the atrocities and disregard of life by the poachers, and continued with the job requirements and compensations.

Must be an exceptional shot, able to handle all sorts of firearms, and have no qualms in making arrests and disposing of the confiscated trophies. The job offered a lifetime pension, catastrophic insurance, survivor benefits, monthly jungle rations, equipment, and bearers. For the right man all these benefits awaited. With guaranteed FORTY EIGHT POUNDS A MONTH, just to patrol the banks of the 8 river and make an end to this senseless slaughter.

With the new baby in her arms, Mara thought he was totally insane, listening to his ravings. But she had never seen him so enthusiastic for a long time. He of course sent in his application. She could only smile and listen.

"Just think of it, my love, forty-eight pounds! A small fortune! I know there would be thousands of applications, but they would consider my mounted police experience. I just hope I'm not too late, the paper was a week old already." The more she listened, the more she began to see the possibilities.

At work he discussed it with the men as they labored over a large stump that just wouldn't budge, even though they had laboriously chopped through the entire root system. Their last resort was bringing in oxen when the mules failed. Sitting around discussing their next move, one of the men asked, "How do you know you are even going to get the job?"

Another said, "Alex, you're crazy! Listen to yourself, catastrophic insurance? Survivors benefits? tell me why do they want another game warden? What happened to the other one?"

A third man laughed, "Perhaps you should first enquire what happened to the other guy, before you go traipsing into the jungle with your young family after poachers. Survivors benefits? That's a laugh, would there be any survivors after the poachers kill you? Do you think they would leave your family alone to tell the tale?"

No amount of questions, advice, or teasing could sway my father's determination to get out of the situation he found himself in. Trying to get the damn stump out had only intensified his feelings. If his application was not accepted he was going to look for something else that didn't destroy body and

soul for a mere pittance. He could feel the sweat pour in streams down his back into cleavage of his buttocks as he shoveled more soil and stone away from the roots that clung to the earth, unyielding.

He slumped back into the mud of the root hole. "I QUIT! I'm leaving! I've had it with this slavery! Anything would be better than this!"

Two days later the letter arrived; of the more than two hundred applicants, his turned out to be the most qualified. He was accepted! He could not contain his joy.

He suggested that he would go first, to establish a camp and then send for Mom and us. But she wouldn't hear about it, quoting: "Where you go, I will go, your people will be my people"

There wasn't much to pack. But Mom insisted that her zinc bath, iron pots, and sewing machine would go, and she wasn't going without a bucket and an ax, and of course sheets and her favorite pillows. Daddy just laughed. "We're going into deep jungle mostly on safari, in tents, and I'm not sure that we will get carriers once we get there."

But Mom insisted, "Then I'll just have to carry it myself!"

2

First Safari

It was a three-days journey by covered wagon that would take us close to our destination and into the veldt, where at a destination point we found our welcoming committee, selected from the Mavenda tribe, who would escort and take us and our belongings to first camp.

Before our coming the drums had talked for days on end about our coming. Beside the cooking fires the word spread that Bwana Mokulu (big man) and his wife and children were coming to save the animals. It always had a ring of sarcasm if drums had that capability. Charlie wondered about this white man, and he had met many. The one before him hadn't lasted very long before he took off and they never saw him again. This one couldn't be any better, and he was indeed very poor, because the poor man had only one wife, unlike himself, who was richer by far, with twenty-six wives before going to Johannesburg. And after he was able to buy four more from the money he earned in the mines. Three of the new wives were already pregnant. He was considering giving him one. Perhaps knowing the white man's ways wasn't so profitable after all.

The sender of the drum messages was the chief of his own established tribe, separated from his father's statuesque Mavenda tribe. He himself was not a big man, burdened with the imposing name of Orrukurere Tombolele. Chief Tombolele had the opportunity to go to the big city of Jo'burg, to the gold mines, to seek his fortune, and to learn the white man's ways and philosophies because he deemed himself a good scholar.

At the mines, he was well liked, but unable to say his name, they called him hey Charlie this, hey Charlie that (they called everyone Charlie). He liked the name, and that stuck.

I was too young to realize all the dangers that surrounded us. It was my father's adventure that grew ours as the first few years passed all too swiftly. The jungle days found root in my soul. The chirring of the chickadees and the melodious sound of the bush doves *coer, coer, dook* became my cradle song. Tucked snugly beneath the mosquito net in my makeshift jungle cot, the roar of the leopard and the hyenas laugh held no more fear for me than the sound of a passing car going past the house of a sleeping city child. They only became background sounds to the child upon waking.

Where the city child learned to cross the streets with man made signals to keep him safe, Sis and I learned the signals of nature to protect us from the dangers of the bush.

Mom Mara, 5-foot-8, solid build, born from a hardworking farming stock, was used to changes, and had early in life learned survival techniques. She had courage, inventiveness, resourcefulness, artistry, and endurance enough to conquer the harshness of the bush and still come up smiling. She managed to hide her fear and concerns for the safety of her husband and two small children.

The second camp was on a rise, where Dad had a perfect view of the river. The Limpopo divided the Transvaal from Zimbabwe. It crawled through the dense bush like a giant boa constrictor, branching out into fourteen streams that formed many islands where the crocodiles lay basking in the sun, mouths wide open allowing the crocodile birds to peck the meat trapped between their teeth. Two miles from its source near the Indian ocean it ran together. The river, lifeblood to the surrounding jungle and its countless inhabitants, showed signs of drying up. It had been a long dry summer. Large sand banks already lay exposed. Tribes on the Zimbabwe side made frequent raids to safari camps along the Transvaal side. Once a proud people dating back to biblical times, Their legends tell of King Solomon, who chose himself a bride from among the daughters of Zimbabwe. In the song of Solomon he sings praises to his many concubines including his Nubian loves. Like the parting of the Red Sea, it made it all too easy for the bad men to cross over. Ignoring the gray basking bodies, their greed was their protection.

For months the poachers had run rampant before Dad's arrival. So they relaxed, not expecting any arrests. They killed whole herds indiscriminately— senseless slaughter to meet the demands of the souvenir trade. The biggest horror was their disregard for life, and the terrible toll they left in their wake. Then there were the snares that mutilated, causing slow torture and lingering death to bush buck, dik-dik, kudu, nyala, eland, sable antelope, reed buck, hartebeest or anything and everything that fell into their traps. Sis and I found the snares and traps and Dad dismantled them. Sometimes we were not so lucky and found the remains.

This was all mindless carnage. The carcasses of their victims lay rotting in the sun. The stench of death hung heavy over the veld. Fat gray vultures weighed the trees down, beaks dripping blood from the latest kill. Hyenas, over fed and bored, ran around in circles, playing tug-of-war with intestines pulled from a sable antelope who had been killed for his magnificent three foot horns that would no doubt be turned into walking sticks.

They also did their killing stealthily in the night, sneaking up on the sleeping monkey troops, blinding them with floodlights, slitting their throats, taking only the heads to mount and the hands to make key chains. In the daytime, they killed openly without shame.

"My God!" Dad sobbed in camp one night. "A whole herd of elephants, I'm telling you! Bulls, females and their calves butchered, twenty of them I counted. Their feet cut off at the knees to make umbrella stands, tusks chopped out with axes. The earth was soaked with blood!"

The days stretched long and lazy. Shimmering heat caused mirages, making everything in the distance seem as if it was floating three feet above the earth, the thermometer reading 120—it seemed impossible but was true. To prove it to someone in the camp, Dad took an egg and broke it open onto a flat stone. Within seconds it sizzled then turned white, the yolk thickened, and we had ourselves a fried egg.

The coolest place was among the branches of a wild fig tree on the edge of camp, or down by the river where dad had found a perfect pool for us surrounded by high rocks. It was impossible for crocodiles to enter, but just to be safe he or Mom sat nearby on the rocks with a gun, while we splashed in the buff to our hearts content in the cool water.

In the beginning, moving camp was a chore done by the bearers. Usually an open spot in the bush was selected, the brush cleared with panga, buffalo-thorn branches placed in a circle around the camp perimeter to keep out unwanted night visitors.

In the center a large bonfire, on which food was prepared, was fed with logs that burned till morning. Logs that would feed the fire were dragged around the fire for seating.

As the logs tumbled, sparks shot up into the night sky. We made wishes on the wood ash stars going up to meet their brothers the heavenly stars. Tossing pebbles or small sticks into the fire had the same effect, so we made endless wishes.

Beyond the thorn fence there were always eyes watching us. Every now and then a hyena, attracted to the smell of venison roasting on the spit over the fire, would run forward, stop short at the thorn fence, and burst out in a cackling laugh as if taunting us. The steel jaws that could crack a giraffe's bones, daring us to come away from the fire it feared. Sometimes Dad would toss a bone across the fence just to see them fight for possession, and be witness to their awesome strength.

After dinner it was usually story time. I would listen intently; some of the stories were not for children's ears, but Mom and Ethel stayed and I didn't want to be alone in the tent.

This particular night there were visitors in the camp, and Dad was telling about the day's happenings. For a birthday present he had made a coffee mug out of a tin can for his patrol-mate, leaving it at his surveillance point as a surprise. Then he went back to the river where he was waiting for some poachers to cross. Dad and he had devised a way to communicate with one another through the use of two small pocket mirrors and a simple Morse code. They could then send messages from the one point to the other by flashing into the sun.

"Crossing now."

"Intercept."

"Heavily armed."

"Danger—help!"

"All's well."

"Coffee's on."

Van Black was on duty on a hill about a mile from the river. He had made a small fire and made some coffee, and was about to signal him when out of the corner of his eye, he spotted a signal coming from the hill where he had just left. He could not make out anything in the message. Could Van Black have decided to come and help him, but was intercepted by the poachers on his way and was now in trouble? He could have been kidnaped and tied up and this was his only way to let him know. It was a very confusing signal, with long intervals between, a code like none he had ever seen. Something was drastically wrong. Some poachers, when apprehended, would rather kill than give up. He did not hear a shot, but there were other ways to get rid of an unwanted witness. The devil was telling him all sorts of things. His patrol-mate was in trouble and he was going to help him. He checked his gun and his ammunition. He had no idea how many of them would be there. One good thing was that the signals were still coming every once in a while. That could only mean that he was still alive. Carefully, Dad made his way up to the hill, without as much as stepping on one dry twig, dodging from one bush to the other, then he crawled forward in the long grass. When he had a clear view of the area where Van Black was supposed to be, he suddenly burst out laughing. There was a young bull elephant taking out his revenge on the shiny manmade object. His wrath was spent and he was now using it like a toy. He would pick it up, then toss it in the air, and when it came down, stomp on it. Every time he tossed it in the air the sun would flash on the shiny metal creating the strange signal.

Van Black thanked Dad for coming to his rescue, and for his birthday present, and everyone had a good laugh.

From out the thorn fence, a set of eyes suddenly left the darkness into the light of the fire. The laughter cut short. Finding its way barred by a forest of grownup legs, the creature scampered left then right looking for the smallest target; I was sitting on the ground near Mom's legs. The tarantula with three-to four-inch leg span was gigantic with thick red hair covering his gruesome body. "Don't move!" Dad yelled. I sat frozen in terror as the thing ran up my chubby four-year-old legs and over my shoulder, back into the darkness from which it had come. That's when I moved, jumping straight into Dad's lap, crying from the shock. Dad tried to laugh it off: "You're too big for his dinner, he's harmless." He did his best to pacify me, but the glowing eyes and hairy body were already imprinted into my memory bank, never to be erased.

What Dad omitted to tell me, because I was too small to understand, was that when a tarantula was hunting for prey or was suddenly aggravated, its two down-curved fangs lunged forward, impaling its victim. An enzyme was then automatically injected that paralyzed and tenderized its meal. He then ingested it while it was still living. It was true that I was too big to be his dinner. When a grown up would be bitten, it would not cause the damage that it would to a small animal or child. Such an injection would produce some paralysis, some breathing problems, and a possible heart failure. Dad certainly sighed a sigh of relief; it didn't happen, but it could have. Before he tucked me in that night he checked my cot carefully, several times at my request, before tucking the mosquito net deep in under the bed mat, to make me happy.

Staring up at the flimsy net wall, the only protection between me and the night, I curled myself up into the middle of the cot, into the smallest ball I could muster.

The countless bugs, moths, and everything that collided with the net always held a fascination. That night I saw everything in a different light. The countless moths that collided with the white net haze tumbled downward, attracted and dazzled by the white light from the fires. Spiders ran down from the tree onto which my net was anchored to catch the bounty. Out in the darkness beyond the fire, a swarm of fire-flies carrying their magic lanterns flashed their mating signals on and off, oblivious to the small dramas taking place on the net.

Through the lacy branches of the mimosa tree, I could see the bright path of the Milky Way. Stars were so bright I lifted my hands up, sure I could touch them. They are the brothers and sisters of the fire-flies and the wood ash stars, I thought as I slowly dozed off, dreaming of animals, baby animals that were all my friends.

Mom had other thoughts as she tried to fall asleep looking at the stars. The story that Alex had told around the fire was funny but close to the truth. It made her worry about the mysterious disappearance of Dad's predecessor, who up till now was never found. She knew Alex never worried about it. He believed the man simply couldn't deal with the hardship of the jungle, and took off never to be seen again. The fact that he didn't worry worried her more; she was afraid that he, too, would never return from one of his patrols. Poachers were always seeking revenge. Arrests and confiscation of the hides and trophies cost them a fortune. So it wasn't unusual the natives said that game wardens disappeared quite frequently. The authorities circulated the story that it was the climate ranging from 100 to a broiling 120, and the demanding schedule of constantly being on the move, snake bites, etc., that simply made them walk off the job.

A routine patrol was to prove otherwise only a few days later …

3

The Discovery — Game Warden Found Murdered

Dad was off on patrol, as usual, following the game path he always took down to the river. Half way to his lookout point he usually stopped at a place he called the mushroom rock to scout out the rest of the way. He had given it that name because it had a small rock perched on a base boulder, on the smaller one rested a large rock that resembled the cap of a mushroom. It would move slightly, but no matter how hard one pushed, the cap would not fall off the smaller one. Climbing onto the rock, he had a perfect view of the rest of the path and of the bend of the river from the Transvaal side.

He had done it so often that it never occurred to him that he always went up the front, in full view of the pathway, and if it was easy to see the poachers, it would also be easy to see him. At the back there was only one drawback. The bush and creepers grew dense up against the rock and getting on top wasn't easily assessable. He could remove the bush or simply pull it away. Groups of rock hyrax the size of a marmot scampered away into various crevasses. They were used to him being there because they usually sunbathed on the larger rock.

Beneath the heavy undergrowth there was an unusual rock formation,

leaning up against the overhang of the boulder, covered in creepers and weeds. His first thought was that there had been a rock slide. Then he realized a rock slide would have tumbled every which way. These rocks looked like they were neatly piled one on top of the other. It wasn't natural. A hyrax face peeped out of a hole where one of the rocks had tumbled inward. He shooed it away and tried to look inside. It appeared hollow, but he couldn't see anything; it was too dark. With his gun butt he knocked a few more stones out. They fell with a dull thud into the hollow. Now he could see inside as the sunlight streamed into the artificial manmade cave. His neck hairs bristled at the gruesome sight. Hyrax pellets lay deep over the decomposed skeletal remains of a man, as if they tried to bury the evidence.

Dried pieces of flesh still clung in places to the bones. Hollow sockets stared blankly back where maggots and ants claimed their share. The rotted bush jacket had spilled the contents of the pockets onto the dung pellets. Whoever did this had no regard for life and disposed of the body with all evidence. There was a photo of a woman and child barely visible, and a small book still intact. It looked like his own patrol logbook. Wrapping his hand in his handkerchief, Dad stuck his hand into the hole, and careful not to disturb anything that could be used as evidence, he withdrew the book. Inside the cover he could barely make out the writing faded by the elements and animal urine, but the man's name was clearly visible. He was about to put the book into his pocket, when he stood back to reflect what he was seeing. It would be selfish, but this was not something he wanted to get involved in. He carefully replaced the book where he had found it. His eyes, now used to the gloom of the interior, sized up the scene.

There was a gaping hole between the eyes; an execution style killing with a close range shot. The hands and feet were tied together with rope, some of which was still visible and not used for nesting material. The man's gun lay beside him, and on the skeletal arm was a wrist watch whose time had run out. Who knew when—at precisely twelve midnight or noon; no one would ever know except the one who did not rewind it. A quick summary told him that this was not a tribal killing. The gun and the watch would have been claimed as well as the boots and the buttons. No, this was white man's doing. Murder pure and simple. Who had covered the deed so cleverly that not a trace would be found, and who hoped that nature would do the rest? The realization made him feel faint. He sat down, leaning his back against the cool of the boulder. He had to think! What would be the best? This was undoubtedly the missing game warden. His predecessor! There was fierce competition among the

poachers. The log and the police issue gun spelled out a man who had definitely given the poachers a hard time and paid for it dearly with his life. He found himself talking aloud: "I would have to make a full report of my find; the repercussions would be insurmountable. There would be security men called in, swarming in camp, investigations, inquiries. The media would get hold of the story. This in turn would reach the ears of the poachers. And before I know it I would be the next target, or taken off the job to ensure my safety. What am I to do now?

"No! No one must know! Not even my patrol-mate, least of all my wife, whose worries would increase one hundred percent. I will just have to be more alert, and very careful!"

He got up and carefully repacked the stones the way he found them, even replacing the soil and the uprooted plants, then pulled the creepers back over the place and released the bush he had tied back. With the bush back over it, no one would ever know, unless they stumbled over it the same way he did. He would avoid mushroom rock in the future, as it still may be targeted. Instead would take a game-path a little way farther up.

For the next few months my Dad's arrests almost doubled. No one knew why. Only he knew it was in revenge for the cold-blooded murder of his predecessor, and because he felt guilty knowing what happened. It gave him immense pleasure to make a bonfire of their hoard of horrible trophies and watch their faces as they calculated their monetary loss. Then he logged what he burned, shackled them, and under guard, marched them two miles to the pick up point where there were holding cells on vehicles that would take them to Mezina, where the law took over. He knew there would be others in their place. As long as he was alive, he would do everything in his power to undermine their efforts.

We seldom saw the people arrested. Dad tried to shield us from them as much as possible.

Only once did we see a head of a poaching operation up close. I imagined that he would look like the picture in the Bible of the Devil, all red with horns and a forked tail, because of all the terrible things he had done to the animals. He looked nothing like it. But he was burned lobster red by the sun, blistered and peeling. And he was an ordinary man, half insane. During the roundup, he had managed to escape into the jungle, wandering around for days. Lost and starved. Dad searched for him and finally found him coming through the river. Covered in leeches. Full of infected gashes, his clothes torn by the thorn trees. Stung by bees and countless mosquitoes. Tortured by the same jungle that he had tortured and robbed.

Mom was a compassionate woman, feeding his hunger, and patching up his hurts. We felt sorry for him, but remembering the gruesome stories around the campfire, we also knew that Dad had done his duty. Van Black and Dad took turns in guarding him where he was chained to the center pole of a tent. The floor in this tent was Dad's pride. From all the bullet casings he collected at the scenes of slaughter, he had planted a smooth mosaic floor a thing of art. Coming back from lunch, he noticed the ranting and raving of his prisoner had stopped. There was a deadly silence inside the tent. He had either fallen asleep or run away again.

Looking in he found the man sitting spread eagle on the floor, with half of the floor already dug up with a bullet casing he had pried loose.

"What in heaven's name are you doing to my floor?" Dad yelled at him.

"What do you think I'm doing? You think I'm an idiot! I know where you have hidden the diamonds, and I'm going to find every last one!" This is where Dad realized that the jungle had taken its toll, the man was stark raving mad—or was pretending to be, to lessen his sentence.

The drums 'talked' about the arrest. Everyone was happy when reenforcements came to collect him.

With the arrest of the leader, there was still poaching, but not like before.

4

Permanent Camp

My earliest memories were of the base camp at Kruitfontein. Before that it was blank; I was too young and we were always on the move. Dad decided that we had enough of tent living, especially after the last incident with the man digging up the tent floor. The same spot was ideal to establish a more permanent camp. This was a favorite crossover point for smugglers and poachers. It was proven by the amount of arrests he had made during the last few months. The riverside rushes grew dense on the river bank and provided him plenty of protection in which he had hidden a scans to surprise them.

The local Mavenda tribe were proud that Dad was getting rid of the poachers and offered to build him three huts as a gift. They would also donate the building material. Wood was plentiful, and grass grew abundantly for thatching.

The day for the building had arrived. The young men came first to clear the place with pangas where the huts were going to be constructed, a little bit higher up from where the tents were erected. The razor sharp blades cut through the bush like a knife through butter; they terrified me because should a fight start, these same blades could cut through a man, child, or anything that is in its way.

When the area was cleared to their satisfaction, one of the women marked three circles on the ground. Two were approximately ten feet in diameter and another was a good distance from the other two, twelve to fourteen feet in diameter with practiced precision.

The young boys who were still living in the women's compound and were thus subordinates, doing menial work for the women, brought the building materials and put them near the building site. With short spears they stripped the bark off the poles. This was all they were instructed to do, and that was all they would do. Building the huts was considered women's work. Some of the men helped with digging the holes for the poles with short lion spears. The rest of the women and children scooped the sand out of the holes, depositing it in a woven basket, where it was later mixed with fresh cow dung to insulate the inside and outside, and lay the foundation of floors. The whole process was called mud-and-daub because the mud was smeared onto the poles after they were set into the holes and secured with strips of bark.

The women sang a rhythmic working song while planting the poles.. The poles were so close together that not even our fat little hands could fit in between. After the poles were in, they tied a bundle of thinner branches into the shape of an open umbrella over the top of the wall, and anchored that to the wall structure. Through the thinner spikes they braided even thinner sticks, onto which the thatching would later be attached. The children who came with their mothers, together with my sister and myself, were running in and out of the grown ups, getting in the way. Mom quickly found a solution. She sat us all down in the shade of a tree, cut some thick slices of cornmeal mush from the morning's breakfast left over, poured some honey over it and passed it out. With us out of the way, it wasn't long before the other two huts were ready for thatching.

After taking a small break for food, which our camp cook provided, they were to hang the first layers of the roof.

The roofing was hot work. The women stripped their outer coverings, unselfconscious about the reaction their partial nakedness caused. In Africa they were judged by their inner beauty and not the size or shape of their breasts or bodies, which ranged from virginal Venus firmness, to exaggerated pendulosity that resulted from the peculiar habit of passing the breast over the shoulder or clasped under the arm to the baby tied onto their backs in a goat skin sling. On their lower bodies they wore a three foot long by one foot wide softened rawhide skin tied to the waist with a thin strap—an article of clothing that served several purposes. It was beautifully decorated with bead work; worn on the outside it enhanced, worn in the inside it acted as an undergarment that they pulled up through the legs and tucked into the strap at the back while squatting at the cooking fire. It was also used for sanitary protection during menstruation, packed with absorbent moss or soft cured rabbit skin. Now it was tucked in for modesty while climbing crab-like around the roof, attaching the beautiful grass thatching. Their fat smeared ebony bodies glistened in the sun as they tied the grass onto the thin anchor twigs. They moved like acrobats, masters at their work, and in no time, the two sleeping huts were done. Hut number one was for the Bwana Mokulu and his number one wife. The other sleeping hut was for the other wives and the children. They had openly assessed his loins and come to the conclusion that there would be many more children.

Now only the communal hut needed doing. Normally at that time a small opening would be cut as doorway to crawl in and out of. Something was strange. During the planting of the wall poles, the bwana had asked that they omit six poles. Now they watched as he took those same six poles, split another in half and hammered them across then he attached thick raw hide hinges at the bottom and top, and to their amazement the thing swung back and forth in the opening. Proud of his door, Dad Mom and us children had to try it out. Dad picked Mom up and laughingly carried her over the threshold. This brought on lots of laughter, and everyone had to try out this new 'door'

35

thing that one could walk upright into the hut without the back-breaking crawling. While the doors were being manufactured, Mom insisted that there also be windows. On a circular wall it proved a bit of an engineering problem. But that too was soon achieved, and with mosquito netting over a wooden frame, light streamed into the dark interior. All these holes in the walls were strange to the ladies who worked on the huts. But then they found everything of the white man strange: their music that came out of a box, their clothes, and the paint they smeared over their faces. When the doors and windows were in place, all the women and girl children mixed the dung the young boys had been gathering, with the sand we had scooped out of the holes till it made a thick mortar smelling like red earth and grass. We had fun mixing while the women smeared the clay between the poles on the outside. Mom smeared it onto the inside walls till smooth. Then putting on a thinner coating, she scooped shell patterns with her hands. Took out a comb and zigzagged between rows of shells; this gave a nautical impression. Like the finest wallpaper, when it dried in a day or two, she could white wash it. That night we would sleep indoors for the first time in a very long time.

On completion of the day's work, everyone was invited to a feast!

Crombi had spent the entire day preparing. On a homemade spit, an entire side of Venison was roasting over an open fire, smelling mouth-wateringly good. In a hole beneath the coals, a porcupine encased in clay minus the dung addition steamed, while corn meal mush bubbled in a huge three-legged, black cast-iron pot. In a smaller pot, the cut up entrails and some fat cooked smothered in onions and marog (wild spinach), for mush dunking a special *shesheba* treat.

Sweet tubers with the familiar taste of sweet potatoes baked in the coals, some of the charcoaled outer skins had already burst open, exposing the steaming sweet yellow interior.

The hut warming turned festive. Mom brought out the records and the gramophone. She instructed Sis and me to wind up the handle, she then lifted the arm and placed a Vienna waltz record on. Dad made an exaggerated bow asking her to dance, and they danced around and around the fire. When the music stopped, he turned the record and tried to teach some of the building ladies to do the waltz. They only giggled. Some of their men had brought their own musical instruments, and soon they were gyrating in a long snake resembling a Conga line holding onto one another's hips. Mom, Ethel, and me joined in much to their delight. Now they in turn tried to teach us some of the hip movements. During an exhausted break, the porcupine clay shell was broken open, the quills encased in the hard baked clay shell came off together with the skin revealing tender white meat somewhat like pork. Succulent pieces were handed out to our guests on a quill like the finest hors d'oeuvre. When the appetizers were gone, Crombi the camp cook with a sharpened spear, and Dad with his hunting knife cut off generous portions of venison and everyone sat down in a circle chatting, dunking, and enjoying malala beer, passing the gourd around till all the food was gone. The dancing continued till well into the night, and those who didn't return to their kraals stayed and slept next to the fire. Before my parents retired they received the title of 'honorary Mavenda' for our hospitality. This they said entitled us to their protection for the duration of our stay.

Before crawling in under the net, Mom thanked Dad for her new 'home' and added, "The meal was wonderful, but don't you think it needed a thick slice of home baked bread to dip up the gravy? If only … I had …"

"Do I detect a hint?" Teasing her, he said, "Wouldn't you like a bed first before I make you a baking oven?"

"That would be nice, and a table, and some chairs, and—"

"I promise you, my love, before the week is up you will have at least one of the things you desire." Then he kissed her goodnight.

The following week, Mom white washed the walls of all three huts on the inside. To finish off the interior, Mom sacrificed one of her dresses and a petticoat to make curtains for her 'windows.' She stood back and said, "It is good," and it was good!

True to his promise, Dad started on the furniture the day after the hut warming. And within days, there was a double bed in Hut One (The Master Suite). We went down to the river with the mattress sacks and re-stuffed them with the fluff off the river reeds. They felt like featherbeds after the solid rawhide mats. There were two single beds in Hut Two (The Nursery), Mom said so that she didn't have to listen to stories of who kicked whom. All the beds had their own mosquito nets, now anchored to the roof beams. The nets afforded security against scorpions, snakes, and other crawling things becoming our bed fellows.

In the communal hut, where some indoor cooking was done on a Primus stove and we sometimes ate, the supplies were kept. Here Dad put the Morris chair with adjustable back. He reckoned the chair to be his best work. It was as smooth as any furniture maker's, and quite a miracle if the primitive ax and hunting knife tools were considered. He also made a table with the same tools that was so smooth that a glass placed on it stood without spilling. Several three-legged stools stood round it. Around the walls were shelves for everything. Also in the sleeping huts were shelves and night stands and pegs to hang clothes on. Hooks were added whereon the hurricane lamps could be hung. Mom chose the communal hut to do her crochet work while Dad sat on his Morris chair woodcarving animals and a statue of Mom.

Two other luxuries soon made their appearance. With us not moving around, Dad dug a latrine pit and erected a wood structure around it with a seat over it. For privacy he erected a pole wall with door.

The other luxury was a makeshift shower.

Dad enclosed four slender trees standing close by with reed mats, made a platform among the branches where on rested a large water drum with a plug that could be pulled, spilling the water from the drum into a can perforated with nail holes. The water was warmed by the sun. We still had the zinc bath tub, and the option of bathing in the river. But the convenience of having a shower within the confines of the camp was a blessing, for Mom and Dad not having to stand guard at the river with a gun while we bathed. Also for visitors to the camp, not that we had many of those, it seemed more civilized.

5

Daily Bread and Scorpion Bets

Dad had not forgotten the baking oven he had promised Mom. A little to the left of the communal hut at the edge of the camp stood a four-foot high anthill. It looked like it had lost its colony, but when Dad shoved some burning rags into a hole dug by an ant-eater, they started pouring out. So did a small snake, flickering its tongue in and out. We all moved back, giving the snake some distance so that he could escape back into the bush safely.

When all the inhabitants of the ant hill was out, Dad lopped off the top. A honeycomb of passageways appeared. In some of them there were still tiny white pupa, the ant babies. I carried as many as I could on a leaf, to where I saw the rest of the ants had disappeared to carrying a large bloated queen. I hoped they would come back for their babies. Dad started digging out the clay from the interior till a thick shell of clay remained. He put some aside to make a door and some toys. I took some and rolled it between my palms, placing two round balls on top of each other on the top one I pinched out some ears and added a tail.

"Look daddy! I made a monkey!" I shouted. Dad just smiled; he had the same thing in mind.   Then he flattened a piece of clay for the door, and slightly overlapping it, poked two holes through the door and the outer shell, and bent some wire for hinges. Ethel and I went to look for kindling while he cut open a large paraffin can to fit over the top to make a stove top, where we barbecued or made coffee while waiting for the bread. Next he cut two smaller cans in half lengthwise to make Mom four shiny bread pans, which he made sure the sharp edges were carefully folded over with a pliers. Then he built a large fire inside that baked the clay oven as hard as pottery. When all was done he stood back with a self-satisfied grin, as if he was the first person to invent a baking oven.

Then bursting with pride he said, "Go call Mommy!"

Mom, who had from the corner of her eye seen the goings on the whole morning, tried to act surprised, but was ecstatic. She couldn't wait to test it out.

That night by the light of the hurricane lamp, she pulled out a small can from one of the shelves and took out two cakes of starter yeast, which she placed in a mason jar with a cup of tepid water. Then she measured out the other ingredients. I watched the miracle of bread take shape as she sifted the flour through a makeshift wire-net sieve into a large enamel dish. Then she tied a kerchief over her hair. I was allowed to make a hole into the center of the flour, and standing on a stool, pour the yeast into the hole that looked like a volcano. With a big wooden spoon she mixed it all up till it formed a ball. She then lifted the ball onto a clean linen cloth spread on her new table, sprinkled some flour on it, and I watched fascinated how she kneaded the dough, pulling it from the outside and punching it together in the middle. Round and round she went, till it looked like a shiny big pumpkin. She sprinkled the enamel dish with flour and lifted the dough into it patted some flour over the top and folded a large white bleached flour sack double over it to allow the bread to rise.

Early the following morning when Dad left on his dawn patrol, he woke Mom and Sis and me. He made the fire in the oven, so that by the time her bread was ready, the coals would also be ready. Mom instructed Sis and me to wash our hands, too, so that we could learn to knead. She sprinkled some water over the top that had risen to almost double its size. To me it looked like a mountain of dough. We struggled but the dough would not yield to us. With her hands over ours she showed us how. I could feel the dough all squishy as I pushed my little fist into it, bursting with pride that I, too, was part of the bread making. When it was ready, she cut the dough into four even parts, smeared and floured the pans. Then she rolled them into four oblongs and lovingly placed them in the pans Daddy had made for her. With the corner of the flour sack she spread some lard over the top of the loaves to form a nice brown crust.

The wood had already burned down to coals; Mom raked them even with a dry branch. The coals glowed red when she lifted the pans with a wooden spatula onto them. Without us seeing, she also placed two dough babies and little clay wagons Daddy had made for us into the oven before she closed the door and secured it by placing a stone against it.

My sis, Ethel, was the one who could count to one hundred by then, so Mom had her count to sixty. Then I pulled a line on the ground, and I asked Mom why sixty? She said, "Sixty seconds make a minute, sixty minutes make an hour, and that is when the bread is ready to come out." So I ran around and around chanting sixty seconds make a minute till I drove Sis quite mad, trying to keep up with her counting. I was to go and call her when we reached an hour. We always thought it was our counting that determined when the bread was ready. But it was just Mom's clever way of keeping us busy. She knew when it was ready by the smell. Just before the bread was baked, she filled the coffee pot's linen filter sack she made specially for the pot with coffee she had ground herself and put it on top of the oven. She thanked us profoundly for our 'help' and sent us to get the condensed milk, sugar, and honey. While we were gone she took the bread and our surprises out. Daddy had made us each a little wagon from the clay he had set aside. And Mom made the dough babies. While the shiny gold bread sat cooling in the pans on a stump, Mom poured herself a cup of steaming coffee, lightened and sweetened it with condensed milk, dipped our dough babies in honey and gave them to us. We couldn't decide whether to play with them or eat them, so we rode them around in our little carts, and ate them limb from limb like little cannibals till only the heads remained. This we saved till last. The remaining coffee she put into a thermos, cut several thick slices of bread, took Crombi a slice in the communal hut and told him we were going to surprise my Dad at the point, which was at the river that day.

The bread making became a regular part of camp life. Dad made two more pans, and once a week six golden loaves stood on the table cooling. Mom exchanged two loaves at Charlie's kraal for two gourds of milk, which we churned into butter. The butter we exchanged afterward for more milk to drink. The butter churn Dad made by hollowing a three-foot log. On top it was a fitted lid with a hole in the middle through which a stick fitted. The milk and salt were poured in and we took turns bumping the stick up and down. This action solidified the milk; the butter was then put into a clean linen cloth and the salt water pressed out with a spatula.

The butter making went hand in hand with the baking, and had to last while the bread lasted. So Dad's inventive genius took over one more time.

He built a cool-box. It looked like a small chicken coop. With a double layer of chicken wire on three sides, the fourth side was hinged and could open. Between the two mesh layers he filled it with charcoal, then hung a large can above it with fine nail holes that dripped water onto the charcoal. This contraption he hung in the shaded cool of the fig tree. With the wind blowing through it, it was cool enough for the butter and other foods that might have spoiled otherwise. Mom was very happy, It wasn't an icebox, but it served its purpose.

Mom was an excellent cook with what was available. She and Crombi, the camp cook, usually went on their shopping walks. She usually came back with a partridge when game wasn't available. They knew just where to find the wild onions, marog (tops of plants that tasted like spinach), and where the wild rice and sorghum grew. Waterlily hearts were equal to artichokes. Tubers that looked and tasted like sweet potatoes could be dug up along with small black tubers with a rough skin (brother to the French truffle). There were also the small fingernail tubers on the roots of tall saw-grass that we loved to dig up on our walks, they were crunchy and tasted like nuts. Eggs were plentiful. There were ostrich, wild duck, wild fowl, turtle, and birds eggs. I loved to punch a hole in them with a buffalo-thorn and suck them out. Any kind of eggs if not fertilized were good enough to eat. Fruit, too, was plentiful if one knew where to look—coconuts, small wild growing bananas, passion fruit, dates, maroella, wild figs, wild grapes, and berries of all kinds. Once they discovered a tomato patch, an obvious gift from another safari camp. Then of course there was the exotic fruit of the baobab. The fruit was pale green with velvet fuzz on the outside, five to six inches long, shaped like an avocado. When broken open with a stone or hammer, it revealed snow white clusters of powder. That when sucked produced a shiny black seed that we strung between scarlet lucky beans for an exquisite necklace. We never lacked in meat due to almost daily poacher kills that we shared with the African natives. Then there was of course wild fowl, porcupine, wild pig, turtle and of course fish.

Although Mom and Crombi were excellent cooks, I still sneaked off to the native cooking fires, to sample their food, where I could dip my fingers in the pot of steaming *mielie pap* (white corn meal mush) without a grownup telling me, "You'll burn yourself." I could also sample the strange things we did not eat normally. Elephant liver fried in crocodile fat with wild onions, turtle steak, snake, eel, and nutty tasting mapani-worms, and locusts that were dried in the sun, ground up, and put on the porridge. They taught me how to make a snack of them by twisting the worm's head off and popping the crunchy tasty morsel into my mouth, or wrapping it in a coating of mush, securing it on a stick and roasting it over the coals like a marshmallow. Marog (wild spinach) and ground up grasshopper was also put on the mush as *sheba*. I loved the music and chanting of stories that accompanied the meal even though I could not understand; they were stories of happenings in the past or legends passed on from generation to generation Daddy said.

After eating there were the games to follow. Usually it was a primitive sort of checkers. Holes were dug in a patch of hard earth and it was played with sand pebbles, stones, or seeds. There were also games of skill, like manipulating a round seed on a curved stick into a small gourd attached to the end. And jacks played with pebbles or seeds.

Only one game I did not like! It was a betting game, played with two deadly live scorpions. Earlier on in the day the camp crew caught two scorpions in a trap, keeping them in separate cans. They were marked with berry juice or white ash. Bets were placed as to which one would be the winner. Then the game began. A deep iron skillet was placed on the coals, and the two scorpions tossed in. As the pan gradually heated up, the scorpions would dance around each other till the pan really heated up. The macabre dance speeded up as they tried desperately to escape, something like running over scorching sand with your bare feet, but unable to escape and unable to fathom the source of their torture they began to attack one another. First with the front claws, but soon one weakened, and off guard, his opponent's deadly stinger penetrated the vulnerable spot behind the head on the soft part of the body. There were hoops and hollers from the winners. The dead one was removed, and as the heat became unbearable, the remaining one did a strange thing. In desperation it lifted its stinger and impaled itself behind its own head, committing *harakiri*. It never failed. They found this very amusing, because then there was no winner or vanquished. But if that last drama did not take place and the remaining one simply burned to death, the losers had to pay up. If the game did not proceed as planned, the game was off and both scorpions were simply tossed into the fire with no fanfare.

6

Threat from Across the River

One morning after Dad left for patrol, Mom gave us the usual warning, "Don't go away from the camp, so that she could go on with packing away the supplies that arrived the previous day.

I found a lizard, chased it around for a while, got bored with that. Then I got on my imaginary horse, a bent limb of the fig tree that nearly touched the ground. I rode to faraway places, with "strange sounding names" like Daddy's gramophone record sang about. Soon I was bored with that, too. A fast movement on the ground caught my eye. Oblivious to anything around him and the scorching sand beneath his little feet, the dung beetle rolled his dung ball to an unknown destiny. Little sticks, seeds, leaves, and blades of grass clung to the still moist core to form a hard crust on the outside. They call them nature's clowns, and by his actions it was obvious. I got off my 'horse' to look at him more closely.

At first he walked upright, pushing with his front legs. It didn't seem to work so he turned around and started pushing with his hind legs, walking on the front ones. This way he couldn't see where he was going. The ball rolled so fast that he became disconnected. Bewildered, he stumbled around like a clown looking this way and that way, till he bumped into his treasure accidentally. I don't know if he was performing a little dance out of joy finding it, but he ran round and around the little ball trying to find a foothold. He finally ended up on top of it, balancing precariously on it like a log-walker. It started to move, he tumbled down right onto his back. He lay there kicking. I picked him up and put him on his feet. He kicked his feet up against the little ball and took off blindly, rolling across the clearing right into a log. Unaware of the obstruction, he continued pushing, getting nowhere. Perhaps he was on his way to the river, I thought. All little creatures usually head for the river. I turned him around with a little stick guiding him in the direction of the river. Intent on my mission to help him get to his destination, I clean forgot about Mom's warning not to leave camp. Then I realized I was on the rise outside of camp.

I could see a lot of activity at the water's edge, on both sides of the river. The men getting off the raft, looked anything but friendly, were naked and covered in paint. The ones on the other side were constructing a second raft.

I ran as fast as I could to tell Mom about the unknown tribe I had spotted by the river. Mom ran to get her gun and binoculars. None of the men from our camp were there except Crombi. She told me to find my sister and the two of us were to climb as high as we could into the wild fig tree, and to stay there no matter what happened. If something bad happened we were to be as quiet as mice, otherwise it would happen to us, too, and then we were to wait in the tree till Daddy came home. There was no time for all of us to go to our special hideaway.

From the rise, she counted a group of at least twenty natives constructing a second raft. At that moment they did not spell trouble, but those who were already on our side of the river did! They were in war paint. She wished that Alex would be there, but he was on a ten-mile patrol hike, and too far away to know what was happening. Then she spotted the advance group sneaking through the bush toward our camp.

From our vantage point through the dense foliage, Sis and I could see the strange natives overrun our camp. I wanted to cry when they killed the two kid goats Chief Charlie had given to us. Sis put her hand over my mouth, because she was afraid they would kill Mom, too.

Mom remained calm; stopping them would just anger them. She went into the communal hut, and came out with a bag of sugar. Calmly she handed them some sugar in their palms, put some in her own, and proceeded to lick it from her palm. They took the hint and did the same. Crombi, who had made his appearance, told Mom that they were from Zimbabwe, and that he knew their dialect and spoke some of it. He acted as translator. Through him she told them they could take the goats they had killed and the sugar as a gift, but if they did not signal the ones on the other side to go back, she would be forced to use her thunder-stick. They only snickered. She walked to the rise. The second raft had just come into range. She waited a few more seconds till they were closer, cocked the gun, took aim at the man pushing the raft with a guide pole. Did a silent prayer. The ones in camp looked, silent spectators. They continued to lick their sugar. They had seen men using a gun before, but this was a woman.

Mom hesitated for a moment. To kill him would mean war, but if she even hit him from this distance it would be a wonder. When the shot rang out, the man on the raft screamed, blood gushing out of his arm that held the pole. She turned around to them. They saw it but did not believe it. But now fear showed on their faces. She nearly burst out laughing. In the door of the communal hut stood Crombi, legs spread apart, looking as threatening as he could muster, with the rusted old elephant gun no longer in use to his shoulder. He cocked the gun.

"I order you to go back where you came from. I do not shoot with pity, like the woman, to wound. I shoot to kill! GO NOW!"

They took their spoils and departed hastily. Just to make sure they did not return, Mom reloaded and shot several shots over their heads and into the water at the raft. Mindful of the danger, they dived into the water and swam for the raft that had turned around to pick them up. On the sand banks, dark shapes slid into the water. This was easy prey!

7

Theft of the Clay Oxen and Wife #30

All hell broke loose the day we stole the clay oxen. We had gone to play in the hideaway like usual, when it happened quite innocently.

The hideaway was a giant, hundred foot high, 300-year-old baobab tree that had rotted halfway up when it was struck by lightning. It was in no ways dead. Dad hollowed the dead part out still further till it made a fair sized cave ten by twelve- foot in diameter. Convenient lianas that could be pulled inside gave us easy access, but prevented others from entering. Dad filled the inside floor with soft white river sand. Around the walls he strung wires on which he hung jerky to dry; there were also cans of water and bags of dry rusks. "Survival foods for emergency," he told us. Several times the tree had been our sanctuary. High in its shelter we would be safe from animal stampedes, or when there were veld fires, and if we had the time to get to its safety in time, the invading tribes from the other side of the river.

One time a runner came from a nearby kraal to report that a herd of elephants on the rampage had flattened their village and were headed in the direction of our camp. Rather safe than sorry, Dad didn't hesitate: he put Ethel on his back and Mom put me on hers, and we hid in the hideaway till the danger had passed. Another time when the river flooded, overflowing its banks right up to our camp, we stayed in there till the river receded.

The tree was also our playground away from the camp. When there was no danger, Crombi escorted Sis and me to the tree. We played there for hours in the cool interior, building sand castles. Or playing with our corn cob dolls. But as soon as Crombi went back to the camp, we climbed around in its vast branches playing "monkey." But sometimes we left our comfortable hideout and explored our surrounding environment to pick maroellas, the succulent yellow-skin fruit with its wax-like interior that hung temptingly in a nearby tree.

In one of our ventures, we discovered a stash of beautifully crafted clay oxen hidden in a hollow stump. We looked around to see if it belonged to anyone, but when we saw no one, we declared it ours, chanting, "Finders keepers, losers weepers!" For the rest of the day till it was time for Crombi to come and fetch us, we played with our new toys, building stick kraals, huts, and compounds for our cattle. Late afternoon when Crombi came, we took the toys with us back to camp. Everyone admired our sudden artistry. They especially admired the clever way we used thorns to make the horns, and ash and charcoal for the skin markings.

Mom, however, thought we were just a little too clever. She expected trouble, which came about a half an hour after our return to camp. She was looking out the window when she saw the surrounding bush come alive with action. Every now and then a brown head and shoulders appeared over the bushes, watching us play with 'their' toys. Soon we were surrounded. They were carrying bows and arrows. To them, the theft of their toy oxen was a serious thing, and Mom was afraid that the tips of the arrows could be poison-dipped. When the arrows suddenly started raining into the camp, she grabbed the old elephant gun went outside and waved it around, shouting in Mavenda, "We have no quarrel with you!" That was all that was needed, and soon we saw bare bottoms bolting into the bushes. That was not the end of the story.

When Dad got back from patrol, Chief Charlie himself walked into the camp with a group of his *indoena* (warriors) in full paint and adornments. Sis and I were terrified, because we had heard of tribal justice. The chief took Dad to one side; there was a lot of whispering and a lot of nodding, then they returned to where we cowered behind Mom. They looked very serious. We expected the worst.

When we were called up, we tried to explain that we thought the oxen were abandoned and that we looked to see if the owners would come forward, but no one did, so we kept them. We did not tell them of the "finders keepers"; that would incriminate us even further. And least of all, we never suspected the grownups to be in on the scam.

Dad did a little more whispering to the chief who in turn spoke to his indoena, then Dad said, "We will now see who the rightful owners are." He told us to bring the toys. He then placed them inside a circle he drew on the ground. The indoena surrounded the circle, holding their spears aloft. Charlie then asked the rightful owners to step forward and make their claim. Which the chief's children did, of course, without hesitating. We were too afraid to move. The dispute was over. We made a public apology, and we were off the hook. We had learned our lesson.

Mom brought out the malala beer (sap of the palm tree, tapped into gourds like maple syrup) for the men and cookies and sugar treats for the children. And we were given permission by the chief's children to play with "their" toys.

To reciprocate, the chief invited us over to his kraal to meet his beautiful number thirty wife. The ebony skinned Mavenda women were indeed beautiful, statuesque. From his ravings about her, we expected to see someone out of this world.

Our arrival at Charlie's kraal a week later was expected. The compound was freshly swept, The main hut freshly smeared with dung inside and out and Mom's shell pattern duplicated, speckled with red ochre and white ash. Everyone was bedecked in their finest beadwork, faces and bodies glistening with butter.

We were led into the soft gloom of the main hut by the second wife. Ornaments of goat sculls, antelope horns, and skins adorned the walls. Coming from the bright sun outside into the hut lit only by the light of the fire that burned inside a ring of stones in the center, we were blinded at first, until our eyes got used to our surroundings. A thin spire of smoke rose up through a hole in the roof that acted as a chimney. A savory smell came from the two pots on the fire. One contained a crumbly *pogotklo* porridge. The other contained roasted goat meat, marog, and wild onions. We were surrounded by a potpourri of smells, each one trying to out do the other. The cooking smells mingled with smoke, human, the almost pungent smell of perspiration, the grassy smell of the newly dunged walls, and the skin-covered floor.

On a mat by the fire sat a woman in her mid thirties. She was anything but beautiful according to European standards, with a large protruding rear, flat pendulous breasts, and flat feet with pigeon toes. When she smiled, we also noticed that all her front teeth were missing. Charlie, bursting with pride,

introduced her to us as his number thirty wife. She had a name that none of us could understand let alone pronounce. Mom had always tried to explain the importance of inner beauty to us. Here was an important example. But five minutes in her presence reflected her inner beauty with a radiance that was hard to ignore. It showed in her kindness, and gentle caring for everyone around her, and in her childlike wonder at everything in the world.

On the other side of the room, in the heat of the fire, wrapped like a mummy, lay a six-week old baby, it wasn't difficult to notice the baby was very sick. His mother explained that her milk just wouldn't come in, and the baby vomited up the goat milk. To illustrate, she dribbled some into the mouth of the baby, who immediately vomited it up. The mother was frantic. What could she do? Mom analyzed the situation in a blink of her eye. With the interior heat of the hut and being wrapped up like a mummy, the baby was overheated and dehydrated from the vomiting and diarrhoea because the goat's milk was too strong for it s little system.

Mom picked up the limp little bundle, gently unwrapped it, and suggested that she take the baby to our camp, where she would find out what the matter was. After dining and the visit, Mom took the baby back to our camp. The second wife came along. There she bathed the baby in sun-warmed tepid water to cool her down and make her comfortable. Then she dressed her in one of my petticoats, and gave her to Second Wife to hold. She boiled some water with a touch of salt to help the dehydration and diluted some condensed milk into it, waited till it was cool enough, and fed it to the baby in small amounts with a small spoon. The baby took it hungrily, and kept it in. Every two hours she repeated the small amounts. Miraculously the vomiting and diarrhoea stopped. Within days the baby showed improvement, within a week it was smiling and gurgling.

Mom sent a note with the runner to the point where the supply truck usually came asking for baby supplies, a bottle, some nipples, baby formula, and baby clothes. A note from the driver read, "Congratulations, I never knew that you were pregnant, but it just so happens I have on hand a canceled order, which I'll send back with the runner."

In the weeks to follow, Mom trained Second Wife in how to boil and clean the bottles, boil water, and mix formula. The baby was strong enough to go back home. Regular visits to Charlie's kraal ensured that the baby stayed healthy. In a few more months the baby was eating mashed banana and corn mush and thrived.

Mom's reputation spread. She was often called out for her healing power.

Her red hair just added a special touch to her magic. Her magic consisted of some tender loving care, a mustard plaster for a chest cold, lancing a boil, or disinfecting a festering wound that was treated with incantations, and goat intestines. She healed a cut wound by cleaning it, sewing it up, and applying aloe ointment and clean bandages instead of cow dung patties and spit. The only magic was that the wound soon healed with this sanitary treatment. Also, the story of the miracle of the dying baby that was brought back from the brink of death spread, and Mom simply helped mothers to understand child care. Mom never charged for her healing, but gourds of milk and baskets of corn were left outside our supply hut.

The witch doctor watched all this, fuming from the sidelines as his customers dwindled. Also the "gifts" he expected in payment for his muti. He had to do something to scare away the white witch, to gain back his customers' confidence.

I remember waking up one morning. In front of my parents sleeping hut was a circle of stones smeared with blood. A headless chicken, with some strategically placed bones and other paraphernalia lay in the center of the ring. Mom came out of the hut. Her flame red hair hung loose over her long white nighty. Her first reaction was shock, but she could sense that the one who staged this little show was still close by to see her reaction. Fear of the unknown consequences often killed the accursed at first encounter.

If whoever was responsible was still around, she would give them the show of her life. Suspecting the witch doctor himself, she immediately fell to the ground in a mock death, flaying her arms and kicking her legs. Then lay still for a few moments. It would certainly bring a smile to his mouth if he thought he had killed her outright, but then came the resurrection. She raised her hands to the sky and got up, giving a scream that would curdle milk. Then she proceeded to dance around and around the stones. She suddenly stopped, and pretending to pluck hair out of her head, she rubbed it onto the first stone, picked up the stone, and threw it with all her might into the surrounding bush with the hope of hitting the one who placed the curse on her. Not hearing an outcry, she repeated this with the rest of the stones, throwing them in the direction they were laying into the bush. Then she stepped into the dreaded center of the circle, she twirled around as fast as she could, and when she stopped she had the chicken in her hand (the hand is faster than the eye). She started plucking out the feathers, blowing them in all directions, and when it was cleanly plucked she chanted a hocus-pocus incantation, swung the

53

chicken over her head, and threw it in the direction where she had seen a slight movement in the bush. This time she hit someone. A blood curdling scream came from the direction where the chicken had landed and the bushes crackled and bent as the one on the receiving end tried to get away, running for his life. She most likely reversed the voodoo. Mom could not contain her laughter any longer.

Knowing the psychology behind the curse, Mom treated this experience as witch against witch. Voodoo in Africa works on fear of the unknown, psychologically acting on the individual's superstitions and the visual intensity of the curse. Fear was known to stop a person's heart beating, helped out by the curser who made sure something awful happened. A deadly mamba snake just accidentally crawled into someone's bed. Or a rock became dislodged when the accursed was walking on a foot path. Fire destroyed his hut. He was seen entering the water to bathe and turned into some kind of animal. Go to sleep and not wake up. Comas were induced with the help of medicinal bark or blowfish.

From very young on, children were told about an evil spirit, the dreaded *tokkelossie*. Too many times they had seen the results. A woman who committed adultery and got pregnant was visited by the *tokkelossie*, and when the baby was born it was substituted with a hairless cat, or salamander, or snake. Of course, all these things were brought about by some one who kept everyone in line by evoking fear.

8

Witch Doctor's Theatrical Tactics

Soon after the incident of the headless chicken, Mom was summoned together with every man woman and child to the witch doctor's compound to find the person or persons responsible for the disappearance of some goats. No one in their right mind dare stay away. To stay away would immediately show guilt. They had been forewarned that the *tokkelossie*, who saw everything, was sure to pay them a visit, Not turning up, they would surely die an unspeakable death. So heads bowed in reverence of the witch doctor's magic, they flocked to the compound, keeping their eyes cast down, lest their eyes declared guilt. They searched their conscience to see if they or their goat herder didn't accidentally bring home a goat that belonged to some one else. When all were seated, the witch doctor made sure that they all witnessed the preparation for the judging. In front of his hut he had made a fire on which he placed a large three-legged cast-iron pot. With generous incantations and dancing, he tossed all kinds of impressive things into the pot, a pinch of this, a pinch of that, and some brains taken from a goat while still living, sacrificed in front of the people that would tell him who the guilty person was.

Chief Charlie was also summoned. He sat a respectable seven-foot distance away from the witch doctor on his carved mahogany chair of state. Watching the procedure of preparation. He could see through the witch

55

doctor's charade, who really could have left it up to him. He no longer believed in this mumbo jumbo, but the ceremony needed all the clout of his official capacity as chief to succeed. The goats had been disappearing almost weekly, so he agreed to be present. However, he refused to wear his official chieftain robes of jackal tailed skirt and G-string, boars tooth necklace, and leopard toga. Instead he was allowed to wear his "big city" clothes to show off his worldliness. This in itself was very impressive to those who had never left their own kraals or hunted farther than the Limpopo river.

He was a man of small stature with dark chocolate skin as opposed to the darker skin of his brothers and sisters. No one looked directly at the witch doctor; they had their eyes riveted on the chief who would be giving the signal for the trial by fire to begin. He struck an imposing figure in his Johannesburg "store boughts."

His shirt was striped and had a starched collar buttoned at his Adam's apple with a rhinestone stud. The long sleeves were rolled down. One of the sleeves boasted a gold cuff link, the other one had a fastener especially admired by women—a treasured impressive two-inch safety pin. This modern device was worn through their noses, through their ears, and as an ornament in their hair threaded with beads. And it held up their loin cloths.

In spite of the sweltering 110 degrees, Charlie wore a genuine hand-knitted woolen, Fair Isle diamond-patterned pullover over his shirt. And just so that everyone should know he had mastered the white man's ways, he had his toothbrush and a fountain pen in the top pocket, showing.

To top it all off he also wore a stunning rhinestone batwing pair of black sunglasses with the price tag still attached to the ear piece. He had sacrificed nearly a whole week's hard labor pay deep in the belly of Johannesburg's gold mines for this luxury, behind which his eyes now hid.

That was not all. His skinny legs with knobby knees comparable to the secretary bird reached down out of the khaki shorts into a pair of virgin white tennis shoes. Virgin white because he made sure that they stayed in their 'genuine' shoe box they came in, and only were taken out for extremely important tribal occasions. He was not a domineering figure, but in a modern art sort of way he was quite a … It's difficult to really find a descriptive noun that did him justice, all that came to mind was quite picturesque!

Charlie had a deep insight into tribal superstitions, real beliefs, and philosophies. For a few moments his thoughts wandered to his becoming chief. Even though his father didn't think so, he had always considered himself to be leader material and could not wait, as the first born, to inherit his father's chiefdom—a custom that had been passed down from generation to generation in his family. He couldn't wait for the day when he would reach his manhood, so that he could break away from the women's compound.

Suddenly he became aware of the silence. The witch doctor had stopped his chanting. The sulfur he cast into the fire had given him time to switch the hot pot for a cold one. Charlie couldn't help but think him awesome in his face and body paint, grass drapes, and other paraphernalia, with a necklace that looked peculiarly like baby skulls around his neck to round out his ensemble—the ones he most likely replaced with hairless cats at birth, he wouldn't put anything past him. He stepped out of the smoke, scowling at Charlie, who he noticed had not paid attention. Charlie, remembering why he was really there, stood up. With great authority, he lifted his staff above his head, and handed the staff to the two men flanking the witch doctor. They lifted the pot up with it, placing it in full view of everyone on a stool in the center of the square. Charlie loosened the safety pin-cuff link, rolled his sleeve up ceremoniously and stuck his hand into the pot almost to the elbow. The hand came out dripping-wet but unharmed. He showed it back and forth to the crowd. He was INNOCENT! The command was given to all to start the judgment, by the innocence of their own chief. They knew that if they were innocent the water would be cold, if guilty the water would boil and burn the hand with the fires of hell itself, that it would eat the hand itself away, and so reveal their guilt. Not in their wildest imaginations did they know it was games of the mind. The *muti* was strong, and the verdict true. The sentence was an unspeakable death that would catch up with them in their hut or during the hunt.

Slowly the people approached the pot, with the terrible thoughts—*what if their own innocence didn't work?* Cautiously they stuck their hand in, trembling in anticipation of the terrible unknown. Their hands touched the water. Almost in disbelief it was cold. Their faces glowed with relief. One by one they came forward, one by one the same reaction. Not guilty … not guilty … not guilty …

Charlie, bored with the procedure, slipped back into his revelry. Back to his boyhood. He remembered his mother's hut, when his mother's goats were the most important thing in his life. Because he was committed to guard them with his life. Losing even one through theft or a lion's killing would have meant a disgrace even, though he was only four summers old and had to guard along with his father's second son. Pasturing the stock taught responsibility and accountability. From seven to ten he had protected his father's cattle. And at ten, when his father could no longer tolerate his presence in his mother's hut because he hung around the cooking fires too much instead of going hunting with the other boys, his father started calling him a girl. He wanted to please his father and become a great hunter, but he simply did not like killing animals. His father at that stage had doubts of him ever becoming the future leader of his kraal. Not yet a *murani* and still considered a boy, he graduated him into the men's hut, thinking that would toughen him up. He was given the responsibility of the most prized labolo cattle—the bride price his father received for his many sisters. In time he would be given a share to pay for acquiring his own brides. He couldn't wait for his fourteenth year to have his manhood ceremony so that he could pass the cattle tending to his brothers, because fate had opened his eyes to other possibilities!

He had seen the camps of passing safaris. Saw the people's affluence. This evoked his curiosity. He learned from their bearers about a city with buildings reaching up into the clouds. A city built on gold, they said, where men went below the earth like ants and dug the gold out got paid in trinkets called money that could be exchanged for cattle, goats, and wives. He wanted some of that 'money' and to learn about the white man's ways so that he too could become a wealthy, worldly man. So after his *murani* ceremony of circumcision and becoming a man, he no longer cared to follow in his father's footsteps. He handed that birthright over to his second in line brother. The city beckoned and he slipped away to the place called Johannesburg.

Four years later as the prodigal son, he returned to his father's kraal, only to discover that he had died and the second son had taken his place. But confident now of his own abilities, he went up the river and established his own Kraal. Hearing of that, his boyhood friends also became breakaway, acquired wives, and also joined his kraal.

The commotion of a dog barking in the square brought him back to the present. The action of the dog caught his attention.

Apart from the crowd sat the true guilty person. The thin dog also knew. He approached him, sniffed him, smelled the fear in his sweat. He alone knew he was guilty because they both were hungry and the man had shared scraps of the stolen goat from his fire. The dog understood hunger, he licked the young man's face like a Judas, then slunk away like a traitor, with his tail between his legs.

With every 'not guilty,' the guilty young man's heart beat like thunderous drumbeats. His mouth was dry with fear. He visibly trembled when everyone had passed and only he was left. The witch doctor, too, had watched him; he had also watched the dog point the guilty one out. Saw him approach the judging pot several times, and then withdraw. The others had approached with confidence in the knowledge that their innocence would stand the test. He knew he would fail because of his guilt! What the guilty one feared most was the unknown. The curse of the witch doctor was strong medicine. He would be better off putting his fate in the hands of his chief, whom he knew was a compassionate man. Before being summoned by the witch doctor, he jumped up and ran across the compound. All eyes were on him; they pitied him!

He threw himself down prostate at the feet of Charlie shouting, "I was hungry! I was hungry! please save me from the anger of the tokkolossie!"

"Get up!" commanded Charlie. "Kneel, and stick out both your hands!" Everyone waited in breathless anticipation; they expected the worst, yet still hoped for leniency.

"Will he lose both his hands?" they whispered among themselves.

When Charlie spoke again, there was deadly silence. Even the birds stopped twittering.

"You will return to the man you stole from as many goats as there are fingers on each hand. And you will work for him as long as that would take. I have spoken! Go now!" A smile appeared on the guilty man's face.

"NO!! I COMMAND YOU TO STAY!" the witch doctor's voice thundered. That was not the response he expected from Chief Charlie—what example did that set the others?

"You will never steal again!" He felt rejected, that the chief had taken over his show. He was very good at special effects; he would teach them both a lesson. He was still the boss, and his *muti* was still the strongest! He would show them all!

On a flat stone, the witch doctor picked up a large glowing coal. The young man had seen his cruelty before. He felt paralyzed with fear. Would he be blinded? This time he was asked by the witch doctor to stick out his hands. Hatred showed in the eyes of the witch doctor as he grabbed the young man's hand ,and forcing his palm open, he dumped the glowing coal into it, closed the hand around it, and pressed it down onto the coal, holding it there till a sickening smell of burning flesh rose in the compound. He did not stop there, but took the other hand also and repeated the cruel act while the young man

59

was screaming, held by the witch doctor's two helpers.

The onlookers stood back in shock. The witch doctor had won again! The sentence was imprinted on everyone's mind. There would be no more stealing! The guilty man would wear the scars as a marked man for the rest of his life. As silently as they had come, they left.

9

Mom's Survival Lessons

Mom's lessons were simple; she taught us basic survival skills—how to find and identify edible plants, roots, and tubers, and how to prepare it so that it becomes edible.

"The first lesson is to watch the birds and the animals. They have tried and true knowledge of fruits, mushrooms and berries, and which green plants and grasses and tubers are edible. They seldom put things in their mouths or beaks if they aren't sure.

"The second lesson is to study behavior patterns of the animals, also their characteristics, and their habits.

"The third very important lesson is never to take baby animals from their nests, lairs, or environment. NEVER! ... Remember! Never handle them! Or bring them back to the camp. Some birds and animal mothers will destroy their young if they find human smells on them."

Our blackboard was the moist sand along the river bank, where she wrote the alphabet, and we copied it underneath. This was also where I first learned to write my name, by tracing over the one she wrote. After she taught us how to write, she started teaching us about the writing of animals.

"Who teaches them?" I wanted to know.

"They write with their tracks that tell a story of where they are going and where they have been. Their tracks can even tell us how long ago they were there," she explained.

"First you must know who you are tracking, now watch." She pressed her hands into the damp sand duplicating each of the animal tracks. Holding her hands together in prayer, she pressed only the sides of the palms from the wrist to the tips of the little fingers into the sand.

"This is a *duiker*," she said.

Pressing just the tips of the pinkies into the sand was the track of a small dik-dik. Two hands pressed together, made into a fist, was a wildebeest.

An open palm with clenched knuckles pressed heavily into the sand was the closest she could imitate a lion. "This one is very important to know because small animals and small children like mine," she smiled, "are easy prey for the old lions who have lost the use of some of their teeth and find the tender meats more delectable. That's why they are called man-eaters."

"He won't get me, I can climb a tree very fast!" I said.

"That, my little one, would be your first solution, because lions don't usually climb trees, unless the tree was so bent that they could easily walk up it. And what are you going to do when you get to the top of the tree and find a leopard there hanging his dinner up in the tree? They are good tree climbers. They also sleep in the cool of the trees during the day, draping themselves over the thicker branches. Their tracks are similar to the lions', but the toes are more spread." She continued, "Snakes also live in trees, except for the boa."

"How can they tell us when they were in a certain place, and where they are going?" my older sister asked.

"That's easy, you look in which direction the prints were facing, turn around and head in the different direction. When is another story." She picked up a small grass stalk, pulled little streaks, and made little dots across the tracks she had made. "If you see these smaller markings of worms, ants, centipedes, it is an indication that the larger animal had been at that very spot about two hours ago. Most small insects will not cross a track if the smell is still fresh, but will do so when the smell has dissipated, which is around one or two hours. So if the tracks are still clear, you can bet on it that the animal is still in the same area. Find out in which direction the wind is blowing and make a hasty retreat in the opposite direction to which the tracks are pointing.

"There is danger everywhere, and the most dangerous are not always the biggest. One of them is about two and a half inch long. The black scorpion. At least he will always give you fair warning. Watch his tail. If it is down you can walk round him, but when he is provoked and angry, he lifts his tail in a defensive position. The poison is in the shiny heart-shaped point at the end of his tail. That is why I make you carry the little snuff box full of anti-toxin." We were really too young to understand about the seriousness and about anti-toxin. The venom in the two glands lying just below the heart shaped stinger of the scorpion contained neuro-toxins, another big word that caused paralysis of the heart muscles, which usually caused death within minutes. So it is important to get the anti-toxin from the little can directly into the sting wound. The red scorpion is not as dangerous and will only cause severe pain and lingering infection. When the red one's tail is up, it was simply that she was carrying her babies, up to twenty at a time, that clung to the tail and one another during the free ride. She tried to explain all this to us. We listened and absorbed only that which we could understand, like putting the stuff from the little tin can into the place where it bit us, and especially the fact that scorpions like to sleep and nest in warm dark places like our shoes or clothing lying around.

Both Daddy and her drummed it into us to always shake our shoes out before putting them on.

I was so glad that I never wore shoes, except the time when we went to visit our prim and proper English grandma and I was forced to wear them then—with socks, even. Besides, I reasoned there would not be enough room in my small shoes for her and her twenty babies to live, remembering "the old woman who lived in a shoe, she had so many children she didn't know what to do."

"The other dangerous predator is the crocodile that lie on the sand banks, so still and unmoving. That it is deceptive—when they want to, they move extremely fast. They also wait at the water holes for their prey and for the water carriers."

We were not afraid of them, because we spent most of our time in our safe little cove, surrounded by big rocks.

The cove was a miniature wonderland. While Mom sat guard on the rocks with her gun, Ethel and I hunted around for tadpoles and other treasures. We tried to catch the small minnows with string tied to a pole, using a safety pin as hook and bread or berries for bait. I was always afraid that one day I would actually catch one. Then when I did, I cried. Mom carefully took it off the pin and helped me to put it back in the stream.

Small wonders happened around us constantly. When we were tired of fishing, Mom taught us how to play jacks using river pebbles. Or we simply explored.

The waterside held endless fascination. We watched the dragonflies with membranous gossamer rainbow wings hover over the water, laying their eggs on aquatic plants by skimming the surface of the water, washing the eggs off her abdomen where they either caught on submerged plants or sank to the bottom to become fish food. Sometimes they were caught by a floating leaf and hatched by the sun. I loved to watch the pond skaters walking on water. They scurried across the water this way and that way, feeding on drowned mosquitoes and bugs. Under their feet the water made little dimples. Mom laughed and said they were tiny glass boats that kept them afloat. In actuality the middle and hind legs had a wet-table hair-pile under the foot pads and under their bellies, enabling them to float. Ethel and I tried to catch one so that we could get the little boats for our treasure boxes. They, too, lay their eggs on plants sticking out of the water, their young fending for themselves right from the start. One day we found a dead one floating on the water and were terribly disappointed when there were no little boats.

Wonders unfolded by the hour along the river beach. Tiny sand crabs played at war brandishing one giant claw that looked very menacing. They wandered around sideways holding the giant claw aloft as a warning, defending their holes. As soon as I approached they would zip back into their holes only to appear again a few seconds later.

Sis (Ethel hated me calling her that, she said that *sis* in the Afrikaans language meant "yuck") and I would run away and watch the crabs come out of their holes, then just when they were all out we sneaked up on them clapping our hands again and again. Time and time again they would retreat as if they had an unspoken signal among themselves. It was a silly little game that amused us and I'm sure frustrated them.

Sometimes we would find little eggs that had fallen out of the weaver birds' nests into the rushes. This particular day we were looking for eggs when we came upon two strange eggs, unlike anything we had ever seen. They had rough shells. So we picked them up and took them to Mom to identify. They were still hot, so she immediately asked us to go and show her where we had found them and to please put them back. Then she told us. "You have found something very rare, they are the eggs of the Basilisk—a legendary serpent dragon. He walked upright, wore a crown on his head, and could walk on water, with a lethal breath and an evil eye. If it hatches in our presence and sees us first, we would be the first to die, but if we are lucky enough to see it first he is sure to die. So we don't want either thing to happen and that was why I asked you to go and put it back." I wondered if it was real, or just like the little glass boats. As little as I was, I knew that the story of the dragon would be one I would one day tell my child. Deep in my heart I knew, though, that it was Mom's way to preserve a life and prevent us from cracking an egg that was so rare, and destroying its contents that were equally rare. Many years later I would actually see one 'walk on water'—it was in Mexico. The local people called it the Jesus lizard. It had been raining and the fields were wet. Above his head there arose a crown and he ran off walking upright with such speed through the puddles that it looked for all the world if he was walking on water.

The bush offered hundreds of lessons, we need only keep our eyes and minds open to the things around us.

In the mud footprint craters left by countless animals at the water hole, wasps came to drink and gather their building material. They sucked up tiny globules of mud mixed with a drop of water, then carried it drop by drop to their building site. We found one of their architectural wonders on the rafters of our supply hut, and another on a branch of our baobab tree, where the mud was deposited and constructed into a perfect igloo, globule by globule. There were other wasps too, smaller with vicious tempers. They were called the paper wasps because they chewed little pieces of leaf and bark into pulp then mixed it with water, copied the honey bees, and formed perfect paper honeycombs. They preferred to attach their combs onto the leaves of a low bush. However, the ants soon discovered their stashes, so they painted the backs of the leaves and around the comb with a sticky black liquid. No one could tell me where they got that from, but one thing was certain—it did keep the ants at bay.

The most wonderful miracle of nature to me was the butterfly's metamorphosis from egg to caterpillar then to butterfly. Sis and I would go looking for the tell-tale double row of tiny dimpled eggs on the bottom of the leaves. We would mark our find, and for two weeks we kept going back to the spot to see the miracle unfolding. Soon equally tiny caterpillars gnawed their way out of the eggs and immediately started eating till they reached an inch, at which time they became a target for the birds and other worm-eating creatures. The ones that survived went into hiding underneath leaves, continuing to eat until it became time to go into the sleep of transformation. During this time they carefully selected the spot to anchor their chrysalis. When ready, it first made sure that the anchor rope was strong enough, then spun a single thread, wrapped it round its middle, much like a cliff climber. Then wiggling and squirming, it started to spin itself into a neat little package called a pupa. That hardened and took on the shape of things to come. There it dangled, on its slender thread, like a Christmas present one was not allowed to open till that special day. To me it seemed like forever. We went daily to see what was happening. Sometimes when the moment arrived when the dorsal splitting occurred, we missed it, even though we took turns watching. But at another time, through weeks of tedious watching, we were awarded with the ultimate wonder of the pupa bursting open, and actually seeing the fully mature butterfly emerge from its glasslike shell where it had been sleeping. It would sit for a moment quivering, then slowly unfold its crumpled wings, which were soon ironed out by the warm sun. And then without drum-rolls or applause, it would spread them and glide to the nearest flower, guided by nature and their instinct to begin the whole process over again.

The cicadas also shed their outer skin. When its time arrived, a large crack appeared down its back. Holding on to the rifts of the tree bark, it started to vibrate. With the constant vibrating and wiggling, it emerged. Free at last! Then it did a free fall to the ground, where it existed for a while if it was lucky enough not to be eaten. Then it climbed back up the tree to sing its endless chirping love song, mate, and lay its eggs in the protective rifts and valleys of the tree bark. The old skin, down to the finest detail, still clung to the bark. We carefully pried the feet loose, and removed the delicate glass-like replica to lay it in our treasure boxes, next to the butterfly's discarded pupa.

My box held crab claws, pupa, dried centipede body rings, snail shells, bird eggs, a weaver birdnest, a dead shiny rainbow-shelled rhinoceros beetle, and one of my favorite creatures—the hard, black shell of a dung-beetle. And a neat bleached crow skull. There was also an assortment of lucky beans, from the thumbnail black ones with red caps to the tiny red ones. And a piece of the skin from the snake that almost killed Daddy.

During our lesson sessions down by the river's edge, we watched in fascination how the weaver birds wove their nests on the slender swaying stems of the river reeds and rushes. Snakes were the only enemy of the weaver birds, so anchoring their nests in the tips of the reeds and rushes ensured that the snakes could not reach their eggs or their chicks.

To make their nests, they started to pull long strips off the leaves of the reeds, then anchored them to the top of the reed in the form of a pear, through which they carefully wove thinner strips in and out, which allowed air to circulate through. On the front they left a small opening big enough to crawl in and out of. The measurements were derived from their own general body size. Customized to fit themselves. To the opening they attached a long funnel, ensuring that their little chicks wouldn't fall out. They built the nests with such precision that one could measure them and find that they were all the same. The weaving displayed great craftsmanship, giving them their name, weaver birds. The inside was then lined with soft plumes from the reeds, fallen feathers of countless birds that frequented the river banks to drink, and finished off with soft feathers they plucked from their own breasts to customize their nests with their own scent. A whole colony usually built their nests together so that it was quite an orchestra of twittering as the wind gently swayed their nests. The bush doves sitting in the trees on the bank usually joined in.

Snakes were also our enemy. Mom usually warned us to look out for them, in the trees, under the cool of the trees, and along the game paths. Boa constrictors, the largest of them all, usually lay along the game paths; they ranged in length from seven to twenty feet, family of the American python.

These snakes have a reputation that is often exaggerated. Stories circulated of them swallowing a baby whole and someone cutting them open and finding the baby alive. This was an unlikely story as their method of ingestion would not allow for that. They usually go for smaller prey, but usually crush and break the bones first to allow them to swallow it. The larger prey they also crushed, then covering it in mucus, slowly swallowed it. Then they lay motionless beside the game paths where they killed their prey, for days till the contents of their stomachs were digested, at which times the snakes are quite vulnerable. Only in extreme danger they would convulse and regurgitate their ingested meal. They usually slunk away from man, but when suddenly surprised, they attacked with great speed. A fact my Dad could attest to.

One morning strolling along a game path, Dad surprised one of the big ones, and in turn was surprised himself when the snake coiled itself around his legging and soon wrapped itself tightly around his waist. The pressure was tremendous, but keeping his presence of mind, Dad loosened the head's grip around his leg, and holding onto the jaws, carried it still wrapped around him back to the camp, where Mom calmly took a sharp carving knife and decapitated the snake. Only then she was able to unwrap the coils that still clung around Dad's waist. We kept the skin, but it made a tasty meal for the natives that night. And that is how I got to tasting snake.

Usually after a period of digestion the snake regurgitated undigested parts and fur-balls, snatched up by the witch doctors to use in their 'magic' to invoke fear. Another myth was that they attack you with their teeth to inject poison, but that isn't true. They do grab with their teeth, but only to get a grip to aid them in crushing their victim.

The other myth was that they fed again as soon as their food was absorbed. They have a very poor appetite and can exist for a long time without food. In Dad's case the teeth penetrated the legging and not his leg. So he was able to pull the head off him.

The difference between the boa constrictor and the American python is that the boa produces living young, which it abandons as soon as they are born, and the python lays eggs that she abandons as soon as the eggs are deposited in a safe place, because even snake eggs are edible. They are hatched by the sun and fend for themselves right away. The third myth is that the boa's meat tastes like chicken, but only the texture resembles the white breast meat of chicken, but tastes more like eel, which I can attest for, having tasted it at Crombi's cooking fire. To prevent being caught and crushed, we simply stayed off the game paths. Snakes were everywhere.

We loved to swing on the lianas, but there the vine snake could easily be mistaken for a liana. They had poisonous fangs in the back of their mouths and liked to drop down onto their victims. Then there was the boom slang (tree-snake) that at least distinguished itself in its bright green coloring. It usually sat motionless, body extended, camouflaged like a tree branch, awaiting its prey—tree frogs, birds, lizards, and chameleons. When ready, it lunged forward, distending its neck. Just a scrape of its fangs caused paralysis that affected the breathing, and death was evident if help was not available. For that reason, Dad always wore a neck scarf when entering the heavy bush. Mambas were also tree dwellers. These we were taught were the most dangerous. Their attacks had no warning and were done with unbelievable speed. It had front fangs, and its victim usually died within the time blood circulated through the body. No one ever survived. We never heard of anybody!

Then there was the cobra, cousin to the Indian cobra. It spat in the eyes of its victim, and if the eyes were not washed immediately, the acid burn was so severe that it could cause permanent blindness.

The coral snake looked very much like the harlequin snake, only one was harmless, and the other—the Coral, small and beautiful, was deadly. I remember trying to pick one up one day, not knowing the difference, when my Dad, standing nearby, saw it and his boot came crashing down on it. He told me a little rhyme, to look at the colors. If yellow was next to the black, you're a lucky fellow, but if it's red against the black, you're dead.

There were many warnings and rules in the survival lessons Mom gave us that Sis and I had to follow. One of these we often ignored, and that was "NEVER bring baby animals back to the camp." It was all done in innocence. Often the baby animals would follow us home, especially when the drought set in; then they came to the camp to drink out of the zinc bath we put out in the sun to warm up for our nightly bath. On this particular day we ignored two warnings, never to stray away from the camp, and the baby animals thing.

We wanted to go and see where the tribal men were hanging the calabashes to collect the palm sap that would be turned into malala beer, but when we got there, there were no men in sight climbing up the trees (the main attraction). Knowing that we were naughty, we turned around to get back to camp before we were missed, then we heard soft grunting noises that emanated from nearby where a palm had fallen over. On investigating we found two little lion cubs a few weeks old. They poked their little heads out, obviously not afraid of the invading man-cubs, and they were so cute we were not afraid of them. As we started to walk away, they clumsily wobbled after us. We could not resist. We each picked one up, not even bothering to see if the mother was anywhere around. We ran back excitedly with our find to the camp to go and show Mom.

Instead of sharing in our excitement, she was very angry that we sneaked out of camp, and on top of that ignored her warning never to bring baby animals to camp.

"Come and show me where you found them, I hope we get them back before their mother returns from the hunt," Mom said through clenched teeth.

When we got to the spot, there was no sign of the mother. Mom put them back among the fallen fronds, but as we left they immediately followed us again. Mom picked them up, rubbing them down with some sand this time to remove the human scent from them and put them back. This time they stayed put, and we made a hasty retreat.

We were about 20 yards away from the nest. Suddenly Mom froze in her tracks, pulling us behind her back. A few yards from her stood the lioness with a rabbit carcass in her mouth returning to her cubs. For what seemed an eternity, the two mothers stared at each other. Mom was very protective of us but in her haste to put back the cubs, she had forgotten to bring her gun with her. I remembered her words: *during the time that they have cubs, they are very dangerous*, but now it was too late. Standing there I could feel Mom's body tremble. Then to our amazement the lioness passed us within a few feet, stepping out of the path and ignoring us, her eyes cast down and her tail up as a signal that she had already eaten; her concern was more for the safety of her cubs. As she passed, Mom slowly turned us around and walked backwards to show respect and also not to be attacked from behind. When we got a safe distance away she didn't look back, but told us to run as fast as we could back to the camp.

10

Dad's Show and Tell Lessons

Dad's lessons were more like 'show and tell.' On the days that he was off and had no patrol duties, Ethel and I accompanied him on reconnoitering trips to study animals in their habitats up close. He had erected several blinds at strategic places where the animals gathered and we could watch them without being seen. My favorite place was near the bank of the river, where all kinds of animals came to drink, as if they silently declared a truce amongst one another. Except for the big cats and the elephants that had the right of way, everyone mingled.

"The first thing you need to know when you are in the veld, is to know in which direction the wind is blowing," Dad said. Then he continued, "The reason to know that is if the wind is blowing from you toward the animal, then you will be in trouble, because the wind carries your scent toward them. But if it's the other way around, the wind coming from the animal towards you, then you are safe. If you can't pick up some soil to throw into the wind to see where it is blowing, then you can stick your finger in your mouth and feel which side gets cool." So we dutifully stuck our fingers in our mouths trying to figure out if we were safe or not. It usually ended up in giggling, because we were never sure. We were still giggling when Dad put his finger over his lips, indicating total silence. We immediately obeyed, sat scarcely breathing waiting for the first animal to arrive. My heart pounded in my chest as I caught a whiff of elephant blowing in our direction. I could also hear a low rumbling sound coming from his stomach.

Dad whispered, "It is part of a silent language that Elephants speak that we can't hear, but they can hear over very long distances. Usually it is the poetry they recite to their sweethearts."

One solo elephant only approached. He stood still for a moment his ears erect, listening intently. He preferred not to wade into the water, instead he did a peculiar thing. He scooped a seep-hole out of the soft sand near the edge of the water. One tusk was shorter than the other, so it dug sideways like a shovel. Soon the hole was around four feet deep. Dark brown muddy water filled the little pool. Self-satisfied, the elephant felt around the edge as if to say, *I've done good for myself!* Then with all the time in the world, he filled his trunk and drank till he was satisfied. Filled it again and started squirting it all over himself. He stopped for a moment, listening again. Hearing nothing he trumpeted loudly, declaring the little pool his. He lay down over it, wallowing in the mud, scooping trunkfuls of the seepage-mud over him. This mud bath would insulate his skin from annoying bugs. When he got up the pool was already flattened, but just to make sure, he trampled over the indentation till there was only small craters of seepage left where his feet had trodden. Satisfied with what he had done, he walked away. I could swear there was a smile on his face.

Next to arrive was a family of warthogs. Like little soldiers they marched in a single file, from the eldest to the youngest. The sow leading was making little assuring grunts to tell them that they were safe. A coarse, thin mane of hair ran the length of her back, with a small bare patch in the middle. The rest of her was covered in short, dark gray bristles. She had thick curly tusks protruding on either side of her face, below them she had two large bumps like fat cheeks, hence the name "warthogs." Her babies were little miniatures of her, but they were black in color. At the side of the water they knelt down on their front knees in a neat little row, from the biggest to the littlest in their marching order, slurping noisily. Between the sow's drinking, she kept up the grunting warnings even though their tails were now hanging down. Then suddenly the mother's tail shot bolt upright, she gave a warning shriek, and they took off running the way they came in, in a single file with their tails up in the air. There was imminent danger and their hole was far away.

We had often seen them feeding. They dug up roots and tubers, chewed grass, and even plucked berries, and sometimes when everything else was scarce, they chewed pieces of bark off the trees. They mated for life, and normally nested in abandoned fox holes or armadillo digs. In danger the piglets first went in and the parents then backed in, so that their biggest defense, their tusks, were facing out. They were vicious fighters, because their piglets were tasty morsels, and they themselves were chosen snacks for lions and humans. They had a mean uppercut with their tusks, and caused damage that left their enemies with broken jaws to starve.

The reason for their hasty retreat approached stealthily.

"Shuuut!" Dad's finger motioned again.

Camouflaged by the river foliage, a leopard made his appearance. What a magnificent cat. The background of the leopard's fur was a light ochre color. The shoulders, back, flank and haunches had dark kinky-shaped spots of black in rosettes of threes. Its chest and throat had smaller spots that faded out into a soft white belly. The leopard was mainly nocturnal, but ventured out sometimes to hunt if it was unsuccessful in the night, where it rested in shady rock areas, or draped itself over sturdy branches in the trees awaiting prey. It also carried its daytime kill into the trees. Often the prey weighed more than itself. There he could eat in peace without having to battle others who vied for his food. It moved sinuously and silently. It killed for food and not for the sport of it. Larger prey, like deer, wildebeest, and antelope it killed by strangulation, holding on to the neck till the animal stopped breathing and dropped down dead. Smaller prey was killed by a single bite to the neck. Its favorite snack was still warthogs, or wild pigs, but in an emergency it killed domestic goats, chickens, rabbits, and even baboons and monkeys. The males walked alone and hunted alone. They only got together with the females when they wanted to mate. And then it was not a friendly encounter. Unlike the lion, they were not family oriented. Usually took off right after his procreation duties were performed. To him it was undecidedly "the female's business" to raise the offspring, which luckily was never more than two, and on very rare occasions a triplet, which seldom made it into maturity. This male was big and well fed, belly bulging as he slunk forward.

Little did Dad ever dream that in the very near future he was to have a close encounter with one, perhaps the same one, fighting him with his bare hands almost to the death. The last rays of the dying sun reflected in the leopard's shiny golden ochre coat. He crouched down, the shoulder blades nearly touching. Unconcerned and with confidence in his awesome power, he lapped contentedly with curled tongue at the water. Silver drops reflecting in the sun glistened on his whiskers, then fell back into the stream, making little circles that widened into ever-growing circles, which turned to gold as they mingled with the sun's last rays reflecting in the water. Like an overgrown house cat he straightened out, paws forward, arching his back, and yawned with wide open mouth exposing the almost four inch-canines. He lingered a moment longer for our pleasure then moved off silently into the surrounding bush.

A small turtle at the water's edge, who had thought it wise to pull his head into his shell for the duration of the leopard's drink, cautiously poked his head back out, sipped daintily, then sauntered off to who knows where to spend the night.

With the leopard's smell still hanging leaden in the air, a whole herd of spring buck with orange-yellow glistening skins edged with white came to drink. Thirst had taken away their fear. With the sun fast setting, Dad motioned that we should go, just as a troop of baboons arrived. I begged to stay a little longer, because there were little babies with the troop.

If I could have looked into the future I would have known that one of these babies through a very cruel fate would very soon become mine. On the back of one of the mothers rode a month-old baby, holding onto her tail for dear life. As she bent forward for a drink, he lost his grip, slipped clumsily over her back, and fell shrieking into the cold shallow water. She let out a the warning sound of *bohoggom* as a reprimand, picked him up out of the water, and held him wet and still shrieking against her breast. Then cradling him with her one hand, she bent down again to drink. The baby, remembering that cold wet stuff he had just fallen into and wanting nothing more to do with it, searched her soft belly for a pacifying teat and drank, too. This time he didn't go back to her back, but stayed where he felt safe, clinging to her belly

Then suddenly without warning all hell broke loose! The whole troop scattered in all directions. Some went up the nearest tree as a second leopard approached the water. He lifted his head up, looking at the departing baboons. He was hungry and some of these would have made a tasty snack until he got his evening meal. He gave a "GET YOU NEXT TIME" roar. Dad gave a shudder of premonition. We didn't move a muscle, staying silent as field mice. Just before he drank, he suddenly tensed up. He looked across the pool in the direction of our blind. We were well-camouflaged among the reeds. But the thought was there. Did he see us? Dad instinctively put his hand on his gun. He never killed unnecessarily, but the wind could have changed in the meantime. Ethel stuck her finger in her mouth and held it up, then motioned to Dad that the wind was coming from him.

The leopard felt uneasy, his instincts told him that something was wrong, but he was thirsty and the night was long, so he drank warily, with a faint whiff of humans in his nostrils. A fish glided past in the shallows. He slapped it out of the water. But while it still flapped around, he lost interest. Fish were his last resort. He could wait! The night still held many promises. We waited for a few minutes after the leopard left. Dad became paranoid as soon as the sun started setting. To him the bush was taboo after sundown.

"So what did you learn today?" he asked.

We didn't know how to answer him, but in our inner being we knew that all creatures had one need—water, and to appease that need they called a truce, no matter at what price.

11

Boggom and Mercy Killing?

A few days later after Daddy's lesson on the riverbank, I met Boggom, my baboon.

I was only four years old, but to the natives I was "little mamma." I had an uncanny repose with small animals that often followed me into camp. Especially during the dry times, when our zinc bath tub became their drinking trough. It was not unusual to see an assortment of animals in our camp drinking together, peacefully, then leave. This caused Mom some frustration because they would also get into her little vegetable garden. In desperation, she dragged thorn branches over the garden, but they would still find a way to wiggle in and eat up what she had planted. They would on occasion allow us to pet them, but always returned to the wild.

Boggom became my first *baby* that didn't leave. He got his name from the sound baboons make—*bohgomm*, a word in their language that has multiple meanings.

When Charlie entered the camp compound, he was carrying a sack. He explained to Mom that there had been a raid by the poachers on a troop of baboons in some trees near the river. No one was spared in their quest for 'monkey paws,' needed to make lucky key chains, except for one little baby who fell out of the tree and escaped miraculously to become my pet.

Charlie put the bag down on the ground, loosening the top. We could see movement inside, and soon a tiny head with enormous ears made its appearance. It struggled out, blinded by the sunlight for a moment after the darkness of the sack where he had cried himself asleep. He let out a mighty shriek. He looked around; he was hungry and wanted his mother. He remembered her warmth and the comfort of his teat. He remembered there was the blinding light when she dropped him, he fell through the branches, stunned, then he awoke in the darkness of the sack, but after crying for her he fell asleep. Where was his mother? Across the open courtyard he spotted a small human creature, standing upright just like his mother did when she was picking berries. He hesitated for a few seconds, then crawled across the hard ground, clambered up my leg and onto my hip, searching for a teat that would alleviate his hunger and give him the comfort he needed.

There was no welcoming teat and no hair to hold onto, only the welcoming arms that held him tightly.

I loved my mom's inventive genius. She quickly sewed a triangle rawhide bag like those she made for mothers who could not nurse their babies, diluted some condensed milk, and tied the bag closed on the broad side, leaving only a small opening at the triangular point. I clasped the bag under my arm, he smelled the milk, tracing it to the drip on the triangle, and was soon sucking contentedly making soft *hurrumph, hurrumph* noises. When I tried to pull him away from the bag, he cried with a sharp squeak. Then settled down and drained the rest of the milk and fell asleep in my arms.

Every morning when I awoke, I would see to his needs first before I attended to my own. He became one with me. He slept with me, ate with me, and within weeks I was feeding him some of my corn meal mush from my plate, and pieces of fruit he took out of my mouth like he would have done with his mother whenever I was eating some. He had different sounds for different needs, which I imitated, convinced that I was talking his language. He had no mother, who would have been his role model, so I became his surrogate mom and teacher. I turned over stones like I saw baboon mothers do for their babies. They would then rub the insect they found in the dirt to stun it and hand it over to the young. I found slugs and grasshoppers, which I pretended to eat, smacking my lips, then handed them to him. He rubbed them in the sand to kill them, then ate them. I climbed up the fruit trees with him on my hip. I in turn taught him everything my mom taught me. He learned through watching me, and learned well.

One day, though, Ethel and I wanted to play a game of marbles, and the shiny yellow Sodom apples were just the thing. We picked enough for our game, not paying attention to Boggom. He must have thought it was for eating and didn't know that these fruits were deadly poison, and I couldn't tell him that. From the corner of my eye I could see him stashing his cheek pouches full of these deadly yellow balls. I screamed, "NO! NO!" I made a mad dash at him. He knew the word "No!" But unable to make the connection what he had done wrong, he started making his 'I'm mad' faces at me, his brows flipping up and down as if to say, "What have I done now?" I didn't have a moment to lose before he would start chomping down on the ones stashed in his cheek pouches. I pried his mouth open stuck my fingers in and extracted everything from his cheek pouches. He screeched and fought back and made threatening bites without piercing the skin, but I finally succeeded emptying his cheeks from the deadly poison.

Boy, was he mad! Sticking my fingers into his mouth at that stage posed no danger but it would have been an impossibility in another year or two when he reached young adulthood, weighing in at 6 to 10 pounds and having exchanged his baby teeth for 1- to 3-inch fangs. Perhaps he wouldn't have attacked me remembering his bonding with me. What happened was just something that couldn't be explained or reasoned about. But that was in nature. I had become his surrogate mom and my family had become his troop—a far cry from the strict rules he would have been subjected to.

Baboon family ties are very strong, but so is their rank placement in their social structure, which became a life long commitment. The strongest bonds exist between parents and children. A mother never severed ties with her children, and often her rank was inherited by her offspring, unless they lost the ranking through challenge. Shifting took place constantly in the troop as young males vied for position.

If Boggom's troop had not been slaughtered, they would have consisted of a polygamous mixture of about six to eight superior ranking adult males, and a harem of different ages of females and their offspring of both sexes numbering around twenty-five to thirty. Baboons, often referred to as monkeys, are really a species on their own. They are easily distinguished by their long dog-like snouts and do not have the flat faces of monkeys. As babies, the hair on their bodies is almost black and silky. Then as they grow older it becomes dark gray with lighter gray speckles.

There is also strong bonding between females, who rely on one another to share responsibility in teaching the young, and protecting them from aggressive males, jealous of the attention infants receive. This bonding is often mistaken for lesbian behavior. But the females also have platonic friendships with younger males to teach them to be accepted into the troop, and to learn social and parenting skills, which would become the key to their acceptance. There is a lot of grooming among all ages, under the guise of removing vermin from one another, but it is in reality touch therapy. Boggom as an adult male would have had to prove himself in strength both physically as well as mentally to determine his superiority and placement in the rank. That would also have given him leadership and mating privileges. He would have selected several female friends, from whose offspring his future harem would have been established to prevent inbreeding. His baboon family, vegetarian mostly, would live off roots of grass, seeds, berries, pods, tubers, fruit, flowers. Their protein they derived from crabs, snails, and insects that they found in rotted stumps or under stones. It was observed that they sometimes deviated from their strict diets and ate meat left over on carcasses, but no one ever saw them kill for it.

As Boggom's role model, he at first expected me to select fruits, berries, and other edibles for him. But as he learned, he became bolder and in his food gathering he started turning stones over himself. He grabbed at the insects that scurried out. At first it was a game. Then later he would slap the beetle or lizard between his hands, and if it didn't move like all infants, it ended up in his mouth. Thus he discovered that these toys were also savory morsels. His favorite food was grasshoppers, and desert was ripe maroela fruit. This was also my favorite. The skin was soft and could easily be bitten into, rewarding one with a sweet-sour wax-like fruit that could be sucked or chewed off. The shiny round black seeds we used for the game of jacks.

Looking for his food, we never went too far away, staying within sight of the camp, but quite often we found ourselves by the river, conveniently forgetting the dangers that lurked there. Several times when Dad was obliged to shoot a crocodile when it became too much of a menace to the water carriers, he would find some of their copper bracelets or ankle rings inside their bellies.

One day we found an abandoned reed cornucopia used for catching fish, and I turned it upside down over Boggom and we weighted it down with a log. He couldn't escape. We hid behind a rock making lion noises, which drove him crazy. After a while we freed him. Not knowing, he immediately was on my hip *goh-gohing* contentedly. Within a year he had outgrown my hip, but as big as he was, at the slightest scare he would take a running leap and jump on my hip, knocking me over in the effort. I couldn't stop him doing that.

Sometimes out of devilment I still dislodged the food from his cheek pouches. I would simply wait till it was stuffed to capacity, then poke my finger on his cheek and everything would pop out. He must have remembered the incident with the Sodom apples, because he closed his lids over his amber eyes, grab my arm, and bit, but instead of his fangs sinking into my arm, he gave me a gentle love bite knowing I was his human mother.

Daddy decided then and there that it was time that he started to live on his own. When he was little he was allowed to sleep with me and eat with me, but Dad explained that now he was becoming too dangerous. Dad planted a pole in the courtyard in front of our hut with a box nailed on top. I gave him one of my dresses to cuddle in. Dad, making sure that he stayed in the box, put a leather strap around his waist with a rope attached that he tied onto the pole so that he could climb up and down. After a while he didn't need the rope anymore; he had accepted his new sleeping place and we undid the strap. Now I knew he no longer needed me because he would grab his security blanket, my old dress, and climb up into the box.

A week later I saw a strange troop foraging near our camp. I was afraid that Boggom would try and join them. That would endanger him, with the human smell all around him. I asked Dad to tie him up. He hated the strap around his waist and the rope he had to drag up the pole. He sat at the base of the pole and sulked, giving me disapproving looks, even showed me teeth. He refused to eat, and when I tried to groom him to pacify him, he scampered up the pole and refused to come down. The more he heard the sounds of his kind, the more restless and irritated he became.

Then one morning he was gone. He had chewed through the rope. We went to look for him but the strange troop had moved on. We could only presume that he had gone with them. I was sad but in a strange way happy for him.

That night just as we were getting ready for bed, Boggom crawled into camp, very weak and covered in blood. He was partially disemboweled, his intestines trailing behind him in the sand. He was in terrible pain, but came back to the only place he had ever known as his home. He wrapped his arms round my legs and tried to pull himself up onto my hip, then fell down in a faint. I screamed, "HELP HIM, DADDY!" I Sat down with Boggom's head on my lap.

Crying and begging, I said, "Please help him, Daddy!"

He opened his eyes and lay softly groaning. Daddy just looked and shook his head. Daddy picked me up ever so gently and took me to Mom. I thought he was going to help, but just to make sure I asked Mom. "Please sew Boggom, Mommy, he's torn." Just then I heard the shot. That to me meant death!

Mom held me close, kissing me, "That's the best way, Poppie (my little doll). He was suffering too much." I wiggled out of her arms and ran to the lifeless body of my surrogate 'baby', wrapped him in his security blanket, and held him on my lap. I sat glued to the spot crying till I fell asleep. My dad put me in my bed, then went outside and buried Boggom under the big wild fig tree.

Early the following morning when the camp was not even stirring, I ran around looking for him. Daddy came out, picked me up, and tried to explain mercy killing to me. I knew the word *killing*, Poachers did that all the time, but I didn't want to understand the word mercy, because that took away someone that I loved deeply. Dad knew it was the kindest thing to do; there was no way of saving Boggom with such severe injuries. I pounded my dad with my fists. I knew the worst thing I could ever call him. "YOU POACHER!" Then I let fly with my fists, my fury had no bounds. "Let me go, let me go!" I didn't have a pole to escape into, so I climbed up the tallest tree in the center of the camp. Staying there the whole day, every time when someone was sent up to get me down, I swung over onto the thin branches so that they couldn't get me. When night came, Mom sent Crombi the camp cook up the tree to watch over me. Because by now I was very hungry, he was able to talk me down, to go and eat something at his fires. But I didn't want to forgive my dad. Later when I fell asleep in his arms, out of sheer exhaustion, Crombi took me back to Mom, who tucked me in.

A few days later fate had the upper hand. The troop that so brutally murdered Boggom because he smelt like human were themselves brutally murdered by humans that they hated. The poachers!

Dad discovered the scene of the massacre, but spotted a baby up a tree that had managed to escape. He went after it and finally trapped it into his backpack. At the camp he told me he had a present for me. I could hardly wait for him to open his backpack, and when he did, the scene of Boggom was repeated. I did not even say thank you, instead ran straight to Mom for a new rawhide bottle. While the new little one was feeding, Mom asked me what it was going to be called, and I answered, "Boggom Two," of course.

Boggom Two had quite the opposite personality of Boggom One. He was more tolerant and gentle. He didn't mind me dressing him up in my clothes, and when he got a little bigger he became quite a clown. He copied all our actions. He looked very comical with my cloth hat on, walking upright. He watched Daddy go off on patrol with his gun. Then he would fetch the old elephant gun which was at least four times bigger than him and drag it around camp till Crombi relieved him of duty and put the gun away. I had to train him like I did Boggom One, but soon he became a self-declared Nanny for my sister and me. He would take things away from us if 'he' thought it wasn't good for us. He regularly shared his food with us, trying to feed us little bits of bugs and lizards that he thought were good for us. We were his sisters. And when we strayed away from camp, he alerted us to danger, steering us away from snakes or other predators. Mom felt at ease when we were with him, even though he could sometimes be an alarmist.

Boggom Two was 'good medicine' because I finally forgave Daddy and learned what mercy killing was, when there was too much suffering and no other choice. I think I forgave him mainly because I found consolation in my new 'baby.'

12

The Leopard Attack

The event that sent us all back to civilization started with the arrival of a tourist called Miller, who with permit in hand was determined to "bag himself a lion" ... But ended up with him wounding a leopard, jeopardizing everyone's life, and Dad eventually fighting the leopard with his bare hands, but here I graciously hand over the story telling to my dad, Alex:

With the poaching under control for a while, I had nothing to do but welcome the sudden influx of legal hunters into our camp. It was a change in routine that I both welcomed and dreaded. They came with permits in hand for a two-week-long safari, determined to fill their quota, and they were mostly inexperienced. I was asked to stay on and watch over them. They followed me around daily, with their own hired line of carriers into the bush. Their dream was to take back big game trophies, like Hemingway, but at night they returned disappointed at having such bad luck. They brought back small game instead, and this they cooked over the camp fires while bragging about other times when they had better luck. There was meat a plenty and the malala beer flowed freely, fresh calabashes were replaced daily in the surrounding malala palms as the fermented ones were brought down. Because of the fruity coconut-pineapple flavor when it wasn't fermented it could be given to

children, but when fermented it had the strength of raw gin. The men drank it like a fruit drink but as the night wore on the voices grew louder, the gestures animated, and the stories that were legendary among hunters, became their own.

One man showed his left hand was without a thumb. "I lost this thumb when a rhino pinned me with his horn against a tree, and I had to use my pocket knife to cut off my thumb to escape him goring me."

"Au, that's the story everyone tells about our first President Paul Kruger," I corrected him, but to avoid a fight starting I started telling them a real story about the tourist, who after ingesting a little too much beer, made a bet with one of his buddies that he knew the direction of the wind so well that he could paste a postage stamp on the rear end of an elephant, then run through its legs and get away without him even noticing. "So they set off looking for an elephant. He tested the direction of the wind, put a postage stamp on the tip of his cane, and managed to paste the stamp, but just then the wind changed or the elephant felt the sting of the cane, turned around, and he was trampled into the earth. We had to scrape him off the ground and mail his ashes home."

"Now THAT sounds like a lie," everyone chorused.

"That was the truth, but if you want to hear a tall story that an old man told me and swore it was the truth, I'll tell you. He said he was sitting on a log one day, and it was a big log because his feet didn't even touch the ground. Suddenly the bushes started moving around him, and soon they were speeding past him like a freight train. He tried to get down from the log, but discovered he was sitting on a giant snake that was going so fast that the bushes looked like they were moving. Now didn't that sound more like a lie?" I excused myself; I'd had a long day wandering around after their big game. Listening to their tall tales.

I wasn't really sleepy but I undressed, folded my clothes, and placed them together with my boots at the foot of my cot to make sure that they didn't become a scorpion bed. I checked on, Mara, my wife who had gone to bed earlier on to see if her net was still safely tucked in. I rolled my own net down and crawled in. I lay down and listened to Mara's gentle deep breathing. The night noises drowned out the voices round the fire.

A gray owl hooted in a giant acacia tree nearby. It was a familiar sound and pleasing to my ear. Far away the drum beats told about the days happenings, the pulse beat of Africa. The drum 'newspaper' beat in regular pulses. I could distinguish different individualized Morse codes that were understood by each of the tribes sending the message out on the drums. Over time I learned to read their codes, too. This one unfortunately was too far away to hear.

The owl continued its lonely call, then suddenly fell silent, interrupted by loud roaring and growling coming from the direction of the river. From the angry tone I could determine that it was not over a kill; this was undoubtedly between two leopard males over the possession of a female. The fight would go on till submission in defeat, or till death, when the victor would take possession of the female. For any other reason the fight would have stopped long ago.

The fighting had woken up a whole family of black faced makek monkeys, who to show their indignation, shrieked and jumped wildly around in the branches. This in turn woke the birds in the tree tops. They shifted uneasily, but being used to the high strung loud mouth group of makeks, they did not move from their perch. They calmly folded their heads back under their wings and continued their already disturbed sleep, safe in the knowledge that they were far out of reach of the danger below.

The roaring had not stopped; this meant only one thing, these were equally matched males and one was sure to submit and slink off. I sent a silent prayer up that I should never get into a fight with one of these cunning cats.

A little to the left of the fight a spotted hyena coughed. I could just picture him. He stood a safe distance away from the rolling snarling dust, then started his sickly *heh ... heh ... heh ... heh* laugh. His keen sense of smell had already told him that the argument was not over a kill. It started laughing again hysterically. Its raucous barking laugh had a cursing ring to it. These cats had cheated him out of a possible meal. With tail clamped tightly to his hind quarters, a grin on his brutal face, he stood with crooked short hind legs posed to run at the first indication that the fight should turn his way. The hyena had spent the entire day in his lair without eating, and then followed the sound of the leopards in hopes of sharing a meal with them. Sometimes if he was lucky, with his powerful jaws he could snatch away the leopards' meals, who would just give it up without a struggle, but these leopards had no pay off. It turned in disgust and ran off in search of something more promising.

Familiar with these sounds of survival, I lay listening with almost indifference. They were close, and they most likely had smelled the men and their meat, but they had no quarrel with man at that moment, only with their own libido.

I felt almost arrogant of my superiority in the safety of my hut. The pole door was strong enough to keep them out.

My eye caught a sudden movement. Something black was moving stealthily across the net over my cot. A huge tarantula halted every few inches as if he was aware of Mara and me in our cots. It must have come down out of the thatching, I thought, snuggling deeper into the center of the cot. The dreaded spider halted again on the net, at least two feet away. To me it felt like it was two inches from my face, studying me for sudden moves I might make towards him. Then attracted by the thin strip of light streaming in from the glow of the fires, it let go and fell to the dung floor with a dull thud. There was deadly silence. I wondered, where was it? The devil told me the net was untucked, and he was right at that moment crawling in somewhere under my sheets.

I lay heart pounding, almost paralyzed. Then with a sigh of relief I spotted him at the base of the door pacing back and forward looking for a place to escape to the outside. At the widest gap it squeezed through. An involuntary shudder ran down my back. I had hunted all kinds of big game, yet this four-inch black hairy tarantula still sent shivers down my spine.

With the spider out of sight I relaxed. I became aware of a dull rumbling in the distance. The veldt had been very dry. The water in the river was low. The elephants dug their own wallow holes but selfishly covered them up again, making it necessary for the game to search for water lower down the stream. Crocodiles attacked anything that came near the shallows to drink. Just the other day I found a dehydrated gemsbok that was so weak that she couldn't get up the banks of the river to go and search for water somewhere else. I took my helmet, dug down to make a seep hole, filled it up, and presented it to her. She quickly slurped the water, and then with renewed energy tried to get up the river bank but kept slipping back down in the loose sand. I gave her a push from behind. She accepted my water and the push, but as she reached the bank, still turned on me, and if I hadn't jumped aside in time she would have gored me with her sharp horns. I thought what an ungrateful animal, but as she sauntered off, she did turn around and give me a 'thank you' look before running off into the bush.

I was glad of the thunder. It could only mean one thing—some rain. I tried to fight the drowsiness to hear the next roll of thunder. Then disappointed, I realized it wasn't thunder after all but the staccato beat of drums coming in on the wind. Before I fell asleep, I heard snatches of the message. "City man wants to find lions." The wind distorted most of it, but I could make out something about lions and a "painted woman." Still concentrating I fell asleep.

Tourists Arriving

A commotion in camp woke me up at dawn. The bearers were running around babbling excitedly at the generosity of the strange looking bwana from the city. With their hands across their mouths to prevent their souls escaping in their merriment, they giggled about his funny clothes, and about the strange woman with man's clothes, whose mouth and fingernails looked like were covered in blood.

At the mention of a woman, I was curious to see this one. I wondered about the mouth and nails covered with blood. Few women ever came on hunting parties, especially not vampires, I laughed. I hurriedly put on a pair of shorts and shirt, pulled on my boots without stockings, and stepped out into the morning sun just rising.

I cast a quick glance over the small group who had just come into the camp clearing. They didn't look anything different from any other group. Only this group had seen a Hollywood Tarzan movie, and dressed accordingly. The woman was far too dressy in fashion magazine clothes. She was poured into pants that looked like riding breeches. The fine silk blouse she wore had the top four buttons deliberately undone, exposing her full rounded breasts and ample cleavage. Which spelled trouble right away, not among the natives who were accustomed to naked breasts. But trouble among the other hunters who were still in their tents after last nights drinking. She was laughing just a little too loud, which automatically focused on her mouth. She had scarlet lipstick on, this of course matched her nails, which resembled the claws of the vultures after a blood feast. So figuratively they were correct. She was waving her arms dramatically around, belting orders out. "Take my trunk in there!" She pointed to the second hut. Like the entire world belonged to her.

I had to interrupt. "Wait a minute there! My children are still sleeping in there. This is not a tourist camp, this is a government working camp! And if you behave yourself I might just consider having my men set up a tent for you." She looked at me in stunned silence.

The man with her looked like he, too, had stepped out of the same movie and was certain that was the latest thing everyone was wearing this time of the year in the bush-veldt. His dazzling white safari suit was immaculately creased in just the right places. He too wore jodhpurs more appropriate for horse riding than for hunting. His helmet, too, was white with a strip of leopard skin around it, and to round that off, a partridge feather stuck in it. He had his monogrammed handkerchief out and was mopping his brow continuously in the already sweltering heat. The woman was absolutely under his spell, and he under her spell, the adoration was almost theatrical.

"Tell the brute, darling, I can't sleep in a tent! And I want a bath right now!" she pouted, ignoring me all together.

Van Black, who was the first one to greet the party on their arrival, now introduced them to me and Mara coming out of the children's hut. She was not aware of people in the camp and was standing in the doorway in her nightdress. Her natural beauty a total contrast to the painted glamour of the new woman. Her red hair, braided the previous night, hung disheveled over her right shoulder, the sun catching the copper glow.

"Mr. Miller, let me introduce you to your host, who also happens to be the game warden. So if you would be so kind as to show him your permit, he in turn will see if he could accommodate you and your demands."

"Mrs. Miller, I presume, this *brute* is called Alex, and his wife is called Mara" he added sarcastically, "the host and hostess."

The woman's voice softened as she approached Mara and the children, but my youngest immediately began crying, afraid of the long scarlet nails, which I just know reminded her of the carnage we had seen too often.

"Where can I have a bath?" the woman asked.

"You can go down to the river with me after breakfast" Mara told her sweetly. "Or you can have a shower. It's cold water of course; the sun hasn't been out long enough to warm it yet."

"I'll take the shower, just show me where, we have been in a truck for two days, and I can't wait till after breakfast."

It was a precious moment when Mara showed her the shower. It was made up of a reed mat wrapped around four slim trees, with a platform suspended over it whereon rested a tub that dribbled water into a second can. I had ordered one of the bearers to fill up the can. The shower usually lasted as long as it took for the water to dribble through into the lower can punctured with nail holes. Mara explained that she had to soap up first and save most of the water for the rinse off, otherwise she would have to wait till the top was refilled, and left her at that—

Only to find her screaming her head off when a half an hour later all soaped up, she had used up all the water and had to wait for one of the men to go and fetch more water from the river to finish off her "shower."

In the meantime, Mara prepared breakfast for the new arrivals, which of course was cold by the time she finally was able to complete her shower. One of the tents was vacated by the previous group and amid a lot of moans, her trunk was moved into the tent.

During breakfast, Miller produced his hunting permit and wasted no time to let me know what his intentions were. To impress me, he talked incessantly about previous 'shoots' and all his trophies back home. Looking him over, I silently doubted he could shoot a rabbit, never mind going after a lion.

"I'm not leaving here without a lion skin, to have it stuffed with head with mane still on. I heard there were plenty around for the taking." Perhaps he got his information directly from the poachers, because they didn't care to disrupt whole families of lions. I thought of the talks of the other hunters round the fire the previous night who said they knew where there was a "whole lair of man-eaters." I found that very amusing. They knew nothing about lions. Firstly, man-eaters always walk alone because they were old and their teeth had worn blunt, and usually they have to rely on domestic goats, rabbits, and such, and their last resort would be man. And when they start roaming, they cause havoc in the native villages, and on occasion I had to kill one.

I laughed. "I suppose you've heard of the pride of man-eaters?" I thought he looked at me as though I was insane.

It was true that there was a whole pride of lions not too far away. It consisted of two families with young cubs. I had marked the area with bleached skulls in the trees, but I would make sure that no one found out where they were while there were cubs. Unless someone stumbled across them accidentally, their lair was well hidden, and they were safe.

I could do nothing but listen to him brag for the next few days. They all bragged that way in the beginning. The silent ones were usually the ones with the best luck; they got their quota on their permits and moved on. But I was up against the grand master of blowing his own horn. My inner thoughts were, he would run at the first signs of trouble. And boy was I wrong; in days to come he was the one that would actually endanger my life, but then save it. It all happened this way.

First Encounter with the Leopard

It was Sunday. Usually I didn't like to shoot on a Sunday, but with the extra mouths to feed in camp we had run out of meat, and it became necessary to go out and shoot something for the pot. Perhaps he was saving his ammunition for that lion he hoped to bag. Up to then I had not seen him shoot anything but some coconuts up a tree. I wondered just how good he was. Bursting with curiosity, I invited him along to go and get something for our evening meal as I knew where a whole herd of impala usually grazed before going down to the water hole. For the rest of the day I avoided him by keeping busy around the camp.

Two hours before sundown, we set out to get some meat for the pot. I had no desire to drag it out, so I headed straight to where I knew the herd would be. Along the way I thought I would test out his skills with the gun before I would go anywhere with him as his guide. A short way out of camp a small steenbok dashed across our path, and before I could even cock my gun, Miller had already brought it down with one perfect heart shot. He was not such a braggart after all, but it could have been beginners luck. The steenbok wasn't big enough to feed everyone, so I sent it back to camp with the gun bearer to prepare it for their supper. They usually provided their own—I didn't worry about them, but they showed more cooperation with a gift of meat. It certainly would help if I was to take them on the lion hunt. So we proceeded to the spot on our own where I had last encountered the gemsbok.

Near the spot where the herd was grazing, there were three large anthills, six to eight feet tall. It provided us with a perfect lookout. I scrambled up one and motioned to Miller to climb on the other anthill. It would be sad if we stampeded the herd before we could even get one shot off. The wind was in our favor and the herd suspected nothing. I could hear contentedly *kge ... gehh* snorting sounds coming from the other side where they were gazing. Peeping over the top, I saw a small group that had separated from the larger herd, plucking at the tender new shoots of maboekie grass. It would afford us a perfect shot. I looked over to where Miller was supposed to be, but he was not there. The next moment he was up beside me, and whispered "snake." I understood because it was a favorite place for snakes to hang out. For a few moments we sat there staring at the peaceful scene. I felt almost sorry to disrupt the herd, let alone take one of their lives. Miller, intent to prove himself the better shot, shrugged his shoulders, lifted his gun to his shoulder, and took aim. Before he pulled the trigger he whispered to me with a smirk, "Like shooting ducks at the carnival!"

Suddenly there were a few snorts of alarm, eyes wild, and bodies a quiver. They perked their ears, listening and looking.

"Dammed, they must have heard us," I whispered. I noticed, though, that their attention wasn't focused on us, but on some bushes to their right. Then seeing nothing, they relaxed, lowered their heads again, and continued eating.

The leopard stalking the herd was hungry; he had been watching them and biding his time. He crouched low. With the wind blowing toward us, also watching the herd, the leopard was unaware of our presence just as the herd was unaware of us, and Miller and me, of the leopard. Inch by inch he slunk forward, belly touching the ground, muscles tucked into the shoulder blades, ready for the pounce.

With the herd again calmed down, Miller selected one to his taste, and lifted his gun. At that very moment the leopard jumped! Miller turned his gun on the new target; the shot rang out. The leopard staggered into the bush. The herd milled around for a few seconds, then spooked, and took off. There was a strange silence as the sound of the hooves died down. Except for Miller, who was shouting at the top of his lungs. "I GOT HIM! I got him! Let's go get him!" He was beside himself with excitement.

The leopard, unaware of where the stinging pain had come from, darted into the bush. Near the spot where Miller had shot the leopard, there was indeed blood on the grass where it disappeared. He wasn't dead, but certainly wounded; how badly or how little was anybody's guess.

"You got him all right! But nobody's going to 'get him,' at least no one in their right mind goes after a wounded leopard with night approaching!" I warned Miller.

"You're a coward!" Miller said sarcastically.

"No, just cautious. I know the nature of nocturnal animal behavior, and going after a wounded one would be suicide."

"I still say you're a coward!" Miller continued.

I took the ribbing in good humor. "You may call me what you will, but I have seen too many deaths of people putting on a show of bravery for the sake of others or to satisfy their own ego. There is a fine dividing line between logical bravery and cowardice, and I'm no coward!"

Ignoring Miller, I headed back to the camp. On the way I tried to explain the implications of his deed, but all he did was laugh.

"Coward! Coward! Coward!" he sang.

The sun was behind us, hovering over the horizon, and for one last glorious display painted everything with bold strokes of gold. Perfect for a waiting leopard to hide himself. Birds who quieted down for the sun's descent now started up their squawking again, fighting over bedding down for the night. And warning us about impending danger!

Miller kept up his mumbling and pouted like a naughty boy who had been reprimanded because he could not have a certain toy. To appease him I promised. "We'll go out and track him in the morning." As the golden shadows turned to dark menacing shadows, I began to see leopards behind every bush, rock, and clump of grass. A wounded animal often back-tracked his aggressor against the wind and pounced in revenge.

I was glad to be back in camp; the fires were already lit. Miller immediately blurted out the story of the hunt, and of wounding a leopard.

"And would you believe it? He turned coward and wouldn't allow me to go flush it out!" He turned to his wife. "Darling, and what a great coat that would have made you!"

His wife, who had been sampling the malala beer the whole afternoon, giggled, threw her arms around him and said drunkenly, "Letsh go get him, honey."

Turning away from them in disgust, I went to have dinner with my family in the communal hut. Two hours later when I went to join the others round the camp fire, Miller and some of the bearers he had bribed were gone. So was his wife.

"The idiot has gone after the leopard!" the others informed me. They said he had been drinking heavily from his own private stock, resented my interference, and determined to get what was due him, claiming the leopard as his.

I was furious. Now the idiot, no, the drunk idiot, and his equally drunk high-heeled silk-clad wife and bribed bearers—who would run off at the first opportunity with the backup guns, were out there in the jungle with torches to "go get the leopard" while it in turn most likely was stalking them.

The hour of sharing at the water hole was over. It was night. Night was made to kill or be killed. I felt like saying to hell with them, but they were in my camp and I was unfortunately indirectly responsible for them. Now I would have to go out there and risk my own life for them.

When I caught up with them, they were laughing and joking as if they were out for a moonlight stroll in some city park. As I had predicted, there was no sign of the bearers, who knew the bush and its dangers and had turned back almost immediately.

"What a dumb thing to do, bribing the bearers! And endangering your wife! And if you're still convinced I'm a coward, I invite you to go with me after the leopard in the morning, without tracking dogs, and now due to your folly without the bearers as well. Just you and I. And if I show any signs of cowardice, you can shoot me!"

He was suddenly sober, realizing what a fool he had been, but not wanting to look foolish he said, "You're on!"

"I'm coming, too. I can't miss out on getting a real live leopard skin coat!" I don't know what annoyed me most. Her lack of feelings or her appearance. This painted woman thought that this was a game, and any time Tarzan would be swinging through the trees if danger was imminent. She had obviously not understood a word. I was rude, but I didn't care!

"NO! This is no game we're playing, we're not in a zoo, these are wild animals! You could have been killed tonight. A wounded animal seeks only revenge and is a deadly force to contend with!"

We walked back in silence. They were made aware that danger was lurking everywhere. They didn't say anything further, perhaps realizing the severity of their senseless action. Like children caught with their hands in the cookie jar. Back in camp, they slunk off to bed.

"We leave at five!" I shouted. I heard him mumble something to his wife as they entered their tent to justify his actions.

I wouldn't be surprised if he doesn't turn up at all in the morning, I thought. I was tired and hoped that I would fall asleep quickly, but sleep evaded me. I found myself tossing and turning throughout the night. A strange premonition gripped my heart in a vice, chilling me to the core. I tried to shrug off the fear that accompanied it. Tried desperately to think of other things and fall asleep, but still sleep evaded me almost till an hour before morning when I finally fell into a fitful sleep halfway between waking, tiring me even more.

Was it morning yet? I listened for the birds' morning songs and for the rest of the camp's waking, but none was up yet. Not even Crombi, who was always up at dawn preparing breakfast for the guests. My eyes felt scratchy and raw from lack of sleep. The cot felt unusually lumpy and uncomfortable. The sheets clung sticky and damp with perspiration to my body from my tossing and turning. It was no use lying in bed.

My body refused to move, but I decided to get up anyway, got dressed, fumbling with the leather leggings, but ever since the incident with the snake, it became a ritual. I kissed my sleeping wife and kids and walked to Miller's tent. There was heavy dew on the grass; I reckoned it would have washed away the tracks. I was about to call out, when I spotted him by the fire. He had stoked the logs that were still glowing from last night's fires, made some coffee in the blue enamel pot, and was drinking a steaming cup.

I obviously had underestimated the man's enthusiasm. He looked fresh and well rested, as if the previous night had never taken place. Even gave me a cheerful greeting.

"Ready when you are!" He definitely didn't have the same night that I had. Cool as a cucumber he stood in front of me in a new khaki safari suit, less blearing than the white one, but still more suitable for a fashion shoot. The pleats in the shorts looked freshly pressed. The jacket was personally monogrammed with his initials and partly unbuttoned, showing a pale hairless chest. He had forsaken the helmet, instead on his head he wore a tropical soft brim hat, left over from some tropic island excursion. I burst out laughing.

"Are you planning that the leopard laugh himself to death?" It relieved the tension.

"Hey, don't laugh at my hat, just call it my good luck hat!" he explained in good humor.

We certainly looked like the odd couple. I wore well-worn khakis, with leather leggings. Mara's knitted scarf was round my neck, a safeguard against snakes dropping from the trees. I had my shirt fully buckled against the sting of insects. And I even wore a tie, being on active duty. In contrast to his office-white skin, I was dark-leather tanned. My helmet had an inside leather strap to provide me cooling and prevent heat exhaustion.

I poured myself a mug of coffee, took a few sips. Anxious to be on the way before the sun was fully out, I put it down.

"Come let's go! If we're lucky he bled to death, and we could be back before breakfast. If he is still alive, let's surprise the damn cat!"

The dew had not washed away everything, which I half expected. We picked up the blood trail beyond a clump of mapani bushes near the ant hill where we saw the leopard disappear into the bushes the night before. Tiny drops of coagulated blood clung to the bent wet grass. About fifty paces further, the grass was flattened where he had rested to lick his wound. We found our own tracks of the previous night's drunken folly crossing over the leopard's.

Three prints were heavy and the fourth back leg had soft imprints with an occasional trickle of blood. From this I deduced that it was the hind leg that was wounded. Farther on his prints crossed over ours, which showed that he had followed us almost back to the camp, but then it branched off. We found two sets of tracks—it looked puzzling, but a wounded animal often walked in circles, crossing its own tracks. The circles widened, leaving the tracker confused. I just knew that whichever track we took the leopard would have the advantage on us. It was like playing Russian roulette. We didn't know which side of the gun was loaded. I tossed a coin and Miller took the set of prints that led up the dry river bed; he was convinced that he had the real set of tracks, and the leopard would be his.

I got the one going into the bush where the track was the fresher of the two. I knew already I had drawn the suicidal deal; there were unlimited hiding places for the leopard in the bush. At this stage, the mongrel dogs from the nearby kraal would have been an advantage; they would have gone in and flushed the leopard into the open, and it would have been easy to shoot it. But I had made that foolish choice and did not even take Jock, my own companion dog. The only suggestion was that we track it to where the blood drops became fresh and then shoot off a warning shot and meet up to continue tracking it to where it came to rest for the night and finish it off.

I started off on my elected trail and already missed Jock; he had gotten his name from a book that had recently appeared on the market. He wasn't a bull terrier like in the book, but he was very good at tracking and very brave when confronting danger. He always made me feel safe. I was carrying a .22 hunting rifle with reload action. I immediately cocked and loaded it, so that it was ready for the first shot, just in case. I need only lift, sight, and shoot, should he jump me right then.

I wondered how Miller was making out? As for me, the deeper I went into the bush the more I felt the same cold sweat of premonition of last night. The leopard must have licked the wound very often, because just here and there were indications of the path he took. A few fresh drops of blood on some fallen leaves, and some on some dry grass. The wound must have opened up again with all the walking. Here the bush was beginning to be almost impenetrable, but traces of him resting were evident in the flattened underbrush. I became aware of the unnatural silence around me. Where were the birds? Normally around this time of the morning they were already making a lot of noise. But it was a deadly silent. Gripped by the sudden fear, my finger automatically crept to the trigger. Should I fire the warning shot that I was close to the leopard? Miller surely will think me a coward then, should I be wrong and just acting on my fear. I put the safety back on. The faint click sounded like thunder in the strange silence.

Pushing the foliage out of my way with the gun barrel, I suddenly stepped into a large clearing. The yellow earth was hard packed with loose black and white gravel rocks spread around. Every few yards there were large sandstone boulders eight to ten feet high. They stood like silent witnesses with clumps of dried yellow grass at their bases like a scene from some forbidden planet, and not the bush I loved and protected. Around the boulders a wall of jungle rose like a wall, surrounding the forbidden open space like an arena that awaited the show to begin.

The tracks led right into the arena, loose gravel crunched under my boots as I walked into the center disturbing the eerie silence. I was full of apprehension. Up to now the track continued to tell a tale of small details. Then vanished! He could be anywhere; in this setting there were a thousand possibilities where a wounded leopard could conceal himself. My blood ran cold, and I lifted my gun to my shoulder. Should he come out of the wall of bush, or from behind the clumps of grass, or from behind the boulders, I would be ready for him. My finger on the trigger trembled with anticipation. I felt like a thousand eyes were looking on in the jungle wall, waiting with bated breath for the drama to take place.

On a large boulder in the center of the arena the leopard crouched, hence the disappearing trick. His hind leg hurt madly the whole night. No amount of licking had eased the throbbing pain. Now right below him stood his mortal enemy, man! His hair bristled on his back. His muscles contracted, ready for the pounce, and sweet revenge.

Battle to Stay Alive

There was no trace of the cat. I could turn around and go and get the dogs. *SHOW YOURSELF!* I thought, not realizing I had actually shouted it.

Triggered by the shout, the cat leaped directly from ABOVE me! I heard a guttural sound, turned swiftly around, expecting him to come from behind the boulder and not from above. The impact blow of the three-hundred-pound leopard knocked me over, the gun went off with my finger still on the trigger, the shot went wild. The force was so hard that my helmet cracked, but saved me from losing consciousness. In a horrifying second the leopard was on top of me, the angry amber eyes flashed KILL! His claws ripped into the bush jacket, looking for a hold. His nails went through the cloth and into my flesh as hot as hell. From the corner of my eye I noticed my gun laying a mere foot away from me. If I made a grab for it, I could at least use it as a club against my attacker, but I would have to get on top of him. I tried to get out from under him. The gravel, embedded into the flesh wounds caused by his claws, dug deeper. I was aware of a detached kind of pain, but more aware of my survival, cutting off the thoughts of pain. Grabbing onto the loose fur around his neck, I struggled for supremacy. I didn't know where he left off and I began, we were so entwined—flesh and fur had become one. Inches from my face his gaping mouth dripped stinking warm saliva. My eyes were riveted on the three-inch, sharp-as-a-dagger yellow teeth, his foul breath coming in rasping sounds warm over me. I got free for a moment, grabbed the gun, and kneeling next to him swung with all my might. The leopard curled away and the gun butt splintered into several pieces as it hit against a rock and not my target. This made the leopard more angry. I fought with fury to keep the flaying claws from hitting flesh. And his mouth from reaching my throat. My head turned aside for a second, and at that very second he made a grab for my throat, an instinctive move. Larger prey were usually strangled, and in smaller prey the throat was torn out, affording an instant death. I got hold of his ears and pulled his head away, but the incredible strength in his neck pulled forward and muscular jaws clamped down on my collar bone. I heard a sickening cracking sound as his jaws closed. Then suddenly he let go. A bilious vomit welled up in my throat, and automatically expelled over his fur, mingling with the other smells. There was no time to think, no time for strategy, no time for pain! I was acting on pure instinct, and the need for survival. The leopard had momentarily let go to try again for my throat. His healthy hind leg was scratching at my legging trying to get a foothold. Then it found its mark and dug into the calf muscle of my leg just above my legging, where it got stuck. Still holding onto its ears, I tried to keep his mouth away from my throat.. With my free left hand, I tried to knock him out. At such close proximity I had little leverage. My blows to his head became just an irritant and hardly effective. My fist slipping in his drool ended up in his open jaw. He bit down on it, and kept chewing, right through the hand. I heard the sickening sound, like a dog chewing on bones. It was a scene from HELL! Frothy red bubbles came from his mouth. I pulled my hand or what I expected was left of it, out of his mouth, and saw to my amazement that it still had fingers on! The left side was now totally out of action, and hung limp, blood pulsing out of the hand. It oozed out of the shoulder, coloring the bush jacked crimson, which was already in shreds. The collarbone, in my effort to knock him out, had snapped and a point of the bone stuck through the skin like a cork, stopping the blood flow temporarily.

My mind was delirious with rage, the adrenaline pumping orders were coming in fast and furious. Logic said; He strangles his prey, this is MY only chance, too. His left leg was wounded, his right leg imbedded into my calf. If I want to live, I would have to do it now. My right hand that had a grip on his ear slipped down to his windpipe. I held him down with my right knee in his chest. I squeezed with all my might down on the windpipe and on the chest, trying to cut off his air supply. A rumbling sound came from his throat as he struggled to free my vice-like grip.

"GOOD!" I shouted. My thumb dug in deeper. I squeezed harder. The leopard's breath came in wheezes. He was feeling what he usually did to his victims. I was strangling it, slowly … too slowly! I started worrying about how long I could last. I applied every ounce of my strength. As my hold increased, his trapped claw in my left calf muscle dug in deeper. I had no time for pain. This only renewed my strangling grip on his throat.

After what seemed never ending, but was only minutes in time, I could feel the leopard's breath weakening. HE IS DYING! flashed through my tired brain. For the first time I felt the pain throbbing through me, I was one big trembling HURT! And then also for the first time I thought about Miller. Did he hear the shot that went off accidentally? Had he given up and returned to camp? MY HAND STARTED CRAMPING! … Not now! Not now! I prayed.

"Die, you bastard!" I shouted in the terrible nightmare zone. There was an echo, "Die you bastard!" It sounded far away, it was unreal, but sounded familiar—my God it was my own voice!

Below me there was little movement. The wheezing had turned to a death rumble. I thought of my oath to 'protect endangered species' and here I was killing one without mercy. Then reason took over. *Was I not the endangered specie at this moment?* And was this not self defense? Surely it was him or me, and he had his turn.

I could feel my grip weakening; there was a small pool of blood forming on the ground. It was fascinating. Red and glistening like a ruby. But if I for a moment let up on my guard, small gulps of air entered his lungs.

My ears began to ring, a cold numb feeling crept up the back of my neck. "God I can't faint now!" *I have failed.* I shook my head. *You can't faint now, you can't faint now,* I kept telling myself. Logically I should've been dead by now, but the fight for survival and the will to live endures incredible odds. "I'm alive! And I'm going to stay alive!" Then I started talking to the cat. "I can't hold on much longer, you know it's you or I. And I choose to live!" I bent forward and whispered into his ear, "You got to die ... NOW!" I felt the faint coming in waves trying to engulf me. I wasn't going to give in. To give in would spell my death, and I had a wife and children that needed me.

"You got to die now, you gotta-gotta-gotta die now!" I was sobbing, "I can't hold out any longer."

Then I heard another voice quite close by say, "All you got to do now is hold on a little longer!" I wondered, was it me again? Only this time a shadow fell over me and the leopard. A gun barrel pressed up against the temple of the leopard. There was a click of the trigger, and total silence followed and not the explosion I was expecting.

And there was the voice again. "Don't let go now, my gun jammed, and I have to reload."

I couldn't understand. "Why don't you shoot?" After what seemed hours the gun barrel was placed inside the leopard's ear. This time the shot rang out like a cannon right through the leopard's brain. I felt the body beneath me jerk spasmodically, then go limp. Even at that moment I didn't believe that it was finally over.

Millers' voice came gently to my ear. "*Now*, you can let go!" It didn't make sense, I couldn't let go! He dug the claws out of my calf, and pried my fingers one by one off the leopard's throat, which held on like a vice, even though my body had finally succumbed to the peace of the faint, which blocked out pain for the moment.

Later, much later, after six months in a coma in a hospital in Johannesburg, Miller told me the rest of the story, and Mara had to fill me in on what happened in the hospital.

Miller told me he had heard the shot, but the trail he was on was very confusing. He lost his way several times and had to backtrack; it seemed the cat had walked in circles. He then went back to where we had tossed the coin and followed the track that I had taken. When he entered the arena, he half expected to find me with a dead leopard and a big smile on my face. Instead he found me kneeling on top of the leopard wild-eyed, delirious, strangling it, my body and clothes ripped to shreds. I was covered in blood, and a small pool of blood had formed on the ground from the wounds on my left side. A bone stuck out of my left shoulder, and the left hand and wrist was chewed into a bloody crimson mess. His greatest shock came when he tried to shoot the leopard and the gun jammed. After he killed the leopard, he stood there for a few seconds, not knowing what to do next. I clung to the throat in a death grip after I collapsed. He then pushed the collarbone back in position and with the tie I wore, made a tourniquet for the worst bleeding, and with the shirt that looked so out of place that morning, he ripped it up and made pressure bandages for the rest. I was blissfully not aware of this.

Then he thought, *How the hell can I get this bleeding six-foot-three, two-hundred-pound man back to camp?* If he left him there to go for help, the blood would draw other predators that would finish him off. He looked up and could already see the vultures spiraling above them. He would have to make some kind of conveyor. He hastily pulled some thorn branches over the leopard carcass, and searched for three long pieces of wood that would support my weight and something that he could use to tie it together. He had read a few books about American Indian migrations where they made biers to convey their property dragged by their horses; he didn't have a horse handy, but he could pull it. Stripping some bark from the branches, he tied it into a triangle with a few cross pieces for body support and his conveyor was complete. He then placed it next to me and rolled me onto it. Then stepping into the tip of the triangle, he started dragging me. He was amazed at how easy it went and soon he entered the camp, where pandemonium broke out. The only ones who kept their cool were Mara and Crombi. She poured a quart of disinfectant into the water of the zinc bath warming in the sun. They lifted me into it while Crombi heated his spear point, and while I was unconscious, he cauterized most of the smaller wounds with the red hot spear point, while Mara did some stitching to the larger wounds. He then took some bearers to retrieve the leopard skin. When he got back I was all bandaged up and strapped to a camp cot. Crombi had set the drums up and was sending a message out to the other kraals for help along the way. Then the runners started off in a slow gallop to the connection point where the supply trucks usually brought our camp supplies. It was a good 100 miles. Like the Pony Express, at every kraal along the way that received the drum message of their coming, they switched with fresh runners. Miller stayed with them all the way, resting only at the connect points. He told me he did it because he felt guilty. Lucky for me the supply trucks had come early and were already camped out, waiting for our camp to collect our rations. When I arrived, they put me in the truck and raced me to a small town called Waterpoort, where there was a railway line for cattle transportation The cattle were already loaded and were going out in minutes when they got the word to hold up the train for a badly mauled man, who needed to get to a hospital in a hurry. The next stop for unloading the cattle was at Germiston where there was a clinic. Here they checked me out and shook their heads. They didn't have the equipment or the skills to treat me. So they loaded me, together with a doctor, Mara, and the kids, who had arrived in the meantime on a waiting train, for the five-hundred-mile journey to Johannesburg.

Here Mara continued the story for me:

"The doctor on the train was unable to do much but monitor your progress, redress the wounds, and set up a blood transfusion to keep you alive. He had little hope that you would make it alive, so he just kept you comfortable. Arriving in Johannesburg, they rushed you to the hospital with screaming sirens. But here the doctors also shook their heads; they had never seen anything like that and after looking at the multiple wounds, they told me that you would expire soon if they did not amputate. The limbs had turned blue and were swollen to giant proportions. The other wounds required a thousand stitches, but that was no concern. They told me, 'You see we have no option, the bones in his hand are totally destroyed and the ligaments are all severed, the collarbone has several fractures, which we have set the best we could, but where the nails tore the calf muscle of the left leg, the wounds show signs of turning gangrenous.' They handed me the papers to sign for the removal of both limbs. I took one look at them and tore them to shreds. You were strong, proof was that you made it up to then, so I told them, 'You see I have no option but to refuse. I'm sure if he was able to talk for himself, he would not want to lose his limbs and would rather die. So do what you can for him. I'm not signing, sorry!' They could not understand my refusal, and I could not explain my decision to you because you were in a coma, but I knew that would have been your decision also. For weeks they did nothing except lay the effected limbs in a saline solution in a metal trough, and gave me a cot in the room adjoining the intensive ward so that I could be near you when the inevitable happened. But you survived!

"The hospital held meeting after meeting about the improbability of your still being alive and then handed you over to a young intern—Doctor Green, who took on the challenge to do something about the patient that everyone had given up on. Mainly to boost his own career."

When he first went to see his new patient, he also shook his head and wondered why he had taken on the challenge, but when he saw Mara's concern, he knew the sickening smell coming from the troughs was not the answer. He had the troughs immediately removed, opened and cleaned out the wounds that were spear-point cauterized and stitched by Mara, and took scores of X-rays to show the extent of the bone fractures. He got a supportive team together and they set to work to correct the damage.

The X-rays showed several fractures including a clean break that was clumsily pushed together at the scene by Miller. This would never heal unless the bone had a support. He consulted a 'plumber' friend of his to see if it was possible to open up a copper rod and clamp it around the still intact but fragmented bone to heal. And also to place a plate in the left hand wrist where the bones were lost, then sew the ligaments that were severed, which would enable the fingers to still work, as the fingers still miraculously had most of their bones intact. The leopard's teeth had only pulverized the wrist and hand bones.

"When he explained his plans in detail to me," Mara recounted, "I was overjoyed. I didn't know if you could hear me, but I explained it all to you, and even though you were in a coma I know you would have been pleased. He also explained that the wounds had become infected through the sudden closure of the wounds, and reopening them and cleaning them properly they had a better chance of healing than the monstrous methods they had used before. The left leg where the leopard had imbedded his claw to control his prey had multiple gashes, the deepest had almost shredded the; calf muscles, but they were carefully repaired. He also planned to take skin from the inside of your inner thigh to restructure the hand when the rest of the repairs had been done, by cutting a flab and putting the hand inside, suturing it onto the hand, like a living craft. He said, 'You understand what I plan to do is mostly experimental and I will have to have your permission to go ahead with the procedures.' This time I signed the papers readily. You would have bionic implants but you would be intact. These were papers of reconstruction and not destruction. The young Doctor Green had performed all the miracles of reconstruction and bone crafting. Still you stayed in a coma, as if the body had gone into stasis to help it recover from the traumatic encounter with the leopard. Still he believed that, too, would pass, and you would come out of it. He started to encourage me to bring the children to see you, to speed up the process of your awakening.

"The shock was that you did not recognize the children or even open your eyes."

When Mom first took Ethel and me to see Daddy, he had lost a lot of weight and we hardly recognized him; with all the paraphernalia around him we were actually afraid of him. Mom in turn could not understand our indifference. But it took something else to awaken Dad from the long coma, it was like the proverbial "hair of the dog that bit you," only this was the leopard that bit you. The real miracle happened one day when Miller showed up. His dress code had not changed one iota, but as a joke he wore the same clothes, minus the shirt, of course, that he sacrificed to make bandages. And on his head he wore the tropical 'lucky hat.' He also brought the clothes Dad wore on the fateful day, which his wife had stitched together with black thread. There were hundreds of rips; it looked like patchwork. He carried a mysterious package under his arm, which he immediately started unwrapping. Out poured the leopard skin.

"Hey, you can let go now! WAKE UP COWARD! I brought you a present!" He hadn't seen Alex since the day of the attack. He could see the man had gone through Hell and back, and felt guilty because he was indirectly responsible.

Slowly Dad's eyes opened and looked in wonder at us. "What happened with the leopard?" Not with a glazed look that did not recognize us, but fully cognitive, yet unaware of his surroundings.

"Mara, where am I?" Mom was ecstatic, he was out of the coma!

"My love, you have been near death, but it is over now. You are in a hospital in Johannesburg. You have been in a coma for the past six months while Doctor Green repaired you. Welcome back to the living! We have been here for you." She bent down and kissed him passionately as she had done for the past six months. Only this time he felt it!

Dad looked at Miller, "You haven't changed a bit, still wearing the hat? I want to hear all about it. The last thing I remember was sitting on top of the cat trying to strangle it with my bare hands, and then your gun misfiring."

"You mean cat?" He spread the skin over Dad; it was beautifully cured, with head still attached.

"I went back and found the carcass still intact where I had covered it over with thorn branches, and one of the bearers skinned it for me. I of course claimed it for myself, but you fought for it and it really belongs to you. As for what happened after that, your wife would be able to tell you. You're a lucky man to still have all your limbs, thanks to her. She refused to have them amputate your arm and leg. She is a remarkable woman!"

Dad touched the softness of the fur; it looked so much smaller than the terrible fury he battled with to stay alive. He stuck his finger through the bullet hole in the head, which ended his agony, and then into the hole in the left hind leg, that started the whole thing. He suddenly looked very thoughtful.

Miller took his 'lucky' tropical hat off his own head and placed it on Dad's head.

"Perhaps you should have been wearing it instead of me. I really came to apologize for my behavior. I'm sorry, man! from the bottom of my heart! I feel responsible, but I'm glad you survived the ordeal. You are in fact the bravest man I've ever come across. But you owe me. I went there to bag a lion, so you better hurry up and get well because you'll have to take me back to fulfill my dream!"

Dad laughed for the first time, and he looked at Miller. The man looked pathetic.

"I forgive you, but I think my career is over. I'm going to find myself a softer job." Just then Doctor Green walked in. He was delighted to see his patient was finally awake, laughing with the silliest tropical hat on his head. And the skin of the leopard that caused all the damage, draped across him. He introduced himself to Dad.

"I always believed that you would make it! You have a strong heart and constitution. Now the battle is half won. It was a long six months of touch and go. Now comes another six months of intensive therapy, and its success is entirely up to you!" He handed Dad a regular tennis ball and said, "Squeeze!"

That was the beginning of the therapy; it was as inventive as his treatment.

And so it was that three months later Daddy was out of the hospital. Walking on the leg they wanted to amputate because it was gangrenous, and using the fingers of the arm they saw no hope for and wanted to amputate. The plate in the hand and the metal pipes in his shoulder did not bother him at all. He joked that he was the first bionic man and would never get arthritis. And Mom was eternally grateful to a young intern who did not write him off, but saw him as a challenge.

13

Back to Civilization —— Culture Shock

During Dad's prolonged stay in the hospital after the leopard's mauling, Aunt Lena's guest rondavel (round hut) became our temporary accommodation. When circumstances beyond our control dumped us back into civilization. The word *civilization* is defined in the dictionary as 'a people who are urbane, cultured, polite and refined.'

Mom had commuted by train during the week between Pretoria North and Johannesburg when Daddy lay in a coma, and to her bush-babies on weekends to help us in our induction to city life. Determined to turn her two rough stones into diamonds, she enrolled us into everything cultural. I was tossed out the first week of piano lessons, because the teacher said I was incorrigible and in her opinion could not be tamed. Besides, I dirtied her pianos ivory keys, because I was either up her trees or digging up her garden As for elocution lessons, I simply refused to come out from under the bed where I escaped to with one of Charlie's daughters who was sent to us to learn the white man's ways. People frightened me with their city ways, which were far from cultured, refined, and polite. Mabalel was in total culture shock. Knowing only her native language of Mavenda, she could not speak to anyone or understand anyone except the kitchen-Mavenda we all had picked up in the bush. We both longed for the music of the animals and the veld. The closest we came to that simplicity was the circular shape of the rondavel (round hut)and its rough ceiling poles and thatching.

Mabalel was away from her tribe and familiar faces. She hated to wear the things called clothes. They itched and scratched, restricted her movements, and smothered her innocent body that had up to then, known nothing but naked freedom, warm sun, and beads. She could not understand why her father had given her away. Her tribe was gone. She missed the stories round the cooking fires, and her twenty brothers and sisters from her father's other wives. She even missed the water carrying chores, which she hated. She only knew what her birth mother had explained to her: that she was to go to Bwana Mokulu's kraal and learn many things, which she would bring back to teach her brothers and sisters.

She knew many things taught to her by the elders, and she knew that she did not like the new world. It was full of strange magic. The sun came up inside the hut whenever you wanted it; you need only touch a small berry on the wall. It was captured inside a small bubble that looked like water but could turn the darkness into light. Outside on a very broad and long footpath within the new kraal with many strange huts there ran things called cars with round legs that ran as fast as a cheetah. Along the broad footpath stood very tall, branchless trees with the same magic that turned night into day.

She wanted to die! She thought if she held her breath long enough it would work. But it always failed. If she could only cry enough, the bush spirits would come and get her and take her back in the belly of the big rumbling snake that puffed smoke and brought her to the other world.

When she cried, I cried with her, and we clung together like my Boggom babies did to me when they were separated from their troops. My latest baboon was tied up to a pole in the back yard, because Aunt Lena said it was too dangerous for me to play with and wouldn't allow it in her rondavel. Mabalel and I retreated to a safe place, under the kitchen table or under the bed. Car horns and street lights were more frightening to me than lions' roar, or stampeding elephant.

Mom sometimes would crawl under the bed with me and in the cool half dark try and tell me about all the wonderful things I would be able to learn in school and the many friends I would make. I did not like the word *school*. It might as well have been called 'confinement.' Sis had already gone to school at Alldays, but I remember she got very sick and very thin, and they thought she had malaria. But I also remembered her crying in the night when it got time to go back to school, and I remembered the marks on her body when we went swimming. And Daddy taking her out of that school and putting her into a school in Waterpoort, because he suspected that she was being abused at Alldays boarding school. So she was enrolled in school as soon as we arrived in Pretoria North, and I missed her because she was at school most of the day, and I could not play with her.

Daddy taught me to be humble in the face of nature's greatness and to respect all living animals. But here the trees grew behind other people's fences, and I was not allowed to climb them. And the only animals that I saw were the two vicious Doberman pinschers that Aunt Lena kept chained up in the yard, keeping them away from people, and nobody could touch because they had even more vicious temperaments than the leopard that bit my Daddy. They attacked Mom one day because she wanted to pet them, but instead had to defend herself from an attack with an opened umbrella. I classified them as brothers to the hyena.

I missed my Daddy. The few times Sis and I had been to the hospital, he did not know us because he was in a coma. It was like sleeping, Mom explained. He smelled funny because of his festering wounds, and he couldn't talk. Since then I never wanted to go back there. But Mom came back one week and explained that a miracle had happened, and Daddy awoke from the long sleep and was coming back to us within the week. I didn't believe her, how could he come back to us if he didn't know us? She explained that he was the same Daddy I always knew, a little thinner perhaps, and with some marks the leopard left behind as a reminder of their encounter.

I remember seeing him come up the garden path at Aunt Lena's. He was so handsome. He had lost a lot of weight and was clean shaven; often at the hospital they had neglected to shave him. He looked like the portrait we had of him in his police uniform as young man. Only now he was dressed as a civilian. He had on a black and white herringbone sports jacket, with charcoal slacks, and a black sling. He limped a bit, but Mom was right—he was well again. For a while longer we would have to endure one-armed hugs, but his lap was always available to cuddle on, and he knew us!

The first thing he did was get an escort for Mabalel and sent her back to her family. The second thing was he took one look at the cramped place we were in and told Mom. "We are going out house hunting!" As an after thought, "Today!"

Two blocks from Aunt Lenie and two blocks the opposite direction from the school and a general store, we found a house with a 'FOR SALE' sign. It also included an adjoining property, which had a small dam with a water pump. And a water well, which had to be hand operated.

It was love at first sight, and amazingly cheap. The only drawback was that it had a outhouse instead of indoor plumbing. But coming from the bush, to us that was considered a luxury not to be constantly digging your own hole.

There was nothing outstanding about the house, and it looked small at first sight, but it had character as Dad put it. And to our surprise, it had ample space. It was a long building running almost the full length of the property toward the back, giving it the appearance of being small. The front door was slap bang in the middle of the front wall, on either side it had a large window with half shutters that looked like two sleepy eyes. The front section pyramid roof had an extended piece over the front porch, and a large potted fuchsia hung from the porch overhang on either side, giving it an appearance of curly hair coming out of a cap.

Mom stood back toward the gate, already planning her garden. She was pleased with the added touch of fuchsias, her favorite.

"Yes, I like it!" Dad said.

"And I like its face, too!" Mom said.

The Realtor led us through the open mouth door. A long passage ran the entire length of the house from the front door to the back door onto a back porch. As we entered we counted four bedrooms, two on either side of the passage, then a larger one doubling as dining sitting room, also a large eat in kitchen with a big friendly black iron stove. Leading off the porch were two more rooms. One as guest room and the other was a bathroom in progress but not completed, because street planning did not provide for indoor toilet facilities. The outhouse stood in the backyard next to a corrugated iron shack that Mom said reminded her of the place where I was born.

Street lights were just put in a month earlier and the house had electricity, the agent told Dad. While they walked toward the dam, he explained that the former owner used the little dam for fish breeding and could be used if Dad wanted to start an orchard and garden. He turned the pump on and a clear stream of water came pouring in. "A fresh underground stream provides the well water. The added property of course is an option, and comes with an addition to the quoted price."

To Dad, who had been dying to start an orchard and garden, this wasn't an option, it was a must! "Where do I sign?"

Days later we moved in with just the basic necessities. While Mom concentrated on furnishing the house, Dad started clearing the overgrown second property to start his garden. It was while he was busy with this that Kondoweh arrived. Charlie was determined that one of his children should come to live with us, and he sent one of his sons named Kondoweh in exchange for Mabalel.

Kondoweh was a magnificent specimen of African manhood—about twenty-five years old, blue black in color, with four raised scars on either cheek, and V shaped dotted scars on the strong calves of his legs—a trophy in recognition of his excellence as a tribal stick fighter. He stood proud and muscular like a black panther. He didn't like clothes either, but was proud to wear Dad's old khakis and bush jacket. Unlike his little sister, he thrived on the excitement of the lights and new ways of the city, but he also reminded us of the jungle and the life we were forced to leave behind. And we loved him as a brother of another time. He played games with Ethel and me, and even inspired me to go to school by piggybacking me there every day. He didn't want to eat with us, so Dad got him the necessary cooking gear, and he made his fire behind the coal shed and prepared his meals there. But Mom insisted that he sleep in the vacant room on the back porch, where she put a cot and table and fixed it up for him. Dad gave him a minimum salary, his food, schooling, and weekends off.

Besides working with Dad to plant the peach and apple orchard, he helped with the upkeep of the house. He loved to polish the wide, smooth as silk, red verandah at the front and back of the house to a mirror finish; it became Kondoweh's pride. Ethel and I used to take our shoes off and skate across it in our socks. When it rained it would amuse us for hours. Large rain puddles formed on the high gloss surface, and didn't evaporate or run off. The fuchsias reflected in each drop, causing an upside down garden. We then traced our fingers through the puddles playing connect-the-dots till we had a larger mirrored garden. Then we scooped them all together till it made a big reflecting pool in which we could see our faces. Then we made ugly faces to see who could make the ugliest.

After the limited space in our African mud hut, the house seemed like a palace with its many rooms. Mom was very house-proud and took immense pride in furnishing it, "With real furniture," she loved saying.

The master bedroom was the first room on the left of the hall. The big double brass bed, its brass polished till it gleamed, was a magnificent thing to see. Sis had helped Daddy to bid for it at an auction. It had a pristine white pom pom candlewick bedspread, with Mom's own crocheted shams on the pillows. In the one corner, Mom's large brown sailor's chest stood. It held her special linens and mementos. Also, her secret love letters tied with a ribbon and the family photos in a flat heart shaped can with a picture of Lord

Kitchener on the lid, some of our sentimental baby clothes, and the few pieces of jewelry she possessed from her past. Things we were only allowed to touch in her presence. In the other corner of the room stood a hand-carved double wardrobe with a full mirror on the inside of the door, which always scared me when we played hide and seek and I hid in it and saw my own reflection. Next to her bed stood a white candle stand, boasting a white and blue designed candle stick edged with gold, which she still lit in the night out of sheer habit, forgetting that we had the luxury of electricity. Near the front window on a stand with open waterlily bass relief tile backsplash stood a deep dish porcelain washbowl with matching jug and soap dish. Hidden in the inside stood a beautiful matching chamberpot. She never used it except when someone was sick, but it was there just for the show.

A box of powder in a black box with a Spanish lady on the lid with a red dress on that read 'full-nana' or something like that, a small ornament, and a small bottle of Evening in Paris and larger bottle of 4711 Au-de-cologne, and Mom's silver brush and comb on one of her hand-embroidered cloths were the only things that graced her dressing table.

Directly across the master bedroom Sis and I had ours. We each had a single bed with a double drawer, and there was a double mirror dressing table between the beds separating them. On either side of the mirror it had a row of little drawers for our personal stuff, hair ribbons, hankies, and socks. We had a smaller version of the master bedroom's wardrobe, only ours had a drawer below for our undies and no inside mirror.

At the end of the hall opposite the kitchen was the dining room, seldom used except on Sundays and when company came. The most impressive feature of this room was its elegant simplicity. Also, the giant Queen Ann table that could be changed with sliding panels to seat at least fifteen people. The second piece of furniture was a sideboard carefully selected to match the table. It had plenty of room for the newly acquired china and silverware, plus a few secret compartments where the best crystal and other valuables were kept. Round about Christmas, Daddy kept the imported Madeira, Cape Marsala, crystallized fruits, cheeses, and chocolates in one of these secret compartments. The best of all were his homemade dried fruit twists, masterpieces of dehydrated apple, peaches, and sugar coated dried figs. These goodies were always there, but only came out on special occasions.

In the sitting room there were two love seats, and a low mahogany coffee table covered with a hand crafted Battenburg lace runner on which stood the most spectacular Venetian glass centerpiece. One of Mom's most treasured possessions. This incredible piece had no function except to make everyone nervous and provoke a lot of "Oohs" and "Aahs" from visitors. It had a transparent hollow doughnut shaped pale pink glass bowl base, which was edged with transparent glass ruffled lace. Sprouting from the center were three two foot high trumpet-like lilies edged with the same delicate ruffled glass lace. Twisted around the fluted lily stems were delicate colorless tendrils with pink leaves. To clean this treasure was a hallowed experience. That job was given as a reward and a show of trust on Mom's part. So when it was my turn to clean it, I approached it with the cleaning cloth with held breath and palpitating heart, fearful that even the lightest touch would let it crumble beneath my fingers.

In the corner, quite out of keeping with the rest of the furniture, stood Dad's handmade wing-back Morris chair he had salvaged from our last jungle camp. This old chair held many memories and now stood without pillows or adornments to show off Dad's wood carving skills. Under the window was a red velvet chaise lounge, draped with the leopard skin from his encounter. In the other corner stood a Pembroke table with foldout wings on which stood our gramophone and records, faithful companion on first safari. The titles were ingrained in my memory.

"Did Your Mother Come from Ireland?"On the flip side was "Irish Eyes."
"Man on a Flying Trapeze," flip side " The Donkey Serenade."
"One Has Brown Eyes," flip side "Far Away Places."
"Wagon Wheels," flip side "Beautiful Dreamer."

In a special cover was Dad's opera with Tito Gobbi and a new Italian singer called Mario Lanza. Daddy knew all the songs and often sang them to us. When we had company, Sis and I took turns to wind the handle and put on the records. To stop it from being too loud, we usually stuffed a sock in the voice box to muffle it. But what I always remembered was the look of wonder and amazement when we first played it for Charlie's warriors on safari. On the wall above the gramophone hung a portrait of Grandpa Austin, dressed in his full 'Star of India' Grand Marshall Free Mason outfit of dark-blue velvet coat with gold epaulettes. Across his left shoulder down to the waist a broad off-white taffeta ribbon, which displayed his medallions of his many good deeds toward humanity, ending in a beautiful rosette the color of his and my Dad's eyes, sky blue. Next to him hung Daddy's portrait in his mounted police uniform with helmet and chin strap. Two very handsome men indeed. Opposite the mahogany chair hung a painting of a beautiful waterfall. Daddy would sit in the old Morris and stare at it for hours with a far away look. We all knew it was a special place. We also knew that was where he grew up, but he never talked about it, and there is where the story ended.

The kitchen was the same size as the other rooms. Around the white scrubbed pine table with two long benches and two chairs on each end, we gathered for socializing, had coffee, and family counseling. There we did our homework, and with special guests played snakes and ladders, fiddlesticks, or put puzzles together.

In the winter we sat round the black iron stove to warm up, listening to stories. Or had a book read out loud for all to enjoy, while watching and smelling the food cook.

On rainy days, Mom flipped pancakes or made fat cakes, sprinkling them with cinnamon sugar. My job was to put them in a plate, and cover them over with another plate 'to sweat' I was told. I loved watching Mom's dexterity with the frying pan as she tossed the pancakes up in the air then caught them. I admired her because she never missed!

On Wednesdays and Saturdays, Ethel and I had our bath in front of the glowing stove, without thoughts of modesty, in the same bath that went with us into the jungle. It was quite a production. The water had to be warmed on the stove in gallon drums, we were allowed one bucket each, but that produced very low water line, so we opted putting the two buckets into the bath, and Ethel, who was always the cleanest, had first choice. We all looked forward to seeing the indoor bathroom completed. Mom and Dad took the bath into their room on bath days.

Having unlimited freedom in the bush, I had a hard time adjusting to new rules. I was forever getting in trouble, both in school and at home. Things that I thought were admissible were just not 'done' in the 'civilized' world. In school I would sit on the writing section of my desk to listen to the teacher, or climb the trees in the school yard. I couldn't understand why they wouldn't let me do that because I was a good climber!

Civilization had one bonus, I thought. The movies! Even though Mom was the censor of everything we were allowed to see. Near the highway a billboard advertised the following week's movie. Sis and I would walk there to see what was showing, and if Mom approved we would go. Escaping for an hour or two into the fantasy world of film. If it was a Shirley Temple or a Tarzan movie, we were sure that we would go. But James Cagney, Bella Lugosi, and certain cowboy movies, were far too risky in her estimation. I remember one day coming back from the billboard. It was a sure thing. We had ironed our best dresses and starched our ribbons and got dressed, full of anticipation. It was a risky movie with Janette Mc Donald and Nelson Eddy, in the *Merry Widow*, but it passed because it was a musical and the life story of a composer.

I was determined to look my best, so I decided to make myself a flower lei like the ones I wore in the bush on special occasions, when Mom made grass skirts out of brown paper and we danced the hula-hula for the visitors in the camp. I looked around for wild flowers, but the only flowers that were available happened to be Mom's climbing roses on the front verandah. I fetched Mom's sewing scissors and cut every rose off and made the lei, and I proudly hung it round my neck. Mom was shocked; she had struggled to get the roses to grow and was overjoyed when they finally bloomed. So I had to be punished! She said I couldn't go to the movies until I tied every rose back on the vine where I found them. I refused and found her slipper on my bottom, but I still had to tie the roses back on the vine. While the others went to the movie, I went and sat on the coal bucket next to the stove, picturing myself as Cinderella, and of course Mom became the wicked stepmother, whatever that was! But from then on, every time I felt wronged, that was were they could find me. A martyr to my own cause.

14

The First Taste of Prejudice

In spite of adjustments, we were happy! In less than a year, there was a seasonal garden in front of the house. Mom's vegetable garden was thriving without the interference of Springbuck and Deer to destroy it.

Dads fruit trees, he and Kondoweh had planted, were blossoming. He delighted ordering from the gardening catalogue; the peaches were called 'blushing brides', the oranges, 'Valencia's', and the apples were rosy with a different variety of names for each one. He was happiest when he was cross hatching, crafting, or emulsifying. He stacked the dam with fish, which grew to an amazing size, and we cut out the thought of ever eating them. They acquired pet names, and he actually stuck his hand in the water, and they came to him to be petted and hand fed. It was an endearing sight seeing him stroking a 3-foot long fish and talking to it. But it was also not surprising because he was a gentle and remarkable man. Behind the house Dad and Kondoweh built Mom a dreamy red brick oven. We simply refused to eat 'store bought' bread. Dad called it 'ghost breath.' When we asked him why he replied, "Because it has no nutritional value, and is with out substance or soul."

Mom spent her time crocheting, making curtains, and piece by piece put in another piece of furniture, till one day she surveyed her work and simply said, "Now it no longer is a house, it is our home.

116

The only thing we did not like, were the fences that separated us from our neighbors. To the right of us was a ten-foot fence. At the back of us was a four-foot barbed wire with an eight-foot hedge. Between us and the corner house was another fence. This didn't stop us, though, to crawl through and visit the Dingles and the Potgieters

Everyone was fenced in. Like animals marked their own territories in the jungle. The city dwellers declared the fences as their private boundaries. But the biggest restriction came when we found out who we could and couldn't associate with. We were told. The Indian lady from the "Coolie" store on the corner was to be treated like a merchant but not to be invited to one's home. The Greek on the next corner no one spoke to because he married out of his race. The people across the street used a skin bleach to whiten their skins so that they were not classified as Negro. We soon found out that it was not just the ethnic background but the color of the skin that had a lot to do with it, too.

On Mondays, a lady came to do our washing. Mom, being a sociable woman, invited her into the kitchen for coffee, which she accepted but would rather sit on the back steps of the house. Mom simply thought it was that she was an outdoors person and sat with her on the back steps to talk. One day while they were talking a neighbor turned up to visit, but refused the coffee and wouldn't sit with Mom and the lady. We always walked guests to the front gate, and while doing so the neighbor told Mom that her behavior was frowned upon. Mom could not understand and asked her what she meant.

"Do you want me to spell it out for you? You're socializing with the washer woman."

"So is that a sin?" Mom asked. The neighbor replied.

"She is BLACK! And there is another thing they have asked me to speak to you about. The 'savage' that is living in your house—he is far too intimate with your children, and they are afraid for the safety of their own children and want him gone!" Mom was shocked! In the jungle we had not once encountered prejudice; we though we were the minority because we did not fit in with all the black tribes around us. Now she was blatantly told that the neighbors did not like her behavior. "Remove him off the premises, or we will have to report you to the authorities."

A few days later Mom came up from where she was tending her flower beds, and told Kondoweh to go and hide in the coal shed, she suspected trouble, and he may be the cause. We went inside the house and all peeped through the curtains.

A uniformed policeman was opening the front gate. It made the familiar squeak that Mom had refused to let Dad oil, because it acted as an alarm and gave her advance notice about unwanted visitors, like solicitors and parsons, and now, she whispered also, "Policemen." The policeman's boots crunched on the gravel path. Mom went out to meet trouble before it had time to knock.

"Good morning, officer," she greeted him cheerfully.

"Good morning, Mevrou (ma'am), I have come about a complaint."

"Come in and have a cup of coffee, and we can talk," she interrupted him.

With such a cheerful greeting, he felt a little embarrassed at what he had to tell her. They walked through to the kitchen, she thought it would be less formal than have him sit in the sitting room. Mom gave him a cup of coffee and some of the rusks she had dried the previous night. She could see he was uncomfortable, and struggled to get out what he had come to say.

"Mevrou, I'm just doing my job, you must understand I have nothing against the black folks, but I received a complaint from the neighbors that you are allowing a savage out of the jungle to live with you in your home. You must understand that we have laws against that, and there are restrictions against fraternizing with your black employees. I will have to take him to jail if you continue to disregard the law. But you seem a reasonable woman, and I'll give you until Monday to find suitable accommodation for him and to report at the police station to register him for a working permit to stay. Otherwise we will have to send him back to where he came from or incarcerate him. He must also get a pass if he is to stay in your employment."

I looked at Mom's face; she had the same look she had on her face when the witch doctor had tried to put a spell on her to show his superiority. That time she had shown her anger at kicking the stone ring to pieces and tossing it at the witch doctor hiding in the bush. She was steaming inside, but she kept her thoughts to herself. *How dare he dictate How I should live my life. The government has no right to dictate whom I should associate with, or whom I wish to accommodate in my home. I feel like giving him a piece of my mind!*

Thinking it over, she switched to her humble face, and instead said, "Forgive me, I've been away for so long in the bush, I did not know what was going on in civilization. We will see to it that he moves out today, and Monday I will come myself to see that he gets his working papers, that is if I could speak to you personally because you are so compassionate and kind. What is your name officer?"

He obviously did not detect the sarcasm in Mom's voice, because he answered. "I'll arrange for it myself if you can give me his name and tribe and where he comes from, but you must realize that because he can't sign for himself, you will be responsible for him not to get into trouble. He was seen down by the river doing stick fighting with others of his sort."

"Oh, yes, he received a trophy for that, after all he is the Mavenda chief's son. Another cup of coffee? Another piece of biscuit?" This time her smile was forced. Deep down she felt like kicking him like she kicked the witch doctor's stones.

"No, thank you, but you DO understand that I'm just doing my job, don't you?"

Mom always saw her guest to the front gate, yet this time she didn't even get up from the chair, almost as if she was glued to it. Instead she told me in her sweetest voice, "Go and open the front door for the officer, and make sure he closes the front gate—we don't want to have more savages coming in."

His parting words were the final twist of the knife. "Remember, there are restrictions to this sort of thing!"

She knew, and he knew, that the only true restrictions there were was in the ignorance of their narrowminded thinking, but then perhaps they never had the freedom we had. Growing up they were brainwashed by the dictates of a prejudiced few who had forgotten that "God had created everyone in his own image regardless of race, creed, and color." In our eyes all peoples— white, brown, yellow, or black were simply people.

She called Kondoweh aside and as diplomatically as possible she tried to explain what the policeman was all about. When Dad got home from errands, he and Kondoweh hurriedly built a coal shed against the outhouse wall and swept out the coal room. Under the coal dust, to our surprise, he discovered it had a beautiful red concrete floor the same as the front verandah. He was thrilled! The room was ten by twelve feet with a fair sized window. After the room was scrubbed, and the walls whitewashed, Kondoweh polished the floor with his beloved 'Oxblood' red floor polish he used on the front porch. They moved the furniture from the back room into his new room. Mom added a mirror, table, and throw rug and curtains. When it was done, Kondoweh stood in the middle of the room surveying his private quarters, proud as a prince. The room to him was luxurious in comparison to his bush hut, which he had to share with several of his brothers.

15

The Foster Home

Three years had passed, war had come into Central Africa. Dad so wanted to join the troops in Central Africa at El-Alemein. But he only qualified for the Army Reserves, as B Category. Soon making the rank of corporal, he became shooting instructor in spite of his injuries. He came home on weekends from the army camp to be with us and putter around in his orchards. When he was away, Mom missed him and kept busy with her countless projects and gardens. She had many charities, many were the same neighbors who had reported her before. She never denied anyone anything. Everyone used to come to her to borrow. "Aunty, my mother asks if you would lend her an onion, to give the stew a taste," or "Aunty, my mother needs a candle, we will give it back next week," "Aunty, do you have a cup of sugar." "Aunty, a few slices of bread, to pack my father's lunch box."

She was very generous and sharing to the point that they took her for granted. Her vegetables and fruit from the garden were shared. When she canned, part of it went to the needy. When she baked a pie, another one had to be baked for the man up the road who didn't have a wife to bake one for him. Children came to her to see to their scrapes and hurts because their mothers were working in the factories. They came during meal times to share from our table. I would see her work for weeks on a milk doily, and someone would say, "I wish I could do that," and she would reply, "Do you like it? You may have it then."

Mom used to joke, "If I charged for everything they borrowed I would be rich, but in the eyes of God, there go I. One day I may need something." And that happened one day.

Mom had planned on doing some canning of Dad's peaches, and with sugar being rationed for the war effort, she had been carefully hoarding her rations and hiding them in her big old wardrobe. But someone must have got wise to her and the entire hidden stock was stolen. So she said she was going to go around the neighborhood and collect the many cups of sugar they borrowed from her and never returned so that she could go ahead and do her canning. She jokingly took the wheelbarrow and went around the neighborhood. After about an hour she returned with only one candle.

I remember her as a very compassionate person as well. She would take the dress off her back and give it to someone who was in need.

One day while taking a walk along the highway, we found a woman badly beaten and almost naked. Mom took her own dress off and put it on the woman. She did not care whether the woman was a prostitute. She was just a woman hurting. She walked the woman to our house wearing only her petticoat, amid stares from everyone in the street. She cleaned her up, let her rest, fed her, and provided her with clothes and shoes and money so she could have a new start.

Another time, an escaped convict, whose crime was not carrying a work pass, came to us looking for sanctuary. Mom fed him and told him she was unable to give him shelter, but he was so grateful that she trusted him, he blessed her and was on his way.

Soon after coming back from the bush, Mom became very ill. The doctors shook their heads. Some said that she had sleeping sickness and most likely had been bitten by a tsetse fly because she slept excessively. Her disposition had changed, her temper would flare up for no reason, and I became the scapegoat. Being the wild one, I did everything wrong in her eyes. But before she could get to me with her slipper, I always slipped away up the mimosa tree and onto the roof. She would send Kondoweh up the tree to get me down, then I would simply climb to the thin branches and swing over onto the roof. By the time he had gotten a ladder to get on the roof, I was back on the tree. By then she had forgotten what I had done. And everything was back to normal. The irony was that when the doctors finally agreed that she had Parkinson's, she was convinced at one stage that the witch doctor's spell that she disrupted had finally caught up with her, and Dad sent for a nearby witch doctor to remove the spell. Totally out of character, he came in civilian clothes, spread the magic bones and stuff on our kitchen floor, removed some coals from our iron stove, and put them in an iron skillet of Mom's. Then he poured some blobs of amber stuff that looked suspiciously like the gum off our backyard acacia tree onto the coals and had Mom, sitting on the floor, sniff the spiraling yellow colored smoke emanating from the blobs. Strange mucus dripped from her nostrils, and tears ran across her cheeks. He stood up and danced round her every time, tapping her on the head. Then he told Dad he wanted his payment in cash, and she was now cured. Unfortunately it only gave her a very bad headache.

Even though she was ill, she concentrated on keeping her home in order. Dad hired someone to come in and help Mom. The woman was of the Mapog tribe, covered on the arms legs and neck with copper rings, and wore her traditional heavy patterned blanket, which made her sweat excessively, and wherever she went, the loathsome cloud of body odor hung in the air. Mom walked behind her with her bottle of Evening in Paris, sprinkling it like Holy Water. This in turn made it more obnoxious. So finally she had to let the woman go. Kondoweh helped wherever he could, with her supervising as he loved sugar and had a tendency to put sugar into all the cooking; with the result we had sweet potato and carrot candy quite often. She tried to teach Sis and me all the skills she was capable of: sewing, cooking, baking, and I wanted to know how to crochet. But slowly she became incapacitated. Her tremors were so severe that she could no longer dress herself or feed herself. She tolerated no one but me to help her. I became her sole caregiver. Daddy came home weekends, and she made an effort to let everything look normal. But it was obvious that she was regressing rapidly, she walked haltingly, drooled, and suffered severe headaches. More and more she found relief in sleep when the tremors miraculously stopped. For hours I would sit with her holding her hands to control the shaking, which exhausted her. Sometimes my hands got so tired I would sit on her hands while reading to her till she fell asleep. Although I loved her deeply, tending to Mom became an unbearable chore. Especially when I could hear the children play outside and wanted desperately to be out there with them playing. My silent thoughts bordered on a love-hate relationship. Dad would sometimes relieve me, but I saw the embarrassment in her eyes and felt terribly sorry for her. After several hospital stays, Sis and I were taken away to live in a Foster home for a while to take the pressure off her in the hopes she would improve. Unfortunately it had quite the opposite effect on her because she worried about us, especially after she was taken to visit us one time, and our caregiver refused to let her eat at the table with the family, saying she slopped over everything and made her sick. They would not allow me to feed my mom, either.

Dad came to see us on his own after that. He was always impressed with our care. We were always scrubbed and immaculately dressed at such times. And she was the perfect hostess to him. But beneath that exterior lurked a Jekyll and Mr. Hyde. And as soon as he departed she turned on us. We lived in a regimented world, which I'm sure she followed out of a book, "How to raise children." We were girls, and girls had to show decorum at all times. We were not allowed to play hopscotch or skipping, because girls didn't jump around like animals, and heaven forbid did not spread their legs apart. If we did that we were punished. The punishment usually fitted the crime, cleverly thought out by her using her imagination. I remember standing for hours sometimes in the corner with my legs tied together, having to learn endless Bible passages. What was strange, however, was that she allowed Sis and I to bathe together, even though she would not allow us to undress in front of one another; she did not want us to see each other's 'private parts.' We had to sit back to back in the bathtub, and in our room undress behind a screen. It was strange indeed to us, who in the jungle had swum naked. So the moment she was out of the bathroom, we would immediately flip around and act like normal children. If she caught us, one of us would have to go to bed without dinner.

After the bath she usually reviewed our homework, and night after night I had to learn a lesson. She rapped me over the knuckles or the top of my thighs where it would not show because of my spelling. I hated her! Sis would try to help me but then she would get into trouble. Being away from Mom she thought that she had to look after me. Usually after that humiliation was over, Dr. Jekyll took over, dressed in our lightly starched nightgowns and dressing gowns, she would pamper us with what she considered love by lovingly rubbing glycerin and rose water on our faces, arms, and legs, still stinging from the object we were reprimanded with. I hated glycerin and rose water for the longest time, associating it with her.

When Dad came to visit, she would accept the gifts of candy he would bring, and then throw them away. There were so many things that made our lives hell, but one thing in particular stuck in my mind, never to be erased. It all started in innocence.

The day had gone smoothly, we had been 'good little girls', and for a treat we were even given a bowl of ice cream before dinner, and she told us we could do what we wanted to. I knew she didn't mean the things she had already forbidden us to do, so I chose to draw, something that I knew would not get me in trouble. Sis chose the safe way out, too, and decided to read. I sat down at the table and thought about what I wanted to draw. In the next door yard there was a big old rooster who always sat on the fence post and crowed. So I proceeded to draw. I had not heard anyone come in, but the next minute I felt a stinging blow across my head.

"You filthy little slut!" These were words I had never heard before. "I will not allow such filth in my house!" She grabbed me harshly by the arm, dragging me outside.

"What did I do?" I started crying.

She answered under her breath, teeth clenched. "You know, and you'll have enough time to reflect over it." Sis, too, wanted to know what I had done wrong, but she told her to go back into the house and wait.

I was dragged, by now screaming, into the coal shed. Here she emptied out the coal from a large sack and shoved me into it. I had stopped screaming because I was terrified what she was going to do to me. She tied the sack above my head with some cord, and after some shuffling around, I felt myself being pulled up over a ceiling beam, off the ground. The sack swung around precariously.

"You will hang here until you apologize and tell me why you drew that filthy picture, or until the rats eat you!" Then I heard her footsteps withdraw and the door shut and I heard the bolt close on the outside. And the next thing I heard were stones falling on the roof above my head. I held my breath, was it stones or the rats to come and get me? I did not know that she was out there pelting the roof with loose gravel stones, smiling sadistically. I started to cry, softly calling for my Mom. After what seemed an eternity, I heard the gravel stones crunch under someone's feet, as if they were tip toeing toward the door. The bolt made a screeching sound and the door creaked slowly open. I was about to scream when I heard Sis whisper, "Shu, it's me, I've come to help you." I found a small hole in the sack through which I could look. She had pulled some coal sacks toward me, and was standing on them, but the knot on the beam was too high for her to reach, and if she did manage I would fall very hard and get injured. It was more than four hours since she had been sent to the room for aiding and abetting, and had no dinner, but had climbed through the window, having witnessed what went on, to save me.

Not being able to get me down, she picked up a piece of firewood and vowed to protect me from the rats, which she heard the woman say would come to eat me up. Several hours had passed and she fell asleep, only to be rudely awakened. "So you want the same thing!" The woman slammed the door shut and left the two of us in the shed for the rest of the night. The following day we heard arguing outside the door, and the next thing the door slammed open and the rope cut and I was lifted down. As the sack opened I saw a very welcome face looking down at my coal-smeared tear-stained face.

"DADDY!" We both clung to him as he piled us into a taxi to take us back home. We never went back there again! What she told my Dad was that I had drawn a man's privates and I had kicked and bitten her.

16

Back to the Bush — "Bar X Ranch"

A year had passed, and Mom's health had not improved; there was no cure for Parkinson's we were told. The war was over, and Dad was home to stay. He had done four years of duty and received a letter from the government informing him that he was entitled to a pension or a homestead, rent free, provided he help with getting the people who went to war back on their feet by giving an eighth of his crops to feed the hungry.

After careful consideration and discussion, Dad thought that the farm life would help to cure her and even made Mom believe it. He had a reasonable pension from the police and considered renting the first house out while we went to check the farm out. I think it was the name that eventually made him decide, The sections of farming land were named after the battle field, Ambalagi, etc. But it was El Alemein that attracted him.

The only drawback was that the school only had the lower grades, and Sis was entering the higher grades. So my mom's younger brother offered to take her in. I was afraid for her remembering the ordeal we still had fresh in our minds. But my uncle was a dear man, and she agreed to live with them and go to school in the city. During the time since coming into civilization, we had accumulated quite a lot of furniture, crockery, linens, and stuff, and two of Dad's brothers came to help us pack as Mom said this time everything was going along. Dad thought it wiser to leave some of the things in storage because the letter said that the house was partly furnished. But Mom said that she was never going to live primitively like when we were on safari.

Everything was finally packed and ready for our new adventure, Dad said.

He had hired a moving van to take our belongings to the new house, approximately three hundred miles away. We would follow in my rich Uncle Ernest's limo, riding in the luxury of an air-regulated car with plenty of leg room.

It was a long and tiring ride for Mom, but I found every mile a treat. And time passed very quickly.

The billboard on the edge of town boasted 801; the added one was due to a new baby born weeks before. Now they would have to add three more I thought. A main road of hard packed well-traveled red dirt traversed the length of the town. Our long limo looked like a vehicle from outer space in contrast with the other vehicles in town for the day. It threw up a cloud of red dust as we entered. It was Saturday, corporation day. The town was bustling with people; farmers brought their wares in and brought their families along for shopping with the money received from their crops. Tied up in front of the main road's few buildings stood an assortment of local transport.

Small two-wheeled wood carts with puny abused little donkeys, heads bent, spirits broken, ears drooping, stood sweating in the heat and red dust clouds. Next to them stood a shiny new buckboard with restless full mule team, loaded with bales of hay and assorted baskets full of vegetables for the market. Across the road, a sharp looking surrey pulled up in the shade of a jacaranda tree sporting a well-matched horse team. Uncle's limo pulled up in front of the only one-story hotel in the center of town. The townspeople had never seen such a grand car. A small group gathered around it while we sat on the long verandah sipping lemonade from tall glasses with clinking blocks of ice. Daddy had pulled someone aside and was asking him for directions to the settlement.

"When you cross the bridge at the end of town, follow the sand embankment for two miles, till you pass the Cloete farm. Turn right at the big blue gum tree, continue another mile till you see the clinic. After the clinic the road forks, take the right fork onto a corrugated road for another mile. Here you will find a large irrigation dam; follow the wall of the dam. Where it ends, turn sharp right and go past the animal camp, and that's where the farms start, you can't miss it." The man took a deep breath. This direction giving was a very important thing, and he took it serious.

"Thank you," Dad said, and joined us on the verandah. "Did anyone get that, the only thing I remember is that we have to keep turning right! Did you notice he didn't take a single breath through all of this?"

Collectively we stumbled through the directions. Found the blue gum tree and the clinic, and the corrugated road was no exaggeration. It looked like a rusted sheet of corrugated roofing. Even though there was excellent suspension on the limo. it nonetheless felt like our brains were being shaken loose. One time a rickety school bus painted bright green trembled past us, carrying a group of farmers singing drunken songs; they looked oblivious to all. Celebrated a little too much and were homeward bound.

We passed the dam, and turning sharp right, just over the ridge, we looked down a long straight dirt road that stretched for a long way down to the river's edge. On either side of the road ran a barbed wire fence, and behind a big iron gate fifteen acres apart stood the farm houses. Identical in their drab appearance, with the same impersonal architecture.

Away from the house were some out buildings and a two-story high flume-barn. On each of the iron gates hung a name board with the farmers' name on it. The people—who hadn't gone to the corporation, were in the fields, waving at us as we passed. At least they were friendly. At the first farm we stopped to ask which one was ours. The farmer said ours was the second one on the right. We couldn't miss it. it was owned by a Yankee, we would find it a little different than everybody else's.

Nearing the gate it was blatantly obvious. "Boy was he right!" Dad whistled.

"Ours definitely has character, that's for sure."

"Are you sure we haven't stumbled on a movie set? By accident?" Uncle Ernest asked. Everywhere were signs of the 'Yanks' ingenuity, starting with the wooden arch over the gate made from split pine planks with 'BAR X RANCH' burnt into the wood.

The stables were surrounded by log corrals. In a shed stood an absolute masterpiece of a buckboard painted black with brightly colored tole paintings around the edges, and on the back rest of the driver's seat, 'Bar X Ranch' done in beautiful script across the back of the seat.

Near the corral stood a wheat stack, some wheat tied in sheaves stood leaning against the stack. The fields were covered in golden stubble. It was an artist's dream. As soon as we stopped, I ran around on a discovery tour of the surroundings. At the back of the house were the remnants of a vegetable garden and a small mulberry tree that was loaded with berries. In the shed with the buckboard I found a basket, picked a cabbage and some tomatoes, found a hen wandering around, and under some knolls of grass discovered her laying place and some eggs. In the fields there was some corn still on their stalks; I plucked a half a dozen and headed back home with a big smile on my face, and everyone was amazed at my finds. I put the basket in the kitchen, which had a big black iron stove.

It was a two-bedroom house. I counted there were four army iron beds, with army issue rough sheets and blankets, two to each room. Two homemade benches in the hall. But that was the extent of the "partly furnished."

The house had no electricity, but Dad had packed a box of provisions, with a hurricane lamp. So we had light. I went looking for wood and found a stack of ready chopped wood by the tobacco barn. And soon there was a glowing fire in the stove and a pot of coffee brewing on the stove.

Mom and I packed the basket with vegetables and other supplies in the pantry. Dad was very resourceful. He packed cornmeal, salt, condensed milk, sugar, and some mugs and blue enamel plates and two cooking pots. In one the corn was already cooking.

I needed to go to the outhouse, so Dad lit the storm lamp and went ahead to check for snakes and spiders before allowing Mom and me to go inside. This one was not like the one we had in town. This one had a seven-foot pit with a seat built over the pit, so sometimes snakes crawled in and lay on the ledge around the pit. I did not mind the daddy long-legs spiders that always lived in our town one, but any black spider I always thought were black widows, which were deadly.

When we returned to the house, our new neighbors came to call to welcome us.

The man was a course type; he was wounded in the Desert war and walked with a limp, using a cane. He was about forty-five. His wife, half his age in her early twenties, carried a small bucket of milk. Holding onto her dress and onto one another, followed five shy little girls, from seven down, a year apart. The oldest carried a candle and a box of matches. The lady looked tired with dark rings around her eyes. Her hands were callused and rough when she greeted us. She gave us the meager gifts, and told Mom that she had washed the sheets and blankets on the bed and swept out the out-house. Dad didn't know if he should pay her or thank her so he settled for the latter, and they sat down on one of the benches that Dad had brought into the kitchen. He also found a large packing case in the barn that wasn't needed by our 'Yank' and brought that into the kitchen to serve as table until our furniture arrived. We used the milk for the coffee and shared some of the left over sandwiches we had packed for our journey and the corn with our guests, who ate it as if it was cake. The woman introduced them as the Winter family and told us that the milk came from a cow that the 'Yank' had left in their care until we arrived, so it was really our milk. The cow was very difficult to handle and was kept in the paddock next to the dam. She had the strange habit of crawling under fences so she hoped that the cow would still be there in the morning for us, and had not wandered off into the 'koppies' behind the dam.

Mr. Winter suggested we keep her in the log corral when we did find her. They told Dad they would help us with what little they had till our things arrived, but just looking at them he knew they had very little to help themselves, and thanked them profusely and said that he had planned to go into town the following day and buy some provisions.

When they went home, Dad went to the outhouse and told us we were lucky—he found a snake curled under the seat. And in future we should hold the lamp into the hole first to see if there were any crawlies. He was forced to kill it with a shovel. He also found the hole where the snake crawled in and promised to fix it the following day. But till that promise was fulfilled, Mom and I went into the field to relieve ourselves and squatted among a chorus of crickets instead.

The following day while Dad and Uncle drove to town, Mom and I found a field full of unharvested potatoes. We harvested as much as we could, walked over to our neighbors and gave them a basket full of potatoes for their kindness.

Dad came back with two more oil lamps and candles, decent sheets and pillow slips, a broom, soap, a dish, and some towels. Also food staples and seeds for a new garden. We walked to the camp next to the dam and found the cow just like they said. She was lying on the ground lifting the wire up with her short horns and was trying to wiggle out of the compound. A few minutes later and we would have had to go and look for her in the adjoining hills. After getting her home, Dad put her in the log corral, and we found out how impossible she was. She stood in the middle legs spread, and snorted into the ground digging with one foot, just like a bull. Then she butted the log fence. When Daddy tried to approach her to milk her, she actually tried to kick him. He called her a hermaphrodite. I asked him what that meant and he told me that it was someone who was half man half woman, only she was half cow and half bull.

"You mean, like a mermaid that is half fish, half woman?" I asked. Not to go into detail, that was good enough for him.

So I told her, "I'll call you half that then. Stand still Aphrodite, and give us some milk for our coffee." She just stood her ground snorting her disapproval of being in the corral. That night she was standing close to the poles and Dad lassoed her and pulled her against the poles and we milked her through the poles. The first bucket she kicked over, after that Dad tied up her hind legs and we got about a pint. For a time we did not take her to the camp, but fed and pampered her in the corral, thinking we could win her over. But it didn't help, so we started taking her to the camp to feed. And one day when I went to find her she was gone. Other people had seen her near the upper camp. I knew that was where they kept the corporation bulls. It wasn't long before I spotted her; she was having a show down with a red bull, butting him with her short little horns.

While she kept the bull at bay, I investigated a sound coming form a ditch near by. *Hee-haw-hee-haw!* It sounded desperate. A donkey had fallen in the ditch and was exhausted trying to get back out. I had brought a rope to bring Aphrodite home, but I was too weak to help the donkey, so I took Aphrodite home in a hurry and begged Dad to come and help. I told him the donkey did not have any brands so he must be homeless. We were able to pile some stumps in the ditch, which gave him a foothold to climb out. But Dad said we would have to find out first if he belonged to anyone before we could keep him. I wanted to call him Charlie after my friend, but he eventually was called Houdini. For like Aphrodite, he too was an escape artist. There was nothing he couldn't get into or out of.

When he came into our lives, Daddy already had a beautiful garden going. Around it he had a chicken wire fence and a gate. But the donkey soon found out how to open the gate, go in pull carrots up and then open the faucet, and in the morning Dad would find the garden violated and flooded.

So he too went into the corral to change his ways. He and Aphrodite became close friends. He would simply lift the cross beam off the corral gate and they would go to the front gate, and like a gentleman he would open it for her, too, and they were off. We were baffled because he not only opened the gate but also knew how to close it. We were accusing one another of leaving the gates open when one night Dad caught the donkey doing it. That's when he became Houdini, and Dad put pig tail locks on the gates, but it wasn't long before Houdini was opening those, too. The two of them would set off to the koppies, where the grass was perhaps sweeter. Now in the upper camp all the bulls were kept, including the corporation's stud bull that was hired out to the farmers for a very exorbitant price. They made quite a lot of money off him, but didn't know about Aphrodite and her accomplice. Houdini would open the gate for her to go butting the bulls and close it after her out of habit, then she would crawl under the fence to get back out.

Usually after her nights out, Dad would watch her very closely for a month to see any signs of pregnancy. And then it happened she wasn't getting fatter, she was indeed pregnant. The superintendent called the corporation in and in turn they called Dad in.

"We have a problem Mr. A., we've been told that your cow was seen in the bull compound, and you know she was sired by our bull and you will have to pay for servicing or give us the calf!"

"That's a matter of probability, I can't deny that she is pregnant, so we'll just wait and see. I'm telling you, your Bull wasn't in that camp when I found her."

As the pregnancy progressed, she became calm, even allowed me to milk her and stroke her head. She stopped her strange behavior altogether. Houdini, on the other hand, became very aggressive and irritable; he felt rejected, because his friend no longer was interested in their night wanderings.

To take his mind off Aphrodite, I started riding him to school. He became spiteful and resented me riding him. He tried to rub me off under low hanging thorn branches, or against the barbed wire. I would simply swing my legs to the other side and he would scratch himself, then he tried to throw me off by kicking up his hind legs. Daily he escaped from the compound reserved for the school children's donkeys, letting theirs out as well, till eventually it became too unbearable for me. I preferred to walk the two miles to the bridge to wait for the bus, and after school walk home from the stop at the bridge.

On the day of Aphrodite's calving, the superintendent and the corporation boss were there to either claim the money or the calf, and much to Dad's relief the calf was red.

"See I told you," was all Dad said. "It was the red Hereford." Their stud bull was black and white and so was Aphrodite. So if the calf would have been theirs, it would either have been black or black and white, but it carried its father's genes and was a little red bull calf.

Aphrodite's changes and her involvement with her calf, really broke Houdini's heart. One morning he was just gone! For weeks we searched for him in all the places where we usually found him.

Two weeks later Daddy went farther up into the hills where he spotted some wild mules. He was tired of borrowing or worse, paying for a mule team when doing work around the farm, and was going to check them out and see if it would be possible to capture them when he accidentally came upon the remains of Houdini in a narrow crack in a gorge. The first time he fell in a gorge, we found him, changing his destiny. This time alas it was too late. Poor Houdini, clever Houdini to have come to such a tragic end. This was the only place he couldn't escape from. More tragic was Daddy had to bring the news home to Mom and me. We all went to the sight, gave him a eulogy and planted a cross with Charlie-Houdini carved on it, and I felt better.

Then in a valley on the other side of the hill we saw the wild mules, almost as if Houdini had led us to them. They looked more like wild horses, So we mentally made a selection, and went home to prepare for their capture. But it wasn't till much later when we could do that.

Aphrodite hadn't crawled a fence since her becoming a mother. But she did miss her donkey friend, because sometimes I would find her at the farm gate giving a woeful, *Moooo, mooo,* calling him to open the gate when the wanderlust called her. She tried one time after the calf weaned, but her udder was too full of milk and she gave up.

Now call it cow-fate, but as soon as the calf was able to eat on his own, Aphrodite did have her day with the champion stud bull.

It happened this way. My sister, who had stayed behind in the city because the farm school only went to the fourth grade, periodically came to visit us on the farm. We had taken Aphrodite in the morning to the lower camp for grazing, and had gone to fetch her home before the sun set. Sis had picked up a small branch and was tickling her on the rump to hurry her up on the long sand road. At the same time we were admiring the glowing sun set at the end of the road. We were unaware that someone had left the upper camp's gate open where the champion was kept. He followed us unnoticed and just as we entered our gate, there this magnificent beast stood, with a mighty erection and the hots for our Aphrodite.

Aphrodite, who never really liked him, took off in the direction of the haystack, trying to escape him. My sister Ethel stood between him and his lady-love, waving her branch calling out, "Shoo—shoo!" She had never seen such a large show of affection, and stood still. Mesmerized. Staring.

She was in imminent danger, so I shouted!

"RUN FOR THE HAYSTACK! The haystack NOW! and get on it!" I ran at the bull, waving and shouting to give her a chance to get away. Sis and Aphrodite got to the haystack almost at the same time. Sis started climbing, sliding back down with every step she took. But finally made it to the top. I jumped onto the buckboard to distract the bull, but he noticed Aphrodite trying to get up the haystack, and with a mighty bellow of victory he mounted her, as she tried to mount the haystack. My poor sister was trapped, and had no option but to witness the whole mating. After the bull was done, he stayed by Aphrodite's side, not because he wanted to show his gratitude, but because he wanted to share the succulent bale of peanut tops with her, which she started munching on to hide her embarrassment. Every time Sis made a move to get down, the Bull charged at her. So she stayed put.

When he finally was satisfied in all ways, he simply turned and walked away, out of our gate, down the road into the sunset. He never once looked back at his lady-love.

17

Mom's Premonition and Untimely Death

Sis went back to school, and now it was just the three of *us* again. Dad, Mom, and I. For a time we thought that Mom had shown some progress, but she had slowly become weaker and weaker. I did as much as I could to keep her comfortable. She now depended on me to help her dress, bathe, and assist with the most *personal* needs. I attributed her menses and the bleeding as part of her illness; for some reason she never explained to me that it happened to all women. Perhaps because she thought I was too young. So because I loved her, I washed the soiled bloody cloths and hung them up to dry behind the barn. She didn't want the men to see it.

She could no longer help with the housework and cooking. I carried the full burden of the household and also worked in the fields. I was exhausted and my schoolwork suffered, because I no longer cared. All I cared for was for my mom getting well.

One night I heard her tell Daddy that I needed help, would he go and get my cousin Nellie. He went the following day to send a telegram.

Two weeks before Mom's birthday, Nellie arrived on the bus with my cousin Fred in Tow. She took over the household while I tended to Mom, who had become so ill that she had a hard time now to swallow, and could not metabolize what she ate. With the excessive drooling, she lacked saliva to mix with the food. Animals pre-chew their young one's food. I reckoned I could do the same, and after chewing it, placed it in her mouth, and she washed it down with milk.

She felt better on her birthday. Better to even get up, listen to some of her favorite records, even laughed when we showed off our dancing skills. Dad even sneaked a little dance with her. And she was able to eat a piece of her birthday cake that Nellie and I had baked for a surprise. This made us all think that she was over what ever had made her so sick.

On the thirteenth of October, the day after her birthday, she had a peaceful day. Hardly had any tremors. She had fallen asleep and I sneaked out to the barn to go and feed the little puppies we rescued, which were sitting on the bloated body of their dead mother, drifting down the river. I was feeding them with an eyedropper because their little eyes were not even open yet. I placed them in a box and brought them into the kitchen, placing the box in the corner. I had just picked up one of the little puppies and held it in my hand; it squirmed about and started to nuzzle between my fingers. How helpless, and how terribly sad that it had to lose its mother so early, I thought.

I heard Mom call me softly from the bedroom. I put the little puppy down and ran to see what she needed. She motioned me to lie beside her. I snuggled into her arms, smelling her warm sleepy smell. She hugged me tightly and softly said: " I'm going to die."

"Please don't say that, Mommy," I cried.

Then she continued, "Go and fetch the puppies. I want to see them." I ran to get them and placed them tenderly on her chest. She wasn't trembling when she picked them up one by one by the skin of their necks like their mother would have done. They yelped softly.

She looked at them for a few seconds, then kissed them lovingly.

"They are so small, I wonder how they survived. It's a miracle, I'm just sorry I won't see them grow up."

"Don't say that, Mommy, you will see them grow up, you are going to get better!" A cold hand gripped my heart, by now I was sobbing.

"Hush, my child, it is true. On the 24th of October at five o'clock I am going to die." She hesitated a moment, " I want you to listen carefully to what I'm going to tell you now. You will be richly rewarded for taking care of me. Go and fetch the Hymn book for me and a pencil and paper so that you can write down what I tell you. For my eulogy I want the words from the Hymn

Oh for a thousand tongues to sing."

My heart was bursting. "I will remember."

Then she continued."I want to go out of this life the way I came in, naked. They can put a sheet round me, and cover my chest with my white lace hanky. I want Daddy to comb my hair, and tell him to leave my tortoiseshell pin in my hair," she smiled, "I don't know what I will do without it where I'm going. Tell him he must take my wedding ring off, so that you can give it to your daughter one day. Yes, you will have a daughter one day and she must have my name. I will not see her, but I will guard over her. I don't want them to paint my face, I want to stay the way I am. On the 23rd when they take me to the hospital, you can put my lilac nighty on me. When Daddy leaves this earth one day, I want him to lie with me. Ethel will understand and will see to it."

Two days before the 24th she complained about terrible pains in her stomach. The district nurse came and gave her some castor oil. Daddy wired for a doctor on the 22nd. The district nurse came again and gave her some more castor oil. Daddy took the bottle from her, and threw her and the bottle out the front door.

"How do you know it isn't her appendix, and that would surely kill her!" We sat with her till she fell asleep. Then we went outside and sat under the Mulberry tree. I told him everything Mom had told me.

He got annoyed with me. "It's no time to tell me such ugly nonsense, aren't you ashamed of yourself making up such things?"

Early the morning of the 24th the doctor's car turned into our gate, and after a thorough examination he confirmed our suspicions. "I must take her now to the hospital, there's no time to lose. It may already too late, the appendix had already burst! Who the hell gave her castor oil? I'm afraid peritonitis had already set in. It's a four hour drive; bring all the pillows you can spare, and you can hold her in the back seat. We have to leave NOW!"

Mom lay on the bed, legs pulled up in pain. The doctor gave her a pain shot. I changed her into her lilac nighty and brushed her beautiful copper hair for the last time, making sure to put her hair slide back in. "Thank you, *my pop-lappie*." She used her pet name for me and smiled weakly.

Daddy carried her out, her arms around his neck, and her gold wedding band shone like a beacon on her finger. He lay her gently in the back on the pillows got in and supported her head on his lap. I kissed her warm face. "Good-bye, my child." She took my face in her hands, they were not trembling. She kissed me. "You're so young, but look after him."

I watched the car till I no longer could then ran to the barn, climbed into the rafters, and cried till I had no more tears left. Like the little puppies, I felt totally abandoned.

When I got back to the house Nellie and Fred were playing records and dancing in the kitchen. This made me furious. I saw it as disrespect, and grabbed the record off the gramophone, smashing the record to bits on the concrete floor.

"Don' t you know she is going to die at five o'clock? She told me so!" I screamed. I ran into my parents' room, and pressed my face into her old day dress hanging behind the door. I drank in her smell hungrily. Everything she had ever taught me flashed before my eyes. I remembered the good times and the bad. The times I hated her when I handled her sanitary napkins and put them in a bucket of salt water to soak out the blood, but later I accepted it the same way that I accepted the chamber pot, and emptying its contents as a labor of love, when she no longer could get up and go to the outhouse. But saying I'm sorry was forever too late. I now only wanted to remember her warmth, and have her back! That made me cry even more. I looked at the bedside clock. I didn't want five o' clock to come and tried over the distance to console her with the words she always used when the burden of her care became too much for me to bear. "Your reward is in heaven, and not on this earth." With that in mind I fell asleep and dreamt of us being together, bathing and laughing in the clear waters of the Limpopo.

I woke up later in the night, the door of my room stood open. My dad was sitting on my bed, his head in his hands, sobbing. I got up and started walking toward him.

"Daddy, please don't cry!" But when I got to where I saw him sitting, he was not there. It was an illusion. I got into my own bed trying to remember if I had just dreamt of him being there. It was so real!

It was two in the morning when a policeman and the superintendent brought him home.

He could only hold me. "She is gone!" he sobbed. "I didn't want to believe you, but she knew, she knew the exact time, didn't she?" He sank down onto my bed with his head in his hands, sobbing, just like I had seen him two hours ago. This time it WAS real. I went over to him and touched him. "Don't cry, Daddy, please don't cry," I told him. "I promised her I'll take care of you."

He calmed down, quietly telling me what happened.

"A quarter to five I went out onto the balcony for some fresh air. She was sleeping peacefully for the first time in weeks. Her lips were parted slightly like they always were when she was in a deep sleep, dreaming. I thought about what you had told me but seeing her so peaceful, I honestly thought that she had made it. Five minutes before five I went back into the room. A nurse was checking her out.

"'I'm sorry' she said, 'Your wife has just passed away.'

"It's not five yet," I objected.

"She looked at her watch. 'It's five minutes past five, your watch must be slow.'

"It was then that the things you told me she had said, had impact for the first time. You were right and Mommy was right. Then I did as you told me." He placed her ring in my hand, and closed his palm over mine. "Like she said, the ring will be for your daughter she wasn't able to see. Take good care of it, and perhaps I will be more fortunate and get to see her some day!"

It amazed me how many people's lives she touched with her caring and generosity of herself, her time, and her possessions she shared. The funeral line up was nearly a hundred cars long. They had come from far and wide to attend her funeral. Daddy had taken her body by train to Pretoria so that she could be near her family. Her sisters provided the mourning clothes and the wake. I had cried so much, that there was no more. She was covered in a sheet with a beautiful lace hanky across her chest. Everyone thought it strange that I, who had been so close to Mom, did not shed a tear.

I wanted to kiss her one more time. She lay so quiet. No pain or tremors. Somehow I expected that she would feel warm in her eternal sleep. But when my lips touched her cheek it felt cold like pottery. She had always said that the body was only a vessel in which the soul spends its time here on earth. To experience the things of the flesh so that it could enrich itself. I kissed that vessel one more time, then ran to hide. Somehow I got through the rest of the funeral.

After the funeral, Dad and I alone returned to the farm. Now I did not have Mom to look after, but the chores became more. While Dad took on the out door chores, I had to take over the cooking, washing, and cleaning without modern conveniences. The sheets and work clothes were too hard for me to handle. So dad built a wash place with scrub board under the Mulberry tree. I filled it with a hose from the garden faucet, grated some home made blue soap into the trough, and let the water warm in the sun. Or made a fire nearby and boiled water in the big three-legged pot. I then scooped some hot water in the trough, added the heavy things, washed my feet, and got in with the washing and started dancing on the washing, moving it around with a big wooden spatula till the clothes looked clean. The worst dirty things I boiled in the rest of the water in the black pot. Then I dumped them all in the trough, pulled the plug and ran clear water in until the washing was all rinsed. Pulled the plug again and danced on them till most of the water was trodden out. And I could hang them up.

On wash days, the fire in the iron stove stayed on the whole day where a half dozen iron triangle irons heated for the ironing that took place on a blanket on the kitchen table.

Dad and I took turns to light the stove in the morning. When it was my turn, I raked the ashes out the previous night before I went to sleep, and packed it with kindling, then corn cobs crisscrossed and a larger log that fitted the fire compartment. At first we had coal, but as the finances dwindled we went into the hills to look for dead trees to use for firewood, sometime before Mom no longer could bake the bread herself. Dad and I had taken over the bread baking and butter churning. Everything was from scratch, from grinding the wheat to making the leaven. And because we both had a very demanding schedule, we made enough corn meal porridge to have for breakfast and enough left over to slice and have with vegetables, and after dinner as a treat with condensed milk. After the dawn breakfast, I opened the sluices in the canal, and manually with the help of a shovel irrigated the part of the wheat fields assigned to me, while Dad did the rest during the day while I was at school. Then I took my homemade book bag and headed in the direction of the bridge two miles away, meeting up along the way with children from the adjoining farms. At the bridge the bus waited to take us two miles farther to the red brick school house in Groblersdal. The school held very few pleasant memories for me. I missed a lot of schooling because of working in the field and in the house. I was poor and was unmercifully teased about wearing Mom's recycled clothes. And as I outgrew my shoes, at first the toes were cut off, and later I made sandals from old harness and a motor car tire I found on the highway. Some of the girls called me a boy, because I took woodwork instead of Arithmetic which I hated and could never grasp.

At home we discovered we could get as much concrete for home improvement as we wanted, and we began making changes. We got sick of bathing in the wash troth, so Dad and I built a concrete bathtub in the room that was supposed to be the bathroom in the first place. Enameled it inside and out and brought pipes in from the outside faucet. Then we built a brick kitchen cabinet and made a kitchen sink. Now we had water inside as well. Then we made pathways and a three-tiered fish pond with spouting water and a perpetual waterfall by sinking the pipes deep enough to create gravitational forces that would recycle the water. Through the property ran a fast flowing canal that made crop watering easier. This, however, gave Dad the idea for a waterwheel that added to a motorcar battery created a generator that would light up at least one bulb in the front room. We still used candles for the bedrooms, but now we also had that convenience and he could work on his wood carving and I could draw to my heart's content.

At first the old superintendent made objections to our modifications, but ours was soon becoming a model for future tenants, and they regularly came to show what could be done.

Sis tried to visit more often now to help me get over Mom's death. I loved her visits because she brought the sunshine back into Dad's and my lives.

During one of her visits, she brought along two very fancy evening gowns that someone had given her. So we decided to dress up and perform an opera for Dad's amusement. She had put some lipstick on me and made herself up and we piled our hair on our heads. But then nature called, we took the lantern and 'went to see the man about the dog.'

Dad had in the meantime received important visitors. So we came back in swinging the lantern, singing our made up opera at the top of our voices, unaware of Dad's visitors. To our surprise we were met with applause and "Bravos." And there stood the old super, introducing the new superintendent, a handsome young man in his early twenties.

Dad in turn introduced us. "Meet my two operatic daughters." I was thirteen in a few days, and Sis was sixteen going on seventeen. She was breathtakingly beautiful in the dress she was wearing. And I looked far older in my getup and makeup. The supers were there on business, but it turned out to be a social call. In a place with such a small population, word quickly spread when a pretty girl steps off the bus, and my sister was news. That night, Henning, the new super asked my sister to the local dance at the school, but Dad said, "Only if my youngest can go, too." So the following night we put on the dresses that we wore the night before, but this time washed and neatly pressed.Of course minus the exaggerated makeup, and thanks to my sister I went to my first ball.

When my sister left, Henning became a regular visitor to my dad, pretending it was business, but he invited us to most of the other functions that happened in town. Dad teased me and said that he was really visiting me. I always considered myself to be the ugly duckling, and besides was only thirteen. Then one day Dad's suspicions were confirmed. Henning turned up with a box of chocolates and a bottle of perfume and asked my Dad if he could take me out alone. Dad saw the difference in our ages and told him not until I turned sixteen. Henning then said that he would wait. But although he was a very attractive man, that was what he was to me: 'a man' ten years older than I was. Then he left to go back to college, and I didn't see him again till I was seventeen.

18

Wild Mule Roundup

With everything that had happened after Mom's death, we had clean forgotten about the mules on the other side of the hill, that is until it became time to plow again. This time Dad was determined to have his own mules and not pay for the use of other people's. We weren't even sure if they were still in that same vicinity. So we packed some overnight food and some camping gear and waited for them to turn up.

The following morning they were grazing not far from where we camped; two of them had wandered away from the rest. That was just the situation we had hoped for so making a lot of noise we drove them into a ditch with no exit. Dad dragged a fallen tree across the other end and they were trapped. It took another day of trying to get the harness onto them. Dad finally succeeded and we tied the harness to the tree and drove them home and into our corral. Two weeks of harnessing them to the tree and dragging it around, we were able to inspan them to the buckboard, and no longer relied on borrowing mules from the corporation.

They were beautiful, almost black, and looked more like horses with smaller ears than the local brown mules. These two had terrible tempers. Harnessing them was very difficult. I was the climber, so I would climb into the rafters of the shed, leading off from the corral. Dad would send them in one by one. I would then put the blinkers on over their head, so that I could get the bit into their mouths. It seldom failed, they would rear up and try and bite me, and while the mouth was open I slipped the bit in, and once the bit was in Dad was able to put the harness on and connect it to the buckboard.

I soon learned to handle the reins, and when they weren't used for transportation, we got them used to plowing. Using a single blade plow with the reins hung over my shoulders, I could help Dad out with the plowing. I even became good at it. I loved the smell of new earth as it opened up in brown waves in front of me. I also took turns driving them to town on occasions we had to take our onion crops in, and for the monthly shopping trips for supplies. They seemed fully adjusted, except for the single car span bridge they hated with a vengeance, and always became skittish the moment they reached the part where the road dipped steeply toward the beginning of the bridge. They would push their hindquarters back into the front of the buckboard and refuse to go forward. Dad did not believe in using a whip, but at times like this he would crack the whip just over their heads and across their rumps to show that he meant business—the next time it wouldn't just be noise, but they would feel it. This usually worked. It was as if they knew that the bridge had a history of accidents. Floods usually followed the rains coming down from the mountains, so the river was known for its unpredictability. Almost without warning, except for the thunderous roar that preceded the red muddy waters, it was known to overflow the bridge and sweep everything away in its path. But when a empty school bus with its driver and two donkey carts were washed off the bridge, the mayor decided to have poles planted on the bridge with a single steel wire on either side. It was flimsy but was better than nothing.

For days Dad had worked on plowing the sweet potato vines under. It was our bonus piece of land; whatever crops we planted between the compulsory wheat and corn crops that went to the government, was ours. There was only about an half acre left to do. The night before we had discussed what we were going to plant. Most of the other farmers had made quite a bit of money from tobacco, so when his neighbor asked if he would like to accompany him to town to get his seeds, he agreed, taking our onion crop in to sell because we needed the money. Dad told me that he was going into town.

"I really wanted to finish plowing that last piece of land where we harvested the sweet potatoes, but I suppose it can wait till tomorrow."

I had plowed on my own before using the single blade. So I suggested to him that I continue where he left off.

"You're sure? Then I can hoe it when I get back from town. I'm quite confident that you will do a good job, but must warn you that the root system is deceptive, they look light, but often are deep and tough. The best way would be to stick the point of the plow into the main stem and let the mules pull it to the surface. But if it's too hard, just go around it, and I will chop them out later. If you can manage I will appreciate it. Just be careful. I'll harness them before I leave."

I was grateful that he harnessed them for me, because they were still a little skittish when I harnessed them to the plow, but were more calm when Dad did it.

They behaved well on the way to the lower field where we usually planted the cash crops. Peanuts, onions, and in this case sweet potatoes that were fast growing and profitable. As soon as the one was harvested, the other one went in. Each one's foliage plowed under as a land renewal.

I took one look at the field, the thin vines spread across the land like a spider web. I thought they would just cut away by the plow.

For two hours everything went smoothly, as I had anticipated. The vines broke away easily, curling under into the damp soil the plow share folded over. The reigns were draped around my shoulders as I usually did to free my hands. Up to then I had not found one stem. Perhaps Dad had got them all. I was going to stop, but it was the last stretch and I wanted to surprise Daddy when he got back.

Suddenly the unexpected happened. The plow was caught in what looked like the mother stem. The mules struggled forward but could not move it. A piece of paper hidden in among the vines flew up, spooking the mules. It hit the one closest to it on the flank. He snorted and reared up onto his hind legs, when he came down the front legs got caught in the cross harness, tripping him, he went down dragging the other mule with him. Just in the nick of time I released the reigns from around my shoulders, otherwise I would have been dragged in under them. I tried to calm them down, so that I could untangle the mess or get to the buckles to undo the harness, but with the kicking going on I was unable to get to the buckles. The lead mule tried to stand up, but in doing so he made the situation worse; he pulled the harness tight around the other mule's neck. It was strangling. I had to do something. I ran as fast as my feet could carry me to the shed and brought back the pruning sheers. The mule's tongue was hanging out. Without hesitation I cut the offending straps. As soon as the one in distress was free, he ran off toward the fence. The other one, still entangled, took off kicking and dragging the plow. I could see the first mule heading straight for the barbed wire. I ran to turn him away, and at

145

the same time I saw Daddy running across the field trying to prevent the same serious accident and also to turn him around. This scared the mule straight into the wire. He kept running parallel with the wire for about ten feet. Daddy managed to grab some of the straps still on him, but when he got him away from the wire, the wounded mule's eyes were as large as saucers. A red gash ran all the way from the neck to his front leg. The cut was about two inches deep, but miraculously had just missed the jugular vein.

While he was still able, Daddy led him to a big tree at the side of the field and tied him up against it. Retrieving the plow and the other Mule that was also heading for the wire, he yelled instructions to me as I ran toward the house.

"Bring that four-inch sharp needle we sew the bales with, and some of the thread treated with bees wax, and bring the red pepper from the kitchen. I'll go and get some chloroform and a sheet and some scissors and antiseptic.

Dad ripped the sheet into bandages, and poured some chloroform on a rag and pressed it to the mule's nostrils. Not sure how much to use, it showed little results so he added some more on the rag, and this time the mule was knocked out and slumped down against the tree. Next we washed the wound out with antiseptic, and Dad poured the whole can of red pepper along the full length of the wound, we were happy to see that it had cut cleanly through the outer skin and flesh without damage to arteries or muscles. I thought it was horrible to put the pepper on, but Dad explained.

"It acts as a painkiller and coagulant, and prevents blue bottles from laying their eggs in the wound."

I threaded the four-inch needle and while Dad pulled the wound together, I sewed it. I was amazed how easily it went through living skin, much easier than when I was making myself some shoes. Soon the two-foot gash was closed up with my best buttonhole stitch, for added strength, and only a reasonable amount of bleeding. Dad was right the pepper did act as a coagulant. Before the mule came to, Dad attached a long piece of hessian to a stick and looped it through under his belly and over the branch above his head, and with the help of the other mule we pulled him upright with the hessian providing a hammock. Then we bandaged the whole neck and chest, tied the hessian up in the tree so that his hoofs barely touched the ground, just for balance with little strain on the wounded leg and shoulder. When he came to, he struggled for a while, but then must have realized that we were trying to help him and calmed down.

For two weeks we fed him by hand, checking the wound that showed no signs of festering and had closed up very well, healing miraculously. He refused to drink water from a bucket, so I filled a bottle, lifted his lip, and poured it down his throat. Gradually we lowered the hammock till he stood on his own legs. At first he avoided putting weight on the wounded leg. Then when he could, we led him to the dam and into the shallow water, increasing the depth till he was forced to swim back out, providing him with good therapy.

For two months we had coddled and nursed him. Finally the day arrived when the wound was fully healed and he trotted off full of renewed spirits. But still we did not want to harness him, putting it off because we thought it would bring up remembered trauma, and we would be the ones to suffer an accident if it acted up.

With the mules out of action, we hand planted onions again instead of the tobacco crop we anticipated, which would have brought in much more income. But Dad arranged to go with our neighbor again to take the rest of his onion crop into the corporation. I found a note telling me to finish my chores, and if he wasn't back by dark to please milk the cow.

I had finished my chores, done the milking, ate my dinner, and put a covered dish for him in the still warm oven, did my homework, and finally went to bed.

In the middle of the night I woke up, went to his room, and found the bed had not been slept in. A cold fear swept through me. He was carrying a lot of money. What if the neighbor and he had an accident? The devil told me all kinds of ugly stories. I dressed hurriedly, lit a hurricane lamp, and ran to the neighbors' farm. I pounded on the back door, half expecting the neighbor not to be there. It took a few minutes before he answered the door.

"What the hell are you doing here? It's two in the morning!" he said angrily.

"I'm looking for my dad, he went into town with you, where is he?"

"How should I know? He said he was staying and would walk home, perhaps he met some friends, and decided to stay over. He will turn up tomorrow. GO HOME!"

I went home but I couldn't just leave it at that. "What if the river had come down and he was washed over the bridge?" The mule was well enough now. I was going to look for him.

They blinked in the light of the lamp as I led them out of the stable into the courtyard where I had laid out the new harness. I would have to back them up to attach the harness to the shaft. They were very skittish because of the dark, but after what seemed like hours I had them harnessed to the buckboard and ready to go. I ran and opened the gate. It would have to stay open, because once on I could not risk them taking off without me, even with the brakes on. I hung the lamp between them on the front of the shaft, but there was a bright moon in the sky lighting the yellow sand road, bright enough for them not to need the lamp. The lamp threw a ring of light around the mules that however provided some comfort for their unsure footing.

The bush on either side of the road looked dark and ominous. We had just learned about highwaymen a few weeks ago, and I imagined a highwayman to jump out at any minute. The mules strained against the reigns and the closer we got to the bridge the more I dreaded the crossing. As the buckboard came to the steep descent, I tried not to think of it as I struggled with both hands to place the brake handle in a lightly restraining slot. At last the brake blocks screeched against the wheels. It was slowing them down.

The solo wire on either side of the bridge gleamed for a moment in a solo flash of lightning that appeared from nowhere. The bridge hung like a fragile path across the black abyss. At least that was what it looked like to a terrified thirteen-year-old who was trying very hard to control two equally terrified mules. To others it was a mere twenty-five feet to the water.

The mules hung back. I tied the reigns onto the brake handle and climbed down. I took the sacks I had put in the back of the wagon, slipped them over their heads, and took the lead rope. I had put just enough strain on the brakes to slow them down, but I was I in front of them now. I started for the bridge, talking calmly to them. I was so engrossed in leading them that I didn't notice a bad storm brewing, till another bolt of lightning hit the wire near the middle of the bridge. A blue flame crackled as it traversed the length of the wire, then exploded as it hit the end pole, dragging the wire and the pole into the water where it hung sizzling. Now the right side of the bridge was totally unprotected. Large drops of rain hit the dirt road. As their hooves hit the concrete of the bridge, they sensed the change even though they could not see it, and instinctively reared up, refusing to go forward, then started pushing the wagon back and nearer to the unprotected side. "Oh God, they are going to trample me to death, spook, and go off the side of the bridge that now is unprotected." I stood fast and started pulling them forward inch by inch across. When we got to the place where the lightning struck, I pulled the sacks off their heads, hoping they would take it from there. It had the desired results, they immediately pushed away from the drop, and I got on and released the brakes. They proceeded across with no more trouble. By the time we got to the other side, the rain was pouring down in sheets. Two miles farther on, at the edge of the town, the rain suddenly stopped.

The town was deserted; it was about five in the morning. I rode up and down the main street and side roads looking for Daddy. And there in an alley behind one of the buildings I found him lying in a pile of trash. I had seen drunk men before, but never saw him drunk. Over friendly perhaps at Christmas after a few glasses of Madeira, but never out of his mind drunk. He was trying to tell me that they had spiked his drink, then mugged him and took away his onion money between bouts of laughter. It sounded more like desperation. Whatever it was that made him laugh didn't sound funny to me, mugging him and tossing him penniless into the alley just would mean more hardship for us.

He tried to get up but couldn't. Supporting him with all my strength, I helped him onto the back of the wagon, but he insisted taking the reigns. I tried to prevent him from climbing over into the driver seat. He reached for the brake handle to pull himself up, and the brake handle slammed back into a brake slot. I heard a crunch. I jumped up on the driver's seat and released the brake. Blood squirted over my dress.

I could only scream, "Daddy, the brake cut your pinkie off!" His pinkie looked mangled and hung at an angle half way off.

"LESH, PULL IT AALAWAY off!" He tried to pull the finger off, but I grabbed his hand as I pulled my ribbon out of my hair, I pushed the flesh together and wound it tightly, then put his handkerchief around the hand so that he couldn't get to it. He tugged at it but finally gave up and fell asleep or passed out on the back of the buckboard..

This time when we reached the bridge they didn't hesitate, it was already full daylight; they could see where they were going and wanted to get home and out of the harness. But in the middle of the bridge they suddenly stopped, something else was happening. I could also hear what they were hearing. If they didn't go right away, we would be lost. I had never used the whip, but now I screamed at them hysterically and whipped them across their backs. I heard the terrible rumble to our left and saw the wall of brown water rolling towards the bridge. As if sensing their own danger, they did not stop again till we reached the other side, only then did they slow down. I looked back and the water, brown and ugly, lapped angrily against the pillions. By the time we reached the high ridge, there was no bridge visible anymore, only the wires still standing could be seen over the foam and debris that had hooked onto it.

Daddy did not wake up through all of this, nor when I pulled up on the shady side of the house, quickly unhitched the mules, and put them in the corral. Daddy was still asleep, but just to make sure I used some of the chloroform we had used on the mule, fetched my sewing kit, and sewed Dad's pinkie back on. I tried to not think of it as Daddy's finger but a doll of mine I was repairing. I left him there to sleep off the chloroform. He slept way past noon. When the sun hit the shady side of the house, he woke up with a terrible headache and an unknown pain in his pinkie. But cold sober.

I brought him a cup of strong coffee. "How did I get here?" he asked stupefied.

"When you didn't come home in the night, I went to look for you," I told him about the journey there and the river that came down in torrents just as we reached safety.

"And this?" He winced in pain.

"I sewed it back on. You were drunk and wanted to pull it off. I thought if I could sew up the mule, it would be good enough for you; you didn't feel a thing because I also used some of his chloroform on you. But, Daddy, tell me this, why did you laugh when you tried to tell me what had happened? Mugging and being robbed is not something considered funny."

"I laughed because I was such a fool and completely caught off guard. After collecting the money for the onions, I decided to go and have a drink to celebrate. I saw some out-of-towner's watching me, and when I paid I must have displayed a little too much cash, because they came over to me and asked if I would like to have a drink with them. I thought they looked quite decent and friendly and agreed. But they must have put something in that second drink because I immediately felt sick, and while I vomited in the alley, they attacked me and beat me up, took the money, and left. I must have passed out because I didn't come to until you found me."

After losing the money, we had to work extra hard to replace the crops that brought in the money in the first place. Usually I missed a lot of schooling and the "Hookey Man" came looking for me to see why I wasn't in school. I just hid in the corn rows till he left and then went on with what I was doing— plowing, irrigating or whatever. To recoup the lost money, we decided to plant tobacco. It seemed everyone was smoking and it would yield the most. We used a weed the natives called *marruwanna*; could we have looked into the future we would have seen that this weed brought in millions. The natives sometimes smoked it because it was free, and tobacco was too expensive. We plowed it under because it renewed the soil and helped us to get more for our sweet potatoes, onions, and peanut crops. When Mom was alive, I often helped Dad with some of his chores. At ten I learned to irrigate and use a one share plow, so by the time I was eleven I was already an old hand at it. Sometimes people on the road going past the farm would stop and take a photo of 'the child' plowing. I had also learned how to use the sickle during wheat harvesting, because we could not afford the expensive machinery. Dad would hire some reapers and I usually led the teams, setting the pace, because we hired by the day. Dad would give a bonus to the team that finished first, and this gave them incentive to work faster. They never realized that in doing the work faster it was really a loss for them. For the duration of the harvest he provided shelter usually in one of the sheds, and food, cornmeal and meat, and anything they could reap from the field.

Soon I would be fourteen and my thoughts were on asking Dad to go back to our first house so that I could attend high school. Our last crop would be tobacco. We couldn't hire the help, so we decided to work it on our own. Just the two of us from tending the seedlings, to planting them, and later we plucked and prepared the leaves for drying. It was a long and tedious process. The flume barn already existed on the farm, so we had only the cost of the seed and the labor to consider, and because we did it ourselves, the money was good! The barn was two stories high, and on the front wall there were two ovens built inwardly that had to be stoked for two to three weeks during the drying time. The selected plucked leaves were braided onto a five-foot long stick with the help of two strings. In the inside of the barn poles were built into the wall from one side to the other horizontally approximately four feet apart, right up to the two story ceiling with vents that let out hot air. Dad was unable to climb these poles because of the plates in his shoulder and left hand, so I became the official hanger-upper. I would climb up and hang the braided sticks across the horizontal ones. When I reached the top, I would send down my rope with a hook on, pull the braided ones up and hang them.

Once they were hung, we camped in the lean-to that Dad had built over the ovens, taking turns stoking and watching the heat monitors. It was a wonderful time bonding with my Dad; he was a known story teller and I loved to hear the stories of his youth. It was usually about the five brothers, and getting into trouble.

"We would go to the corner of the street, where there was a small water furrow. It was the spot where the ladies had to cross the street. There was nothing unusual about that, except the fashion at the time was very long narrow skirts down to the ladies' ankles. We would sit and wait, and when a lady came along, she tried to hop across the furrow with the narrow skirt intact, but the bolder ones would lift their skirts up and we would see a leg, and if lucky we would even get a glimpse of a soft inner leg or even spot a garter, or frilly undergarment. That always evoked talks among us of the wondrous things to come." Once started I would urge him to continue. "Sundays we were marched off to Sunday school, in our black knickerbockers. Short pants that were gathered at the knee with long black socks that tucked into the knee band. I hated those socks because I was always getting holes in them, and not having sisters, we had to darn them ourselves. I hated that more than the socks, so if I had a hole, I would simply stick my finger in the black boot polish and paint the spot black on my leg so that my mother wouldn't notice. Of course I got in trouble for it, but then I always got in trouble. There was the incident with the cat. My mother had a beautiful long-haired cat. The hair was always hanging in its eyes, so we decided to do something about it. We caught the cat and I took an elastic band off one of the canning bottles and tied the hair into a pony tail. The cat ran away and up a tree. That night the cat was missing and we went looking for it. When we found it the elastic band had slipped around the cats neck when he tried to get it off and got caught on a branch and there it hung, strangled. We of course denied it was our doing, but it always stayed on my conscience." During the story time, we roasted corn off the field still wrapped in its outer leaves in the ovens, eating it with butter brought from the house and kept cool in the ice cold water of the canal. Then he continued. "Did I tell you about the time my dad nearly lost all his horses?" Even if I had heard the story before I always said no, just to hear him tell it again. "That is he almost lost them all, if it was not for our neighbor's daughter who happened to weigh nearly three hundred pounds. The fire was started by a lamp that slipped off a nail in the stables. We did get all the horses out, but as soon as we got them out, they panicked and went back in. The half doors in the other stalls got warped as it got hotter, and we couldn't get them open to let the others out, but it was then that the neighbor's daughter took over, and ran like a fullback straight into the doors, and those that didn't pop open, she simply sat on the half doors and wiggled till they collapsed. Unfortunately it grew too hot to continue, and we lost about a third."

"Now tell me again how you met Mommy." I never tired of hearing him tell me that story.

"Well as you well know, I was in the Royal Mounted Police, and long after the Boer War was over, we were still patrolling the Boer farms. One of them was where *she* lived, with an extended family. She had five brothers and four sisters and three adopted girls, who had come over on the ship her mother came on from Holland. My brother and I arrived at the farm during the celebration of someone's nineteenth birthday, when I asked whose birthday it was, they pointed out a tall vivacious girl, with the most beautiful long copper hair, which hung halfway down her back. It just knew it was love at first sight.

"The party was in full swing, they were playing blind man's buff, and she was blindfolded. She stumbled around the ring. I was standing to one side looking at her every movement, totally enchanted by her outgoing personality, when the sisters opened up the ring and she caught me. In more ways than one, I pulled the blindfold off, and suddenly shy, she ran off. I knew from that moment on that she was meant for me. I tried to get close to her for the next half hour, but she avoided me.

When I started to leave, her younger sister, who had worked for an Englishman, came over to me with a bag full of cookies to take with me. She spoke some English. She said, 'I'm sorry Mara avoided you, but she isn't over the tragedy of losing the man she was engaged to, but she said she liked you and wouldn't mind if you came to call.'

"She was nowhere to be seen when we rode off. Stopping later by a stream to water our horses, we also tried out the sugar cookies. I remember telling my brother, I hope it was her who baked the Birthday cake and not the cookies. Because this is the girl I'm going to ask to marry me. It was the hardest cookie I had ever bitten into, and simply couldn't bite through them. We packed them under some stones in the river to soften them before we could get a taste. When I told my mother I had met my dream girl, she was disappointed that she wasn't a well- bred English girl, and asked if I was aware that not long ago the English were fighting the Boers. She was against that union, but I ignored her, and after a very short courtship I married her."

During the baling of the tobacco, my art teacher, who encouraged me to take art seriously, presented me with a box of oil paints and some brushes that would influence me for the rest of my life. Dad cut me a piece of canvass off the roll and mounted it in the braiding shed, and with the help of some animal pictures taken on first safari, I made a panorama of what else, a safari. Regretfully I had to give it up when we ran out of the pre-measured canvas. Daddy held out till the last bale before he finally used it. It broke my heart to give it up.

Several weeks later a large package arrived at our house addressed to "The Artist." In it was a letter from the tobacco corporation, telling how they exhibited it for all to see, and returned the money Dad had spent on the purchase of the whole roll of canvas. And there was extra clean canvas for me and my panorama back, so indirectly that counted as my first sale.

Just before my fourteenth birthday, Daddy had a long talk with me.

The farm work was becoming too much for us, and the funds were running out, besides I would have to get to a high school soon, and perhaps concentrate on a career in art? He considered going back to our first home, what did I think about it? I was excited, I would see my sister again, but instead of studying art, I told him I wanted to become a veterinarian. "When do we leave?"

19

With My Dreams of Becoming a Vet

Coming from the farm, I felt different, and everything around me was different. The high school on the hill was unsure of which grade to place me in, because I looked older than my fourteen years. So they gave me an IQ test and placed me in seventh grade. Aunt Ciellie had taken me on a shopping spree before entering high school and that helped a bit. I was the new girl on the block, but didn't really belong in their groups. All the children I had known before going away to the farm were young adults now. They were also more mature, in their makeup and high heels.

Beaulah, who was my best friend, and two years older than me, was sixteen and dating a nineteen-year-old college student. She ran around with the older groups. I tagged along on her invitation, but felt more like a unwanted younger sister.

Opposite the old general store, a Greek had opened a soda fountain, where we all hung out after school to gossip, flirt, and drink the latest soft drink from America, Coca Cola or the South African cheaper imitation Cola Rita. The girls talked about boys and the boys talked about owning a motor bike, Paul and Gerrit, two of the older ones sixteen and seventeen, had their own bikes. Their thrill was to go on the outskirts of town on the dirt road and do some drag racing. I would usually ride on the back of Gerrit's Harley Davidson. But Paul had the stronger bike and usually won. So I told Gerrit to teach me to drive in secret, and when I was ready I challenged Paul. He said, "You can't even handle a bike." But I did outwit him because his strategy was to cut whomever he had challenged off and slow them down, then win. I had seen what he did a few times and wise to his tricks, I was ready. On the night of the race, when he passed me to cut me off, I didn't slow down, I circled around him to the left, cutting him off. That was something he didn't expect, and I won. The ultimate humiliation for him was the teasing of everyone that a mere slip of a girl had beaten him. And the fact that he also had to pay for anything I wanted to eat or drink for two weeks.

At fifteen after I completed eighth grade, I dropped out of school when Daddy decided to give up our first home and move into the big city where he got a job.

I moved into the Young Women's Christian Association, taking an ushers job in a movie house to pay for my boarding. I could not wait to go to veterinary college, but discovered I had to be seventeen to enter as an apprentice.

I begged Dad to write me a letter, to tell the veterinary department we were waiting for my birth certificate and he can testify that I was seventeen.

I bought myself some high heels and makeup and went for an interview at Onderstepoort Veterinary College. To my surprise they accepted me. They had a bus specially for the students and staff that picked me up at the Y. At first I was content just to be there and do odd jobs, running errands for the veterinarians.

While I longed to work with and learn more about the animals, in three months I was upgraded to the laboratories where vaccines were developed and distributed. I worked in a small glass cubicle, with unspeakable diseases like anthrax, contagious abortion, Rift Valley fever, protected only with protective clothing, a mask, and gloves. My task was to drill a small hole into bred eggs and inject a chicken embryo with one of the diseases. Some of these horrible diseases I also had to inject into the artery in the tail of white mice, then keep a diary of the development of the disease. I found it ironic that I should destroy one animal to save another. One day they approached me, "How would you like to work in the stock improvement project?" That couldn't be worse than what I was doing, I thought, I would be working with real animals. Till I discovered that *The Island of Dr. Moreau* was a reality. The project was a genetic experiment of species cross breeding. The first animal I saw was a cross between a dog and baboon, It had the characteristics of both species, and was alive. It was monstrous. It was so vicious that it was

156

kept in a steel cage, it had the face of a dog and the hindquarters of a baboon. Insane, vicious, and frothing at the mouth like a rabid dog. Experiment two was still born; it was a sperm mix of a lamb and a dog. It had two siamese bodies of a lamb, on which three heads where attached, melted into one like some gross flower. The brain had no crania and was surrounded by six dog ears. Experiment three was a chicken bred and hatched in ultraviolet light. Although it lived till maturity, its bones where soft and pliable, to the point that one could tie a knot in them, It also was albino with no color. Experiment four was a cow with multiple legs, two of which protruded out of the belly and one on the back. This put the nail in the coffin. I was completely disenchanted with the idea of becoming a vet by then.

Fate had a way of correcting things that didn't go my way.

20

First Taste of Show Business

One morning I was called into the main office. There was a strange looking Englishman, with knobby knees and baggy shorts who introduced himself as Bladon Peake, Film Director. He didn't beat around the bush.

"I would like to cast you as the lead in a film called *Transvaal Tale*; it's a period film, about a man who loses all his cattle and had to destroy them because of an outbreak of Rift Valley fever. I hear you are good at handling horses and buckboards and such. Because it is a film that would benefit the veterinary department, they have agreed to give you three months leave to complete the film. We would be filming on various locations. We would pay you of course." Again I thought, well this cannot be worse than what I was doing right then. I did the screen test, and got the part opposite a charming veterinarian that looked a little like Clark Gable.

In the hopes that they too would also be recognized, I suddenly had scores of friends who hung around me on the set. Right after completion of the film, I turned seventeen, and they naturally wanted to celebrate.

"We know just the place," they said, "and we have arranged for a blind date for you. He is an older man but you'll easily pass for twenty. He would call for you at the YWCA."

At eight when I went down to the lobby, I was surprised to find an older man in his early thirties waiting for me. He was charming and elegant, but I thought I had made a mistake and that they had sent somebody's father to fetch me. I felt completely out of his class as we got into the latest model convertible Studebaker. I must have looked scared getting into a strange man's car because he laughed and reassured me. "Relax, I'm not a monster! Your friends are waiting for us at my club they have a surprise planned for you I believe." *Little did I know that was exactly what he turned out to be— a Monster.*

At the Jockey Club, everyone seemed to know him. He was throwing money around as if it grew on trees. They talked about the racehorses he owned, and I was quite impressed. He even lit a girl's cigarette with a rolled up twenty dollar bill, something that would last me a week.

I noticed that everybody besides myself was drinking hard liqueur. They all tried to get me to drink something, too; I refused and said that I would rather not.

They started teasing. "Poor little virgin, she doesn't drink either." I felt embarrassed. "I don't find that funny, you're just jealous that I'm still one and that I'm also still sober."

"We'll just have to see to that," and they winked at my 'date.' Like they had a secret with him. Which they had, but I was too innocent to see it.

"Don't mind them, I'll take care of you. Would you like another Coke? It's the latest import from America." I felt flattered when this handsome worldly man should take so much notice of me. But when he brought me the Coke, it tasted funny. I told him so, but he only laughed.

"It's nothing. I think they just wanted to play a trick on you. They put a little rum in, it won't hurt you. Drink up." I had never tasted rum before, and trusted him that it wouldn't hurt me. Seconds later I started feeling strange, and asked one of the girls to take me to the cloakroom.

"I'll take her home," he said, and this time I could clearly see him wink to the others. By now I could hardly stand up. With his arm around my waist he guided me out of the club. I was hardly in the car when I passed out.

I came to stark naked, in a beautiful room with a oversized circular bed. Everything was wrong! I was fully aware of my surroundings, but I could not move or speak. I was paralyzed. He came into the room naked with a drink in his hand, put his drink down on a bedside table nonchalantly as if he had done what he was about to do many times. He could have slit my throat at that moment and I wouldn't have been able to prevent it. He flipped me over onto my stomach onto the edge of the bed, and brutally sodomized me. I tried to scream, but couldn't. When he was done he left the room. I could hear a shower, tried again to scream and desperately to get up, and my brain responded but my body wouldn't. Then in my living nightmare he came back in again, turned me over and dragged me fully onto the bed, spread my legs and raped me repeatedly. My brain registered, "It isn't real, this isn't happening to you," but there was blood everywhere, and it was real! At last he was through, And fell halfway across me asleep.

I did not know where I was, but instinct took over and I knew I had to get out of there if I wanted to stay alive. Some of my feelings were coming back. He was snoring and fast asleep. Like awakening from a terrible nightmare, I slid off the bed, and crawling, dragged myself toward the door, where I found my dress he had torn off me. I slipped it over my head. Like a beaten wounded animal I slunk out the door, minus underclothes or shoes, down some stairs and into the street, where I lay slumped against a wall till I could regain full mobility. People passing by shrugged their shoulders, and whispered, "Isn't it terrible that such a young girl could be so drunk?" They just surmised that, but no one asked me what really happened?

When I was able to walk, I wandered around trying to find my direction. Terrified that he might come after me to finish me off, I hid in hedges, bruised and bleeding, tears streaming down my face. At last I recognized something! I was near the little park with the giant magnolias where I spent a lot of time, dreaming of the day when I should meet some knight in shining armor who would carry me off into the realms of true love. It was only blocks away from the YWCA, but I dare not go there because the doors were locked and I would have to explain where I had been the whole night. The brutality of the terrible ordeal I had just gone through dawned on me, yet I felt guilty that I accepted the invitation because I thought the so-called friends were going to give me a surprise birthday party. One part of me said, *You should go to the police,* and the other part of me that was degraded, drugged and raped said, *No, nobody must know.*

For weeks I wandered around like a zombie, afraid that I might be pregnant. I performed my work with extra care, so that I did not reveal the dirty secret. I moved out of the YWCA into an old house with three of my loyal friends, who had no idea why I had suddenly become so withdrawn. Indirectly I found out that for a price I was sold to Mr. F.J., who added me to his collection of conquered virgins, like a trophy. The drug he used on me was Rohipnol, used by animals like him who used unsuspecting young woman for their own sick gratification, but were coward enough to use paralysis to achieve their goal without a fight.

I wanted to tell my sister, but too ashamed, I decided that she was the last one I could tell. She had married a wonderful man, and was awaiting her first child; it would be too much of a shock to her.

As the months turned into years, I learned to live with my secret. To boost my self-esteem, I took up ball room dancing. Won many competitions. Became a finalist in the Miss South Africa Competition. Even tried dating, usually shying away from the first signs I detected of intimacy. I tried to excel in all that I did to show myself that I was worthy.

At twenty I was already a department head at the veterinary department. Had reorganized the entire department to work more efficiently, so when I was offered the opportunity to go to Cape Town, one thousand miles away to do the same for their branch there, I did not hesitate for a moment. Grabbed at the chance for a new beginning.

21

Cape Town — A New Beginning

After the first movie, another followed. Now I had other dreams to pursue, the stage! set design perhaps? Pretoria had nothing more to offer me. I had heard the place to be was Cape Town, abounding with theaters and opportunities!

Parting was indeed sweet sorrow, as I bid good-bye to friends and family at the station.

The train clicked past desolate sweeps of grassland, desert, and forests. Passing small neglected towns where tattered children ran alongside the tracks, shouting greetings and begging for handouts or cash. They were dangerously near the tracks, so I tossed out a handful of change as far away from the slow-moving train as possible. Laughter and pandemonium broke out as they scrambled after the change, in among the shrubbery to get at it.

We passed colorful land tapestries, thrown haphazardly against the rolling hills, made up of freshly plowed fields, new green growth sprouting through the black burnt earth, and seas of golden wheat moving in rhythmic waves like some sleeping dragon's breath, exhaling wave upon wave.

A few clicks farther we were climbing high into the mountain ranges with sheer cliffs and deep valleys. Small waterfalls tumbled in glistening abundance over the rock walls into emerald fern below. Then with train brakes screeching over well worn tracks we descended slowly into shaded forests, lorded over by giant yellow-wood trees. Soon it became too dark to see, but I was distracted by the slim blue suited porter walking along the narrow hall, playing a melodious gong, calling al diners to the dining car.

The blue-train, with it's private compartments and plush red velvet seats, panoramic paintings and crochet antimacassars on the compartment backrests, outdid itself in decor in the dining salon. It also boasted starched white damask tablecloths, with artistically folded matching napkins and fresh flowers on the tables. The menu was outstanding, with a selection of Cape wines on the wine list.

My well-traveled companion ordered a wine from Stellenbosh.

"We will pass Stellenbosh in the morning, unfortunately you will miss some of the most spectacular scenery during the night, but make sure you wake up early for the sunrise as we enter the Cape with backdrops of folded mountains that is equal to Scandinavian splendor." I wanted to linger longer after dinner, but if I was going to have a wake-up call for sunrise I decided to have a early night.

The night porter had already been, pulled down the bed and made it up. On my pillow lay a goodnight message and a small chocolate. During the night I lay with my face pressed against the window. In the light of the moon following us, I could only make out dark cathedral-like shapes, and black expanses where deep gorges dropped precipitously into deep valleys. I fell asleep with the sound of the wheels clicking the travelers tune of "sugarbags-cornbags-sugarbags-cornbag-sugarbags-cornbags" I sang on the train to visit Grandpa and Grandma a long time ago. Now it sang me asleep on another track as it carried me to another destination, and other adventures.

I was awake long before my wake-up call. I got up, folded the quaint copper basin out of the wall, washed and brushed my teeth. I dressed hurriedly and went to the observation car, not to miss anything. My dinner companion of the previous night had not exaggerated. The passing scenery was breathtaking. A wonderland of mountain ranges both near and into the distance. As I enjoyed a full South African breakfast of eggs, bacon, and sausage, we passed gems of wine farms, lying side by side with unique Dutch architecture. Within an hour I would be entering Cape Town.

While I gathered my belongings together, I kept my eyes focused on the window.

And there it was! In the distance loomed the awesome majesty of Table Mountain, shrouded in a cloud tablecloth, in whose bosom, Cape Town was just waking up.

"So this is it?" I said out loud as we steamed into an unimpressive gray painted station. Along the platform stood the strangest collection of people with the greatest collection of complexions I had ever seen gathered together in one place. I was told to expect a rainbow of peoples from all over the world, because it was a port city, but never expected them all to have gathered at the station! I marveled at the selection.

Pale brown skins with long black hair, brown skins with blond hair, sallow yellow skins with slanted eyes and blue-black hair, dark brown skins with broad noses and short fuzzy hair. The rest were made up from white, ruddy and pink skins and all shades of hair, either natural or dyed, who were descendants from the Dutch, French, and Portuguese who came originally with three ships to the Cape with Jan Van Riebeek to establish a colony as a stopover for ships traveling to the far east and provide them with fresh fruits and vegetables to prevent scurvy on their long journeys around the Cape point. This together with the inhabitants who were already in Africa and the later offspring resulting from indiscriminate mating turned Cape Town into a true melting pot. The ones coming from Europe were categorized as White or European. The true in habitants were called Kaffirs, meaning black, with the dictionary specifying only the Bantu tribe, but later became a descriptive noun that applied to all African tribes. Because of sensitivity already existing between tribes, it lost its simple meaning and being called a Kaffir became an insult much like the word Negro in America lost its meaning, and became nigger, and an insult and offensive. The last flavor in the pot were simply called coloreds because of the unlimited variety of ethnicity. Children of slaves and their white masters, and children of international transit sailors, who passed through the Port of Cape Town, also children of colored and the Malay import slaves were called "Gammat" with their own slang language. Derived from Afrikaans, it was flowery, almost poetic in its misuse of the original, with English thrown in. I tried to follow a conversation taking place between some people on a bus and it went something like this.

" Maan raai tjog, toe kryg die tjeent de greep."

"Haai foei tjog, ek is sorrie Martjie, wat's to do?"

"Sy wil glad nie eers meer aan de tet suip nie."

In this conversation they were using a combination of Dutch, English, and their own slang. There was no direct translation, but it all boiled down to a child who contracted a chest cold, the second person was sorry, and the mother was concerned that the child would no longer suck her tit.

Afrikaans was the bastard language composed of Dutch, German, French, and Portuguese by the first European settlers who arrived with Jan Van Riebeek from Holland. And who had to cope with the babble of languages brought in that no one could understand. Like the tower of Babel of the Bible.

English, that came later, was the language held over from the invasion of the British who saw the trading potential and conquered the Boer settlers, throwing them into concentration camps to achieve their takeover.

Cape Town was the Mother City of the first white settlers, a city of mushroom growth, that stretched out to the ocean and up into the slopes of the mountain, it was both dignified and cosmopolitan as any European port city. Its rainbow population and mountainous setting gave it its unique charm.

I looked around. Dr. Morton on the Cape Town staff was to meet me and take me to the hotel situated in the botanical gardens a small walk to the Cape Town offices. He had a description of me, and as soon as I stepped off the train he was there.

The hotel was a terrible disappointment. The proprietress came out from behind the counter to greet me. She was wearing a scruffy, wrinkled day dress, on her feet that looked unwashed she had on a pair of torn and trodden down slippers. Her hair standing on end looked uncombed, as if she had been in bed for a week without pulling a comb through it. As Dr. Morton brought in my luggage, she called into the kitchen for a porter. He, too, looked unkempt and obviously doubled on duties. He had on a coat that at some time must have been white. He hurriedly wiped his hands on his jacket, took one look at my luggage, and sulked, as she instructed him to take it up to the second floor. There was no elevator in sight, which accounted for the sour face.

I almost pitied him as it was a large trunk; out of breath he deposited it into a small and dingy looking room. I immediately noticed that there was a wash stand with dish and jug, but no bathroom. When I got back downstairs, I asked Dr. Morton who was waiting for me to go and introduce me to the rest of the veterinary staff, who had selected the hotel.

He said, "I'm sorry, this is the first time I've seen the place. Onderstepoort had written and said that it was only temporary, the brochure looked good. When I phoned to confirm, the proprietress told me it was paid for a month. In that time I'm sure we can find you somewhere else."

On the way back to the hotel after the introductions, I bought a newspaper, and looked through the accommodation section, but not knowing Cape Town I realized that I would have to grin and bear it. In the week I had off to settle in, I would take a bus and check out some places. In the meantime with the hotel paid for, I could check out the dining room, because the last meal I had was on the train that morning. I was hungry.

There were still a few people in the dining room. I was seated at a table by the same woman, who still had not combed her hair, at a table equally unkempt.

She informed me, "Lunch is over in fifteen minutes, I'll go see if I can still get you something."

She came back from the kitchen with a broad smile, "You're in luck!" She was followed by the same young man who had taken up my luggage. At least he had made a noticeable change in his appearance. He had washed his face and hopefully his hands and had changed into a faded red jacket, with one button missing.

There was no menu. He was carrying a plate that he plonked down in front of me. "Roast beef, cabbage, and potatoes," he announced proudly, trying to be friendly. "And tonight we are having my meat loaf!"

I didn't want to think about what went in it. But I had the answer to his change of costume. He was not only the porter, but also the cook and the maitre d. I had a vivid imagination and could just about picture the preparation of that dish, and how the ingredients were mixed. He was desperately trying to be friendly anticipating a tip.

"That would be nice." I smiled thinking, *I'll definitely try to avoid that meal!* as I handed him the cutlery to go and rinse, still smiling not to offend.

The cutlery looked as if someone had just licked it clean.

He brought me still damp clean cutlery, and then took position against the wall watching me, as I choked down some of the food, trying not to think about it's dubious preparation.

"On my way here I saw some people dressed up in some carnival costumes, is there going to be a parade?" I asked trying to distract him.

"It's the beginning of the summer season, and District Six usually has a carnival up Adderley Street to De Lorentz Street near the base of the mountain." I thanked him, went up to the room, unpacked only the essentials, and changed into more comfortable clothes. It was really very hot and I still had on my travel clothes. I locked my door and walked into the botanical garden to a tea garden I had seen earlier on, to reflect on what to do with the rest of the afternoon.

Adderley, the main street, started near the docks, past ancient buildings decorated with scrolls and gables, past tall new office buildings, and new modern shops. A hundred years ago Adderley Street was called "Heerengracht" which meant gentleman's walk. It continued into the long red gold hard packed soil promenade, which ran the full length of the remnants of the original botanical garden where the markets of the East India Company once thrived and provided the world's ships with fresh fruits and vegetables. Though very little remained of the fourteen acres of the original gardens, the 100-year-old oak trees stood like sentinels along the promenade where beaux and belles met in secret rendezvous in the gardens in the time of our pioneer forefathers.

To the Cape-tonians, it was simply known as the 'Avenue.' The promenades still continued with the exception that the modern guys and gals both wore blue jeans. To the lovers the dense tropical vegetation still provided a secret hideaway to steal a few kisses.

At that hour the avenue was full of people taking their lunch breaks in romantic outdoor tea gardens hidden in among the trees. The children of families out for the day delighted in feeding bushy tailed squirrels darting back and forth across the walks that branched off from the main avenue. I passed a Japanese aromatic garden, made specially for the blind, with descriptive plaques in Braille. Chains guided the sightless from one delight to another. There were beds of herbs to rub and sweet smelling flowers. Stone statues to explore. I closed my eyes and took hold of the chain. Stood still for a moment, aware of the incredible smells that surrounded me. I felt the shapes of the stones and their textures. Some were in the shade and felt cool and smooth, while others were rough and hot having been in the sun the whole morning. I retraced my steps, still with my eyes closed back to the herb garden, rubbed them one by one in my hands. Identifying several, proud of myself that I did not have to look at one of them.

I left the garden of the blind. Whichever path I took, I marveled at the plants and trees from all over the world.

A shrill sound suddenly pierced the air, drowning out the sound of the birds, and people strolling along the Avenue.

"PEANUTS! P E A - U - N U T S!" A scrawny boy, no older than seven, waved his wares into the faces of the passersby.

I sat down, several bush doves, pigeons and squirrels approached me eagerly.

"Peeeeeee-nuts!" It came almost in my ear. His life's ambition at that moment was to sell the six bags he still had in his hands, because to day of all days he wanted to be somewhere else where all the action would take place.

When I bought them all, he looked at me in disbelief, and when I said, "Hou die kleingeld," his jaw dropped. No one had ever told him to keep the change. A penny here or there perhaps but never the whole thing. He ran whooping and hollering, and somersaulting down the Avenue. I handed the peanuts to some children, and followed the boy.

As I exited the gardens, the air suddenly pulsated with a cacophony of sounds.

Colorful bands, bells, and laughter. The marchers were broken up into groups of fifty or more. The costumes over all were in the brightest colors imaginable. The first group was in top hats and tails. Dots, diamonds, stripes in two tones with faces painted to match, a small boy looking very familiar was leading the group dressed like the rest. So that's what the urgency was to sell his peanuts. He paused for a second and waved to me. I waved back.

The second group was dressed like Carmen Miranda, all frills and bare waists with skirts flaring out behind, covered with sequins. They tried to outdo one another with the turbans and hats covered in fruits. In front of them on the shoulders of a man rode a small girl mascot, behind the man followed four little charmers twirling their batons. They somersaulted, tap danced, and twirled their batons like pros.

Some one in the spectators looked at me and said, "Aren't these guys fabulous?"

"What do you mean guys?" I couldn't believe my ears.

"Yes they are Men!"

On closer inspection I saw they were indeed men, cleverly padded and painted. Between each group marched the spectacular costume creations, that sometimes needed three to four people to support just the incredible headdresses and trains. Made up of every conceivable bauble, feathers, mirrors and glitter.

After them came the bands each performing their own compositions, competing for the top prize that would pay for the following years creations. A crowd of about two thousand coloreds marched behind doing their own thing, singing their own songs. To enjoy this uncensored spontaneity, one must know the song or the language. I recognized one of the songs, which we sang in secret behind the school. I repeated their words softly to myself.

"Jou kombers en my mattras, die slaap nie eners nie, die slaap nie eners nie! Emma kom lemma, se ma vir jou gremma, emma wil 'n baby he."

"What are they saying?" an onlooker asked me.

"It's just a nonsense rhyme," I tried to explain.

"But what are they saying?"

"They are talking in Gammat slang, it goes something like this. 'Your mattress and my blanket, never sleeps the same, never sleeps the same. Emma come lay with me, you can tell your grandma you only wanted a baby.'"

I was slowly carried away by the crowds watching the show, and where the parade turned around I found myself deep in the heart of District Six—the slum area that I was warned about, and found out that no sane person would ever enter on their own. If I was awed by the ethnic melting pot at the station, here there were no color barriers. Poverty and prostitution played the center stage. Morality was definitely not their highest priority.

A sailor in milk white bell-bottoms stumbled out of a dilapidated building, puked the cheap wine and meager supper over the filthy pavement, staggered a few more paces and fell flat on his face, his head hanging in the gutter. Several rainbow children jumped back and forth over him, making a game out of his misfortune. Some of them saw it as an unexpected gain and were going through his pockets, supervised and encouraged by a large woman sitting on some steps, scratching herself. She was grossly overweight and sat with her legs spread apart; her stomach hung in folds over her enormous thighs. She was dressed, or rather undressed, in a cheap see-through nighty. Breasts the size of watermelons fought against the flimsy material and popped out at every broken stitch opening. She eyed me curiously.

Minutes later some sailors strolled by, possible customers I thought and shuddered. Could someone actually find her attractive?

Some of the "Carmens" from the carnival danced by at the opposite side of the street. The sailors, mistaking them for broads, and not aware of their gender, made a B-line for them. The cross-dressers played along for a while, then tired of the deception, one pulled out the stuffing from his bra, and removed the turban from his head, then in a very masculine voice asked, "Do you still want me darling?" He embraced the sailor, rubbing himself against him. Annoyed at the deception the sailor shoved him away. For a moment it looked like there was going to be a fight, but the sailor wasn't going to spend his shore leave on a fight, he had other things in mind. He shrugged his shoulders, and joined his sailor-buddies, and they took off in another direction.

The fat lady who stood up and started preening when the sailors came into view said, "DAMN!"And sat down again on the steps, focusing her attention on a bunch of children pushing a soap box cart down a slight incline in the road, oblivious to possible cars. Screams of either pain or delight emanated from several clinging to the side of the contraption, like flies to a spoon of honey. All at once they let it go! The cart careened down the slope out of control, spilling the occupants along the way. The ones at the top of the road showed no concern, they had another distraction.

In a cobbled side street stood a horse-drawn cart. The worn out old horse, more bone than flesh, hung his head low from weariness and whip lashings.

The man was shouting, " BOTTLES AND BAGS! Bottles and Bags!! a penny a bottle." He had no idea that he was helping in the recycling project, he only knew that he would get five cents himself at the recycling place, that would mean a full four cents profit on each bottle. "Bring your old bottles!" A woman came out the house with a sack full of wine bottles. The bottles came with her profession. To the man she was a regular customer and always worth at least fifty pennies. Sometimes she would bypass the penny a bottle for some of the flea market junk he got for free when they asked him to haul away the left-overs from their days market. Sometimes they would even pay him to haul it away, then the profit was all his. He put on his charming face and tried to persuade her to take something from the back of the cart. She turned to the back of the cart, and selected two of the cast off dresses; she would make triple what the man made with the next ship that came in, but for now she needed a dress, and to get rid of the bottles that were filling up her room. He could be generous with her, so he handed her two other items to promote a good relationship. The only problem he had with the free merchandise were the children helping themselves while he was busy with a client.

As he got on the wagon, he caught some of the children getting on the back, throwing some of the things down to retrieve later. "Get off, *Verfloekte vabonde*!"(you dammed delinquents) he screamed, waving the whip at the children. Then he whipped the thin, overburdened horse, who tried to move, but was either too hungry or too tired or discouraged to move. This angered the man even more who took the pause of the animal to mean, lazy. Immediately the whip rained unmercifully down. In my imagination, I set the old horse free. I saw him gallop away, young and free, over rich green fields of clover. The beating had taken effect, slowly the beast walked along.

"BOTTLES AND BAGS! BOTTLES AND BAGS!" The children mimicked the man, "bottles and baaaags, bottles and baaaags!" as they retrieved the stolen goods that would assure them a seat at the *bioscope* on Saturday

By now I had taken so many side streets, I knew I was lost. Further up the street, someone had tried to bring a festive atmosphere to the street by hanging colored rags interspersed with wilted flowers on a string from one telephone pole to the other. People were laughing! I wondered how they could be so cheerful surrounded by such squalor.

Out of a dark corner, a famished, obviously ill-treated kitten appeared, his wet caked fur pulled out in patches. Haunted sad eyes popped out of it's pleading little face, his tail dragging behind him in the dirt. A soft almost inaudible mewing came from deep within his wounded little insides. It was trying desperately to escape its torture, staggering aimlessly on to nowhere.

"Oh my God, please help it!" I prayed out loud. I was just about to pick it up when an equally scrawny child came from out of the same darkness and grabbed the kitten by its neck. The defenseless bundle of bedraggled fur hung for a moment in the child's hands. Who swung it back and forth, and with obvious hatred, he flung it against a wall. It made no sound, and lay still where it landed. I ran to the boy. "What did you do that for?" He shrugged his shoulders. At that moment I felt like picking up that child and flinging him against the wall, without thinking for a moment that he was taking his hatred of what he himself was enduring out on that poor little thing, for the simple reason that it was smaller than him. Instead I picked up the little kitten; it lay limp in my hands.

A strapping woman appeared, "*Baster!*" (bastard) she addressed the child, "Come here!" She spewed some more vulgarities at him as she hit him without question or reasoning with resounding slaps across his head, he fell back against the same wall he had thrown the kitten, and for a moment I recognized the same astonished wounded look on his face that the kitten had earlier on.

"What the hell are you doing with my cat?" she yelled at me, snatching the kitten from my hands. She grabbed the child by the neck, and took both inside, where the child screamed as more blows fell on his body. I stood rooted there but couldn't do a thing. I don't know who, or what I hated more at that moment. Poverty, the government, or the ignorance that came with both. And understood the child's anger.

I prayed again, silently. *Please God take this kitten into your loving hands, and teach the woman compassion spare the child from the world's anger.*

I had to get away from there. I tried to retrace my steps, looked for landmarks, but one dilapidated building looked much like the other. Finally I found the hotel.

That night I could not sleep; there was a wild party going on in the room next to mine. I heard a click of a key in my door. A drunk stumbled into my room. I recognized him as the man with the red jacket. So he also had access to the room keys. I jumped up and shoved him outside, so hard that he almost fell over the balcony. I pushed the wash stand in front of the door packed the things I had unpacked and lay wide-eyed waiting for the noise to stop, but sleep did not come easy. In the morning I checked out. I was prepared to spend all my savings but could not tolerate another night in that hotel. I did not care when the woman told me she could not refund me. I called a cab.

"Take me to a hotel please." I think the cabby understood, as he took a look at the woman who was still in the same dress and slippers, and this time her hair definitely had been slept in.

Hotel Geneva in Bantry-Bay was beautiful, with the beach a stones throw away across the street.

"The others had already checked in." The man behind the counter said and handed my key to the porter who loaded my trunk on a cart and escorted me to the elevator.

"Thank you," I stammered, "I'll check in later then.?" I didn't know who the others were, but it was obvious he had mistaken me for someone else. I was sure to find out later, but for now I was satisfied just to be out of the other place.

The room was spacious and luxuriously furnished. I had my own bathroom with thick monogrammed towels, and a telephone by my bed side. I felt like a queen as my spike heels sunk into the plush wine-red carpet

That night, I dressed for dinner, and after being seated, I saw who the *others* were. Earlier on in the lobby, I had read an article that the Follies Bergere was staying in the Geneva. Just looking around it was obvious. The showgirls were beautiful. I felt flattered to be mistaken for one of them, and was basking in the attention. I wasn't going to let them know. I still had a few days before starting work and wanted to enjoy the limelight while it lasted.

I even had room service, with a fresh rose on my tray. It would cost me a fortune, but I didn't care! I scanned the papers at night for cheaper accommodations.

At the end of my 'Follies' week I saw a room advertised in a bungalow on Fourth Beach. The price was right; I would be able to afford it on the salary Onderstepoort was going to pay me. But I didn't know where Fourth Beach was. So I asked around and someone said it was on Clifton. Busses ran at regular intervals there and back to town. That was wonderful news, because it would solve getting to and from work in the gardens.

Clifton was a half an hour away by bus from where I was. I had obtained a brochure from the hotel lobby. It said it was a surfers paradise. As the bus turned the corner, it was obvious that it was not only a surfers paradise, but a paradise for sun worshipers, and artists. Clifton's natural rock formation divided the salt white beaches into four sections. First through fourth beach.

"End of the line!" the bus driver shouted as we reached Fourth Beach. I inquired from a person heading to one of many stairs going down to the beach where I would find a bungalow called "Far Horizon." They pointed out a black wooden bungalow anchored onto the side of the biggest rock I had ever seen. Like a giant sleeping whale it stretched from the beach out to sea.

A woman in her sixties opened the door when I knocked.

"You must be the young lady who called about my ad, come right in." There was a big fat tabby cat sitting sunning itself on the narrow window sill. "This here is Tabby, I'm Molly." The cat was obviously regarded as family otherwise there wouldn't have been the formal introduction.

"Hi, Tabby," I greeted the cat and held my hand out to Molly.

"I don't give meals, you can get that at Mount Pleasant, a boarding house across from the Clifton Hotel, I don't tolerate loud music, and I charge for overnight *visitors*, if you get what I mean. I'll show you the room now."

The room was fairly large, plain and pleasant with a large window that looked out to the far horizon. There were no protective bars at the window. The sun streamed across the polished plank floor. I opened the window; as I leaned out it made me dizzy, there was just a sudden drop and the sea washed foamingly up against the rock below. To the right I had a seaman's view of all four beaches. The big rock was full of seagulls resting between flights of fancy on wind currents playing on ten-foot surfer waves. I paid Molly and moved in the following day.

I was in love with my surroundings, loved the sea. Every free moment I spent climbing the rocks, and wandering along the four beaches. My feet carried me dancing around the beautiful Clifton drive. Sometimes I would get off the bus a mile away from home and skip down the two hundred and odd wooden steps, blackened by the elements that started behind the Clifton Hotel down to First Beach, stopping only occasionally to smell the wild oleander and arum lilies that grew in wild profusion against the cliffs. The steps, defying privacy, wound through backyards without fences like a snake. My business became their business as I looked through windows opened to the world. Most of the old bungalows had romantic names like Wind Song,

Cliff Side, and Mandalay, which belonged to the most famous leading poet of South Africa.

There was one house built on concrete pillars over the rocks at water's edge, on First Beach, that had me fascinated. It had the wonderful name of *Laughing Waters*.

It had a tropical room filled with ferns and exotic orchids. The amazing feature of this room was that it had a floor entirely made of glass that was suspended over the rocks below. Standing on the floor with bare feet gave one the feeling that you were standing on the wet rocks, and walking on the water. It was the peculiar behavior of the water through these very same rocks that gave the place its name. Through time the sea had carved large holes into the rocks that were deeply buried in the sand. As the tide rolled in the rocks sucked in the water, then like a sea dragon blowing out flames through its nostrils, with a surging, gurgling and whistling, it blew the water with enormous force out through the holes. As the waves receded it sucked the water back through the holes into unknown crevasses below the sand, sounding for all the world like a low giggle, as if the stone freak of nature had turned human and was laughing at the elements that created it, inspiring the beautiful original name.

No one had prepared me for the beauty of Cape Town. Many said that it reminded them of Rio De Janeiro, but never having traveled, I couldn't confirm it.

Cape Town lay in a bowl of mountains starting with Table-Mountain, then Lions Head, and round Chapmen's Peak Drive that was carved out of the side of the Twelve Apostles Mountains that stretched all the way to Cape Point where the Atlantic and the Pacific Oceans met in a wild horse mane.

During the week I worked in the botanical gardens in the shadow of Table Mountain, and commuted with a double decker bus to the beaches. But weekends I explored, my feet and my senses never at rest, as if I was wearing the enchanted red shoes that never stopped dancing. I roasted to a deep tan like all the other sun worshipers as I went hiking over the beaches and up the side of Lions Head carpeted in lilac heather, mixed with fields of daffodils contrasting in their bright yellow tutus. I brought back arms full, filling every bottle glass and hollow thing, with still plenty over to give away.

I was restless, with a strange passion growing in me! I spent hours on the big rock that was my back porch, where Tabby and I played. I became part of Tabby's life and love affairs, ignoring my own growing passions.

Tabby revealed she had a dual character. In front of Miss Molly, she was the sophisticated refined house cat who was particular about who she associated with and finicky about what she ate. Miss Molly fell for this part of her, pampering to her likes and dislikes. She lay on her special pillow on the window sill, looking out over the horizon. Occasionally she licked her lips secretly, when a bird alighted outside her window.

Miss Molly was very excited when the tortoise shell tomcat from next door came to call. She wanted Tabby to fall in love with the beautiful tortoise shell.

"You know he actually comes from a long line of tortoise shells and has the pedigree papers to prove it, *His Emminence Big Red.*"

Molly enticed Big Red with tidbits of sardines, also saucers of cream its owner recommended, which it simply adored. Naturally, Big Red called regularly with such fancy cuisine. Tabby usually sat to one side to share the final lickings, but whenever *His Eminence* tried to make a move on her, the fur flew. She wanted nothing to do with his advances.

The snacks naturally attracted a lot of unsavory characters, that Molly patiently shooed away. Only I knew that Tabby had already made her selection. I dare not tell Molly. When Tabby took her nightly moonlight walk on the rock, I'd see her with one or the other of the "unsavories." There would be a lot of hissing and slapping, but she had chosen the scruffiest of the lot to sing her love songs to.

Tabby became pregnant; Miss Molly was overjoyed and convinced that Big Red was going to be the daddy. But when the kittens arrived it was obvious that they were the offspring of the alley cat with no name or pedigree.

Three Prophetic Dreams

The big rock was full of dimples and holes. Huge waves slammed against the side of the rock, but sometimes the waves spilled over onto the rock, filling the deep holes with water. When the water receded, it left behind glistening aquariums filled with small sea creatures trapped in the fragile swaying green fingers of the water plants. I usually waited till the bubbles and froth broke and it became clear to see what treasures the waves had brought in. On the side of the rock pools there were barnacles and brightly colored sea anemones. Between waves I would lie on the wet rock dipping my hands into

the cool depth, teasing the anemones, who when touched withdrew their tentacles till the coast was clear. Sometimes whole pieces of seaweed would end up in the rock pools. I would search for tiny transparent little creatures with semi colon eyes, which turned out to be minuscule baby shrimp. I left them in the pool, to prolong their little lives by keeping them away from fish. One day I found clinging to a piece of sea weed a most amazing little animal. A brown dimpled sea horse. Miniature dragon of the sea. This one had a full belly. He was undeniably pregnant. I felt sorry for him because once the pool evaporated it would dry out and he would not be able to have his babies. The rock pool was definitely not the place to be, in his condition. I ran
 inside and got a dish, and after a lot of evasive maneuvers on his side and trickery on mine, I was able to scoop both him and the sea weed into the dish, I climbed down to the waters edge where there were larger rock caves were I carefully deposited him into the water, hoping that the shock of my capturing him wasn't too much to survive and have his little family.

It was during one of these rock climbs that I accidentally discovered the *cove* that eventually became my "Shangri-la." Against the side of the cliff, past fourth beach and the big rock I could see what looked like a small cove. I immediately started planning how to get there. I reckoned I would be able to reach it by going round the dividing rock separating fourth beach from it. But the tide was too strong and washed me up against the rough side of the rock. If it was impossible from the beach side, it looked even more improbable from the road above it. I would climb halfway down the steps and make my way slowly across the steep incline, where they were landscaping, hold onto the fig tree growing lower down and let myself down onto the cove's little beach.

But as I scrambled crab-like along the incline, the soil suddenly gave way, causing a landslide. To break my fall I made a grab for a branch of the fig tree. I missed and tumbled between the branches into a dark hole. When my eyes got used to the darkness and the little bit of light that came from above me, I realized I had fallen into a room-sized cave. Had I come down on my head on the sharp flat stone in the center of the cave, I would have been badly injured, but luckily I landed on my feet in deep, soft beach sand. The advantage of the rock was that I could stand on it grab the lip of the mouth of the cave and swing myself out, with little difficulty. Which I promptly did, but instead of having a soft landing I went head over heels, about five feet down, straight onto my bottom. I hadn't hurt myself, but I felt silly sitting there. When I got up I was surprised to find I had fallen in the little cove I was able to see from my window. On a rock wall on the outside of the cave there was a deep hollow like a basket chair, where I could sit through all kinds of weather. I would have a perfect view of everything without being seen from the outside, or from above from the road. The only thing wrong was that I couldn't reach it or the mouth of the cave unless I built some kind of stairway to both, but how? There were a lot of loose big rocks lying around to do it with but they were too heavy to move on my own without some sort of leverage. Wedged among the rocks I spotted a large pole the tide had deposited there a long time ago. I pried it loose, and after about two hours of back breaking work, I had moved some of the bigger rocks in position under the cave mouth and the hollow. Then I piled other rocks onto it to make a simple stairway.

Feeling like a queen, I ascended the stairs and sat in the hollow rock chair. Thick velvet soft moss, covered the inside walls. Tiny flowers grew on it. The view surpassed anything I could imagine. I could see the mountains to the right and above me and the ocean rolling in from horizon to horizon.

"I hereby declare this my *Shangri-la*, and this will henceforth be called my throne and that my castle," I shouted to the waves as they echoed my declaration to the thousands long lost beneath the sea. *Now I need only my prince to come to me and claim my heart for all eternity*, I thought, dreaming of the soul mate who was still to enter my life. That is if he could find the hidden gate to my kingdom. Then I saw it. The big rock that divided fourth beach from my Shangri-la wasn't totally planted into the sand, it leaned at an angle against the back of the cliff. With the high waves breaking against the front of it I could not see that opening, that was below the water line. If I waited between the time of the breaking of the wave and the withdrawal, there was a few moments in time that the water withdrew with the wave, and the hole was big enough to run through. I grabbed my things and timed several waves before the door of opportunity presented itself again, and stooping slightly, I ran through to the fourth beach side. Moments later it closed when the waters settled down behind me and hid the magic door.

That night I lay awake thinking about my private place, the cave, and what I was going to do. I must get a flashlight tomorrow and some supplies to fix up my cave, if I scooped some of the sand out I would be able to stand up in it. When I finally fell asleep I dreamt. *I received an invitation to a Ball. Like Cinderella I had no one to go with and my clothes were in rags. But with my Golden Invitation I go. Just to look. I could hear the music inside, but every time I try to enter I am turned away. Despondent I sat down on the steps. A*

177

hand reached out to me. "Come with me," he says; he is dressed for the ball. I notice his silver hair and mustache and pointed beard. I start to object, saying, "I can't go in like this," but when I look down, I'm dressed in a beautiful billowing gown. He takes me in his arms and we glide off together, our bodies in perfect harmony. "Who are you?" I ask, but before he can answer, a strange blue mist envelopes us, and I find myself dancing alone. He is gone!

I woke up in the morning, feeling sad, remembering the dream in every detail, his image indelibly etched as if in stone in my mind. It puzzled me why I felt sad. I attributed it to my little fantasy trip in my "Shangri-la."

The following day after work I hurried to a hardware store, bought a small storm lamp, some rope, candles, matches, a small shovel and some shelving planks. As an afterthought I bought a note book to start up my diary again. I couldn't wait for four o'clock to come so that I could go and fix up my cave. The bus was very slow. I hurriedly changed and went to the time gate; there were very few people on the beach. I had the timing off pat so it didn't take me long to get through.

Once in the cave I lit some candles and then the storm lamp. The cave was about eight by ten feet and I could almost stand upright. I took the little shovel and dug down; there was about three feet of sand on the bottom before I hit solid rock. The water level must have at one time covered the little cove to be able to deposit so much sand on the bottom. I started shoveling, tossing the sand out through the tree branches. If someone was looking down from the road at that time, it must have looked funny seeing the sand flying out of the tree. Finally I hit rock bottom. Now I could walk upright. Some of the sand I piled up in a corner for me to lie on. There were some natural hollows along the walls. I lay some of the planks in there and hit them in firmly with a rock. I should get some things to snack on next time I went out, I thought, but for now I left the candles, matches, and other things on the shelves. I dusted off the flat rock in the middle; it would be my table. I put my towel on the sand pile and took out my notebook. In it I wrote about my strange dream, and a love letter to the unknown man in my dream. Satisfied, I put the book on the shelf. Stretched out on the sand. It was cool and dark and smelling of sand.

A thought hit home. What if the earth on the embankment shifted more and covered the Cave. No one would ever find me, I would be buried for a very long time before someone would discover that I was missing, and because no one saw me enter through the star gate they would presume that I had run away because I had not told anyone about my secret place.

There was a soft soothing sound as the waves came rolling in, in organized monotony, *shoooz, shoooz* they broke on the soft white sand below, which squeaked when I walked on it like running my finger on the edge of a crystal glass.

The digging had tired me more than I thought and soon I fell asleep.

I dreamt I was in a dungeon; *I was a slave about to be put on the auction block. The slave traders took me naked and in chains out to the block. The bidding started, and I'm aware someone was going to buy me, but I was afraid. "SOLD!" the auctioneer shouted. I looked around but see no one, then a man stepped forward; he was tall and tanned with silver hair and a small pointed beard. His voice was soothing as he took my chains.*

"Do not be afraid, from now on I will take care of you." I woke up feeling strangely content, but confused; where was I? The lamp had gone out, and the candle standing in a draft had burned very low. Was I still in the dungeon? I don't know how long I had slept, but when I pulled myself out of the cave, it was dark and the lights on the bungalows glowed like Christmas lights along the mountainside.

I climbed up on my throne. A heavy sea mist had come up. Far away around the big toe of Moulli Point the light house marked off the minutes as the yellow beams of light revolved, searching in the mist. At intervals the mournful siren wailed its lonely sound over the breaking waves at my feet, the farthest waves building up till they looked like solid walls of green glass in the light of the rising full moon. A silver phosphor glow appeared on the cap of the waves as they folded over and broke into a thousand lacy fragments on the beach moments later with whiplash precision. I had no concept of time. I was part of the elements around me.

My landlady was an old maid who took enough notice of me, not to let me feel neglected, but not too much to make me feel uncomfortable, but going through the time gate in the light of the moon was difficult, and it was late when I entered the bungalow. I thought it wise to take my shoes off; Molly was long ago asleep as I tip toed to my room. Only Tabby lifted her head up off her pillow, yawned, and went straight back to sleep

The next few days Cape Town gave me a taste of unpredictable weather. It rained every day for a week and the south easterly wind played havoc with Cape Town's inhabitants. The streets were crowded with colored raincoats, umbrellas, and rain-sodden people. The wind ripped round each corner, and people were bending into the wind to maintain a firm foothold. Everyone was clinging onto something or someone. I, having no one to cling to, clung onto the telephone poles and onto my clothes to prevent them from blowing over my head. In that brief moment of decision about the clothes, the wind popped my umbrella inside out, tore it out of my grip and it took off like some heaven bound missile. I got drenched going home, and stopped over at Mount Pleasant for my supper.

The landlady there brought a towel and helped me dry of a bit. "Why don't you just move in here? Then you wouldn't have to brave the rain and wind daily, between *Far Horizon* and here. She showed me a room facing the mountain side, it was cheaper, and I wouldn't have to brave the elements daily.

Molly was a sweetheart when I told her the news that I was relocating to Mount Pleasant, changed out of my wet clothes, and opened my window to the night. A thick mist entered uninvited, flooding the room. The mountain and sea were also covered in mist, which had its own identity. I couldn't see the waves through the mist, but knew they too had a passion unto themselves. I felt the bungalow shake in their fury as they hit the pylons anchored on the rocks below. The daffodils on the table trembled in fear. As I climbed in bed, I, too, trembled, listening to the thunder of the rain I fell asleep

Once more I dreamt of the stranger who had visited me on two other occasions, in the nether world of *le petite mort.* The little death of sleep.

I was walking on a mountain path. The path was unfamiliar to me, it was night, and I was afraid. In front of me blocking my path stood a lone wolf. I turned to run, but as I turned, first one, then a whole pack of wolves gathered, glaring at me with teeth showing. If I ran they would surely attack, so I froze in my tracks, praying that someone would soon come and rescue me. Far away I heard the sound of horse's hooves coming in my direction. Then I saw the man. Sitting tall in the saddle his hair reflecting silver in the moonlight, he looked familiar with a little pointed beard. Seeing my distress, he didn't hesitate and pulled me onto the back of the horse. As I looked back I saw the solo wolf, leader of the pack, had joined the others and gave chase. We headed toward a lighthouse where we could shelter, but arriving there discovered that a storm had washed part of the light house away, but the spiral stairs were still hanging half way up.

He pulled the horse up under the stairs and helped me to stand on the horse's back, making it possible for me to reach the stairs and climb up and out of danger. I shouted down to him to come up, too. But the higher I climbed, the stairs began to crumble below me and fell onto him, and soon he was completely buried beneath the rubble.

I woke up shaking and crying, "He is dead, he is dead!"

I couldn't go back to sleep. The heavy rain had stopped. I crept out of the bungalow and walked to the edge of the big rock. Below me the sea was twisting and turning in foamy anger and it's inability to reach me. Below my feet the sleepy giant stood high and proud in all its magnificence. A loud thud announced each breakers end against its solid mass. In the dim moonlight, the once silver white sand, now wet and covered in sea weed, ripped from the depth of the sea, looked like a neglected maiden covered in rags. Yet even now there was an indescribable beauty in it. A deep mist still hung over the water. The lighthouse hadn't crumbled under the storm's impact, but scarcely visible performed its duty, going round and round in the fine drizzle of the sea spray.

The unabated fury of the sea knew no bounds, thundering, raging, overwhelming, triumphantly it had reached the top of the rock. I got drenched in the spray, but did not care. I got up, water running off me, wondering who could ever know all its secrets, penetrate its true depth, unfathomable like my own. If I could not understand my own depth. how could I, beholding its awesome power, understand the effect, when I was too overwhelmed to know its cause.

Still caught up in the emotion of the third dream, and the loss of the stranger who was after all just a phantom in my dream world, I started to cry softly, not knowing the reason. I felt so alone. For how long I stood there with the salt of the sea spray mingling with the salt of my tears I don't know. It was the cold of the wet night dress clinging to my body that finally made me realize that he was not real and it was only the emotions evoked by the dream that sent me out to the big rock in the middle of the night. The dream was over, and I had a conventional home, and a warm bed to return to.

With the rain letting up for a few weeks, I was able to move over to Mount Pleasant, and also get back into my cave. I stocked it up with supplies and found that no animals had visited because the crackers and cheese was still un touched, and in the cool had stayed fresh. I had brought along a flask of tea. I filled the screw-on cap and took the diary from the shelf. I read some of the entries I had made, and the letter addressed to the phantom of my dream. And with two more he had much more substance. I took my pen down and remembering the two followup dreams, I wrote them into the diary as well. Was the stranger a foreboding of things to come, or someone from another life time I had known, or an alternate reality from an alternate universe? Was he the soul mate I was waiting for? Or was I just an incurable romantic that came with the restlessness of my age. In a few days I would be twenty-two.

22

Kismet —— Continuation of the Dream

The day broke warm, but the skies promised rain. At first I didn't want to go to the beach. I felt the same elation I had felt in my dreams. Dreams had a tendency of getting lost on awakening, but mine for some inexplicable reason had stayed with me. I simply could not get them out of my mind.

I had a sense of something great about to happen, but didn't know what. My steps were light and happy as I descended the weather-worn steps two at a time leading down to Fourth Beach. This time I did not stop to smell the flowers, afraid that I might miss something. The beach was full of people, but I managed to slip through the time gate unobserved. I started piling up a sand pillow to lay down, when I caught sight of a pair of brown legs sticking out from behind a rock. I wasn't alone. How could it be? It had taken me what I thought forever to get into the cove. Could this intruder have stumbled upon my Shangri-la the same way I did, or did he come through the time gate?

I would go in for a dip, and when I got out I would inform him that he would have to leave.

The water was freezing but invigorating; I couldn't stay in for long. I was shivering as I shook the water out of my hair that hung like limp seaweed down my back. I peeped behind the rock. Whoever it was was still there, covered up with a folded open newspaper.

"How's the water?" a voice inquired from under the newspaper.

"Why don't you find out for yourself!" I answered sharply. "The water's the same on Fourth Beach." I wanted to add *what are you doing in my cove?* But I really held no claim to that strip of beach, except that I had unofficially claimed it for myself.

I stretched out on my towel. I could feel the warmth returning to my body, the sun rays creeping through every pore. If I wasn't careful my nose would peel. I pulled my hair across my face as a shield. Behind the rock the newspaper stirred. *Ah, he is leaving,* I thought. I peeped through my hair. He was standing on a rock at the water's edge, dipping only his toes in. With his back toward me, I could barely make out his shape. The sun was blinding, but what I could see pleased me. The body matched the legs. He was tall, around six-foot-two, tanned, and well proportioned. Not overly broad shouldered or too muscular in the legs, with a slim waist and narrow hips and firm buttocks. In few words, he was perfect! The sharp sun behind him made a silver halo around his head. A shiver ran through my body. The shiver turned to shock as he turned around and approached me. As if time stood still. Or was the sun playing tricks on me? It was not the sun's reflections, but his hair was silver and he did have a pointed beard and mustache.

"IT IS YOU!" I shouted. He looked puzzled at what I had just said. I added, contributing more to the confusion of the moment, "I have met you before!" To myself it sounded just as ridiculous as it must have sounded to him.

He looked almost pathetic trying to recall where we might have met. "I don't recall us ever meeting, but I would like to know you." He held out his hand, "My naam is *Pieter*," he said in Afrikaans. Then as an afterthought he added, "My name is Peter, perhaps we met in a dream."

"Yes" was all I could stammer. It would be crazy to try and explain. I was visibly shaking when his hand touched mine, the shock of reality going through me like a thousand volts. He WAS real! Or had I fallen asleep on the beach and this was just another dream? Through my mind ran a refrain. *I have found you, I have found you!*

He mistook my trembling for cold, took his towel, and wrapped it gently round me.

"Don't worry, I will take care of you!" It freaked me out! It was the same sentence he used in the dream. A déja vu manifested in the flesh. I tried to sound calm making small talk, nervously stumbling over my own words. I told him my name, and then couldn't stop, words bubbled out. We talked feverishly like two people who hadn't seen one another for a very long time.

There was so much to tell. We tried to cram a whole lifetime into an hour, as though there had been no silent interval, no separation. We carried on in our divided lives where yesterday we left off. Like a frozen river that after a long winter unthawed and followed its well-known route. I loved his voice and the way his mouth like a cupids bow turned up at the corners; I wanted to kiss those corners. My eyes averted his strange green-flecked eyes, so that I wouldn't reveal my desire for him.

Suddenly the sky opened up with one of those showers that lasted only an hour and then was gone. We became aware of it only when a few heavy drops hit our sun-warmed bodies. I grabbed his hand, "Come with me! "He didn't object, or didn't know what was happening as we gathered our stuff and I led him up the stones to the entrance of my cave. When I disappeared over the rim and into the dark, dank hole he followed. I hurriedly lit a candle. The surprise was obvious. For a long time we sat in silence listening to the rain outside. He rummaged through his stuff and came up with an old pipe. He lit a match, and then lit the pipe. The match slowly burned toward his fingers, the flame going out just before burning his fingers. I sat mesmerized, the movement of his hands were like music.

While he puffed on the pipe, I took the journal from the shelf and read the three dream entries to him. He looked stunned.

"So we did meet in a dream?"

I handed him the envelope I had on the shelf. "The letter is for you. I'm sorry I did not know your name" He didn't open it, but sat staring at it, as if the reality of it was a dream to him, tapped the pipe that had gone out against the rock; the cave now smelled faintly of Beechnut and him..

I realized the rain had stopped so we blew out the candle and sat outside under the overhang of my throne. I broke the silence by announcing, "Tomorrow is my twenty-second birthday."

"Then starting midnight tonight we will go out and celebrate. I know a place you'd love! It's a small fishing harbor called Houtbay."

"How did you find Shangri-la?" I asked him.

"I turned around when I saw how crowded the beach was, and was about to walk away, when something drew me to the rock at the end Of Fourth Beach. The water had receded and I saw what looked like a door opening. I slipped through into this small paradise."

"You mean you came through the time-gate." I then told him how I literally fell into the cove, and how I spent hours piling the stones, and how I annexed it as my own, and how mad I was when I discovered him there, and the shock when he turned out to be the one in my dreams.

There was a golden glow over everything that came after rain. A small ant had fallen in an ant lion hole and with every step was sliding down into his ultimate doom.

Suddenly the sand closed in on him. Peter, who had been watching the little drama, dug frantically in the sand where the little ant had disappeared and lifted it out with his pinkie, and put it on solid ground. With a gentle, ever so gentle smile he watched it scamper away. A tear welled up in my eyes. I felt deeply touched. "Thank you for not letting him die." I whispered.

I watched the afternoon folding back casting long shadows into the approaching night. And I didn't want the day to end. Oblivious to the crowded beach on the other side of the rock, we held on to the last of the day. We discovered we both were raised in the Bushveld, We loved Africa with the same passion, loved ancient history, the same books, philosophy, nature, and both wrote poetry, he had taken ballroom dancing and so did I. I loved classical music, especially Vienna waltzes, and so did he. This was Kismet!

The sun was setting, he looked at his watch. "I must go." I didn't ask why.

A great sadness came over me, I didn't want him to leave me. *What if he disappeared like in the dream?*

"Just remember, we have a date for tonight. I will pick you up at eleven, that is if you give me your address."

I left with him and pointed out Mount Pleasant to him. As he drove off, my heart went with him. The feeling I had wasn't infatuation, or an attraction that wouldn't last, it was LOVE!. The kind that skeptics thought wasn't possible, love at first sight. Only in my case it was *LOVE AT FORESIGHT!*

It was only seven; there was an eternity to wait till I would see him again. I was so excited that to go to dinner would be a waste, I would not be able to eat anything. So I set the alarm for ten, this way I would have a full hour to get ready. I fell into a deep dreamless sleep this time, and woke with a start when the alarm rang shrilly next to my ear. I lay there in the darkness reflecting the happenings of the day. No longer wondering about his reality. The green-flecked hazel eyes, his silver hair, his pipe, the sound of his voice, his mouth was real. And I have a date with him to celebrate my birthday in just an hour! I ran out onto the balcony. Nothing had changed! Except me! The night still smelled like oleander and seaweed and clung moist, hot and humid around me. The moon a full silver ball hung in the sky, just like my new love who carried the full moon in his hair. It was a magic night, I could see every rock clearly defined on the four beaches.

"Do you hear me moon? He is real, and he has come back to me! Do you hear me stars! I am in love! Do you hear me rocks, THIS IS FOREVER!" I shouted to the night.

I had to get ready. I filled the bath and sprinkled an ample supply of bath oil, turned the tap on high, and watched the bubbles form. As I stepped in it tickled my bare skin and made me aware that I just had a little too much sun. But I felt spoiled and special for him. I was humming excitedly as I tossed my soft white chiffon over my head. I took particular care not to overdo the makeup, settling for my own natural look. I surveyed the end results. The billowing white that so flattered my tan also made me look like a young girl. Perhaps I should have chosen the dark-blue dress that matched his more mature look. He would prefer the white. Now I just had to do something with my hair. I piled it loosely on top of my head in a soft Grecian style. A soft golden curl escaped and fell over my shoulder I let it.

I kept running onto the balcony, impatiently searching the moonlit road for his coming. Below on the stairs a movement caught my eye. I prayed softly; *O God it must be him.* My heart beat uncontrollably. I just knew I was going to make a fool of myself. Slamming my door shut, I ran down the steps, stumbled and lost my footing, nearly knocking him down as he was coming up. He caught me in time with open arms to break my fall. "Glorious night for your birthday!" he greeted me.

As he opened the car door for me, "I hope you don't mind the long drive, but in the back seat you will find some gifts that I hope will amuse you on the way to our destination."

Each little gift, twenty one of them, was carefully chosen and individually wrapped; pencils for sketching, brushes for painting, a proper diary, beautiful bead work and trinkets from different tribes, each one a surprise. But for the mistake of twenty-one? I was amazed how he knew all, but then I had that day revealed all. Even my favorite chocolate.

The unsurpassed beauty of the Chapman's Peak drive was another gift in itself. The road lay like a ribbon of moonlight behind and in front of us. To the right the sea came rolling in wave upon wave of foam-capped splendor. The wind blowing the foam cap back like a bridal veil, gently caressing the cliffs far below. To our left the Twelve Apostles Mountains rose like a mysterious cathedral to the sky, getting lost among the stars.

I felt glad he hadn't chosen a crowded smoke-filled night club in which to celebrate my birthday. The road started dropping away to a little fishing harbor where all was in darkness except for a boat with brightly colored lights strung from the center mast to the back and front in a triangle. A barge dance floor was anchored to it and floating on calm waters a little distance from it. A single string of lights tied on poles around the deck swung back and forth. The lights reflected on the smooth water, reaching like giant fingers, across to the far shores. A three-man band supplied the few couples dancing with popular tunes. I caught a few lines of the "Tennessee Waltz" mournfully drifting across the water. The light from the boat cast dim shadows on the ghostly fishing boats resting on wooden cradles out of the water, awaiting their repair or demise. We wound through the dark shapes to a flat-roofed fishing shack, pulling up next to it. A scruffy fat man with an eye patch and luxurious black mustache came out to meet us. I half expected to see a wooden leg. He could have stepped right out of a pirate movie instead of being the owner of, "The best seafood tavern in the whole of the Cape" to quote his own words.

"*Piet, my vriend, alles is reg, kom binne.*" (Peter, my friend, everything is ready, come in). Peter was holding my hand, and if it wasn't for his warm smile and the reassuring pressure of his hand. I would have sworn that I was being lead straight to walk the plank with a cutlass in my back. Only the *pirate* was in front of us leading the way.

Inside the shack, sand crunched under our feet to provide atmosphere; to anyone not used to atmosphere it would have definitely been classified as 'dirty.' Atmosphere was evident everywhere, in the form of fishing nets loaded with cork, floats, blowfish, and other salvaged oceanic paraphernalia. Stuffed fish that won trophies were mounted and hung on the walls. The small windows had curtains of unseamed hessian sacking. On the coarse wooden tables stood fishermen's lanterns. A film set for sure for our host.

We paused for a moment in front of a door hung with hessian. Peter pushed it aside and we stepped into another room, a room reserved for different functions no doubt. It took my breath away; hundreds of candles and sunflowers filled the room. In the center stood a table with red tablecloth, beautifully set up. It was a magic moment out of time never to be forgotten, even though words failed me, the tears across my cheeks clearly showed my emotion.. Moments after Peter pulled out my chair and seated me, a jovial little woman arrived with two giant steaming lobsters, freshly baked bread, and a tossed salad. I was glad that I couldn't eat dinner, because I wouldn't have done justice to this succulent feast.

On the stroke of midnight, she reappeared bearing a large chocolate cake, with twenty-two candles on, and she, her husband, and Peter sang "Happy Birthday" with heartfelt gusto.

After the delectable meal, we thanked our host and hostess for their trouble and walked over to the floating dance floor. The tourists were gone, and the barge pulled alongside the boat; the musicians were making their move to leave. Peter seated me on a bench on the barge and went over to speak to the musicians. I don't know how he achieved it but the next moment I heard the familiar strains of a Vienna Waltz. He walked over to me and with an exaggerated bow said, "May I have this dance?" He pulled me into his arms, and as we floated off our bodies in perfect harmony, I thought of the dream when we danced. Now in reality, our steps blended perfectly. He led my movements with his thighs, the rhythm of his movements flowing through me, his body warm against mine made my head spin. I had drunk no wine, but I was drunk with the nearness of him. The band played a few more waltzes, and we would have danced till morning, but in the middle of one Peter stopped. "Come! the night would not be complete unless I give you your last gift!"

We drove back the way we had come, but halfway we turned off the main road onto a lookout point, a peninsula of land surrounded by water with the tip of a mountain jutting out across the bay. He turned off the motor, we got out and sat on the grass among the heather. There was a slight chilling wind coming from the water, but I felt sheltered and warm, nestling with my back against his chest, his arms enfolding me.

"Now we wait," he whispered in my neck.

We sat in silence as dawn slowly painted the sky crimson and the mountain across the bay deep scarlet, and we watched it turn to copper, and then glow with hues of gold, giving birth to day. I thought, *Only he would give me a sunrise.*

But then the sky turned black, black with thousands of flapping wings, drifting on the currents of air over the bay. Tiny birds almost legless, dipping and falling in a mating dance on the currents.

"I knew they would come! this is my last present to you, my love, now you have twenty-two."

I watched in awe at the movement of black clouds of wings above and around us.

"Swifts, they will rest here for a while in the caves of the mountain across the bay, before they move on to Australia. They come yearly on the same day to this place like clockwork."

We watched in electric silence, hands tightly interlocked. I could feel a faint throbbing of pulses where our fingers intertwined, but was more aware of our hearts beating wildly together. He kissed my hair, the back of my neck, my shoulders, slowly turning me around in his arms, his lips caressing my face. When we kissed, it was an exploding kiss that echoed across eternity, paling the stars. We were aware only of the moment and the hunger of our bodies, which had waited for eons to consummate a love that was always there, and would accept no boundaries. With dawn gently fading into day, we shed our clothes, exposing our souls, joined in the mating dance of the swifts, lost in our own wonder of loving.

"This place and time would be the narrow bridge for our souls to cross, throughout eternity when we are no longer here," he whispered hoarsely in passion.

In the months to follow, we lived in the dream world of lovers. The days were too short to fully experience the joys of each other's company. The nights not long enough to explore each other's bodies. Declaring that love in touching each others souls through our love-making that never became satiated, always wanting MORE! One more touch, one more caress, one more kiss that would fan the fires of our passion one more time. Each parting became a Shakespeare tragedy rewritten especially for us.

In the afterglow of loves tenderness, I cried, fearing that fate would take him away from me just as it brought him to me. He would kiss away my tears, begging me to tell him why I cried, and I could not tell him.

"I fear a future without you." He would then assure me over and over that we would be together for always and quoted me Gibran; *"We were born together, and we will be together for evermore. We shall be together, when the white wings of death, scatter our days. We shall be together, even in the silent memory of God."*

And my fears would go away, and I would reap the golden harvest of love in his assurances. We explored the beaches of Kalk Bay, Bakhoven, Lundudno. We climbed the mountains, bathing in icy mountain streams, went camping, frequented the nude beaches, enjoying the innocence of nudity like children free from inhibitions. We went to the opera and plays, spent hours in my cave writing together, diving in the underwater caves. Went dancing together. Won trophies, because we were perfectly matched.

The drudgery of work and other commitments of living stole time away from us, but every moment we could be together, we were together. Our love was complete; we needed nothing more.

Then one night he told me that he was asked by his firm Trans Africa Safaris, to crisscross Africa from Cape Town to as far as the Horn of Africa and Nigeria, charting future sites for tourist facilities, to build rest camps, hotels, and such.

"It would take from three to six months."

"I would die without you in that time." I cried.

"Then come with me."

There was no hesitation on my part. I gave notice at the veterinary department I had long ago made a decision that I wanted a change. Peter moved my things into his apartment. During our trip we had lots of time to decide what to do, and where we would get married, on the banks of the Limpopo was my choice, so it was just natural that my possessions stay with him.

23

Second Safari

The beginning of our trip would take us through the garden route, where we would turn inland to Botswana and then stay as close to the animal migrating route as possible, then Kenya and Somali to the horn of Africa where we turn across Central African republic, Nigeria, toward the Ivory Coast, and down the west coast to Congo, Angola, and South west Africa, through the Kalahari and the Karoo back to Cape Town.

On the first night driving with the sea on our right past Hawston, we started looking for a camping spot. Onrust looked like the perfect place. Everything went fine. We put up the tent and I lit the Primus stove for coffee. And then it happened, they came in droves. Soon the fire sounded like I was popping corn. The sand fleas had taken over the beach. When I opened the coffee pot to put coffee in, several fleas the size of my thumb nail hopped into the pot. It was too dark to break up camp so we decided to go for a swim and stay till morning, but the beach was covered in smelly seaweed and crawling with crabs trying to get at the fleas. We ate some of the sandwiches I had packed for our first day and crawled into the bed roll, that's when the fleas on the beach decided to avenge their relatives that died in the coffee pot. They crawled in our hair, into our bedding, clothes and everything that was in reach. It was indeed an *Onrustige* night; whoever gave the place its name was right when they called it Onrust (meaning restless).

In the morning we ate the rest of the sandwiches, I put the Primus on top of the car, and we managed to have flea-less coffee. "This is one place that is not being scheduled for a rest stop," was Peter's comment. Ahead of us lay at least twelve thousand miles. Seven miles ahead was Hermanus where Peter wanted to stay the first night. It was a picturesque place, with a mixture of old and new. Many of the houses were built with stone cemented on top of one another. The old Harbor House still had it's original thatched roof, in its window boxes grew orange nasturtiums. Like Cape Town, the homes had the most enchanting names. *Heen en Weer* (Back and Forth), The Big Fish, (where they filmed the Afrikaans version of *The Old Man and the Sea*), Pandora's Box, Spendthrift, Lalaleen, Gold Fish Bowl. We went to the Little Red Hen for lunch, and had a fresh caught seafood salad. Then we took a walk to the small light house beacon. The path we took had rock walls with gnarled trees growing against the rocks forming a cool and shady arbor, sheltering fern and white arum lilies. The inlet was strewn with sharp rocks, but had a network of concrete paths with benches anchored firmly at the end, where wives could wait for their seafaring husbands to come home. Here too was a clear strip of beach for overnight campers. But alas we couldn't mourn the seven miles we didn't make to camp in peace.

An hour later we were snaking our way up through Shaw's Pass. Way below in a green valley, in the shadow of a high mountain, tiny sheep grazed in paddocks adjoining tiny farms. From the height we were, the river below looked like a trickle of silver.

Caledon, a bleak conventional town, was almost devoid of people. It was Sunday and everyone was in the church in the center of town. We wanted to see the Wild Tropical Garden, but found the gates locked because it was Sunday. There was a gatekeeper on duty, but he was not in the mood for *verdomde buitelanders.* As he reluctantly opened the gate he mumbled in Afrikaans, *"Die vroumense in hulle mans broeke maak my siek."* I replied, "I'm sorry Meneer if my slacks make you sick, but we are on a long journey across Africa and it is comfortable." He was amazed that I understood and replied to him in his own language, because he had immediately classified me as 'a damned foreigner.' When Peter explained his mission, he turned all sweetness and light suddenly, very eager to show us around, so that they too could be put on the map.

The gardens were designed around the natural environment. With the addition of several ponds, fed by a natural waterfall, whereon ducks and swans floated, the place was ablaze with indigenous shrub and flowers. Little open-sided gazebos against the mountain provided a place where we could rest and drink in the park's beauty. At the top of the mountain there was a natural rock formation called appropriately *Venster Rots* (Window Rock) through which one could look down at the valleys below, which looked like an artist pallet contrasting patches of pink and pastel, in almost geometric shapes. Blue gum trees framed yellow fields edged with purple and white cosmos on slender stems.

The next town, Swellendam, we passed through in minutes. The whole town burnt down in 1798. They boasted a stone monument declaring it to be the first republic. We were following the route of the pioneers. It also had a historical museum, but being Sunday it was closed. We would have liked to see it, but we had to get through the treacherous Tradouw Pass before it got dark, so while Peter gassed up the car I made a quick sketch of a flat roofed-house surrounded by giant sunflowers almost the height of the roof, which compelled me to draw it.

The road into Tradouw Pass was bad. It was still an earth road with dense bush growing along side it. The river looked like it was climbing up with us, For a while the road dipped down again past meadow and small holdings, mostly Hottentot farmers, the houses constructed of red mud bricks with individual mud walled dams. Picturesque willows and silver poplar grew by the dams. Then as we ascended again we met up with the river. Peter suggested that we overnight in the Pass and tackle the steep descent in the morning. I had seen a dilapidated ruin of a house about a mile back. I was not about to suggest it, but Peter had also seen it because the next minute he suggested, "I think we should back track to that ruin a mile back; it would still be light enough for us to check it out, and we could cook our supper and be on our way early in the morning.

It wasn't long since someone had actually lived in the house, but now it was a true ghost house. The roof was still on, two of the rooms were livable. Peter looked the house over to make sure no snakes had moved in. I swept out one of the back rooms with some branches. It still had curtains hanging on the windows. At the back of the house off a porch there were the remnants of a *vleis braai pit*. While I set up our beds for the night, Peter made a fire in the pit and soon I could smell the steaks we bought at Swellendam sizzling and the coffee brewing. I went to the car and took out one of the bottles of green beans I had canned before leaving, and cut open a can of peaches. We sat on the back porch, where I had spread a clean sheet, eating our dinner, wondering what happened to the people in whose house we were sheltering for the night and why they would abandon the incredible view. Around us the air smelled like pink rambling roses that had gone wild, cascading in wild abandon over everything in sight.

As I entered the room I had prepared for us, the perfume of the roses was there also, because next to my bedroll stood a peach can full of roses. Outside a single bush dove was preparing himself for a night's rest, with soft trilling sounds and an occasional *koer-koer-dook*, as we, too, bedded down for the night.

Leaving the ruin the following morning, I could see why Peter had decided to stay over and not attempt the way down; the pass itself circled around the mountain. On our right there were fantastic high cliffs, on the left, the driver's side, I dare not look down; the shear drop gave the impression we were flying. There was no wall or even stones to mark off the side of the road. Riding with the break constantly being used, the car started to overheat. We pulled over onto the wrong side of the road at a cliff overhang. Here in a deep rift, a small waterfall tumbled into a crystal clear pool at its base, around which a variety of ferns grew thickly. The crevasse ended in a cave. On the cave walls, cave drawings were still visible, partly ruined by graffiti— modern man's desire to also leave his mark to show that they were there, too, with total disregard for those valuable drawings they defaced.

I scooped a handful of mountain water; it was cool and sweet. I filled all our water bottles and the barrel we kept in the back of the car while Peter filled the radiator.

We descended slowly. Way below the river met up with the road. Along its banks, wattles were in bloom. And from its fertile banks small orchards of peaches and apples stretched in neat but untended rows. Reaching the valley below there were already signs that we were entering the low veld. Dusty looking sheep were grazing on the stumpy *renoster bos*. We stopped to let the radiator cool down, and I went to inspect the strange flat little bush with hard branches covered with tiny succulent leaves, and it was hard to believe that the sheep actually lived off these tiny little leaves. I picked one of the leaves discovering they consisted mainly of a bitter tasting liquid, scratching myself on the hard stem.

This was the beginning of the Karoo, a semi-desert with low rolling hills and blue mountains in the distance. Where the farms were few and far between and the houses looked like they were plonked down from out the sky, on barren and dry earth. But then in southern Africa, every hundred miles holds a surprise, and just over a rise in the long road we found ourselves on, we came upon a green fertile oasis, with vineyards and vegetable gardens on either side of the road, irrigated by mountain springs brought by concrete canals from far away.

On the side of the dusty road stood "The Valley Inn," dating back from 1782, handed down from generation to generation, and no doubt it would live on for years to come. It was a long building, two stories high, which was unusual for its time, with a verandah that ran the length of the building on both the floors. The heavy oak doors stood wide open, welcoming the traveler. On either side of the door half wine vats had heather growing in them. There was no sign post or name on the few buildings surrounding the inn. But someone in the street told us we were in Barrydale; if you were driving through you would be through the place in a blink of an eye.

On the verandah was a sign inviting people to afternoon tea, written in Afrikaans. *Agtermiddig tee,* which Peter thought would be a good idea, before we tackled the next mountain looming blue in the distance.

The proprietress tried to maintain the 1782 flavor of the place. It still had most of its original furniture and woodwork. It was like walking into the past. On the wall of the entrance-reception hall hung a framed copy of the original rules and regulations.

RULES OF THE INN
NO Thieves, Fakirs, Rogues or Tinkers
NO Skulking Loafers or Flea-Ridden Tramps
NO Slap and tickle, or propositioning of the wenches
NO Banging of tankards on the tables for attention
NO Dogs allowed in the kitchen or bedrooms
NO Cock fighting or gambling on the premises
FLINTLOCKS, CUDGELS, DAGGERS AND SWORDS
TO BE HANDED IN TO THE INNKEEPER FOR SAFEKEEPING
Bed for the night.......................1 English shilling
Stabling for Horse....................4 pence
Groom.......................................1 penny extra

"With prices like this I think we could stay over for the night," Peter told the proprietress, "but for now we would love some tea."

Tea was served with chunky scones and lumpy apricot jam, in old fashioned china cups, the teapot decently covered in a hand embroidered tea-cosy, and the milk jug with a crocheted doily.

Our stops were less frequent now; in the next couple of hundred miles the scenery changed from Barren to eight-thousand-foot-high mountains, to cutting ground level through dry river beds, then climbing up again through other worldly rock formations into Zwartberg Pass, the road constructed by chain-gang convicts with dynamite, pick axes, and shovels, following the wagon tracks of the Boers, who went across the mountains by disassembling their wagons and carrying the parts across. On a look out point on top of the mountain we pulled over at a rock rest-house. "Where the convicts were shackled together to rest at night," Peter explained. I saw the same type of stone houses along the way as we were going up. Looking back down the road snaking up for thirteen miles I was dumbfounded; it was an awesome sight of engineering and endurance with many people dying in the construction. The little donkey cart we passed had not even reached the first bend, and looked like ants. I was terribly sorry for the little donkey with his monstrous load. At least I was grateful that some of his passengers had got off the overloaded cart and were walking beside it. I have a soft spot for beasts of burden.

The steep descent was still to come. That side of the mountain was covered in giant waxy proteas resplendent in shape and rose colored stamens, complemented by low bushes of lavender in bloom.

I dared not speak to Peter, for to lose concentration spelled instant death. The steep road swung round precipitous bends. I tried to concentrate on the beauty of the place, focusing on the scenery in the distance, but all I could see was the terrifying three-thousand-foot-drop as we hurled through space. With nothing to stop us.

At that precise moment I heard a loud crack as the car ran over some rocks that moments earlier had rolled down the cliff side. The next minute Peter was praying aloud. "Oh God, help us!" He was pumping the brakes for all he was worth, but the car was on the verge of becoming a runaway. "The brakes are not working. I'm going to ram it into the foliage on the rock side! HOLD ON!"

I tried to stay calm for both of us, but was expecting a truck or car to come careening around the bend at any time. We were on the wrong side of the road again, ramming it into the foliage. It slowed us down enough for him to put the car in neutral.

"If this doesn't work," he screamed across the din, "then we will have to jump out and abandon our gear!" Driving in neutral was fine for a while but then that too gave in. He turned the car off and we started to free-wheel down the mountain, breaking against the mountain every time the car gained momentum. After about an hour we reached ground level. Here the engine was overheated, and the car gave up the ghost, coming to a standstill against some protea bushes. Shaken by our experience, we sat in silence. Life went on as usual down in the valley, some men were planting on a freshly plowed field, while some boys were trying to ride a pink hog in a field of scarlet poppies. Throughout the beginning of our journey I had been taking notes, with Peter teasing me about it fast becoming a book. Now the first thing out of his mouth was, "Did you write all this down?" Then to break the tension he laughed, "At least now your story will have an ending, that is if we survive the rest of what is waiting for us once we leave civilization."

"You mean, there are rougher times ahead?"

"My love, you've seen nothing yet. We are going into uncharted jungles where man eating is still a possibility."

"You must be kidding, I haven't heard about cannibalism since I was a child, and even then it was debatable."

"That may be true, but there are other man-eaters—lion, leopard, not necessarily cannibals!" For a while on the mountainside I thought the car would be scrapped and the trip was over.

"I'll go and ask those farmers if they know about a mechanic."

As luck would have it, someone knew someone's brother who had a friend that wasn't "really a mechanic" but pottered around with old cars; he would certainly help us. They would hook us up to the tractor and tow us to him. But first we would have to have some lunch with the farmer.

"It's been a long time since I've had visitors from the outside," the farmer said.

The self-taught mechanic was so enthusiastic when he heard about our trip that he not only repaired the car, but made external modifications. He said he just happened to have a stronger engine that would not leave us in the lurch. He lifted the empty body of the Morris onto a Jeep chassis, with Jeep wheels and engine. The jeep just happened to have had an accident nearby and he salvaged it, The body was scrapped but everything else was in good condition. He removed the back seats so that the front seats could collapse into a sleeping position. Now we not only had a mini camper but more packing space, and a souped up *Chorrie* that could challenge any terrain. The price for all this was an incredible bargain; he said he always wanted to do something as adventurous as we were about to undertake. And he had the parts hanging around that were just made for it.

As if fate had brought us together. He would be with us in spirit on our adventure, and if either of us ever published our books he wanted a signed copy.

We were stared at in our strange vehicle, but it would take to the mountains and rough terrains and never overheat, or let us down again. Before going on to Botswana we decided to go to the Congo Caves that were only fifteen miles farther. But were just too late, the last group to go in was just coming out. There was some sort of *voortrekker* (jamboree). To go into the caves we would have to wait till the morning. We were told that there was a campground close to the caves, also a guest farm. So we stayed and joined in the *volkspele* and *baaivleis* (folk dancing and barbecue). After the festivities we discovered that the campground was full and the guest house too far out of our way. We simply pulled off the road behind some cactus for the night, folded the seats down in our renovated mini camper, surrounded by some curious black and white cows who breathed on the windows to check us out. In the music of the cattle loudly chewing their cud, we fell asleep.

I was up early in the morning, but not wanting to make a big fuss, made a small twig fire and brewed some coffee, and when Peter awoke ate some rusks, and joined the line of cars already at the gate.

We could make out a dark hole against the side of the mountain, but otherwise it was still undeveloped. The narrow entrance looked unimpressive. Here the guide called us together. There were about fifteen people in all including the guide. He was obviously not comfortable with English, but had made an effort to memorize the whole speech.

Out of habit he started in Afrikaans, *"Dames en here,"* realizing he stuttered an apology, and continued. "Ladies and gentlemen, you are about to see one of the wonders of the world, but a great deal of it is yet to be explored. It is therefore full of danger. You are to all stay together in a group and not to go wandering off alone. Some of the crevices have unmeasured depth."

To illustrate he picked up a rock and threw it down a dark crevasse closed off with rope.

We could not hear it drop.

"The caves were first discovered by a Mr. Van Zyl who was hunting a leopard, he saw it go in and not come back out. Curious he went in with a lantern and some rope.

"We have on purpose extinguished all light, and I ask you now not to use flashlights or lighters. There are ropes to lead the way. You will feel your way by holding onto the rope. We will first descend into the Van Zyl Chamber so that you could get the feeling of how he felt when together with some friends, he first explored these caves. There are many chambers, but this one is the most impressive. After which you could climb the Devil's Chimney and see the rest. That is if you live up to the measurement."

In the pitch black bowel of the Earth, we felt our way down, clinging to the umbilical cord of survival. There was no light to guide us, nor any light filtering in from anywhere. I could not see my hand in front of my face, even inches from my eyes. This is how a blind person must feel, was my only thought. Like the blind I was aware of others in front of and behind me, whispering, they whispered to alleviate their fear. The guide's voice broke the unholy whispered silence. "When you come to the end of the rope. I want you to walk six paces forward, making room for others behind you, there is no immediate danger, but do not go farther than what I told you."

As each person left the rope, they groped around finding their own people in the black. Soon we were in a tight little cluster like frightened children, No one was talking. Afraid that talking would interfere with the process of ever seeing light again.

"Now I will demonstrate to you the power of light, it only takes one match to start a fire." There was a sudden hush, a tiny *fiiirt* sound as he struck a match. And in the glow of that one match reflecting from the crystal glow off the walls, we saw a room the likes of which I had never seen. "To give you an idea of the size during the recent celebration of the Pioneer *Trek* celebration. Two thousand people listened to an 80 man Orchestra in here." The match flickered and went out. A strange sensation of loss came over me. I was standing on solid ground yet it felt as if the ground gave way under my feet and I was tumbling into nowhere. Everyone must have had the same disorientation, because though no one moved an inch, frightened voices rang out in a chorus.

"PLEASE PUT ON THE LIGHTS!" In a blinding moment floodlights filled the grand chamber and the dome of which curved three stories above our heads. We could see into every corner, that was covered in spectacular display of pale pink stalagmites and stalactites taking on different shapes, of pipe organs, angels, and whatever my imagination could make out.

A group of people were being measured, I thought it was a strange thing to be doing at that moment, but when I inquired the guide said it was a requirement if I wanted to go up the Devil's Chimney, so Peter and I got measured around the shoulders, waist and hips. We were taken to a small hole that was pointing straight up, it looked no wider than my hip measurement of thirty-six inches. There were no visible handholds or footholds. I called my name into the hole and heard a strange hollow echo of it somewhere, but where? The guide explained that once inside we had to use the bumps, to push ourselves up using elbows, knees and anything to wiggle with. There was a strange pink glow in what looked like a sausage turned inside out; at places the continual drip had discolored it red, it was the devil's chimney all-right— thirty feet of it. And I in some moment of madness was inside, going the lord knows only where. I could hear someone in the narrow tube above me, softly cursing as he pulled himself through the smooth as silk damp tube. I forced my backside up against the one side, searching for a lump below me on which to get some foot hold as I wiggled myself up with my elbows pressed tight against the sides. It was a slow process, and the thought occurred to me what if the person above me lost his grip, would we all start slipping down and get stuck in a lump somewhere. Half way up, the tube started to turn in a downward direction, and I found myself on my belly slithering like a snake head down, using my elbows as a brake, as I was going faster and faster. Then suddenly I got to the end of the tunnel and was expelled into an anti chamber onto a soft sand bank, right onto my face, much to the amusement of the rest of the group who didn't measure up. Peter appeared moments later falling all over me, and someone on top of him. We were handed certificates of our achievement, but with the long road ahead we had to skip the festivities that were to follow. Botswana was a long way off.

24

Migration —— First Signs of Elephants

We had left the garden route, an already established tourist route, behind; soon we would meet up with the migrating herds at Botswana. And from there on it would be mostly uncharted.

An old elephant had fallen ; he was a loner and had died of old age. His was a lonely death, he would have no relatives to scatter his bones. His pallbearers would be nature's cruel balance.

In the approaching night, white glowing eyes, sensing his death, stood around waiting for him to drop. No sooner had the old bull breathed his last breath when one of the bolder Hyenas climbed on top of the carcass of the giant, claiming it for himself.

His coarse spiked hair around his head stood on end; the leader of the pack had a gruesome grin on his face. Several others stood around the flanks of the elephant, waiting for the signal that they too could share in the feast. Unusually patient, like ogres from hell they strutted back and forth, looking up at their leader on top of the carcass, laughing insanely.

Patience wearing thin, they made little dashes toward the tempting mound of flesh, to pluck at tender spots with their steel jaws, where the skin was thinner and more giving. At each approach, digging deeper till their own bodies almost disappeared into the innards of the elephant. Every now and then they emerged to take a breath, their coats and noses dyed red with blood.

When dawn came, they lay around the carcass, full to bursting, but reluctant to give up their prize. The lions were strangely absent; they were either too far away or had killed big in the night and were disinterested. Above us a cloud of vultures soared in circles awaiting the departure of the hyenas. When they finally departed the vultures descended around the carcass, one eye on the feast, the other looking out for other predators. With their sharp beaks they tore shards of flesh from the holes the hyenas had left, gulping it with ferocious greed till they disgorged. During the frenzy, fights erupted, pecking at one another, wings flapping, they charged with scrawny necks arched, dust and feathers flying, an ugly bloody disorder.

Peter and I watched from a distance, with binoculars, careful not to disturb nature's balance. The clean up crew was so full that they were only able to waddle away, some tried to take off and fly, but they were too full. After an hour or so after much effort, some made it up into a dried up tree. For the others successive efforts did not pay off, so they just sat under the tree, flapping their wings awkwardly. Then eventually giving up they just sat there dozing off, every now and then they opened one eye, to see if anything else was going to happen. They were not finished by a long shot, for now yes, but they were ready for a challenge should other scavengers approach. This we knew would not be the end of the story. Nature was by far the most efficient cleaner-uppers.

Soon a few red jackals made their cautious appearance, in general they were shy and skittish, never uninvited guests. The vultures sitting beneath the tree saw their approach. One of them broke away from the vulgar coalition and halfheartedly challenged the new comers, but still too full he returned to his gorged brothers.

This served as an invitation. The jackals ate delicately, allowing one another space. The females were eating a double portion that they would take back to their young and disgorge to feed them. After they left, some meat-eating birds picked up the fallen pieces. Then the blue flies descended in swarms to eat, paying in kind for their meal by depositing their eggs in the left carcass. The eggs in a few days would hatch into maggots. Some of which would provide dessert for the birds, while the other maggots ate away the remaining flesh off the bones. When there was no one else, the wind would follow, sandblasting the bones.. Then the sun bleached the bones to pristine whiteness.

Even then the cleanup was not done yet. Little birds in the process of nest building carried off hairs and fibers. Then last but not least the ants came to claim a share, taking the dried flakes that had fallen to the ground.

During this stage the old bull elephant's relatives would have picked up his bones and carried them one at a time off to the burial grounds, but this one was a rogue elephant who had, during a fight for a female, excommunicated himself from his relatives, so he would not be awarded the honor of a wake; his bones would lie as a monument to his passing, and an example to others of his kind that he had been cast out, denying him his inherent rites. Elephant graveyards were glorified by the film industry that showed thousands of ivory tusks in one gorge or another. It was a fact that some elephants, remembering where they had taken a relatives bones to, would on their own approaching death walk to that location to await his own death. Bone yards were usually found below high cliffs, and around quicksand holes and other inaccessible places.

We were entering the heart of Botswana where game and people lived together in harmony still. Between the grassy savannas and the salt plains lay vast forests of acacia trees. But man's destruction outweighed that of the animal inhabitants. Vast areas were destroyed by farmers with their slash and burn techniques to obtain land. Slowly destroying the feeding ground of the elephant. Black stumps stood everywhere

"Mark my word, if they keep this up in just twenty to thirty years from now the herds will disappear, so will the acacia forests. There's just no supervision. With the coming of independence from Britain, open house will be declared on the game, the approximate 80,000 different species would certainly disappear!"

"I don't think the elephant would ever disappear." I added.

"And why is that?"

"Because I think they are strangely aware of their vulnerability. They were known to go miles out of their way to avoid areas where they knew a slaughter was to take place. Then they warned other herds to avoid the same area. There was no visible or apparent signs to us humans that anything was wrong, but Daddy would find a slaughter field where poachers had killed indiscriminately many miles away. I remember Daddy telling us children that the rumblings we heard was a secret language that many animals knew and humans cannot hear. It was also the poetry emitted by the young cows, calling to the young bulls. Females were the ones that vied for male attention, only coming into estrous once in four years, and that for only two days, and not a full season like other animals. There was no particular breeding season, at which she sang her love songs to attract a male. The males then in musts followed their silent songs—Daddy's poetry' till they reached the object of its origin."

"I suppose you could call it poetry," Peter agreed, "because poetry is a form of procreation's language. For us anyway. It's our secret language to our lovers to convey our feelings to them. So infra sound is their secret language, for their ears only. But the elephants are not the only ones using it. The rivers and the forests are filled with sounds the pitch too high for human ears, sounds that are carried across the miles. Elephants and crocodiles have the same frequency. There are of course exceptions like the sea creatures, the blue whales and dolphins whose frequencies are lower. In the animal kingdom there are other sounds too, barks, growls, snorts, and rumblings bordering on infra sound that can be heard for two miles or more"

"Because the elephants are aware of their own vulnerability, I suppose that's why they like Royalty seldom travel together. Adult males and females live apart you know, each with their own elected leader. This tactic ensures the preservation of their species. Males like to forage on their own often traveling twenty miles or more a day."

From a very tender age I had been obsessed with elephants, always asking Dad about them, he was usually ready with the answers. They were not too difficult to understand, because they were creatures of habit, that in itself was a reason why poachers always knew where to find them, because their actions were mostly determined by feeding and water. They followed the same paths, one of the reasons the natives knew not to build their kraals on an elephant path, because they walked over everything like a bulldozer that was obstructing their way. One could read their body language too, sometimes they showed signs of distress. Their ears would perk up and they started walking in circles. The matriarch would immediately start gathering the babies together in a group, and they would listen carefully, swaying from side to side, waiting for instructions from the bulls, who were perhaps a mile away, reacting to their own danger.

Females were very protective toward the babies who were a precious commodities, because gestation lasted twenty two months, and when the calf was born usually weighing between two hundred to two hundred and fifty pounds, there were many helping trunks to get him or her on their feet. The mother usually holds the baby up with her trunk, nudging him to stand on wobbly legs. Then a ring of *aunties*, who would later on be responsible for his upbringing, stepped forward and gently stuck the tip of their trunks into the babies mouth, so did the mother, as a welcoming kiss, or to leave their scent with the baby. Days after the birth the trek toward water had to start, and the calf had to be strong enough to travel. Unlike human or baboon babies, there was no one to carry him. The birth of twins were vary rare, if it occurred it was through double mating, but they seldom survived because they were smaller and weaker than single births.

The wondrous thing was how these mighty bodies survived, between the terrible toll of the poachers, the long droughts, long periods between gestation and estrous, infant mortality by predators, and great distances they traveled to water. But they DO SURVIVE by forming a strong bond from the beginning of their lives, each looking after and out for the other. Like the baboons, elephants functioned in a selective caste system, protective of one another, yet still aware of their station in life, from grand matriarch to lowest subservient. Each one had an elected task, sharing responsibilities, baby sitting, and supervising the young males that still travel in the female groups, social responsibilities, and caring for the sick and the old

The bulls traveling separately from the females, knew where to dig with their tusks, next to green tipped bushes, deep below the roots they would find water, or in river beds. Having kept track of the females they would call them through infra sound to the wells. During the mating calls they vied for mating favors by challenge, fighting for possession of the females. The strongest bulls competing for the privilege, to ensure healthy and strong calves. At this time the younger bull calves learn by looking, and play at imitating the mating fights, and among themselves imitate the love dances and mating. Always listening for the love songs when it would be their time to leave the circle of the *aunties* and join the bull pen.

Both the females and the males were messy and wasteful eaters, often knocking or tearing a tree apart to get to just one branch of their choosing. Sometimes I had seen them knock over an entire tree just to get to the tender branches at the top, then walk away leaving the tree to die.

In the weeks to follow, as we steadily moved north in our zig zag route, we heard the rumblings of the elephants stomachs in the distance, but did not see them. We followed their trails as they had followed the trails of their fore-bearers season after season, hoping to see them. From the empty water holes their paths spread out like giant spider webs. The thirst was always there, often the bulls going on ahead were weary, because instinct had taught them through past experience that danger lurked round water holes. But then at other times the water holes from previous diggings had widened by many rains and were very deep. Too deep to wade in so when the females arrived, the adults would draw the water up by their trunks and squirt it into waiting mouths and over their bodies; as there were no mud wallows they scooped dust and threw it over their wet bodies, as a protection against insect bites and the ravages of the sun.

The trunk of the elephant was a wonderful appendage, having 50,000 muscles, that was both extremely sensitive as well as versatile. With it they can carry enormous weights, pick up a tiny seed, deposit it in the mouth. Scoop up water and put it in the mouths of babies, they use it to smell, to examine things, and use it for a shower and a snorkel when crossing deep water.

A few days later Peter and I came across a whole herd of elephants on the way to a water hole. Mothers and baby-sitting daughters and sisters and *aunties* with their under two-year-old charges. They were marching in true Disney fashion in single file, from the matriarch down to the babies who could not keep up, with the bigger ones up front.

Suddenly the matriarch stopped, raised her trunk in warning. Behind her the herd froze in their tracks, she had picked up the silent message that several families were on their way to the water hole. But because the danger wasn't imminent, she gave a soft trumpet. She marched on and the others followed. So did we, at a safe distance, all heading for the water hole, they to drink and meet up with their bulls and we to observe.

Some *aunties* held onto the babies tails to keep them in tow.

At the water hole there were several elephants that showed traces of red dirt on their bodies, and others with yellow. It looked like two families had already joined up. While watching we saw a smaller group approach from the east. In the red and yellow group there was a lot of excitement, they ran over to the approaching group, whirled in circles, trumpeting, embracing trunks, scooping sand up and blowing it across each other's backs in anticipation of the same action later done with water. In the ones we had been following, the small ones wanted to join in this new kind of fun, they urinated with pleasure and ran around the newcomers legs. The *aunties* didn't approve of such forward behavior, rounded them up with a few slaps of their trunks, and together with the sisters they formed a circle around them, big legs making a fleshy cage. The new arrivals were a bond group to the red and yellow dust group, but they were also a higher caste group, because the other two groups hesitated at a distance out of courtesy and allowed the dustless group from the east to enter the water first. Our deduction was that it was obviously their water hole, as they were cleanly washed. This courtesy kept everyone in tow.

The red and yellow group left right after the reunion at the water hole going west.

The group we had followed moved a more northerly direction toward the Makarikari Pans, in the company of their bulls, and mature male calves. We found this strange till we saw them hovering around an old bull that was staggering and obviously sick. They were walking close to him, keeping him erect. They were aware of us, but didn't mind us, as if they could read our minds that we were not there to harm them, but were there to observe and learn. It was a slow procession that arrived at the Pans. The entire family was there when the sick bull, who had been well revered, finally succumbed, right up to the last breath, the herd was there to support him, constantly laying their trunks on him, in a stroking gesture, feeling the whole body, even behind the ears. After his death, out of respect for his former rank and position, they gathered around him, trumpeting, and filing past, touched him all over again lingering longer over the ivory tusks, like a subject would have respect for the emperor's bejeweled sword. The smaller brothers and sisters and his offspring put their mouths over the tusks and then chewed on them. Then the young teenage bulls who in times of his coupling, had imitated him, performed a strange ritual. One by one they approached, sniffed his genitalia, and went through the motions of intercourse mounting his carcass. The reason for this I could not understand, except that in their own way they paid homage to his procreation skills.

For a full week they hovered near the carcass, very protective. If any predator came near they raised their tails turning to the predator, defecating on him, fanning their ears, and stampeding the intruders away.

Our minds went back to the old elephant with no relatives, the contrast being this one died surrounded by relatives. We camped nearby so that we could only look. Out of respect for the relatives we never approached the scene. A week later they held a last farewell conference over the carcass, then the family took off. In all that two weeks we never saw them foraging. Out of respect they fasted then on the day of their departure they turned up, each one of them carrying a tender branch which they lay across the carcass, the younger ones scooping leaves and grass over, till it was almost buried. Equal to man's last handful of dust or rose cast upon the coffin. They had done their duty and now left it up to nature's cleaning squad. They would be back again, one more time after that to carry the bones off deep into the heart of the Makarikari Pans. Their original destination was to get to the Etosha Pans. A hundred miles west of the Etosha along the Atlantic Coast lay a strip of shifting sand where many a sick whale had beached. Here too the old and the sick and the no longer in rank of the elephant population, aware of their nearing end had traveled to die. Even from the time of their far relatives, tracing back millions of years, when these noble beasts were but a shadow of their modern counterpart. Hog-sized in the Eocene period, at first with internalized tusks later to externalize pointing over the lip, curving down to dig out tubers. By the time the Mammut developed in the Oligocene period, it had all the characteristics of the current elephant and with shifting earth, migrated via land bridges to all but Antarctica and Australia. The only change occurring during the millennia was by addition of fur and curved tusks during the Miocene period. After the Ice Age, hunting had destroyed many, but in the last thousand years, over-hunting extinguished the elephant in all but Asia and Africa.

" If we are not careful they will become extinct," I said to Peter as we watched the last relative leave.

25

Search for Eden
East Africa — We Drink Blood

In our crisscross journey, Peter was making note of the perfect Eden for tourists. But Eden was everywhere. Only here drought had left the earth cracked and scorched in places by the sun's heat that knew no mercy. There was still grass, but most of it had been eaten down to stumps by the zebra, who always made an early start. Migration was only a month away, leaving no time for the grass to recuperate before the next onslaught was afoot. Now they were in search for greener pastures. The N'Gorogoro Crater was their ultimate destiny.

The giraffe preferred to travel in the company of zebras, because they were the main repasts of lions and thus an insurance against losing a calf should they give birth. Standing fourteen to seventeen feet high, they had already cleaned the tops of the acacia trees to maintain their weight. The cows weighing 2,500 pounds, and the bulls around 3,000 pounds. Without nature and man's intervention the Camelopardalis live twenty-five to thirty years. They were direct descendants of the Sivatherium who lived five million years ago, on the same savannahs of Africa. These ancients stood ten to sixteen feet high, sprouted antlers, but in spite of the variation in height they had the same number of vertebrae as the current species—seven, elongated of course.

Modern giraffe's antlers of course were long gone, shrinking to the small stumps that now adorn their heads, and is mostly decorative. Their necks, a continuous muscle, is their defensive tool, and so are their hooves—the kick was strong enough to decapitate a lion, yet the neck was also the courting tool. To entice the female it would gently wrap his neck around hers and rub it, hence perhaps the term "necking." Like the elephant, they too have a long period of gestation, fifteen months. The calf once born weighs 150 pounds, standing about six feet tall, if it doesn't break a leg on the way to the ground with the five-foot drop. In one week it grew eight inches to a foot. It suckles only till about a month then already starts to nibble on the tender acacia twigs and leaves, like their parents, by using their long pointed hardy tongues, to pick the new sprouts from between the long dangerous thorns. The acacia being their favorite, has one advantage: it provides seventy-four percent of their water needs. They are their most vulnerable while drinking, because of the precarious position they have to take to get to the water level. They splay their legs, and drop their heads down to the water, and it takes a lot of acrobatics to get upright again. Giraffe babies have a high mortality rate, because they are the second favorite food of the lions, leopards, cheetahs, and crocodiles, because they become independent at a very young age, bonding in groups they are more vulnerable. Up to that time they stayed by their mother's side forming a stronger bond, even a suckling on occasion, depending on their mothers to defend them from their main predator, the lion. She usually aimed for the jaw, breaking it with a swift kick, leaving the lion to die from starvation.

Standing on a rise we watched a mixture of herbivores; springbok, kudu, and hartebeest, all together in their need, moving in perpetual movement, searching for food.

The hundreds now gathered were restless and hungry, nature had no clock to tell the herds when to start the migration, but they knew. When their usual foraging got scarce, they gathered together in droves. Till clouds of dust started billowing under a million hooves milling across the savannas.

We deviated from our own route to visit the site where Leaky had made his discovery of what he called our Anthropoidal ancestor. He also called the Oldevai Gorge where he found the skull, the Cradle of Mankind, which infuriated the churches throughout the world, putting the Creationists in an uproar, toppling their theory and acceptance of the Adam and Eve story as the only truth of our descent. They argued that the Evolutionists were evil in their assumption that man could have evolved from the ape-man-beast, and that anthropologists therefore must accept God to be an ape, as the Bible clearly stated that man was made in his image.

In the shade of the only undamaged acacia tree standing, we found the meager shed, that served as laboratory, and museum, and gathering place of these dedicated men and women in search of a common history. They were proud and excited showing us their finds, but refused us the opportunity to be present at the digging site, guarding it like a national secret, aware of the existing skepticism. And the trickery of journalists to get information. We could easily be mistaken for that; I was making notes.

From far away we could see the snow caps of Mt. Meru, around fourteen thousand nine hundred feet high, one hundred short of fifteen thousand feet. For all its beauty it still paled in the nineteen thousand three hundred and forty feet of the majestic Kilimanjaro on the border of Tanzania and Kenya.

Near Mwanza, Lake Victoria made a small foot we reckoned would take us at least two to three days to skirt with our vehicle. But there was no visible pontoon that would be able to take our car across. Within Tanzania lived around one hundred tribes, each with his own dialect, but the main language was Swahili. Peter, being a linguist, had no problem communicating with them. We would have difficulty finding short term accommodation so we camped on the lake side of Mwanza, kept everything in the car and pitched our tent up against it. From here we had a view of Kilimanjaro. It was hot and muggy, and we had stripped to the bare essentials, causing curious stares from the local inhabitants who unlike other parts of Africa, were well covered up. Our only relief was to look up at the cool snow-covered peaks of the Kilimanjaro and wish we were there.

Mwanza was a small native city near a shipping route, made up of mud brick buildings surrounding a large open market. What it lacked in architectural beauty, its inhabitants and the market made up for it. We were fast running out of special supplies, and the market looked inviting. If we were going shopping I even decided to put a dress on for the occasion.

We entered the market square on a market day. It was a clash of color, sounds, and smells set up on and among the cotton bales and crates of cashew nuts awaiting the traders in the afternoon. The stalls were stacked high with home produce, beans of all colors, black, red with white speckles, brown, dark green. Red hot and green peppers strung on string. On the ground there were yams and tubers in baskets, peanuts in bags. And on inverted steel drums, on makeshift coal beds, assorted dishes were cooking emanating heavenly aromas. On another one there was corn roasting still wrapped in their husks and peanuts roasting in their shells. The air sweet and pungent with wares and cooking, mingled with the musty smell of spice and exotic perfume extracts, sold in tiny colorful bottles. We wandered among the stalls and the market people. The women who could afford their own cotton fabrics, showed imagination with hand-dyed and beautifully decorated embroidered wrap-around dresses, which had matching turbans with individually thought up knots and folds, like gay butterflies.

Babies that were being *abba'd* on their mothers' backs had a wrap matching the mothers' outfits. A woman was loading her child. She tied two corners around her waist then hoisted the child up onto her back, pulled the wrap up, one corner went under her arm and the other over a shoulder, making a neat hammock, leaving her hands free to carry the fully laden rush basket that she lifted onto her head rolling one end of the turban into a doughnut to balance the basket.

I bought the necessary things like salt, and flour, and beans, but also a measure of material that I would back home transform into an exotic remembrance of one of the places definitely set on the map for tourists to see. And that night we feasted on a variety of edibles we bought directly off the coals, wrapped in brown paper cartouches.

The Earth was dappled black by four legged creatures, thousands swelling to millions moving in the same direction. Year after year they made their way across savannas, through rivers thick with crocodiles who awaited their arrival, migrating from the low lands to graze against the rim of the N'gorogoro Crater rising precipitously two thousand feet up.

A large herd of wildebeest wound their way mile upon mile of living flesh up toward the rim. It was here within the crater that they would deliver their young. They had survived the last hurdle by crossing the Grumeti River, where death waited for them in the form of thousands of crocodiles that slipped like shadows out of the muddied water, where they had tried to slake their thirst for the next step of their journey. They had no chance except for the numbers to escape from the twenty-foot monsters weighing almost a ton, with deadly jaws from which there was no escape. Once grabbed by the nose, reptilian eyes usually dived down to the depth for the drowning of its victim, but with such abundance there was a feeding frenzy and three or four simply tore the live victim apart. And then went on to another. The calves that were unfortunately born before the river crossing, succumbed by drowning in the masses or became a tasty morsel to stimulate the crocodiles for bigger things.

We traveled parallel with them, witnessing the slaughter without being able to do anything. Finally they reached the crater. The floor of the crater, eleven by thirteen miles, contained a blue lake which lay five thousand six or seven hundred miles above sea level. Within the sloping walls and on the outside everything was green and fertile. The grazing around supported a concentration of wild life rivaling the Serengeti Plains.

During the wet season, along the outer rim, the Masai grazed their longhorn cattle and lived in harmony with the migrating herds, taking their chances with predators, who became so overfed and lazy that they did not bother their cattle.

Kenya's Masai lands totaled ten million acres. But lower down in the Flatlands, other tribes started to move in, depleting the land with slash and burn techniques, trying to grow maize. To keep the Masai cattle off their squatting areas, they erected barbed wire fences, blocking the migratory paths that had been there for centuries. The Masai were given the right to graze their cattle, because they neither farmed nor hunted, but derived all their living provisions from their cattle which they named. They seldom slaughtered except for ritual rites. But rarely for consumption. They lived off the raw blood and milk of their cattle.

We pitched our tent on the ridge of the crater where we could look down on the incredible spectacle.

As the herds moved slowly along, their eyes were always wandering, looking for other hungry eyes, which watched their every move searching for weaknesses.

The milling herds, regardless of species, participated in silent coordinated feeding, ignoring the occasional demise among them; it became a interruption only where it was occurring, then they resumed their grazing as if nothing had happened. Each member in turn stopped their chewing at intervals, ears pricked up for listening. Listening for infra sounds, the enemy called man, soft footfalls, creeping through long grass, mating grunts and other animal small talk, too low for our ears. WE were the *voyeurs* in this yearly migration.

Several of the ewes were pregnant and would not reach the inside of the crater in time. We could only watch as they struggled along, bleating. To the left of us a life and death drama now took place. One of the hartebeest ewes had broken rank, her time had come prematurely. Breaking away from the protection of the others left her open and vulnerable. She licked at her rear. Small convulsions were visible as her belly contracted trying to expel the calf she was carrying. She was obviously in trouble. Hyenas standing several yards away, had smelled the blood, and now waited grinning, waiting for the calf to drop. The calf was presenting breach, one of the legs were caught. The ewe stumbled a few feet. Instinct told her that she was in danger. She knew too that she would have to protect her calf, and it was essential that he start running the moment he was born. The contractions were stronger, she pushed but only one leg still presented itself.

Peter and I stood helplessly by. We could help her, but to do so would destroy the cycle of nature. We had to accept nature in the raw, but we could see the hyenas closing in. I looked at Peter, there was pleading in my eyes; he didn't reply but lifted his gun in the air and fired a shot, hoping to scare off the hyena pack.. This stampeded the feeding herd, but when the dust cleared, we saw a gruesome spectacle. The pack had closed in on the ewe, some were tugging at the leg of the unborn calf, while the others had her by the nose and were pulling her down, some tearing chunks from her rump and belly. Eating her alive. This time Peter took careful aim and gave the ewe a brain shot, eliminating her suffering all at once. It distracted the hyenas momentarily, but then brought them back with renewed force and vigor, having tasted blood, the feeding made easier by Peter's shot.

Several Masai bringing their cattle down from the slopes had witnessed the same drama, but they were used to it. It was the shot that attracted them. They were more interested in our strange vehicle, and Peter's white hair and beard, and naturally my blonde hair. They in turn looked fierce in their earth-dyed red wraps, red ochre-painted faces and razor-sharp spears they used against the lion, enemy of their cattle.

They invited us to their *kraal* to share in their riches, if we let them have a ride in our car. We didn't know what to expect, but the riches of King Solomon's mines immediately came to mind, so Peter accepted. Within minutes they were standing on the wheel covers, the bumper, and sitting on the roof. The interior looked like one of those circus cars that were capable of holding numerous clowns. The unfortunate ones who did not fit herded the cattle into the compound surrounded by a circle fence of dead tree branches, braided together. Within the cattle compound there were small holes in which smoldering fires were giving off a lot of white smoke that hung like a cloud over everything. It amazed me that they didn't die from smoke inhalation.

They explained to Peter that the mosquitoes and the tsetse flies were fierce on their cattle, and the smoke prevented the cattle from being stung and getting sick.

Our hosts' families came out of small round *rondawels,* dotted around the perimeter of the compound to welcome their men and the strangers. We watched what form of greeting we should use, not to offend our hosts, and then decided that the handshake would be appropriate. They found this ritual extremely funny, laughing into their cupped hands to prevent their souls from escaping out of their mouths. The handshake was so popular that from the oldest to the youngest lined up to pump our hands. Some pressing with an iron grip and prolonging the pumping with exaggerated movements. The women shyly offered their hands limply, but considered it a fair exchange for the privilege to touch Peter's silver and my sun bleached spun gold hair, being that their own heads were shaved bald, smeared with fat. They left the hair growing to the men and initiate boys, who started growing theirs right after their initiation. Some of the men sported waist-length hair, braided into fine braids, then rolled into spaghetti thin strands of red clay.

The married women wore large rawhide collars reaching from the neck to the shoulders, beautifully embroidered with beadwork. They were either bare breasted or covered in the same earth dyed ochre cloth of the men. The collar flopped up and down with the rhythm of their stride.

One of the women squatted down beside a cow that she had called by name, and politely with eyes lowered asked if she could have some milk for her children, men, and guests. I thought it coincidence when the cow mooed at just that moment, but she was convinced that was her answer. So she started milking into a large open gourd.

Then she asked Peter if he would like some milk. When he answered affirmatively, she again asked if he would allow his woman (me) to have some. He, knowing the protocol, asked me if I would like some milk. I nodded yes. I thought she was quite clean and her milking fine. Then out of the corner of my eye I saw a few young men chasing some cattle around in circles.(I learned later that was to encourage the blood to flow faster.) When caught the young man took the flame sharp point of his spear and stuck it, barely breaking the skin into a vein in the neck of the beast, then stuck a hollow reed into the hole, holding his thumb over the reed's opening. The woman brought him the gourd of milk and when he released his thumb, a scarlet stream of blood shot out of the reed into the gourd of milk. The woman picked up a thin stick, stirred the blood and milk till it formed a smooth foamy pink color.

215

When it reached the color and texture she wanted she nodded to the young man. He removed the reed and plugged the hole. To my amazement there was no more bleeding. Peter asked him what was in the plug he had put on the hole. He explained it was soil, dung and a herb that acted as a coagulant.

The woman who did the milking was leader in the women's rank; she motioned us to come and drink, she also called the warriors. They closed in on us, simply curious. We thought perhaps she wanted to make a point to them, and show off our weakness. They looked even more threatening up close. And we were not at all sure about what would happen if we refused.

She handed Peter the gourd, he accepted it with a nod of recognition of her status. All I could think of was, *Thank God that she considered Peter tops in importance at that moment.* Looking around us at the children and even her husband, with snot noses and swarms of flies feasting off the moisture out of the corners of their eyes and mouths, I was sure I would not feel squeamish about the blood. I was used to blood products. Mom used to take the blood from a kill and bake it like a brawn, but the thought of drinking something from the same gourd as them made my stomach turn.

I watched Peter's face for signs of faking, but he swallowed a few big gulps as if it was the most delectable cuisine prepared by our hostess. Took another few gulps, smacking his lips, which left a pink foamy ring on his mustache. They were highly pleased. Next would be me. I prayed silently that after the first gulp I wouldn't throw up on our hostess. I kept my mind on blood products Mom frequently used to make. I loved the black blood sausage, and the baked blood sliced like liver. But we NEVER HAD IT RAW! I had on occasion sucked the blood from my finger when I was pricked by a thorn; it tasted funny, so I usually spat it out. I could pretend. Peter actually smiled when he saw my hesitation. Then trying to allow me to save face, he told our hostess that I was waiting for his command to drink. He wiped the spot where he drank with the back of his hand for me. I could see the amused look on the faces of the warriors and even the children, and the hostess looked dejected. I took a small taste, it had a surprising sweet milky taste with a tinge of metallic, like sucking on a copper penny. But I knew I wouldn't be able to take more of it, so I dutifully smacked my lips, put my lips to the gourd, tilted my head back, and pretended to drink deeply, swallowing my spit very realistically, then wiped my mouth with the back of my hand, and licked my lips. They were pleased when I, not knowing who was next, handed the gourd over to our hostess, thanking her non verbally by pressing my hands together in prayer. When we finally went after a tour of their prized possessions, their cows, and their children, the whole tribe saw us to their gate, waving and smiling behind cupped hands. We had made friends for a lifetime. I couldn't help thinking, it's rather like insurance. At our camp, when we arrived, there stood a sentinel off to one side, guarding our possessions. And for days we saw the same person at a respectable distance guarding us.

Leaving Kenya, we entered the rift valley, a sort of lethargic low key forbidding place, with some of the most spectacular scenery. Geological Africa could be seen as a rigid rock laid down two hundred million years ago, with dense vegetation, down to oozy swamp. In this amazing topography lies two of these trough-like depressions starting at Turkey, running for four thousand miles into the African Continent, the other rift is about nearly two thousand miles long fifty to sixty miles wide and are a hundred to one thousand feet deep, forming a series of catch basin lakes. The largest fresh water lake, Lake Superior is the size of, say, Ireland. Therefore it is better to think of Africa not in terms of its cities, but by the size of its villages, We encountered many of these rising like ant hills out of the indigenous forests that only enfolds six to ten percent of Africa; the rest are mountainous and savannas.

It took us more than a month to skirt the rift valley, meeting a strange assortment of its peoples living where their forefathers lived. Doing mostly the same things in the same way, largely uneducated except for their own tribal enlightenment. To the rest of the world, Africa is a bewildering realization, which conveniently is called the Dark Continent. Our little vehicle was miraculously holding up suffering the muddy rutted roads and in some places impenetrable bush. We followed convenience roads, carved around dangerous curves, and came upon the Dorze peoples, known in more enlightened circles as fierce warriors. We expected the worst, but were greeted by their more gentler side. We found them musical, with a song upon their lips. This became evident as we passed a funeral on our way to their village. The people were carrying flowers, and gifts of food, both for the diseased and for the living.

Young people dancing stiff legged, along the muddy dirt road, sang of the departed's scandals during his living, but also of his good deeds performed and how many enemies he destroyed. The widow lamenting tore at her hair and her clothes, screaming for all the world to hear: *"Tana wanda ... tana wanda!"* (Kill me ... kill me!)

217

She really didn't want to be killed, but that was the ultimate expression of her grief, because in his passing she would also lose everything she ever possessed. Later we saw a hut burning, and were told that it was his earthly possessions. Nearby family members were already busy building a new hut, with beautiful woven roof. The weaving skills were taught from very small. Some boys were sitting against the side of a hut, using a loom with such dexterity that was surprising, holding the cotton that was brought from Ethiopia with their mouths and gripped between their toes to achieve the end results. They were singing of St. Helena the mother of Constantine who they believed they had descended from.

In the village square, there was a feast of goats meat, ensete tubers sweetened with honey, maize roasted on the open fires and a luxury, coffee awaiting the funeral guests. We were invited to the wake by the medicine man, as living good spirits to bring good fortune to the widow. We gladly accepted.; not only was it a free meal, but it afforded us the opportunity to learn something of these people.

The medicine man got the honors of slitting the throat of the wedding lamb, which played a very significant part at the funeral. Not only was the medicine man the physical healer, but also a soothsayer, and the healer of hearts. The lamb carcass was stripped of the skin, which was then stretched taught by hammering four wooden pegs through the legs into the ground. The entrails were then placed on the skin. Some of it was then tossed into the fire for nibbling later on.

He would then scramble those on the skin, and proceed to tell the future of the widow in the entrails. He told her where her new husband lived, and how long it would take for him to notice her as a future wife. In her case he told her she would not have to wait for very long, because the Big Spirit had seen fit to send her two good spirits, "Before two full moons she would be a bride again!"

I told Peter in Afrikaans, *"Hoe kan die twee goeie geeste haar dan teleur stel?"(How can the two good spirits disappoint them?)*

From our stash we pulled out two pounds and a handful of change and presented it to the widow. The two good spirits did not disappoint the widow.

"SIYA-HAMBA" Became reality a few days later on our way to Cape Horn; it was the farthest point North East of Africa, near the Red Sea mouth where ships sailed past on their way to India. I had read in a magazine about a strange group of people who got ship wrecked at the horn and were living there withdrawn from the world. I wanted to go and see for myself. That

would also be a vantage lookout point I told Peter, who had not planned going into Somalia. To get to the horn we would have to backtrack quite a distance. We soon ran into a snag, because here the roads were non existent. So we secured everything, covered the car with branches to camouflage it, packed some food and took our canteens for refilling, and set off on a long walk. It was several days, the walk was endless, we came across some Somali huts, conical frames covered in skins. They are a nomadic people who move around a lot. When Peter tried to find out from them if they had seen others like us, at the top of the horn, they smiled a lot, but shook their heads "yes" from side to side, which really meant "No."

26

Captured for Gene Pool?

It was late afternoon, we stopped to rest and discuss where we would sleep for the night. That's when we noticed a thin spiral of smoke rising out of the trees some distance farther up. We immediately headed in that direction. High up on the rise we came upon a clearing. Several A-frame roofs stuck out of the ground. We saw no people, but as soon as we entered the clearing, people started to appear from everywhere, and converged on us. They surrounded us in a free for all touchy, feely exploration. I was wearing short shorts and a halter top, and there wasn't an inch of me that was left unexplored, by both men and woman. I tried to stop them but looking over at Peter, they were doing the same to him. There was something very strange about the people. They looked a bit simple and deformed, with cleft lips, clubfeet, even humps, as if some institute for deformity had opened its doors and dumped them all out, as far away from civilization as possible to fend for themselves. At first I thought we had stumbled on a leprosy colony. We tried to speak with them, to inquire where we were, they answered but rather incoherently.

"LOS HULLE UIT !" (LEAVE THEM ALONE!) A booming Dutch voice thundered out orders to leave us alone! A woman joined him, pushing the people away from us. They didn't touch us themselves but their eyes scanned our bodies with unnatural intent. I sent silent ESP messages to Peter

for us to get out of there. The man seemed to be intelligent. He saw us looking with interest at the houses, and invited us to see the inside of one of them. We expected the door to open outwardly but, instead it swung down like a bridge into a circular pit, with seating and sleeping areas dug out of the dirt. There was nothing personal in it except for the bedding, *karosses*, of beautifully soft animal skins on the floor and around the seating and sleeping platforms. The woman also spoke Dutch and offered us the hospitality of the hut for the night. She had just brewed tea; they picked their own herbs she said. We walked down the steep incline of the door into the dimly lit circular room. The man, Peter, and I sat down, while the woman went to fetch the tea. The man told us that his ancestors had followed the same sea route that Jan Van Riebeek took, but instead of landing at Cape Point, the sea drove them off course. After a long time they reached land, crashing against the rocks. Thinking it was the Cape, they tried to go inland, but met up with many obstacles and animosities. They salvaged everything that could be used off the ship, and established their own little colony, hoping that sooner or later they would meet up with other pioneers. But after years, they finally gave up; they could see other ships far off, but had no hope of them ever coming on land. When available mates died out, incest became commonplace, he explained that his wife was really the daughter of his eldest daughter, but she seemed the healthiest. He laughed, "What we really need is some new breeding stock!"

"Where do you get your supplies?" Peter asked, trying to change the subject.

"I have a mule, and go down to the Berbera trading port, where I trade our skins for salt, materials, and simple staples, the rest we derive from nature." Walking away he made the excuse he would go and see why the woman had not brought the tea. He would be back to call us for food, and suggested we stay for the night. The moment he left I whispered to Peter. "If we stay, we might never be seen again, because he practically hinted that his grand-daughter-wife was the pick of the crop to continue their line. They need new breeding stock, and we are it!"

"It's too late now, we should have left when it was still light, but we will never get to the car in the dark; we will just have to take a chance." He put his arms protectively around me. "I suggest we do not drink the tea, and if they offer us food we only eat that which we see others eating. OK?"

The food was quite good; it was a familiar dish called *potjie-kos*. A communal pot with layers of meat and vegetables cooked in the same pot, so we enjoyed it, but I secretly threw my tea out, and noticed so did Peter.

In the light of the campfire we were escorted back to the same room where we had the talk with the leader of the strange motley group. Once inside, the door was pulled up from the outside, and we heard a noise of something sliding into a bolt. There was also a whispering and a giggling. Peter tried to assure me.

"Perhaps they are locking it for our safety and to keep us away from our touchy- feely welcoming committee."

"Yeah, but it is locked on the outside, and that means we are prisoners. I'm more afraid of these people than I was of the Masai," I said.

The door was about seven feet up, but standing on the sleeping platform Peter was able to reach the roof beam. "I'll wait until everyone is asleep and see if I could lift the bolt on the outside from in here."

The long hike had tired me out, and I lay down on the skins and soon fell fast asleep. About dawn I woke up. Peter was holding his hand cupped over my mouth in case I shouted out in alarm. "I was unable to move the lock, but sitting on one of the beams I cut a hole through the thatch near the back. I took a look and there is no one about yet. Come, we must go now! I'll go first in case there is trouble. You hand me the packs and water bottles, and I'll pull you up."

I didn't hesitate as I pulled myself onto the rafters and out the hole, and slid down to the ground with Peter breaking my fall. We ran off into the bush, and did not stop or look back till we reached a safe distance away. Nor did we ever consider in the months to follow that we may have misinterpreted their intentions with us, but to this day I still believe that had we not escaped, they would have kept us there as 'love slaves' to improve their breeding stock like the man said.

27

The Nuba Wrestlers

With all of Peter's linguistic skills, we were unable to communicate with the Nuba except through an interpreter who knew a smattering of French he had obtained through trading. There were more than a hundred languages in the Sudan, derived from the surrounding areas. Arabic and French were only two of the conglomerate of all the dialects.

While in Ethiopia we had heard of the Wrestlers of Nuba in Central Sudan, and made our way there. They competed with the Mesakin and the Karongo, who were top of their list for their competitive spirit; they were their neighbors but couldn't understand one another's languages because they were so profoundly different. But they had other things in common. They shared a common culture and origin.

The roads here were game paths, that were widened to accommodate the peculiar habit of the Korongo, who moved with their homes. The Mesakin, however, built their mud houses permanently against the hills in the shape of castles and tall towers and turrets, pieces of living art, similar to the Dogon of Mali. While all the other tribes lived on the plains. The Mesakin Nuba, approximately five to eight thousand, were divided into ten to fifteen hill communities. Each of them had their own *mak* (chief) and their own *kudjur* (medicine man and priest).

The Mesakin were the poorest of the Nuba, not as tall as the Korongo. The

Korongo were a head taller because their diet included meat as they were cattle breeders, and had more milk and animal proteins. Yet it was the smaller Mesakin that were to be watched during the famous wrestling matches.

Our strange converted transport caused a sensation, equal to the landing of a UFO. It was approached with extreme caution. The elders and the brave came to greet us on our arrival. The lack of clothing did not bother me, but I had to refrain from laughing. They were dressed in of all things, boxer shorts, one even had polka dots and hearts.

We too were strange to them, once the elders had established that we had come from our world to theirs for the wrestling. We were accepted. The rest of the people stepped forward to investigate. They felt my blonde hair, they pinched my arm to see if the color would come off. We most likely reminded them of the wrestlers who colored themselves white to ward off evil spirits. Ours did not rub off so we must be either gods or spirits, or eternally in good terms with the spirits, which made us an asset to them. They immediately made us mascots for the upcoming festivities.

The preparations for the *sanda* (wrestling) had started a month before. Messengers were sent to invite the Nuba clans to the gathering. It was just after the grain was harvested. The *sanda* acted as a sort of harvest festival, and a time for sharing and socializing and for selecting a mate. Polygamy was still encouraged, to ensure the survival of their own tribe, but outside the tribe. A man could have four wives, but even that small amount of wives sometimes posed a problem keeping track of the progeny and often led to incest, when children of a third or fourth wife got separated from one another, and brother and sister got together or even sisters and brothers of a man's other wives, necessitating a social event to select marriage partners from another Nuba tribe. The women flirted outrageously with Peter, his silver hair too was a fascination, because only their very old had silver hair. Both men and woman either shaved their hair all off or had very close cropped hair.

We set up our tent outside the perimeter of their *kraal* this way we could observe and be part of the preparation, without infringing.

I joined the women in harvesting the millet. My farming experience came in handy with the long handled sickle; we carried it to a clean-swept area, where it was thrashed with stick brooms, then scooped up in a ladle calabash. The chaff was tossed up into the air slowly, the breezes sorting out the chaff from the grains. These were transferred into a larger gourd, where smaller pieces of chaff were hand rubbed and sorted out. They marveled at my skill to grind the grains, but Mom often let us help out with grinding the corn into flour. From these grains they brewed quantities of beer, with honey, marisa, and hops in large earthen pots. A few days before the event, milk was gathered into clay pots, covered with cloth, and hung up in the cool of the trees, away from dogs and children, to thicken into yogurt, as a special drink for the wrestlers and old men. The rest of the milk was churned into butter, not for eating but for cosmetic purposes and skin beautification. Some buttermilk was saved for the children, with honey added, or drunk in its natural semi-sour state by the women. Wild fruit and berries were picked and saved as a treat. The maroela, a small round fruit smaller than a hen's egg, with wax-colored fruit in the inside, was lain out in the sun to ferment, which turned the fruit into a simulated alcohol potency. It reminded me of the elephants in my childhood my Dad told me about. They shook the fruit off the trees and left them to ferment then they would come back to the tree when the fruit had fermented and eat them. This would make them tipsy and they would dance around the tree and act quite silly.

At least a month before the happening, the newly initiated started their body scarring that would enhance their beauty and declare their maturity and availability for courtship. I had seen the freshly healed scars, and in a strange way it was artistic. I had missed seeing it done, but I was curious about the pain that went with it, and the fear that must accompany it. This was their cultural heritage and they wore the scars on their naked bodies with extreme pride. Through the interpreter I was told that a girl with no scarring was considered almost obscene. They asked to see my scarring, and when I couldn't produce any, logic told them that was why I had to hide my body in shame under the clothes that I wore. I told them that in my culture, scarring was considered ugly and was removed. Except a thing called Tattoo that Sailors on ships do to their bodies, and those pictures drawn on their arms and bodies were considered attractive. They then asked if I had any of those pictures on my body. When I said I didn't they were very sorry for me. They said that if I wanted to attend the wrestle gathering I would have to go as a subordinate to one of the elderly ladies. I would have to be her carrier. I thought that to mean that I would have to carry her. I had looked them over and they were all skinny, and if that was what it would cost to go to the *sanda*, I'd be happy.

"Show me the one that I would have to carry?" I demanded.

They only laughed, and told me, "You don't carry her, you carry only what she takes to the festivities—the food or beer that she contributes, and you would have to see to her needs. There is only one more thing, you would have

225

to shed your clothes and would have to be symbolically scarred with *a tutu* like the men on the ships." I wanted to go to the wrestling, so I agreed to do that also. They explained that they would draw on my body with berry dye, which would wear off in time.

One of the girls who had helped me harvest the millet and was initiated together with the others, had not yet been scarred. She did not know when she was born, but remembered it was during the big storm. Her breasts were not yet fully developed, but she had turned a woman during her withdrawal with the others when she had learned all there was to know about being a woman and how to please a man. And her mind told her that she was ready, if the gods are kind, to be a bride, but she would have to show that she was by scarring.

She decided on a double "V" that started on her shoulders and ran over her breasts down to her navel, and from her shoulders across her back down to her coccyx.

This gave me the opportunity to see an actual scarring ceremony.

Early on the appointed day, we went down to the river and scrubbed one another down with branches of *looga* (soap bush that produced foam like soap).

She had chosen a cool spot under a tree, and the local performer of the cicatrix surgery had taken her sharp fingernail and traced the pattern she requested over her perfect black body, leaving a faint white mark on the skin. I thought, this is where she surely was going to change her mind. But she showed incredible composure for someone who was about to undergo several hours of torture. I on the other hand sat stripped down to my panties waiting to have my bloodless tattoos in their familiar tribal patterns all over my fully developed breasts, and over my back belly and arms, everywhere that was exposed, except my hips, which would be covered with a wrap around sarong.

I felt slightly nauseated by watching the old woman pinch the girls skin together with thumb and forefinger and hold it with a strong thorn, then cut two small cuts with her prized possession—a razor blade that had been sharpened many times, on either side of the thorn. Then to my horror she spat on the newly made wound and rubbed it in. The girl made a small cringing movement, chanting a special song softly to herself as the woman deftly proceeded down the marked "V" making cut after cut, a small trickle of blood ran parallel with the "V." She rubbed it away with the back of her hand and spat into every new scar she made. I saw the girl grit her teeth when she reached the tender breasts, and the tears run down her cheeks, but she didn't cry out or even moan when it was finally over on the front and the back, and the woman rubbed the speckling wounds with sesame oil and rubbed salt into the wounds. God that must have burned. I cringed at the unsanitary procedures, and was glad for the girl when it was over. She had been very brave to endure such pain for the sake of beauty.

The young girl stood up calmly, thanking the woman, her young body colored scarlet where the blood was wiped away, with no signs of suffering, only a wise smile on her face, thinking of things to come. She would have normally showered; the Nuba are a very clean tribe and behind each hut there was a shower pot similar to the one we used in the jungle with a plug hole in the bottom through which the water trickled, and of course there was the river. But instead she picked up her music maker; it was a simple instrument consisting of a thin rawhide string with a four inch hollowed stick attached to the end. The stick was a gift from an admirer, and was elaborately carved. She walked through the village, swinging the rawhide in circles above her head, till the hollow stick made a soft musical hum growing louder and louder with the force of the swing. The blood had dried on her back and front, but she wore it proudly, like a girl graduating would show off her graduating dress, only this was living material. It showed others her endurance, and made her more attractive to the young men, who gave her admiring glances. One in particular walked all the way behind her. I thought that might well be the one who carved her music maker. And I was proven right later when I saw him again at the festival.

The day of the *Sanda* had arrived. The women, including me, had loaded the food into woven grass baskets. There was thick millet mush cut into thick slices soaked in honey. Round crunchy millet cakes roasted on a flat stone. Wild fruit, cakes of honey still dripping from the honeycomb. Clay pots full of yogurt, and other delectable goodies.

The newly scarred freshly bathed were all rubbed with butter and shone like polished ebony, adorned only by a short skirt and hip bead work, not to distract from the patterns of Cicatrix that declared their availability to the young men at the wrestling. Some of the girls had other additional body piercings through the nose and bottom lip. Through these holes they wore lip plugs, made like small drums from wood or ivory, or burnt or carved hollow whistles, they blew every now and then to attract a certain boy's attention. These rested on their chins. Others preferred miniature bouquets of delicately braided grass and flowers.

It was dawn and already a hundred and ten degrees, the mercury still rising. I was almost grateful that I wasn't obliged to wear any clothes.

I couldn't help but laugh when Peter came to tell me that the men would be separated from the women, and were going in advance to prepare the site and themselves. He had been elected as a good spirit. The men partaking in the wrestling, and their *entourage* were dressed in their birthday suits, except for the bark jock straps. I complimented him on his outfit, and he in turn on my berry tattoos, of squiggles and dots and stripes. We had gone naked in our expedition, and were proud of our tans, but now we looked pale in comparison to their glistening black bodies.

At the elected site, the men partaking in the wrestling and those who walked in the shadow of their fame had dug a shallow pit, filled it with twigs, and set it alight, refilling it when each layer had burnt down, till the pit was filled with fine talcum white ash.

Our challenger, together with his *entourage* was the first to arrive at the pit, because the winner was from our village, and that was his right. He had not lifted a finger since his victory, but built up muscle and strength together with his assistants who had been challengers in the past, but were defeated, and so became his subordinates. To stay in the game, they devoted their whole year to care for the victor. He was massaged, and provided with a vegetarian diet of mush, nuts, sesame seeds, fruit, yogurt, millet cakes, and honey, and buttermilk. He was in top form physically, walking tall like a fighting bull.

A helper dipped a small branch in an earthen pot and flicked it deftly over the magnificent, statuesque body. He then lay down in the cooled off ash and rolled around until his whole body was covered in white. Coming out of the pit, a chosen man dipped his finger in a bowl of milk and made a distinct pattern in the ash clinging to his skin. In his case it was a symbolic scarring in honor of a certain female debutante. Where the ash was removed it looked like polka dots. Now a solitary colored strip of cloth was tied around his waist. This strip of cloth meant nothing for an outsider, but definitely held meaning for the wrestlers and their opponents. And because they were totally naked, even without jockstrap, the strip of cloth offered a hand hold. On the cloth of the previous year's winner hung a small calabash, a symbol of his previous fights, to show that it was unbroken, and he was never defeated. After the challengers were through, the pit was open to all, and it was a mad scramble for everyone to roll in the ash. I watched from the outer ring where the woman were supposed to be, but I had my binoculars and it was amusing to see that no one was laughing as they clashed and thrashed, ash flying in white clouds. This was serious business. Peter too rolled in the ash, they had chosen him as a living spirit mascot. Something to scare off their challengers, as it had never been done before, we just happened to be there at the time. And they just happened to like his white goatee.

The assistants had no restrictions in their mode of dress or undress, but they leaned toward the bizarre. Tied to their outstanding manhood they had tied the tip of a lions tail, a hollow piece of bamboo in a permanent erect position, and a G-string of beadwork from a female admirer, while others settled for the more conservative of boxer shorts, or leaf skirts.

The spectators had arrived in droves. They were milling around eagerly to see what they could see, and to be seen. Flirting and showing off with acrobatics, stick fights, and mock wrestling challenges.

To set perimeters for the crowds, a large circle was drawn with ash in the center of the undeclared arena. Around this circle the crowds stood or squatted, claiming ring-side seats. As the Wrestlers arrived they were escorted to a smaller circle, providing some shade, from a leaf canopy, where only they and their helpers were allowed in. Everything proceeded very orderly. No one entered the larger or smaller circles. The men selected for crowd control watched carefully, and if anyone tried to approach their heroes too closely or tried to touch them, they slapped the ground with a paddle staff near the offender's feet, making them jump in fright. The young boys deliberately made a game of it, taunting the crowd controllers, to show off to the newly scarred girls, who had been given special privileges to be on the outside of the inner circle of men, and only entered when refreshments were called for.

The women did not mingle with the men but stayed in the shade of the trees, guarding the food, and supervising the needs of the elderly. They discussed the men and their attributes openly among themselves, which could be plainly seen, and spoke about their own marital status, hoping that the word would spread.

The village I was with got a secret kick out of the stares and remarks cast their way, by having a mascot of their own, me! Against the ebony black of my adoptive sisters, my body was pale except for the elaborate designs. They approached me timidly to admire the living artwork. I was naked except for a very short wrap-around skirt on my hips. White people were never seen at the *Sanda,* and that made me and Peter quite an oddity. Like the initiates I was buttered, and my hair made into thin spaghetti strands around my head, festooned with flowers.

The noisy crowd without any prompting suddenly became hushed., when the first challenger stepped into the arena, surrounded by his helpers. After depositing him in the center, they proudly stepped out of the ring carrying symbolic spears and clubs, and boughs of luck bringing branches. Respectfully a group of men sitting ringside got up and moved back, allowing them ringside view of their charge. He bent forward, spread his legs and placed his hands on his knees and waited. The second man entered with his support group, they then walked around the first man sizing him up, loudly declaring that their man had nothing to fear. With a lot of taunting they then tied a calabash onto his colored waist cloth. Then they too were given honored seats ringside. The second man took up the same stance, their heads touching. His calabash was the same color as his waist cloth, declaring to the crowd, that he was a first-time challenger. A ripple of comments ran like wild fire through the crowd, then like one man there was silence. There was no referee except for the crowd who watched every move. No gong or drum roll, but an unspoken mutually agreeable signal from the two men in the inner circle. They stuck their tongues out at one another, and the fight began. Like two fighting cockerels they danced around stiff legged hands on knees displaying rippling muscles, sticking their tongues out at one another, till they both seized the other's colored belt. Holding onto the belt, they then coiled and twisted, standing upright. With their hands never leaving the belt, which would mean an instant disqualification, working only with their legs, they tried to trip one another, throwing him off balance down on his buttocks, The one left standing then broke the downed one's calabash by stamping it with his foot declaring him a loser. The winner, with an unbroken calabash, remained in the ring getting into the beginning stance. Then one by one he was challenged like the game of "King of the Castle." When all the challengers had a turn, and the last calabash was smashed, the one who still had his calabash unbroken was the all time winner and would remain so until the next year. His helpers immediately ran in and lifted him onto their shoulders, and a chorus of *lah-lah-lah-lah-lah- lah* broke out among the initiates and the women on the outside. The winner was paraded through the crowd. The fires were packed in the inner circle and the food brought in by the woman for all to share. It was time for celebration! The victor was glorified, his year of celibacy was over, he had the pick of the maidens. After the feasting, the ring was cleared for dancing, losers forgetting their defeat as they watched the gyrating of the girls to the drumbeats. I joined in, directing my dancing to the special spirit mascot of our host village who carried off the unbroken calabash for yet another year. The dancing went on till morning. Till one by one the groups gathered and lit their torches by the fires and in a single line made their way back to their villages, some with conquests made, others with only promises till next year. For the reluctant to leave, a horn sounded to let them know that the party was over.

As special guests, Peter and I stayed over for a few more days in a hut assigned to us, a hut that reminded me of my childhood with the smell of dung and ochre that insulated the pole wall that surrounded me.

28

The Mopti — Niger River

Leaving the Nuba behind, we crossed Central Africa and the Cameroon, arriving at the mouth of the Niger River that started near the Cameroon basin, ran through Nigeria, Niger, into Mali, turning near Timbuktu in a south-westerly direction down the Upper Volta. Our arrival at the Niger River caused a stir as usual. We were mistaken for buyers, but were only inquiring around for a means of getting our vehicle across the river, which stretched like a sea in front of us. We were swamped by merchants.

A man in his forties dressed in a western suit in the unbearable heat, with a traditional shawl, which could be used for all purposes draped around his shoulders, had been observing us from the moment we arrived in Mopti. He waited until the swarm of merchants left, then approached us.

"You are looking at *Joliba*," he said with a very British accent. "At least that's what we call the Niger River." Then he continued with the rehearsed speech all guides usually use for outsiders. "She is unpredictable like a woman, sometimes she is a gentle stream, nourishing her children from her breast, flowing quietly like a lullaby, and at other times she is angry, screaming at the top of her voice, roaring along her embankments, destroying our crops of sorghum and millet growing along the banks with no regard for the humans and their dwellings, carrying everything away in her rage!

"But we love her most when she becomes pregnant with the waters of the lake at Timbuktu, swelling up with many fish."

"Timbuktu?" I laughed. "That sounds like the place people were always sending people to that had done them an injustice. As a child I would ask them where it was, and they would always reply at the end of the world."

"Perhaps it is, because it is not far from the Sahara Desert."

"What does *Joliba* mean?" Peter asked.

"*Joliba* means, the big river, it is sister to the Zambesie in the east, the Congo in the west and her big brother the Nile in the north." Then he went on. "When *Joliba* was pregnant like last year, we ate well! We caught just under 200,000 tons of fish from her 1,000 mile journey to the sea."

It sounded a bit like exaggeration, but we noticed that Mopti had a large fish market, so presumed the Niger was pregnant again. But Mopti was also an alternate market, overflowing with all kinds of produce, and house wares, pots and pottery, polished amber, and if you had enough money, exquisite gold jewelry of fine filigree and bold earrings the size of tea cups. We bypassed these and bought our meager essential purchases. Our new friend, who found it unnecessary to introduce himself to us, was a little disappointed at our purchases, till Peter explained we had come a long way, and had still a long way to go, with limited space. He explained that we would open the routes we mapped to tourists and merchants that would follow. (In 1954, Mopti and Nigeria had seen very little Tourists, only traders that came and went).

I saw a man wrap a large white block with cloth made from pulped bamboo, and load it on a Camel that objected loudly with a course guttural *gaah -aagg*, trying to take a nip out of its owner. The same blocks were stacked side by side and up like children's building blocks. Before I could ask our friend said. "Salt! better than money! They bring it from the salt diggings and barter it for wares, cooking pots, hand-woven material, sorghum, goats, chickens, and fish of course, then we sell it again for money." Our friend was both informative and articulate, and from snatches of conversation, we gathered that he had attended college in England but came back to his birthplace. He told us that he was named after a leader *Kwame*. Kwame told us that the man who was loading the salt had bartered for wares that he would take with him on a sampan to the Niger mouth and then to Cameroon for export. Or take the crossover and go up the Gold Coast. Peter was about to ask him how we could get our vehicle across, when there was a shrill warbling sound coming up the street. It was a colorful procession of women dressed in gaily colored dresses, with immense full flare skirts standing out like giant morning glories. Kwame said they were celebrating the end of a period of "abstinence." The predominant religion was Islam, but the Moslem fishermen who knelt down as much as five times a day in prayer to thank Allah for their daily bread, which of course was fish, would conclude the month's long fasting by killing some chickens. My scantily clad body up to then had not bothered Kwame, but now faced with something that represented a religious act, he became concerned and removed his all purpose shawl off his shoulders, and handed it to me.

"It would be wise, if you want to continue to participate and watch the festivities, that you cover your shoulders and body parts so as not to offend anybody. It would also please me for you are a very comely woman." I thought it funny that not a month ago, the body tattoos now gone, I was asked to take my clothes off so as not to offend everyone, and here I had to cover it. It was fine for Peter to show his body parts, and he had such fine ones, too. But here I was considered a mere woman, and needed to be covered.

We entered a compound, where there was a round arena, much like a water-less swimming pool. The walls on the outside made from mud bricks, were about four feet high. I could easily see over. The walls were colored in dark brown splashes. Inside a holy man was killing chickens for the feast. With one swing of a long flame sharp knife, a cross between a sword and a panga, he beheaded the chickens, purifying them, by ironically draining the blood out of their bodies and mumbling a prayer over them.

The amazing thing was how long they continued to stay upright after their heads were off. A few of them that were already beheaded were dancing a gruesome death dance, flipping and stumbling around reminding me of the directionless bumping into the walls of the dung beatles, the blood squirting out of the necks, coloring everything in its path red. I realized that the dark brown designs on the walls were not decorations, but old blood from previous slaughters. The color drained out of my face. I walked in a haze to where the women were dancing a different kind of dance yet symbolically reminding me of the macabre dance of the chickens I had just witnessed.

Their dance with all the whirling had taken on a kind of individual hypnotic effect. They hummed in a strange monotone something about *raaam-ah-daaan*, over and over. Two broke free from the rest, crossed their arms linking hands, they continued their whirling, round and round like when we were children and the twirling made us drunk and we fell down, they went faster and faster till they became a blur. Faster and faster they spun in a timeless frenzy, till they dropped down tumbling over the other dancers and the onlookers, till all were lying on a heap laughing on the road.

The men, not used to the women (who were generally very conservative and reserved), enjoyed for once the uninhibited display of abandonment.

Other women who were enjoying the reckless display covered their faces not to show their pleasure, and stood looking from a distance, and just to show that they were supposed to be shocked, exclaimed. "Aren't they ashamed?" or "And that in a public place."

The sun made the earth feel like a giant sauna, and with the wrap around me, big pearly drops of sweat stood out on my arms, and I could feel a trickle run down between my breasts down to my navel. I needed to get into shade.

Peter and Kwame had joined some people under a makeshift canopy of braided sorghum leave. This turned out to be an outdoor eating place. What I noticed though was that all the people under the canopy were men. They sat on the ground or squatted around a communal pot with a mixture of boiled sorghum and rice, and a pan of fish, boiled smoked herring and fresh caught salmon. They interrupted their eating for just a moment to stare at me. It wasn't a friendly stare, so putting two and two together I discretely withdrew and joined the women who were gathered a round a similar pot under a canopy nearby, so as not to embarrass my Peter in front of the men.

It was midday and the market was alive with activity, from the celebration as well as trade. The street we were on was the main highway to the barges, and the take off point to the Sahara of the salt caravans, fully loaded on the backs of camels, who loudly bellowed their objections.

We were scarcely finished with our meager meal, listening to the last minute negotiations among the men in languages that equaled the stock exchange, when suddenly everyone grabbed whatever was in reach, and made a run for shelter, including me. I half expected the arrival of a giant one-eyed cyclops, with the urgency around me to get away. Everyone scattered to the sides, like the parting of the Dead Sea. Mooing, bellowing, and bleating filled the air, as a large herd of humped back Brahman cattle stampeded up the road followed by a noisy bunch of goats driven by a group of men in pristine white loose-fitting pajamas. Behind them followed a group of women, bedecked in embroidered silk flowing robes and magnificent gold jewelry draped in abundance round their necks and heads, together with golf ball-sized pure amber beads. Some of the gold jewelry was handed down from generation to generation, as far back as Biblical times. On their ears they wore the entire fortune of the family, in the form of gigantic cup-sized earrings. I had seen imitations in the marketplace, but this was the real thing. Pure gold of generations' wealth smelted together and hammered into strange shapes, supported by a chain or rawhide straps looped over their ears.

With a respectable distance between him and the women, a man walked.

I guessed he was the owner of the cattle. He wore a white loose fitting robe down to his feet, his head was covered, and round his neck he wore three fine gold filigree pouches with his favorite verses of the Koran inside. Ten paces behind him his wife followed, with a man who carried a elaborate umbrella that he held over her head. Her bou-bou and head covering was richly embroidered with gold thread and gold coins, clinging to her dress was a two-year-old boy with a short tunic down to his naked little bottom, for convenient potty training. Kwame, who had a dark skin, told us that those people claimed they were descendants of Noah. They looked down on anyone who had darker skins, saying they bore the curse of Ham, whom they claimed had intercourse with the animals of the Ark.

We wanted to be on the way, and Kwame informed us that he had arranged for our vehicle to do the crossing on the barge the following day. He was sorry to see us go as he enjoyed practicing his English again with us. He wished us well. Peter wanted to compensate him for his time, but he blatantly refused, saying it would be an insult. So to say good-bye we went to a stall and Peter ordered three bamboo tumblers of the local *kai-kai.*

It smelled familiar and when Kwame said it was the sap of a date palm. I drank it! Within minutes my head felt like it was on a flag pole. Peter found it amusing, because he knew me to be a teetotaller.

"Oh I know this, my father had the men tap it from the malala palm, and before it fermented he gave it to us children to drink."

"Only I don't think your father would have allowed you to drink this, because it is distilled much like whiskey by boiling it and catching the steam through reeds drop by drop, and it is very potent!"

"Peter, then perhaps you shouldn't be drinking it because you would have to drive the car onto the barge." We said our farewells and drove to the barge landing site to sleep in our car, so that we would be the first on, and the first off. Our destination and turning point was the Ivory Coast.

29

The Leopard Men

When we started our journey, it was decided that the Ivory Coast would be our turning point in our return to Cape Town. We had encountered many strange people, with strange legends carried over from generation to generation. We had also seen many species of animals that were part of their folklore. But here on the Ivory Coast the panther was not only a legend, but a reality incorporated into their tribal rituals. It featured prominently in their stories. Their witch doctors used the fear of it in bringing their predictions to fulfillment.

My fascination with the Panther Men began when I saw my first Tarzan movie. I sat in a dark movie house watching men dressed in leopard skins, the head pulled over their own to hide their identification with metal claws on their hands, attacking safari camps, and Tarzan coming to the rescue shortly before the victims were eaten. I thought it pure fiction.

That was a far cry from the existing peoples. French was the predominant language, brought into the Ivory Coast round 1890 when merchants heard from the slave runners about the rich soil and tropic climate, and French coffee farmers started plantations and harvested the hardwood forests to finance their ventures and furnish their homes. We skirted several villages where people still were using handheld wooden picks to till the soil. They were descendants from the slaves of the coffee planters, but among them there were pale-skinned direct descendants from the French as well.

The people of the Ivory Coast had strict social and moral codes and were searchers of knowledge. To maintain social order, they followed strict social codes, bordering on passed on tribal philosophies. The elders were revered for their past experiences, and respected for their contributions to their village. They began their teaching in the last phase of their existence to pass their knowledge to the children.

A man's life was judged not in regular yearly birthdays, but in seven year phases.

1—7: The birth years, for developing coordination skills.

7—14: To learn passed-on knowledge obtained from the elderly.

14—21: The reaching of maturity and becoming a man or woman and the time for experiencing that what you have learned. Time to procreate.

21—6x21: The last phase. Standing on the brink of the river of death, and crossing over to join the spirits of their ancestors. This too is the time of teaching to the children what life had taught you.

So it was that we saw the old man with snow-white peppercorns take the children of their village into the bush daily, to a secluded quiet place beneath a big tree. Here we waited for him to arrive.

"What do you want with me, children of another father?" he asked.

"We ask to observe what you teach the children today," Peter told him in French.

"I will teach them only the things that I remember from things passed on to me."

"Is it well then that we learn that knowledge, too?" Peter asked.

The old man shook his head from side to side as he answered: "It will be difficult for you to learn anything new. I have seen your knowledge fly like magic birds through the sky, while our knowledge is still planted among the yams in our fields with wooden picks."

"We will sit at the feet of him that remembers, and learn many things," Peter told him and sat down under the tree a little way away from the children, who showed fear in our being there. I sat down with Peter, and the children stood around waiting for the old man to be seated on a fallen log, then sat down themselves.

"Listen well, my children!" The old man said softly. "Listen well, because we live but a brief day and a night to learn all there is. Respect the taboos of our traditions, and the many magics of living. The first thing you must learn is to treat your relatives well and respect them, because you WILL meet them across the river of death, and it will not be a good thing for you to be met on the other side by a bunch of angry relatives.

"You must be good to strangers, because you were not the first people here. Long before you, long before the coffee planters came, there were little brown men who hunted for their food, and hunted the elephants for their tusks and carried their ivory to the coast to trade with people with pale skins who came in very large boats from across the big salt waters. But there were traitors among us that stole people from other tribes to give to those on the boats in exchange for things that were not of the spirit, but only temporarily lifted up the spirits. Then when there was no more people to trade, the men from the north came with people they brought from other places, and the boats ate them, because they were never seen again!"

The children listened in open mouthed wonder as he explained the powers of their deities that overshadowed the gods of the plantation owners, and the missionaries who came after and before them.

"I heard them myself tell of a man who could heal the sick, and even raise the dead. But the people were afraid of the man, so they nailed him to a tree." He paused for a moment to scratch his wise old head and continued. "There were so many stories that I myself did not know whose god I was believing in. Listen, my children, you know nothing if you do not understand the supernatural that hides in the womb of a woman, and the seeds that water the womb that flows from the loins of the man. The spirits are many! They live in the trees, and the water, and the soil, and there are many gods, from the north and the west and the east. But we need not believe in their gods to know that our teachings tell of two distinct deities of good and bad." He grew silent for a long while, reflecting. The children did not interrupt or ask questions. They knew that he was very old and he would tell them when he had rested. So they waited in silence. Then he continued.

"The good is to have enough food for yourself and your children, many possessions, wealth of spirit and body, the power of healing the sick, fertility to have many children, abundance of water, good crops.

"The bad are all the uncontrolled elements. Floods, lightning, the unpredictable nature of man, killing, theft of others' possessions, dishonor of the elderly, and disrespect of father and mother." He paused for a moment, then added as an afterthought. "Also stealing of wives." He waved his hand in dismissal. "Yes you have heard, now go and remember what was said, so that when you reach the river you may tell the story."

239

When the children left him we asked him about the legend of the Panther Men.

He hesitated. "There are spirits too strong to speak of in front of the children, their time will come." He stroked his hair. "That magic is not of the past, but is still with us in the future, and still walks the forest. But it is not for telling, it is too strong medicine."

We walked the old man back to his village, thanking him in the traditional way.

His words were imbedded in my mind. *"It is not of the Past ... and still walks in the forest."*

I asked Peter that we not set up a tent, we were parked too close to the forest. I would rather prefer to sleep in the car that night. We folded the seats back and rolled out our sleeping bags. I locked the doors and turned up the windows, wide enough for air, but not enough for creepy crawlies or other kinds of *magic*.

In the middle of the night we both woke up with loud thumping on the roof of the car. I didn't know what was up there, and I definitely wasn't dreaming because Peter was wide awake too. Then one by one the rest of the Leopard Men came out of the forest, till the car was surrounded. I was terrified. The men were naked, painted with white spots. They wore leopard skins draped over their backs, the leopard's head pulled over their heads, blood-shot eyes peering through the eyes. The leopards' paws tied over their hands, the claws extended. They scratched on the car, the nails screeched across the glass right near my face. I rolled the windows all the way up. But when one started banging on the window I screamed. They were unimpressed; it was only when Peter grabbed his gun that they seemed to understand, growled, and slunk back into the bush, as silently as they had come. Peter wanted to go after them just to scare them, but I wouldn't let him out of the car.

"You know, neither of us thought of blowing the horn." I pressed my hand hard on the horn. There was a commotion on the roof and a spotted body jumped down, and ran on all fours into the bush. We were both in shock. They say they start acting like the animal they portray. What was this solitary one planning?

"Do you think they will be back?" I asked Peter. He didn't say a word, just started up the car and drove through the veld, through potholes and around giant ant hills, to the village where we escorted the old teacher. We pulled over to the side and waited for morning, because sleep would not be merciful.

In the morning he came out of his hut and sat by the fire.

I ran over to him and shouted excitedly. "We saw the Panther Men last night!" Peter was right behind me.

The old man looked at Peter sternly. "Did you not teach your woman manners? It is the custom in our village to first greet the person you are addressing, and inquire about his health and family before any other matters."

"I apologize. Good morning old father, you are well? Your family I hope is well? I will see that my woman shows more respect." He told the old man in French. and he told me in Afrikaans.

"Nou is jy veronderstel om sy voete te soen."

With a smile on my face, I told him. "I'll be dammed if I kiss his feet, the old geezer most likely hasn't washed them since the last big flood."

Peter turned to the old man and translated. "The woman says she is sorry, she says she saw the Panther Men last night. She is ignorant of your magic and wanted to know more about this very strong medicine, but she does not know your tongue. I now speak for her, she will know her place in the future. I will teach her how to speak to her elders, if you will teach me the magic of the Panther Men."

The old man laughed. "You are wise. I knew yesterday when you joined the children, that it is not their learning you wanted to know. But you wanted to know more about our magic. It is easy to know the ways of my people, but the ways of the ones who walk in the forest takes time to learn. The tortoise cannot carry the elephant on his back, he is too slow, and not strong enough. Long time back the panther hides in the shadows and does not show his wisdom. But kills many, so the young men want to know. They entered the forest alone for seven months to learn his ways and to worship his magic. Till they became one spirit. Like him they hunted and killed, and like him they ate raw flesh. The ritual was very dangerous. Sometimes the panther does not want to understand, and the panther deity turns on them and steals their soul, and they do not come out of the forest, and their earth mother mourns her son. And it is those who stay behind in the forest that steal the bodies and souls of the unwary, to compensate for the soul taken by the deity.

"Are the men who frightened us last night dangerous to us if we should see them again?" Peter asked.

"They are and they are not. The old women tell stories that long ago, the Leopard Men ate those who saw them during the seven months of their rituals, but no one knows if it is so. Those who come back from the seven months of being the panther walk among us. But they do not tell. I think the ones you saw learned about the curiosity of the cat, and of watching your reaction, and you would benefit knowing their curiosity. It is rare that the white spirit brother and sister had ever seen them during this time. I too have learned something. You were not eaten, and you are here to tell the story. It will be a story for my children and your children."

I thanked the old man, knelt down at his feet, lowered my head, and asked if I had his permission to leave. Peter translated. "Go well with you and your family, till we meet again on the other side of the river." I touched my fingers on my lips, and gently touched his feet. A big smile appeared on his face. " You have done well, daughter of the white spirit, go in peace."

30

Congo — Rain, Rain, Rain

Nearly a month had passed since leaving the Ivory Coast. We were becoming experts at finding crossovers for our vehicle, but here there were very few roads, except elephant paths and loggers roads hacked out of virgin forests. We made it across the river with a logging expedition near Lake Tumba. We had to abandon our vehicle because the jungle became impenetrable, covering it with branches to hide it. Carrying our camping gear on backpacks, we entered the unpredictable Congo forest, home of elephant, and chimpanzee and higher up into the mountainous areas, several families of gorilla. People described it as a rain forest, which it really isn't, but with the dense vegetation, condensation was a factor and it dripped continuously.

The giant trees towered over the undergrowth like green beach umbrellas, cutting out the sun. The upper leafy canopy interlocked shading the second layers of lesser trees. Only when the wind stirred, it allowed daggers of sunlight to pierce through. Distributing the much needed nourishment to the lower levels, sucking up the natural condensation held like a sponge into the canopy a hundred feet up where it formed droplets that constantly rained down on the dense six- to eight-foot-high ferns with their velvet soft branches and animal-like curled fronds. An emerald twilight hung over everything on ground level. Nestled in their softness second growth saplings grew, and exotic tri-color bromeliads and heavily scented phaius orchids with incredible leaves three to four feet long with clusters of buff-yellow flowers, rose purple in the center, the lips marked red. The flowers were 5 inches in diameter, they thrived on filtered sunlight, their roots never touching soil. Hidden among the fern, the stunning bird of paradise plant. Tried to compete with the bird of the same name. The path beneath our feet gave with every step, our footsteps cushioned by soft layers upon layers of decayed leaf, oozing a musty perfume.

Black ribbons of lianas like Christmas tree streamers were draped from tree to tree, on which swung small black-faced monkeys. On a fallen tree, steps of bright orange and red mushrooms grew. On another one leaning against it lilac orchids hung in profusion. A blue black loerie bird with harp tail feathers trailing softly behind him glided silently among the branches while green and red and yellow and blue parrots flapped their wings, squawking loudly, evoking the wrath of the monkeys. We hiked through the dark-blue mud pools and dense undergrowth, till we came to a natural clearing next to the lake. It took an hour to set up camp in the space we cut among the ferns. A black crow, having never seen a human being, watched me with his head cocked sideways as I dug a hole in the leaf mold and filled it with fern fronds to form a soft bed. Everything was wet around us so I brought a flat stone into the tent, and prepared our food on a Primus stove. This was Utopia.

After a good night's rest, Peter took me to where the elephants had formed a game path by pushing through the trees. The evidence of them being there was everywhere in the torn off limbs of trees and flattened undergrowth, creating a highway for the banded duiker and the tiny dik-dik and other game that had stumbled upon the path. On either side of the path a thick wall of jungle rose to the sky in which a variety of birds, tree frogs, fruit bats, monkeys, and other forest dwellers lived including a troop of chimpanzees that were seldom seen, shying away from human contact, because they were choice meat to the natives who came into the jungle to hunt them, then sold their meat in the market place.

"To truly become one with the forest, you must walk through on your own," Peter suggested. "The elephant highway is about two miles long. The elephants are very noisy, and according to the loggers, the herd has shrunk to about twenty. They are short-sighted and you can easily dodge them by disappearing into the thick underbrush; as for the other creatures you need only stand still, and they will go on their way. I will enter from the other side and meet up with you halfway."

He removed the belt with scabbard and nine-inch razor sharp hunting knife from his waist and buckled it round my waist.

"There you'll be safe now!"

With those reassuring words, I entered the gloom of the forest, my heart pounding with apprehension. The ferns curled way above my head. Small stagnant brown pools glimmered through their stems. My footsteps fell silently on the thick carpet, each step sinking deep. I wondered if some people had ever disappeared. Above me in the emerald depth in the streaks of sunlight, I spotted flutters of butterflies and hundreds of white tiger moths flitting around like falling leaves. And then among them appeared an incredible shimmering blue, king of the butterflies with a four to five inch wingtip and swallow tail. Seen alive perhaps for only once in a lifetime, the crown-jewel of the collectors! And I was honored. I stood completely mesmerized by its incredible beauty, but glad that this one would not be crucified by the collector's pin.

The spell was broken by a whirring sound near my head. I ducked instinctively in case it was a tree snake. But was pleasantly surprised when a small black rhinoceros beetle descended onto my shoulder, folded his little wings nonchalantly under the hard shell of his outer wings, and stayed there, mistaking me for some strange upright animal. Behind the horn, in a glimmer of light I noticed a faint blue-green glow. I let him sit on my shoulder and continued my walk.

In the silence that was around me I became aware of the myriad voices of the forest inhabitants. There was a chorus of birdsong, chirping, croaking, and the *tap-tap-tapping* drumbeat of the woodpecker searching for grubs in the hardwood. But through it all I became aware of twigs snapping in the fern on the outside of the walk. It wasn't noisy enough for elephants, but it definitely was something or someone sneaking through the forest. "A leopard perhaps?" I quietly unsheathed the knife. The snap that held it in place sounded like a gunshot, it was as if everything including me was holding its breath. My hand clasped the knife firmly, my body tensed, and was poised for action. This is how my father must have felt when the leopard was stalking him. My shoulder passenger did not stir. He sensed no danger. That did not pacify me. Perhaps he had no sense of danger? I waited, heart pounding for the danger to confront me. The ferns parted, and a small gazelle stepped onto the path in front of me. Its big eyes focused on me. I suddenly felt quite stupid, slowly hid the knife behind my back and froze to let him pass. Perhaps he too, like my shoulder passenger, simply thought of me as an upright animal, or he had never seen a human and therefore had no fear of one. He pushed past me, going where I had just come from. I quietly replaced the knife in the scabbard, but left the snap open, just in case real danger should suddenly show its face. Twenty feet further on, I discovered the reason for his detour. A large log had fallen across the path, it must have been standing alongside the path and tumbled or pushed by the chimp population, because there was moss all over the trunk, with tiny white flowers on it, and where the bark had rotted away slender stems of orchids were blooming. A narrow tunnel branched off around the base of the log, trampled and pushed by many feet that came to the detour. I was just about to crawl into the detour when I remembered my jungle teachings. *The forest was full of creepy crawlies. The python, wild hogs and leopards hung around paths for prey.* So I climbed over the log instead, and in passing gathered some orchids and stuck them in my hair. I met up with the beginning of the detour on the other side. A slow tortoise was exiting. The path continued uninterrupted on the other side. Walking along I became more and more aware of the towering giants around me that had not yet caught the loggers' eyes. I felt insignificant in their presence, I felt unborn in their age. A tree frog clung to a branch, a glistening live jewel. In front of my eyes within touching distance a small forest eagle swooped down and the frog was gone. I was so engrossed in this unexpected drama of life, and the brevity of it, that I did not hear or see someone approaching till I saw the fern fronds part for a second time. This time my reaction was faster and the knife flashed in my hand.

"Relax, it's only ME!" Peter shouted. His voice sounded unreal, like it didn't belong, and deep in the trees I swore I heard an echo. *It's only me!*

"I'm making us a raft, I found a natural little harbor, right next to our camp, were we can dive off and swim, and there is plenty of small game and guinea fowl."

He sounded so cheerful. Where I was so worried that we would become the hunted instead of the hunters.

He finished our raft, and anchored it onto the lake. There was not a soul within miles and the only village was a half a day's walk away, we had no cares in the world and shed our clothes, the bugs played havoc with the unexpected smorgasbord of two naked bodies cavorting in the forest, but we were gloriously happy. The sun baked us strawberry red as we lay on the raft, preoccupied with nothing but making love and listening to nature's sounds, diving off the raft when we needed cooling off.

We had long ago gone out of staples and ammunition, so Peter took a backpack and left me at the camp with his gun and hiked to the logging road to where our car was to fill the car with gas and get supplies at the village. I wasn't worried because in the weeks we were there we had not encountered real danger, besides I was expecting him back before nightfall. It was the anniversary of our meeting and also my birthday, and I had prepared the two guinea fowl, ready for roasting. But I wanted to decorate the tent, so I set out to gather some orchids to hang inside and around the camp. Every time I plucked one I heard a faint click, and became aware of eyes staring at me. I swung round, and there up a tree was a man sitting on a branch taking photos of me.

"What are you doing?" I shouted.

"What are you doing, walking around, alone in the forest in your birthday suit?" the man asked answering my question with a question.

"I'm not alone, and I'm preparing for my birthday celebration!" Just then Peter came into sight, surprised by finding a stranger in our camp.

The man explained he was a photographer for a nature magazine taking candid photos of people in the Congo when he came upon the naked wood nymph gathering orchids in the forest.

"And I couldn't resist the temptation. I will let you see all the proofs, and to compensate let me at least contribute to the party."

He came back with a can of peaches, some condensed milk, and a bottle of wine. I put on some clothes and prepared the meal. He talked about his travels, and Peter about ours. He stayed for another week, putting a damper on our Utopia. But taking many photos of me, in the presence of Peter they were fully clothed. He told us he lived in Cape Town and had a studio there, planned a trip to Europe for a year, but had a problem with getting someone to look after his cats. I said I loved cats. He was willing to let me use and stay in his studio for free, if I took care of the cats. Peter and I had planned to look for a bigger apartment when we got back. "Because we plan to marry as soon as we get back" Peter explained to the man. And when he left us, I just meaning to be polite said I would think about looking after the cats.

Days later, paradise became Noah's flood. The heavens had opened up, and it rained and rained without letting up! At first we tried to see it as fun, running and dancing in it, but then, the mud oozed on the paths, and leeches appeared in our lake. We stayed in the tent, trapped. Everything was soaking wet. I couldn't change into something dry because everything smelled musty in the backpacks. I hung them out in the rain to wash, but the sun stayed hidden, and they wouldn't dry. We withdrew into our own, I read and Peter worked on his novel. The book I was reading couldn't hold my attention. I read each paragraph over and over; instead I listened to the water falling on the tent.

A small vein of water ran down the pole onto the handle of the hurricane lamp hanging on the center pole. It sizzled as it met up with metal then splattered on the hot glass steaming away. The trickle suddenly turned into a splash, shattering the glass and drowning the wick. We were dumped into complete darkness. I heard a soft "Damn" as Peter fumbled around trying to find his matches.

He removed the broken glass and tried to relight the lamp, but time upon time it fluttered and died, the wick was too wet and the matches didn't want to strike. His lighter was somewhere in the tent. But in the dark we were unable to find it. The water pouring down the center pole had turned our bedding into a sodden mess. He tried to plug the hole where the water was coming in, and it helped for a while. We found a dry spot in the tent, covered ourselves with the damp musty clothes from the backpack, and holding one another for comfort spent a very uncomfortable sleepless night.

Morning found us cramped, cold, and stiff. We had witnessed many wondrous things in our journey, but now on our way back home found we had very little tolerance for simple mishaps.

"Let's get out of here." I wanted to go somewhere dry and catch up with the stragglers of the migration.

"It's a very good idea! We'll head for the Okovongo Delta."

We hurriedly shoved everything into the backpacks and tore down the tent. The wet stuff weighed a ton. Strapping it to the frames of the backpacks in the pouring rain was a challenge, and a revelation how well we could control frayed tempers. He couldn't find his compass in the mess.

Tramping through the rain, we reached the car, exhausted, where Peter had left it on the edge of the forest. He rested for a while then went to see if he could find the compass. I found some dry clothes of mine I had left in the car, and we shared what I found. When he returned he dumped the soaked tent in a tarpaulin and stripped. I rubbed his hair and body dry and helped him change in the cramped space. He looked a silly sight in my short shorts and a pink fluffy cardigan, but we were dry and comfortable. We curled up in each other's arms and slept for several hours. Later in the day we awoke. Peter drove south on a logging road till we were out of the rain belt.

A thousand miles later we were in the Okowango Basin at the bend of the Zambezi river near Lake N'Gami. It was a key watering hole for the traveling cape buffalo that were always on the move. Lake N'Gami was almost dried up and the last of the migration had gone lower down to the Makarikari Pans. The earth around the lake seemed lifeless, grazed down to the root. Billows of dust swept across barren earth. Small *dwarrels* spiraled dancing funnels in the dust.

With the growing influx of people, the cattle herds grew in alarming numbers, cutting off resources for the animal migration. To give the earth a chance to restore itself, the preservationists had tried to fence off certain sections that were badly damaged, hoping the rains would come and restore the grass to its former glory days. But the rains stayed away, and the fences lay down rusted. The elephants abandoned the area and moved north to the Chobe river, away from the threat of man who harvested ivory with such fever to swell their money coffers that they were blind to the threat of extinction.

We had hoped to see elephant, but caught only the last of the stragglers. There was constant movement at the low water line of N'Gami where they usually turned North to the N'gorogoro where they could calf in peace, but they were three months late in starting, and some had already calved and that slowed them down, even though they realized that they did not stand a chance in the open savannas. The lion, wild dogs and hyena preferred the open with plenty of running space. The wild dogs even more so, because they hunted in packs, and like a football team they used strategy. They had crossed the Okowango River to get to the Delta. A few days before crossing the river a ewe had calved, they made it across, the calf had been right behind her when they stepped out onto the bank, but now he was lost, running in circles bleating for his mother. The others, fearing for their own lives, had butted him away. The ewe had called for her calf, but couldn't hear it in the melee. But a pack of wild dogs who were waiting for just such an opportunity did hear her call, they were just abiding their time, closing in on him.

I felt sick knowing that he would soon be torn apart. By the edge of the river there was still an abundance of sweet grass, and the others remained unconcerned and continued grazing; they felt safe in numbers, but here in the open there was a fatalistic unconcern.

The herd was fully aware of the predators that had been following them in the background, waiting for the weak, and the sick, and the weary, so that they too could eat. But now it was their turn and they had to remain strong to survive. It was the savage law of eat or be eaten that they obeyed. They had to take advantage of the opportunity that presented itself. Often it was not the strong going after the weak, but a matter of the strong and the swift that conquered. The wild dogs killed indiscriminately, not selective of the weak, not relying on their own strength, but rather on strategy and ambush in packs that they achieved their goal. Today they go after the calf. Tomorrow they pull down the ewe.

We headed inland too; we knew that where there was water, the animals would go.

The Makarikari Pans fed by the Okavango River spread into two parallel faults; seasonally it overflowed into a fan shaped delta. This was sought out by thirty to forty thousand cape buffalo always on the hoof. The water carried rich silt, with the swamps forming little islands—a rich oasis with lush green grasslands awaiting the hordes passing through. It was a total contrast to the harsh Kalahari sands farther south. Part of our route still to come.

To our east rock cliffs rose out of nowhere. Migrating zebra took flight as our vehicle cut across the grassland. There was a soft rumble of hoof beats that sounded like far off thunder. We skirted the beds of papyrus that grew abundantly, redirecting the water.

Reaching the rock cliffs, I saw a ledge.

"There must be a cave in there, if it has no currents residents it will be ours." I told Peter, for here we could observe more game than we ever thought possible. We parked our vehicle near the lip of the cave. It was higher up on the cliffs than what we expected. But we were both avid rock climbers, so it didn't take long to scale the rocks.

The cave wasn't very deep, but way on the back of the wall I saw signs that it once was inhabited. Rock paintings faded with age told a tale of hunters with poisoned arrows hunting cape buffalo. There were also drawings of running impala and zebra. I ran my hands across the drawings.

"Just to think they camped in these same caves. Can you imagine it was here where they waited for the animals to miraculously appear overnight. Sent by the rain gods where there was no life in the dry months. It was here where they gorged themselves with daily kills, and still had more animals come the next day and the next."

"And that's just what we are going to do tonight, gorge ourselves, because

I'm starved for meat!"

We sat by the mouth of the cave. Thousands of animals could be observed from our vantage point by the naked eye. And zoomed in for a closeup using our binoculars. Within fifty to a hundred feet below us a group of Thomson's gazelle grazed, their black flag tails shot up as a lioness came into view. But the tails went down again, and they continued grazing.

"That was strange, they are ignoring the lioness."

"It's not so strange, in the animal world there are courtesy signs. You see the lioness gave them a signal that she wasn't interested, and wasn't hunting. She had her tail curled up showing she had already eaten."

"I know that! That was one of our jungle lessons."

Lower down on the savannas I watched a troop of baboons through my binoculars. I always had a soft spot for them, since raising the babies whose mothers were murdered. They were pulling up the buttercups and shoving the flowers in their cheek pouches. As a herd of wildebeest moved into their feeding ground, they moved off unwillingly. Herds of 200,000 congregated at the end of their trek here on an ecosystem so fine tuned that nothing was wasted. The black and white zebra grazed shiny fat in the company of their travel companions, the wildebeest and black cape buffalo near some overfed lions just lazing in the tall grass. Uninterested surrounded by overabundance.

It was an orgy to my eyes! The subtle colors all around us were a painting of nature's finest Cubist abstraction. I did not know where to look first, without becoming overwhelmed with the color!

The golden yellow of the Thomson's gazelle interspersed with the white rear circles of the lilac fawn color of the Grant's gazelle against a backdrop of vivid green grass shoots. Above them a cloud of a thousand pink flamingos rising up out of the blue water. It was a sight so incredible as to leave the mind numb. Combined with the spectacle and drama of a million animals assembled in one equally incredible spectacular place.

My exclamations of "Look there!" and "Did you see that?"—I had to move away from Peter to save him the embarrassment of telling me to "SHUT UP!"

We felt like *voyeurs* seeing them, but unseen by them in our shallow cave. A rank of impalas slaked their thirst, ignoring the lion at the end of the pan drinking. I looked for the telltale "tail up" but his was down, then I saw the red dried blood on his face—he had just eaten. But I knew that night the impala would sleep in the dense underbrush, too difficult to penetrate by the lions who had not yet eaten.

It was getting late, so I started looking around for dried wood, while Peter climbed down and soon came back with a gazelle slung over his back. While I made the fire and set the pot boiling, he skinned and cut up the meat; choice pieces soon hung sizzling on the iron spit we brought along. The other he packed in salt in the big bucket we brought along. I purposely made our fire on the lip of the cave where we could sit and eat and watch much like they did thousands of years back.

"Peter, in all the rock paintings, I never saw them showing fire, or was the fire only women's business, and they didn't think women's business art?"

"What makes you think that these rock paintings were done so long ago? The bushmen still come from the Kalahari to hunt, perhaps they made the drawings." I knew Peter was just teasing me, because I was a dreamer, and an incurable romantic.

Nothing stopped me, though, to relive the past. I tore with raw emotions into the flesh of our hunt imagining their passion. Only in long ago days, Peter would have had first choice, and I would have had to wait my turn till all the hunters were fed before I would get a share. Now I had an equal share.

As the sun went down, our little fire became a weak security blanket against the harsh voices of the night, calling out, "Beware! I'm going to eat you!" Up on the ridge we felt secure and that danger was canceled out by the beauty that surrounded us.

Flocks of ibis announced the end of the day. Flying over the swamp bush like white ghosts were the white egrets, vying for the best foothold where they noisily had come home to roost. Their almost adult lazy offspring made throaty raucous noises, begging their belabored parents for a last disgorging before going to sleep.

The impala after leisurely slaking their thirst slowly ambled off to a selected sleeping place. Deep in the underbrush they felt safe, sleeping in shifts, in a clump all facing outward. The ones on guard listened for the warning grunts from the antelope, whose survival technique was to wade deep into the pond almost up to their nostrils, a routine that had kept them alive for as long as the night hunters had called out: "We are hungry!"

Against the cave rim, the moon outlined the deep purple bush of the flowering amaranth, romantic flower of love, opening only to the night.

Below the cliffs the voice of the lion declared his sovereignty, so we dragged another dry log, which lay in abundance outside the mouth of the cave, onto the fire. Soon the flames licked warm and assuring. It would last till morning and give us warmth as well, for even though the days were muggy and hot, the nights still dipped down several degrees.

All animals had their survival tactics; ours were the flames of our fire that shot high up declaring to the predators. "You are not going to eat us; if we see you first, we will kill you!"

With all our intentions of being vigilant, smug in each others arms in our cave we slept like logs through the night, unaware of the dramas that played themselves off below us.

I awoke with the sun's first kiss upon my cheek; for a while I sat looking at my beloved's peaceful sleeping face, remembering our unbridled passion, before we finally fell asleep, astounded at how much I loved him.

Leaving him to sleep some more, I stirred the fire, poured some water from the canteen into the coffee pot and hung it onto the tripod. The night before I had seen a small waterfall gushing over the rocks at the far side of the cave. I stripped and sitting on a moss-covered stone scooped the water over my body with my hands. It was icy cold but refreshing. The coffee ready, I poured myself a mug, and sat down on the rock lip of the cave to dry in the sun, dangling my legs over the edge.

The water lilies had opened with the first rays of the sun, greeting the day with their soft pastel colors, contrasting with the yellow, rust, and green of the papyrus reflecting back out of the water, which was no longer muddied. The antelope had cleared out at dawn before my awakening.

At another pool I saw movement, took my binoculars, to see what it was. A black egret was fishing in the shallows. I had seen them shading the waters with their wings when they couldn't see the fish gliding below among the lily stems to soften the glare. Every now and then his head would penetrate the water, and he would come up with a fish. I was amused at the success of the bird. A few feet from the black egret, a slender darter bird standing on a lily pad was getting his breakfast, unaware of a scaly black log drifting toward him.

I could see the danger in my binoculars, but I was unable to delay or prevent what was about to happen. As the snake-like slender neck rose out of the water, silver drops tumbled back in, making circles. He too was successful. A silver fish impaled in his sharp beak, wiggled and squirmed trying to free itself. Before the darter bird could swallow its catch, the waters churned for a moment, the bird flapped its wings wildly as the crocodile rose out of the water, opened his mouth, and snapped. Sharp white teeth impaled the bird, with the fish still in its beak.

Silently with hardly a ripple *lalela* sunk back into the deeper water, leaving only a water ring that widened and widened till it disturbed the black egret's fishing domain. He had lost his last catch and once more waited patiently for the darter bird to leave, and therefore he had no concern for the darter bird's demise. I was surprised to see a crocodile in these waters.

I scanned some of the other pools. The group of large boulders lying in the middle of the pool, stirred and rose out of the water, turning into four tons of rage that tossed one another around like rag dolls in a terrifying fight over a female hippopotamus. She surfaced shyly a little way off, watching the show of force with almost indifference. For some time the fight went on. Then abruptly as it started it was over, all but the victor and the object of his affection remained; the others slunk off to a safe distance.

The victor without any foreplay mounted her, the fight alone was his arousal. His weight bearing heavily down on her, pressed her under water. Without the water to give him buoyancy as heavy as what he was, he would be unable to achieve copulation. Soon the mud bubbled up in his trusting. His head alone was visible above the water, hers stayed under water. This went on for some time longer. I knew they were able to stay under water for long periods of time, but this seemed unusually long; she hadn't come up once for air during this time.

Just when I got worried his amorous advances came to an end. I felt relieved when I saw her head surface. She looked around, and I could swear she took a sigh of relief as she breathed deeply. Then she swam to the shallows where she rested with only eyes and nostrils showing, unimpressed that they fought over her, and she was the recipient of the victor's love play.

My love was still asleep, so I made the porridge and poured him a mug of coffee, and gave him breakfast in bed, grateful that I didn't have to be submerged to receive his favors.

31

Lost — Mirage in the Desert

Leaving Lake N'Gami there were no roads. Losing his compass had not helped. So taking his bearings from the hanging of the southern cross, we headed in the direction Peter was sure was south. We followed that direction for the next week, seeing soon we finally realized we had swung west into south west Africa.

"We are lost! Peter confessed. We stopped and he filled the tank with gas and the radiator with water that we kept in the back of the car while I took a walk over the nearest dune. And there right in front of my eyes stood a sign. *MINERALE BADDENS* (mineral baths), almost buried in the sand. I ran back to Peter grabbed him by the hand and pulled him to where I had seen the sign.

It had swung around in the mean time and on the back it read: *IN SEISOEN HALFKROON PER DAG* (in season a half a crown per day). An arrow pointed to the what we thought to be the west.

"Well we struck pay dirt who can pass up an offer of mineral baths, and for that price!" Peter laughed.

"We sure need a bath, and everything we possess needs washing, and it also means there are people who could direct us, perhaps it is the Kalahari we stumbled upon."

The arrow pointed left, but there was no road in sight, and had there been one the sand would have covered it. So we headed in the direction the arrow pointed. Fifteen minutes of traveling we ended up back at the sign. It was still pointing to the left, but from the deep tracks the car made it was actually pointing to the right.

"I think we'll just go opposite to our tracks; the wind must have swung it around again." Peter's deduction was right because just over the last dune, a sight straight out of some twilight zone met our eyes. Round an enormous Olympic-size swimming pool stood five brightly painted log cabins. And to one side a small house and some out-houses, and places to disrobe. There was no one in sight, so Peter called out.

"ANYONE HERE?"

I followed it up with "IEMAND HIER?" After all, the sign was in Afrikaans. Out of the empty pool a woman's voice replied.

"*Ja, ek is hier, maar ons is nie oop nie!*" (Yes, I'm here but we are not open!)

We got out of the car and looked down into the pool. There was an elderly woman on her knees, with her long dress tucked in her bloomers, scrubbing the bottom of the pool with an ordinary scrubbing brush, some blue homemade soap, and a bucket. *Like scrubbing a football field with a tooth brush,* I thought.

When I called down to her, she continued with her scrubbing.

"*Goeie middag Mevrou, ons het die uithang bord gesien!*" (We saw the sign.)

"*Ek se mos vir jou ons is nie oop nie!*" (I told you we are not open.)

She stood up pulled her dress out of her bloomers, and in German said, "Can't you see the pool is empty, we were not expecting anyone. This is out of season."

"We traveled for thousands of miles, we were on our way to the Kalahari, and we got lost. The sign said you have warm baths, do you have warm baths? We will appreciate a bath and then we will go." With Peter addressing her in her own language, she changed her mind, and came out of the pool.

"Yes, the baths are in the cabins but they haven't been serviced for months, I will have to go and speak to my husband. Pull the car up to the red cabin."

"It looks like we're in, it will be nice to rest for a while; we are almost home."

"I'll clean it myself!" I called after her. A few minutes later she was back.

"You'll have to pay season prices and do the cleaning yourself. I have no time to do it. Put your things in the cabin and my old man will come and fix the bath when you're ready."

"God, it will be good to sleep in a bed again, and have a bath and wash our clothes!" It just bubbled out of me. "Not that I regretted sleeping in trees, in caves, and on fern frond beds in the forest."

The thick wooden door crunched when I pushed it open, resisting against a thick bank of sand that had seeped through the logs and sifted through the mesh near the roof. There were no windows, only the mesh to let in light. Inside was a single room about twelve square feet, but no signs of a bathroom or bath. Against the side of one wall stood a bunk bed, rough hewn from logs, and a small table and stool. Everything had about two inches of sand on it, including the bunks that had sacking mattresses stuffed with straw. I first shoveled the sand out with a shovel I got from the *oom*. Then took the mattresses outside and beat them with a stick. Outside by a barbecue pit I found a twig broom, which I used to sweep the rest of the sand out of the room. I was surprised to find a plank floor under all that sand, but wondered if the old man would carry in the bath, perhaps it would look like the zinc bath we carried on first safari. Peter helped me take the table outside, and I was just about to start our dinner when the two old people arrived with bed linen, a black iron pot with some *mielie pap* (corn meal mush), a plate of lamb chops and a tomato, and a pot of coffee and two mugs. They apologized that there was no milk for the coffee. So we presented them with two cans of condensed milk as a present for their kindness.

While we ate, we heard strange noises coming from the inside of the cabin, squeaking and then some banging. Then he came out to where we were eating and announced that our bath was ready. And under his breath he mumbled something about waiting for about an hour before entering the water, because it was boiling hot and the minerals tend to knock one out. The moon was full and we had all the time in the world, so we went and lay down on the dunes and watched the stars, which were unbelievably bright without city lights and forests to hide them.

After we thought the hour was up, we entered the cabin to find a strange transformation had occurred. There was a gaping big hole blasted by dynamite out of solid bedrock, on which the cabin was built. It was seven foot wide by four foot deep in the center of the floor. A hole was drilled into the rock where the mineral spring was and when the water level had reached its mark the old man had plugged the hole with a thick wooden plug. The floor was hinged and stood leaning up against the bunk beds.

There was one candle standing on the rock wall of the bath. I took out all the candles we had and dripping wax on the rock ledge, I pasted them down. Heavy steam still hung in a cloud in the room and made a rainbow over the light of the candles. We shed our clothes almost reverently anticipating this unexpected new experience.

The stone felt rough and hot under my bottom and against my skin as I slid into the steaming hot water smelling faintly like sulfur. The water swirled sensually warm around me waking every pore. There was a strange buoyancy in the water. In the dim flicker of the candles I could see Peter floating on his back, his eyes quietly watching my every move. Tiny globules of water had formed on his chest and on his magnificent brown thighs. Gliding over to him I kissed his feet, playfully rubbing his toes against my breasts till the nipples stood erect. I slowly kissed his legs; they tasted salty. My tongue continued to caressed every inch of him, I knew so well. He closed his eyes, lost in my caresses. He did not move, but I was aware of his body's responses, and he shuddered as I took him gently into my mouth and tasted the small drop of almond that usually preceded his ecstasy, but selfishly I wanted this time to last forever. So my mouth continued to caress the rest of him with gentle kisses on his chest, and on his neck and arms till it reached his mouth and we were lost in a soul kiss that brought tears to my eyes.

There were no sounds except of the water from my movement, gently lapping against the stone. There were no words between us but silent interaction. His mouth in turn searched my body's responses, his hands flowing over every curve and crevice. Slowly the fires of our passion in the strange, gentle yet intense foreplay, built up like a volcano, till I could no longer contain my desire to become one with him, to enter his very soul, and be lost in him forever! When he lifted me almost harshly onto his velvet steel, the sensation was intense, unreal! I did not know where he began and I ended. Our movements rhythmically orchestrated by our bodies to please, blending with the warmth of the mineral water swirling round us. Our love felt boundless, ethereal. There was no explosion when we came together, but rather a soft flowing together, and the knowledge that we were one and would be together till the end of time.

We dropped the floor back over the pool, and pulled the bedding onto the floor, we could still feel the warmth of the water coming up from beneath us. The rough beds felt like a cloud as we held one another sleeping like contented children till noon. Still half awake we opened up the floor cover. The water was still lukewarm, so we repeated our bath, only this time soaping each other up resulted into a playful romp of splashing that left us gloriously clean yet exhausted.

Our hosts were not surprised.

"We knocked several times with your breakfast, the water must have really exhausted you, after your long trip."

The lady concluded, *" Ja, die water put mens uit!"* She winked at me.

I echoed her sentiments, "Yes the water certainly exhausts one."

Peter's eyes crinkled up and a small all-knowing smile played around the corners of his mouth, his flecked blue green eyes looking straight into mine. "Exhausting, but unforgettable. I think we would have to stay on another week to recuperate."

We did indeed stay on another two weeks, accumulating more nights never to be forgotten! I could have stayed forever, but there were other responsibilities awaiting our return in Cape Town. When Peter paid the bill, I heard him say: "What? That much for all this time?"

The old man seemed embarrassed, "If you think a quarter a day is too much, I warned you that you would have to pay season prices."

Peter laughed. "I'm not objecting, I'm amazed. If this is your seasonal price, how do you make it off season? I'm going to pay you what I think it was really worth and not a penny more!" He handed the man three times what he asked.

"But this is far too much!"

"No, not hardly enough for the pleasure it gave us!"

"There's only one favor we would like to ask you," I interrupted. "Sell us a compass and a map or point us in the right direction."

With the new compass and map we were soon back on track; this was the last lap of our extended safari across Africa. We had time to recuperate, and to wash and dry all our belongings, and were eager to make a start on our journey home.

South of the delta, the Kalahari Desert stretched to beyond the southern borders of Bechuanaland, we had made a wrong turn after the Congo, which turned out to be a blessing in disguise. Now we were again headed south.

Beyond the luscious vegetation of the delta swamps lay a barren landscape comparable to Mars. A total contrast with red gold scattered boulders, interspersed with golden sand dunes and mile upon mile of cracked parched land. Dotted throughout the landscape towered giant baobab trees. The grassland long ago dried up. This was *Boesman land* (Bushman Land) or *San* as they were called in long ago days. It was here that they lived their prehistoric nomadic lives, with temporary shelters, hunting with poison tipped arrows and gut-strung bows. Their lives in 1954 had not changed an iota. They hunted for food only. Here roamed with desert antelope together gemsbok, and herds of golden springbok blending in with the environment, all getting their moisture from low growing vegetation and tubers they together with the Bushmen scratched out of the earth. In turn their predators the lion, leopard, cheetah, and hyena survived off the body fluids of their victims till the next time the rains came and water was plentiful.

The wildebeest and hartebeest, not as hardy as the former, preferred to trek northeast with the migrating hordes when the water became low.

Driving aimlessly along, out of boredom of the bleak scenery, we followed some ostriches, timing their speed. They had no restrictions in the wide open spaces and clocked in at thirty to forty miles an hour. In the Twenties they were sought after for their feathers. Now the eggs have become the prize.

32

Trapped up a Baobab Tree by Lions

We drove to one of the baobab giants that looked vaguely familiar, pulling our car up against it, to prepare our camp for the night.

The Bushmen believed that these trees existed from the beginning of time, but the gods had made a mistake and planted the trees upside down, with their almost bare branches resembling a root system. The bark looked rough but was really very smooth. It is unbelievable but true that some of these old giants were alive when Rome was in its heyday and when Jesus walked the Earth. No wonder the Bushmen called them the *Earth Spirits*. They said that within their branches they carry all the secrets of the world.

I threw a rope up into the lower branches, pulling myself up into the outstretched arms reaching to the sky. The branches spread out like fingers around an open palm. The center of the crest was wide enough to spread our sleeping bags, and still have room left. I dropped the rope and Peter tied what we would need for the night on the rope and I pulled it up.

Then He started the fire, with brush wood; it was just enough for the food preparation as wood was scarce. I climbed down and started the staple porridge and cut strips of meat from the leftover carcass of our meal from the previous night, packing the rest of the meat back in the salt barrel. Peter had gone up to rest a while from the day's driving.

He dropped the rope and said: "Please send up my binoculars. I've spotted some lions about a mile away, they have not picked up our smell yet, because the wind is coming from them. But it looks like they are coming our way!"

I found a fairly large log and dragged it to the fire, braided the meat onto sticks, leant it against the log over the fine coals to slow roast, and started the coffee.

Peters voice called down to me. "Don't be alarmed, but they are much closer than I thought. That smells good! Let's eat early and sleep up here tonight under the stars, close to God."

The sun had gone down, but the deep red of the sky still lingered on. It was difficult to see where the red parched earth left off and the sky began. Slowly the darkness descended around us, the time for being hunted had started. Our little fire crackled and hissed, the flames dancing along the dry bark only, and wouldn't burn into the heart. The log would not last for another hour. It would die as soon as the bark was burnt off.

I called back to Peter, "I have no desire to sleep down here tonight anyway, besides the fire won't last for more than an hour, it's already smoldering."

We ate more hurriedly than usual, and through the lip smacking and chewing came the roaring of the lions, quite close now, the wind had changed and was carrying the smell of the meat in the barrel to them. They had not yet discovered the source. And we knew they were out there. The moon in Africa is always as bright as day, and hung like a giant ball in the sky. A perfect hunting moon. And we were the prey.

We hurriedly packed the leftovers in the car. I even put the still steaming porridge pot inside. By morning it would be cold, and I loved cold porridge with condensed milk. We locked the car and climbed back up into the tree, hand-over-hand on the rope, about thirty feet off the ground for safety.

We lay down beneath the stars in the gods-of-the-spirits-hand, and fell asleep.

Later in the night I woke up. A cool breeze was blowing across the veld.

Giant eight-inch white baobab lilies swung back and forth like silent cathedral bells above our heads. I expected them to ring out the secrets the Earth spirits had told them, but they only whispered a heavy perfume of silence to the moon. I plucked one to smell, immediately regretting my action.

Below us something was sniffing and scratching at the trunk of the car where the meat was packed. I lay down quietly so as not to alert whatever was down there about our presence. Then I remembered the story. The bushmen believed if you picked one of the flowers of the gods, a lion would eat you. I replaced the flower in the fork of a branch where I picked it, like sacrifice.

Peter was sleeping peacefully and whatever was down there would go away soon. Crawling forward on my stomach, where I could look down, I saw a lioness clawing at the trunk, two others joined her circling the car and the tree. I prayed that there was no easy way up on the back of the tree. Peter too had woken up by the sudden roar of frustration when they were unable to reach the meat. He slithered over to where I was laying.

"I didn't want to wake you, do you think they could reach us here? I've heard of lions clawing their way up a tree to get at a leopard's stash," I whispered.

"I don't think so, the trunk is too steep, besides they are more interested in the meat in the car, and if they get clever enough to climb thirty feet straight up then we can always get onto some thin branches. For the moment we are outnumbered; there must be at least ten of them. I was an idiot to leave my gun in the car. One shot in their direction would have scattered them. We are trapped till they decide to leave. They haven't hunted last night and they will be hungry soon."

One of them had climbed up on the roof of the car, and lay lazily draped over the strange thing with a familiar smell. The others had also tired of trying to break the metal skin to get to the meat and lay around the base of the tree.

There was no indication that they would soon be leaving. The wind blew high up above them and carried our scent away, but by now they were overwhelmed by the human smell emanating from within the car. Peter pulled me over to him, kissing me to assure me that everything would be OK and that they would be gone in the morning.

"The best thing we can do was to go back to sleep."

We woke up with the sun baking through the leafless branches. I pulled one of the sheets out of the bedroll and tied the four corners onto some convenient branches. It made a neat canopy. The lions had not gone away like we expected. With the shade and a breeze blowing through the branches, we now simply had no alternative but to wait out our unwanted visitors' departure, hoping that they would be hungry enough to go daylight hunting.

My stomach by noon was so empty that I was convinced the rumblings were loud enough to wake the sleeping lions. I lay with my head on Peter's tummy, it was growling too.

"At this moment my survival tactics are uppermost in my mind, and cannibalism is not far from my thoughts. If they don't leave soon, you look good enough to eat."

I started nibbling all the delectable parts I would start with first; he couldn't stop me once my mouth started its assault. In a heart beat I went from an easy slow seduction, too almost devouring him. My tongue traced a thin line of hair from his navel down to the place that gave him untold delights, I was heady with his smell and at the same time from below a strong animal smell wafted up, awakening thoughts of lions' mating I had witnessed. At first the male was un-aroused, but then the female repeatedly drew her mate passionately to her. Peter's passions were now fully aroused. The blood from his head went straight to his loins. Faint with desire. Eager for more, he dragged me closer to him, his lips deliciously cruising my body. Flicking his tongue over my nipples, they immediately responded by becoming erect. A shock of sensations sent shudders though my spine and into the mount of Venus. While his hand caressed my inner thigh, I arched in response begging for that certain erotic touch. He didn't hesitate, he knew just where to touch to please me. But then his mouth sought my pleasure spot, he nibbled and caressed it with his tongue and as he increased pressure and speed, my need for him to penetrate became almost animalistic. I forced him hungrily into me. The movement of our bodies seemed to pulse in greedy waves. Forgotten was time, forgotten was danger. We had become those far off ancestors, two brown bodies moving in rhythm with the swaying branches of the ancient tree.

This must have been how CroMagnon men and women must have expressed their sexuality, copying the animals they hunted and in turn hunted them. Feelings that welled up, and they didn't understand and had no other way to express. Feelings that overwhelmed without reason like ours. Our needs knew no boundaries for satiation. Recuperating just long enough between session of loves expression and lust, his body resting on mine, his head pillowed between my breasts, I rocked him gently from side to side between my thighs till well-spent he slept the sleep of lovers.

When we awoke the lions were gone. Another hunger now gave me the bravery to swing down. A half an hour later, I had a blazing fire going, and the meat that was in the belly of the metal animal the lions were unable to conquer hung on the spit roasting. Once more I became aware of a world outside my body as I ravenously tore into the food, realizing that we had been up the tree for two whole days. Later as we brought down our sleeping gear, we saw them about a mile away, ravenously tearing into the carcass of a gemsbok after all they too had also not eaten for two whole days.

33

Return from Second Safari

After coming back from 2nd Safari, I needed to find work. For months I had been hanging around the theaters, hoping to break into show business. Time had passed, I bought tickets to all the plays done at the Labia Theater and the adjoining Little Theater. I became a member of the film society. During all this time I studied every aspect of the productions, from producing to lighting and set design. I came to the conclusion that I had found the career I wanted to pursue.

Sitting in the audience was not enough anymore, so I started attending rehearsals. It gave me the opportunity to study everything up close. And I thought, *I can DO that!*

Cape Town was indeed the place to be, there were weekly productions. Cape Town unfortunately also had established set designers who passed their positions to their own families. An outsider had as much hope of breaking into the design field, as my mother used to put it "Like a snowball in Hell."

Then one day I saw the perfect opportunity, and grabbed at it like an eagle its prey, and wouldn't let go. I overheard a dispute about a price for a set between the current god of sets Manka, and the production manager Roy Grant of a newly formed company. Manka was shouting at the top of his lungs: "What do you take me for? I'm worth twenty times that!"

Roy felt embarrassed. "Would you at least think about it?"

"I don't have to think about it I'm no fool, besides I'm doing *Ruddigore*."

He was just out of view, when I ran up to Mr. Grant and told him I would do it for half the price he had offered Manka.

"That's just it, we have only forty pounds, and that was why he was insulted. Could you really do it for that measly sum?"

"If you provided a place where I could work on the sets?" I hoped he could not read from my expression, that I only had book knowledge and that I had never built a set, except in scale and in my imagination.

"We open the same week as *Ruddigore*. You're on! I've heard of an old piano factory that other companies have used for set building, I'll look into it. If you are successful the rest of the season is yours!"

I thanked him profusely and went home floating on air. After reading the play, I did some preliminary sketches, made a mini working model for the three sets, and went through the price catalogues. The shock almost made me withdraw my offer, but even with the knowledge that I wouldn't make a cent out of it, the song in my heart sang out: "I'M IN! I'M IN!"

The following morning I went to check out the piano factory. Part of my financial problems were immediately solved. In the backyard lay an endless supply of scrap wood for making the flats. I contacted the owner of the factory, and he said I could take as much as I needed and to give the old man who came to check the grounds once in a while a small compensation.

"And provided of course my family received tickets for every play that you put on from sets manufactured in the factory."

In constructing my mini set, I had used paper to cut out the scene of the log cabin in the woods. Now I needed only to solve the need for canvas. It struck me that perhaps it would be possible to make the sets out of paper, seeing I had no money to fund the supplies. But where to find that much paper? The Sunday paper delivered to my apartment solved that. It was thick! I took the pages and lay them side by side across the floor. They covered the entire floor. Three or four layers would do the trick.

The Monday morning I called the newspaper office, and asked them what they did with the leftover papers. "We recycle them of course! why do you ask?" When I explained what I wanted them for, they thought it was a wonderful way to recycle and also get publicity. I could have a truck full if I wanted, where did I want it delivered? I couldn't believe my luck.

"Would you please deliver it to the old piano factory on Broad Street?" They complied, not asking me a cent. So production could start immediately.

The factory was vast, and with limited time left, I could work there on three sets at once. I had the electricity turned on, using only the minimum high voltage floodlight bulbs for lighting.. The Italian Opera Company's flats and props were still standing there against the walls. I had the perfect prototypes for my sets. The props would also come in handy. Othello's bed had a real mattress, so on the long nights I would be working there I could rest on it and even sleep over. There were other props from other plays, including a very realistic gun from a period play, and some lamps that still worked.

Working there alone was really spooky, but in three days I had made double-sided book flats that could be opened like pages, the first of their kind, instead of flats that one stacked, which naturally eliminated cleats. I cut out the forest, making it three dimensional. By the time the producer and some of the actors workshop came to see how the work was progressing, I had almost completed the project. I used total realism and they were impressed.

Now my greatest challenge came when I discovered we were working in "The Little Theater" that had limited lighting. To give life to the burning forest I experimented with yellow and red silk scarves tied onto a bicycle wheel with under lighting, and I blew smoke through a cut off hose-pipe; it gave the right effect, even looked realistic.

Knowing that Manka was just across the road with the opening of *Ruddigore*, I was terrified with our opening. And as I expected, he was there to see what I had done, his criticism was very unkind, but I didn't care; this was the one that he turned down, and it was taken over in his words by "an amateur." He took one look at the book flats and said, "It will never work!"

But it did! The book flats were easy to handle and needed limited bracing.

Everything went off fantastic. When the reviews came out that morning I naturally went to Manka's reviews first.

His read "Too box-like, could have used a little more imagination!" I did not even read any further. Right next to his review mine read "Ramona's set—the bungalow in the Essex woods—displayed both creative and theater sense, but a more imaginative use of lighting would have helped." I thought it fantastic, and was not surprised about the lighting remark; there just wasn't anything to work with. But a professional lighting company who happened to see the play offered their help for free, installing the proper lighting for the fee of advertising their services, and I was promised a larger theater for my next production.

Night Must Fall put my name on the books. But the thing that touched my heart was the support of the producer and cast, for whom I did many other plays, lighting, and sets after that.

Now the offers started pouring in, and sometimes I found myself working on several projects at once. I painted backdrops, designed and constructed sets, made props, and costumes, even helping with the posters. The money also started rolling in. For a while after returning from my trek across Africa, I moved into the photographer's apartment situated in the theater district whom I'd met on 2nd safari to be closer to my work, looking after his 30 cats but with money no object anymore, I was able to move into a penthouse in the botanical gardens. I even designed my own furniture, something I always wanted to do. In the middle of my move I received a contract to produce *Anastasia* with actors from the cream of the crop. Following that came *No, No, Nannette*. I felt honored because in America it ran for years as *The Boyfriend* on Broadway. I also designed and made the new costumes. The sets were a delight. I still used the factory, so naturally that's where Nannette was born. It was set in the 1920s period, but because it was sprung on me at the last minute, I brought bedding and stayed over in the gloom of the old place sewing the costumes, and between naps painted scenery till early in the morning.

One night I was working late as usual. I had a deadline to meet so naturally my hair sometimes went uncombed, and hung wild like Medusa's snakes over my head. I couldn't remember when last I had had a decent bath, or even eaten. It had rained the entire day, and the roof was leaking. Every now and then thunder that preceded lightning flashed and lit up everything through the windows. Every time it did that it made me jump. I had placed buckets on the floor where the water came in with a continuous *drip, drip, drip* that seemed to get louder by the minute as it hit the bottom of the buckets. I was tired and jittery, but determined to finish the set I was working on. Two of the electric bulbs with water dripping from them, had threatened to die on me, so in case they did I lighted two of the prop lamps. The remaining one bulb and prop lamps cast an eerie shadow over the sets against the wall. It was too dark to continue working. Just then the remaining bulb popped and went out, I was left with only the two dim lamps. The red paint on my hands had dried and going down to the bathroom down the rickety spiral stairs to clean them, was out of the question. The spiral stairs were loose somewhere and had the tendency to swing out and hit the back of the wall when I was on it. I had meant to fix it but never got round to it, because the scraping noise was nerve wracking. I was expecting it to break down at any minute.

It was still raining and I was aware of all the sounds. The leaks falling in the buckets. Wind howling outside, and the rattling of the windows. But above these noises I suddenly became aware of the downstairs steel doors opening up with a creak. I no longer was alone. Footsteps were coming up the stairs, slowly and carefully not to make a noise. Someone had seen the light was on. When the person or persons reached the place where the stairs swung out and the bolt scraped against the back wall, I tiptoed over to where the prop gun stood leaning against the wall, reached for my flashlight, and blew out the lamps. My head was wildly pounding.

As he entered, the lightning flashed revealing a big black man standing in the doorway. It also lit for just a few seconds a mad looking white woman with wild Medusa hair, holding a very large gun in her what looked like blood-stained hands. I let out a bloodcurdling scream and made a mad dash at him. He gave a scream in fright and practically fell down the stairs two at a time, trying to get away, before "being blown away."

I flashed my flashlight after him, and heard the lower door slam shut. Then a deadly silence followed. I hardly took a breath so scared I was.

He'll be back! the devil told me.

Listening intently for his return, I took a few beams of wood and hammered them crisscross across the open door leading to the larger room. If he came back he would have a hard time getting to me!

Minutes later, I heard soft mumbling and the steel door opened once more downstairs. A flashlight beam played against the upper wall.

"Oh my God, he is not alone! But they won't get me without a fight." The steps moved. I moved into the shadows and hid behind the flats. I heard someone say "Shu" but then followed a familiar voice.

"What happened to this door? It's nailed from the inside, but she must be in there!"

Then I heard someone kick and tear at the planks to remove them. And when it was done, several people burst in.

"SURPRISE! SURPRISE! What's going on here?"

"I just had an intruder, I thought you were his reenforcements."

"So that's it. We saw a man running down the street, with eyes bulging as if he had seen a ghost. No wonder you scared him out of his wits. You look like a demon out of hell!" We all had a good laugh. They told me they had been rehearsing late, and thought it would be nice to surprise me with a midnight snack and hot coffee. I relit the lamps and turned the lights back on, and we sat on the floor and had a picnic. Some of them volunteered to stay. Feeling safe, I resumed my painting, and completed the sets.

My intruder never came back. I felt sorry for him, he most likely was just a simple soul who wanted to get out of the rain.

During my breaks from the theater I wandered into the botanical gardens, lunching at one of the outdoor cafés nestled among giant oak trees.

Large concealed aviaries blended in with the vegetation, in which a collection of finches, parrots and other exotic birds lived. The cages were large enough to allow them the freedom of flight. It gave the illusion of freedom, yet they were not really free, comparing them to the birds I saw in the Congo.

The pigeons living in the trees had more freedom, begging for crumbs off the clientele. After lunch I visited the art galleries, or browsed the flea markets at the entrance to the gardens. They had a variety of stuff, old books, nicknacks, handmade native bead work, and wooden effigies. On Mondays and Wednesdays it included a farmers market, with fresh vegetables, which I delighted in. Also sold flowers. I bought for myself and my friends.

One day at lunch a young portrait artist, dressed all in black with a French beret on her head asked if I wanted my portrait done, because she paid for University herself, and needed the money. I agreed and while she was drawing she told me that she had done several plays at the "Little Theater" and belonged to the Gilbert and Sullivan Society, who were soon opening at the Labia with a new production; they also needed other help with sets and costumes.

"They are doing *The Gondoliers*. Why don't you come and audition?"

I had never thought of my voice being professional, but just to please her, I promised that I would go and try out. If I couldn't get in the chorus, I would try for the sets.

The following week I not only got a part in the chorus, but also the opportunity to do their sets, costumes, posters, wigs, and props. As a break in the routine the Light Opera Company went on tour. It was fun and offered a chance to again see the enchanting little fishing village, Hermanus, that Peter and I visited in our tour of Africa.

The mayor gave us the key to the city, and provided a wonderful buffet with flowing wine. The men in the company took full advantage of the wine and in no time, everyone was just a little more than tipsy.

Before the show started the pep talk was to make sure to "Come in on your cues, and for heavens sakes, if you lose an earring on stage, don't make a fuss about it, just act natural pick it up, put it on and continue singing." The earrings were made from brass curtain rings, and fitted over their ears by means of an elastic band, which was giving them trouble. They nodded that they understood, but as fate would have it, one of the men lost his earring. Looking around he thought he spotted it, and as natural as he could muster under the circumstances he made his way to where it lay on the floor. He bent down and tried to pick it up, but the ring stuck and without making a fuss he tugged at it, and to everyone's surprise the floor gave way, and half of the sailors in the chorus disappeared down the trapdoor. The audience roared with laughter. We were front stage and couldn't see what was happening behind us, we thought, *What a rude audience*, till they started pointing. All we saw were some disheveled faces peering out of the opening of the trapdoor dragging themselves up out of the pit. Then they calmly took their places on stage, and started singing with straight faces. This made the audience laugh even more. But the comedy of errors was by no means over yet, because just in the next act, as the curtain opened, two guards were seen in short Roman skirts kneeling on one knee, on either side of the stage. Again there were ripples of laughter, as the audience started pointing and at one of the guards. The women in the front row were madly motioning the guard to get off the stage. He ignored them and stood steadfast at his post, not aware of what the fuss was about. Then when his cue came to exit, he left. Only then he discovered that in his drunkenness he had forgotten to put his underwear on under the short skirt, and in that kneeling position, the front row had an eyeful of his family jewels. After that the whole thing turned into a major comic opera.

The audience even laughed at the serious parts, but so did we.

Not long after this notorious night, the mayor asked for a repeat performance. He added that the trapdoor had been secured, and they put an apron to the footlights. The producer agreed to give another performance provided that receptions with alcohol be given after the performance and not before. And he promised to personally check that all the performers wore underwear.

34

Betrayal

During our trip across Africa, Peter had proven his love for me over and over. I had no reason to doubt that he loved me. His words were chiseled in granite in my memory. We had made our vows under the moon; "I will love you for ever, even after death I will still be with you."

He said in the eyes of God, we were really married. We continued where we left off. I to my career in show business, and he to African safaris.

We still went mountain climbing and hiking. Sometimes Phil and Hugo, Peter's friends, would go along. We would pack our backpacks, hiking across the rugged mountain trails, or across the rock strewn beaches to Hout Bay where we camped in a little cove on the beach at the bend of the road. Usually during the long walks the three of us would challenge one another composing poetry. Hugo, being a recognized published poet, usually won because he had an impeccable memory; we often were suspicious that he was simply quoting from things he had previously written. I could only remember from moment to moment as my ideas came and went.

Walking ahead one day, Hugo slipped up. "How are things getting on with you and your young poet?" he asked Peter.

Peter did not answer but motioned to Hugo to hush up. I did not suspect anything because I thought he was referring to me.

At that time however I did not consider myself a poet yet. Inspired by Peter to express myself, I was simply just dabbling in that art. But a conversation I had with Phil suddenly came to mind. A month earlier he had told me that Hugo had introduced Peter to a mutual friend of his who was also a poet. She had insisted on meeting him. He thought Peter was quite infatuated by her. He warned me that while I was blinded by my ambition to establish my career, I was slowly losing Peter.

I never confronted Peter with it, because I believed in him and trusted him with all my heart. Had he not promised to marry me? When we got back from 2nd safari. When I asked Phil about it he said Peter told him that he only admired her work and found her cute, but there was nothing between them, because he told him that he only loved me. That put my mind to rest; in his arms there were no changes. Our lovemaking was a pure expression of our love for one another, I needed no other proof. Still Hugo's slip up put doubt in my mind. I loved Peter with all my heart, body, and soul. But if there was anything between him and the young poet, I needed to find out the truth for myself. That would mean only one thing, I would have to confront him with it. And it could not be done over the phone.

To give me time to think things over, I did not call him to tell him I was coming over, but walked the four miles from the botanical gardens to his apartment we shared together before going on second safari.

His light was on. He was home, my coming would be a nice surprise to him, because we were together just the night before, and he was not expecting me and was most likely working on his novel. I wondered whether I had not jumped to conclusions too quickly and misjudged his loyalty to me. What would I say to him? My heart was racing. But then it always raced being near him, or just thinking about him. I should just turn around and not make a fool of myself, but then I would never know the truth.

No, I will knock, and if he is alone I have my answer, and the subject would never come up again.

Seconds before I knocked, I heard soft voices and muffled moans coming from within. *HE IS NOT ALONE!* my mind screamed out in silent agony.

I couldn't breathe, if I did, he would know I was there. So I stood glued in stunned silence a foot away from his front door. Like one of my nightmares, where I wanted to run, but couldn't.

Not wanting to eavesdrop but unable to move, I stood there and sobbed silently visualizing his every move. *My God! it was unreal, only last night we had made passionate love, and here he was making love to someone else!*

There was no mistaking the reality of it. It must be the young poet.

It seemed like an hour had passed before I heard their climax, and then silence. I pictured his head resting between her breasts. Minutes later the bed creaked. It always creaked! Then I heard her giggle again and they went to the shower together.

I almost fell down the stairs, trying to escape. Suffering intense pain, like a moth with singed wings, still drawn to the flame, fascinated with its own doom. I ran down to the beach, but I could not leave. A heavy mist rose out of the sea. I sat down on the beach wall, detached. This wasn't me! Perhaps I had died back there in front of his door. The light from his bedroom window was still mocking me. He liked the light on. I knew their lovemaking would continue till morning.

Some time near dawn the light went out. The door opened and they came down the stairs, his arm wrapped around her waist.

Intimate and beautiful together after a night of lovemaking, like I had seen him countless times with me.

For a moment, a passing car's light shone full on me. Preoccupied, he didn't see me. I felt guilty somehow invading his privacy. I dropped off the stone wall and hid among some hibiscus. They stopped a few feet from me, and kissed tenderly. I felt fragile in my pain, at THEIR happiness.

I wanted to scream, "I'm here! The one you pledged your love to, can you remember? Can't you feel my presence?"

But they were wrapped in the moment of now, and I was forgotten. His promises were forgotten, would they be there tomorrow again? As if nothing happened?

Long after they were gone I sat beneath the lighthouse and let the overpowering loudness of the foghorn carry my sobs tearing out of my soul to the far reaches of the universe!

I HAVE BEEN BETRAYED!

So there I was, suddenly without a future with him. When we were together I did not lie awake in longing, because in the morning he awoke beside me. I didn't hurt because I was one with him. But now the tables had turned. The hurt and the longing was unbearable. He was with her! Out of my reach! But because I loved him, I wanted him to be happy; that meant I would have to let him go. Even if it meant losing him. I went home and wrote a letter, returned, and put the letter under his door, hand delivered so that he would know I had been there. While the tears flowed freely, I told him what I had overheard and what I had seen, and wished him nothing but happiness in the future. I would always love him. I would look upon our separation as gray weather, under which my love would continue to grow, because he had given birth to my love, and he was my life.

The night he married Ingrid, Phil, being loyal to me did not go to the wedding. He took me home and stayed with me. Peter had instructed him to look after me because he feared that I would take my own life. I wanted to go and stop the wedding. But she had won him over, and I had accepted that as my fate. I kept thinking that I should hate her, but how could I if she pleased him? Within a week of the wedding it turned out that I was not the one to be watched; she had a history of wanting to take her own life.

During their honeymoon she told Peter that she did not love him, and had made a mistake in marrying him, because she only did it to make the man she loved jealous. He also found out about her manic depression and her previous attempts of self destruction, which turned her to drugs and addiction.

Her first attempt followed soon after the honeymoon, when she said she felt trapped because the little affair they had made her pregnant. She hated to be pregnant because it was "his" child. To help and rehabilitate her, he committed her to an institute.

Peter's letters started to arrive soon after, hand delivered in my mailbox.

I left them unopened till I no longer could, fearing what I would find out. Then taking the letters with me to my private cove, I sat in my cave and opened the first one. Trembling, I read.

I love you with all my heart and soul and I have made a terrible mistake. Yet I'm torn in two; I could annul the farce of a marriage, and ask you to come back to me, but your love is too pure and true to have anything but that which you deserve. Physically I have betrayed you, and I will suffer for that. Only now I can be spiritually true, and continue to be true till the end of time, because I too have been betrayed and misled. Emotionally I'm in a mess. SHE IS PREGNANT WITH MY CHILD! Forgive me, you can only place a curse on me for what I had done, and what my conscience now dictates I must do.

In your letter you nobly said that all that matters is my happiness. But now I know the tables have turned; you are the only one who holds my happiness in your hands. I don't know how I can ever undo what I have done, but now she is carrying MY child, and I will have to stay with her so that I can keep her drug free to save the baby. God forgive me, the baby you wanted and in all rights should have belonged to you, and she doesn't want because it didn't come from her true love. Now I will think of the baby as yours, that will protect my sanity. You are and always will be part of me and nothing on Earth

276

will ever change that because our pledge beside the lake means more to me than the piece of paper I signed to become part of her life.

I'm going to suffer agonies and horrible heartbreak longing for you. Last night I stood by your window, just to hear you breathe. I have been near you again.

My tears washed the words together as I read the letter over and over again. I wanted to fly to his side and into his arms. But knew it was too late.

The letters came daily! I let them pile up in a box, and when I finally had the courage to read them, his words washed together, with my tears into a soggy mess. In the long night I called out his name, like a prayer.

Now more than ever I threw myself into my work, but everywhere I ran into Peter. I tried not to let him see me, but was overjoyed at seeing him again. At the opera, or in the botanical gardens where I had my lunch, he sat in the farthest corner when she was with him. Sometimes our eyes would meet, and I would tremble and slink away.

On Fourth Beach I went through the time gate to escape from seeing them together. He had moved into a flat on First Beach with her after her dismissal from the institute, swearing that she was drug free. Hugo, who lived on Third Beach kept me informed about the progress of her pregnancy. And one time with them away, he invited me to go with him to feed the cat.

I walked into the apartment hoping to see evidence of him and her together but found nothing there that even said he existed in her life. Only the inlaid wooden tobacco holder I had given him, his manuscript he was working on, and his pipe. In the corner of the bedroom stood a wicker baby bassinet. In it was an old fashioned patchwork baby quilt. Hugo said it was from when Peter was a baby. I ran out of the room crying.

It was getting closer to her time of delivery and I simply had to get away. I took some time off from the theater and my career and took the Blue Train to see my family, a thousand miles away in Pretoria.

I thought telling my Dad about Peter, he would understand and give me sympathy. But instead of being sympathetic, he condemned Peter for being uncaring and breaking my heart. I tried to explain the circumstances of the marriage and her feeling trapped because she was pregnant with Peter's child. But Dad only shook his head and said. "He is no good, he is just using you! So he made a mistake, he made his bed and now he must lie in it! Don't get involved! Come back home! You must get away from him. You have no other alternative! Next is he will expect you to become his mistress, using the baby as his pawn when it is born."

I protested, "SHE doesn't love him! She told him so. And she hates the child she is carrying. He is the only man I will ever love! And if he asks me to be his mistress I will, because he told me he will always love me!" I ranted and raved.

My dad was disgusted. "Now I've heard everything, you will commit adultery? The greatest sin for him? Just shows what a character he has, or rather lack of character, to expect you to give up your principles for his satisfaction!"

Nowhere did I find a sympathetic ear. Except my dear Aunt Cielie, who had a similar secret affair, understood, and when she said I should try and get away for a while so that I could see perspective, I listened.

"Perhaps it would do you good to really get away for a while, even out of the country. Your career is already established in South Africa, you could always return here later. London is the place of opportunity. You could go there.

"I will support you for three months as a try-out, if nothing happens in that time, you can come back home. Think about it, put a little spending money together, and when you're ready let me know and I will book passage for you on an ocean liner."

When I discussed my aunt's proposal to me, the family was happy it would solve their problem nicely. "You would be free of Peter," they said, justifying their own thoughts about the whole affair.

I went back to Cape Town but the more I thought about it, the more I disliked the idea. If I traveled over the waters, he would be even more lost to me. Here at least I could see him even if it was at a distance. As time went by, the more her pregnancy progressed, the more depressed I became. Dreading the pain it would cause for me to see this child I coveted, I wrote to my aunt and told her to book the trip but to give me three more months to get my affairs in order and to get letters of recommendation. Now I was ready and wanted to get away as soon as possible.

35

Leaving for England

On the 28th of November, my birthday, just before his baby was born, he came to me. I didn't question why he was there! I flew into his arms. Like soft rain falling on parched earth our bodies fulfilled all our silent promises, blending as if it was the last time, and there would never be another time to manifest our love for one another because I was certain the world would end in the morning! Between the pain of tenderness and sobs of passion, I told him I was leaving South Africa for good and moving to London, and I would never see him again! This was my final good-bye. We cried together, and loved together, falling asleep in each others' arms, like so many times before. And in the morning he left to welcome his new daughter, my dream child who arrived on the 1st of December. And I continued packing to leave him. Knowing in my heart that no matter where I went, distance and time would never make me forget him. My love for him defied logic, because when the world was made it already existed, and would exist to the end of time, when we will be together for all times like I had promised him.

It was pouring with rain the day I left Cape Town for London. I thought, *How appropriate, the Heavens are crying for me.*

The people I had worked with, painted scenery for, given parts in plays, appeared on stage with, everyone in the Gilbert and Sullivan Opera Company seemed all to be at the ship, to see me off. The ones who knew me well came with fruit baskets and flowers. For the others, my leaving simply presented the opportunity to get on board the magnificent ship, *The Southern Cross*.

They stayed till the last call came for visitors to disembark, then lined up on the pier to wave good-bye, and break the silly streamers I tossed out to them, as the ship sailed off.

In all this time my eyes searched the crowds for him. Would HE come to see me off? I had told him not to come, but I was hoping. In vain I searched. While my heart was being ripped out of my chest I threw the silly streamers to my friends, smiling and waving as if nothing was wrong. The departing horn sounded and slowly the ship began to move out of the harbor. For a while after, the flimsy streamers broke off in the hands of those who came to see me off as a token of a last farewell. The crowd dispersed. The decks emptied out into the lounge for the bon voyage party.

I stayed behind on deck, and when the ship turned I ran to the other side. Blinded by tears I still hoped he would turn up. That's when I saw Cricket, his Carmen Ghia, speeding to the end of the harbor and coming to a screeching stop, the door swung open.

The sun highlighted his silver hair like the first day we met. My heart sang out, *he came, he came!* I jumped up and down, waving and shouting his name. We were already some distance out. And I knew he couldn't possibly hear me.

I could see him, but could he see me? Even if he couldn't hear or see me, he didn't leave, and I stood alone on deck, staring at the spot where he was, till he was only a speck on the receding pier, which turned the scenery of Table Mountain into a Postcard. I clung to the view for just a moment longer, and then stepped inside the lounge with all its gaiety. Smiling but with a broken heart.

36

London with High Hopes

Every one was up at five in the morning to see the coastline of England looming through the mist of the green waters. I was not impressed but was rather excited at the thought of what it might hold in store for me.

Was it indeed going to be a new beginning for me, or would I become obsessed with my star-crossed affair on the other side of the ocean?

There were all kinds of people on deck, in all stages of dress and undress. Some were in pajamas and plush new dressing gowns, while others like me had hastily put on their coats over whatever night attire they wore or didn't wear. In my case nothing, so I held tightly to the coat, to stop the playful wind from revealing my secrets. There were head scarves that concealed hair curlers and pin curls. While the over anxious were already fully dressed with hair styled in the latest beehive style, rock hard with hair spray, to look their best for the disembarking.

Even though we were still at least four hours from reaching shore, they stood on deck with hand luggage already slung over their shoulders.

How silly they looked. After the first view most people went back to their cabins, or to the pursers to fall in line to retrieve their valuables and their deposited money. As I had everything with me, I stood watching the crew for a while preparing everything for the docking. They moved the gang plank to the side of debarkation, secured and stacked deck chairs, and tidied up. Then they proceeded to bring the luggage out of the hold piling it in no particular order on the deck. There was no system, they simply piled trunks, boxes, and suitcases one on top of the others in long rows, so that the people could walk in between looking for their belongings. As the last piece of luggage appeared, I wandered through the rows and soon was able to find my two trunks, which I dragged together and made a mental note of location. Then I went down to my cabin to get another two hours of sleep.

Loudspeakers awoke me. They were telling us about landing procedures and passport inspection. I got dressed, took my purse and hand luggage and headed to the selected deck. How and when the passport agents boarded I did not know, but they at least had a system. There were cards with the alphabet on them. My surname starting with "A," got me through in no time. So I headed to the top deck to see what was going on as we neared Dover coast.

The loud speakers were announcing that we would have a splendid view of the White Cliffs of Dover on the starboard side of the ship. I saw the people milling like ants trying to find their multiple pieces of luggage. But saw only water. As I moved to the other side of the Ship. Which had to be starboard.

We were passing some gray cliffs that looked more like the walls of a quarry than the magnificent White Cliffs I had seen on postcards.

So this was the White Cliffs, I thought disappointed. Perhaps the gray color had something to do with the fog.

The same voice who announced the splendid view, now told the people who had passed the Duanna and passport procedure, to collect our tickets for the boat train to London at the exit ramp where people were waiting to assist us with getting our possessions on board the train. The boat train would arrive alphabetically in relay for the others. I was glad again that I was in the "A" line because my aunt had written and told me that my cousin Johan would be waiting at Charrington Station. I wasn't sure how they would know what time, because I had no idea how it worked.

The boat train arrived an hour later at Charrington station. The soot-encrusted clogged aorta to the rest of the world. I had read so much about London's history, and about England's beauty, and about London being the fashion capital of the world. I made sure to dress in my most elegant outfit to make a good first impression. Everything I ever read about London's fashion sense disappeared in a moment as I looked around and saw only nondescript tweeds, galoshes, and dull gray raincoats and head scarves. Looking like they were eternally dressed in advance for rainy weather.

I also heard about the smog. I had already seen fog hanging over the White

Cliffs. Smog was a combination of smoke and fog that accounted for the very unfashionable clothes the people were wearing. It was a beautiful day according to the locals. I looked up at the sky. It looked completely clouded over with a weak sun straining to peep through the blanket of thick clouds.

My cousin had sent me a photo of himself, so that I could recognize him. As the train slowly steamed into the station, I searched for the face on the photo, while I gathered my hand luggage together. There was no one that looked vaguely like the photo I held in my hand. Perhaps he had not received the information of my arrival that day.

What if he didn't turn up at all? I had the address of the place where I was to stay with my cousin, he described in his letter to me as being in the suburbs of London. I started planning an alternate to get there; the bobbies would know. They said the bobbies knew everything. They also said the bobbies were tall but this one stood at least a head taller than everyone around him. They hadn't exaggerated. I would ask him how to proceed further to my destination. I was still considering the alternative when I heard my name called by a handsome young man running up and down the station. He looked vaguely familiar even though I hadn't seen him since he was four years old.

Something in his enthusiastic mannerisms told me, this is family. He in turn was looking for a grown up blonde girl of four. After the train stopped and poured out its paisley contents onto the platform, the same young man ran up to me. "You are my cousin?"

When I confirmed, he grabbed me in a warm embrace. Only when the guard started blowing the whistle to stand clear, I remembered my trunks were still on the train, at least they said they would place them on the train, so we ran nearly the length of the train to the luggage compartment. We snatched my trunks off just as the final whistle sounded for the train to depart. As our train pulled out and the smoke cleared, another train pulled in. The gold plaque on the side of it read EXPRESS PARIS ROME. "Must be the boat train to Paris, from here you can take a train anywhere in Europe." He still had the guttural accent of South Africa, but now spoke fluent English to me. It was easy to understand him. The people around us were also speaking English, but blimey I found myself constantly saying "pardon?" I just couldn't understand them, even though they spoke the King's English. Their pronunciation was appalling. They slurred their sentences, and dropped their Hs. I found it amusing that Johan, who previously didn't speak English very well, was interpreting for them what I said to them in English, and what they replied.

Johan had arranged for a friend of his, who drove a taxi "till his big break in show business came," to pick me up at the station and show me a little of London and then on to go on to Woodside Park, where everyone was waiting to welcome Johan's actress cousin from South Africa.

The London taxi was a very impressive, quaint, square black vehicle.

It had large comfortable sliding doors. With a low floor almost level with the ground, one could and I did, almost stand upright in it. I stepped directly into it without having to step up or down. The high ceilings were made to allow for men's black toppers or bowlers. The passenger seat next to the driver was cut away to accommodate space for luggage or parcels. It was big enough to hold both my trunks. Inside there was enough space to seat six people in non sloughing upright seats with two more fold down ones.

"I hope you don't mind, there is a subway, and a train going out to Woodside Park, but we would have had difficulty with your luggage, besides you wouldn't have been able to see anything of London. What would you like to see first?" Johan asked.

"That's easy, I want to see Trafalgar Square first, and then you can surprise me with everything I had ever read about."

There were years to catch up with, so we proceeded in silence, the past could wait till we reached home. This was my NEW present, not to be wasted.

As we left the station we entered the mainstream rush hour traffic.

The driver turned off into a narrow cobbled street to avoid the traffic. This was the London of the "old curiosity shop." The quaint street lights of Jack the Ripper I thought as we wound our way past foliage covered courtyards, old squares, and graveyards. The city rich in history consisted of many distinguished neighborhoods crammed with cathedrals, old hotels, museums, pubs, and mews.

We reentered the traffic flow through Piccadilly Square where Eros stood in a pose of just having released an arrow from his bow. On the steps below him two lovers were billing and cooing as if to confirm that his arrow had reached its mark. His friend was oblivious to the honking of the traffic as we circled the steps.

We were in the Theater District, the Broadway of London. I saw famous names like Windmill, Lyric, Apollo, Palladium. Theaters I had only read about where everyone who became someone got their start in show business. It gave me high hopes, that London was indeed the place where I perhaps would have a chance. Johan, who was studying theater makeup in London, was as excited as I was of that same prospect, but had not as yet had the opportunity of proving his worth. We stopped at a newsstand to pick up the aspiring actor's Bible—*The Variety Theatrical Newspaper* that was brim full of addresses of agents I could look up. Then we went on to Trafalgar Square, the hub of London.

We parked near the museum and took a walk onto the square, which was called square but was really a large inverted circle. To one side stood a very tall column; Lord Nelson was covered in pigeons. He was dubbed by the Londoners as "King of the pigeons." Here he looked down on the nation's children and grownups being photographed on the backs of four giant black lions gracing his pedestal. Around the base of the column, the battle of Trafalgar was depicted in bass-relief, ending forever Napoleon's hopes of invading England. Within the circle two fountains squirted water high up into the air, around which screaming children darted in and out among the pigeons that fluttered in total disarray around the square looking for handouts. Some were so tame that they landed on the heads of people and ate out of their hands, to the delight of the children, while proud parents took pictures for the family album. A bag lady handing out crumbs was covered in pigeons. This in turn was photographed by the tourists for their albums back home. Every time she waved her hands, the pigeons descended on her in clouds, ate from her hands, then lifted off and made a wide circle around the column, settling to rest for a moment on Nelson's hat. Waiting till the next group of tourists arrived. Then they swooped down again to repeat the same thing over again.

We left the pigeons and took to the streets again, passing the Tower of London. It seemed peaceful enough but rumor had it that the ghosts of the two princes murdered there in their sleep still played in the Tower, which now held the Crown Jewels behind walls of four-foot-thick glass.

We stopped briefly to see a cloud of black crows swoop down onto the grounds.

"They say that the crows are the souls of people who were executed in the Tower for offenses both private and political, and when they finally leave, London will fall."

We saw remnants of the old Roman wall when the city was walled in.

Everywhere London's Roman heritage was still evident, starting with the architecture surrounding Trafalgar Square. Old horse troughs around the base of the wall still serviced the police on horseback and the horses from the horse guard.

We passed Westminster Abbey with its spires and gargoyles, and ancient cobbled stone roads near the mews that were stables long ago. These stables were now converted to prestigious apartments for royalty, lords and ladies who left their drafty palaces in the country preferring to live in the city. We stopped briefly in front of the palace to see if we could get a glimpse of royalty, but while waiting a Rolls Royce stopped next to us to make a turn into the palace, and we didn't even notice the Queen herself in it till it was almost in the gates. I sat staring at the palace guard, to do what everybody else did, try to catch him moving. He looked carved out of wood, like the famous toy soldiers. I couldn't even see him breathe, tried to catch his chest swelling underneath his scarlet mohair jacket with black epaulettes and collar. I counted eight silver buttons while waiting for him to inhale and exhale. I gave up on the breathing and tried to count how many times he would blink his eyes. His eyes barely visible below his carefully combed bearskin hat. He stared steadily into nowhere. Thinking perhaps of steak and kidney pudding and his "bird" waiting for him at home in Manchester.

Near the palace gates I saw a group of people dressed entirely in black. Their clothes, hats, and shoes everything was covered in white buttons. Thousands of buttons, small and big, forming intricate mosaic patterns.

"Who are they?" I wanted to know.

"They are London's other royal family. The Pearly King and Queen, the tradition is passed on from generation to generation.

"There are all kinds of stories how it originated, the most realistic is that it was a simple way of advertising their trade, the mother of pearl buttons, which then escalated to the present day of button 'royalty' because they usually hung around the palace."

For a while we drove along the Thames river. It was a working river.

Everywhere there were incoming or outgoing barges, pushed or pulled by small courageous little tugboats with serious faces, laboring away. Half of all cargo went through the Port of London. We left London, crossing over London Bridge, singing, "London Bridge is falling down, falling down, falling down! My fair lady!"

Johan stopped the singing and got serious for a moment. "There are several giant man-made caves underneath the bridge, constructed by French prisoners during the Napoleon War, that stores at least 80,000 gallons of wine and spirits, and who knows what else?"

Leaving the city of London behind, we entered the suburbs where the council houses start. People who earned substandard paychecks made applications for these drab looking government houses. We passed rows and rows of dirty, brown brick, soot covered houses sandwiched together like a stretched out concertina.

Occasionally a house stood out from the others by showing a little character. The walls were painted and the windows and front door had a bright color. The front doors all opened directly onto the sidewalk. At the back of the subdivision, each house had a room-sized enclosed courtyard, with a coal shed and small glass house to grow simple staples like tomatoes, carrots, and lettuce. A throw back from World War II when food was scarce, and they had to grow their own. Sometimes these glass houses were used as storage because space within the house was limited. Most people called these houses "two up and one down," meaning two rooms up and one big one downstairs that was a living room and kitchen all in one. In every back yard, soot-speckled washing flapped on lines or umbrella dryers in the feeble sun, or hung inside the kitchen on a pull-up clothing dryer to avoid the soot in the air from tainting the wash.

The Boarding House

Woodside Park was pleasantly different from the brown brick council houses we just left behind. It had single family middle class houses with lawns and flowerbeds.

Along the well-kept streets grew green oak trees.

We stopped at the only two story building around. It was an old private home that because of the change in the zoning laws had been turned into a boarding house for "theatrical people" who formed a commune and jointly paid the rent and other expenses. We entered through the side door into a giant glass house the height of the building. This was transformed into a sun room, for added space, it was covered in hanging plants, and quite charming. In the middle stood a large dining table and chairs.

"This is where we dine in all sorts of weather, except when there are lightning storms, then we eat indoors in front of the telly."

Entering the house itself I had to let my eyes get adjusted to the gloom, intensified by the dark woodwork, closed curtains, and warehouse furniture. Everyone liked to describe the furniture as early Victorian antique. Knowing the difference I diplomatically agreed with them, not to get into an argument.

Johan and I dragged my trunks up a narrow staircase, to a temporary room he had prepared for me. It was an attic room that slanted so drastically that walking crab-like, one could reach the broom-closet at the end of the room which would serve for the time being as a sort of wardrobe. It obviously was built for that purpose only, because it had no room inside. The bed filled half of the room and was pushed up against the overhang of the roof. I would have to crawl onto the bed to avoid bumping my head. It didn't bother me at all. It was cheap and I would not spend a lot of time in it, except to sleep in it.

"I plan to start circulating the agents soon," I told him. We put my trunks at the foot of my bed. My cousin was full of apologies and explained it was the lowest rent in the house. I laughed it off, "Don't worry, I won't dance in here, I will only sleep in here. I'll just think of it as an extension of my cabin on the Southern Cross."

I left everything in my trunk, unpacking only the necessary things. I felt claustrophobic with no windows. And after the boat train's sooty ride, and the long taxi ride home, all I wanted was a nice long warm bath. On my orientation of the house I noticed an old fashioned bath in the bathroom at the end of the hall. Johan had pointed it out as the communal bathroom.

I approached him about having a special schedule, and he said, "The pennies take care of that!"

"What do you mean pennies?" I wanted to know. "I don't have any."

"I'll lend you some pennies, remember to get some, because if you have them then the bathroom is yours, that's what I meant by the pennies take care of the schedule. Let me show you what you do to get hot water."

I couldn't imagine what pennies had to do with getting a bath, then I found out that everything in the house worked by putting pennies in a slot attached to whatever you wanted to use. "The house has been modernized since the law came in to block some chimneys. We have cut down on our coal consumption to help stop the air pollution. The house now uses electricity.

"The water tank above the bath heats the water when you put pennies in the slot. The room heater and the artificial fireplace work with a shilling, and the telly is the most expensive it uses a half a crown."

"I thought I could just turn on the faucet. I hope they don't get rid of all the chimneys, I think a blazing fire in a fireplace is very romantic, and the chimneys are very charming."

Johan gave me a roll of pennies and told me, "Enjoy your bath."

With each penny I put in the slot, the water ran into the bath for a few seconds, and by the time the next one was put in the first pennies worth was cold already. Twelve pennies gave me about two inches of tepid water, but I bathed and changed to something sexy to play the part my cousin had selected for me, by telling everyone I was an actress from South Africa. It was a half truth. I had done two movies and about twenty plays, but I was really in London to continue with set design and execution.

Everyone was in the sitting room when I walked in, discussing the live show direct from America that was going to be coming on. I had heard about television, but had never seen one so it would be something to look forward to.

"Tea is on!" I heard someone call out. Tea would be nice, I was kinda thirsty but I was really hungry; the last meal I had was on board the ship. In the hot house all the borders were seated around the long 'Victorian' dining table. Tea consisted of a lettuce, tomato, and onion tossed salad. In a serving plate there was bread, cut up spam slices, and boiled eggs. A large pot of tea brewed under a crochet kitty tea-cozy. There was food! A pleasant surprise because I expected just tea. I found out there was all kinds of "teas." Social tea, six o'clock tea, and high tea. It sounded simple but was eagerly explained to me. Social tea was when one goes visiting and crumpets or cookies were served with regular tea. Just tea was just that, tea on its own. Six o'clock tea was a light uncooked meal. High tea was served later and was usually a full-course cooked meal. I didn't really care what it was called as long as it was food. I also found that during tea, everyone did their talking because during telly time no one was aloud to talk. So the table talk became chaotic. Everyone tried to talk at once. They mostly talked about their dreams of getting into a play, each one had big dreams. of making it into the "Big Time" But now things had slowed down and some of them had to take menial jobs to survive. I found out that out of the eight people living in the boarding house only two had theatrical jobs, bringing in real money, the others depended on family handouts. Or government subsidies. I changed my mind from my thought of the morning. Listening to them at that moment things didn't look too promising.

After tea we all went back to the sitting room. The set was small. 9x11, someone had put the required quarters in and soon the screen flickered on.

It looked blurry like snow, and then fed by another quarter turned clear. The picture was black and white.

"Show's on," somebody shouted, and all conversation stopped as if people were turned off. I wanted to talk to my cousin about our childhood memories but again it had to wait. I got my first taste of television watching. It was some sort of shrine. "Where can you get to see a whole show for a few quarters?" someone said during a commercial break. I could not believe what power this 9x11 inch box had on people. They turned instantly into obeying zombies the moment the picture came on. No one talked, except during commercials when conversation flamed up, but then cut off in mid sentence when the show returned. It annoyed me rather than entertain me, so I gave the excuse in the next commercial of course that I was very tired and could I be excused. I was still lilting after two weeks on the ship when I stripped and crawled into my bed. It was cold in my attic.

Although I was exhausted I did not fall asleep immediately. My brain tossed around the reasons why I found myself in London. I left my country, sold my possessions, gave up a flourishing career, and gave up my soul mate to please my family, who will forget why they objected in a few years from now why they were against Peter and my union with him in the first place.

Tossing and turning I fell asleep, dreaming that I had fallen overboard and the ship had sailed without me. And Peter swimming out from the pier to rescue me.

The following morning I awoke with a start. The confined space felt like the ship's cabin. I felt disoriented, for a moment I thought I was still on the ship.

It definitely wasn't my spacious penthouse in the gardens. From the money I received from the Broadway play *The Boyfriend* I was able to design my own furniture. I had built a sunken bed in the corner of the pie shaped forty-foot bedroom and hung safari net over it to remind me of the jungle days.

In the morning the warm sun would break through the wall-size picture windows and gently wake me with its warmth, Now I awoke in semi darkness without a single window. Shivering from cold and the realization of what I had done.

I ran away from a man I loved, and left him looking after his baby daughter, with a suicidal wife in a drug rehabilitation institute. But I could not escape my true feelings.

There was a knock on the door. "Come in" I called out in my friendliest voice. Johan came in bending a little in the waist, he couldn't help it he was tall and it was the only way to stand in that room. He handed me a tray. On it was a typical English breakfast of eggs, sausage, bacon, kidneys, fried tomato, and toast. It was my first day in England. They must have all chipped in to welcome me. Johan had asked his friend John to take me for a drive into the countryside after breakfast. I felt guilty getting breakfast in bed, got dressed, and took the tray into the dining room. Just to feel even more guilty.

They had given me the royal treatment. And were all eating corn flakes. During breakfast, Johan, John, Frank and the others confessed to me that things weren't going too good with them financially. Johan had made no progress with his career as makeup artist, "Westmore" had their own clique. John, who wanted to open a antique shop, had run out of money, and Frank, who was a dancer, was clearing tables as a busboy because the theaters were not hiring boy dancers. He recently lost that job too, and had no luck with the agents. They were all collectively broke. They explained they were often asked out to high tea and that was a blessing. Judging from the previous night's tea I thought it was obvious that money wasn't flowing like water.

After breakfast, Johan, John, and I took a drive into the countryside.

The clouds of the previous day had dispersed and the sun was out in full glory. It looked and felt like summer. "When is summer?" I asked.

"About seven days."

"And the rest?"

John laughed, "It is foggy or it rains. So 'carpe diem!'"

The English countryside was as picturesque as I had seen on calendars and post cards. We drove through narrow country lanes that allowed only one car at a time. Old thatched cottages were bursting with country gardens, rambling roses draped over trellised doorways. Window boxes full of petunias behind fluttering lace curtains. It was at one of these cottages we stopped later that evening. I knew that Frank was gay, but never suspected that John and Johan were an Item, till when John's friends, who obviously were aware of it, talked to them as a couple. Somehow it didn't matter to me, they were good together.

The table was elegantly set for dinner, candlelight and flowers.

"You are all staying for high tea, of course?" John's friend inquired. Just hearing that morning how everyone was broke, I wasn't sure if I should accept and started making an excuse that I wasn't really very hungry.

John interjected. "Of course we'll stay. She should be starving by now, we ate breakfast last."

High tea really turned out to be a three-course dinner. I wondered why they don't just call it dinner and avoid the confusion. To them there was no confusion, perhaps it was the intonation in the voice, but everyone knew exactly what they meant. This meal started with a hearty hot soup, and bakers bread. Then a tossed salad, followed by a steak and kidney pie slow cooked in sweet onions and carrots, topped with a golden brown, mashed potato crust, with fresh garden vegetables on the side. Just when I thought I couldn't eat one more bite, our host brought out a large crystal bowl of trifle as only the

English can make it. Layers of home made custard, fruit compote, lady fingers, nuts and whatever else is deemed to make it more delectable. In this case it was pound cake slices saturated with liqueur. After trifle, we retired to the sitting room where a blazing fire crackled in an old fashioned fireplace. In a corner of the room stood a telly but our host was gracious enough not to turn the damn thing on, and we had a nice conversation about travel and books while the tea brewed under a most unusual knitted tea cozy with leaves and blossoms all over it. Our host took the compliment I gave him with a smile and proudly said, "I knitted it myself. Would you like the pattern?" Tea was the secondary drink only to beer. The "pint" was the undeclared social drink of England.

After high tea we went to the local pub, to drink in a bit of night life. It seemed that every town, suburb, district, city's, social life revolved around the local pub. Here whole families met to while the hours away drinking foamy pints of warm beer tapped from a keg with a handle much like a slot machine when not working or sitting around the telly.

In the pub we went to I even saw a baby in a carry cot sleeping in a corner while the mother made merry. For the younger people and the teetotallers there was orange juice till the day they turned sixteen and were allowed a pint like their elders. I nursed my orange juice or ginger ale, to avoid going to the public toilet, that smelled sickeningly like, "what else?" Beer of course.

I appeared a little stand-offish to them for not drinking, as everyone drank! It was part of their everyday lives. It was dubbed as "social drinking," and the fact that it was done daily to excess and they were really a nation of alcoholics was vehemently denied.

It was at the pub where business was discussed, contracts negotiated and signed. It was where Jack met Jill, or Jack met Jack, and where dates were made and dates were kept, or broken. Where weddings were celebrated, and later where husbands got away from nagging wives. They nagged that the husbands whole paycheck went to the pub and not to the household. It is where the husband had an unspoken understanding with the barkeeper. "If the missus calls tell her I had just left." And then he drank a few more just for the road. When she stormed into his pub to find out why her Jack had not come home when the tea was already spoiled. The pub owner sneaked his customer out the back door, so that it wouldn't turn into a public brawl, and the pub owner didn't lose his longtime customer.

There was a strange loyalty among boozers. It definitely had something to do with supply and demand. It was as simple as when the demand stops the owner of the pub is out of business. So he resorts to all kinds of gimmicks to keep the customer coming back for more. The customer is supplied with all kinds of freebies as long as his glass stays full. And when properly hooked and reeled in, there was free psycho-logical advice, which every barman had mastered in years of listening to sob stories and dealing with-in-house therapy. Marriage counseling and the occasional free beer to keep the spirits up or down whatever the circumstances may be, were on the house. Then there was the opportunity also to launch a career.

Bands and singers hired for the nights entertainment, often were picked up by potential managers, hoping to get that golden 25%. On that night there were no hired entertainers, but with an open mike, a spontaneous "sing along" erupted. The songs were all old and well known, and soon everyone joined in, vying to take the mike and show off their talent. It continued till LAST CALL, at midnight. When drunk or sober, everyone stood up and sang the National Anthem. And we headed back to the boarding house.

37

Walking Tour

Not having much luck with the agents, on my first month in England, I decided to take some time off and take a walking tour to see more of the country. I was told that it would be dangerous to do it on my own, so I placed an add in the variety paper for a male companion to walk with me.

I had about thirty replies to my ad. But to test their sincerity I asked everyone the same question to see their reaction. The answers I got determined my decision of who would accompany me. The one I finally chose was a tall skinny pale Englishman, with a broad English accent, dressed in a black suit, carrying a black umbrella, and sporting a round bowler on his head. One request was that each prospective companion write a one page bio. He shook my hand and handed me his bio; the others did not bother, this made him one up already.

I took his bio and read:

The reason I applied was that I love walking, I'm a true romantic, I write poetry and love acting, but currently am out of luck with the agents. I was educated in Oxford, studied languages, I'm fluent in Russian and Chinese in case we ever have a third World War. I have very little funds, but love an adventure and I know the country very well. I can assure you I'm sincere in my intentions, and you will be quite safe with me.

He signed it Watson. I liked his bio so I put my question to him. " If we are in an inn and I ask you to share a bed with me, what would you do?"

His answer was, "I would get in bed and go to sleep."

That was enough for me, it was the answer I was waiting for; the others immediately told me about their sexual capabilities and what they would like TO do TO me. They also bragged about the size of their organ without blushing. He was the only gentleman in the lot. I didn't ask him out right if he was gay, but his answer assured me I wouldn't have to fight him off. I wanted to see the country, and not England's genitalia.

"You're the one, we leave within the week, I will meet you in Trafalgar Square. I will call you to confirm the time and date."

When he arrived at our rendezvous, he looked quite different from the man with the double- breasted black suit. Watson was dressed in knee breeches golfers normally wore, tucked into brown knee socks, a tweed coat with leather elbow patches, an outfit straight out of a play about the life of Sherlock Holmes. I had guessed right. He borrowed the suit and the name from a play. He thought we would get further if we pretended to be from a foreign country.

He chose to speak Russian and I would speak Afrikaans because I was from a foreign country.

Once out of London we followed the same road I had traveled with my cousin Johan. Narrow roads, rolling hills, there were cool breezes and it was pleasant walking.

We were both talkers and had amusing conversations to share. Needless to say I was worried about the first night, so near sun down we started looking out for lodgings for the night. That's when we spotted the "FOX AND GOOSE" against the hill nestled among apple trees, covered in blossoms.

To save money I suggested that we pretended that we were married and get a single room. At the desk we rang the bell. The landlady came out and took one look at Watson. "Where are you from?" I was about to ask for a single room when Watson started to talk to the lady in Russian. She shook her head, I turned to him and pretended to hold a conversation in Afrikaans with him.

"You'll have to pay in advance, it will be ten bob for the night." She took some change from her pocket rattled it to indicate she wanted money.

Watson pulled a hand full of change from his pocket and handed it to her. She indicated more. I started digging in my pocket and produced a few more coins. It amounted to about half of what she asked for so she indicated more, we both dug around and came up with a few more coins. This game went on for some time.

Finally she gave up, and led us upstairs. When she handed us the key, she mumbled "These bloody foreigners."

Once the door closed behind her, we could not contain ourselves, we got away with murder. We were screaming with laughter when there was a knock at the door, and to account for our hilarity, we grabbed each other and started to dance. When she came in she apologized that perhaps we couldn't hear her, we repeated what she said in our respective languages and continued to do our dance laughing.

She shook her head that she couldn't understand and left the two cups of tea on the table with some scones and blueberry jam. She made a motion to eat, handed me some towels and pointing down the hall made signs of washing, shaking the change again. When we looked at her strangely, she went to the wash stand and poured some water into a dish and demonstrated to wash, mumbling, "Don't you wash where you come from?" Then she fluffed-up the already fluffy feather bed and left.

The pub was directly below us and conversation drifted up. The customers were openly discussing us.

I tried to avoid going to bed for the longest while but was dead tired; we had walked at least twenty-five miles the first day. Then I stripped into my petticoat and got into bed, he took off his clothes and true to character had on a long john, and climbed in beside me, and within minutes we were both asleep. The test was over! He didn't touch me. I reckoned I was the wrong sex.

In the morning before going down I looked around to see if I could find something that resembled a wedding ring. The curtains had small brass rings, so I took one down and put it on my right hand where foreigners wear theirs.

With our backpacks on we entered the dining room, the land lady motioned us to sit down. We greeted everyone in Russian, insisting on kissing them. This really shocked everyone into silence. I made a grab at someone's breakfast. The woman said "No, dear, in this country everyone gets their own. She handed me a full plate. Watson promptly took it away from me and put it in front of him, she gave him one, he scraped the one she had given me onto the one she had just given him. They all stared at him strangely, but he ignored them and started eating. I made a movement to take some from his plate. He shouted "Niet!" and lifted his hand as if to slap me.

I got up and went to sit in the far corner of the room. She brought me another plate, I ate. When he had enough he took a billy can out of the backpack and scraped the leftovers into it, took a piece of bacon out of a woman's plate and ate it loud and open mouthed. The woman left in disgust.

He took her food and scraped it into the billy can smiling at everyone.

Someone said, "I hear they eat dog in Russia". Some more people left. He took all the leftover toast and popped it in the bag, then grabbed me by the arm and marched me out the door.

Well out of earshot, "Very good acting, a bit overdone, but we have our lunch, and perhaps dinner as well."

We acted our way through Cambridge, Leeds, and York, saving a lot of money. Then camped in Sherwood Forest, for free, pretending we were Robin Hood and Maid Marion. When a Bobby tried to stop us from roasting a chicken on an open fire, we talked in our own respective languages and he gave up finally and shared some of the chicken when it was done.

"Damn good chicken even if I didn't understand a word of what you said." We left him to ponder these strange Gypsies, going onto Chester where we encountered the best loved scenery with rolling mountains, lakes, and unbelievable green valleys. Skirted the shores of Lake Windemere on the way to Grasmere, where we slept under the stars because it didn't rain, and Watson surprised me by quoting several of Wordsworth's poems. I was able to include Hadrian's wall, Cardiff in Whales, and had a taste of Scotland, while listening to Frost. And on the way back to London, Bath, and Stonehenge, Shakespeare was on the agenda. He was such a delightful companion that I was sorry it was too soon over, but I needed to get back and continue my quest.

We were about ten miles out of London, footsore and hungry, when a car stopped and offered us a ride. Watson accepted but nudged me in the car, and for some reason started talking Russian to me. When the driver turned around and stared at Watson.

"Why are you speaking Russian, don't you know me, I'm the deacon in your Father's Church."

"My girlfriend here doesn't speak English."

"What a dish! Since when do you go for women?"

I couldn't help it, and blurted out in my best English. "Since Watson and I have been sleeping together, on our hike across England. And you better not tell his father." I didn't know how Watson would take it but he immediately took me in his arms and lay the biggest, wettest Hollywood kiss on my lips.

"Tell him, darling!"

Later when we were having our last meal together before separating, I asked him why he did that. He said because the man was vulgar, and what gave him the right to judge his sexual preference when he knew nothing about him. After lunch we walked across Hyde Park, feeding the ducks. He told me he insinuated he was gay because he overheard some of the other applicants, and he wanted to walk with me. As a young man in an all male college, he had for a time wondered if he was gay because several of the young men came on to him.

"But to be honest, being in that bed with you in your petticoat just knowing that your feminine softness slept so close me, I could feel your warmth radiating through me. I just knew for certain in which direction I was heading. The realization came to me, how could I be gay if I desired you, a woman?"

"Some times I wondered?"

I told him I was glad that he contained himself, and hoped that one day he would find that special someone, but I had fled my country to escape a very complicated affair and could not enter into another one just then. We could remain friends, though as long as I was in London, I had come here for the sole purpose of furthering my career in show business.

38

I Finally Get a Break

Soon after my walking tour of England I started up the rounds of the agents. The lines were still as long as when I left, the answer was still, "Sorry, not at the moment, come again."

I got into the habit of going to read the notice boards at Max Rehearsal Rooms. Then going directly to the theater's auditioning. But this time there was nothing except a handwritten note on a bulletin board next to a room used for auditioning. WANTED: YOUNG LADY TO BE GROOMED FOR THE OPENING OF *The Modern Miss de Milo*. Below the note was scribbled "see Mr. Mitch Revelly, Talent Scout." If I suspected that somehow this could be fraudulent, I did not want to admit it. I was desperate. I couldn't live off cereal and salad for much longer, even if it was doing wonders for my figure. I was also tired of sharing the little I had left with all the other hopefuls in the boarding house, waiting for breaks, but not doing anything about it.

I knocked on rehearsal room 5. The room was empty except for a desk in the far corner and one straight-backed chair. The room had a warm up bar and mirror running the length of it. Behind the desk sat a man with spectacles. He stood up when I entered. He was about five-foot-four.

He handed me his calling card. It read, "Certified Agent, Talent Scout, Placements Guaranteed."

It seemed genuine. We talked about my theatrical experiences and I showed him my portfolio. He browsed through the introduction letters, and when he got to the one African Theaters had given me to White City TV, his eyes lit up. That must have been the opportunity he was waiting for.

"Strange coincidence, this is where they are going to shoot my production of *The Modern Miss de Milo*." He promised that he would give me the address as soon as I was ready. It did strike me funny that every day it would be only the two of us. He taped my voice, walked me through my steps, taught me some what he called "camera tricks." He wrote a song I was to sing for the taping. After two weeks he told me I was ready. He would launch the publicity. But I needed a proper photo layout that would cost me.

He reassured me that because he had faith in my capabilities to play the role he would do the layout himself. He wanted to style me as the new sex-goddess that would put Jane Mansfield to shame. He made an appointment for the following day. He turned up with three cameras around his neck. I got the impression that he had borrowed them and that they did not even have film in them because he used only a hand-held camera. With it he shot a few head shots then proceeded posing me in provocative poses, suggesting I showed more cleavage and legs. Up to then he had not touched me, but suddenly during the photo session, his hands were all over me like an octopus. I objected and demanded that if we were to proceed that he keep it professional, by keeping his distance. He laughed it off and said he was only testing me, then added, "Luv, you MUST learn to relax, you know in this business it's give and take, you will find out that to get anywhere you will have to sleep with a few to get where you want to get, so it might as well be me!" I was shocked. I talked it over with the people at the boarding house. But he gave me the address of the TV station. They agreed that I should at least go check that out, because one never knew. Besides it would show whether Mr. Revely was legitimate.

At White City TV what I suspected became reality. No one there had ever heard of *The Modern Miss de Milo* production nor of Mr. Mitch Revely. They thought I had concocted the whole scheme to obtain access to the studio, then declared my introduction letters from South Africa were fake also.

Was my face red when security escorted me out of the TV station. I felt like having the man arrested then and there, but luckily I had not paid him a cent.

I was just furious that he had wasted my precious time.

My money was running out. I needed to get real serious. With my last allowance from Aunt Cielie, I asked Frank, the aspiring dancer, to go with me for dance poses I needed to complete my portfolio. With this added to my portfolio I went in to London. On my previous visits to the agents I had dressed low key not to offend anyone, but I decided to change my strategy.

It was Monday in the land of the drab. I put my white sexiest cross-my-heart Marilyn Monroe dress on with sheer stockings and high heels. Did the usual agent rounds, got some wolf whistles, and looks, but had no luck.

I had missed the early train and was sitting in the local actor's hangout ACT ONE/SCENE ONE in Leicester Square, nursing a cup of coffee. Hoping that some one who was involved in the theater would notice me. I think everyone noticed me only because they were sick of drab. I was the exception dressed in white, and there was no raincoat to hide my 36,24,36 figure. However, none of them looked as if they were about to give me my big break.

Across the street a sign caught my attention. With my budget as low as it was it pulsated the message to me loud and clear. *"This may be your chance of a lifetime!!!"* I left my coffee and followed it right into the theater.

It was a small theater, the size of Little Theater in Cape Town, I judged at full capacity perhaps seated around five hundred. The seats like a Roman theater slanted steeply toward the ceiling. The stage too was small.

The people who were auditioning were seated in the first three rows while others were still signing in. Most of them were properly dressed in leotards, holding their music and professional looking portfolios.

I stood out like a sore thumb, totally unprepared. Discouraged, I didn't even sign in but mounted the steps into the auditorium and sat down halfway up to watch the audition from a distance.

The theater owner with a heavy Indian accent was conducting the audition. With little enthusiasm he went through the line up systematically.

When he had seen enough he said politely, "Thank you, you may go, NEXT!" Obviously he had someone special in mind, because the "Next!" command suddenly speeded up. I thought the people he dismissed had real talent, I looked around, *I don't stand a chance!* Besides I didn't even know what they were auditioning for. I watched a few more minutes then decided to just sneak out. I stood up quietly looking for the exit, not to disrupt the proceedings. But too late the man with the Indian accent had noticed.

He shouted.

"You there, with the white dress on. What do YOU do?"

It was as if lightning had struck me. I froze in my steps, my knees visibly shaking. Now everyone's attention was focused on me. In my clearest theatrical voice I replied, "Sir, I do sets, design costumes, production, props, lighting, or anything that is required."

"That's not what I'm looking for, but do you sing?"

"I do, but I don't have any music with me."

"Do you read?"

"I do."

"Do you dance?"

"I do."

"Well then, come down here and show me what you CAN do."

As I descended the stairs, the others stared daggers at me, they had been waiting for hours for an interview, and I who had just walked in was getting preferential treatment.

The stage director gave me his hand to help me onto the stage, this personalized touch angered them even more. *I silently sympathized with them; it was nearly three months and I had not even had an interview yet never mind an audition.*

"Play something for her," he instructed the band.

They looked for the easy way out and played the first popular tune that came into their heads. Luckily I knew "Blue Moon."

"Is this OK?" I had seen "The Blue Angel" only a week before. The band started with an introduction, and I immediately started with the song. When they realized, they started over and this time I waited. The third try we got it all together. There was no applause when I finished. "Now let me see you walk, go across the stage and back." I had done some modeling, so I did some rhythm walking from one side of the stage to the other.

Halfway back he shouted, "Stop!" I was taken aback thinking he was displeased and stopped short.

"Let me see your legs." I raised my dress to above my knees.

"Higher," he commanded.

I raised it higher, it was dangerously near to the tops of my stockings. Now I was already showing parts of my garter belt ribbons.

"Higher," he commanded again.

I blushed. I was wearing the briefest of see- through panties, a lace garter belt and a French strapless bra. But I complied and wiggled the tight dress all the way up to my panties.

"Take it off!"

I thought he meant my stockings, and it dawned on me that this could be a strip club. I had heard about those in South Africa. *I'll give them something to remember if that's the case, before they dismiss me.*

Just below the stage stood a piano. I sat down on it and started to peel down my stockings very sensually. The piano player got into the act and started to play bump and grind music. When I got back onto the stage minus my stockings and the garter belt, he laughed.

"It was a good show, but what I meant was to take off the dress so that you can move. I want to see you dance. You can dance can't you?"

This time I took off my dress with no fanfare, and tossed it to a little man sitting in the first row, thinking surely this wasn't what the requirement was for getting the job.

So there I stood on the stage in my briefest of underwear, when the band started playing dance music. To hide my embarrassment, I automatically started dancing. I improvised along with the music like I had never done before. When the music stopped, I prayed that he wouldn't ask me to repeat. But instead he tossed me a thick script and commanded, "Now, read!" I was out of breath but I opened the first page and it so happened to be Shakespeare. I read it straight.

"That's fine, I want comedy" he requested. I immediately switched my style of reading.

"How fast can you learn?"

That was easy I was hungry and broke, so I answered, "How about yesterday?"

He turned to the others who sat through my private audition, I'm sure as hope ful as I was, and said the unbelievable.

"Thank you ladies, that will be all, please leave your name and address at the door when you exit. Don't call us, we'll call you."

He turned to a short stocky man who caught my dress and had been sitting quietly in the first row in the auditorium.

"Bert, when the young lady is dressed please take her to my office."

In the office I took one look at the oversized couch, and remembered Mitch's words. *"Sometimes you'll have to give out a little if you want to get somewhere."* I avoided it on purpose, instead sat in a straight backed chair near his desk.

"So you are multi-talented, but I would not be using your other talents, for now, but may I see your portfolio?" He flipped through it. "Very good, but that's not why I really chose you. It is because you react spontaneously, and you are good at improvising, and according to you a fast learner. I see you have done many straight plays. This however is a revue. But you are adaptable. We do not have a lot of time to rehearse. The young lady you are replacing has eloped to get married and the show has to go on. It's a lot to learn, but I will give you the tapes for the duets. There are thirteen pages in all. Do you really think you can do it?"

"I'm sure I could, but what about costumes, will they fit me?"

"I'm sure it would fit, your measurements are I guess 36-24-36! He looked me up and down, smiling "Yes I'm sure it would fit." *Now comes the couch,* ran through my mind. But instead he pulled a photocopied two page document out of his drawer.

"Read this and sign where I put the 'x.' See what you can do with the script. Take in consideration, it is a combination of Vaudeville and revue, and should be easy to memorize. Report back tomorrow morning at eight, and we will run through the show with the cast."

As I got up to go, he called me back. "Wait there's something more." *Now comes the couch.* Instead he handed me a fat envelope.

"Here's two week's rehearsal pay, that's what I would have paid, and how long it would have taken, if I hadn't picked you."

I didn't question or refuse him, I took the envelope the scripts and the tapes, and thanked him wholeheartedly.

With my first London contract safely tucked in my bag, and the money burning a hole in it, I walked out stunned. Had I bitten off more than I could chew? I didn't care! It would work itself out. Outside the theater I looked at the posters advertising the show. The costumes were extremely brief, no wonder he said they would fit, there wasn't much of them.

So this was revue!

I stopped in again at the ACT ONE. This time I didn't count my pennies for a cup of coffee, but ordered a thick steak and vegetables. Then I hailed a cab and picked up some groceries for the boarding house.

There was much rejoicing at the boarding house. The fact that I had a West End contract spread like wild fire, but what I had to do to keep it was a shocker. I had less than 24 hours to know the scripts. It was Frank who became the realist.

"Well if WE are going to help her learn her lines the whole night, I think I will go and make a large pot of coffee."

Frank and Johan alternated with the others to drum my lines into my head. By about 3 that morning I could parrot my lines, and prayed that expression would come with delivery. I was totally hyper with coffee but that didn't stop me from catching two hours of sleep.

At the theater I was introduced to A Company, who were amazed that I knew all my lines and with their help and a lot of improvising I breezed through the show. The only problem I encountered was that the man I was to sing the duet with was at least a head shorter than me, and the script read I'm standing in a garden with my arms around him looking into his eyes. I quickly solved the problem. The scene was set in a garden with falling blossoms with a love seat. We simply sat down on the love-seat with our arms around each other. When it was his turn, he got up and sang his part, and I did the same, when our lines were together we stayed seated. The audience would not be able to see the difference.

The costumes were all see through or paste-on and minuscule, so everyone's attention was focused on that in any case. As a nudist it didn't bother me. What bothered me was the intense scrutiny of my body by the first row, which normally consisted of mostly men.

At my stage debut that night, I gave free tickets to the entire boarding house. Naturally they applauded the loudest. During the show I stumbled over some of my lines, but suddenly there was a loud cue from the audience.

The audience thought it was part of the show, because it was a solo of a telephone exchange girl, making mistakes. The audience laughed. But then Frank, being a ham, stood up and took a bow. And when I then repeated the line there was even a bigger laugh and applause.

The rest of the show went off easy. After the show everyone came back stage to congratulate me. Even the cleaning lady at the boarding house and her family was there. The others in the show were impressed with my popularity; they were unaware that it was all my friends.

Mr. Chanduri was doubly impressed that I pulled it off in less than 24 hours.

He sent champagne. There was one person though that wasn't impressed. She immediately threw a temper.

"I'M THE STAR!" she shouted over all the celebration. "And you never gave ME champagne! If she's so damn good, she can have my part too, I'm quitting." And she walked out.

I didn't think it real, but Chanduri looked at me and asked, "How soon can you learn her part, is it still yesterday?"

"Well, I'll settle for tomorrow." I wasn't quite sure what exactly happened.

"Then the part is yours." He explained that she really did quit!

"I better leave now then." I was exhausted but I spent yet another night learning lines. The following night I stepped into the shoes of the STAR. I always thought that it only happened in movies. But it was real! And my first week's pay reflected it. I worked every second night as we alternated with B Company. So I had an easy time.

We changed shows every twelve weeks. The choreography was simple, walk, walk, kick, kick, twirl, twirl, kick, kick. It was a breeze!

They wanted me on points in one scene. I took the ballet slippers home and practiced walking on my toes, found it easy; as a child for fun I used to do it with bare feet. The show although supposed to be written specially for us, reeked of plagiarism stolen from the old time Burlesque shows and silent movies.

It made fun out of British Variety. In Shakespeare, I played all the female characters, as a quick change artist, talking to Shakespeare in a mirror, with a dresser in the wings helping me with the changes.

"Oh, Mr. Shakespeare, fie-fie-fie, why did all the pretty ladies have to die?" The scripts were witty and everything had double meaning, depending on how I delivered the lines. The songs were ditties that rhymed; that was easy.

To get through them I simply imagined my self singing in the shower and that there was no audience. When the tour busses came, the ladies laughed harder than the men. But on other nights of course our audiences consisted mostly of men. They came as regulars, and came to every show change.

And then there was Bert. Good old faithful Bert. He was an institution and the show's greatest admirer. Bert had attended so many shows that he had his own seat with a plaque, permanently reserved for him alone. He seldom missed a show and when he did we all worried about him, but no one knew where he lived. When we asked he was evasive. Bert was there for every rehearsal, helping with lines. Bert saw every first night show, if he didn't like it, he showed his dislike openly. We watched his face for approval.

Mr. Chanduri trusted Bert's opinion and expert eye. If there was a number he found distasteful, the number was scrapped. He was our sensor. His saying was, "Nudity is not crudity" Bert knew every girl's birthday, and sent her flowers. If anyone needed money for lunch, he gave it willingly. He drove the girls to costume fittings and shopping. He never was fresh with anyone. Respected us as much as we respected him. He chaperoned the photographic sessions, preventing any deviations from the norm, and believe me they did try and get us into compromising positions to make a buck on the side, selling the photos to the tabloids.

Bert was short, fat, bald with thick glasses and had an IQ not much higher than the room temperature, but we always made him our honored guest.

He was always surrounded by showgirls at our stage parties. He always turned up in his threadbare tux, wearing a white carnation.

There were rumors that Bert was rich, because he spent most his money on showgirls. But most of the girls suspected that he was really the theater's janitor, and lived somewhere in the dark basement, like the *Phantom of the Opera*. Bert was there when we arrived and was there when the last person left. He locked up. We never stayed to see if it was true, and never caught him cleaning the dressing rooms or the toilets. We simply did not want to embarrass him, because he was Bert.

39

Helping the Needy — Meeting Jack Kerouac

During my Leicester Square Theater days I became the one woman benefactor of the forgotten and the homeless. I visited the homebound and the sick. Norman, a very talented violinist, came to my attention one day when I visited a quadriplegic who became blind later on and had only the use of one of his fingers on his left hand. Unable to talk, he typed his thoughts on a typewriter. One day he typed for me:

"Why waste your time with me, this is my world! Go and see Norman, he can still be helped, but I think his mother is virtually keeping him captive, smothering him with protection. They tell me he has given up doing anything for himself, even given up on practicing his talent of playing the violin.

"When I first met him in the hospital he was in bad shape, but he was lucky enough to only be paralyzed from the waist down. For therapy, a nurse there brought him an old violin and had him practice to strengthen his upper body.

"He displayed natural talent. And on leaving the hospital he gave up all together. But now he is confined to his room day and night, when he could be up and around if only he could have a wheelchair and someone to take him out. And someone to see to it that he works on developing his talent further. He needs someone like you to believe in him! GO!"

When I arrived at the address I found it was just as Max had typed.

Norman's mother was sweet, but overbearingly protective. Through the years she had become the martyr for her son who needed her for everything. I explained that is why I came to help lighten her burden a bit, and teach him to do more for himself. At first she was reluctant to step out of his shadow and lose all the attention she was getting for her silent, yet very vocal suffering. Then she submitted but became very alarmed when I brought a wheelchair and took him out for walks in the park.

"Norm's never been outside, he will surely catch a death of a cold."

Later that week I took him on his first train ride and to the underground to see the Buskers perform. They are fire eaters, musicians, and other artists performing on streets for a living. One man with no arms had a one man band. The cymbals were tied between his knees, a mouth organ on a wire contraption round his neck, the drumstick tied to his head, and the drums tied to his waist. It was a cacophony of sound, but the hat by his feet soon filled up. This intrigued Norm. "He's earning his own living!" He saw the other acts too, tap dancing, fire eating, and one man's attempt at playing a horn. But he was more interested in how much they earned. By the end of the day he was impressed enough to ask me if he could do it too. I pretended not to know about the violin. He said, "I'm not too bad with the violin. I haven't practiced for a long time but I think I can still do it."

"OK if you're sure, the only thing to do now is select a good spot."

Right after rehearsals I went to pick him up, and we selected a place in the station where there was both incoming and outgoing traffic. The acoustics here were fantastic, even drawing people from the street in. When he started playing I was amazed at his talent. In an hour he had earned twenty five pounds, without tiring himself. Not only was I amazed but so were the people who stopped to listen. "He is good enough to play in the Royal Albert Hall on amateur night, with a little more help of course. The man handed me his card—Professor Friedricks. I handed Norman the card.

"God has sent you a helper!"

After several weeks of personal tutoring by Professor F., I went to hear Norman play in the Royal Albert Hall. This in turn lead to auditioning for the Royal Philharmonic Orchestra. They thought that the wheelchair would be a hindrance. But he later graduated from wheelchair, to have a specially constructed car, and took his first trip to Europe to play in the orchestra there. Seeing all this happen in such a short time made me happy, and I went on to my next person to help.

There were so many homeless in London. I found HIM sitting on a street corner, unshaven in dirty rags. He looked pathetic and it immediately triggered my Pygmalion instincts. SAVE! I reasoned; *If I gave him money he would just use it to buy some booze, and what he needs was food.* Across the station I found a great soup kitchen with the best homemade soup I had ever tasted, with a very generous helping of fresh baked rolls to go with it. That was the answer. I took him by the hand.

"Come with me, I'm taking you to go and eat something." He didn't object, came willingly and ate everything I put in front of him up. He didn't say a word, but listened with the faintest glimmer of a smile beneath the grime and dribbled soup, while I went on lecturing him about sobriety and taking care of oneself.

In a slurred drunken voice he said, "Dere' sh sho little time fo living, in dis beat genarasi-on."

When he was through eating I handed him 5 shillings for a Salvation Army cot for the night.

Then as he walked away from me, he stopped and turned around. Gone was the slurred drunken voice.

"I would like to reciprocate, would you meet me here tomorrow at the same time?" It was most unusual, but I looked into the dark eyes and saw only sincerity. I loved stories, and this one I wanted to hear. He had a cultured voice, and I thought I detected an American accent.

"Thank you, I'll be here!"

The following day I waited at the soup kitchen a little before the appointed time, waiting for my "bum" to turn up. He was nowhere to be seen.

A shiny Mercedes pulled up. Behind the wheel sat a gorgeous man with clean black hair, but with the same haunting black eyes of my "bum."

We stared at one another. Then he got out of the car and approached me. He looked taller, because he wasn't walking slumped over. He was clean shaved, and sharply dressed in casual clothes. My jaw dropped. It couldn't be! Gone was the dirty slumping gray-haired, raggedy bum. In front of me stood the metamorphosis of bum to gentleman.

"YOU'RE my bum?" I stammered.

310

"So? Do we still have a lunch date?" He opened the car door for me, and inside the car he handed me a rose. We rode in silence to a suburb of London, and pulled-up in the driveway of an elegant old house.

Inside the table was elegantly set with finest linen, silver, and lace, and red candles in silver candlesticks. He seated me by pulling the chair out for me, lit the candles, and put on beautiful music. Then with a starched white napkin draped over his arm, he brought me my lunch. A bowl of soup kitchen soup and a basket of their finest baked bread.

"I have been eating there for the past month, and believe me, they do have the best homemade soup."

I introduced myself to him, telling him a little of myself and why I found myself in London. He then introduced himself.

"I on the other hand have multiple identities. The bum you met was Percipied. But otherwise I am known as Leo, and if ever you go to Paris I would be Jean Mauries or TiJean. But the one you are having lunch with today is the real me, Jack Kerouac, born in Massachusetts, America in 1922."

"The author? I read your book only weeks before I left South Africa. Tell me was it really autobiographical? Because it was filled with liquor, sex, and fights?"

"Let's just say it was the shocking candor of the possibilities of life that so few see because they go through life blindfolded. Wondering when they are ever going to experience life, while life passes them by. On the other hand I live and research my characters I write about. Just a moment. You just happened to catch me in one of my researches." He left the table and came back with his "then" current book *The Beat Generation*. "I received only a few for distribution, I'm still trying to promote it in London, but because you are aware of the possibilities, and have made peace with your life, and live on the edge of the Beat Generation. And you have your eyes open to life because you 'saved' me without asking, so this one's for you."

"Then the master of words will surely autograph it for me?"

"Me, 'bum', master of words?" I took the book from his hands and opened it at random, reading quietly the part where, after making love to someone named Mardou he writes about sounds in the night, sounds that course through his mind. I read out loud.

"I lie in the dark, Mardou seen in this light is a little brown body in a gray bed sheet, and the vision of great words in strange rhythmic order, all in one giant archangel book go roaring through my brain, so I lie in the dark also seeing and hearing the jargon of the future worlds—damajehe eleout ekeke dhdkdk. Poor examples of the mechanical needs of typing, of the flow of river sounds words, dark, leading to the future and attesting to my madness, hollowness, ring and roar of my mind which blessed or unblessed is where trees sing."

He sat mesmerized as if hearing the words for the first time. I continued skipping through the pages, eye catching poetical phrases.

"Pure poetry, master of words, pure poetry." I said.

"STOP!" He took the book from my hands and wrote. "To Ramona, for romance, in romantic mood, of that Beat Generation, Jack Kerouac." He got up and gently but passionately kissed me.

The house and the car were on loan to him, till his friend came back from France. And so it was that he was experimenting on being a street bum to see reactions from different people. The ashes in the fireplace made the gray hair and dirt on his face believable. To find compassion in one person was his goal. "Because you saw my need and responded to it, I am convinced that it was effective, now I could go on to other studies for another book."

"But what if I saw you, and didn't accept you?"

"But you did. Who knows our paths may cross again someday."

"And if it doesn't, what a story I would have to tell my children one day, of the metamorphosis of the bum in London, that's if I wrote my own book and had enough 'damajehe eleout ekeke' to write about it." In his own made up words.

40

The Big Break — Las Vegas or Paris?

I had been under contract in the Leicester Theater for nine months and everything was going fine. It was the first evening show.

There was an unusual activity back stage. The rumor was circulating that there were two scouts in the audience. Everyone was bustling around, putting their best foot forward, and their best stage smiles on, to impress the scouts. Except me it seemed—I was once bitten and twice shy, after the episode with Mitch Revely. I mistrusted all scouts, turning a few down along the way. No wonder I was not impressed with the two that they all said were in the audience. But as fate would have it, not one but two cards were delivered to my dressing room. On the back of the card was a request for an interview the following day at the Max Rehearsal Studios.

The following day I showed the cards to the girls in the show, they were a little jealous but all agreed that if I was lucky enough to get into the Leicester Square Theater overnight, perhaps I would have the same luck.

And who wouldn't want to go to America or to France? They suggested that I at least go and check it out. They would cover for me. The rehearsal rooms were only blocks away. It was the break between shows. I was in heavy stage makeup in my tights and a skimpy costume. If I changed I would be late for the second show entrance. So I hastily threw my coat over my costume, and ran up the road dodging the traffic and the stares. I bypassed room 5 in a hurry where Mitch Revely had gypped me and looked for Studio B where the serious auditions took place. I knocked and pushed the door open. There were voices inside. A tall overdressed, over perfumed woman with too many teeth and black hair severely pulled back into a sleek French roll was talking to some girls she had already selected from the group of girls who had turned up for the audition. The selected ones all looked the same as if they had been cloned. They were all between five-foot-ten to six-foot.

Same facial and body features, with perfect noses, blonde with blue eyes. The menu of the day! They were all giggling nervously not wanting to disappoint her in any way. They agreed to everything they thought she wanted to hear. She in turn was lapping it up. She saw me and beckoned me to approach her.

"Oh yeah! You're the one I saw work last night. I was quite impressed, let's see what we've got!"

She had an American drawl as deep as the Grand Canyon. I thought it was put on but found out it was real. She looked me up and down, told me to remove the bra, and put my hands on my head and walk up and down. She felt my breasts and nodded to someone in the room that was taking notes. That angered me inside, but the next thing she did definitely determined things for me. She told me to open my mouth, and stuck her finger in my mouth exploring my teeth. I felt the compulsion strongly to bite her finger off.

"Yeah that would do nicely, but that nose! Yuck! It has to go! A nip and a tuck here and there would do the trick."

As if my nose and everything else I had been living with for my entire life was something that somehow belonged to her, to do with what she wanted.

"Buying a horse?" I asked her.

She resented me saying that but she went on to explain that one of her sets of twins was quitting to get married, and I was the closest match she had seen in her search for a replacement. But she would have to make a few alterations through plastic surgery to get me perfect. Then to add Insult to injury she added, "The adaptation of personality is up to you, but is necessary so that you can step into the shoes of the missing twin." I couldn't believe what she was saying.

"The troop would be performing in Las Vegas, where you could be done, and it would take a few weeks of recuperation before we could use you." It was unreal but she meant it. I was simply considered a commodity to her.

"I'm sorry, but I think I'd rather be me. Thank you, but NO THANK YOU!" I said, walking out. The clones could not understand my attitude.

I looked at the other card, Studio A. France. I only had twenty more minutes left. I swore that if they poked at me with their fingers or asked to see my teeth I would walk straight out. I knocked with some hesitation. A beautiful young woman with short blonde hair and a warm smile said, "Come in," in a heavy German accent. "I vish you come, tomorrow you go with to Paris for my show, jah?" I waited for her to tell me to dance to sing or to walk but instead she said, "I see you work, now from close, I vant you for my show. Please you say jah."

PARIS, GLORIOUS PARIS, HERE I COME! my mind flashed in bright neon.

Then the bubble burst. I started to explain to her, "But, I am still under contract with Leicester Square Theater."

"Is OK," she said. "We fix."

"Andre," she called to a man in the back. He was very French. She introduced him to me, and they talked enthusiastically among themselves. I could not understand because I did not speak a word of French yet.

"He go with you now to fix. You give him your passport."

Andre walked with me to the theater. While I did the show, Mr. Andre and Mr. Chanduri negotiated for my immediate release. The money that changed hands obviously pleased Mr. Chanduri, because when the final curtain came down that night he came to my dressing room.

"It seems that you have been chosen for bigger things, and I have released you from your contract. I can't stand in your way. We will miss you, but we wish you luck in the future. Don't worry, B Company will stand in for you till we find a replacement. I just hope they learn lines as fast as you did."

I felt a little sad as I greeted the people in the show and packed up my makeup. I had enjoyed working with them, but I did not know what I was getting into. The experience gained in this small revue prepared me for the bigger things to follow, and I was grateful.

As the familiar stations flashed past during my train ride to Woodside Park that night, it dawned on me that by tomorrow night I would be in another country altogether.

The first one I told was my cousin Johan. I woke him up because it was past two in the morning. He knew about the calling cards but did not expect such fast results. At breakfast the word soon spread and everyone came to wish me well. These people were all theater hopefuls and reveled in my success obtaining a contract in such a world famous place as the "Moulin Rouge." Why only a week before we had discussed the movie by that name, and now I was to appear in that same place, in what role I still didn't know. I also remembered each one of these people as true troopers who stayed awake helping me learn lines so that I could get into the show I was now leaving behind to go to France. When the phone rang to tell me that Mr. Andre would meet me at the station to hand me my passport and the boat ticket to France, the reality hit home.

"Bigger things! Just exactly how big? Not even knowing the language, how will I cope?" I confessed to Johan. I suddenly felt very inadequate, and afraid.

"What do I pack?" I asked Frank the aspiring dancer.

"Everything that would knock them off their feet, sweetheart."

"And what do I wear?"

"I would start with that adorable number that got you your first break in London."

"Which one was that?" I had forgotten what I had worn.

"The Marilyn Monroe dress, darling. The other things you can pack in the trunk and I will bring it to you personally if you promise to get me an audition in Paris!" We started packing.

"I promise, but what if things don't work out in Paris?" I laughed self-consciously.

He just looked at me. "But you know things will work out for you, it did here? Didn't it?"

In the kitchen there was a lot of fussing going on, I thought they were preparing me a last breakfast, then someone came in.

"Tea's on!" The table was filled with things that reminded me of my first "tea" when money was extremely scarce. There were tomatoes, margarine, lettuce, bread, and a can of spam. There was also a box of Corn Flakes and milk. Things we lived off because it was all we could afford. We were soon laughing and sharing

"You realize your support team would not be there for you. You're on your own, baby." No truer words were ever spoken.

316

41

Pare — Moulin Rouge Buys My London Contract

At the station I looked out for the other girl who I was told would be traveling with me to France. Standing to one side I noticed a stunning redhead, with loads of designer luggage. I walked over to her and introduced my self, explaining that Ms. Doris had told me that she would be traveling with me.

"I'm not traveling with you, so go away!" she said and turned her back on me. I told her that was extremely rude. She said, "So what? So now get lost." Andre arrived and thinking we had not met, he introduced us and handed us our travel documents and a wallet each. It was a cold meeting. When the train came she deliberately got on the train in a different compartment. She struggled with all her luggage but I left her alone because she had made herself clear.

Coming into England I had seen the white cliffs of Dover from a distance; it was very disappointing. But the ship for the crossover to France was a bigger disappointment. I entered the ship through the car hold where private cars making the crossing were parked and new cars were stored. The walls of the hold were dirty and oil splattered. A deep chugging sound came from the direction of the engine. Loud squeaking noises followed from the side of the hull as it scraped against the giant tires that were tied to the walls of the docks, onto which our ship was tied. I climbed some steep metal stairs that felt slippery from oil slicks, which stuck to soles of shoes of people trying to get to the lounge deck, where people who looked a little lost and uncomfortable in their new surroundings were milling around. Most of them were apprehensive over the prospect that they might be seasick. So they searched for the nearest rest rooms, just in case. The others who tried their best not to look like rookies, traveling abroad for the first time, sat nonchalantly at the tables either reading or staring out at the unmoving sea. I looked for the exit door, so that I could see us sail off. It was a heavy steel door with a foot high threshold. A sailor standing nearby said it was to block the water from entering into the lounge. I couldn't imagine waves coming up that high, on the open sea perhaps but not on a crossing.

I looked over the side. Bilge water was spilling out of a hole of the ship, causing a dark green foam to gush up against the grimy dock wall. Below me the men were cranking a thick anchor chain around a block that looked like a giant cotton-reel, getting the ship ready for sailing.

As the ship started moving, I felt a definite lilting as I stepped over the doorstop into the lounge area. I felt disoriented as the ship suddenly dropped away from under my feet. Seconds later it rose up again.

Not being a very good sailor, I immediately sought out a more stable place from where I could watch the coastline recede without focusing too much on the waves that suddenly changed from lake smooth to turbulent.

In a dark corner someone had the same idea. She was ghostly white and thin. She looked vaguely familiar, but try as I may, I could not place her.

"They say that eating or drinking something helps to steady the stomach," I told her, trying to make conversation. " I think we both need it at this time to survive this crossing. It's also good not to look at the land mass we left behind." I said this more to appease my own feelings than hers.

Then she said something strange. "To think I'll never see England again."

I went over to the bar and got two orange juices, and brought them back to her table.

She did not object, so I sat down.

"Of course you'll see it again, surely you'll be coming back here after your visit to France," I tried to re-assure her.

"No! This is my last trip, anywhere!" She was obviously distressed but continued without hesitation. "You see, I have a month to live. I am dying of cancer."

I was shocked into silence. People with the big C don't like to talk about it usually. What could I say?

She continued, feeling my discomfort. "You don't have to say anything, and don't feel bad for me. I am going to Paris, my favorite place, to do a film with one of my favorite people, Yul Brynner. It's called *Once More with Feeling*. It should be fun, it's about this orchestra conductor who can't find time for his wife."

Suddenly I knew who she was. I had read a recent article about Rex Harrison's wife, Kay Kendall, who was traveling by boat to France because she was very ill and disliked flying. Rex was back in London doing *My Fair Lady* and couldn't take the trip with her. I thought perhaps he wasn't aware of how seriously ill she was, or perhaps he knew and for that reason allowed her that privacy. I told her what a big fan I was of both gentlemen with whom she was currently involved with.

"I stood for TWO hours in the rain to get an autograph from your husband."

She laughed. "Don't feel bad, I cannot remember that he ever gave out an autograph, because he said he never felt worthy of a fans' admiration. I was always amazed that he felt that way because I always thought his work was remarkable." She then changed the subject telling me about her co-star whose work she also admired.

"And now, imagine I am to play his wife. I just hope I can complete the picture. But uh …" I cut her conversation short so that I could lead her thoughts away from her fatalism.

"I recently made a life-size painting of Yul, and hoped to give it to him some day. I too am enamored with him. I've seen most everything he ever did."

"Then I shall make sure that you get to meet him in person. I'll arrange for a gate pass, and send you an invitation to one of our shoots. I'm sure he will be delighted. He is a very caring person." I told her I was bought out of a show in London and given a contract by the Moulin Rouge and didn't know what kind of commitment and rehearsal schedule I was on, but I appreciated it. I reciprocated and invited her and Yul in turn to the opening night at the Moulin Rouge. We sat quiet for some time, but then knowing that she had found a listening ear, she went back to her dying. "I actually have no fear of dying, but I'm fond of Earthly things, and feel sad that I'm leaving it behind. I can't imagine not smelling the flowers, or seeing a rosebud develop into a full-blown rose. And not to see the fading sky after a glorious sunset. And seeing the mood changes of my husband. I'm most concerned about him."

She sat silent as if reflecting what she had just said. Then continued softly, "I know I really shouldn't worry about him, his career is doing well, and there is talk about a movie follow-up, after the stage play of *Fair Lady*. Now there's, a part I would have loved to play opposite him, but they say it could go to Audrey Hepburn, and not to the young lady Ms. Julie Andrews, currently starring in the play *My Fair Lady* in Drury Lane. You know she first did Eliza in New York in Bernard Shaw's original *Pygmalion*? Right after she became a success in the West End production of the *Boy Friend*. So it was just natural that she acted in the London production of *My Fair Lady*. But Julie has her mind set on continuing her career in movies and letting her singing rest for a while. I was surprised they didn't offer her the movie role. Rex wasn't too happy about an almost unknown doing the part of Liza. But she told Rex she had other offers pending."

She was silent for a few more minutes then she said: " I think I was fourteen when I first saw Rex in the movie *Anna and the King of Siam*. I think I was in love with him then, right from the very start." She reminisced for a while, and went on telling me how they met; she talked dreamily about their times together. "Now I must let him go, don't even know if I will ever see him again. The doctor has given me such a short time, that's why I am living it to the fullest. Doing what I like best."

I let her talk on and on. I almost had a morbid fascination with someone who was about to die. Talking so matter-of-factly, like she was going on a trip without destination, and was wondering who was going to water the plants and feed the puppies. "I'm so glad I'm not traveling with an entourage. I sneaked off, they exhaust me so, and usually attract the publicity-hounds, something I wanted to avoid at all costs. They can be so blunt and heartless, and would have made a tragedy out of my dying."

I felt so sorry for her; she suddenly looked so frail and tired. I tried to put a lilt in my voice. "I don't know about you, we both have a full day ahead of us tomorrow. Can I walk you to your cabin?"

"Thank you for listening, I don't usually talk that much. I will appreciate you walking me to my cabin. I suddenly feel extremely tired."

On deck the following morning going through La Duane formalities, I saw Ms. Kendall step into a long white limousine. I was glad. It must be wonderful to be so famous that all the drudgery of formalities are waved, as I struggled with my luggage and wondered how I was going to cope with a language I didn't know, in a ballet of eighty I was never trained for.

Paris Nights

42
Moulin Rouge

What a change stepping off the boat train in Paris. I was sure English had died on the ship. A swarm of locust characters descended on me. All of course saying things in French I did not understand. When I said something in English they shook their heads, laughed and mumbled "Je comprend pas," so I got nowhere.

"Porte votre valise?" the guy nearest me said, and made a grab for my luggage.

"Leave my stuff alone!" I yelled at him. "I need a taxi cab."

"Ah! Un taxi?" The first man let go of my "valise." I made a comparison and recognized the word. He whistled and waved the second taxi to pull up.

A taxi pulled up next to me. The two of them had a conversation in French, having a good laugh. I saw the "valise" man wink at him as he loaded my luggage. I somehow knew that I was in for the scenic route.

I did not know where I was going. "Ou aller?" In the intonation of his voice, I presumed he wanted to know where I was going. I looked for the scrap of paper Andre had pasted in my passport, with an address on it. I read it to the driver, and even though I was sure it was the correct pronunciation, he looked at me and said, "Je comprend pas," and shook his head. Which clearly said, *I've got myself a patsy, boy is she going for a ride!*

He naturally turned the meter up right from the start. I didn't mind because I was seeing the City of Lights for the first time.

What worried me was not knowing how far I was going out of my way, and how much it would cost me. The country was in a transition stage of changing their currency from thousands to hundreds, and there were both in the wallet of advance money I got from Andre to last me till my first paycheck. We circled the Arc de Triomphe several times. I thought it strange till I saw the other cars doing the same thing. Later I found out that Paris was laid out like a wheel. Every second spoke was a one way, so most vehicles circled the hub till they sorted out the street they wanted to enter to get to their destination. So if they missed out the first time they simply went around a second time, There were no set lines to follow, so it was natural to cut one another off. Tempers flared. Several times we stopped, the driver got out and yelled at the people who seemed directionless, to untangle the mess.

A car side-swiped our taxi; he inspected the damage. The two involved shook fists and yelled some more. Some money exchanged hands and we were on our way. All this time the meter was tickling away. The near miss brought my unsolicited tour to an end. We entered the correct turn off and he pulled up sharp in front of a small hotel in a dead-end street.

"Voila, arrive!" He dumped my luggage on the sidewalk. I had no idea how much I should give him, so I handed him the bigger of the two notes, and in good faith waited for him to give me change so that I could tip him. He grabbed the note, and the next minute his wheels screeched in reverse out of the alley as he made a hurried exit, laughing all the way.

"My change!" I screamed after him.

"Ca c'est Pare!" he screamed back.

Shocked, I watched the smoking tail pipe disappear round the corner of a large circular building.

"I saw that! How much did he get you for?" asked the manager of the hotel in English.

"I don't really know, I think it read 'mille'! He also shouted something as he drove off in a hurry. It sounded like 'sah say pare.'"

"He shouted 'This is Paris,' but this isn't what Paris is all about, it's creeps like this that gives Paris a bad name. He really gypped you." He carried my luggage inside the lobby. "You must be Ramona. Andre was here early this morning to book the room. The other girl has already checked in and has gone on to the Moulin Rouge. He left a message for you to come to the Moulin as soon as you arrived. They have an orientation at ten." The hotel manager asked me for my passport and checked me in.

"I'm sorry, we don't have a porter, and you're on the third floor."

I looked at the wall clock, it was nine already.

"How far is the Moulin Rouge from here? I hope not a taxi ride away?"

"No, we're only five minutes away. Turn left at Cliché, about five blocks up, you couldn't possibly miss it—it has a red windmill on the roof."

He didn't have to describe the building. I had painted murals of it, seen it on post-cards, and in the movies.

"Then I have just a few minutes to freshen up."

I picked up my case, I was glad I had not brought my trunk, slung my hand luggage over my shoulder and started up the steep narrow stairs. The carpet was a thread-bare imitation of a real Turkish carpet. With the added weight, the stairs creaked precariously beneath my feet. Two more flights up and I was dragging the case *bumpity, bumpity, bumpity*!

I stood in front of 304 huffing and puffing. When I shoved the door open a heavy cloud of expensive perfume knocked my senses for a loop. It was the same smell that hung in the air as the girl who refused to travel with me walked away from me on the London Station. *It must be the redhead.*

I opened the large old armoire, every hanger was taken. The drawers in the dresser were full too, and more things spilled out of her trunk filling the middle of the room, and another stack onto a large four poster bed. She was not only rude, but selfish too.

In the corner of the room stood a small daybed, at least that was still unoccupied. I put my coat and suitcase on it. Perhaps she was not briefed that the room was supposed to be shared. Next to the small bed stood a strange little bath, with the name "Biddy" on it. I turned the faucet on and a fountain of water shot straight up into the air with such a force that it nearly hit the low ceiling. We had no bathroom in the room, so I stuffed one of my stockings in the hole, and freshened up as much as possible. Down the hallway I discovered a public toilet, also a bathroom with shower, but no bath. It was a communal bathroom. Perhaps that was why they put those little foot baths in the rooms. I had never seen one of those before.

When I inquired at the front desk about the little bath. He laughed.

"The thing you call a foot bath is called a 'Bibby.' It's there to do personal ablutions."

"What do you mean?"

"Exactly what I said; let me tell you the story of the American lady who asked the hotel manager the same thing, on seeing it for the first time.

"'Is this a bath to wash the baby in?' He replied, 'No, madam, it's a bath to wash the baby out!' Get it?"

"Why doesn't this hotel have bathrooms in the rooms? Everywhere I've been hotel rooms always have bathrooms."

"It's because this is a very old hotel, and goes back to the time when people still used public bath houses; some still do—there is one on the corner next to the Cirque Medrano, that big round building at the end of the road."

I left the hotel. The alley on which the Hotel Stevens stood had a dead-end with an elaborate old fountain that no longer spouted water. On the opposite side of the street there stood a dark brown building that looked like an apartment building. The narrow dirty windows had shutters on the outside with drawn lace curtains on the inside. I was born curious, and liked to look and eavesdrop into other people's lifestyles. My imagination usually ran off with me like wild horses. The interiors of these apartments were the perfect setting for a mystery novel. Dark and sinister, with gloomy furnishings. Except for the pristine white lace curtains that allowed me to look in. *But I must hurry!*

As I turned the corner there was a broad boulevard with a walkway down the center. Silver oak trees were held Prisoner in wrought iron cages, which protected them from lovers who carved their names on thick white-flecked stems. Between the trees stood wooden benches bolted together back to back on which several old people sat feeding pigeons.

Mothers with baby carriages strolled up and down, or stood in babbling clumps. Although it was early morning, still there were couples who either had not yet gone home from the previous night's loving sessions, or were so in love that they didn't care who saw them openly declaring their love for one another in the street with heavy smooching. Oblivious to the clicking of tourist cameras photographing them. The nighttime scene changed to accommodate the daytime crowds.

On the right side of the boulevard in front of the shops, the stalls of daytime vendors spilled half way over the pavement, displaying all manner of wares. Loudly encouraging the colorful groups of tourists to, it sounded like they were saying, ashtray—"Ashtay! Ashtay!" but really meant, "Buy! Buy!"

Next to the stall with a sign that read "Best Fashions in Paris!" with cheap looking dresses swaying in the breeze from hangers hooked over the overhang of a shop there stood a three-tier box filled with ice, selling smelly dead fish with glassy eyes and half-frozen, slow-moving live crabs trying to escape out of the boxes, the vendor pushing them back onto the ice with a stick.

Every twenty steps I was propositioned with lewd gestures, some were outright funny. Sticking their tongues in and out.

"Hey, lady, wanna eat my banana?"

Some sleazy character pulled at my sleeve. "Real French postcards, very dirty, very sexy, you buy?" They were indeed very dirty because dirty hands were handling them. His voice in whispered tones hinted that they were pornographic. This normally made the sale for them to unsuspecting male tourists. But out of the corner of my eye, I recognized the Venus and other nudes from the Louvre Museum of Art.

I had read somewhere about "The notorious Ladies of the Night" who paraded the boulevards. I would be walking to and from the Moulin Rouge nightly, and I sincerely hoped that showgirls were excluded and not mistaken for the ladies of the night who plied their trade in front of the strip clubs of the boulevard that have barkers calling out the speciality of the club and offering sexual favors.

The only club that was an exception was the Crazy Horse, near the Champs-Elysees. They specialized in doing exotic stripping, but did not offer themselves for gain, and were considered high class strip artists in their trade.

I approached a large open square. Looking up my eye caught sight of the famous red windmill on the roof. An indescribable thrill ran through my body. I pinched myself. This was the place I dreamed that I would go and see one day when I could afford to travel. And there I was standing in front of it. And was going to work there. This not only was a dream come true, but a psychic prediction come true.

Before leaving South Africa, my singing teacher invited me to a psychic show with him. I was a true skeptic but thought it would be interesting. The hall was full of people, hoping to be called because that was what the psychic did. Told people of their future. She was on stage calling a Mr. Jones. Above her head there was a strange sound like bees buzzing. I thought she was wired.

"Mr. Jones, you are about to negotiate a contract. I want to warn you, it will turn out fraudulent. Don't sign!" She stepped down from the stage and started walking down the aisle.

"Charlotte B. Please stand up. I have a message for you." A woman raised her hand and stood up. "You have withdrawn from your children, claiming they have forsaken you, and lost contact. I see you standing in front of a blue door. It is up to you to go through. Behind it your children are waiting with open arms to welcome you. The first one you will see is a granddaughter who was named after you."

All the time she was talking the buzzing emanated out of her head or thereabout. I laughed and whispered to my teacher, "It's rigged, she must know them and the information is being fed to her through a radio hidden in her clothes." She walked fast to near the back of the hall to where we were sitting. Almost as if she had heard me. I got goose pimples when she stopped right in front of me and stared into my eyes: "You know someone by the name of Alex, he has a stomach problem. But don't be alarmed, he saw a doctor. And he is OK!"

My jaw dropped. "That's my father," I told her.

She said, "I know, but wait, Ramona!"

I couldn't believe that she knew my name. "I see something else. You are going on a journey across the water! Your career I'm afraid is NOT going to be in design!" She started laughing. "This might embarrass you, but listen carefully." She stopped and asked me if she could say what she saw in public. By now I was fully convinced, because no one could have told her any of the information she had given me nor my name.

So I told her, "You may."

"You are standing in a circular place. It could be circus, no! It is a round room! It is in three tiers like an inverted wedding cake. There IS A LOT OF RED around the place. You are naked, covered in diamonds, on your head you have a very large hat with feathers. I see more travels, to the Far East, maybe."

I was stunned; at the time I had only dreamed of travel, but had no idea that it would really happen. Soon after though, the over water thing happened when I left for London, and my career did take a turn when I didn't get into set designing. But that building was square.

Now as I opened the wine red curtains, I was looking at a large circular room. It had three inverted tiers. On each of the tiers, there were tables with red tablecloths. From the ceiling hung hundreds of red pendants, with flags of other countries in between, also flags with names of people who had worked there. It dawned on me that what I was seeing was exactly what the psychic had predicted nearly two years before. There indeed was a "lot of red." In a few hours I would be starting to work there. During my career in Cape Town I had painted murals of the Moulin Rouge and made sure that I learned everything about it.

The Moulin Rouge was inaugurated in April 1889 as part of the Worlds Fair. It was here where the Can-Can was born with quadrilles composed of dancers like La Goulue, Jane Avril, D'Egout and Monsieur Valentin le Desosse. At first they were known as dancing ladies of ill repute. With the event of the NEW dance craze Paris artists started flocking to the Moulin Rouge for inspiration, a drink, or simply to be seen, spreading the name of the Moulin Rouge and its growing fame to every part of the world. One of the Artists who stood out from all others was Toulouse Lautrec, a four-foot-tall man of noble birth, dwarfed by fate. As a child he had fallen off a horse. This stunted the growth of his legs and left him deformed. Unlike the other starving artists of Paris who bartered their art for food, he had no financial worries and could enjoy his artistic talent. He became an avant-garde artist, being an observer and recorder of facts, copied many styles, which later stylistically categorized him as Impressionist, even as he was against it, calling it *le belle peinture*. He used his art to earn a living even though he was considered independently rich. He inherited his fortune from his father's noble family, Count Alphonse de Toulouse-Lautrec. His charm and mischievous personality came from his beloved mother, who taught him to value his spirit more than the body in which he was trapped, artistic talent, according to him, came from his Grandfather Alphonse. His other attributes were legendary too, because he was well liked by the ladies, not just for that aspect, but for his known monetary generosity. He fitted in among his contemporaries. Indulging in all vices. In all of his drawings and paintings he made fun of his subjects, showing them often as cartoon caricatures. But he became famous for his posters of coming events, and for the realism depicted in his paintings of the ladies of the brothels. Also of the quadrilles showing off their bloomers. Other famous contemporary artists followed; Degas, Raphael, Renoir, and Forain. Searat and Gauguin of his generation. They often had open disputes about who was copying whose style. So each developed their own. Degas worked with speckles, and at some time shared the same living quarters with Lautrec when they both lived at 19 Bis rue Fontaine. The only similarity in style was that both artists painted from life. Toulouse was known for his excessive drinking and visits to sanitariums; he died September the 9th, 1901, at the age of 35. Already world famous.

The entrance hall to the Moulin Rouge was long and narrow and had not impressed me, but the long curved walk that led to the stage did. I was wide-eyed at the beauty of the interior. The gilded statues and frescoes in bass relief circled the rounded back wall. The top terrace was divided into cubicles, depicting tableaus from the past, with statues of girls in can-can positions forming the pillars. On one balcony it felt like sitting on the porch of a little house. I could see through the window into a kitchen. The table had cards and a bottle of wine on it as if someone had dropped everything and left in a hurry. There was a note on the table which read: "Gone to see the can-can." Above the second cubicle set with table for the tourists. There was a large sickle moon hanging in the sky, on which a statue of a life-size sailor sat strumming his guitar and serenading his girlfriend sitting on the moon with him, leaning her head on his shoulder She was dressed like a dancer so I naturally presumed that she was the one the sailor had gone to see, leaving the cards and wine in such a hurry.

I could picture this rounded hall empty, as depicted by the paintings of Lautrec the way it had been in the 1800s. When it was first established, it had drinking booths around the walls. At first it was only the serving maids, *femme de menage*, and working men who flocked to the place to relax after work with a glass of wine and small talk.

To entertain the crowds it was where the first boulder foursome showed their particular skills that were more acrobatic than dance. The three ladies would challenge one another to kick a glass of wine out of Valentine's hand, the males hollering and whooping to encourage them. They would pull up their dresses, aim for the glass and kick high up in the air. Everyone clapped for more, eager to see more of their frilly bloomers. Night after night they became more inventive to show off their acrobatic skills by doing back-flips, tumbles, and somersaults. Soon others from the circus joined in to make a lineup, which culminated the evening with the very suggestive and risky splits. Free drink for the ladies and their companions were served as compensation.. When the interest of the girls to perform dropped, the managers gave a special monetary incentive to continue. Soon not only the working class went to see the "spectacle," but the elite of Paris started dropping by in droves to see the scandalous new dance craze that became synonymous with the Moulin Rouge. And "IF YOU CAN, THEN I CAN— BECAME THE CAN-CAN!"

To accommodate the new crowds, a stage was added so that everyone could see, and chairs were added to watch the budding shows. Other acts followed. Fire eaters, jugglers, even bareback horse riding tricks had a legitimate place to show off their skills and get paid for it.

The management started charging an entrance fee. People who saw the show spread the word. Lautrec posters advertised it. People touring came in package deals from other countries. And the tourists still continue to come till this very day.

But this is the present, and I'm in it! The engineers were busy testing the lights and the mechanics of the three stages that ingeniously locked together. The top one moved slowly back, fitting under the stationary one on which the band sat. For the first day there were only three members of the forty-man band. Just to give us support. When the first stage was safely tucked in under the band stand. A third glass stage rose up from a twenty-foot pit in the center of the round public seating area, the glass softly changing color as it slowly came up. At the same time a trellis rail rose out of the floor to prevent accidents from happening.

Curious tourists often leaned too far over to see what was happening. Rumor had it that several people had at some or other time fallen into the pit. So they added the railing.

Most of the cast for the new show, plus others held over from the previous show, had arrived by then. Some were looking around like me, while the others who were no longer rookies, sat nonchalantly at the tables discussing the new arrivals. Waiting for their briefing.

A beautiful English-speaking blonde came to me and asked me where the lady's room was. One of the French girls explained where it was, but said there was no sex discrimination, and we should call out first. I went with the English girl; being very nervous before the orientation, I too had to go!

It was dark backstage, but so far devoid of cables and scenery. A small passage light gave just enough light to see by. There were some crutch-high men's urinals anchored to the back wall. Next to it, there was a three quarter door. I knocked and then looked. The interior did not look like a toilet to me, but it was either that or more urinals. I opened the door. I had never seen anything like that before, but if they said it was a toilet it must be there for that purpose. It was empty. With no seat. The floor was a giant funnel with an outlet hole in the center, inside the rim of the funnel on either side there were steel footprints. From the water closet above my head hung an old-fashioned chain with a handle. I could only imagine what to do next, and looking at the pencil slim skirt and stiletto heels of the other young lady, I volunteered to try it out first. The trick was holding onto the walls and getting one's feet positioned onto the footprints. But once I had achieved that I discovered that in the spread eagled position it was impossible to pull down my underwear. So balancing on one leg I was able to do so. But logic told me that if I stood up doing it, it would be a disaster, so I squatted down, alla bush mode, and aimed for the hole. BULLS-EYE! I was actually proud!

Now to flush? I reversed the entire procedure and balancing on one leg pulled up my underwear. Hoping that there might be a delayed action while flushing, I pulled the handle while leaping for the door. I made it just in time, as a flood of water gushed over the footprints where my feet had been seconds before. I looked the girl up and down, besides the other clothing she wore a three quarter length mink coat. I couldn't imagine how she was going to cope.

"Good luck!" I said, trying to explain to her about the mechanics of the FUNNEL THING.

Quite unprepared, she stepped in. Seconds later the coat came over the door, followed by the skirt, then the spike shoes. After that there was a string of curse words emanating from that sophisticated young lady's mouth and she tumbled out the door in next to nothing to avoid the flooding, looking totally disgusted from her experience.

Just then there came an announcement over the intercom for everyone to form a line on stage. She quickly dressed, and we hurried onto the stage.

The lineup was spectacular! It consisted of around fifty international beauties, each one stunning in their own right. Equal to any world caliber beauty queen. These were the results of international scouting-roundups in Europe, and auditions held by Miss Doris at the Moulin Rouge.

Miss D. made her appearance, together with a tall good looking Latino man in his thirties, and a smaller man and lady from Cuba. After welcoming us, she introduced the tall man as Mr. R., the person who would be assisting her in the choreography of the contemporary and Latin numbers.

The smaller man, Anibal, and his companion, Miss Inda, would be responsible for the exotic Afro-Cuban and underwater numbers. We were then introduced to a seventy-year-old lady called Suzanne who would be our costume coordinator in house as well as on tour. She was a feisty multi-lingual little lady. She spoke to us in French, but also spoke German and English with ease and told us that the sooner we learn French the sooner we would be able to help ourselves. She would be attending to her duties and could not translate for the rest of the shows It would have been an impossible task in any case, because there were Russians, Scandinavians, South Africans, and even one from Helsinki. The rest were all French, and the majority always wins. So in the future she would only speak to us in French.

"I was a dancer myself, long ago," she said, and to prove it she did a few high kicks and a perfectly executed split. I thought she was remarkable for her age (seventy). Then she calmly continued.

"I run a tight ship, I will not tolerate slovenly dressed girls. All repairs must be reported by the end of the rehearsal day, as heavy fines will be imposed for holes in working stockings, missing parts to costumes, broken chains and elastics on headdresses. There will also be fines for late arrivals because you would have to dress in a hurry, and could not do justice to my costumes.

"Your seats in the dressing room are assigned alphabetically, 'A' starting in front going to 'Z' in the back. Your names are above your mirrors. These seats cannot be switched and will be yours for the duration of the show. The dressing rooms have confined space and it is expected that you get along with one another."

She handed out black rehearsal leotards and told us to go upstairs and change. "These and only these will be worn for rehearsals, and do not let me catch you wearing shorts or private clothes during rehearsals, they will not be taken off the premises, and will be laundered by Moulin Rouge. One more thing, G-strings will be laundered by yourselves. Now go and get into your leotards and be back on stage in ten minutes."

Our dressing rooms were one flight up some iron stairs. On the level below the showgirls were small cubicle dressing rooms off the side for acts like acrobats, jugglers, contortionists. Below them in the basement were the animal acts. Trained seals, tigers, dancing dogs, and the doves, rabbits, parrots, and a fox of the magician. There was also snakes and a baby elephant that actually lived in a private room floor level in the hotel where I was living.

To the right of the stage there were five larger, carpeted rooms, with the luxury of a washbasin and private toilet. The only way to distinguish these star dressing rooms from the others were they were painted bright green, the same as the door leading from outside into the backstage area. But they each had a brightly polished brass star on the door. And at the end of their hallway hung a sign that said NO ENTRY.

Suzanne really did not exaggerate. The dressing rooms, one for the boys and one for the girls, were long narrow rooms, with counter tops along each side of the room, subdivided by a four-foot space allotted to each performer. Individual makeup mirrors were mounted along the wall. Each place had a drawer for our brushes and makeup and to hold our private "bootsan"(paste-on titty covers) and six flesh-toned G-strings. Above the mirror there was a shoe rack that held a dozen pair of our dancing shoes. Each girl also had a straight back caned kitchen chair. We learned to hate them in time. First because they were very uncomfortable, noisy, and had cane on the seats, which imprinted a crisscross pattern on our legs and bottoms where the costumes were very brief, which set us up for a fine. Adjoining the dressing rooms was a curtained-off area where there were lockers for private clothes and stuff. But another curtained area exclusively with rods that would later hold our costumes, wigs, and head dresses. Near the descending stairs there hung full mirrors to check costumes, stocking seams, and last minute makeup touch ups, before going down stairs to the warm up rooms and on either side of the stage.

Looking for my space, I sent up a silent prayer that I would not be seated next to the rude redhead, but mine was the first one in and walking down the room reading the names I saw that she was "H" and halfway in on the far side.

We all felt a little self conscious about our bodies at first getting undressed in front of one another. Those who had been in the previous show were less concerned than those in the show for the first time. I was in a semi-nude revue, so it didn't worry me. I got into the rehearsal outfit in a hurry. It was my first day and I wanted to make a good impression and not be late. The intercom announced "SUR SCENE S'IL VOUS PLAIT" followed by "ON STAGE, PLEASE. Five minutes." It startled me. And I started down the stairs. There was an earsplitting clanging behind me as everyone rushed down the stairs. Totally ignoring the BIG sign in four languages that read.

"S I L E N C E   P L E A S E."

Girls taking cues from those who already knew what to do started lining up. How unlike the Blue Bells these girls were. Not cloned, but carefully selected for parts, already thought out. Instead we were sorted by size.

Miss Doris ordered us to remove our shoes. Everyone 5'4 to 5'6. Step forward. Next, 5'8 to 6'. I was in that group. Out of that group she then selected eight girls, and told us to form a separate line. She told everyone else to sit down in place and watch. "Now I want you eight to watch me carefully and copy the steps I'm going to show you once. I won't repeat it." She said this in French and Suzanne translated it. The count was in eight beat time, and I was already familiar with it from the London show. So I tried to imitate her in every detail.

"TRES BIEN!" she said to me. I thought it meant "Sit down." So I sat down. "No, get up," she said. "You did well! Get up, you're not through yet," Suzanne said. Next came dips and walking I was also familiar with, when I was modeling in London. Miss D. called us mannequins; I thought that she thought we looked like, and behaved like dolls in a shop window. I felt a little insulted, because I thought I had done rather well. But she said "tres bien" again. And I knew it now to mean I did well.

One of the girls whispered to me, "She keeps saying you're good—she must favor you." Slowly she had all eight mannequins go through their paces one by one.

"In line, everyone!" Everyone formed one line again. The foreign ones did not understand. She smiled and took them by the hand and placed them in the lines she previously selected.

This time the three on duty musicians started playing.

"Now we will see how much you can endure."

The warm up exercises were extremely strenuous. Some tried to fall out, but she simply put them back in line. I did not realize, but I had grown lazy in Leicester Square Theater because our exercises usually consisted only of a few stretches. I was using muscles again I had not used for a long time. We the showgirls were not exempted from any of the exercises because in certain numbers we were expected to fill in for the dancers in the 5'6-5'8 lineup. My

legs refused to go into a full split. Some others had the same difficulty. But she pushed us down until I felt like I was being torn in two. Luckily she concentrated more on the dance lineup to get them perfect.

Soon we were huffing and puffing, and sweat ran down in rivers between my buttocks and breasts. She gave us five minutes to rest. We just fell over where we were, and then she resumed the next hour with more aerobics. Exhausted she gave us a lunch break. I was the only one who stayed behind. She wanted to know why? I told miss D. about the cab driver taking my money. She told me to go to Andre and get an advance. We all clubbed together and bought some foot-long *jambonne* sandwiches (goose liver sandwiches) that were delicious but fattening. In the dresser's estimation a definite no-no!

The Latin and Afro Cuban choreographers then took over. Ruggero spoke Spanish. Another language I did not know. I recognized some bad words he seemed to use regularly. I was worried about the choreography but I watched and learned he was doing some Latin numbers that included the Meringue and the Cha-Cha. Here my ballroom dancing classes came in handy. He also used ballet terminology. I got lost in the terms. Not having had formal ballet training, I made notes in a little note book. In my own form of "ballet" shorthand. I simply drew the moves in little stick men, with the counts written underneath.

I thought I had trouble, but the girl from Helsinki was constantly crying. I spoke to her in Afrikaans, and it somehow consoled her, or she found it similar to her language, which I think was Swedish because she calmed down. When I showed her how I coped with my little stick ballerinas, she started doing the same.

The redhead in turn just giggled and gave up after the first try. Mr. R. simply cursed under his breath after he had taken her hand and gone over the steps for the umpteenth time with her. Every time she fumbled the whole troop had to do it over again. After several tries that involved all of us. He lost his patience and blatantly cursed her out. I could understand what he said, but could not speak the language. And really couldn't blame him. He had seen me communicating with the Swedish girl, and I had not given him any trouble, so he naturally thought that I understood. He pointed to me, expecting me to translate, "Tell this blah-blah she is blah-blah and wearing my blah-blah patience thin, and she is blah-blah hopeless!" I saw Miss Doris looking at her watch; the girl was also wearing her patience thin. I thought the best would be to use diplomacy.

So I replied: "I didn't quite understand, but I think some of the words you used were not in my vocabulary."

Miss Doris walked over to the redhead. "Emily, don't disappoint me, you have to pay more attention. We cannot waste so much time. Otherwise you will end up with demerits, or dismissal before the week is up. And we don't want to do that, do we?"

She then turned to Mr. R. and looking at her watch again, and then at us said, " I think we all need a rest. It's five now; go home and take a rest and be back here at eight. Also take a look at the bulletin board for rehearsal times and anything else you need to know.

"There were a few things I've already noticed that I need to bring to your attention. When you all came down, the most important sign was totally ignored. The last time I read it, it clearly said SILENCE PLEASE in three languages.

"That means at all times, you might as well start doing it during rehearsals as well to get used to it. The next time you come down the stairs you will not talk, and if you cannot tip-toe then you will come down with shoes in hand and put them on downstairs."

Besides the warnings Miss D. had given us, the bulletin board had a whole set of rules to follow. I read the pencil written note on the bottom of the board first. Special tickets for entrance to the solarium please talk to Andre.

THE FOLLOWING PENALTIES WILL BE IMPOSED BY MANAGEMENT AND WILL BE SUBTRACTED FROM SALARIES FOR NON COMPLIANCE.

1. Hair not properly styled.................................. 5 N.F.
2. Unmatched nails and lipstick............................ 5 N.F.
3. Holes in stockings and crooked seams...............5 N.F.
4. Inappropriately dressed................................. 10 N.F.
5. Late for rehearsals... 10 N.F.
6 Late for the makeup call............................... 20 N.F.
7. Uneven tan or bruises.................................... 20 N.F.
8. Fighting and inappropriate behavior.............. 50 N.F.
9. Soliciting.. 50 N.F.
10. Not showing up for the SHOW......................... Immediate Dismissal

———————REHEARSAL TIMES ———————

Dancers and Mannequins Grp 1 10 a.m.—12 p.m.
Dancers Lineup Grp 2 1—3 p.m.
Specialty Groups Grp 3 3—5 p.m.
Entire Show———Run through for Performance 8—9 p.m.
Makeup Call.. 9—9:30 p.m.
SHOW TIME.. 11 p.m.—2 a.m.

I wrote the particulars down and hurried to the hotel. In the room Emily had completely taken over. I knew then that it was face off time. I told her the room was for sharing and if she wanted a single room there were other options. I would gladly share with someone else who was a little more considerate, less selfish, and less rude.

She didn't like my direct approach, but reluctantly gave up some of the drawer and wardrobe space and I was able to unpack. I stuffed a cloth in the biddy and calmly sponged down. I filled it afterward and soaked my feet.

And then I lay down on the day bed and rested till seven.

Before leaving the rehearsal, Miss D. had told us that we no longer would come in through the public main entrance, but should use the stage entrance. She described in detail where we would find the magic button in the side road that would give us access to the performers' back door of the Moulin Rouge.

Seven thirty I was looking for the magic button. There was an old metal door with MOULIN ROUGE on it with a sign that read "SORTIE de SECOURS—NE PAS ENCOMBRER CETTE PORTE." Almost next to the door it said, "Emergency Exit, Don't block this door" in English. There was the green door she described. Under a crossbeam I found a small rounded bell with a nipple button. I pressed it. It miraculously opened up to a courtyard, at the end of which I found another green door with a similar button. I pressed it and it too swung open. This let me in backstage. There an old man called Banan greeted me and let me sign in, placing the exact time behind my name when I arrived. (Reading the bulletin board I wondered how they would be able to tell whether we were late or not, now I knew.)

Everyone, that is everyone who read the b.b. commandments and the penalties were there promptly at eight. The few who ignored it were handed a pink slip that indicated the amount that would be subtracted from their weekly pay.

We went over the already rehearsed morning routines. Miss D. marked the special choreography high points, and key positions with an X on the wooden stage with chalk. Future sets were indicated by laying down some chairs in their positions. This helped to eliminate some of the confusion.

Showgirls, chorus boys, lineup dancers walked through their routines before the actual dancing was incorporated. The dance routines that still only existed in the minds of the choreographers, with preconceived dreams of the whole, were then slowly drummed into us, leaving us stumbling through the moves in total confusion. Different groups rehearsed out of sequence without help of the music in different areas, while the best way how to bring it all together was tossed back and forth among the choreographers.

At that stage all I could see was chaos and wondered how they would ever bring it together. But after two weeks, routines that looked chaotic and impossible slowly fell into place, and started to melt into the whole. The tableaus took shape and started to get a story behind them. We still only worked with recorded music and some days only with a piano. But after two weeks, one day half of the orchestra appeared. The musicians seemed to have no interest in the score of music but to score with the new girls. They flirted outrageously. It was strange at first to find our musical cues directly from the live music, but once found, everything became easier.

With rehearsals in full swing, wig makers, costumers, shoemakers, and hat makers all descended on us like locusts. With it came still photographers, and the media to photograph and write up the progress.

We were prodded, and poked, and handled, and sometimes marked with colored chalk, for the ones who came after to take our measurements. They whispered it to us, but then in the same breath, shouted it across the stage to the costumers sitting in the front row, who wrote it down in their little black books for later. Our names naturally were called out with the numbers.

Soft whistles came from out the darkness, where visitors and family sat at the audience tables, also from the musicians stage with every announcement of our measurements, especially the ones who caught their fancy. Those who missed the measurement made up their own loudly and tried to match it up with their rightful owners. In the dancer's lineup they had a hard time matching up. But in the showgirls there was almost one standard 36-24-36, with slight variations of an inch plus or minus here and there. The headaches usually came when the costumers had to even up the dancers. A waist-nipper here, a padding there, feathers to hide imperfections. A padded headdress that added another inch. An inch or two added to the heels till they all evened out. Plaster casts were made of our feet to assure perfectly fitting dancing shoes, which were handmade. The heads were also measured, and individual scull caps were pinned to assume the size and shape of our heads, over which our hats and elaborate headdresses were shaped by the hat makers. A week later the headdresses or rather the wire frames that would eventually become the spectacular creations that would enhance the costumes, were tried out for stability and workability. Duplicates of our costumes, made in rough muslin lining material, were tried on over our leotards to give us the feel of the real thing while we rehearsed and helped with choreography and adjustment to the moves. Within a week the headdresses were back, covered with brocades and velvets to match our costumes. The plumes were added, and the pearls, "strass" (diamonds), and other additions were left off till later. I tried some of the more difficult moves with my various headdresses. The ones too difficult to move in were fitted with metal shoulder struts or back supports to equalize the weight. When all was added some weighed as much as thirty pounds. If the balance worked out, they were camouflaged by feathers, embroidery with pearls, or diamonds. Next we worked with costumes that required underwire and battery boxes, sewn into muslin bags that would be added to the costumes later.

Long trains, heavy capes, and giant fans were rehearsed with existing old ones from previous shows to give us the feel and help to stabilize our moves.

Near the fourth week the stages were crowded with prospective set builders, who measured and measured and measured again with pen and pad, lingering among the scantily clad showgirls and dancers just a little too long. Staring and stretching the job to the utmost. They got in our way, and we tried to ignore their open flirting. When they left, blinding flashes of spotlights crisscrossed the stage, while the technicians mapped the lighting from notes given to them about the color schemes that would be used for the different sets and their respective costumes. The ones they were unsure of they marked with white or amber jellies till the arrival of the costumes expected the following week.

43
Stage Door Johnnys

With time becoming critical, we worked through the day and sometimes deep into the night, with few breaks. Miss Doris provided box lunches so that we could continue. Waiting for our cues, while something else was happening, we lay down for a short rest in the semi-darkness of the auditorium with our feet up on a chair. On occasion we got away from the stage, and were allowed to go out to eat. The Stage Door Johnnys were waiting at the side door stage entrance with gifts of flowers and candy, asking for autographs and the more bolder ones asking the girls out to dinner in the hopes that they would get that free ticket for the grand opening. But also to be seen with a showgirl or artiste around town.

We were on rehearsal pay and the running joke was, "Have you snared yourself a Meal-Ticket yet?"

Up till then I had not snared my meal ticket yet, nor had someone asked me for my autograph, but I had noticed a tall, handsome Frenchman nightly, watching from the side, not frantic like the others. As if he was shopping for the right time and the right one. On the third night, after midnight as I came out after rehearsals, he walked up to me and said in broken English, "I like you dinner with me? Yes?" Then he said in French. "Avez vous faim?" I hoped it meant was I hungry.

I was starving, had missed all opportunity for a food break since early that morning, so without any hesitation I replied, "Thank you, yes, I will dinner with you."

As I would find out in the next few months, Jacques was a most remarkable man, and a very tall one for a French man. He knew enough English to get by, and knew all the local watering holes. From the lowliest cafés where the artists gathered, to the five-person-capacity-step -through-the-kitchen-window- and-eat-what-the- femme- du-maison-cooked-for-the-day place. But he also knew and frequented the elite restaurants where the rich appeased their inner man with the latest of Nouvelle Cuisine. The place he took me to that first night had no category. It was across the road from Rue Ravigna at the foot of Mont Martre. We entered a small general store that stayed open all night. Here a meal could be had for whatever you had in your pocket, or what you bought off the shelves. I thought we were going to just buy something and take it to the steps below the Sacre Coeur where the students, the night owls, and an occasional tourist gathered to while the night away. There were quite a few people in the store. I was amazed how many people were still awake. (No wonder they called it the city that never sleeps.) It was a non-descriptive store with the regular paraphernalia around. It looked like things from a time capsule out of 1920. It had apple and pickle barrels. Bags of rice and baskets of potatoes leaning up against the counter on which stood jars full of spices, homemade peanut brittle, and cake. In a large bottle there were blue-white pickled eggs and a smaller bottle with sweet-finger jerkins. On a chain from the ceiling hung cured bacon, some sausages, and large blocks of cheeses. On some shelves stood canned goods in mason jars.

In a curtained off room stood a large old ion stove burning "boulets" (egg-shaped lumps of coal dust) with an assortment of pots and pans hanging from hooks on the wall. Here a buxom lady was preparing some thick slices of bacon she had minutes ago sliced off the one hanging from the ceiling together with some eggs a man peeping round the curtain had just handed her. A large pot of stew stood on the stove simmering. I chose the stew and some French bread. And for desert a generous helping of home-canned peaches and a café au lait.

In the center of the store stood a long wooden table with carafes of wine and cut up loaves of French bread in baskets, around which the strangest collection of people sat talking and eating at the same time.

The man with the bacon and eggs came through the curtain and sat down beside us.

While we ate, he and Jacques had a long conversation about astronomy, because that was the only word I recognized and because it was my favorite topic, but I soon became very bored not able to participate and trying to figure out what they were saying. I realized the middle-aged man wasn't really into the conversation, but when the word *Moulin Rouge* cropped up, he could not keep his eyes off me and it made me uncomfortable, so I wandered around the store looking at the wares.

A big man sat on a closed pickle barrel, his dirty feet resting on a store shelf. He was feeding a large skinny dog with sad begging eyes with leftovers from various plates still standing on the table, helping himself to the larger morsels, which he ate together with the free bread and wine that stood on the table for the customers. He was drinking directly out of the carafe, but no one stopped him, they just ignored that particular carafe. His hair was so matted that it hung in slabs and long ropes down his back. It looked like the dread-locks of Jamaicans I had seen in magazines. But he spoke a language that could have been any one of those spoken in Africa. Except for the hair, he looked like the Sanda wrestlers I had seen in the Sudan. The same blue black strong features and build, except the Sandas' hair was totally shaved off.

When he hesitated too long to give the dog a handout, the dog licked his feet. It must have tickled because he suddenly burst out in a hoarse laugh, almost neighing with pleasure. He didn't like the look in the man with the eggs' face. He stood up, and producing a mean looking knife from nowhere, walked over to the man. All conversations stopped, expecting the worst. But instead he reached up to the hanging cheese above his head and cut a large chunk off. The man in the suit instantly lost his appetite because the big man's body odors were overwhelming; he handed his uneaten plate of food to the man with the knife, who took it eagerly and ate with his fingers, sharing it with the dog. It was then I noticed the dog was tied to his ankle with a dirty rope.

After eating he took another of the carafes of wine and downed it with few noisy gulps. Nobody stopped him and all sighed a sigh of relief when he and his dog sauntered out.

Life went on. Here the artists from Mont Martre came to hang out to discuss their work. Or hoped to peddle their latest creation. Everyone shared. If you had money, you chipped in to buy someone who didn't have any a can of beans or some eggs, or just drank in the atmosphere. I loved the atmosphere, but felt uncomfortable because I could not participate in the conversations, and was becoming a little frustrated. Jacques understood. "Si vou voulez apprande eh perfectionner votre Francais. Il faut necessaire du etre plus possible avec un Francais, moi!" I understood that! If I wanted to learn and perfect my French, it is necessary to be with a Frenchman, him!

The following night we climbed the stairs to the heart of Mont Matre where we ate a wonderful meal at a sidewalk café on the square and where Jacques tried to teach me French in one night, while he practiced his English by telling me a little of the history of Mont Matre.

He explained that the Place du Terte, the little square in which we sat, used to be the village square and early morning market place in the days when the surrounding hills were still farms. And the place where the Sacre Coeur stood was where St. Denise was put to death by guillotine in the third century, when he tried to convert Paris to Christianity. It was then called the Hill of Martyrs (Mont Matre). On the side of the hill, little farm houses sprung up for the farmers in the valley. Later years they became homes to anyone who had the stamina to climb the hill in search of seclusion from the center of Paris that kept on expanding.

It was also cheaper lodgings that attracted writers and artists. Nothing had changed since then except that the hillside became more congested. They started building one over the other, and then devised an easier way to get to the top by adding 290 steps. There was also a winding road from below that they built to take the building material to the top of the hill to build the magnificent Sacre Coeur Basilica in honor of the martyrs, around which grew the present day artist colony. The road is seldom used except for an occasional car, cab, or tour bus that brought visitors to Paris and to the hill.

Some of the artists who turned Mont Matre into legend were Utrillo, Picasso, Gauguin, Van Gogh, and of course Toulouse. One of the farm houses that still stood was the Lapin Agile, the agile rabbit, where these often starving artists gave a painting away for a bowl of soup.

On the days when I didn't have rehearsals I took my sketchbook and headed for Mont Martre where I joined the regular artists who drew the narrow cobbled streets year in and year out, hoping that their mastery would rub off on me. On every corner in the square a color splattered profusion of artists worked. The genuine artists worked on pieces that fed their souls, while the superficial painted the same scene over and over in different colors. To a mirrored perfection, till they could paint it with their eyes shut calling each reproduction an original for their tourist clientele, who not knowing the value of real art bought it with the same closed-eye knowledge in good faith as "absolumo" original, and declared it so when they got home, because the color matched their sofa or curtain. Unaware that their "original" appeared in tasteless homes as well as in mansions scattered across the four corners of the Earth.

While the artists' true originals mildewed in dark rooms to be sold posthumously as legacy to their progeny, they continued to paint the few tried and true, commercialized ones that paid the rent and put food on their tables.

They even dressed the part to impress perspective clientele in paint splattered smocks and berets famous for France. Some hand-to-mouth artists not wanting to prostitute their art painted their masterpieces on the walls of houses facing the dead-end alleys. On a wall of a house near a cul-de-sac, a perfect reproduction of the *Mona Lisa* was framed over with glass. The patron of the house had whitewashed around it for years, claiming it was done by one of the more famous artists. It was surrounded by tourists photographing it with the same enthusiasm, had they permission to do so in the Louvre, while other modern art reproductions did not make it to the first whitewashing.

I resented repetitive drawings. Day after day the same artists sat in the same spot doing the same scene. Like people in an elevator always turn to the door out of habit, and think it strange if someone turned around to face the back wall. I would deliberately turn in the opposite direction and draw, finding the opposite view as beautiful, or even more so than the tried and true. They would walk over to me and ask me why I did that.

"For the same reason I should ask you why you continue to draw the same thing when you have so many options?" I would tell them. But it would irritate me to no end when they asked me what I was drawing, even though my drawings were total realism, and they could see it for themselves if only they looked. The other question from the tourists was, "Are you a famous Artist?" Getting their cameras ready.

And when I answered "No, but I hope to be, someday," They put their cameras away, and said, "Why are you painting then?" It normally warranted no reply. One day a man approached me, looked at my work, and said he worked for the magazine *Noir et Blanc* and because I worked in black and white, he would like to do an article about my work. I was very flattered that he chose me out of all the other black-and-white artists, and saw no harm in it. I did the interview.

The following week, it showed some of my sketches and mentioned that I was currently rehearsing in the Moulin Rouge.

When the Article came out, even though I thought it very innocent, the Moulin reprimanded me severely and told me to read my contract over again. I must have not read the contract very seriously because there it was.

THE ARTIST SHALL NOT APPEAR IN CINEMA OR ANY OTHER MEDIA WITHOUT THE PERMISSION OF THE MANAGEMENT.

I went to management and explained that I did not understand. They let me off with a warning as they said they read the article and there was nothing derogatory about it, in fact was good publicity for the establishment, but to consult them in future, should it happen again.

After the last rehearsal, which normally ended at about two in the morning, Jacques would pick me up for a snack, or if I missed dinner to eat. I never knew where he would take me, because Paris never slept, and you could go to one café or restaurant every day of your life and never run out. One place we regularly went to that served food throughout the night was at Les Halles, the farmers market. I swear it had the best onion soup in the whole of France.

The Place, a small satellite café still had a few vacant tables with chairs left where people did not mind sharing space. It was filled to capacity with very loud tourists and some locals trying to get to know one another through the noise.

We watched the market fill up with farmers in their work clothes bringing in their wares for sale the following morning. The market was alive with sights and sounds. An orchestra of people's voices in a cacophonous harmony. Here was a foreign group trying to outdo one another with their worldly knowledge, shouting to be heard over the din of unloading trucks, and people calling out instructions. The farmer's children who had slept through the day were now awake with play in the floodlights that switched their night to day. They were tossing a cabbage around like a ball, and playing tag among the bags of onions.

Through the din I recognized arguing voices, hysterical voices, anxious voices, affected voices, foreign voices, cooing voices of lovers, and bargaining voices, all blending to make it the showplace of culinary beginnings.

A man walked past carrying a dish full of shaven pigs' heads, peering down at nothing with their dead eyes over the rim. Were the glassy eyes perhaps seeing the milling crowds like we were? Our eyes in turn saw the beauty of the plump red tomatoes carefully stacked into a pyramid that would become magnificent salads complemented by the delicate green of the lettuce that was being tossed from the wagon and deftly caught by someone who turned them into art masterpieces, together with peas in the pod and green beans that would be served across Paris by noon. The pigs' deaf dead ears standing cleanly scrubbed attentively erect looked as if they were listening to the same sounds that we were.

Our onion soup arrived steaming hot in brown earthenware containers. Thick, sweet brown onions were hidden under a crust of cheese that pulled into long spaghetti strings as I spooned the delicious contents into my mouth, drooling with anticipation. While we ate there was a floor show going on of juggling done with vegetables. A man using a flame sharp sword tossed the cabbages up one by one over a big basket deftly snapping the stems off in midair, then catching it before it fell, and tossing it to another man who stacked them into a round pillar. The cabbages would end up in cooking pots of housewives as well as famous restaurants, one served up as common cabbage soup and the other with an exotic name.

In time we would try many of these restaurants, from Le vie Cosshon where all the dishes served took on the form of genitalia. My favorite of course was a thick brown six inch sausage and two golden brown roast potatoes. "The Golden Cockerel" specializing in "Poullet au Creme," and had booths with curtains for the Elite's privacy with black table cloths, crystal and gold plated knives and forks. They also specialized in truffle dishes extraordinaire. Then there was "Tete du Negre" with the best "Trout au blue," pan fried, and a dace-like fish called "Goujon" baked whole, with head and all. Also "Callimari con pitti poivre."

Of course not to forget the world famous Maximes, where the ultra rich met for tea and petit fours. Just to be seen! It is here I couldn't resist riding the stair rails down to see the reaction of the ancient ladies who insisted showing off their furs and hats no matter what the season. It caused quite a stir when the picture ended up in the local newspaper. The picture was a classic with my skirts flying, and three ladies holding onto their hats with shocked faces.

We also went to the Luxembourg Gardens for the plat du jour or for the chefs tournedos with sauce béarnaise and café creme glace (hot coffee with ice cream), and naturally a French custard layered Napoleon.

Jacques kept his word, to show me "The City of Lights." My first impression was anything but lights. It was an old city with gray crumbling walls and ancient cobbled streets; the Roman influence was evident everywhere. With the exception of Les Champs-Elysees that was six cars wide and tarred, at the end of which stood L'Arc de Triomphe (the hub of the wheel).

Etoile, to the first time visitor to the city, looked dirty and gloomy, like an unkempt young girl who saw life too soon, but still retained her girlish innocence.

But to others she was a street woman hiding behind that innocence.

Paris was full of mystery and intrigue with a ratatouille of choices and lust for life. There was something for everyone. For the old and the young, for the perverted and others who preferred different lifestyles. By day the street markets appeared as if by magic, street puppeteers amused the children while parents mingled with the tourists and shopped. Old people sat on the boulevard benches feeding pigeons or looking after their progenies offspring. Everywhere there was evidence of food, artistically displayed on stands. Colorful vendors part of the still life of life, shouted out their wares. Packed on the mountain of ice among seaweed in a trough, crabs moved in numbed macabre slow-motion, ignorant of the boiling pots that awaited them. I tried to help, by pulling them out of the troughs hoping that they would find their way into the sewers and back to the ocean. But moments later they were tossed back onto the ice by a vigilant vendor who sold them to someone who had no other thought in mind but to boil them in garlic and spice for their supper.

Food was an art in Paris, and a celebration of life. When a grand master chef prepared a meal, it was a creation that was worth exhibition and applause, equal to the finest choreographed show. When the chef introduced his dish it was with aplomb, his brainchild to be applauded, admired, and then eaten with reverence to its creator. After an appropriate pause, the chef would then circulate among the gourmands to make a personal appearance for some more accolades. He took his cooking seriously and personally, insult was not even dreamed of, because he believed that failure was impossible. He joked around with his long standing customers, letting them know that behind the stiff formality there beat a warm heart that was capable of the exquisite artistry.

He expected those who came for his creations to admire, drink in the beauty, to savor the smell, enjoy the color combinations, in other words experience the food with their five senses. Never to rush, shove or gobble, and heaven forbid pour extra salt or ketchup on and just EAT IT!

These last five things were frowned upon and lent a punishment equal to execution by guillotine. The insult was unpardonable as the food was literally created by the gods, for the gods, and not for pigs who shove or gobble.

To submit your mouth and tongue to his creations was an honor. To even think of their source, a mortal sin. Take the musty black-brown fungus, the truffle, equal in price and taste to gold. In reality it was dug up from dirty earth by a pig's snout. Or "sweet-breads." Castration of a bull's sex organs? And lambs brains, and veal, the sacrifice of baby animals! And what about the ordinary but gourmet delight the lobster? Plunged head first into boiling water, can you imagine the excruciating death. Science determined with instruments that at the moment of death it emanated a scream that can be picked up in an adjoining room, as infra sound that cannot be heard by the human ear, so we presume that it's death was painless.

I would rather think of bread. And there was a lot to say about bread, because the French believe contrary to the Bible, "that you CAN live by bread alone!" Especially the breads of France. The taste of a fresh crunchy farm loaf molded lovingly by human hands. Bread-making had been passed on from generation to generation from father to son, from mother to daughter, and family to family. With additions to the dough that indeed made it an entire meal, eaten with a flask of wine. Or in its natural form nurtured and kneaded till pliant, then baked in wood ovens with love to be a complement to every meal in every restaurant or just to the ordinary man or woman's pot-au-feu (hot-pot) dunking.

Walking to Mont Martre daily I could smell the warm sweet yeasted dough browning and baking in underground bakeries. The mouth watering aroma wafting up through pavement grates. The artistry to be displayed later in the day in bakery shops, still hot! Round plump loaves cross cut across the top, with crusts curled open at the cut smiling at the world. Braided wreaths with brown leaves and berries baked in dough. Cigar-shaped loaves. Round balls. Triangular loaves with small golden balls on top accentuating. Large round balls with a smaller round ball on top.

Then to top it all there was the enticing, irresistible decadence of the tempting French pastries. To name only a few, fluffy chocolate and custard eclairs, and the king of them all—the Napoleon with crumbly gossamer layers filled with thick custard and a thick layer of white icing crowning it. I would bite into one and the filling would ooze out the sides and onto my chin. Oh and not to speak of the delectable petit fours, tiny two-inch square tea cakes, frosted and decorated with icing-roses or tiny mini leaf wreaths that would tempt even the most serious dieter. But the staple and lifeblood of Paris was still the two-foot long slender French bread. Crunchy on the outside but tender as a kiss on the inside. The world has tried to imitate but never could. The loaves were everywhere. Carried off by the hungry masses. Clipped on the back of bicycles, tucked under armpits, under hats, protruding from back pockets, knapsacks, baby carriages, or tied with string across backs of day laborers, and a bouquet of bread stuffed into shopping bags to be turned by street cafés into subs, stuffed with paté, ham and with smelly cheeses that smelled like weeds crushed under foot and wild flowers that the cows eat to produce the milk that produces the cheese, or the vile smelling Camembert with the distinct smell of sweaty sneakers, but was creamy and delicious if you remembered to pinch your nose shut, at least that was what I did. The stink of musty Roquefort blue streaked with aged perfection smelled like a rose in comparison. Or the gentle Dijon spiced because of the subtle taste. The bread was made for dunking too, because French cooking specialized in gravies. Every Frenchman dunked and sopped up to clean their plate, and tourists discovered and copied.

But it was also eaten au natural, by workers in the fields who simply tore off a chunk and dunked it in a mug of wine for their lunch break.

Wine of France was synonymous with its people, used at the table instead of water. Conjured from the grape. They believed the grape to be a living thing to be nurtured and treated like a woman, with understanding and due respect. Handled with sensitivity and loved with their deepest passion. The trade of wine making was not only a profession, but harbored on being a cult, passed on from generation to generation like its bread making.

Over four million acres of France is used for growing grapes. Burgundy prided itself as the family vineyards. And a yearly festival is held in Darcey dedicated to the wine god. The festival started off by having an old-fashioned foot-stomping incorporating the pickers and their families in the first pressing, making it a happy event. Occasionally they were infiltrated by tourists. Wine produced had exotic names like Chateau-neuf-du-Pape.

As night fell, the other side of Paris emerged. Jacques explained that it changes from Hyde to Jekyll. Or from Good to Bad, whatever one's taste is in entertainment.

It amazed me to see the innocent day stalls disappear, and the shutters behind them lifted to reveal the darker side of the boulevard. Sleazy nightclubs and strip joints appeared in their place, with barkers in uniforms and epaulets that whispered the deep secrets of strange Acts, and other talents of the girls inside, to passers by who cared to listen. Shocked but curious. The whispers promised, She can actually smoke a cigarette with her anus and has such muscle control in her you-know-what that she can squirt water two feet in the air with it! Come in and see for yourself. This usually got them. And in walked the curious to see the strange and amazing things he had just told them, so that they could go back to their country telling stories that would astound people about what the human body was capable of. And they in turn whisper, "Boy and you won't believe what she does with a donkey." I usually hurried away as fast as my feet could carry me, embarrassed about what I had heard.

Jacques whispered in my ear, "Let me go and show you the true Paris."

"Venn avec moi pour un promenade sous les Ponts." To see the lights of Paris by night from the deck of the Bateau Mouche.

Soon the boat purred along the Seine. Jacques leaned up against me by the rail. I thought, *Here I was with a handsome man in Paris and I was not even thinking about Peter and Cape Town.*

It was all so romantic I still had to pinch myself to know that I was really in Paris.

A voice over the intercom announced. "L'Ile de la Cite. Over 2000 years ago a tribe of pagan fishermen lived on this little island. Julius Caesar wrote about them in 53 BC. He called them the Parosii people, and the little island Lutetia. But after Atilla the Hun overran the rest of Gaul and thought the Parisii people were insignificant to spare them, they built a bridge and spread their community to either side of the river. On this very Isle the Notre Dame was begun during the Gothic Revolution under King Louis VII who consolidated his powers at the expense of the feudal lords. Notre Dame with its thick walls was the most impressive structure in the world, an architectural wonder. Against the night sky its lacy stone arches soared, a monument to artists whose mastery of stone masonry supported the cathedral walls long before structural steel. In 1240 the west front was completed and in 1250 the towers. In a few minutes the lights of the cathedral will be turned on. We will stop our engines and turn off all our lights. So have your cameras ready!" As all was engulfed in pitch darkness, Jacques pulled me to him and kissed me. "Mon cheri," the voice interrupted.

"OK all you lovers, don't fall for the old trick that if you kissed in the shadow of Notre Dame, you'll have endless good luck, and don't believe any promises that go with it."

Suddenly the cathedral floodlights bathed the building and its surroundings in a strength that was as bright as day.

"Note the flying buttresses, pointed arches and rib vaulting. As the cathedral grew, revisions grew with it, such as the stain glass windows. The flying buttresses curving between them were added not just as a decoration, but because the cathedral was plagued by high winds. The buttresses absorbed the wind's thrust and were built through trial and error to put it bluntly, and not as calculated engineering. On the facades there are more than

500 figures. The nave took sixteen years to complete, funds coming from merchants of wine, clothing and dyes. The vaults unsupported by modern fortifications rose 139 feet. I implore everyone to make a daytime trip to see it in all its glory."

One of the tourists asked, "Tell us about those ugly figures we saw on every corner when we visited it yesterday?"

The guide replied, "I hate to burst your bubble, but there is no romantic story behind them. These ugly faces called gargoyles were added less than a hundred years ago through necessity. During the restoration of the cathedral when rain water was damming up on the walkways along the spires, something had to be done. A conference was held how to overcome the problem and prevent further water damage to the walls. Everyone agreed that gutters were needed, but would spoil the beauty. It was then that stone carvers were commissioned to come up with an idea how to conduct water away from the walls. They suggested to use the same idea that appeared on fountains all over Europe. So each carver tried to outdo the other. You must have noticed that each grotesque figure was really a water spout, with a distinct characteristic of it's own. But I do hope that you would not just concentrate on those but that you would pay special attention to the magnificent stain glass windows. They trace the genealogy of both Joseph and Mary."

As we left the Grand Dame of Architecture I looked back. *I will always remember this!*

With the floodlights extinguished, the cathedral looked like it floated on the water in the darkness. Paris was indeed the place for lovers.

Every once in a while as we went under the bridges, the boat would switch on a floodlight. Sometimes it would spotlight a homeless person bedding down for the night, who would be startled and curse thinking it was a police boat to arrest him for loitering. But mostly it was lovers, strolling or kissing, and sometimes, on a blanket in compromising positions melting into one. They would quickly switch off the lights. Jacques would take my hand and kiss it and say, "Je teme."

I knew by then that it was a big come on, and tried to explain to him,"But I love someone back home, and will always love him."

He would just laugh. "Je suis la, and he is over there."

He would hold me very close, so close that his desire for me could be felt mounting through his clothing. And I was fully aware of him as he kissed me in the nape of my neck whispering sweet nothings in a most seductive language. At which time I almost forgot my Peter and thought, *I could easily get lost in his arms!*

After the boat trip, we visited the booksellers, and browsed the art exhibits on the bank of the river. Jacques loved to talk, most eloquently, he talked about art books he had read, archeology, travel with such passion that made me want to cry out of frustration trying to follow his conversations. In my time off I frequented the movie houses reading the subtitles so that I could catch the drift of what people were talking about. I wished he had subtittles.

Jacques had a Pygmalion way of teaching me, with repetition and patience.

I would easily get distracted, because he was very attractive. He oozed sexuality from every pore. Sometimes while showing me how to pronounce something he would pout his mouth, and hold my face in his hands to keep my attention focused on the word in question. I tried very hard to concentrate, but it was difficult looking in those deep brown-black eyes, with slightly disheveled black hair that looked like he had just got up out of bed.

I would then dash off to rehearsal and have wild fantasies about him that always turned out to be funny instead of romantic.

Marie was told by Miss D. to understudy me; she wanted to teach her my parts to get to know them on her own. So I was given a 24 hour pass.

Jacques wanted to go and see his parents, so he asked if I would like to accompany him. I had nothing to do, and thought going into the countryside would be a wonderful distraction from the up and coming shows preparations.

He picked me up early the following morning bearing southeast in the direction of Dijon, where we turned off onto a small road shaded by lacy beech and popular trees, past fields where tranquil cattle grazed, being fattened for the market. Most small villages had disappeared, Jacques explained. In 1950 most small farms began to go under and could not support themselves, so they subdivided and parceled off the land, and people moved into the cities, looking for work. He continued. Darcey where his parents lived survived. At least two to three hundred people held onto their properties, including his family. It was near Burgundy. All over there were small holdings that grew grapes for wine making, and it was ripening.

It was near lunch time, so we stopped at a small café for lunch. The menu had solid food with rich sauces, but we chose two dozen escargot each and a salad nicoisse served with the local wine and a baguette. The owner of the place was starved for intelligent conversation, and we became his captive

audience. He told us while serving Jacques the wine, that he no longer made his own vin ordinaire but now got it from one of the other farmers. Then he went on a tangent, and before we left, we knew everything of everyone, because he loved to gossip. We tried to escape, but just as we got ready to go, he had another anecdote or juicy little gossip about people Jacques knew, but I would never know.

By the time we got to the farm it was already late afternoon. Jacques' mom welcomed us into the kitchen. She was a woman of gentle old village charm. Beautiful in her own right. Her dress, obviously homemade, protected by a white apron with hand embroidered flowers around the edges.

The house was well loved, and well lived in. The kitchen was a little too warm due to the good fire going in a big old iron stove, whereon a large pot sat bubbling.

"My mother is famous for her pot-au-feu" Jacques said proudly, and sneaked up behind her, lifting her clean off the floor and swung her around and around. She felt a little embarrassed by his demonstrative behavior, shrugged him playfully off, took the corner of her apron, and lifted the lid off the pot. Steam engulfed her for a second. She stirred it with a large well-worn wooden spoon. Lifted some out and blew it cool, then tasted it. The pot roast smelt strongly of bay leaf and garlic, but the cook knew it needed something more. She pulled a basket filled with fresh vegetables out from under the large old kitchen table, pulled a bunch of carrots from it, Wrung the tops off, and scraped a few more clean, cut them into thick chunks, and pushed it with the spoon directly off the cutting-board into the pot. Then pinched off a piece of thyme hanging on a string from the sideboard and added that too, to the pot. I drank in the smell, remembering Mom's stews.

She said in French, "We grow our own vegetables, and still have a few vines up the hill for our own wine making. And if my husband gets here in time with the cows, we will have milk for our coffee. We have enough milk, enough over for me to make into cloth cheese and yogurt." Jacques translated this while his mother spoke, with the same fire and enthusiasm that his mother used. It was obvious that he adored and admired her.

"Je arrive, cheri!" Through the window I saw a man bringing the cows home, he was talking to them like little children.

"He knows them all by name, but I wish he was a little more careful around my flower beds. Fete attension mon shoo!" she screamed through the window. I noticed the cows had no regard for the small but beautiful little garden that I noticed when we arrived. It had a profusion of colors all thrown together with no evidence of any planning. Yet they grew in total harmony with each other. Like the many characters of the quaint little village. There were dalias, geraniums, sunflowers, daisies, multi-colored peonies, and shy violets and pansies that peeped out from under the dense foliage. But overshadowing the "garden" with its beauty was a peach tree in full blossom leaning up against the stone wall that separated the family dwelling from the back courtyard where the cows entered a long milking shed.

I helped with setting the table. In a short while a man looking like a carbon copy of Jacques only about twenty years older and graying at the temples came in carrying a bucket of milk which he strained and poured into containers and placed into the cold pantry. One earthen ware jug he placed on the dining room table, together with a family-sized carafe of wine.

Although we had a late lunch the pot roast was tender, succulent with thick gravy, just the way I like it dark brown with onion and potato bits floating in it. And lumpy pieces of beef.

Jacques' mom held the large freshly baked farm loaf lovingly against her breast in an earthy way while she cut thick slices from it without cutting herself and passed it impaled on the sharp knife point to each of us without mortally wounding us. Jacques had told them before we came for the visit that I was a showgirl at the Moulin Rouge. They were curious, and a little surprised, but what surprised them most was that I preferred milk instead of wine. And they insisted that I at least take a mouthful just to taste their homemade wine. Just to please them I did. But even the sip went directly to my head. At least that was what I thought, but it really was the company and hospitality that went to my head.

After dinner Jacques and I made our excuses and went for a long walk into the vineyard. His arm around my waist felt comfortable. While we walked he told me the story of his youth on the farm. It was one of those magic nights. The full moon hung low reflecting the bunches of grapes in their transparent fullness. I stumbled for a second and his arms encircled me warmly. It was inevitable that we kissed. It was too easy to respond, his kisses were long and sensuous, our tongues awakening other awareness. He spoke softly, "Je vous couchez avec toi." I knew by the action of his body and the sound of his voice that the words were propositioning. The feeling was definitely mutual with every tongue kiss and every step that took us back to the farm house. When we entered the kitchen his mom spoke to him, which he translated to me.

"She said she fixed up the upstairs room for us." I had heard that the French don't beat around the bush when it came to cohabiting. As long as there were consenting adults, sex to them was as natural as eating. The menu was up to the couple. To them two attractive young people together spelled sexual attraction, so why sneak around, when everyone knew that eventually they would get together.

I felt uncomfortable knowing that his parents knew how I felt. And at the same time wondered, with it being so matter of fact, how many others preceded me. Jacques on the other hand simply thanked his parents, took my hand and lead me upstairs. I climbed the stairs unnatural but with anticipation and excitement mounting.

It was a small room, his at one time. Now the furniture covered two thirds of the room. The big Iron bed dominating everything was covered with a feather quilt that rose like a farm loaf. My overnight bag stood in the center of the room like a sore thumb. The bedroom door stood wide open. He took my hand, planting warm circles with his tongue in my palm, working his way up the inside of my arm, and lifting my dress over my head, he kissed my waist and stomach.

His tongue, gently circling my navel, gave me a foretaste of things to come. It left me feeling faint. I couldn't believe it but at that moment, I was concerned that the door was still standing open. I could barely talk, and instead of words of passion I said, "Ferme le port sil vous plait."

Jacques, expecting words of passion, softly laughed and whispered back in a soft seductive voice, "My sweet, your French is definitely improving, but no one will disturb us, my parents respect our privacy and have gone to bed." He went and closed the door. When he took me in his arms again, my body automatically responded to his every move. There was no denying now that he wanted me as much as I wanted him; the last man that made me feel like this was Peter, and Jacques was right when he told me on the boat that he was here and Peter was far out of reach. Frantically we tore off on another's clothes, barely made it to the bed, our passion exploded into exploration of each other's bodies, hungry for consummation.

Then at fever pitch we melted into each other with sweet abandon, savoring the penetration that slowly built up into hot rhythmic movements. With every responding movement, the bed responded back with a deep creak! But we were so overwhelmed with uncontrollable feelings, that the *CREE CREE* of the old bed fell on deaf ears, and became one with our movement. It didn't stop us. Then in the last throes of passion, as if the old bed no longer could carry the strain, right at the moment of earth-shattering ecstasy and my suppressed scream, it too gave a final *creek* and gave up the ghost, folding in on us with a loud bang!

Shocked into the reality that we actually broke the bed, we lay there in the mess laughing uncontrollably. I put my finger to my mouth signaling Jacques to be quiet, that only made him laugh more. Then we realized that the noise of the creaking during our lovemaking and the collapse of the bed was louder than our laughter, we burst out anew laughing hysterically.

I expected his parents to come up and investigate, but they didn't.

They either were sound sleepers, or were making more noise than we did, or the old house was really sound-proofed. We pulled the mattress down onto the floor, and continued where we had left off, this time a little more aware of noise.

In the morning I surveyed the damage, and felt shy enough to try and wiggle out of going down to breakfast and facing his parents, but he assured me that everything would be fine. They did not ask what happened. So Jacques explained that there had been a small accident.

"The old bed had seen it's days, and it was just not strong enough to support both of us, and finally collapsed, so we pulled the bedding onto the floor and had a very good night's rest."

They looked at us smiled sympathetically, but behind that smile hid the knowledge that they heard every creak, every bump, every whisper, every giggle, every moan, and the uncontrolled laughter. They relived their emotions in our wanton passion. And accepted it simply as "doing what comes naturally."

44
Opening Night Jitters

We were working almost around the clock before the opening, getting only short breaks to eat and take cat-naps. Living only a few blocks from the Moulin Rouge, I gave up an invitation for dinner because I was too tired to eat and just wanted to sleep. I hurried home. When my key turned in the lock, I heard some giggling. There was movement under the blanket on the big double bed. My first thought was that Emily had met a man and was having a romp. I apologized and said I will go and wait in the Lobby. But then from under the blanket, appeared first the head of my roommate and then the face of Jasmine, another girl from the show. They were both naked. I was stunned. I had never expected it. But now I knew why she was so nasty to me. I didn't want to wait in the lobby, so I asked for another room, checked in, and took the key and climbed directly in bed with a wake up call in for two hours.

I did not want to face them, so I moved my things out after the last rehearsal into the new room. It was way past midnight when I finally settled down.

It was a small single room, but cozy with a small balcony at the back that looked out over some artist studios, and a front balcony that looked into the alley where I first arrived and an old fountain that no longer worked. Here an old man lay sleeping on some rumpled newspapers. The front window had a window box where the remnants of some unidentifiable plants still desperately clung to life, in soil that was cracked from drought. I just couldn't

362

go back to sleep until I had helped the poor plants. I loosened the soil with my nailfile and pulverized a few of my vitamin tablets and mixed it into the soil, then wet it. Within a week I was rewarded with green leaves and geraniums. I was happy in my little room.

For the next week there was a lot of activity on and around the stage.

The sets were ready, the master carpenters and set designers were busy making small adjustments. I spent as much time with them as possible. I was envious! Set design was my first choice of career to pursue before fate put me on stage instead of behind it. They did an incredible job. I remembered the cold drafty nights I had spent in the abandoned piano factory where I worked with primitive tools and lighting, putting together my sets. But in the spectacular setting of the Moulin Rouge Cape Town seemed an eternity away!

Off the Champs-Elysees in the heart of Paris the rag trades famous Couturier Houses stood, usually making fashionably custom made clothing for the very rich. These same houses also designed and sewed the costumes for the larger shows like the Lido, Pigalle and the Moulin Rouge.

Weekly we visited the Couturier Mme Vionnet, whose venerable strass work made it's peak in the 1920s and 30s, now made our costumes.

To us in our mid twenties, she seemed ancient, even though she was only sixty-five in 1959. She worked out of the lower floor of an old house, and lived upstairs in her own apartments.

The salon downstairs with stained wallpaper peeling in places from water damage smelled of must, which mingled with other smells of feathers, muslin, taffeta, tulle and starch. The wall damage was covered by giant murals of ancient tapestries that came out of some castle long ago depicting knights on horses and ladies dressed in their finest with wreaths of flowers in their hair.

The windows were draped with thick velvet curtains covered in dust, concealing louvered windows that never let sunlight in.

In the hall stood two suffering palms, reflected in a eight-foot gilded ornamental mirror that filled the entire wall. A maid answered the door when we entered and told us to wait inside for Mme Vionnet. Inside the main room stood a magnificent Renaissance sideboard, with applied gilded ornaments and carvings, applied swags, molded pediments and incised lines.

Scattered over its surface lay water color costume designs, swatches of material and a partially finished head dress, dripping with garlands of strass reflecting like diamonds in the light of a dusty chandelier. There were a few chairs against the wall. They looked very much like the Louis XV I had seen in antique magazines. They could have been sub style because they were covered in new brocade, but I didn't want to be the one who sat on it, and had it collapse under me. So I stood in the middle of the room, where I could do no damage.

The door opened on the left. I saw someone enter the room she walked straight and tall. It was obvious that she tried to keep the boyish figure she had in the twenties. She was dressed in the twenties style in a form-fitted outmoded art deco outfit. That looked like a silent movie stars, reject. I turned fully around to face her. Her lips were deep wine red outlined with a darker lip liner in exaggerated lines, making her mouth hard in contrast to the sun-starved, heavily made up, powdered spook-white face. Her natural brows were completely plucked out. Thin penciled-in, rainbow-arched ones substituted her own, almost two inches higher up, giving her a perpetual look of amazement.

My first impulse was to laugh, but I stifled it graciously with a smile.

She embraced us one by one, kissing us on both cheeks.

"Bon jour, mess enfants," she greeted us, looking us up and down. Then she declared, "As long as there are beautiful bodies, I will be there to dress them." As she went about her business, a heavy cloud of perfume lingered behind her, like a scented ghost where she had just been seconds before. I don't know whether she wanted to cover up the must odor of her environment, or of herself. As she fitted me my eyes downcast traced patterns out of the worn carpet where cut-off multi-colored threads sprouted like grass.

I got through the fittings, choking in perfume and fine feather fluff that spiraled in the air like snow particles.

When I finally got free, I ran down the Champs-Elysees breathing in the fresh air, clearing my lungs of the impurities it had just tolerated in the name of art.

A week later Suzanne the costume director, also chief dresser was arguing with some men who were carrying three large wicker costume baskets across the stage. They were supposed to bring it back stage, but had brazenly brought it in through the foyer. And annoyed at being reprimanded, they dropped the baskets right there and refused to take them up the stairs to the dressing room area, till she apologized. Then and only then, they lugged them

up to the costume room. Here the private dressers unpacked and hung up the costumes in their respective places. The intercom called all to their dressing rooms announcing the costume try-out.

The costumes were spectacular. We had been working with the muslin substitutes for so long that the real thing took my breath away.

Having designed costumes myself I drank in every detail. The material was of the best quality, in comparison to the costumes I wore in the London show, these were fit for a queen. Lame, brocade, velvet, metallic weave, silks, satin, French lace, tulle, chiffon, magnificently embroidered with, pearls, gold thread, feathers, and diamante, so real that they looked and sparkled like diamonds.

Starting from the opening number, "Frou-frou," one by one we were called on to try on the costumes, and just parade in it to accustom us to the weight and feel of it. The two male dressers, Jules and Pierre, assigned to me were fawning over me like mother birds. We also tried on the custom made dancing shoes. A month before plaster casts were made of our feet, and the height of the heel was determined in the day of the lineup. My heels were two and half inches. The shoes were made out of soft pliable leather and satin. Being custom made, they were as comfortable as old worn shoes and as light as a feather.

Whereas most of my headdresses weighed between ten to thirty or forty pounds. The heavier ones had concealed struts that provided stability and took some of the weight off my head. The struts placed the load onto my shoulders, but added even more weight. For weeks I had practiced with the framework but now I was not prepared for the real thing. I tried on the costume I called my pony outfit there wasn't much of it, a brief thong with a large cascade of red and orange feather boas. The towering cylindrical hat was formed around the shape of my head with more feather boas trailing down to the ground. Standing still I was able to balance this, but silently wondered how I was ever going to dance with it. Miss Doris read my mind or thought the same thing, because she put on a tape of my entrance and instructed me to do the dance. I smiled my best stage smile because I knew there were people in the audience who were watching my every move including some reporters who were there to get some candid pre-opening night shots. Moving forward onto the stage was fine, but with every back step the boas swung back, pulling me back with them. I tried my best to keep my balance, found it impossible, and went down without dignity straight onto my fanny.

Suzanne rushed forward and before anyone could say or do anything she trimmed off at least two feet from each of the boas. I tried again and this time they swung like bells but I was able to do the dance and enjoy doing it.

A voice rang out from the audience.

"Damn you, you have ruined my creation! You should teach your dancers balance before you take artistic license with my costumes."

Miss D. pretended to be mad with Suzanne but out of earshot of the designer she said, "Good job!" I couldn't help but feel for the costume designer, because I remembered a few of my designs for *The Gondoliers* in Cape Town being violated because a dressmaker altered them to suit her own taste.

Next came the La Goulue dress with a tight underskirt and hundreds of tulle-frills edged with satin ribbon in different shades of pink that flared out into a train, the bodice beautifully embroidered with gray, black and pink pearls. The hat was the same pink as the dress in a large dish style filled with a cloud of pink tulle on which rested black roses, and around the edge of the dish bird of paradise feathers curled over into the center, anchored with black roses. It was beautiful, but extremely difficult to dance in, so without changing the design, they put a slit in the lining up to my thigh, and I was able to do the moves without losing too much of the choreography. This time Miss D. was unhappy and the dressmaker was smiling.

The next costume was a very wide cape that I used to swirl into intricate patterns. It was aquamarine color, covered in the inside with black lace. The sleeves were in four shades of ostrich feathers, and were very awkward to work with because they flared out, and making the swirling patterns was very difficult because I had nothing to grip it with so they sewed elastic arm bands into the inner seam, and I asked that a rod be added, that I could grip it made working easier. The cape's movements were similar to the moves a bullfighter uses on teasing a bull. Only this cape was ten times larger and heavier, which made me the only person who could handle this heavy costume. I loved working the cape but every time I moved the sleeves, it knocked the feather cone headdress off, so Suzanne sewed a broad flesh colored elastic on that fit under my chin, and a few lead weights at the base of the cape, and it turned out one of my most spectacular numbers, stealing the show.

After all the costumes were tried on and altered, the dressers sorted them into the running order of the show while we had a short rest and coffee and sandwich break. Then the full band arrived and took their places on the band stand behind the moving stages and a drop down gauze curtain where they could not be seen, but could see us, otherwise it would be too distracting for the audience. The break was all too short. We were told we could experiment with our makeup, to get into the routine for the following night's dress rehearsal with a select audience, but that it was optional. So I preferred not to put on makeup, I would have enough of that in the coming year.

For the next few hours, we changed into costume after costume and ran through the routines over and over. Tempers were flaring up like bush fire among the staff, choreographers, scene changers, especially the band for having to repeat things over when they thought it should have been shelved already. To add to the confusion, Suzanne was packing the outgoing show back stage between scene breaks. Some of the costumes were being packed for revamping of our travel company. Others already sold were put into large trunks that would be shipped to far away places like Tokyo and London.

Then the band left, and we did a simple walk through with full costumes so that the lighting could be focused and set.

When all was set and done, dressed in street clothes, we were given the usual "pep" talk, and some cried while others chatted excitedly about the following night. I could only repeat in my mind again *I did it!* as I headed home.

45

Dress Rehearsal Show for the Homeless

I was amazed when I looked through the peephole in the curtain that the place, at least the lower two tiers of the place, was crammed with people.

The preview audience consisted mainly of family and friends of the staff, stage hands and performers. A few select people from the media were also invited to take discreet shots and formulate a pre-show review, then submit it to the management for approval and release to the papers as publicity for the grand opening of the show.

I of course had invited Jacque and his family. As I entered the main dressing room I was delighted to find a small bouquet of wild flowers from their garden at my place, with a note that read "creee-creee." Someone had draped my ceinture de chastity on top of the flowers. This was my London good-luck G-String, a 3x4 inch triangle that covered my private part, and the only thing that offered a bit of dignity between costume changes. I immediately attributed it to Emily and jealousy.

I put it on and slipped my tan nets over it. Picked up my bootsan, the two inch sequin cups that fit over my nipples, then remembered that I had stated in my contract that I would work topless in a number of my stage appearances, and the opening number was one of them. I put them down again and proceeded with putting on my makeup. I did not have to experiment because I had found out in the London show what suited me best. I removed the street makeup with Albolene cream and smoothed the base over my face and neck, blending it well into the skin so as not to make a mask. Next I applied a soft blue on the upper lids to complement my hazel eyes, and gently blotted some of it away, to prevent it looking like a racoon. With a sharp paintbrush, I pulled a thick line above my natural lashes, then glued the stage lashes onto the line, and blended the natural with the artificial with a heavy block mascara. Dipped my brush in again and curved the black line up at the outer corners of my eyes. Then I added white on the inside bottom lid and a small red dot near the tear duct. This little trick under the lights made one's eyes look bigger. Then I outlined my lips slightly bigger than my natural lip line, curving it ever so slightly upward into the corners, then filling it in with stick pillar box red, I dabbed a speck of white in the middle of the lower lip to increase the fullness of the lips.

I was ready, and pulled on the tail part of the costume. I now had a private dresser. He was afraid that I would fall down the stairs with the heavy headdress, so he carried it down and put it on in the cue room back stage where I waited to open the show, which would be followed by a dance group number which would give me time to get into the Can-Can costume in time to do my specialty during the challenge.

The girls were already in costume and were warming up. They were in the new costumes that had wale bone ribs in the bustiers. During the tryouts for alterations, they had complained that the whalebones were stabbing them, but the couturiers put their foot down after the 'mutilation' of some of their costumes the night before, and would not allow them to take the offending whalebones out.

As they warmed up the complaints became even louder:

"I can't do my cartwheels!"

" I can't do my high kicks without being stabbed in the ribs!" It all fell on deaf ears. Miss D. argued with the couturier standing in the wings.

"You have ruined enough of my costumes already, I won't allow it!"

I thought even if they tried to take them out now it was already too late. My cue came up, I gripped the curtain, moving with it as it opened. I could hear them still arguing through my music. As I exited the stage, the Can-Can lineup ran in with their deafening yells. Jules was waiting in the wings with my Can-Can dress for my quick change, when things started happening on stage. Four girls had already fainted and the stage hands were carrying them off.

Miss. D. And Suzanne themselves slit the pockets that contained the whale bones and old Banan pulled them out with a pliers. One of the side acts

filled in while this was happening. We all lined up again, and within minutes the Can-Can was back on stage. With no more strangling whale bones. The Can-Can went on without a hitch. The audience rewarded us with a standing ovation, after having witnessed the fainting earlier on.

A few minor things went on. In the number of the Frog Prince, the showgirls were all exotic birds. I had a five-foot circular feather contraption that had a thousand little lights on hidden in the feathers with the electric box strapped to my back. I was supposed to be a peacock. I was scheduled to enter through an archway in the back but couldn't, so they literally shoved me on from side stage. Every time I kicked my legs up behind, the round frame swung forward and hit me behind the head. As soon as I came off sage the "Scissors Team,"we secretly called them that, remedied it by cutting a "V" out of it at the back so that I could move without it hitting me in the head.

Amazingly we went through the rest of the show with no more mishaps, many of the costumes were altered as we went along because of the remarkable Suzanne, who knew everyone's entrances and got them on stage in time with many a saving stitch; what she couldn't sew she temporarily pinned with safety pins, to sew later. Nothing escaped her eye. She never seemed to tire either as if the show regenerated her energy.

Although the lighting was set the night before, there were still glitches, which were noted by management and then passed on to the lighting director, amid a loud denial. We tried not to notice the nervous pacing both in the lighting box, back stage staff, and the nervous fingernail biting as the choreographers watched from the sidelines.

The band was overwhelming. Mr. R. Cursed under his breath at the individuals who missed a step or cue. Sometimes the directors got in the way of the performers or the stage hands setting up. And Suzanne stepped in and told them in no uncertain terms that they were getting in the way.

In spite of the little mistakes, the audience gave us a wonderful ovation. But then they were prejudiced, they were friends and families.

They asked for autographs, and congratulated everyone. Jacques wanted to take me out on the town, but we had received direct orders not to accept, and I had to graciously decline.

When the backstage visitors left, Miss. D. called a meeting on stage.

We hurriedly dressed and dragged ourselves on stage. To be met by the full staff. With everything that went wrong that night we expected the worst. But never what followed. Miss D. looked serious: "Everyone into your rehearsal leotards, with a few more rehearsals, we might just make the opening." All the faces dropped.

Then she burst out laughing. "Formidable mess enfants. There's only a few little things to iron out, but we fix." She motioned to some caterers to come, and they walked in with silver trays and a veritable feast. "After you've eaten, go home, there won't be a rehearsal tomorrow morning, you can sleep in, but we expect you here at 5 p.m. We have one more invited audience for tomorrow's matinee before the opening." A sigh of relief went through all of us; we were dead on our feet. I felt sorry for the production staff, who were invited to share the eats with us but then had to stay. At the stage entrance Jacques waited patiently for me. His parents had gone home. I thanked him for the flowers and asked for a rain check for the dinner. I told him about the surprise catering. He walked me home.

Sleeping in was a luxury! I took full advantage of it, waking at midday. I ate the fruit and sandwich I bought on my way home, took a leisurely bath and was the first to arrive at the Moulin. There was a lineup that stretched around the block, it was indeed a SPECIAL audience. I pushed my way through the line and entered into the stage entrance. Inside the tables were set each with a bottle of champagne, and on each place a bag of foodstuff. I learned that a thousand free tickets were handed out to this very special audience.

My jaw simply dropped when I came on stage. This time I wore my "bootsan" as requested by Suzanne out of respect for the nature of our audience.

Just as well, in the first row sat about twenty-five priests in full robes, who had accompanied the people from the old-age homes.

The whole of the two layers of the inner circle was crammed full of groups of the elderly from old age homes, and the homeless from under the Bridges of Paris, and the subway bums and the bag ladies! All smiling broadly with heavenly toothless smiles, waving and whistling, with thunderous applause for each number. Some drank directly from the bottle because the glasses were too slow. They were by far the most appreciative audience we have ever seen. The eyes of the priests were popping at the grandeur of the costumes, or lack there of. Tears were flowing from the eyes of the less fortunate, when they looked at the food gift bags provided by the owners. Even though I had on my fixed stage smile, there were also tears in my eyes for those same reasons. We had our first standing ovation when the show was over.

On my way back to the Hotel I passed the Metro Pigalle.

Because of the hot air rising from the underground, this was a favorite sleeping place for *le monde pauvre*. There on the steps sat the usual motley group, feet wrapped in rags, each with their bundle of worldly possessions, ready to retire for the night. These were the ones who didn't make it into the show. On the first level between steps stood one of the ladies who did make it to the show. She was giving them a detailed description of everything she saw.

She had gathered up some of the broken feathers in the hall after the show, and had one in her hair and the other stuck in the back of her dress. I stopped and watched. She pulled her dress up as high as modesty allowed and did a mighty fine rendition of the Can-Can, followed by a showgirl, which she exaggerated with a lot of added wiggles. Her audience, enjoying her performance, were laughing, forgetting their troubles for once. I went across the street to an all night *tabac*, got some food and a couple of bottles of wine and went back where her show had acquired more ladies who joined in with a line up and some high kicks of their own. When there was a pause, I applauded and handed out the food and wine. The star was so happy that she kissed me on both cheeks. Next I found myself swamped with hugs. She had recognized me, from my back flips and asked me to perform one for them.

So I pulled up my dress and did a few high kicks and a full back-flip. That sealed our friendship. Some nights they would leave their bundles and carry my makeup case and see me safely home. They told anyone who wanted to listen that I was their ami from the Moulin Rouge. Basking in the shadow of my fame.

46

The Goldfinger Number and I Refuse a Date With Elvis

Someone once said: "Nudity is only indecent if indecency is the intention." In the following number it certainly proved it. It was one of the numbers borrowed from several old movies.

This one was supposed to be set in America. On a long platform stood all the tall buildings, mimicking the skyline of New York. This was really girls dressed in blue body stockings with golden buildings on their heads. They stood unmoving. The lighting focused on the buildings alone.

Behind them I stood unmoving on a high pedestal, painted gold from head to toe, in gold chiffon drapes, representing the Statue of Liberty spotlighted behind a blue net backdrop. In front of the net, on stage two a street scene took place. The setting was supposed to be Central Park. People were homeward bound or just standing around talking. A ballerina danced across the stage her shoes slung over her shoulder. Against a lamp post a lady of the night was plying her trade to some sailors. One sailor wanted to go with her but the others were trying to pull him away from her, resulting in a tug of war.

A clock struck 12 midnight. Slowly the crowds dispersed. Now buildings, trees, and fountains—all nude people in frozen poses, came alive and started dancing. Then the spotlight fell on me, coming alive, walking down on a staircase of clouds. The gauze curtain went up, and I descended onto the stage, removing the drapes around me, throwing away the book and torch. By the time I got to the lower stage, I was totally naked except for a gold G-string glued with rubber cement just above the hairline of my crotch and up between my buttocks so as not to show an elastic band. This was my only insurance of decency between me and the audience as I performed a very classic dance among the "buildings."

The gold number was a sensation. It seemed simple but there was a lot of preparation to be done preceding its presentation. All the men envied my dresser, a young man in his thirties. He had the job of painting me, and afterward scrubbing the paint off me. For the paint mixed with glycerin he applied with his bare hands to go on evenly, so as not to cause streaking. This was where the decency came in.

To him painting a showgirl gold was as much a job as was getting me into my costumes, and strapping on the halters and electric boxes that went with them. He ignored the remarks because he took his job seriously. I had more trouble emanating from the band. After I was painted and blown dry I waited in the cue room till the blue gauze curtain dropped then took my place on the pedestal situated in the center of the orchestra. The idea was as soon as the spotlight hit me to stay as still as a statue. It was a little embarrassing because I had my gold painted naked bottom practically in the face of the orchestra leader's face.

Mr. Renay took full advantage of the situation to amuse the orchestra, making kissy, kissy noises behind me. He tried all kinds of things to make me move, but the worst was one night when he stuck a feather between my buttocks after I had already removed the drape; the audience luckily could not see what was happening. I tried to release the feather by pinching the cheeks together to dislodge it, and this amused the band to no end; they had made bets whether I would be able to release the feather before descending. Then just before I reached the audience they graciously removed it.

The gold number also poisoned me. Suzanne usually bought the plastic gold powder at a theatrical supply shop, which was then mixed with glycerin. This time we had nearly run out of it so she sent my dresser to go and buy some. He had no idea where to go but he came back with a gold powder that looked somewhat similar, and painted me as usual.

A few days later I started having nausea, and started vomiting. I knew I wasn't pregnant, and became very worried. Usually when he scrubbed me with a soft brush after the tableau to get me ready for the next number, The water ran clear but this water turned green, sometimes leaving a greenish tint on my skin.

When I blew my nose it was green. My urine was green! I knew I was being poisoned, but this time I couldn't blame Emily. I knew milk was supposed to counteract poison, so just to be on the safe side I started drinking gallons of milk. But I also took a sample of urine to a chemist for analysis. He said I had metal poisoning and ordered the number stopped. But it was too late to substitute the number, so they painted me with glycerin and threw gold sprinkles over me till the real thing could be found. My dresser had gone to an art supplier and got metallic gold paint.

I knew I was over it when all my body functions no longer turned green. And the Moulin Rouge was happy because it was one of their best production numbers, drawing Americans in particular.

I had no qualms about the nudity, or the topless numbers as I never expected any of my relatives to ever turn up in Paris. But one night in the middle of my "gold" dance I looked down into the audience and there at the first table sat my beloved Aunt Cielie who had made my trip to London a reality. She had gone to visit my cousin in London and heard the whole story of my "good fortune" of getting the French contract, and flew over to see me. I knew she was very broad minded, but I wondered how she would react to my topless appearances and the gold number in particular. So I sent a note inviting her backstage.

She was thrilled to visit me backstage, and swore secrecy not to tell my father and sister who knew I was in showbiz but was not aware what I really was doing. With that reassurance the worry was out of the way, and I spent the following day happily showing her Paris.

Before she left she said, "I never told you what I thought about your performance. You were great on stage, but my favorite was still the girl in the gold paint." I didn't know if she didn't recognize me naked or was pulling my leg about "the girl" and left it at that.

The gold number stayed in for the rest of the season. The biggest problem was always to get the paint dry before I got draped on stage. I usually dried it standing in front of a fan to speed up the drying process, and Jules or Pierre would wave a towel over my body while I waited in the cue room before taking my position. Then rush off to get my next costume ready. Usually if I wasn't dry yet they would toss the towel to anyone who was waiting in the cue room.

No one was allowed to go into the "inner circle" unless their cue was coming up soon, or they had permission from management. Usually only a celebrity or a personal guest of management had that privilege.

This particular night there was a lot of excitement backstage. In the warmup room there was a bunch of strange men. Everyone seemed to pay them extra attention, and they loved the fuss made over them. All I could make out was "Where is he?"

I wasn't paying much attention, concentrating on getting myself dry.

It was dark in the cue room. I could make someone out in the darkness. There stood a man. My dresser tossed the towel to the man, mistaking him for a stagehand.

"What do I do with this?" the man asked. There was a familiar ring to his voice, but I just couldn't place where I had heard it before.

"You are supposed to wave it to dry my paint." Then he stepped forward and started waving the towel. It was then I recognized it was Elvis Presley himself.

"What do I say to a naked lady? And a beautiful gold one at that?" he whispered.

"Well I would start with hello for a start," I replied.

Just then the Colonel appeared. "Boy, you got to get me HER autograph." He handed Elvis his little black book. I took Elvis's pinkie, dipped it into my navel where the paint was still wet, and wrote "LOVE RAMONA." The Colonel then rushed out to show the rest of his "guys"' in the warmup room his book.

While I was being draped for my appearance, he told me he was hiding there in the dark because he felt sad, going back to America for the anniversary of his mother's death whom he loved very much, and to arrange for the schooling of a young girl he met in Germany and wanted to take back to America. There was a deep sadness in his eyes. I wished him well. He was more handsome than I had ever dreamt him to be with his dark hair and deep blue eyes. His whole group stayed for the rest of the show and the Colonel tried to persuade Andre to arrange for a date with Elvis and me after the show. When Andre spoke to me about it, I told Andre that Elvis had told me he just wanted to rest. And I refused. The girls all thought I was crazy to refuse a date with Elvis. And I tried in vain to explain that he was a different person beneath that veneer. Not long after that I read an article that he brought a young schoolgirl to live in Graceland, promising her father he would look after her till she was old enough for him to marry her.

We were well into the third month of the new show when I insulted a pornographer and nearly paid with my life. At the close of the show three of us living at the Stephen's Hotel walked home together, believing there was safety in numbers.

Paris was under the attack from the Liberation Army. The streets were overrun by some very unsavory characters who had very little respect for women, and much less for life. They were indistinguishable from the rest of Paris's inhabitants, who were made up of all nations.

Perhaps their mission in Paris accounted for their unsavory behavior. Several car bombings had already occurred, including one tossed into an all-night café near where we lived. The Fille de la Nuit had had their fill of the riffraff manhandling them, but they also found it amusing when these low downs walked straight up to us showgirls on our way home, and grabbed at our crutches and breasts for a change, then as we turned around they slapped our bottoms, all to show their disrespect. So they were glad that they left them alone for a while the L.A. were comparing us to their own women who were covered from head to toe, if and when they were allowed to go outside their homes.

It got so bad that I would hold my steel makeup case in front of me when I saw them approach, and then covered my behind with the case when they passed. Sometimes one of the girls would take a swipe at them. This usually brought about a belly laugh from the "Ladies of the Night."

That particular night, we were happily walking along discussing the events of the show. There were no tormentors in sight, and we deemed ourselves lucky.

Out of nowhere a man approached me. He was different; he was missing a leg and used crutches to walk. He was bitter at losing a leg in one of their bomb attacks and had an even meaner demeanor than our usual tormentors. He was cursing a stream in what I presumed to be Arabic because that was where they were from, we were told.

We were about two blocks from the hotel. One of the girls ran home, while the other one stepped behind me, expecting me to deal with the situation.

The man had a framed picture in his hand. At first I felt sorry for him, perhaps I had jumped to conclusions and he was not one of them, but a drifter who was begging for money for a meal, or it was a picture of his family back home and he wanted to show it to get sympathy. I smiled and waved him away with a friendly gesture, which worked at times.

But my smile turned to a frown when he suddenly grabbed me by my collar in a stranglehold. His breath reeked of cheap booze. I knew I was in trouble when he shoved the picture in my face. "You like?" I was shocked. It was a pornographic picture of a girl having sex with a donkey! The girl clinging to my back somehow thought the picture funny because she started laughing. This made him angry. I tried to shove him away. He wobbled a bit but held onto my collar.

"Take the filthy thing away!" I shouted, trying to pry his hand off my collar. He let go and hit me with his fist. It sideswiped my temple, and burned like hell. That's when I hit him with my steel makeup case. The picture dropped from his hand and the glass shattered into a million pieces on the pavement. This angered him even more and he took another swipe at me. This time I ducked in time. Some of the prostitutes had left their beat and gathered around us, their body language indicating that they detested this character. "COSHON! Sallo!"they were screaming at him. At the same time they were egging me on to fight back. When he lunged forward again, I hit him full force over the head with my steel makeup case.

He staggered and fell back, landing on his bottom, his ego hurt more than the bump on his head. By now quite a curious crowd had gathered. I had hoped a policeman would come, but there were no police in sight. A cheer went up from the bystanders, and the "ladies" pointed at him, laughing and jeering. That's when we ran. Looking back, I saw him waving the crutch and then made a slit throat signal. Cold shivers ran down my back. *What if he does come after me?* I thought.

The whole incident had an unfortunate repercussion sooner than I thought.

The following night I was invited to dinner in Montmartre by some people who had seen the show and came to see me backstage. I accepted and made an appointment. I was early for my appointment and I slowly ascended the two hundred and ninety steps to the top of Montmartre.

On either side of the steps the windows of the houses were already lit, people were moving around preparing their evening meal before stepping out on the town. I was happily anticipating my own meal as the savory smells wafted out at me. I had no thoughts of danger, nor did I think about the previous night's encounter with the one-legged man. Several people pushed past me in a race against themselves, determined to reach the top in one go, huffing and puffing with a lot of teasing and good humor.

The quaint old-fashioned street lamps on each landing cast a yellow glow over everything, painting everything into a memory picture of charm and romance, erasing the possibility that there in the dark spots, evil might lurk.

My hosts were so entertaining and the dinner so pleasant that I almost forgot that it was a show night and had to be at the Moulin for makeup call at nine, remembering, anything over would impose a stiff fine. So I hastily bid my hosts good night and thanked them for the lovely dinner. Because I was in a hurry to get back, I refused their offer to walk me down the stairs.

I started my descent with two steps at a time, but was soon winded. On the second terrace I noticed something peculiar. Most of the lamps that were on when I arrived were now out. Here all the houses too were in darkness. What a time to have a blackout! I thought. I could hardly see where I was going, so I slowed down my pace. I would rather be late and pay a fine, than fall down the steps and break my neck.

I became aware of shuffling footsteps behind me. I was not alone in this predicament, someone else was also inconvenienced by the blackout. But it seemed strange that every time I stopped the footsteps also stopped. The scene that seemed so romantic earlier on suddenly had a very threatening appearance.

Where had everyone suddenly disappeared to? There were no sounds in the houses, everything seemed in a deadly silence. Except the footsteps behind me. My heart started pounding, someone was stalking me. Then I tried to rationalize it and relaxed for a moment. But why hadn't the person passed me by now? If they wanted to rob or rape me, surely if I screamed someone would come to my aid, with houses on either side of the steps.

On the next terrace I stopped; whoever was behind me had to pass or attack. I steeled myself and turned to see if I could see anyone, but like a stalking animal he was on me, grabbing me from behind by my hair. I sank to my knees to unbalance him and throw him over my back. It always worked in defense classes. Instead of throwing him off balance I stumbled, and as I pulled away I saw a bloody handful of blonde hair in his hand.

My God! He has scalped me! I thought as I felt my head. His kick landed full in my stomach, knocking me down. I was stunned for a moment. He straddled me, pinning my arms down with his knees. Blow after blow rained down on me. Dull *whop* sounds fell on my breasts and stomach, somehow sparing my face, as if he was saving that for something special. Like a vice his hands were round my throat, his nails dug into the flesh. Flashes of my father's strong hands strangling the leopard came to my mind. I couldn't breathe! " GOD HELP ME!" I shouted. This wasn't Africa, this was Paris.

A trickle of blood ran from my scalp into my eye. I had to get his hands off my throat before I blacked out. I couldn't move my hands. But my legs were still free. Kneeling over me, I had a target. I pulled my knee up sharply from behind him and it caught him full force in the balls. It had the effect I hoped for.

He let go of my neck and grabbed to where he hurt. I broke free and ran down the remaining stairs. Now it first dawned on me to scream for help. "HELP! HELP!" I screamed. But no one came to help. So I stumbled down the last set of steps.

I also noticed that here all the lamp lights were on. Tourists were wandering about. I ran up to a policeman and rambled on in English about the attack on me, but he simply shooed me away. It was understandable; this was the boulevard they always filmed on and where there were street fights between the prostitutes and their pimps. And there were street performers, and fire eaters, and occasionally a café explosion.

BUT COULDN'T THEY SEE THE DIFFERENCE? I had blood on my face and hair, and had just fought for my life. They ignored me. I ran screaming into the stage entrance and fainted in the doorway. Mr. R. and a doorman carried me inside. The house doctor checked me out and gave me a shot to calm me down. While I was telling them what happened, the makeup artist came and patched up the bruises. The doctor said I was fit to go on stage, and he would remain there throughout the show to check me out again. I couldn't believe that they actually wanted me to go on with the show after my terrible ordeal.

By the time I came off stage after the first production, there were at least a half a dozen plainclothes police to take my statement in detail, and they asked the description of my attacker, and whether I knew him. One even spoke English. I recognized one as the one who shooed me away on the boulevard.

"Where were you all when I ran to you for help?"

The one who spoke English said the officer didn't know I was working in the Moulin Rouge, as if not knowing that excused him from helping me on the street.

"You ran away so fast that I couldn't help you."

I told him about the previous night, and the man with the crutch. How his ego must have been so wounded that he contracted someone to go after me for revenge.

"Well we now have a good description, and we should be able to make an arrest soon." But it never happened!

For the following weeks the fingermarks on my neck and the body bruises turned blue then brown then green, hidden by body paint. And I struggled to forget about the physical violation. I thanked the police who escorted me home, and even pointed out the man with the crutches. But no arrests were made and no charges brought against the man whom I suspected orchestrated my attack. But I did change my route home, and always kept a lookout for either of the men. But they had disappeared, and I resumed my old routines.

47

Blood and Lace Tragedy

A new hair-care product called Le Oreal approached the Moulin Rouge to do a promotional spectacular for them. They agreed and it was put in the hands of Andre to select the person who would do it. Andre suggested to them that I had the sage presence and the long hair required, without even consulting me. I was insulted and flattered at the same time and also apprehensive about what the hair care product would require. I did not want my hair cut.

All I got from Andre was, "Not to worry, they told me all they want to do was build a swan on your head, made from your hair." I thought he was making up the story. Then later I found out what it was all about. It was a spectacular that would also involve the Paris City Ballet and eight Dior models. The making of the swan and the show would be televised and I would get double pay.

The dress I was to wear was used by Grace Kelly in a movie called *The Swan*. It had come all the way from the Movie Archives in America. It was magnificent, consisting of two hundred yards of lace and tulle layers with a twenty-foot billowing stole.

As Jules slipped the hoop petticoat over my head, he said: "You can be proud to wear it. Did you know you had the same measurements as Grace Kelly and the same height, so they did not have to alter it?"

The Oreal Spectacular was scheduled for one time only. There were only two rehearsals scheduled with costume because of the exorbitant price of the dress, and the salaries of the Dior Models who were paid by the hour.

The first time we rehearsed with substitute props till the throne I was to sit on was made. On the day before the presentation we had a full cast call. Myself, six eight-year-old boys, twenty young ballerinas from the Paris Ballet, and the eight Dior Fashion models. Before the rehearsal started the children were warned about the glass stage coming up from the pit, and also of the railing that came up around the pit; they listened intently, but their curiosity overcame the warning.

Down in the pit the men had already set up the steel troughs that held the dry ice to make the mist, and poured in the water. They left the pit area so that we could try it out with the Oreal cast. I stepped onto the glass stage. The mist was already rising.

At the same time the railing shot up around the opening. One of the young ballerinas leaning over to see the dress I was wearing was caught off balance, knocking her tumbling twenty feet down into the pit. On landing her jaw was caught on the corner of the metal trough, cutting her almost from ear to ear. She looked as if she was decapitated. Blood gushed out of the gaping hole beneath her chin. I could see the shock in her eyes, pleading for me to help. I was the only one in the pit.

The steam issuing from the troughs had already started to spread across the glass stage. I tried to get to her, but the floor was as slippery as ice. On top of that I was aware of the terribly expensive dress I had on. But I was also aware that if I didn't do anything soon, she would drown in her own blood. I flipped up the dress and its layered hooped petticoats behind me, and crawled over to her. She was conscious, so I tried to assure her. I took her head in both of my hands and tried to hold the gaping hole together under her chin. The warm blood bubbled into my hands, staining the white satin gloves crimson instantly.

The band had sensed the danger and stopped playing. The engineer then turned the stage on, sending it slowly up; there was more danger in reversing it because someone had called emergency and they were already waiting on the upper level. The stage took an eternity rising. I could hear screaming and crying coming from her companions above staring at the drama below them. They were leaning over the rails; I was just waiting for another accident to happen. By now she had passed out, but I knew she was still alive, because I could feel a faint pulse beneath my fingers. With my knee I propped her up, her head hung heavy in my hands. Tilting her head back, I heard a gurgling sound—she would choke in the blood. So I immediately tilted it forward. It amazed me at the amount of blood. I sighed a sigh of relief when competent medical help took over. Everyone was in shock, but it also amazed me at how quickly the concern switched to the dress and the stage. I was on the verge of passing out myself.

But my dresser acted quickly and pulled the bloody gloves off, and deftly lifted the cloud of dress and petticoats over my head carefully, not to let it trail in the blood that stood like a pool on the glass stage. I half expected them to cancel the rest of the rehearsal, but "the show must go on" rang true.

"You can have a fifteen minute break while the stage is cleaned up and reset," came over the loudspeaker.

The accident irritated the Dior Models, mumbling that the whole thing was a monetary loss to them. They were standoffish and demanded star treatment and a separate dressing room. Suzanne told them they could have a section of the general dressing room and that was that.

The morning of the show, a limo called for me at the hotel. The whole process of building the swan out of my hair was to be televised. It would take four to six hours they told me to transform my waist-length hair into the multi-colored hair sculpture. Doing it on TV was the advanced advertising for the presentation at the Moulin Rouge that night.

One of the gofers went to get me some breakfast, and I was given an explanation of the procedure then the cameras started rolling.

First all the color was removed from my hair. Then it was divided into eight sections, to which all eight colors of the new product Le Oreal was added, then he tied them with elastic bands, and back combing each piece, he added a hat-wire armature, around which he started sculpting a beautiful swan. He knotted, teased and sprayed, and slowly there emerged the body and slender neck, of the swan, with spread wings drifting on a rainbow of waves. I had seen the elaborate fourteenth century hairstyles where they even built birdcages into the hair in a book somewhere. But this creation was on MY head, and I wondered how I would be able to dance with it on my head.

When it was done, I practiced walking with it. I had worked with heavy headdresses before, and was able to take them off to alleviate the pressure. But this was my own hair. With a gallon of hair spray, a factory of hairpins and a swan fortified with hat-wires protruding at least a foot-and-a-half to either side of my head.

If I could walk with it, I would be able to dance with it on my head. We stopped for light lunch and when I went to sit down again, I stumbled. At least ten hands grabbed at me to steady me. Not out of concern for me, but rather for the precious sculpture on my head. It would have been a disaster if everything had to be done over again.

It was already sundown when the creation was ready and the filming was over. *Ah, I would have a few hours before show time,* I thought. I was exhausted but they couldn't risk taking me home. I was dropped off at the Moulin. I couldn't lay down to rest, so I propped my sculptured head against my dressing room mirror, and actually fell asleep, to be awoken by my dresser whispering "Show time" in my ear. The models were already in the dressing room. They were white, gaunt, and absolutely anorexic. I actually thought that some of them were trans-dressers; they were totally flat chested from the constant starving.

Opposite them the show girls looked like buxom wenches. Their boyish figures did not impress me, they were just too bony. Perhaps that was why they insisted having a separate dressing-room, they were ashamed to undress in front of us.

My dresser carried the dress down into the pit, where I stepped into it.

I wouldn't have been able to do it otherwise with the hair sculpture. As the dim light of the glass stage went on, I had a flashback of the tragic accident that took place a few days ago and wondered what happened to the little ballerina. I recognized the last strains of *Swan Lake*. The ballet above us on stage two was about over. The troughs had already been watered and the steam was drifting slowly up. I was helped onto the stage, and the ballet slippers I was wearing were slipping and sliding. I asked my dresser to remove them. I would be able to dance better with my bare feet. The size of the dress would cover it. As we reached the audience level, the steam was already flowing into the audience. Under the billowing clouds I waltzed slowly in circles. The audience saw a beautiful swan swimming in the clouds, then as the stage leveled with the audience and the steam drifted softly down. There was a gasp of astonishment; the blue light had changed to phosphorescent white to accent the dress, and a spontaneous applause greeted me, as they discovered there was a living girl dancing beneath the swan. I headed for the magnificent red velvet and gold throne I was supposed to sit on for the fashion show to follow. Millions of flickering lights danced through the audience onto the swirling steam, people reached out to try and catch the little lights. Through the clouds of flickering lights the little boys appeared dressed in little lord Font le Roy suits carrying gold candelabrums with red candles putting them onto the tables surrounding the sage, then went to either side of the stage, each one returning with a model wearing magnificent gowns that matched the Le Oreal color they wore in their hair, which matched the eight colors in my hair sculpture. When all the colors were presented, the little ballerinas came on wearing tutus in the same colors and danced on the upper stage while we descended into the pit.

The audience was still applauding while the big stage closed up over our heads. It took nearly two hours just to dismantle the sculpture with the help of my dressers. Several of the knots had to be cut out, making my hair shorter in front and long at the back. It didn't look too bad when it was finally brushed out, and they promised to color it back to my own color. And my scalp felt raw for the next few weeks, and it was agony putting on my wigs and headdresses.

48
Trapped Between Two Stages

Not long after the accident, it seemed the glass stage took revenge.

During the first act, eight of us were waiting in the pit to have the mechanized five-foot windmills strapped onto our backs. We were rushing to change, but there was still time because we took our cue from the upper stage to moving back. Then we heard a strange rumbling noise. We thought nothing of it, even joked that old Banan had again forgotten to oil the upper stage's tracks. Our cue was coming up, so we put on the plumed hats and stepped onto the glass hydraulic stage to take up our positions. The dressers and stage hands left the pit to prepare the costumes and props for the next number. Only the engineer remained to set the stage in motion.

We were on our own awaiting the tableau above us to come to an end. Their music stopped. And ours began. This was also our signal to stop our giggling and chatting, because soon the top stage would slide back and we would come into view of the audience. Our music started, and we could hear the soft purr of the glass stage as it slowly rose up. We helped one another to switch on the windmill boxes, that would start the blades revolving. Then we heard the same rumbling we had heard earlier on, only this time it was much louder.

Then for a heart-stopping moment we realized the big wooden stage above our heads was not moving, and we were still going up.

It was stuck! The engineer was trying desperately to reverse the glass stage. But being synchronized, it just wouldn't descend. We had three more minutes before we would be crushed. We had to act fast, but it seemed that I was the only one who responded to crises; the others all went to the center and huddled together screaming. I took stock of the possibilities. Around the perimeter of the glass stage there was only a two-foot gap. We could jump down, but we were already half way up, and no one could jump the 15 feet to the ground and not get hurt. The other alternative was to lie down on the glass stage like sardines between the 18-inch rafters that protruded from the stage above us. The engineer was shouting from below, "JUMP! I will catch you!" That was totally out of the question. So I decided on the cross-beams rafters that were about three feet apart.

I quickly instructed the girls to lay down on their stomachs head to toe and unbuckle their electric boxes and windmills and headdresses and throw them down to the engineer, that also meant to remove the corselets in which the battery packs and wires were sewn, leaving us only in our G-strings. They calmed down from screaming when they realized this was their only salvation. We were all showgirls and the biggest hard structure on the skeleton was the pelvic bone and the head, which when laying flat measured between 9 to 10 inches in thickness at the most. It would be a tight squeeze but we would be alive!

In the meantime, the engineer had rushed upstairs and informed everyone of what was going on. Our music had stopped and the band together with some men from the audience were trying to move the top stage manually out of the way with little success; the only thing they could manage was a three-foot gap, into which they wedged some chairs—that would give us some added head space.

Above us we could hear the buzzing of voices, and some screaming coming from the audience, knowing we were on our way up and would soon be crushed. The girls lying in place dressed only in their G-strings and stockings were shocked into silence, except for Emily the redhead, who suffered from claustrophobia. She was praying aloud. Most of them had turned over onto their stomachs so as not to see the impact, which was now about three feet away if the chairs held. We would have to act lightning fast. I instructed the girls not to crowd one another but crawl as quick as they could two by two toward the opening made by the wedged chairs. The house lights were full on and there was an overabundance of helping hands, pulling them to safety. It was like giving birth to octuplets. With each one surfacing, a cheer went up out of the audience. I was the last to get out, seconds before the chairs holding the space open splintered and the glass stage crunched into the wooden beams beneath the top stage. We were so glad to be alive that there was no modesty as we made our way through the audience, clad only in our G-strings.

Everyone was eager to shake our hands., whispering their admiration and encouragement. Management announced: "There will be a brief intermission, and the SHOW WILL GO ON, except for the number canceled by the breakdown of glass stage."

Backstage there was concern for us, and amazement at our calm as we put on our next costumes and our best stage smiles, and went on stage, on cue, completing the entire show on the top stage.

After the finale, there was thunderous applause, and a standing ovation, with numerous curtain calls.

When we left about forty minutes later, we were amazed to see throngs of people lined up at the stage door exit, to hug and kiss us, and again shake our hands.

The following night the management was concerned that the interruption in the shows routine would affect the attendance, but the opposite was true. It was also strange that nothing was mentioned in the media. But it was obvious that the people who saw it the previous night had spread the word. They themselves had come to bring flowers, which were all over in our dressing room. The place was packed to see where and how the miracle of our escape with death had taken place. The mechanics of the two stages had been repaired, and there was no damage to our windmills which were caught instead of us, and the show went on in its entirety. There was only one small hitch, which was not noticeable. Our hearts beat wildly as we rose out of the pit, remembering our fear of the previous night as we rose to our doom.

49
Casino Beirut —World Opening

"Nothing that ever happens later ever equals the first time." This rang true in the next few months.

Rumor had it that the company would be split into two groups. One group would be going to Marrakech and the other to the World opening in Beirut in the Middle East. I went to the library and looked up both places, but there was very little written about both places, and that which I found was very outdated. It showed camels, palm trees, women in black shrouds with only their eyes showing, and men with beards and wild eyes wearing pajamas. It was situated on a crook of an arm to the right of Egypt on the Mediterranean Sea between Israel and Turkey and Iran and Iraq to the north. It was even spelled differently. "Beirut, Capital of Lebanon, Land of Bible History." I couldn't in my wildest dreams imagine or place a nude revue in both those settings. None of us could get any further information.

When we asked Miss Doris, our ballet mistress, she said: "When the time comes we'll tell you all you want to know, and you will know who would be chosen, and learn more; just watch the bulletin board."

A week later I noticed a news clipping that wasn't there before.

"WORLD INAUGURATION OF SPECTACULAR CASINO IN THE MIDDLE EAST. Nestled in the mountains of Mameltein, ten miles from Central Beirut, the spectacular Lido Casino is situated, equal to Monaco in splendor. It's foundations resting on the mountainside, with a waterfall two

393

hundred feet in length, cascading into blue glass lined fountains. The Egyptian motif pillars are covered in blue one-inch mirrored tiles. The surrounding gardens and nature walks, when completed, will stretch for two miles surrounding the buildings which not only houses the casino but has a hair salon, dress shops, jewelers, florists and beauticians. To this beautiful place comes the full cast of the Moulin Rouge with its beautiful girls to perform for the inauguration of the largest casino opening in the northern hemisphere.

"The celebrity guest list includes Princess Grace of Monaco, who will open the Casino, and 400 invited dignitaries and movie stars from America and all over the world, plus a contingent of world press will be there to meet them. A ten-mile long fireworks display is planned to light up the night sky on opening night."

It went on to describe our ballet and the fleet of airlines hired to transport costumes and sets, promising the show to be the event of the century.

Suddenly things did not look so bleak as it looked before, and I reckoned that the place could not be so backward if all that was planned sounded so modern and spectacular. We were taking part of the Paris show and would have two months to add some other productions.

Excitement grew by the day. The group who had previously gone to Marrakech were hoping to go back there to renew old love affairs and make new friends, and mainly they knew they would not have to rehearse a new show or add to the one we already knew.

I had been to neither place, but secretly hoped that I could go to Beirut. It was within reach of the Holy land and places from the Bible I had always dreamt of visiting. I remember sitting in the Mimosa Gardens in Pretoria, where I dreamt of those "far away places," and I started to hum the song over and over again, "Those far away places, with the strange sounding names, are calling, calling me … They call me a dreamer, and maybe I am … But I know what I'm yearning to see, those far away places with the strange sounding names, are calling, calling me …" in the dressing room till the girls started bribing me with my favorite chocolate-covered cherries to stop. But it was catching and soon they too were humming it.

On the night the list appeared, we rushed over like eager school girls to the bulletin board to see if our names were there. Some of the girls were not on either list. They were disappointed and we were sorry for them, because we knew it meant their contracts were dropped and they would be going home.

There were two lists. The M and the B list. We all knew what it meant because we all had our secret dreams. There were shouts of joy as our dreams were realized. And there were tears when they were on the wrong list. My maiden name started with an A, so there I was at the top of the Beirut list.

At the bottom of the list there was a notice; "B-troupe will meet after tonight's show for a briefing about foreign protocol, and information about Beirut and when the new rehearsals will start." M troupe could go home, with a reminder that regular rules and routines still applied, with the show still in residence. The pressure was on.

Like sheep going to the slaughter, the chosen assembled after the show. Our hearts were pounding with anticipation of the new adventure.

Miss Doris did not beat around the bush.

"We have two months in Paris to work and four more weeks there, to work the show up into world showcase caliber. We also have that much time to shape ourselves up. Each girl and boy will be given an additional 400 new Francs on their paychecks from this week on. Use it wisely. Go to a spa, go on a diet, have your hair color changed, get a nose job, fix your teeth. The M.R is willing to pay for other additional plastic surgery where necessary." We all laughed (and later found out two girls had actually asked for booby implants, one for ankle slimming, and one for a tushie tuck).

Eight girls were selected in alphabetical order, to be the first off the plane.

"Their clothes will be provided by the Moulin Rouge, and they are asked to comply with the choices made for them. As there is no time to waste, rehearsals on the new numbers will start tomorrow, at the usual rehearsal scheduled times.

"As far as which numbers will stay in there was a long deliberation, and it was decided that the Afro Cuban number will stay, with a few changes, such as costumes for the underwater tank. At this very moment a tank is being installed in the casino, and we will be able to rehearse the changes for that number the last four weeks before the Beirut opening. 'Frou-frou' satin and lace stay as well as the Can-Can, of course. And a larger finale in pink is planned to match the magnificence of the cascade of fireworks. All this will mean frayed nerves and fatigue, and of course hard work. If you are not well enough or not prepared to accept this, then I ask you to decline now because there would be no time later to find replacements for you.

"The contracts will be issued when you leave the facility tonight. For your convenience it is given in your own spoken language, so that here could not be a misunderstanding. Because of the urgency to arrange visas, accommodation, etc., you are urged to read it tonight and bring it back tomorrow, or a signed letter if you cannot go through with it. Now in closing, I want to tell you that you can be proud, you have been specially chosen for this world premier."

When I got home I decided to leave the contract till morning, but my curiosity got the better of me and I read:

Article 1. The direction has the right to suspend the artist for 4 days without pay if the artist does not comply with the rules and regulations as set forth.

Article 2. In case of the shows interruption due to war, revolution, epidemics, dual national conflicts, religious wars, or any other catastrophies making it necessary to close the establishment, the artist will be paid for the time of the performance up to then, and not the full nine month's contract. In that case also the return ticket to the point of departure Paris will be honored.

Article 3. The artist will travel with the group, unless other arrangements have been made, for which the artist is responsible, also for the insurance of said arrangements.

Article 4. The artist should at all times conform to the instructions given by the director of the ballet, namely Miss Doris of the Doris Girls Ballet and Choreographers and the establishment that employs them. Regulations and clauses of the contract should be respected.

Article 5. Written authorization should be obtained from the Doris Girls Director, who would use discretion for agreement, should the artist be presented on cinema, television, photo sessions for magazine or news media other than for the purpose of the Moulin Rouge. The artist should not engage in any display of his or her talent, in any other establishment other than that contracted for,

night or day, professional or private, paid or unpaid.

Article 6. Any injuries incurred in private or in public under direction orders, will be reimbursed immediately after the injury occurs. However, if the injury is caused through self abuse by suicide, drugs, rock climbing, skiing or water skiing while under contract or during rehearsals, or professional obligations, it will NOT BE compensated.

Article 7. BE IT KNOWN it is strictly forbidden to:

1. Eat, drink, or smoke in the costumes, or near the costumes where they are hung.

2. To sit in your costume other than the tights.

3. To leave the theater in any costume or any jewelry or accessory thereof, including shoes.

4. The artist is responsible for replacing, shoes, costumes and accessories to their proper places at the end of the show before leaving the premises, unless a private dresser is assigned to the artist for that specific purpose.

Article 8. For sanitary purposes, the artist is responsible for furnishing two of each "cas crout" (2x4-inch G-strings) in the following colors: black, white, and flesh tone. Upkeep and laundering will be done by the artist. Rehearsal tights will be supplied by direction, and laundered ballet slippers for rehearsal will be supplied as well. No private rehearsal gear will be allowed, and no excuses tolerated. Hair during rehearsals will be in a ponytail, or in the head covering supplied. During the show, hair will be secured inside a stocking cap, for protection of wigs and head pieces. (We used to first put our hair into pin curls under the stocking caps, so that we at least looked respectable when we were going out after the show, so this was added.)

Article 9. The artist must present him/herself in private, at the scene and on stage dressed and made up, and combed in an impeccable manner. In this regard the direction reserves the right to impose a change of makeup, nail polish, lipstick that has to match at all times. Clothes and color of hair, etc., to present a proper representation of the show.

Discretion rests on the artist at all times not to disgrace the FAME and CHARACTER and HISTORY of the establishment.

Article 10. In case of illness, a doctor certificate is required. Failing to do so with at least 8 hours notice to replace the scene or the performer, the Doris Girls Ballet Director will have the right to replace indefinitely the artist with the understudy without obligations.

Article 11. The direction reserves the right to prolong or terminate 15 day notice of contract according to the all-over performance for the duration as stipulated on the original engagement.

Article 12. By signing Article 19, the signer takes all the clauses herein as a reconcilable between the two parties.

Article 13. The artist agrees with this contract to travel to all countries under the direction of Doris Girls where the engagement leads.

Article 14. If in the course of 14 days after the debut of the show, the artist does not satisfy management by conduct, or just wants to leave,

will not be compensated as herewith agreed.

Article 15. Passports, visas and work permits are the responsibility of the artist. (Here Mr. Andre was always so wonderful and got all our passports, visas and papers ready in time.)

Article 16. The management agrees to pay for 20 kilos of luggage, no matter where the engagement takes place. All supplements is considered the artists expense except for a makeup case and reasonable pocketbook. No other carry-on will be allowed. The Doris Moulin Rouge labels will be visible on all luggage, except personal handbags.

Article 17. If the artist does not respect all the clauses as set forth in this contract it will be understood that he/she waves the tour and all indemnities and compensations. Before the tour starts the management could therefore fire the artist before the month of grace is up, or as the situation justifies.

Article 18. Clothing, conduct, of religious observances, for all countries visited will be complied with and respected. In services for observation and restrictions will be held to assure compliance.

Article 19. I the signer agrees to respect and uphold as set forth, etc.,etc. ...

I signed hoping that they would not find fault with me, because the rehearsals would be 90 days duration. I was also very careful not to offend or break any of the rules ("AS SET FORTH"), and the day before the full tour started a full contract was given to the ones who were found faultless. I WAS ONE OF THEM!

50

I Become One of the Beautiful People

We had eight weeks of solid night and day rehearsals. Plus costume fittings, and photo calls. I felt bruised and my muscles felt tortured. I also wondered when I would ever again have a full night's sleep, without muscle spasms.

Then the miracle happened! We were given two whole weeks off to recuperate before leaving for Beirut.

Being indoors for some time, I decided to get an even tan all over so that I didn't have to apply body makeup, because I was ivory white, and during the Afro Cuban numbers I was always obliged to put on body makeup.

Together with some of the other girls we had followed up on the address at the foot of the bulletin, and gone to the solarium on the Champs-Elysees where we could sunbathe in the buff. It was a private enterprise by someone who saw the possibilities and took advantage of it.

The solarium was simply the entire rooftop of a building. It was enclosed with a reed fence all around, and furnished with chaise lounges on an incline, otherwise it was nondescript. In the corners there were some artificial potted palms. When we checked in, we were given a small plaque with a number that corresponded with one of the chaise lounges. Here we lay down in our birthday suits or wore one of our "cras coutes." Like sunflowers following the sun, we were tended by a bevy of Adonis beautiful gay men with ludicrous looking plastic watering cans painted with flower motifs. The reason for this

I couldn't fathom, all that came to mind was that the owners of the solarium must have thought employing gay men would prevent hankie-panky and scandal. Somewhat like the eunuchs guarding the ladies of the harem.

The young man that watered me was pure perfection, equal to the David statue in Florence. I found it amusing that he was actually paid a salary to walk around the sundeck watering the creme de la creme of showgirls from the Novelle Eve, Follies Bergere, Crazy Horse and the Moulin Rouge.

Some of the watering boys preferred to wear a flowered jock strap to go with their little watering cans. On the other hand, Mr. Magnificence, aware of his godly body, wore only a gold chain around his slender waist with a timer on to make sure that the "live flower" he was tending was turned every 15 minutes. His own perfection demanded only perfection.

Few lady tourists ever turned up; they didn't mind the admission price of roughly twelve American dollars. But they did not shed their clothes; to be compared to the showgirls was too steep a price. So they lay on the chaise in the broiling sun, staring at Nicco's magnificent manhood which was a prize indeed, but to us women, *What a waste!* He made his money from catering to the male tourists. If the tip was big enough he would get them past the concierge for a peek at the showgirls. This too was a source of amusement to us.

To get past the concierge, the tourists had to pose as nudists and had to remove all their clothing. The variety of pot bellies and family jewels were amazing. I had an insight what was usually hidden behind candy striped suits of conservatism. Here the pot bellies could look to their hearts' content at all the girls, but could not touch. Or look at the "boys" for comparison if they so chose.

Nudity never phased me because I was young and proud of my body, and they were simply having fun. And had a story to tell back home.

By the second week I had a beautiful brown even tan. When Miss D. saw it she approved. Because the day of departure for the Middle East was only days away.

When the morning arrived, I couldn't see why we were asked to be in half stage makeup. It was three in the morning. I could not sleep with the elaborate hairstyle they had given me, but I liked the soft golden color. I could hardly see through my eyes to paste the thick mink eyelashes on, but carefully applied the stick makeup on, not as heavy as for stage, but strong enough should there be publicity shots.

I had complied with everything up till then that was asked of me. But I was not going to wear the dress presented to me, even if it was designed by a very well known designer—it was just too florally and full of bows and stuff. I decided to wear an ivory tube dress that flattered my figure, and matched the coat and designer shoes.

Our luggage had to be in front of the Moulin Rouge at four a.m. I was one of the first ones to arrive. One by one the others arrived, looking like one of the fashion shows we did in Milan. While underneath the beautiful clothing there were tired people wearing deceptive stage smiles for everyone pointing a camera in their direction. They were right about the stage makeup. When we reached Orley Airport, the media was there in full force, so were the curious and fans to see us off.

The cameras started whirring and flashes popping. We were the BEAUTIFUL people, and we belonged to the media. We went through the usual posing on luggage carts with porters. And a fair amount of solo pin-up poses showing just enough leg not to look cheap, with the photographers demanding to see "more." We gave them just a little more, but with Article 9 fresh in our minds.

"Discretion rests on the artist at all times, not to disgrace the fame and character of the establishment."

What an incredible entourage. Two chartered Douglas Super DC6s, stood on the tarmac, with "Kelig-Arc Spotlights" focused on them. Behind them were two freight planes to carry the orchestra's instruments, scenery, and costumes. Some of the orchestra and the dressers and staff decided to travel with the accessories. While we would go with the newly pressurized four engine planes with all the comforts of home. Or as Andre told us: "Un voyage dans le meilleures conditions de confort vous est assure." We posed a little more going up the steps. Then finally we were inside. As I had sailed from South Africa, and sailed from England to France, this was my official first flight, so needless to say I was apprehensive. When we were finally seated, I sighed a sigh of relief. Perhaps I could rest. But instead we got a lecture on the dress code. Not to expose too much skin, definitely no spaghetti straps or too tight fitting clothes. (My entire wardrobe consisted of that.)

And then came a suggestion how to handle the media on the other side. We were warned not to be too revealing because everything we say would also hit the Arabic newspapers, and how to answer questions put to us by world press and television.

We would arrive in Beirut between 6 and 7 p.m. the following night, which they said would give us plenty of time to rest up. Miss Doris suggested that we get into our rehearsal tights. We thought she was totally out of her mind, we couldn't possibly rehearse inside the plane. But she explained it would save our clothes from becoming wrinkled, and we would be more comfortable. It was a strange suggestion, but soon everyone had changed. Ours was a chartered plane exclusively for the Moulin Rouge so there were no stopovers or pickups of the general public.

We were all so excited that we dosed off in shifts. I just couldn't sleep sitting up, and was worried about disrupting my elaborate hair style. I was told not to worry as we were carrying our own hairstylist and makeup artist with us to do the necessary repairs before we landed.

After dinner that night we were told that the plane doors would not open till we are ready to descend, and then we would exit the plane in the groups. Alphabetically selected, six at a time. Pose in the doorway for 15 seconds, then descend the stairs halfway and pose till all six are out, leave a distance of two feet at all times between each girl. Then with the police escort we would be taken across the tarmac into a preselected area, where there would be a press conference when everyone was out of the two planes and assembled in the VIP lounge. After which a fleet of limos would take us to the Palm Beach hotel. For the first month, we would have a private suite with a partner. Where there would be a banquet in our honor and another press and media invite to do private interviews. After the briefing we were told to get some rest, and they would alert us when to get dressed.

My surname being "A" I was told I would be the first to exit the plane. I had never really had stage fright but now I felt a strange fear.

Two hours before our descent we were told to get dressed. And soon we all looked showgirl perfect. My heart was threatening to jump out of my throat. Miss Doris was walking up and down the aisle trying to keep everyone calm.

"REMEMBER! No matter what happens SMILE! And please sign those autographs!"

Some distance from the landing strip we could see at least eight giant search lights crisscrossing the sky. Then on the approach in the whole airport was brightly lit up like daylight. The earth looked like it was moving. Beirut, with a population of more than a half million inhabitants, was there to greet us on our arrival. We circled for a while before descending.

As we descended there were loudspeakers welcoming us.

And a radio message over the internal intercom inside the plane with a message of welcome, and informing officials would board the planes to process our passports, then the doors would remain closed for another half an hour, and we would then exit the plane according to our briefing.

As our planes were taxiing in, we could see thousands of people, on either side of the length of the runway. At the appointed place the planes stopped. Here there was a circle of strobe lights placed around the planes.

While the makeup artist and hairdresser fussed with my hair I could see a mile-long police line, their arms interlocked trying to hold back the wildly cheering and milling crowd. I put on the magnificent golden mink coat while the air hostess opened the door. I could hear the thump as the steps locked up against the side, allowing the officials to enter. They immediately started processing us. I forgot for a moment the crowds outside, praying that the human barricade of police would hold. I vaguely remembered Doris saying:

"Remember, you're first out, keep calm, this is world press! SMILE!"

After the officials left, we got into position, Andre counted 15 seconds and shouted above the din of the crowd, when a spotlight illuminated the exit door, "Met Na! Sorrier, Et Bon Chance!" Now! Go! And Good Luck!

I stepped outside onto the steps, smiling broadly. My knees felt like they were knocking together. Flood lights hit me full on and at the same time about 20 flashlights popped simultaneously. I was totally blinded, but still smiling as I felt my way down, trying to remember to keep two steps between me and Mr. R.'s girlfriend stunning in a full Geisha outfit with her jet black hair in matching hairstyle and apple blossoms. Behind her followed Emily in a leopard skin coat and pill box on her flaming red hair. Each girl that followed drew the same gasps from the crowds as I received when I made my appearance, because each was stunning in their own right.

Just as our group took position on the stairs for the last pose, waiting for our police escort to take us in. The people broke through the police barrier, rushed toward us, thrusting scraps of paper, magazines, and newspaper articles to us to sign. Those who supplied a pen I signed. Then they lost control and started pushing. Suddenly I felt myself being lifted up into the air, above the people's heads. I was shocked into silence. Slowly I was passed hand over hand along. Every now and then my human conveyor belt paused for me to sign some autographs.. I signed laying horizontally on a sea of hands. Every time I signed one a cheer went up among the crowd. In the sea of human hands some were gentle and some were rough, taking advantage of my body as I was at their mercy.

When they finally set me down, my hair was loose, my shoes had disappeared. Luckily our hand luggage and luggage would be delivered to the hotel. We were swept up into a vacant hangar.

Now the police turned up in droves to man crowd control because the people were trying to get into the hangar.

Andre kept us there in the shed till things calmed down. Gone was the VIP lounge and orderly press conference. They were moving it to the Palm Beach Hotel downtown. People outside were literally climbing the walls to take a look at us and there were random interviews at our discretion. Later when we got to the hotel it was going on eleven o'clock. Andre handed out our keys to our suites, we freshened up and went to meet the press. Our reception was a little more orderly. The members of the press who couldn't get to the airport was there. They got their stories for the morning paper, and they hung around just long enough to partake in the elaborate food feast. By one a.m. Big Brother Andre sent us all to bed, including the media, who found it very amusing. And it rounded off their day with yet another story, that the Moulin Rouge was just a big old caring family. Then rushed off to get their pictures and stories in.

Exhausted we went to bed, only after consulting the makeshift bulletin board. That announced our 8 a.m. rehearsal pickup to go to the casino.

In the morning, there were two school busses at the back of the hotel to pick us up. School busses were chosen because it would indicate transportation of children. And we would be safer. There were two Jeeps, one on either side of the bus, full of soldiers with heavy machine guns. The soldiers were something we did not anticipate, and at first we thought it was some sort of publicity stunt. They looked so serious that they made us laugh. Andre became very angry, and explained to us that what was happening was no joke. There had been some religious skirmishes right after our arrival, and we were in danger. The army did not want to take a chance that the bus would be bombed. He ordered us to stay low in our seats and if some shooting occurred we should get down on the floor. The possibility existed that we would run into people who either objected to show business or our religious affiliations. After the generous turnout at the airport and being carried by the crowds, we thought it ridiculous. But not so, because when we got to the casino we were told that there had been random shots fired by snipers, and that we better remain indoors.

The casino was as impressive as the newspaper descriptions. But when we got into the show hall, there was raw concrete everywhere. The stages were up and functioning, as well as the tank, but the dressing rooms were not yet ready, so they erected a drip sheet in the corner for us to change into rehearsal leotards. They cleared away some of the building materials from an area where the concrete floors were already covered in deep royal blue plush carpet. This was to be our resting area.

We worked deep into the night, with the builders and decorators working around us over time to finish off the building for the opening set for four weeks after our arrival. Some nights we did not go home, working repeatedly on difficult numbers, catching little catnaps between scenes. Food and drink were brought to us, but sometimes we were just too tired to eat.

Miraculously the show fell into place, so did everything else. On the last week before opening, the exterior and interior became completely transformed. With all the furnishings and trim in place, it was all too glorious.

We only had to test the underwater tank, and learn the secrets of which flowers hid the oxygen pipes, which made it possible to the amazement of the audience for us to stay submerged for the entire twenty minutes the number was on. We were using the ankle length water nymph wigs from Paris, which were giving us trouble by hooking onto the waterlily ankle bracelets. These wigs were sent out to be dyed black for the Afro Cuban sacrificial number in the tank. Men dressed like ogres carried us above their heads and sacrificed us into the water. The show had gone smoothly and we rehearsed the number minus the water to get the feel of the routine. Then they put the water in. And it was decided that the ones working in the tank would stay for two nights, and they supplied us with pillows and blankets so that we did not lose travel time.

The wigs looked beautiful. So did the giant flowers inside the tank. A run through was ordered. Easy! Done—we already knew the number with the dry runs. Everything went fine. Till we got to the part where the witch doctors carried us to the water and threw us in.

Suddenly the whole tank clouded over like some giant octopus squirting black ink. We could not locate the breathing tanks, and totally disoriented struggled against the glass to get to the top, where we were hoisted out. The wrong dye was used on the wigs, so the color came out with contact of the water. What a production to empty the thousand gallons of water, scrub the tank and the flowers and plants, clean and redo the wigs—this time with the right waterproof dye. It came out easily out of everything except it left streaks on our bodies that was very hard to scrub off.

The following night we had a full dress rehearsal for the builders, decorators casino staff, and their families. This time "the tank" and the show were a great success, and we knew we were ready.

We had a few days to rest up. I read all the brochures in the hotel lobby, which boasted about some of the oldest and most magnificent ruins in the world. It was still hard to believe that we were actually in the land of milk and honey. Some of the names I recognized came directly out of the Bible. I planned to visit each one of them while in Beirut. Biblos, Baalbeck, Sidon, the Cedars of Lebanon. The emblem on the Lebanese Flag showed a Cedar tree. The people were very proud that Solomon's wood for his temple came from their mountains.

It was a land of history, legend, poetry, art and recreation. There was the ocean to bathe in, and an hour away up the mountains with spectacular views, there was snow and skiing. And then there was the Wadi El Hani, the birthplace of my favorite poet and philosopher Kahlil Gibran. And of course the Holy Land Israel, and legendary Bagdad just around the border. So much to see and do!

But first there was the inauguration. Everyone had first night jitters. Not because we were unsure of the show, but who we were doing it for.

Every few minutes we were at the peephole to see the celebrities arrive. It was unbelievable but everyone the papers said would come were there in the flesh. Everyone that is but the one I was expecting to see there, Yul Brynner.

The show was at peak performance. We made it to the finale when the massive curtains that surrounded the hall slowly opened onto the most spectacular fireworks I had ever seen. It stretched for ten miles down the valley. We froze in our tracks and the band stopped as the audience ignored us, stood up, and headed for the ceiling high glass windows to watch the fireworks. Their eyes riveted on the pink cascade of fireworks that fell from the roof like a waterfall, blending in with miles and miles of fireworks displays bursting out of the side of the mountain from as far away as Beirut itself, reflecting in the mirror calm of the ocean. It went on for over an hour, one display more spectacular than the previous one. It was a little premature because this glorious spectacle was supposed to start AFTER the finale was over. When the fireworks FINALLY died down, our music started up again and we completed the show with our pink finale, sure that it would be an anti-climax to the incredible sight they had just seen. Instead there was a standing ovation and applause that seemed to go on and on forever—the show was indeed world caliber!

The stage party was a closed affair in the casino. I was amazed by the catering Beirut style, and the magnificent display of the clothes from all over the world. I wore my skin tight floor length white crepe. Its simplicity paled in the spectacular dresses of the rest of the showgirls who were not going to be outdone by movie stars and royalty.

My biggest thrill came when an Arab prince asked me to show him how to do the jitterbug. It was a show in itself, with his robes and head scarf flying all over the place.

The following night my dressing room was flooded with flowers. A note attached read "One night with you for $30,000 is all I want." It was from the prince I danced with. I was shocked. I thought the dance was for his enjoyment only, but all he wanted was to buy my favors. And I felt insulted.

"Take it," the other girls said. I couldn't believe that they were serious.

I told them, "Over my dead body. "Besides, have you read your contract recently?"

He was in the audience again with his whole entourage. I sent a message to him. "Thank you for the dance and the flowers, but I'm not for sale." It did not stop him because the offer did not stop with me. One of the girls did take up on his offer with bad results. Some of the other girls also took other men up on their offers, and even bragged about it.

One of the girls received a gold nugget from a sheik. "Now I can put my kid through college and it only cost me an hour." But it also cost her VD. No one reported them. They thought the payoff was punishment enough. Because a few more were guilty of giving, and receiving favors to put it mildly.

The men in the Middle East had a very strange idea of morality. There were two classifications for women. The pure, and the slut. "Artistes" on stage had no category. They were being touched and screwed, yet classed as untouchable in their own moral code.

The ones considered pure were their own women who covered themselves from head to toe, showing no flesh. They were obedient to their fathers and subordinates to their husbands, they did not touch anything that was masculine except for procreation purposes, they seldom left their homes. They would never drive a man's vehicle or have a job—that was considered for men only. If they didn't obey they were severely punished.

The ones considered sluts were foreign women, movie stars, and showgirls who showed bare shoulders, necks and faces, and even legs and whole bodies on the beaches and on a stage. To the local males they were the lowest of the low. They were not worthy of respect, therefore they could be bought, jostled, molested, and spat on. Yet it did not stop them from looking and even touching.

Now I understood the roving hands on our arrival. I also understood why I was almost run over on the first day, because I wore a sun dress with spaghetti straps.

But WE soon found out that there were two kinds of men. The men who treated women with no respect. And the well educated, well traveled men that showered women with attention. Their families also considered show people elite and invited us to dine at their homes. We never lacked socialization. Hobnobbing with everyone who was someone.

As promised, the first month at the hotel was paid by the Moulin Rouge, and then half of the tab was picked up for two more months if we chose to stay on. But to me the hotel became too busy a place. I did not drink, nor liked parties, and there was a party almost every night. Not being a party animal, and hating being on display all the time because the media was always out for "another story," I started putting my feelers out at the casino for an apartment. One night during dinner, the Italian maitre d' at the casino approached me having heard I was looking for an apartment. He said it was up against the mountain in Mameltein, two miles from the casino, with a glorious view of the ocean and the mountains. He had an apartment there; unfortunately the vacant one was unfurnished, but fortunately it had a stove and fridge, and he just happened to have an extra bed I could have. The little village nearby made quite nice rattan furniture and also grass mats for the floor. I paid him in full.

The following day I hailed a cabby that looked desperate and moved my luggage over to the apartment were I was pleasantly surprised in that it was quite modern. The scenery was fantastic from my porch I could see the ocean to the far horizon. Below me there was a pine forest and large boulders against the mountain. On the right the road winding like a snake up to the casino met up with the road coming from Damascus and Syria. And below the forest a colorful Bedouin Camp had their tents up, with some goats grazing up toward the boulders. I was pleased, we would be in Beirut for nine months and then return to Paris for a European tour, and talks of eventually going to South America and then America. I could be happy here. I planned to explore the mountain above me and do some drawing and painting if I could find some art materials. I was so busy fantasizing that I had clean forgotten the cabby waiting to be paid. The driver was very humbled by the big tip I gave him, and when I asked him to pick me up the following day to go and get supplies and buy some furniture, he was all too willing.

He was very prompt the following day, and it impressed me. I bought groceries to stock up the kitchen, and asked him what he needed. He told me, and couldn't believe it when I bought it for him. We then went and bought cloth for curtains and a table and chairs, and bed linen, and he helped me move it into the apartment. I asked him back again, and after several more trips to Jouni, the place looked quite respectable with room sized grass mats, potted plants and my newly acquired rattan furniture. The cabby had always come when I asked him to, but now I needed transportation to get to the casino nightly. So I asked him what he earned a month. To him it was a lot, but to me it was a mere pittance. I tripled it and he became my exclusive driver, taking me back and forth from the show. The other drivers were jealous, because there were so many of them, that some days they didn't even get any business.

He not only picked me up for the Casino but he arrived weekly at my apartment for my weekly shopping trip into the villages of Jouni or Beyrouth. On those days he was well rewarded with extras. Out of courtesy he always refused, and then on my insistence he would eventually accept.

He never spoke about his private life, so I never asked, but when I found out that he had a wife and several children, I thought it would be a nice gesture to ask them to the show. He had never seen a spectacular. This was the highlight of his working for me when I gave him front row seats to the show for him and his family with dinner and the works. Something a poor taxi driver could never afford. The low point came when I had to let him go; it wasn't that his services were bad, but because I had come into some good fortune, and with a two week rest period coming up I had big plans. So I spoke to the maitre d'. He said he would gladly take him over till I needed him again.

Twice a month the showgirls were allowed to go into the casino. The locals had the strange idea that because we were showgirls and employed there we had the inside information as to what will win. To dispel that myth we were told to keep a low profile while in the casino. We also had to dress formal with full makeup, which meant I would bring evening clothes with me to change into as I usually just wore day clothes. The myth started when men wanting to be seen with the showgirls approached them for numbers. Often those men won and passed the word around, "You can't lose if a girl gives you the number."

Usually I would only watch for a while and then leave because the moment I entered I was swamped with offers, "To come and have a drink." I did not drink so it became very annoying, and I had to stay cordial for the show's sake.

Sometimes a rich undesirable would latch onto me, asking me what numbers to play, or what winning number was coming up. Sometimes out of pure devilment I would tell them a number that "was a sure thing" just to get rid of them. I never stopped long enough to see the results, because I certainly wasn't a psychic, nor even a gambler. Because I never made a bet myself.

Beginners LUCK. One night, I decided to give this gambling thing a try. I would take $20 and if that was gone I would leave. So I went to the money changer and got a hand-full of chips. My card playing wasn't up to par, because my arithmetic was poor. On the roulette tables people simply put chips on a number or on a color or across a corner or a thing called "Banque" that let it ride. So I took a chance and put ten of my chips on a number. I was amazed when it came up and the groupier called out. "Numoro, tres, payee 36!" He shoveled everything off and shoved 36 times the ten that I had put on the number three. I put it in my bucket.

Soon I was getting daring and placed it on several positions at once on the table.

As the chips came rolling in someone said "beginners luck" but then suddenly my bucket started emptying out. I was back to my original $20. I should go! But the gambling devil whispered in my ear "Put half on this table and the other half on table number 2." I put one chip on "Banque," and switched over to table two and put the rest on table two. What I didn't see was a man leaning over table one, and move the Bank Chip over into 0. So when they called out zero I didn't care. I was doing very well on table two.

Twice I had to go and cash in my bucket. But now I had a distraction. That same annoying man who moved the chip to 0 kept coming over to me. I had noticed him watching me at table one, but ignored him because they warned us about the table "Sharks" who watched every move of the rookies, and if one made a mistake they honed in on the mistake, often claiming the winnings for themselves.

"Where do you want me to put the chips now?" he asked, every few minutes. I was so engrossed in my own game's winning that I would just answer to get him off my back.

"Put ten on 4," I would say.

"It did it! What now?"

I was about to leave so I said, "Put everything on thirty-six."

Both my buckets were full again and I decided if it was indeed "beginners luck," it was time for me to cash in and leave. I could hear the little man in the background shout "WE WON! We Won!"Before I reached the check out, the little man caught up with me, tapped me on the shoulder, and said, "I just want to give you your winnings!"

"What winnings?" I asked, surprised.

"I was the one who picked up your chip and placed it onto 0. And just when I wanted to change it back to Banque, it came up, so I felt guilty and continued to play the numbers you gave me, and it really belongs to you because I didn't have any money to start with. It was my first time, I only came to look because we are expecting our first, and I thought if I learned what went on I could try it the next time."

After cashing in we sat down I got him some champagne, and gave him the money from table one for his honesty, telling him about the table sharks who would have taken it all without telling.

"My wife is going to be very happy. We will be able to pay for the baby, and still have some over." I was glad when I gave it to him. I had made enough for myself from table two.

51
Casino Night Out — The Vespa

And so it happened that I bought the secondhand Vespa. I had never driven one before, but one of the ballet boys taught me, and soon I had the hang of it. I was free to go anywhere I wanted, provided of course I tucked my hair into a cap and wore a man's overalls to hide the fact that I was a "woman of the lowest kind" who dared drive a machine.

We were all promised two weeks off, and mine was coming up. I had taken all the brochures I obtained from the hotel and marked the route out on a map. My understudy would take my place on stage, so I had nothing to worry about.

When I moved into the apartment, I had written "CARPE DIEM" on my mirror so that every time I greeted the day, I would indeed "seize the day," and now it meant If I didn't take advantage of every day presented to me in this place so rich in ancient history, I would be the loser.

When my two weeks arrived, I packed a container for extra gasoline and extra spark plugs and a spare tire, just in case. In the other side lock up I packed my clothing, non perishable food and money. At the casino I told Andre and my friends my travel route. They thought I was insane, but said all they could do about it was to pray that I make it back alive.

On the road, I couldn't imagine anything bad happening to me. I thought the safest way would be to stay on the main roads, and those that ran parallel with the railroad, which was well traveled by foreigners.

So I set off on my adventure into ancient history as soon as the sun showed its face over the mountains. Hoping to reach Biblos, 50 miles from Beirut, by noon. Its ancient name was Jebail. This land was all called Canaan in Biblical times, with borders but no restrictions, which I hoped would apply to me.

I had planned my first sleep over to be in Tripoli, then known by the Biblical name of Tarabulus,

With God as my pilot, I felt free as a bird, feeling the wind in my face, driving along the picturesque Mediterranean coastal road. I had given up the idea of following the railroad because it went inland.

It was long before lunch time when I came upon Biblos. I had stepped straight into the past. The yellow dusty road was full of traffic, but not a single modern vehicle. There were donkeys, fully laden with wares, and horses with back packs, and humans pulling hand carts. This was a port city where Phoenician camel caravans brought cedar wood for shipping to Rome and Greece. I closed my eyes, sure that I was in a time warp. When I opened my eyes I could well imagine I was in the ancient city of Jebail. Sitting in the shade of the low sand brick buildings, merchants were displaying their handwoven cloth, baskets of dried figs and bunches of dates, home-baked round flat pot bread and honey cakes, and jars of orange blossom jam. I stopped in the shade of a tree to buy some orange blossom jam, some honey cakes, figs, and dates for the road to find my Vespa surrounded by children; to them my humble vehicle must have looked like an extra terrestrial vehicle, and so many of them had climbed onto it that they had popped the air valve in the back tire. On the first leg of my journey, so much for hoping that nothing could happen to me. I was now with a flat. I spotted an old building near the waterfront, and pushed the Vespa there, hoping to get away from the crowds of curious spectators. I needed a mechanic pronto if I was to reach Tripoli by night and asked around in French. Most of the people spoke Arabic, of which I spoke a few words. I imagined stepping back a thousand years, and asking for a mechanic. One man who spoke French told me they had never needed a mechanic, but he was willing to help me change to the spare if I showed him how. As we started to change the tire, a larger crowd gathered pushing up against me. He saw my discomfort. I don't know what authority he had, but with one magical word "JALLAH!" *I must remember that word!* And with the wave of his hand, he quickly dispersed the crowd. This instantly made him my official guide. He told me the building in whose shade we had changed the wheel was one of the oldest temples in existence, it was of the Byzantine period. The door was standing open so I went in. The inside had nothing except the sand floor and rough stone walls to indicate its age. But in the farthest end of the room there was an ancient pulpit on which rested the most impressive piece of artwork I had ever seen. A giant hand-written Bible, each page illustrated with icons in gold and red. I asked him why no one had ever attempted to steal such a valuable book. He indicated the heavy chain, and said it was simple.

"They would be beheaded. Come, there is much to see." He asked if I would drive him through Biblos so that his friends could see him. I thought it was little enough payment for his kindness. He got on the back, and I made several turns where he indicated. Everywhere there were monuments of the past that pertained to Phoenician, Amorite, Egyptian, Hyksos, and Greco Roman. At the time of the Crusaders, it was an open market port with no forts. With very little protection or resistance, it passed from hand to hand. After my sightseeing and his "being seen," I drove him home, where everyone admired his daring. When I left, I gave him some monetary compensation for "being such a very good guide." This also pleased him, as money was a scarce commodity because they did everything by trade. As an added tip he told me not to miss the Caves of the Dog River.

Not too far along I came upon the Dog River, a name most unbecoming to compliment the incredible discovery I made. The Dog River was the main source of potable water to Beirut and Biblos. Carved against some high cliffs were ancient graffiti of names of different conquerors who ruled Beirut since Ramses the 2nd in th year 13 BC. Here I was beseeched with offers from boat owners to row me on the underground river to the subterranean lake.

While the others screeched and babbled to catch my attention. A young man fourteen or fifteen years old was biding his time, while the older men practically forced their tour on me.

Being a patron of the underdog, I chose the flat bottom boat of the young man.

He could not believe his luck. But it turned out more my luck. He spoke English!

"The whole day they pushed me away, so I just gave up, and now you have chosen me to guide you."

"Everything good comes to those that wait," I told him.

"The river runs 13 miles into the mountain," he explained, "and I will take you all the way if you want." His little boat looked as if it would not take us one mile into the mountain, never mind thirteen. But I had made my choice!

As we entered the gloom of the cave, I was scared witless, but he explained that it was quite safe and not so deep that if the boat capsized I would be able to stand up in places, and at all times one could see the bottom.

"It only gets dangerously full during certain times of the year when underground runoff tunnels run into the river."

About a half mile into the cave we stopped and he secured the little boat to some low standing stalactites.

"This is one of the tunnels that brought water gushing into the river, but now it is dry enough to walk on. You see how smooth it is, the walls of the tunnel are worn smooth from the force of the water, but do not be afraid. We could turn around now, but there is no possibility that the water would come down now; there hasn't been enough rainfall in the mountains." Somewhere deep inside the bowels of the Earth, I could hear a rumbling, and my heart started racing.

"What was that rumbling I just heard?"

"It is a subterranean waterfall that falls to a lower level beyond the lake, that is how far we can go, but I have discovered a sight never seen by anyone. The river continues beyond that but it is blocked by a huge rock."

"I would be honored to see something no one has ever seen, and I am willing to go farther with you, if you assure me it is safe and we'll be able to find our way back out.

"It would be too dangerous to take anyone deeper in if one did not know where you were going, besides I was raised around these caves, but just to let you feel more safe, I will attach a rope to you, because for the next half hour we are going to do some rock climbing."

After tying me to him, we crawled along a narrow ledge with a precarious fissure, and slid down onto a sandy bank. Around us arose scenes from the Arabian Nights, in the middle of a cerulean blue lake, a Herculean pillar reflected in the water, defying nature. Formed through the ages where a stalagmite and Stalactite met, growing still larger with each millennium.

"Do you still want to go on?" He produced a strong flashlight from his backpack. "Very few people have ever seen what I'm about to show you today, so are you ready for a little rock climbing?"

At this stage I had no option, besides I was too curious. We started to scale some large boulders, and somewhere near the roof of the cave we squeezed through a very narrow funnel onto a ledge. "Don't move," he whispered out of respect.

He had turned off the flashlight, and after a few minutes my eyes got used to the strange light that came from somewhere, reflecting like diamonds onto vast curtains of crystalline translucent draperies that hung as if detached from the roof. Diaphanous pink in color.

I had pulled my breath in, afraid that even breathing would make the magic scene disappear and they would crack and shatter to bits. Before I could ask, he answered: "Yes they are crystals, pristine and untouched. I have come in here at times and heard them ring, like tracing your finger round a glass, when the faintest breeze blew through them. The first explorers of these caves missed this because they only got as far as the Hells Rapids from where they could make out a large cavern but could not get over the rock. You are lucky to see it. We just climbed it because it was high water. But you have to know which tunnel to climb through. To this very day, I know of only a few who have made it to this site."

By now my stomach was rumbling louder than the subterranean waterfall, so I asked him. "Is there a place we can go and have some lunch. I will pay you your fee, but I think you need a little more, would you have lunch with me?"

"No one has ever asked me to have lunch before!" he answered in surprise. "Yes, a wonderful café, one that is built over the waterfall where it comes out of the mountain."

"And no one has ever shown me such a wonderful sight as the crystal curtain, you deserve the best!"

And so I treated him to the best. The others I had rejected seeing us going into the restaurant, were jealous, and I know called him names in Arabic.

We had a wonderful Lunch and he told me more about the caves history, and also recommended that I should see the Source of Adonis, a similar cave between Beirut and Baalbeck. I paid him double and he escorted to where I had chained my Vespa, and to my surprise, with the jealousy of the other guides, no one had molested it. I thanked him profusely again, and was on the way to my next destination.

Fifty miles north of Beirut I reached Tripoli the second capital, because it was the second largest city of the republic. It had it's foundation some 800 years before Christ. The city was divided in two.

52
The Little Priest

On top of the mountain stood the Monastery of the Dervishes. It was a place where men congregated and therefore it was frowned upon for women to enter. I was nervous. However, the Church of St. Giles was also perched against the summit. I thought I would make that my excuse, should I be caught.

The Monastery of the Dervish had a very ancient library in their possession, dating even pre-Christ, and I was dying to even have a peek.

On reaching the monastery, to my surprise I found that the priests were all in the fields. There were only a few Anitiates in house. I was dressed like a young man, and at first they did not mind me wandering around. So I took full advantage. They were in a vow of silence so they did not question my looking around inside and out. It was when I retrieved my Vespa and kick started it that my cap fell off. I snatched it up and tried to put it back on, but my hair rolled out and tumbled down my back; there was no denying my sex now. I expected them to shout out in alarm, but instead they stood rooted in little clumps, staring and giggling like little school girls.

That's when I decided I had outstayed my welcome, and they would get into trouble if I was caught by the priests returning from the fields, so I left in a hurry. I was even more nervous going down than when I was going up, knowing that I was treading on hallowed ground. Only this time it wasn't monks that made me nervous, it was the terrible sharp turns and rock-strewn dirt road full of stones that could flip my wheels without a moment's notice and send me plummeting to my end.

Concentrating very hard, I did not notice the little priest waving his arms till I was almost on top of him. My brakes screeched as I came to a halt next to him.

Judging from his sign language and a scrap of paper with El Mina Harbour written on it, it was obvious that he wanted me to take him down to the harbor, which was two miles down the mountain. He was hot, the walk, even though it was down hill, would be exhausting. He was wearing his full robes. I showed him how to sit astride on the passenger seat, but he shook his head and got on sidesaddle, which immediately threw me off balance. I swerved dangerously near the edge of the unprotected drop. He tapped me on the shoulder. I thought he might have changed his mind, and stopped. Instead he gathered up his robes and this time mounted up astride.

But he still didn't want to touch me. So I took hold of his hand and placed it on my waist, as we drove off. His hand slipped and I think this time he discovered I was a woman, because his other hand came around too, and he slid up as close as he could.

He didn't speak, but I could feel his breath on my neck as he prayed silently as we went round the hairpin bends. The sharper the bends became the more serious his prayers became, he would then let go of wherever he was holding on to and I could see him in my side mirror crossing himself.

When we made it to the bottom of the mountain, he motioned for me to stop. I thought he wanted to get to the harbor, but by the relief on his face, I could see that he wouldn't mind walking the rest of the way. He crossed himself a few times, and I think he would have fallen down on the ground and kissed it if he did not think it would be an insult to me.

Or perhaps he was already doing some silent prayers of cleansing and forgiveness for touching a woman. Even though it wasn't his fault. Either way I was also relieved, with no more obligation toward delivering him to the Harbor at El Mina, I decided to go and have a look, and see if the valve to my wheel could be fixed. I took my cap off, braided my hair, and returned it to beneath the cap, while he stood there in awe watching me. I reckoned this last act of mine would at least warrant prayers for the rest of his walk, and ablution, for his thoughts, having been so close to me. It gave me a strange perverted pleasure.

El Mina was a little city in itself, built like a fortress estimated to date back to the fifteenth century. It was in reality the finest specimen of Islamic architecture of the old Syrie. I visited the open air market, comprising of new and old, to my amazement I discovered some mechanical stuff and bought two valves for my Vespa, and a hand pump for in case. But by now feeling terribly unfeminine, I browsed the women's apparel stand and bought the most exquisite pink gossamer hand-made coat with inlaid gold thread and tiny buttons that opened all the way down. The pink reminded me of the pink crystal hidden from all eyes except a few privileged.

I had read about the Turkish Baths, but they were closed, so I sat down at a sidewalk café, and had an infusion of tea so strong that it could eat away the enamel of my teeth to contemplate my next move. It was still early afternoon. I could push on to Tripoli, and overnight there as planned, or go straight through and reach the Cedars before nightfall.

I could feel the change of climate as I entered the narrow road of the Quadisha Gorge. I was warned in advance about not stopping for any reason, because it was notorious for bandits. But I must have not made a profitable target because I got through the treacherous valley without incident, enjoying the view at the same time. All foreigners that I met in Beirut before going on my adventure said: "Be sure to visit the Kadissa Grottos through which gushed the icy waters of the river with the same name." But I had enough of grottos for now and was more interested to get to the Makhmal Mountains where the progeny of the same cedars grew that built barges for the Pharaohs, and built the Temple of Solomon.

What an amazing sight greeted my eyes. Coming in from the warm valleys, seeing the world transformed into a wonderland of snow. People were skiing down the mountainside. I secured a room at a lodge, found a safe place for my Vespa, and took the ski lift to the top of the mountain, from where I had a glorious view of the world's oldest most venerable trees, which were declared, "LIVING MONUMENTS OF THE PAST." At the lodge the man behind the desk described the region as the Swiss of the Orient, making no comments of the historic value, which I thought an injustice. However he was right to say that it was the meeting place for the rich and the famous. But now looking on this unforgettable sight, as I admired these immortal trees, I had a glimpse of Cleopatra's barge sailing on the Nile. At the same time I pictured the destruction of war, and wondered if these historical trees were to survive an angry future.

Silently I prayed for their survival from possible future wars, even though war seemed far away, as peace hung in a soft white glistening shroud over the mountains, wrapping me in history itself.

The following morning I got a small pocket map from the desk, tied it onto my handlebars, and turned back west toward Baalbeck. It too was one of the oldest remaining cities, now in ruins after an endless barrage of conquests.

It was first built as a worship center for the pagan god Baal, over existing ancient ruins of a still older city. Later conquests transformed it into Greek and Roman temples for sun worshiping, with side temples for a variety of their gods, Bachus, Venus, Jupiter. With the Christian period a church was added to honor St. Barbara. After the conquest of Alexander the Great, mosques appeared. It was a conglomerate of religions, each with its own architectural styles.

Here the temperature had changed back to HOT. I settled into a small niche in the wall, where I overheard a tour guide tell the story of two lovers, who when caught, were built into the wall by the irate husband..

As I unpacked my lunch and settled down to have it. I noticed some Arab peasants climbing out of a deep pit they were digging. I presumed it was an archeological dig to find the city below Baalbeck. They settled down in the shade of some pillars to which their donkeys were tied, loosened the four corners of a checkered cloth and fed their donkeys some fodder out of it, before they sat down and fed themselves.

After finishing my own lunch I ambled over to the workers. I addressed them in French, wanting to know what they were doing. One of them explained that they were digging a hole for some men, looking for an old city. They received fodder for their donkeys and rations for themselves, but only received ten cents a day. When they went back to work, I watched them digging haphazardly with short picks, throwing the dirt into a course sieve. They dumped whatever they found between two to four feet into a basket with a number on it, which a man at the top pulled up.

Inwardly I was laughing, "Very scientific." There was no cataloging because they were illiterate, and the stuff they brought up had no intrinsic value to them, because it was old and soil encrusted and the pottery shards were just that, broken shards, where in the village they could buy one that was still whole. The coins in the one heap in the basket were ancient and couldn't buy them anything! Whatever they brought up was saved to exchange it for their wages. As the last basket came up I spotted some broken bits that looked like glass, but among the broken bits, lay a perfectly preserved bottle, I had seen something similar in a museum once. In Cleopatra's time, women had used these three inch tear-shaped amphora to catch their tears in; they believed that tears came directly out of the soul. On another pile they threw different coins that were found on several layers as they dug down. I exclaimed how beautiful they were; the man laughed at me. They obviously didn't know how valuable these artifacts were. I pulled out the equivalent of $5 and asked if I could buy the little bottle; they whispered among themselves, and the interpreter said, "For $5 more to each of us, you I can have the bottle and a handful of the dirty coins that you can scoop up with one hand." I pulled out a $20. This was a tidy sum to share.

I made a broad sweep of the coins and picked up the bottle in the sweep, hoping that no one with any sense had seen the transaction. At my Vespa I took the salt tablets I carried out of the aluminum container and threw the coins in, wrapped the little bottle in some of my undies, and hid them in the lockup underneath my seat.

The men I knew had several months of pay, and they wouldn't tell, but I felt guilty. I knew better, and it was really dishonest. Now I was sitting on a bit of ancient history, because of the lack of proper education and gross underpayment that amounted to slave labor.

The next few days were uneventful so I swung southeast toward the Mediterranean Sea, this time determined to stay parallel with the railroad till I reached the national boundary. I touched on at Saida or Sidon depending on what religion one belonged to. I had other things besides religion in mind.

I wanted to visit the Crusader's Castle, because way back in my maternal ancestry there were 15 knights who fought in the Crusaders Wars across the globe.

Israel was one of the places. The crossover point would be at Haifa to get into Israel. I was a few miles from the border. I knew I was not prepared for it. But that was one place I always dreamt of visiting. There was a line. So I fell in behind the last car. For protection I was dressed like a man.

When I got to the guard he took one look at my passport and shook his head.

"Vous pouves pa passe!! Sa say pour un femme!" "You can't pass! This is for a woman!" he said angrily. Naturally in the male disguise I looked nothing like my picture. My passport also stated that I was "un artiste." It didn't matter, performer or artiste was a dirty word to them because according to them we had no morality.

"An lev votre chapeau!" he commanded. I complied.. My blonde hair, happy to be free, cascaded down my back. Being blonde, too, was another sign of decadence. He pulled me to the side; he decided there and then that he

421

just wasn't going to let me pass through. I watched him argue animatedly with the other guards.

Just then a big official black car flying Beirut flags pulled up. I recognized the occupant as one of the VIPs who frequented our show regularly.

"What's the holdup?" he asked the guard in Arabic. The guard who pulled me aside was speechless in the presence of such a high-up dignitary. He pointed to me, explaining that I was disguised as a man and my passport wasn't good. It said I was an artiste-dancer.

The official took my passport, looking at it.

"This is a friend of mine, there is nothing wrong with the passport, she pays taxes to Lebanon and supports your salary. How dare you treat her with such disrespect?" I thanked him for intervening and explained to him that the disguise part was correct. I did that for my own safety on the road. He winked at me. "I will let them pass you, but they have to learn a lesson to have more respect for women." He turned to the man. "Today I will overlook it, but next time you may not be so lucky, and will lose your jobs. Let her go, and in the future if she wants to make a trip to Israel, you let her." They stamped my passport with no further ado. It would take two days to reach Jerusalem, and I was on my way. I stopped overnight in two villages on the way; there was plenty room at their inns.

The road to Jerusalem was long and dusty. The red brown rolling hills with a few grey patches of olive groves didn't help to break the monotony. Near the outside walls of Jerusalem I saw caves in the hillside that were used for entombing. Here I stopped and changed into a dress out of respect for my Heavenly father, and combed my hair, braiding it respectably down my back. I felt sweaty and dirty, driving through in the heat and clouds of dust, and was tired when at last I entered into Jerusalem through a side gate that was formally used to bring the livestock home. I stopped in the shade of a mosque, leaning against the wall, resting before going farther, when suddenly from the balcony of the minaret a muezzim summoned the people to prayer. Being unexpected, it came as a shock, it was so loud! That made me jump in fright. During shock, my first reaction was always to laugh, that's what I did. To the men coming for prayer this was interpreted as an insult to their religion, and it angered them. They would have attacked me, but I kept shouting "I'm sorry!" in Arabic, which stopped them in their tracks; they couldn't believe their ears, I addressed them in Arabic. But that gave me no excuse to laugh at their religion, and being a woman on top of it.

Unable to take their anger out on me they then turned their anger on my

Vespa, kicking it over."That could have been me, why did you do that?" I asked them, but when they came at me, I didn't hesitate, turned the Vespa upright, got on and took off. I had no idea where I was going, winding in and out through narrow streets, filled with sheep and jaywalkers. I had to use my horn on several occasions not to run someone over. They cursed me everywhere. I found it strange that I saw no women around. I was totally lost. But judging from the local dress code among the men. I was definitely in a very exclusive Jewish section of the city. Groups of men were walking along in the heat wearing long black coats, and flat-topped black hats with a hatband of fur. All of them had some degree of beard, the younger ones still in the process of growing one. The elders with bushy untended black ones, and equally bushy sideburns, camouflaged their ages. The younger boys, were also dressed in black, but instead of sideburns they all had ringlets. It dawned on me that I had jumped from the frying pan into the fire. They too had very strict laws in regard to women and women's behavior. They looked at me with malaise, behaving very strangely when I pulled up. I did not speak Hebrew, or Jewish, only German, which they seemed to understand. It's what I said that made them uneasy; I tried to explain to them that I got lost coming into Jerusalem.

"I'm looking for the Tomb of Jesus?" I asked a man quite respectfully, forgetting that they also had a very negative idea of Jesus. No wonder no one answered me.

Out of the corner of my eye I saw a man bend down and pick up a stone, another one did the same. Before I was back on my Vespa, I felt the first stone hit my back. I kicked the starter and made my second getaway. Then the stones rained down on me; even the children copying the action of their parents joined in. The stones were small but they stung like angry bees where they hit. They ran after me shouting insults as I sped up. The stones that zoomed past me became bigger and bigger. Thank God none found their mark. I had done nothing to them and I couldn't understand their anger!

All the while escaping, I thought of the woman caught in adultery who was about to be stoned. Jesus then asked those who were about to do it, "If there is one among you without sin, cast the first stone." Those men who started stoning me did not even have the excuse that I was guilty of adultery. My only sin was perhaps that I was a liberated woman, and had entered their territory where women were subordinates. I could see their need for rejecting me but could not justify their deed, as I zigzagged out of their reach.

I had entered two areas that were not friendly toward women, and if I was

423

to survive the rest of my tour, I had better change to a more acceptable mode of transport.

I found a garage that would store my Vespa, and joined a tourist group who saw everything from the safety of a bus seat. And for a small extra fee, I was able to see Iran and Iraq. And as a memento of my experience, I bought a Silver pendant with the symbols of both countries. On my return from Bagdad, remembering it for the romantic story of "Ali Baba and the Forty Thieves," I took a guided walking tour of Jerusalem to visit the Holy Shrines before I retrieved my Vespa and bid the place good-bye. I was hurt; I had expected so much love from Jerusalem, but saw so much hate. Perhaps the ongoing feuds were already evident in Jesus' time, because he already preached, "Love your neighbor as yourself." I thought it was such a pity that they could not remember those words said so long ago, because it was evident they didn't even tolerate them, never mind "LOVE" them.

This time I entered Lebanon from a different direction. Because of the animosity, I thought of changing back into mens clothing, but eventually changed my mind. I was amazed that I encountered no further confrontations. I was almost home. Perhaps people closer to Lebanon where slightly more open minded with all the changes that had taken place there, and with the influx of tourists. Or the casino had influenced them to a more liberal outlook, about women driving machines. I had my passport stamped immediately, I had a week left of my vacation and wanted to visit Bsherri where my beloved Prophet Kahlil Gibran was buried in a grotto of the small Monastery of Mar Sarkis where he attended Sunday school as a child. I carried a well worn copy of *The Prophet*, my daily companion with me. I wanted to know everything about him, and touch his life as he touched mine through his many writings.

In Bsherri I had no problem finding the small house where he grew up.

The self-appointed guide, a far related relative, took me to the room at the rear of the house. It was small. Furnished only with a narrow bed a writing desk and a table. He filled me in with stories passed on to him of Kahlil. Some of the rooms shared by family members had been turned into a kind of museum. I was privileged to see some of the rough sketches he did to illustrate his books. Saw the countless letters that passed between him and his soul companion and benefactress. I always understood from others that Mary was a very ugly woman, but the painting he made of her was of a kind gentle woman, who surprisingly looked like an alter-ego of him. Indeed she was the personification of "The spirit that embraced his spirit, and poured out her spirit into his." I finally tore myself away from this hallowed space. The guide

told me that high on the mountain top, the people of the city had erected a memorial shrine, a place where he always climbed to meditate. To reach the top I had to climb holding onto a chain hand over hand. But when I reached the small
stone shrine it was rewarding beyond my wildest dreams. Here was the place he had described in several of his books. As I sat looking over the valley, I heard the wind howling as it had howled to him. Yet this was a place of stillness where he found solitude, above the noises of the houses below, and the noise of everyday living and he thought up the poetry of his words. I at last felt one with this remarkable spirit. I had closure, and could leave this place. I was at peace with myself.

The road from Damascus was usually quiet at four in the afternoon, I had made good time coming back and I was an hour's drive away from home. The road was clear, and I was driving cliff-side, humming to myself, enjoying the view, looking at the waves breaking up against the rocks below. I recognized it as the place where I had gone scuba diving.

When a car slowed down behind me, I thought he wanted to pass me so I pulled over more to the side. A man leaned out of the window, it looked as if he wanted to ask for directions, but when he got close enough, he didn't say anything, instead gave me a hard push. I regained my balance and speeded up a bit to get away from him. I was confused, perhaps I had mistaken what exactly happened. But when he pushed me the second time, there was no mistaking his intentions, he wanted to push me off the cliff! This time it was hard enough to send me flying. The bike had fallen over and on top of me, my right leg was trapped and I was sliding about ten feet across the hot tar straight for the drop. The shock of my impact with the asphalt caught my head right on my temple, blinding me. In my mind's eye I could see my broken body on the rocks below. But suddenly I came to a spinning halt on a sandbank on the side of the road. Moments later a car pulled up next to me. *My God! Now he is coming to finish me off!* I lay pinned beneath my Vespa, waiting, expecting the worst. Without my knowledge the men who pushed me speeded off but were seen by someone who was going in the opposite direction. I was bleeding from the wound on my head, and the skin was scraped off my leg. A sharp pain told me that the foot pinned beneath the Vespa was most likely broken. As a showgirl dancer that was a disaster. I was still trying to think which article on my contract would cover that. When I heard the voice of a croupier who worked at the casino.

425

"Sorry I did not get their plate number, and they are long gone. But I saw the whole thing." He did not even ask me if I provoked them; he knew their mentality. My bike was intact, mainly because I acted as a human carpet.

But I needed help. "Help me! I can't see," was my first response. He was shocked by their deliberateness. Pulled the Vespa off me and explaining what he was doing to ease my mind, he loaded the Vespa in the trunk of his car and secured it with rope. Then he picked me up, gave me his handkerchief to hold over the head wound, and drove me to the nearest pharmacy, where a doctor checked me out, treated me for shock, and patched me up. He checked my foot, and found no break, but by the sudden swelling said he suspected a hairline break in one of the bones. He suggested that I stay off it for a few days after he taped it well. I was very worried about the blindness. He assured me that it was only nerve blindness caused by the impact. "Your sight will return within a day or two." I could only think perhaps he was just telling me that to calm me down. I was an artist, and dancer, what would I do if my sight never returned?

The groupier was kind enough to drive me home, even helped me into the bed, promising to inform the Moulin Rouge of my accident, so that the ballet doctor could come and check me out, which he did assuring me that I did not have a concussion, but had to take it easy. My understudy was doing fine in my position on stage, and there was nothing to worry about.

I don't know how word spread, but I was swamped by well-wishers who brought gifts of food and flowers. Two days later I saw some of the flowers through a haze. And two more days my sight was fully restored. I could also stand on my foot, but with a lot of pain. So for a few more days I enjoyed the pampering and stayed in bed, so that I could be ready to return to the stage.

53
A Hunted Woman

Soon after coming back from vacation I decided to stay for casino night. I had brought along my white evening dress to change into, the last time I stayed I had won enough money to buy the Vespa, and it had given me a lot of freedom, but also a lot of trouble. I had become good at disguise, and defensive driving. Once they even slashed my tire. But I always put it out of my mind the good outweighed the bad.

On this particular night my intention was to stay no longer than an hour or two, but that soon passed and about two a.m I was ready to leave. I did not feel like changing into disguise. At that hour I reckoned no one would be on the road and I wouldn't be seen if I stayed in my evening gown.

It was a beautiful night, the moon hung full over the horizon. Every now and then a few clouds drifted over it, giving shadows. Otherwise it was bright enough to read by. No one saw me leave. The cabbies were all asleep anticipating the mad rush when the casino crowd would finally decide to go home toward dawn. It looked so peaceful. Slowly I drove down the side of the mountain. The wind was playing in my hair caught up loosely into a Grecian style. My apartment was about two miles away from the casino, there was nobody on the road. What could happen? I stopped at the end of the S-bend descent where the Damascus road met up with the road from Beirut. I looked left and right, no cars in sight, and then crossed to the right hand side of the road; to the right of me lay a dark, mirror-calm ocean. I could see a string of fishing boats anchored about three miles in, their tiny lanterns forming a necklace of light. I stopped for a while to take a look. The road ran straight along the beachfront for about two miles, the drop down from the road was quite steep. On the other side of the road a narrow mountain stream ran parallel with the railway line, which cut through large boulders. Higher up on the mountain, a pine forest rose in black relief against the light of the moon. I started up my Vespa, driving slowly to drink in the beauty of the night.

From the direction of Damascus a car approached, passing me. They hadn't noticed me! Or they were civilized enough not to care that I was a woman on a machine all alone at two-thirty in the morning. But boy was I wrong! They had noticed, and about 20 yards farther they made a sharp U-turn. They turned the three hunting lights mounted on the their roof on, heading straight at me. *They are going to run me down!* flashed through my mind. Blinded by the light I swerved to the side to avoid them. My Vespa got stuck in some sand. It was too steep here to jump down onto the beach and escape them, so I threw my Vespa down. In the meantime they turned off their lights and cruised up to me. I was terrified when the car pulled up next to me. The front and back door swung open, simultaneously forming a barrier round me. I was trapped and there were two of them. In the front a large fat man was trying to squirm out from behind the wheel, giving instructions to a tall evil-looking man who grabbed my left arm and tried to pull me into the back seat of the car. On my right arm I wore a four-inch wide silver Egyptian bracelet. As he tried to shove me into the car, I hit him first over the head with it and then on the hand that held mine in a vice. He screamed out in pain, letting go of my hand just long enough for me to slam the door shut on the fat man's leg, who was at that moment getting out of the car to assist his friend.

I ran across the road, made an Olympic record-breaking leap across the narrow stream, and headed toward the Bedouin encampment below the mountain. I had on several occasions taken food and clothing gifts; they surely would help me. I didn't want to scream because it would give my position away to my pursuers. They had turned the car around in the direction where I had gone with the lights searching for me. I crouched down low behind the bushes. In the light of the hunting light I could see them beating the bushes with a long object. A gun? I had never thought of that. I had spoiled their fun of raping me, and now they were going to kill me to heal their wounded egos.

But it must have not been their hunting night, because he was beating the bushes down with a crowbar. They did not see me jump the stream and thought I must be hiding somewhere beside the stream.

I was almost at the camp and safety, when two Doberman pinschers jumped at me like specters out of hell growling and exposing their fangs, choking with foaming mouths, pulling at the unyielding chains that would not allow them to reach their quarry. I stumbled out of their reach just in time. They started barking furiously; surely it would wake their masters. But no one stirred; perhaps they were used to their nightly barking and they didn't care. One of the dogs broke free, dragging his chain behind him. He charged me. Behind me there grew a cactus patch in a circle. I dived into the center. The dog's chain hooked on a stump. He came to an abrupt stop, sniffed the air where I had disappeared. The barking alerted my pursuers that I was on the other side of the stream.

They found a small footbridge higher up the stream, and thinking it was where I was hiding, started to beat the bushes and grass with the crowbar. By now they were so angry that they no longer wanted to rape me, but I was sure they would beat me to a pulp. Sooner or later they would discover my hiding place. If only the dogs would stop barking. I pulled my shoes off and threw it in the direction the dog was barking, He growled and started chomping away at the shoe. This held his attention long enough for me to crawl on my belly out of the cactus patch toward the train tracks. The moon slid in between the clouds, at that very moment.

On the side of the tracks and between the ties there were white stones. I crawled over the rough stones, scraping my elbows raw, and lay down between the rails; with my white dress, the white stones would provide me with camouflage.

From where I lay I could see what was going on below. I put my ear to the rail and could hear a deep rumbling on the steel. I knew a train was on its way, but how far away from me I could not tell. I prayed silently it would be soon, because I could hear them cursing not too far from me. They were almost at the Bedouin camp, because the dog started barking again.

The moon came out from behind the clouds. But in the light of the moon I could see another danger rumbling toward me. I feared the big eye of the train coming round the bend would reveal my hiding place. I lay still, hardly breathing, watching till it was so near that I could no longer hesitate. The driver of the train had not noticed me, so I rolled over the rail up against the boulders on the side of the mountain. In Cape Town, I had scaled steeper rocks than the ones that loomed above me with my bare feet to enjoy the sensation of climbing.

So while the train rumbled past I scaled the rocks, showering loose rocks onto the train as I tried to reach the pine forest above. I selected a tall tree and hastily clambered up into the topmost branches that would conceal me from below.

From my perch I had a view of the camp, river and cactus patch. The tall one discovered one of my shoes. To them I had disappeared into thin air. They obviously did not see me scale the rocks, If they did they wouldn't have believed their eyes because I was a woman. But after the train had passed, they walked up and down the track. The other dog, caught on a stump, started barking. The thin one ran toward the cactus patch. I heard the dog yelp a few times and fall to the ground, and then there was silence. The fat one found my other chewed-up high heel shoe, held it up triumphantly, laughing thinking the dogs must have got me, but finding no blood other than that of the dog the thin one had just killed, became so angry at not finding me that to vent his anger he beat the shoe to bits. A shudder ran through my entire body. That could have been me! I saw them finally give up, get into their car, and head back into the direction of Damascus, which had been where they came from originally. But I couldn't move, fearing that they would be back with reenforcements.

It was nearly dawn, even though about three or four hours had transpired since climbing up the tree. A red glow spread over the horizon. I could see the fishing boats, pulling to shore, and dragging their nets in over the sand. As the sun rose I heard shouting coming from the Bedouin camp as they discovered the body of their slain dog. Finding the shoes, they must have thought the dogs had attacked someone, and they were not going to stay to take the blame. So within a half an hour, their camp was packed and moved out.

My pursuers had not returned, so I climbed down carefully skirting the place where the camp had stood, wondering if I would find my Vespa intact after the anger meted out on my shoe.

To my surprise it still lay where I had pushed it over when they tried to pull me into the car. I also looked for my bracelet, found first one piece then the other. I had broken it clean in half over his head and the hand that held me in a grip. No wonder he was mad enough to kill me.

I picked up my Vespa, looked around carefully, and made the last two miles back home in record time. Giving thanks all the way in prayer for being alive, and able to tell the tale.

54
Liberating the Women

I had written the men of Beirut off for sure, and was about to do the same with the women. At the time I was painting a nude woman (one of the showgirls had generously given me some time to do a live study). This, in a country where the women were veiled from head to toe, caused quite a stir to say the least. And shocked their senses. I could not lock my doors because it was considered an insult if one did that. It showed mistrust, and theft was unheard of because it was severely punished. A lock would surely allow me privacy, and I was determined to go to town and buy a lock regardless whether it would show mistrust on my part or not.

Only to find that one morning when I was granted time off from rehearsals and relished sleeping in, I discovered a row of ladies dressed in black with only eyes visible behind a netted veil sitting quietly against the wall of my bedroom, watching me sleep. I woke up in shock. They were slyly casting an eye every few minutes at the nude painting obviously was enjoying the free show, from the giggles coming from behind the masks.

I decided to go about my business as if they were invisible. They watched me getting dressed, clucking at the brevity of my undies. They watched me brush my teeth, cook my breakfast and eat it, and laughed when I attempted to make their Arabic coffee, and after deliberating in whispers among themselves, they accepted my coffee and pulled faces when they tasted it. One of them then went into the kitchen, motioning for me to come and look.

She dumped mine and made a fresh pot, which the ladies accepted with a concealed smile, lifting their veils just high enough to drink the coffee. I had made it without sugar; their secret was a 50-50 sugar with the infusion.

Later in the morning they left without a word. I knew somehow they would be back. This little ritual became a regular thing. They even brought along a young girl from a mission who could translate. With the addition of the interpreter they had an outlet for their frustrations. The questions started rolling in about equality for women, marriage in other countries, abuse, all the things these repressed women always wanted to know but were afraid to ask.

Through their interpreter I tried to give them honest answers, but realizing that the little girl was getting the answers at the same time, she was too young to understand, which made me feel uncomfortable—she was only ten years old. But what she translated to them would always remain a secret, but judging from their body language of wonder, disgust, joy and amazement, they felt enlightened. They rewarded me with the compliment of removing their facial veils in my presence (something they would only do in the privacy of their homes in front of their intimate friends and family members).

The things they enjoyed most were the sinful things that I shared with them such as my photo album, cookies, and candies. And when I brought my film projector and my travel films, they were overwhelmed that I would share it so freely with them. Films were something they would never be allowed to see.

So I closed the curtains and showed them the silent movies of Charlie Chaplin, and the only other love story I had. They laughed openly and discussed every aspect of the action they beheld. But when they went home at night I somehow knew they were silent as the grave for fear of getting beatings from their husbands. They never shared the wonders they beheld.

But for the duration of my stay in Beirut, they enjoyed that liberation for a few hours.

They also reciprocated with fresh flowers all over. And my apartment was always neatly swept with a pot of fresh coffee when I returned from the casino.

55

Back in Europe and the Little American Sailor in Naples

Before the show left for Beirut, the Countess of Naples had seen the show in Paris fallen in love with it. Without hesitation she bought the whole show to appear in her night club in Naples, Italy.

Andre went and checked it out. She did not tell him how big the whole place was, because on other tours we had played movie theaters, and even ice rinks, so he presumed this was big enough to accommodate the whole show.

Andre was very disappointed and promptly returned with the news to Doris.

"The countess wants us in Naples, the only good thing about it is she is going to provide free accommodations and food for the cast and staff for the duration of our appearance in Naples. And pay us double. The bad news is, there is no stage, and she wants the show Parisian style—topless. Which means you would have to perform on a dance floor with the audience sitting at tables two feet away."

Because the nightclub also served food.

"To accommodate the whole show she promised to break two side walls out to make entrances."

Here Suzanne interrupted, "At such a close range, I'm not allowing my girls working without bootsan!" As if these two-inch nipple covers would give us protection from groping hands.

The first two rehearsals we had an invited audience. A selection of the countess's friends, who became overly friendly with the performers after the first bottle of champagne.

The free accommodations in the Pensioni smelt musty and the bed linen so damp it gave the impression it had just come off a washing line. The food was passable but we were asked to sit down with the clients. Andre objected to this. The countess explained that it was just mingling. But at the end Andre won and we ate separately.

On either side of the dance floor they had broken away a certain amount of the wall. It was more like two large holes in the wall. Through these holes we had to make our way onto the dance floor. It was difficult with the oversized costumes to make a dignified entrance, clinging to our hats or trains. There was no space for the musicians. So the show's music was put on tape and barely audible. The night club's equipment was so old that the tapes came out in slow motion. And we often performed in slow motion.

Marie-L had taken leave of absence to visit her parents in Germany, and Andre found an understudy for me who spoke English and hailed from America. She was stunning with long golden hair. The Italians were mad about her, and she was out partying every night. Andre had her move in with me. She was 19 years old, and he wanted me to keep an eye on her. I tried to take her with me wherever I went, but she had her own ideas. She never told me where she was going, and when she wasn't sitting in on the rehearsals, I came home and found her smoking. That is one of the things I didn't like about her, because the room always had a strange smell of burnt rope. She explained it away as having smoked a cigar with one of her friends. I knew she smoked, so I did not ask her about the smell again.

Before I left Paris, I read in a paper that I was selected as the mascot on a Battleship of the U.S. Navy. That was quite an honor, because I knew about the custom of taking the photos of the showgirls and putting them onto various large transports, trucks and trains, but a ship?

The ship was in the Naples Harbor and I wanted to go and see my picture displayed on their funnel. So I asked Nita and another blonde showgirl to take a trip down to the harbor with me.

When I got to the plaza where the horse-drawn buggies were for hire, the man operating it said he didn't want to go. I asked him then what he made for the day. I said I would pay him very well if he would allow me the use of his buggy for the rest of the day; I would drive it myself. He agreed on one condition—he would charge me double if anything happened to his horse or buggy. I agreed, paid him, and took over the reins.

First I went up the hill to see the Royal Palace on Via Calatabel Verdlo, then turned back to the Plaza del Plebisito where we saw a charming little sidewalk café to have lunch in.

On the way there we spotted a nondescript, thin little sailor standing on the side of the road looking totally lost and bored.

"There goes the love of your life," the girls teased. I promptly pulled over. The look on the girls' faces and the shocked surprise on his were precious when I asked him to have lunch with us.

"They'll never believe me back on the ship," he said in disbelief that three gorgeous showgirls speaking English invited him to lunch in a strange port city.

During lunch he suddenly became very talkative. He was from a small town in America with a population of just under five hundred. He joined the Navy to see the world, but now he wasn't too sure because he had not made any friends on the ship. They never invited him to go on shore leave with them. Instead he got a lot of teasing, about not liking girls. But then, he didn't like the kind of women they were eager to introduce to him, nor did he fancy the kind of things they thought macho, like drinking and picking fights.

Throughout the day he kept saying: "They'll never believe me! What would they say if we took you back to the ship? They would have to believe then, wouldn't they? So that's exactly what we will do!"

After lunch, we stopped at every street photographer, specially posing with him, to give him the evidence that he was indeed on the excursion with us. For the rest of the day he was totally relaxed and we enjoyed his company. He was funny and a pleasure to be with. The biggest coincidence was that the ship he was on was also the ship that had my picture on their funnel.

The ship was anchored at Porto Beverello. When we got there most of the men had already returned from shore leave and were just hanging around on deck talking and observing the arrival of the late comers. They spotted us immediately, we made sure of that. We pretended not to notice the cat calls and whistles coming from the rails. Then they saw him! I pulled the horses up close to the edge of the docks where they would have a good view, then in turn each of us gave him a long and lingering proper Hollywood French kiss, all three swooning over him. We tried to hold him back when he got down from the buggy and as he started up the gangplank, I jumped down and ran after him up the gangplank. Taking him in my arms, I gave him another spectacular kiss, then stopped dramatically at the foot of the gang plank and shouted loud enough for all to hear: "DARLING, YOU WERE GREAT!" through the whistles and the applause coming from the guys hanging over the rail. I saw his lips form the words.

"Now they'll believe me."

That night the show played to a full house, mostly of sailors and officers off the S.S. Gainard ship. Among the officers sat our little sailor, who was suddenly everyone's friend! He was beaming from ear to ear. Naturally we went over to talk to him after the show.

For the duration of their stay in port, they took us on the Amalfi drive and to Pompeii, the ship's cooks packing us wonderful picnic baskets. I in turn took a whole group of girls out to the ship and gave them a farewell show on board. They sailed the day after and promised to see the show wherever they were anchored. And they kept their word whenever they were in port near where I was performing. They came to see the show.

56
The Fur Coat Boycott

A few days before leaving for Milan, Nita disappeared on one of her party binges. Everyone was looking for her, even the police were looking for her.

On the day we were leaving she turned up, very disoriented, looking drunk. She had no explanation of her whereabouts for the past three days. We tried to hush up the whole thing, but Andre found out and was furious and imposed a large fine on her. Being an understudy, she was literally put under house arrest and under probation for the rest of the show in Milan. It was like a paid vacation for her.

But she charmed Andre and persuaded him to let her travel back with the show to Paris. Luckily I did not get in trouble, because he had put her in my care. But I argued that I was not her conscience. I asked him to let her stay with one of the other girls who smoked, making her smoking the excuse.

"She doesn't speak French, so for Milan she'll stay with Rejan, but in Paris she is booked with you."

The usual confusion of getting everything together for our next move to Milan, where we would do a fashion show as well as the show, was up to Suzanne and her very able crew. We did the usual advance publicity shots.

This time we were going by train with a stop over in Rome, so we posed with guards and the train driver sitting on the mountains of luggage showing legs. It was all very glamorous! But inside the train was another story. We had three coaches reserved. Each of the compartments eight people shared. Our compartment included Miss Doris and her Alsatian, Bruce, also Jackie the male lead of the Can-Can group; he had his toy Pomeranian, Fifi, concealed in a large travel bag. He had given her a sleeping pill to keep her quiet, as she had a very disturbing high-pitched yap, and this was a night trip. During our travels, Jackie got in trouble several times taking her secretly on flights with him in the same manner. He refused to let his Fifi ride with the other animals, because she was his baby. So it always cost him a "human" fare when they discovered her.

The compartment had four pull-down sleeping bunks, and we were told to sleep head to foot with a partner. That being very uncomfortable, we just sat up on the bottom two bunks like sardines. Fifi lay in her bag on Jackie's lap, while Bruce the Alsation was curled up at miss Doris's feet sleeping. But soon the tranquilizer wore off and Fifi woke up and gave a polite little bark asking Jackie to come out for her "walkies." This woke Bruce the Alsation up and all hell broke loose. He started barking and jumping over everyone to get at the annoying sound. Jackie grabbed his precious baby out of the bag and scrambled onto the upper bunk screaming at Miss D., "Take the vicious beast off my baby." Miss D grabbed Bruce's collar, nearly choking him and pulling him off us, who were screaming trying to get away from him. He was barking at the top of his voice, determined to get to Fifi, who would not stop yapping.

SUDDENLY the train came to a scrrreeeeching halt, everyone falling over one another.

"That's it!" Doris screamed in German through the din. "Someone pulled the emergency cord on us, making so much noise!" She immediately accused Jackie.

This brought on shocked silence from everyone. We all quieted down, except the two dogs. Bruce with a hoarse *woof, woof, woof* by now, and the diminutive Fifi defending her size responding with a bitchy *yap, yap, yap!*

Looking out the window, we saw the driver of the train walking on the side of the track calling out to everyone in Italian. "Follow me!"

We did not know what was going on. It could be a fire, or worse, a bomb. But we heard no sounds bar the ones coming from within our compartment. The rest of the train looked peaceful. Outside the window we could see Christmas lights on against the hill. We stumbled over one another to get out and follow the driver acting as Pied Piper. Many other regulars who were not asleep, also peeled out of the steaming train and followed the driver up a nearby hill, expecting the worse. *He seemed to be taking us away from the train, for safety.* When he stopped, relieved laughter filled the air.

"Regarde!" he said, pointing to a small cave. Within the mouth of the cave there was a life size Nativity scene glowing with lights. I had almost forgotten that it was almost Christmas. The wonder he wanted everyone to see, and the reason he stopped an entire train, was a mother cat who had given birth to a litter of six within the manger, cuddling up to Baby Jesus.

"Belissimo?" We couldn't believe our eyes. He stopped a whole train to go and show us the miracle of new life!

Milan's Italian audiences, being more conservative, weren't ready for a nude show! So the manager of the Trocadero insisted the upper bodies of the showgirls must be covered. They even supplied ugly regular bras that looked like funnels. This of course made Suzanne very unhappy and our management mad. The costumes were specially designed for being topless. It spoiled the whole look of the tableau, and drew more attention to our being topless, but in a vulgar sort of way. Suzanne removed the bras, and we were instructed to go back to our regular bootsan.

One night I came out with my pony outfit that was supposed to be totally topless but I was instructed at the last minute to glue on my regular bootsan (titty covers). However, the quality of glue I could get in Milan did not hold, and as I reached the front of the stage, my nipples popped, and both of the bootsan popped off into the audience.

The front rows naturally made up of men made a mad scramble to retrieve them. It amused me and the show's staff. I was used to doing the dance without titty covers, so I continued with the dance as if nothing had happened. Everyone was afraid that it would affect audience attendance. On the contrary this did not diminish our audiences. It increased them. The rest of the two weeks remaining I did it without the pasties.

On the last week there, we were scheduled to do a fashion show consisting of "Fabulous Furs." I was totally against killing animals for their furs, and determined to secretly boycott the manufacturers from selling these coats. In a strange way my idea backfired on me.

A long catwalk was constructed across the seats into the middle of the audience.

For the first few coats, a silver fox and a snow fox, I wore a tube dresses below to show them. The last one was a Astrakhan that reached to my feet, made from at least a thousand newborn lambs. Who never saw the light of day. It sickened me. The inside lining was dotted with diamonds. It was really magnificent! Nonetheless, before putting it on I removed every stitch of my clothing leaving only my flesh-tone G-string on. Appearing as if I was completely naked.

I put on my high heels and waited for my musical cue. No one knew or suspected anything. And I knew I was going against my contract and could be dismissed.

All eyes were on the coat I held tightly closed as I strutted my stuff on the catwalk. One of the group of photographers came forward to photograph the coat. At that very moment I was showing off the collar.

Then halfway on the catwalk, I stopped to make a full turn to show off the back of the coat, I turned a full turn and opened wide the coat cut in a full flare. The women in the audience gasped in shock at my total nudity. The men whistled. While the flash bulbs of all the photographers flashed in a frenzy. To get the shot of a lifetime! I stood still on the catwalk for around 30 seconds. Then closed the coat and completed my strut among thunderous applause. Backstage they heard the applause, but didn't find out what I had done till the calls started pouring in to buy the diamond studded coat and anything else the nude model wore that night. I got off with a reprimand and a fine because the fantastic publicity for the show counteracted my action. I thought I would at least be arrested for indecent exposure, and I would be able to voice my opinion about the needless slaughter of animals to supply the rich with their coats. It backfired on me; instead I opened up a still greater demand. The cops standing backstage were unaware of what took place, but when they heard, there were more of them nightly, guarding in case it happened again. We knew better.

57

Helping a Count in Distress

One night coming back from the show, I heard sobbing coming from the room next to mine. The room was open. I knocked softly and walked in. There was a man in bed, he was fast asleep, obviously having a very bad dream. The sobs came from him. I felt like an intruder, hastily withdrew, and went to my room.

The following day I noticed the shoes in front of the door. There were other shoes in front of other rooms. But the ones in front of suite 203 alone fascinated me. They belonged to the man who cried in his sleep. One can tell a lot from shoes.

These were expensive and very elegant, hand made in very fine leather. They belonged to a man with very good taste, not short of money. Although the shoes were very well kept, I thought they were unsuited for the rainy weather of Milan.

There were no ladies shoes next to them, so it couldn't have been a lover's spat. Or on the other hand it could have been because of a divorce.

His sobbing worried me. I don't know why but I had to know the reason for those sobs. Coming from or going to do the show, I sometimes heard him talk to the staff. The voice was deep, with a marked German accent. It had a pleasant ring to it as he confidently spoke to them in a broken Italian. Someone asked him where he was from so he answered, "Bonn, I'o sono Germani." So I was right, he was German.

Passing his door after the show that night, I heard the sobbing again. I told my roommate Christine that I was going to go in there and find out why he had these disturbing dreams.

"You are out of your mind going into a stranger's room in the middle of the night. What if he has a gun and shoots you? Mistaking you for an intruder? What if he is a mass murderer and that is his way of enticing women to come into his room?"

"I don't care, I must know. Perhaps I can help, I wouldn't rest until I find out." The knob turned in my hand and I walked in. I stood there in the darkness with only the light from the passage lighting up the sleeping form of the stranger. He was tossing his head back and forth, sobs racking his body. The agony of his dream showed on his face. Beads of sweat stood in drops on his forehead, matting his hair. I tip-toed to his bedside. Stroked the hair away from his sleeping eyes. He awoke with a befuddled look on his face. He did not ask who I was or what I was doing in his room. Suddenly I felt embarrassed at my intrusion into his life.

I muttered, "Sorry," and turned to go.

"Bitte nicht gehen."

I offered a weak explanation, "You were having a nightmare, and were crying, I wanted to help."

"Yes, I have these dreams over and over," he said in broken English. "Der krieg (the war). Sit down, please." He hesitated for a moment, but being a stranger, it encouraged him to talk.

Slowly he opened up and started to tell me about his dream that was a repetition of the reality that happened to his entire family.

"My friends, being Jewish, were being ill treated. I started seeing the Fuhrer as a fanatic, and the show of force, the spectacle of banners and speeches, were leading to the destruction of the German Nation, who had looked up to him to lead them out of the recession." He told me he was in the German Army, and under cover joined a resistence group to assassinate the mad man. They made several attempts on his life, but failed.

The Fuhrer, suspecting all who were in the bunker, tried to find out who was responsible by choosing a family to face a firing squad. If the person or the group responsible came forward, he would save the family's lives. If no one confessed, they would be shot.

"None of us knew whose family was chosen. We were marched under fire out to a hillside covered in snow. Each with the threat of our own extermination hanging over our heads. The firing squad stood ready. Then we saw a group of people coming over the hill.

"It was impossible to make out who they were. We thought this was one of the henchmen of the Fuhrer's mind games. It was a trick to make us talk, telling us that it was our family. Nobody stepped forward to confess, still thinking it was a mind game. Seconds passed and the command to fire was given. We saw the people fall, their blood staining the snow. We showed no emotion. To show emotion would be the end of all of us.

"They then marched us past the mutilated bodies. I saw my father, mother, and sister lying in a pool of blood that congealed in the cold of the snow. I'm ashamed to say, at that moment, the only thing I felt was the cold steel of the gun against my temple." He burst out sobbing again. "I just stood there and did nothing! I DID NOTHING!" I felt his pain, and putting my arms around his shoulders, I held him and gently rocked him like his mother would have done. After a moment he continued.

"Then after further interrogation of the cruellest kind, some of the detainees confessed. Those who confessed were shot in the basement where they were kept. A few of us endured the cruelty without confessing and were let go. That same night I walked to Switzerland, where I remained till the war was over. I was determined to go back after the war and reclaim my family's business and property."

I let him talk, and as he talked he relaxed.

"Now I have these recurring nightmares where I see my family lying in the snow riddled with bullets, and I feel the same guilt and helplessness I felt then."

I sat there in the semi darkness holding onto a stranger, listening to the bizarre story, not knowing if it was true or not. It was nearly morning when I explained that I had to go. I was in a show at the Olympia Music Hall with the Moulin Rouge and had a few hours left before I had to show up for rehearsal.

He turned on the light; it was around five in the morning.

"My God! I have been talking to you for hours. Forgive me, how can I ever repay you for listening to me?"

My roommate was still sleeping, so I lay down on my bed, thinking about what I had just heard. Thinking, *It must have been true because it took painful emotions telling the story to me.*

It so happened to be my birthday two days later. When I entered my room in the hotel, it was festooned in flowers and on a table in the center of the room stood a beautiful cake with the appropriate amount of candles. A silver mirror stood next to it. The note written in German read, "Dear RA, when you look into this mirror you will be a year older, but you will remember the kindness you showed me, and my gratitude will always follow you. I would like it if you accept my invitation to spend a White Christmas in Germany, next month with me and some friends. If you agree, I will of course arrange for travel, etc., Count Mario M."

I of course accepted his invitation when a large envelope arrived soon after containing my tickets, to Bonn. There was also a wallet containing travel money.

Christina, my roommate, of course was sure that I would never be heard of again. I laughed it off and told her instead about the even stranger story about the proposition I received to deflower Johnny, before going to Germany.

58

The Deflowering of Johnny Jr.

As Christmas drew near, I was thrilled going to Germany but almost forgot that I also had a previous commitment, an invitation to visit the Joanni family for a week before Christmas on the French Riviera. They were a fourth generation act of jugglers and shadow puppeteers. Johnny's Mom was an ex showgirl like myself. We met some time back in Paris when they became a last minute fill-in act. It was then that she came up with the strange request. She never mentioned it again but I somehow suspected that the invitation to the Riviera had an ulterior motive. The Joannis were close to retirement and they hoped that Johnny would find someone nice to marry to carry on their act. Mrs. J. had shown her admiration of me, openly. I suspected that they hoped that I would be the one.

So she invited me to the Cote d'Azure for the week before Christmas. But it was then that the request surfaced again, when she told me there were other concerns that plagued her. With a worried look she told me that she suspected that at 30 plus, Johnny Jr. was still a virgin or had "gone the other way" because besides me, they had never seen him with women.

In Paris I had gone out to dinner with Johnny a few times. He flirted with me, but never tried to even kiss me goodnight. But there was definitely an attraction. So I assured her that he had never shown preference for men, and she had nothing to worry about.

"Perhaps he just never found the right woman."

"Ramona, you are a woman of the world, perhaps you can find out what the reason is behind his hesitancy?" Then the invitation followed.

"You would do me a great favor if you were the one to deflower Johnny." She was so serious and so direct. It came as a shock. At the same time it was hilariously funny. I had never had a proposition like that before, at least not from the family of the virgin. And never from the mother on behalf of her son. I naturally accepted their Christmas invitation, still thinking it a joke, but looking forward to the French Riviera. They called that they were in Monaco and would meet me there.

When I arrived in Monaco where they were appearing. The whole family was there to greet me at the station. At their suite, J. Senior simply took my case into Johnny's room (I suspected he was in on the arrangement because he had a permanent smile on his face when he looked at me).

So it was that I found myself that night in the large double bed, wondering how I was to proceed with my special consignment. Johnny walked in wearing very effeminate satin pyjamas. I didn't beat around the bush, and blatantly confronted him about his sexual preference. I confessed to him his mother was worried that there never would be an heir to carry on their act. She suspected that he was a virgin still, or in her words "had gone the other way."

"You don't mean gay? I can assure you I'm not."

He was shocked that his mother could divulge such a private thing, but more shocked that she could think him gay and suggest such a thing.

"And by the way, I think it was really your father's idea in the first place to throw us together. He was grinning from ear to ear when he put my bag in your room. But I'm a good actress and we could just give them a real show."

He then told me, "I couldn't tell them. I tried, several times, but it was too painful, so I never tried again."

"Then let us just do a lot of moaning and oohs and aahs, and they would get off your back."

"You mean, get me off my back?" We laughed, and it broke the ice.

I kissed him softly, caressing his whole body with gentle foreplay. I felt his body tense up, fearful of what could follow, yet eager to try again. Like a soft symphony, I played his senses. Slowly he relaxed under my touch, and his body looked normal. I saw he was un circumcised; the foreskin which should have pulled back during erection was tight and unyielding. He was eager to proceed with the act, but every time he came close, he would roll off me, remembering the pain.

While he was still erect, I assumed the superior position and gently eased myself down on him. He stifled a cry, and when I saw blood, I immediately stopped.

The foreskin had torn. We hurriedly got dressed and rushed to the hospital, where the doctor completed the minor surgery. He was amazed that Johnny had not had the surgery earlier on, and assured him that after a few weeks of recovery, Johnny would be able to have a pain free and pleasurable sex life.

We were able to sneak back into the hotel suite. I explained to his mother that I had my period when she discovered the blood stained sheet, I tried to wash out, and I could not go through with it. But just before my departure I decided to tell her the truth, knowing that Johnny would not. I told her that her fears were unfounded and that the whole mystery was solved through just a minor surgery. He now just had to find the right woman. He, through circumstances, was no longer a virgin. I also explained that I was not the right daughter-in-law, and wished her luck.

Then leaving for Germany to see the count, I felt guilty, as if I had just been involved in a hit and run accident. And left it at that!

Two days later I was on the train heading for Bonn in Germany. I took a cab from the station to the address on the black folder. The cab stopped in front of a large factory with a sign above the ornate gate. "BASF" I read. The gates swung open to admit us. He had seen the cab and came out to greet me with a large umbrella because it was cold and softly snowing.

Inside he ordered his secretary to bring us some hot chocolate, and explained that they manufactured tape recorders and musical tapes, but at one stage during the war it was used for an ammunition's factory that used Jewish people as laborers. He had reclaimed all of his father's properties, including the castle that was used to house German officers and their families.

After I finished the chocolate he ordered the company car to take me to the castle where the ball was to be held and all his guests would be staying including, he rambled off a few names that sounded vaguely familiar. I had come with no preconceived ideas of what was to happen, or what to expect.

So it was a delightful surprise when we stopped in front of a grey castle straight out of a fairy tale with turrets, and a drop gate over a moat; my jaw dropped.

"You really live here?"

"Sometimes. I reclaimed it after the war. It's too costly. I have a modern apartment in Bonn, but I'm afraid it wouldn't hold all my guests for the Christmas party. You'll like it. I had all the cobwebs removed specially for you." He laughed.

Going through the gigantic doors, my first impression was of a movie set of all the Errol Flynn movies I had ever seen, where he came jumping down the winding stairs, swords clashing. We were in a large hall with walk-in fireplaces crackling and glowing, flames dancing out of large logs. A jovial couple took us in to have lunch, where we were dwarfed sitting in high-backed wooden chairs carved with griffins and vines, with red velvet backrests at an equally impressive wooden table that could easily seat twenty people. Somehow I wished that my suspicious roommate from Milan could see me now.

"I have to go back to work, but I will be back at about 5 p.m. to pick you up for dinner at my apartment where you'll be more comfortable and we could eat alone. You'll have to amuse yourself for a while. I have had your luggage taken to the red wing I hope you like red." He started laughing and in a mysterious voice said: "But I'm warning you, never go into the locked room in tower two." I knew he was joking. In the movies there was always some insane relative kept captive in some tower room.

With everything he told me, I still found myself looking over my shoulder as the young man I had previously seen in the garden carried my bag to the red wing. The door to my room was about five foot three with a gigantic key tied with what else? A red ribbon. I had to duck when entering, and it dawned on me that the people were much smaller a hundred years ago.

"The castle dates from 1400. The Count is from a very prominent German family as you may have noticed from the pictures in the hallway," the young man explained. I certainly noticed His family had the same blond hair and blue eyes as my host. Hitler's preferred race, which had me wondering why then was his family selected as an example?

But the young man obviously did not know anything about that side of the story. And I wasn't the one to tell him.

The furnishings in the room were ancient, but with modern drapes at the window and on the canopied bed. The windows stood wide open to remove the faint musty smell that still hung in the air. The view was spectacular. It had snowed in the night and the snow lay in thin layers over everything. Picture postcard perfect. It must be beautiful in spring was my first thought. I put my things down and went downstairs into the garden. I couldn't stay long, because I was unprepared for the sudden change in climate and was obviously inappropriately dressed. I made some snowballs and tossed them against the damp black trunks of the trees, till my hands turned lobster red and my teeth began to chatter, then I ran indoors where a roaring fire was lending its warmth to no one in particular.

During dinner, Mario (he told me he kept the name he adopted during his escape from Germany) told me how he reclaimed his father's property and business. All guilt of the conspiracy against the former Fuhrer had been dropped after his death, and to justify their actions the government declared the death of his own family as mistaken identity. And his claim was recognized.

"You see why I don't live at the castle and only use it for special events. It is the place where I grew up and it holds too many memories for me. I was lucky though everything miraculously stayed intact only because it was used by the officers and their families for a retreat during the war.

On Christmas morning after a pleasantly social breakfast around the big wooden table with some of the other guests, we watched the staff carry a giant twenty-foot Christmas tree over to the tower and hoist it onto the roof and then hang garlands of greenery on the winding staircase and in the great hall. For a while I got into the spirit of the thing and helped with attaching the flowers to the garlands. When I got back to my room to rest for the ball, I found a wonderful surprise laying on my bed. A beautiful full-length softly glittering evening gown with matching shoes. All in my size. I somehow knew it was from him, but was amazed that everything was in my size.

Later as I got dressed, I felt like Cinderella, expecting everything to disappear at midnight. The dress slipped like a second skin over my body; it was stunning. I piled my hair on my head but then changed my mind, pinning it gently out of my face and let it fall down my back in a Roman style of soft curls. I'd seen scenes like this before in movies. As I graciously descended the winding stairs, he stood waiting for me below dressed in a very regal outfit, becoming a count. A broad sash was over his shoulder with a crest pin at his waist. He called me over to stand with him in the receiving line as his honored guest.

The "creme de la creme" of German society slowly filed past. I smiled and shook hands with the elite, secretly wondering what role they played in the atrocities of the war. After the greeting I was asked to dance by everyone there except Mario.

A few minutes before midnight, the guests all headed up a narrow spiral stair to the roof tower to see the tree light up. It was freezing. It seemed nature was ordered to produce a white Christmas and it started snowing softly.

A group of people gathered around a large barrel with blazing fire on which chestnuts were roasting. Too hot to handle, they grabbed them off the fire and rubbed them in the snow. Then right on cue at midnight, thousands of twinkling lights burst forth on the tree in all their glory competing with the stars and snowflakes landing on our hair. We spontaneously started singing "Silent Night."

Hundreds of packages hung on the tree, each with a guest's name on. To get the guests to really mingle, we filed past the tree, plucked a present and had to go around and find who it belonged to. It was chaotic, but a lot of fun and laughter, and soon everyone was ooh and ahhing at the chosen gift specially selected for them. I received a sparkling Strass bracelet wrapped around eight ounces of my favorite Mollinar perfume. Perfectly matching my dress, I immediately put the bracelet on. At the fire, a gypsy was telling fortunes by melting lead in a soup spoon and tossing the lead into the snow. Then she analyzed the shapes it made.

When it was my turn she said : "You are going on many voyages. I see a marriage to a very short man with black hair and dark eyes." *I heard this before in Cape Town before I left,* I thought. "You will have several children but only one will survive who will give you much pleasure."

"And when will this marriage take place?" I interrupted.

"Very soon, within two years."

I wanted to tell her, "No, you're wrong. The man I truly love is over sea and has silver hair and green-blue eyes," but then my future was very unsure at this stage. The only one with dark hair and eyes was Jacques Elbaz with whom I had a small affair, but he was tall. *This man better make his appearance soon, I'm near 27 and if he doesn't come soon I'll certainly be an old-maid. With no children.*

After the ball was over and the guests were gone, Mario finally caught up with me. "You know I didn't have a single dance with you?" he took my hand and we went up to the tower. And there we danced in the light of the tree and the falling snow while I hummed a tune.

"If only I was younger, I would ask you to marry me," he whispered in my ear. I couldn't help but laugh. "It has nothing to do with age. Besides forty isn't old. But according to the Gypsy you're not the right size—the man I am to marry is short with dark eyes and hair. You are tall and handsome with blond hair and blue eyes. You are a wonderful man, and I thank you. Never sell yourself short. You have spoiled me with wonderful gifts on my birthday and given me this unforgettable Christmas, but in a few days I am going back to Paris to continue my contract, and who knows what will happen? Because I do not know what the future holds for me."

59
Drug Bust — Nita Gets Deported

After the European trip, trouble followed us back to Paris. Doris automatically booked Nita and me into the Stevens Hotel.

"You are older than her, and can guide her. She is only eighteen and Paris has many temptations."

I didn't say anything to Doris, but thought Nita was much more world wise than me, judging from her behavior the past few months. She proved herself as a party animal, was off every night after the show with some very shady characters, and nothing I could say or do stopped her. So how could I prevent her now from doing the same?

"Perhaps you should put her with the party crowd. I'm afraid she is going to get me into trouble, besides I can't stand her smoking."

"What do you mean trouble, she is so innocent?" Doris said with true conviction.

"Take my word for it. She's trouble." I couldn't tell Miss D. how I covered for her when she was off on her night wanderings in Naples. Because she was an understudy, she had more time on her hands than the rest of us and was only on call when the person she was understudying was on call.

For three weeks we had been working on two new numbers; usually I stayed after the show to rehearse till three in the morning, then went home to sleep till show time or went directly home after the show and was called in again at ten o' clock.

This particular morning when Nita got busted, I dragged myself into the room at 6 a.m, totally exhausted, reeking of sweat. I contemplated going down the hall for a shower, but chose sleep instead. Nita was still asleep on the daybed. Picture perfect, like a fairy princess. Her golden hair spread in soft curls across the pillow, complexion like peaches and cream. I undressed and looked at the wall clock; it was nearly seven. I would get about three hours sleep if I was lucky before I had to go back. There was a strange lingering smell like burning rope in the room, the same smell I often smelt on Nita's clothes when she came back from an all night party. "Nita really should stop smoking," I mumbled as I fell into an exhausted sleep.

"OUVREZ LA PORT!!! OPEN THE DOOR!!! JANDARM!!"

My heart was pounding as I stumbled to the door. My eyes were bloodshot, and I was disoriented. How long had I slept? I fumbled for the key, but before I could open it. Someone kicked it open. Two men burst past me, nearly knocking me to the ground.

"GET UP!" One of them shouted at Nita, who sat up, stretched, and looked at them innocently with her baby blue eyes, smiling sweetly.

"What's going on?"

I on the other hand looked like Medusa with my hair in wild array, clutching a sheet I hastily wrapped around me because I usually slept in the nude.

I looked at them with bloodshot eyes and a scowl on my face from lack of sleep, screaming at them.

"Who the hell are you? What do you want ? Is the hotel on fire?" I went to my bed and sat down, visibly shaking now; with no sleep I felt faint. They did not answer, and I didn't know what was going on. Out of the corner of my eye I could see Nita flirting seductively with the men, as if it was the most natural thing to see two men in the room so early in the morning.

"What's going on ?" I asked again.

"You tell me!" the tall one said sarcastically in perfect English, his sharp blue eyes flashing daggers at me. He took a badge out of his inside pocket and held it out to me. I didn't catch the name, but the words *Narcotic Bureau* jumped out at me like a tiger. " I don't get it! Why us?" Nita got up and headed for the door in a hurry.

"SIT DOWN!" Blue eyes ordered.

"I need to go to the bathroom and take a shower."

"You're not going anywhere till we are through in here!"

The second man was dumping the clothes out of the drawers, and pulling

453

everything out of the wardrobe. He found the box with my sculpting project making angel medallions out of plaster of Paris. He stuck his finger in his mouth and took a lick in the plaster. It obviously was not what he was looking for because the next minute he spat it out into the biddy. His eyes kept scanning the room.

He spotted the black bag on top of the wardrobe. "Ah-hah! Jackpot!" he shouted as he opened the bag. It was Nita's bag. I had seen her pull it down several times before. It was a doctor's bag she had carried with her from Milan to Naples, and never let out of her sight.

"Whose bag is this?" the man queried.

"Not mine, I saw her put it there." Nita smiled her angelic smile and pointed at me. Taken aback I protested.

"She's lying, she brought it with her from Naples, never letting it out of her sight." I added.

Blue eyes placed the bag on a chair and opened it all the way. It was full of little plastic bags that had stuff in it that looked peculiarly like my plaster of Paris. He opened another brown parcel that was full of strange looking cigarettes twisted at the end and loose branches of Cannabis, a weed my dad used to plow under to renew our fields. But I dare not tell the cop that.

There was also a variety of pills. He was looking into my bloodshot eyes and addressing me.

"So this isn't yours?" he asked me, while his attention was on Nita's reaction. She was cool as a cucumber, making small talk with the other cop.

"You're both under arrest. Get dressed, I'm taking you in!"

"It's not my bag, I'm telling you!" He didn't care. "Nita, tell him it's your bag, I'm not being dragged into this because of you! TELL HIM! NOW!" I shouted.

She just looked at me. I detected a coldness in her eyes. She didn't say a thing.

"Get dressed," the first cop ordered.

"Get out of here and I'll get dressed!" I shouted back.

"Are you kidding, doll?" And he wasn't kidding as he leaned back against the chair. I worked semi-nude on stage every night, but I sure as hell wasn't going to give him a private show. I tried to dress under the sheet; that amused him to no end. This was the only time I really regretted sleeping in the nude. Anita dressed in front of them. They didn't take their eyes off us for one minute.

"Where are we going?" I asked sweetly this time because I saw them getting handcuffs ready. "You don't need that! I'll come peacefully, but I need to know where, because if I don't turn up for rehearsal, there is a $50 fine, and I want to let them know at the Moulin."

"The Bastille, for questioning." He turned to Nita. "She was your roommate in Naples, wasn't she?"

"Yes." Nita smiled.

I had no idea what was going on, and I didn't like it, but it seemed I was caught up in it and had to play along. The evidence sat on a chair, and it wasn't innocent. I had heard of heroine and pot and this was the real thing. Each one took us by the arm in an iron grip. I automatically added the cost of that bruise in with skipping rehearsal.

They led us to an unmarked police car. I was grateful that no one was up this early. Parisians stay up the whole night, then sleep the next day.

Nita suddenly became very talkative, and continued her outlandish flirtation. While all I could think of was losing my career. I felt like throwing up, and did so as we reached the Bastille over the cobbled courtyard and dark, gloomy passages which conjured up heads rolling away from the guillotine in days gone by.

Coming into the inner court was a black paddy wagon. When it came to a halt, out tumbled a gaggle of brightly, scantily clothed prostitutes, long legged, ample bosomed, some quite stunning under the heavy makeup and rhinestone minis. They could be showgirls if fate had not taken a wrong turn.

The gendarmes doing their paper work gave us a second look as we were led in with the "Ladies of the night." They expected us to look like showgirls. We had no makeup on and dressed hastily, in throw-on clothing, so we did not fit their expected image. It was a nightmare. I couldn't believe that it was happening to me.

In a dull looking room, a rookie Frenchman took my hand and rolled my fingers one by one onto an ink pad and then onto a paper. We were both silent while the procedure was going on. He did Nita and took pictures of us. Then he led us into an isolation cell. There were two wooden cots with padded bedrolls and blankets at the foot. I sat down on one of the cots. Then, without a word, he left us.

"Nita," I begged. "You have to tell them I'm innocent. I worked hard to get where I am, I don't want to lose my career." She just sat there with a silly smile on her face, searching the cell with her eyes, looking for a bugging device.

"I don't have to tell them anything, they already know it's your bag!" She

455

said it with such conviction it could have fooled anybody. I was stunned by her blatant lying without a blink of an eye. I knew she was guilty, I suspected it already in Naples. She wasn't going to say a word to incriminate herself. We sat there in absolute silence for over an hour, when Blue eyes made his appearance, unlocked the cell door, grabbed me roughly by the arm, and when I objected to his man-handling me, he pushed me roughly around some more.

"COME, BITCH!" It was so realistic. *Perhaps they heard her say it was my bag and they now believed it.*

"Where are you taking me?" I started crying for real. He pushed me out of the cell and slammed it shut with a loud bang. As soon as we got into a room at the end of the passage, he smiled and winked at me, "I'm sorry, hun, I had to play the meany so she wouldn't suspect. We know you're innocent."

"Innocent of what?" I sobbed. "I shared a room with her on tour, but the ballet booked us together. I had no choice!"

"We have been tracking Nita since she left America, and finally caught up with her when she joined the ballet as a cover for peddling the uppers, marijuana, and heroine."

"Is that why you tasted my art project?"

"I didn't know it was an art project, but we were looking for heroine, and what a clever way that would be to hide it, so the only way to make sure was to taste it." The other cop walked in.

"Sorry we had to be rough with you and bring you in with her, but you did room with her and could give us a picture of her comings and goings, and perhaps who she saw."

I told them that she was very secretive about who and where, and I did not allow her to bring her many "dates" into our room because I did not like the looks of them.

"All I know was that she was often missing for a day or two at a time and looked like a zombie when she returned, smelling bad and trying to hide it by wearing heavy perfume. I was naive enough to believe her when she explained it away as taking a tour."

"Did you ever see her smoke?"

"Oh yes! She was a chain smoker, lit one cigaret with the other. I thought she smoked too much.

"What did she smoke?"

"She smoked those cigarettes in the red and white package starting with an M."

"You mean like this?" He laughed and pulled out a pack out of his pocket. "I know what they're called."

"Yes" I nodded.

"No, like the ones twisted on the end that were in the black bag."

"Are those the ones that stunk up the room?" His eyes lit up and he winked at his partner. If I saw her smoke those I was their witness, and the case was closed. If I saw.

"No, I didn't see her smoke those, but she must have done it when I was out, because the room always stank, and the smell of burnt rope was always there or in her clothes. What is going to happen to her now?"

"We can only hold her for a time under suspicion of trafficking drugs unless you can help us make her confess. The cell you were both in is bugged and has hidden cameras. We want you to go back in and get her to talk." By now the whole day had nearly passed and I asked Blue eyes to call Andre and let him know what was going on. Andre was shocked, but promised to "Fix."

Before going back into the cell, I rubbed my eyes red, sprinkled some water on my face, and roughed up my hair. Blue eyes took me back to the cell and shoved me so hard I fell down, crawled toward the bed, and sat down pretending to cry, although real tears were not far away.

"You don't know what they did to me. I told them it was my bag to stop them torturing me, you can relax now."

Immediately she started laughing and said, "You pathetic idiot, you know the bag and the contents are mine! I only told them it was yours to get them off my back. I made a fortune out of the suckers who bought the stuff from me." She then went on to incriminate one of the girls who mysteriously dropped out of the ballet right after Naples and some of the very prominent citizens of Naples. She used names and places freely, because now she thought because I had confessed about the bag she would be freed. It was as if she wanted to get it all off her chest. I felt that I deceived her and wanted her to stop talking, but she went on and on about how she also got hooked and used it.

The two cops who arrested us came in. They said Andre had paid the bail. They pointed to me. "You can go now."

"What about me? She's the guilty one."

"I'm afraid not! You see with the information you just gave us, you will be deported, and incarcerated in America for possession and trafficking. The cell was bugged with recorder and camera."

Gone was the innocense.

"You f-----g bastard, you tricked me!" she yelled at Blue eyes.

Then she turned to me. "And you, bitch! You set me up. I've got connections, you better watch your back!"

"Do you want me to add that to your rap sheet?" Blue eyes said with a sneer.

Andre came to pick me up, made sure that my fingerprints were off the record, and also the fake arrest. The chief of police offered me a job as undercover informer, stating that he watched the tapes and my acting was very convincing. I graciously declined. "I don't think I will look good in cement shoes on the bottom of the Seine, I'm already nervous about her threat."

"Don't worry, it was an empty threat. You will have our protection." I found out from Andre that she was deported to America within forty-eight hours. In Paris she would have remained for the rest of her life in prison because her passport lied and she said she was 19, but in America because she was really 17; they would show leniency because she was still considered as a juvenile.

For a while after this incident, I became aware of someone following me. It made me nervous, but after a month I no longer saw them, but my heart always skipped a beat when I caught someone's eye lingering just a little too long on me.

60
Little Man — Big Voice

Two extra numbers were added on to our Argentina show and they were auditioning acts. I chose to come in for the 10 a.m. rehearsal. We had been at it the whole morning in between auditions. Doris told us to take a break. I went to the tabac next door and got myself a sandwich and a mint tea. When I got back.

A trampoline act was busy setting up their gear, arguing with the producers.

"The ceiling is too low I'm telling you we won't be able to do anything without hitting our heads on it!"

"Show me then what you CAN do without the trampoline."

"The trampoline is the main thing around which our act revolves, and it's too low!"

"What do you want me to do, make the ceiling higher? This is not a circus, if you want a circus, the Circ Medrano is just round the corner. They have a very high ceiling!" I had a few more minutes to rest and put my feet up, so I went upstairs to my dressing room, turned on my intercom, and put my feet up.

As soon as the trampoline clatter stopped I heard the producer call out "Next!" Then there was a pause. "Oh God not another circus act!" I jumped up and ran to the peephole. Across the stage I saw a blur as someone somersaulted onto the stage and up to the mike. A strong masculine voice rang out, gloriously filling every nook in the Moulin Rouge circular hall. I couldn't believe my eyes! The voice came from a little man no more than four feet tall. He was singing the song "Personality," then another dwarf appeared, slightly shorter but pleasantly plump. They did the funniest comedy routine I had seen for a long time. To show a little more of the range of his talent, the little man with the big voice next sang "When You Walk Through a Storm, Hold Your Head up High." When he hit the last high notes everyone was silent, deeply touched. Then the musicians started to applaud, and everyone, staff and visitors, joined in the applause. What a voice! Had he been 6 feet tall, Tom Jones would have had competition. I was impressed. I half expected his voice to be effeminate. But then, the only other dwarf I had ever known was a man called Tickey, who was from the Barnum and Baily Circus and had a rather effeminate voice. But this one's voice matched his speaking voice, pleasantly masculine.

After his audition we were called in to work on the number we were rehearsing earlier in the day. During my number, I noticed him, his partner, and another man I presumed to be his manager or agent sitting in the audience watching us rehearse. When our rehearsal was over I got hurriedly dressed and rushed to get home so that I could get some more rest before the evening's performance. I ran down the ramp to the exit door, and in the semi dark nearly fell over the little man sitting on the edge of the ramp. I stumbled then righted myself just in time, quickly regaining my balance. He jumped off the ramp to apologize. I towered over him on the ramp. *My God! He is even smaller than what I thought!*

"I'm so sorry, miss, are you okay?" He had a broad Manchester accent, with completely different intonation than his perfect singing diction. It was confusing.

I mumbled back, "I'm okay. I'm just in a hurry to get home and didn't see you sitting there, are you okay?"

"No I think my heart is broken because you are in such a hurry to get away from me."

I had no sooner reached the stage exit and was busy signing out when his manager caught up with me.

"Excuse me, miss, Dee wanted to know if you were free to join us at the Artist Club for dinner tonight? Before the show? Or for a drink after the show?"

I didn't know how to react to the invitation. Perhaps he was shy to ask me himself.

"I'm sorry, but I have a previous appointment." I was looking for a way out; I was just tired and wanted to have some rest. Most men I had dated before had been taller than me, or at least as tall as me. I tried to visualize us walking into the club together, me towering over him and he looking like a small boy who reached almost to my navel. It was a strange picture. But then curiosity won over.

"Thank you, but tell him I'm free tomorrow night if he came to ask me himself." Some flowers arrived at my dressing room later that same night, with a written invitation. I also notice him in the audience that night.

The following night getting dressed for my special "date," I had several moments of doubt when I was purposely putting on low heels. Then the thought came to me that whatever heels I wore it wouldn't matter unless he was wearing stilts. So I wore my usual high heels. Then when I put perfume behind my ears, it dawned on me he would never smell it there so I added some behind my knees instead of behind my ears.

I knew the club, it was where all the acts hung out in the old Montmartre. He was as attentive and as charming as can be, like his counterpart Toulouse Lautrec, who as a small child fell off a pony and was dwarfed. To make an impression on the ladies, Toulouse charmed them with his art, title, wealth, conversation, and libido.

Dee was no artist, except as a performer, he had amazing talent, as for wealth and title I wasn't sure. As for conversation? He talked mostly of his work and travels with his band, confessed that he had only read one book in his life that wasn't a school book. So right off bat I knew we had nothing in common, except we were both performers. As for libido, I couldn't tell.

The surprise however came when he kissed me during a toast to celebrate his getting a part in the Paris show and another lingering one for getting the contract for Argentina. His lips were soft and warm and the kiss disarmingly sensual.

The weeks that followed he became my constant companion; we went everywhere together. The Moulin Rouge took advantage of the opportunity and built publicity around us. At first it was difficult to adjust to the stares and comments of thoughtless people. But it did not phase him one bit, and I rather admired him for his cool. He had an answer to all their remarks. The media was unmercifully personal and outright rude. The true test came one night about a month after "dating" Dee.

I had gone to meet Dee at his hotel and we were getting ready to go to a Chinese restaurant for dinner. There was a knock on his door. Opening it there stood a man who could look up to Dee. He was under three feet in height. Dee introduced him to me as Billy Bardie, a friend of his from back home. Billy said he was there on a "Little People's Convention" before going to work on a *Star Wars* picture. He said he got the part because he was the only one who could fit inside the robot R2-D2. There was another knock and in came another small person. Billy in turn introduced him to us as Ton-Ton; he was Spanish and about Dee's size, very flamboyantly dressed with colorful waistcoat over a gipsy blouse, open at the chest displaying a gold pendant. But the thing that brought out comment was a thin braid that hung down from the top of his forehead between his eyes down onto the bridge of his nose.

"It's a gimmick and conversation piece to distract from the usual boring comments about my stature. With Ivan Dee's partner, now there were two dwarfs, two midgets, and one lilliputian, and three more uncategorized. When the door knock was answered again, there stood an identical twin, both doctors, and an even smaller man than Billy.

Snow white and the seven dwarfs were now complete!

"Where's the party?" They I'm sure did not have Snow White in mind. They were just a bunch of guys looking for a good time at the convention. And were overjoyed to see Dee's success in getting a contract at the Moulin Rouge and having such a stunning blonde as co-star.

"We were just on the way out to go and have dinner at a Chinese restaurant a block up the road. Care to accompany us?" Dee asked.

The answer was, "Yes, of course." As we started to walk up the road, people started following us. When we went into the restaurant they also entered hoping to see something, a film shooting or something. The restaurant owner was delighted with the crowd but panicked when he found out it was just us who came to dinner. To avoid trouble, a waiter came and handed Dee a key to the owner's apartment above the restaurant, and the waiter to took our orders.

We accepted and enjoyed a peaceful dinner and social time till it was time for me to go to the Moulin Rouge for makeup and do my performance. They naturally came to the show, and after the show we piled into two cabs and went to the Bantoe Club, another watering hole for celebrities, where instead of just taking a bow, Dee and Ton-Ton gave them an impromptu show on the house. I of course took turns dancing with all seven. Dee was an excellent dancer and the people gave us the floor throughout the night. Dee had just signed a contract, and already violated two of the clauses.

That night coming from the club, Dee proposed. With the courage of quite a few drinks behind his belt. He said he had fallen in love with me, and told me he got an apartment on Boulevard de Cliché that needed a woman's touch. He was going back to England for a month before starting at the Moulin Rouge, and then he actually knelt down in front of me and said: "Will you marry me?" I was taken aback. He looked quite sincere, but I was sure it was just the booze talking. I did not answer.

Up un till then I had not told him about Peter back in South Africa. So I told Dee that my love for Peter was the reason I left home in the first place. Peter was waiting for a divorce from his wife who was in therapy for her multiple attempts at suicide, and the law would not allow divorce while a person was incapacitated and could not sign. There was hope that she would be released from the institute, and he would get a divorce, then it would be possible for me to marry him.

I told him that I intended to quit the show and go back to South Africa to see what was going on. I tried to tell him in the kindest way possible.

"So you see, I cannot give you an answer. I admire your talent, but I am not in love with you, because I'm caught up in a star-crossed love affair already, to which there seems to be no solution.

He's answer to me was, "Go to him and find out, I can wait! I have enough love for both of us. In time you will learn to love me, but for the moment my apartment still needs a woman's touch, will you help me? There is a second bedroom. You can move in to there till I leave for England and you go to South Africa to sort out your affairs."

I needed a change in my accommodation, and on impulse I moved in. Dee was pleased, he took it as my answer, but I told him it would only be to help him out with the apartment. He was quite the gentleman, and showered me with attention. I enjoyed the domesticity of cleaning and furnishing it. And thrilled to no longer use the communal bathroom in the hotel; this apartment actually had it's own bathroom

In the meantime I had informed the Miss Doris of my intention to go to South Africa. She said, "Go back and sort out your love life," adding, "it would be preferable than staying with Dee, then if it doesn't work out there and you are ready to join the ballet in Argentina, we will send you your ticket. You have rehearsed the show already so it wouldn't be difficult to step back in and do the show."

Only when I came back with my ticket to Cape Town and the sailing date did Dee believe me, He was devastated. I felt sorry for him, not because of his size, but because he said he would never love anyone the way he loved me. He even cried when he said, "Please don't go!" Then he added, "What will I do without you? Now that I found you I don't want to lose you again. If you don't come back, I swear I'll kill myself!"

He didn't say anything more as the time drew near, but cancelled his own contract in England, to stay till I left. He became more depressed, even though we still went out to the clubs and to dinner. He started going to the rehearsals for the Argentina show In the hopes that I would return to the Moulin Rouge.

A few days before my departure, I walked into the apartment. Dee was lying on the couch; he looked pale. At first I thought he was either sleeping or drunk, but then I noticed the empty bottle of sleeping tablets in his hand. My heart stopped for a second. *No he couldn't have,* was my only thought. *He did threaten to kill himself.* Then I cursed silently, mad as hell; this was exactly what Peter was going through. I knelt down beside him and smelled his breath, there was no alcohol on his breath. I slapped his face and there was no reaction. Then panicking I called his partner and told him that I could not rouse Dee. I explained to him that Dee had threatened to kill himself.

It didn't seem to phase him. "Don't be alarmed, I'm sure it's only an act to stop you from leaving him. He will be okay. He always snaps back."

"What do you mean 'He ALWAYS snaps back'? I don't think this is an act. He's clutching an empty bottle of sleeping tablets in his hand, and I don't know how many he had in the bottle."

"I'll be over shortly, give him some salt water, and try to get him to sit up." There was silence on the other end of the line, then he said, "He's had many affairs before you, and I'm sure he will have many more after you, just try and arouse him."

When Ivan arrived, we lifted him into a sitting position and I forced salt water down him. He heaved once and threw up some tablets, then lay down again.

"No! You have to stay awake!" He was still breathing irregularly. We lifted him off the couch and dragged him around the room till he was forced to walk on his own. Then I poured black coffee into him, till he pleaded for mercy, and confessed he had only taken four and threw the others out the window. He just was sleepy.

The following day he acted as if nothing had ever happened, even suggested that we go to our favorite restaurant, Le Rosary, for escargot.

The name in itself suggests, "Father forgive me, I have sinned." Well that was exactly what it turned out to be to some unsuspecting customers. To us however it was the best restaurant, to have succulent escargot, or stuffed quail with truffles or golden crisp frogs legs at the regular price. We never noticed it before, but it was the haven for food hustling. I never heard of such a thing before, but it happened!

The name "Le Rosary" also conjured up cathedral-like decor, but it was nothing like it; there was nothing distinguishable about it. It had the usual café tables with white tablecloths divided into separate booths. There were bedraggled potted plants (later we found out why), and in the middle of the room on a divider stood a large very dirty fish tank with one solitary fish that swam sideways and had only one eye, most likely because of the cloudy water(we also found out why), so I naturally called the restaurant 'The One-Eyed Fish."

That night for the first time I found out about food hustling. Past the tank several tables had RESERVED cards on. Dee's very generous tips always gave us a booth near there. We usually noticed, though, that there was a large turnover with American tourists in this restaurant.

We had no sooner sat down and our order taken when a lovely sexy young lady came in on the arm of an already inebriated American man. They had no sooner sat down when she turned into a clinging vine; she was all over him with a "cheri this" and "darling that."

When the waiter came to take their orders, the American couldn't understand the menu, so she, being very helpful, ordered the best for them. Starting "naturally" with caviar, then lobster, then quail and truffles of course, with champagne "naturally." Between courses, she massaged his thighs, whispering sweet nothing in his ear about things to come. Telling him all lovey-dovey to drink his "very expensive champagne," seductively taking little sips and bites from him, and hand feeding him, never touching her own food. When he became ready for the fleecing, a rose vender came in from the street with a bunch of roses, telling the man that it was his last bunch and wouldn't the lovely young lady want some roses?

"Of course, cheri," she raved about the roses. He bought it for her, "naturally." This was where she told him sweetly that she needed to ago to the ladies room to powder her nose and put the roses into some water, and she won't be long. She then takes her little pocket book and goes upstairs. NOW, the waiter arrives on cue with an astronomical bill. The American explains he is waiting for his date, but the waiter wants to leave and insists he pay up.

Eavesdropping on this all, we try to warn him that the bill is too high, but he tells us to "bug off" and tears off three $100 travelers checks and pays.

Then he waits and waits, but his date doesn't turn up, but the waiter brings him a phone message, telling him that she had a family emergency and had to leave, but would he meet her in an hour at the X-Y-Z Hotel.(Which "naturally" doesn't exist but is conveniently situated on the other side of town.) The waiter generously calls him a cab on the house. Minutes later after the cab left, the same lovely sexy young lady walked into the door on the arm of her next client. We were intrigued to see what would happen next. The same scene played itself out, like a bad play. Except this one wasn't as drunk as the previous one and insisted she eat her very expensive food, and drink her very expensive champagne. She went through the motions in between the seduction, and while kissing him, she neatly disposed the food into the potted plant and the drink into the fish tank.

When the bill came she argued with him about the size of the bill, saying it was terrible. I wondered how she was going to get out of this one. The telephone page called out "NANETTE," and she motioned to the page that is was she.

Spoke on the phone, and showing a lot of emotion, told her "date" that there was an emergency at home, but would he meet her at the X-Y-Z Hotel in an hour. He fell for it. Even bought her the roses from the vender standing at the door. Besides, she had promised him a "Good Time" and he was going to collect, so he paid the bill and accepted the offer of a free cab.

On one occasion I followed her to the ladies room where the vender was waiting on the roof. She climbed through the window, handed the roses to him, also the share of the sale, climbed back down the back stairs, and went in search of her next client. In the meantime, the food was removed from the plants. Nothing could be done to clear the water in the tank, and by the end of the night the poor old one-eyed fish was swimming sideways, soused to the gills! I suggested to the management that he replaced the real fish with a plastic one. I was terribly sorry for the old thing.

In two hours we saw "Nanette" repeat the same scene four times with different men. The surprise was that she never slept with one of them. She was paid a percentage of the final tab, also a share of the sale of the roses, which were returned and resold to all the girls who worked the "Reserved Tables" in shifts throughout the night. Later we became experts in spotting the girls who used the same scenario and script, and naturally the same exit over the roof.

61
Stalemate in Affairs of the Heart

I felt lousy leaving Dee, but his partner had assured me that he would snap out of it.

The two weeks on the ship, I could think of nothing else but Peter and my family. On arrival in Cape Town I took the boat train to Johannesburg where Peter was working. He came to collect me at the station. From the moment he took me in his arms I knew that he loved me, and I loved him. He had temporarily moved in with friends of his. I was in second heaven just being with him, walking in the park, or visiting him on the set where he was making a movie, or just reading the latest of his publications. But the bad news was that after his wife left the drug habilitation center, she took their 18-month-old daughter and went back to Cape Town. The dark cloud still hung over our heads—even though she was living with one of her lovers in Cape Town, she refused to grant Peter the divorce. I tried to reason it out with him, but there was no way out. He was sure she would change her mind. But I had heard it before. I told him about the pending contract with Moulin Rouge to go to Argentina and that I needed an answer within weeks or lose that opportunity. For the first time words of anger flew between us.

"If your career is more important than my love for you, then GO!" he shouted, and I blew up, blaming his deception, infatuation, and sudden marriage to Ingrid as the cause of my pursuing my career in the first place.

"You promised to marry me when we returned from second safari, and broke my heart by marrying her instead, and now I have waited four years, living off promises that she would grant you a divorce! But it is still the same old story. There is no doubt that I love you, will always love you. But we are caught up in a stalemate that has no way of resolving our dilemma. Perhaps the only way out would be if I left you for good."

The following morning I left to visit my dad forty miles away. Daddy was happy to see me after four years of Europe, even though they felt hurt that I had gone straight to Peter before even coming to them. I wanted Daddy to meet Peter, who was working for Trans Africa Safari, and knew that they would hit it off wonderfully, and he would get to know him and like him, as Dad was a game warden. They both loved Africa. But Daddy refused; he had seen a painting I had made of Peter. His long hair made him see Peter as a hippie with no morals. I tried to convince him that they had everything in common and that Peter loved me, and promised that things would change soon.(I did not tell him about our final fight because hope was still there that before I accepted the Argentina contract, things would miraculously change.) But Daddy just looked at me; "Peter's promises don't mean a thing. You are blind, my child. You say you love him, and he says he loves you, but he has used his wife's instability as a hold on you. It's been four years! I should say that constitutes a definite STALEMATE. Life is too short, you should get on with your life. There are other fish in the sea! Go out and catch another."

I told Daddy that Dee had proposed and was waiting for an answer.

"There's your answer, say yes." *I didn't tell him that Dee was a dwarf, I thought it was complicated enough.*

Next I went to visit my sister. Several telegrams had arrived at her address from the Moulin Rouge and two from Dee wanting to know what my answer was to his proposal. The telephone rang incessantly. I knew it was from Peter. My sister asked me why I didn't answer it, but I did not know what to do, it was now in the hands of fate!

A few days after leaving Peter, we were having morning tea pool side. I looked up, and turning in at the gate and winding down the long driveway was Peter's little sports car, Cricket.

"I'm not expecting anyone, I wonder who that could be?"

"You're not expecting anyone, but I am. All those calls were from Peter, and I hope you treat him more civil than Daddy did, who refused to even meet him." I could see Peter's hesitancy when he got out of his car to approach us at the pool. My heart felt like it would leap out of my throat, and I visibly trembled when he shook my sisters hand and said, "I don't want her to go!

You must convince her that I love her." As if I wasn't there. Then he turned to me and asked me to go to the fancy dress ball with him.

For the week preceding the ball, he drove the forty miles from Johannesburg every night to visit me. We met secretly under the giant old tree next to the house. He pleaded with me to stay and I stubbornly insisted that he give me a reason to stay.

"Because we love each other" was his reason. *But what about her?* raced through my mind. *Will she EVER divorce him?*

With everything appearing so hopeless, I had accepted the Argentina contract, and in a moment of insanity, to convince him that I was going to move on with my life, I told him the blatant lie that I was in love with someone else, and had accepted his proposal of marriage. He was shocked.

On the night of the ball, Peter looked magnificent as Lucifer in red leotards and red body paint, but it was as a raw symbol of the hell to come without him. So I dressed the part in black leotards and lace bat wings, as the bat from hell.

In spite of my impending doom, it was a magical night like the first time we danced on the barge. My body became one with him as we glided across the dance floor. While we danced he whispered in my ear. "Why don't you believe me, my love? I'm finally home."

Even though I had told him that I was leaving him for the final time, he was not convinced.

On the way back home he asked me: "How can you say that you are in love with someone else when you know we were born for each other?"

"Perhaps it is not the same kind of love I feel for you, but he is offering me stability, without commitment to any one else in his life. He knows that I love you, and has accepted that, and time does not stand still. I am twenty-eight years old and still hope to have children, even if they are not yours, and you know and I have known for some time now that your wife will never give you a divorce, out of spite. Yet you made me believe that it was still possible. I came back to South Africa, with the belief that I would be able to marry you, but now I have found out that my hope is shattered and I must move on." He did not reply, but as we parted he took me in his arms, and we kissed. I kissed him back with my whole being with tears streaming over my cheeks.

He kissed the tears away and said, "Now tell me that you don't love me— your whole body tells me that you love me."

I pulled away from him and ran into the house, my soul screamed out in pain, and I could not deny it! *Forgive me, my love,* and with his name on my lips as I fell asleep.

His letters arrived daily, twenty pages long, the pages drenched with my tears. I closed my mind to his pleas.

Weeks later, back in Paris, my sister wrote to me how her heart went out to Peter when she saw him standing alone at the airport, sobbing silently as he watched my departure. She confessed that she realized that all of them had been wrong, she now knew that he loved me deeply, and when they left after the plane was already out of sight, he was still standing there looking out into space where my plane had disappeared. She wanted to go over to him and console him, but it was too late. I had chosen. It was too late. They should have stood by me and believed in him, but mainly they should have supported me.

62

Second Thoughts on the Rebound Marriage

Doris was glad that I was back. And finding myself in the Argentina show had taken my mind off Peter. They made some changes in the choreography but I worked hard and soon had it down pat.

It felt good to work again. The Moulin Rouge capitalized on the publicity of my return, naming Dee as the reason. The media followed us around everywhere Dee and I went. We tried to dodge them by taking the company limo and going to remote beaches, only to find them there waiting for us. We were the "stars" at all the social functions. It was flattering, but at the same time infringed in our privacy. The papers called me the Ruby of the Moulin, and asked us if the rumors that we were getting married in Argentina were true? Dee said we had not even announced our engagement. At which point the media took over and arranged for a public engagement, which turned out to be a circus. The reception was elaborate and held in the foyer of the theater we were performing in.

The public came in droves and were cordoned off by ribbons. We were posed and displayed. The headlines were "THE ROMANCE OF THE CENTURY." It sounded so romantic, but the real interviews were stinging. Their questions were personal and insulting. The champagne was flowing, and soon Dee was intoxicated and replied with some humor to some of the questions put to him.

"How will you make love to her; she is so much bigger than you?"

" Simple. I'll just hang a bucket over her head and hang onto the handle!" Dee laughed. I got into the game as well.

"Actually, he likes to do it standing up."

"How is that possible, he is so little?"

"No, I mean standing up on a hammock!" I added.

Dee, unable to look the reporter in the eyes, focused his eyes on the man's crotch.

"What are you staring at?" the reporter asked, annoyed.

"I was just wondering, how do YOU make love, with yours being so little?"

I burst out laughing, the man was taken aback.

"That's outright insulting!" the reporter blurted out.

"Just about as insulting as your questions about my lovemaking skills, which I'm sure if it comes to comparison, equal yours, or not to boast, even excel yours in quantity and quality. For what I lack in stature, God was most generous with size!"

It amazed me to see Dee so cool; I half expected him to attack the man, because he had a short fuse.

We stayed for a little longer, signing autographs and mingling with the guests.

Doris came over to me, mainly to express her surprise at my accepting Dee's proposal, then she turned to him.

"You are no good for her—you sleep around with half of my ballet, are ill mannered and an ignorant drunk."

To my horror, he raised his hand and slapped her face. She immediately slapped him back. Two men had to restrain him and literally carried him outside to cool off. I was totally embarrassed at his behavior. I apologized to Miss D. She just responded, "You are a fool. I said it when you left for South Africa, and I'm saying it now."

Dee took the media engagement party as his personal victory over Peter. I made him apologize for slapping Doris. He blamed it on the overindulgence of champagne. I should have told him then that it was over, but in my mind I thought I was in too deep, especially when we made the headlines, glorifying our romance. It was only after our engagement that he first made love to me. Like his kisses he surprised me, he was an expert in the technique of pleasing a woman and he did not lie to the reporter, which I had confirmation of soon after. Two girls came to me and told me directly that he had slept with them during my absence in South Africa.

I confronted him then, and he was furious that I believed the wild rumors. "You just see things out of context." He denied their accusations and brought me a bunch of yellow roses, "to cure my unfounded jealousy." To compensate that night he presented me with a beautiful, black sexy negligee to model for him. He cured everything with sex, and I fell for it, having had a foretaste of his ability to satisfy me. I forgave him and dismissed their accusations in my mind as "just stories!"

Our last stop on the South American tour was Mara-Del-Plata. The show was a great success. It was all work and no play, so we had to take advantage of every free minute. Dee had in his youth worked with horses and had even dreamed of one day being a jockey, but even though he had the correct height, his legs were too short to be able to stand up in the stirrups. But here we were in horse country and he could devote all his spare time riding. It was just naturally expected that I do it with him.

Our hotel was situated on a cliff side, so every morning Dee had two horses brought to the back door. He had ordered an English saddle, so they brought the nearest thing, an American saddle. This I graciously let Dee have, being the better rider and the stirrups could be adjusted to suit his legs. I settled for something that they called a saddle, but was far from it. It was an ordinary sheepskin tied with a rawhide girth beneath the belly. The stirrups were blocks of wood with a hole burnt through in the middle tied onto a rawhide strap with wire. With heavy riding boots these things would have been sufficient, but with my flimsy day boots that did not support my ankles it was dangerous to say the least; the wires kept chafing through the shoes. The horse I rode had his mouth spoiled and was a follower as a result; it did not obey the reins, no matter how hard I pulled—having an insensitive mouth it ignored my command.

Dee was following a well-worn horse path, riding dangerously close to the edge of the cliff. It was a magnificent view, and because my horse was a follower, I wasn't paying a lot of attention. So when Dee suddenly reined in to a halt, my horse close behind responded automatically. I was thrown forward with such force that the wire of the stirrup cut into my flesh, and I could feel a warm trickle of blood flowing into my boots. If I did not grab the horse around the neck, I would have been thrown across his head and over the edge of the cliff.

By the time we got back to the hotel, my feet were so swollen because the wire that held the blocks in place were rusted, and I had to go through a series of painful Tetanus shots to prevent blood poisoning. But the thing that hurt most was the large fine I had to pay, for "JEOPARDIZING MY PERFORMANCE."

By now we were openly living together, and the media speculated that we had married in Argentina and left us alone. Doris had never forgiven the slap she received in public, so she cancelled Dee's contract after Argentina.

Lew, our American manager, took over our management and thought it would be a good time for us to get officially married, so he booked a series of shows in England so that I could meet Dee's family.

The showgirls all clubbed together to give me a "Bon voyage" party, as this time I would leave the show for good. They all promised to keep in touch. We had been together for three years and it was sad to say good-bye to the Moulin Rouge Ballet Troop.

Hal, Dee's English manager, wanted to quit. So he went ahead to London and got us a lovely apartment. We were booked to perform in the Churchill Club. Dee's parents and sisters were overjoyed that he finally was making a commitment that looked real. Everyone talked together excitedly to tell me about his growing up.

I looked for signs of dwarfism in his family; with his father six foot one, and five normal sisters, I saw none. We searched his family history. His mother at five-foot-three thought that she must have contributed to his size. He was born normal and genetically sound, but a defect in his pituitary stunted his growth.

It wasn't till later on that his father noticed that his only son wouldn't grow. They tried everything. Health spas and sunshine clubs. Pituitary shots were not yet used to increase growth. They couldn't do anything for him but prepare him for the future, and shield him from the cruelty of people's stares, remarks and ignorance. His mother made him do everything for himself.

"And he had many scrapes and falls climbing on the cupboards getting things down, and I didn't count the bloody noses he had defending himself. But his size never stopped him doing things," his mother bragged.

"He started singing in the church and later entertained in the pubs."

She went on to tell me about his big dream of becoming a jockey, but hated working in the Queen's stables lugging big feed buckets as tall as himself. That was when he had the operation to straighten his legs, when they told him his legs were too short. So he gave up that dream, and one night singing in a pub, a young midget started heckling him, but the people loved it and they became partners doing the nightclub circuit, and soon they had a manager, Hal Monty, which led to bigger things. And the Moulin Rouge where he met me. Soon the photo albums came out. They were obviously very proud of him.

As the wedding drew near, I became more and more nervous. If I believed the newspapers, I would have been very happy. But I couldn't get Peter out of my mind. The media painted a wonderful picture of two people not concerned with size, but being in love with no worries in the world. I spent my spare time digging up any material I could find on dwarfism and reading it in secret so as not to offend Dee, even though his family assured me that there had not been any dwarfism in their family as far as they could track. He had earned my respect as a lover and an entertainer. I thought that in time I would forget all about Peter and learn to love him. But the "what ifs" kept cropping up, and I found myself lying awake deep into the night.

What if I married him and found the difference in our heights affect me after all? What if the constant remarks of the people around us DO matter? What if our cultural differences, language and food preferences, even the fact that he's only read one book and I'm a book lover escalated to dislike. What if he becomes violent? I have seen him slap a woman once, would he do it to me? What if the girls were right and he did sleep around while I was in South Africa, and his partner was right, he had many affairs? But the biggest "what if" was, *What if we married and had children, and it wasn't true that there WAS no genetic throwback, my child was born a dwarf and had to go through what he had to go through? What if I couldn't cope?*

I did not tell Dee of my fears. But now I had second thoughts that I couldn't shake.

Two weeks before the wedding we took the boat to France to pick up our new sports car, so that we could use it on our honeymoon.

And in spite of the "what ifs," on a very rainy day in May (they said it was lucky if it rained on a wedding), we got married with only the immediate family of his in attendance; mine was back in South Africa. It was a late afternoon wedding with reception in the Waldorf Hotel where Dee had booked our fourteen guests coming from Manchester who were attending a sit down wedding dinner. The bride's table looked beautiful with white lace table covers and raised centerpieces of white camellias and snowdrops with green napkins to match the leaves on the camellias. On either side of the table stood a wedding cake in the form of a ballerina, and small ballerinas attached

475

to the cake with ribbons indicated the place settings. After the reception, Dee's youngest sister danced a traditional Irish saber dance. And later the guests were collected by taxi and taken to the Churchill Club to see our late, late 12 a.m. show. After the show there was an English wedding breakfast of eggs, bacon sausage, fried tomato, and English muffins. Everyone who was in the club to see the show stayed. Dancing continued till dawn. That was when we decided to leave and take his sister and her boyfriend back to the hotel.

The new cars gears were still a little stiff so Dee drove very slowly, because he had quite a lot to drink and with his new bride, and sister with her boyfriend sitting crammed into the section normally reserved for luggage, he was extra careful.

About five blocks from the hotel, as we crossed an intersection, a cab cutting a red light and going full speed hit us broadside. The impact was so strong that it shattered the shatter-proof windows, which rained down on us, creating tiny cuts to exposed skin, and sent the car into a roll, not just once but three times and coming to rest against a garden rail of a nearby house.

They say that in a near-death experience, one's whole life flashes before you. That was not the case with me. I was very much in the present.

As we rolled over I had the strangest thoughts flashing through my mind. My head was piled high in a beehive style of curls, done for my wedding. It saved my life. On the first roll over, as my head hit the ceiling of the car, I wondered if the curls would take the blow. I looked at Dee; he sat clinging to the steering wheel with both hands in a shocked trance. I could see the car turn over for the second time. I knew I was too big to catapult through the broken window, but he wasn't, so holding on to the window handle on my side and bracing myself with my foot on the dashboard, I grabbed him by the back of his pants. As we hit the pavement on the roll over I said a prayer. "THANK YOU, LORD, WE ARE ALIVE!" Then as we rolled over for the last time and hit the iron fence, crushing it, the strangest thought came to mind. I was still in full stage makeup with long stage lashes. A picture flashed through my mind, of me lying dead with the makeup smeared all over my face and the false lashes plastered sideways over my eyes. So there on the last moments of my life I let go of the dashboard where I had been holding on for dear life and plucked the eyelashes off my eyes. When the car finally came to rest almost inside the house. I looked around, dazed and badly shaken, surprised that I wasn't dead.

Lots of blood came from superficial minute wounds of the broken glass.

And when the ambulance man pulled me free from the wreck, I had no recollection of the marriage, or my new name.

The car was a write-off, but the manufacturers in France replaced it with a similar model; we were well insured.

63

On the Road Again

By marrying Dee I automatically became a British subject and was able to obtain a work permit that would allow me to work in his show. I was written into his show so that I could travel with him. My travel expenses were covered by our bookings. At first we went to the Steel Pier boardwalk in England to introduce the new comedy skit to see if it would work out, then we did it in the nightclub circuit, and on to Germany to the American military camps. It was completely different from Paris. The skit was cute and people loved it.

While he sang, I came out of the curtains behind him wearing a very daring skintight elasticized dress which was open to my navel in front and slit up the side to my thigh. With it I wore long black gloves up to my elbow. The moment I came out the audience started clapping and the men whistled. Dee pretended that he thought the applause was for him and reacted to it, but by then they were shouting look behind you, I sneaked up close and when he looked around I moved with him, so there was no one there, he shrugged his shoulders and went on singing. I then put my gloved hand on his shoulder and seductively pressed my leg with the slit up against him. Without looking round he felt behind him who it could be, his hand going right up the slit. The audience roared as he slowly felt up my leg and over my hip, stopping short of my bust. I put my hand on his head and motioned "No!" He then stepped back and made the usual sign of a woman's curves and whistled. He then motioned to the audience he had an idea, felt around in his pockets and produced a tape measure, looped the tape around my hips with exaggerated sensual movements, walked up to the mike and announced 36 inches, walked back to me and with his arms around my waist, put the tape around, then stayed there for a moment doing kissy-kissy gestures. The audience loved it and started whistling again. He walked to the mike and announced 24 inches, motioned to the audience that next would be my bust, but he wouldn't be able to reach. I straightened up, pushing my bust into the air. He approached me, walking around me and sizing things up, then proceeded to toss the tape up over my bust, but it kept falling down. He then wrapped his leg a round me, pretending to climb up me with the tape measure in his mouth. The audience shouted out encouragement! He slipped down every time. I then took the tape out of his mouth, put it round my bust and handed it back to him. He looked at it and nodded, went to the mike, and announced, "36 … 24 … 36." Where upon I walked over to him bent down and gave him a big sexy kiss right on his mouth. He closed his eyes and fell straight back on his back in a mock faint.

I exited waiving at the audience with a last seductive gesture with my bare leg out of the curtain. The moment I was off, Dee's partner entered, a three-foot, nine-inch tall midget dressed in drag wearing an identical outfit and blond wig with short black gloves, and the addition of a beard. Dee got up from his swoon, with eyes still closed when he heard the audience applaud, thinking it was me again. He pouted his lips for another kiss. Ivan went up to him and planted a smacking kiss on his mouth, and Dee opened his eyes up, feeling the beard against his face. Then motioned to the audience, "WHAT HAPPENED?" Ivan looked at the audience while Dee went looking for me in the curtains and off stage. Strip music started. Ivan started to strut across the stage doing strippers' bumps and grinds. The audience was roaring with laughter by then when he popped off the dress, dragged it between his legs, then continued the strip till he ended up in an old- fashioned corset and jockey shorts. Now Dee returned and did the same routine that he did with me, but very quickly. And he announced with every measurement, "36 … 36 … 36 …" Then he measured him from head to toe and announced, "36." Ivan did a drag queen pout and took off the corset as a last measure to win the audience over and tossed it into the wings. Dee went up to the mike and said, "You're just jealous because I have two inches more than you."

Ivan looked shocked. The audience laughed. Dee added, "In height!"

This same act nearly caused a riot a month later in an American Camp near the Polish border. I had just gone off the stage when the stomping and shouting started. "BRING ON THE BROAD! BRING ON THE BROAD!"

"Bring on the broad" rang out throughout the hall. The men had not seen a woman in a while, and all they wanted was me back. The commander of the camp escorted me to his office, explaining the circumstance. "You're far too sexy, and I was afraid they would storm the stage and cause a riot. It's so bad that we have to give them paper cups and plastic knives. They break the glass to cut someone with when a fight breaks out." On the table in a side room he showed me the dangerous arsenal of weapons that were confiscated from them before they came into the show. There were hunting knives, flick knives, knuckle dusters, chains, and two guns.

The Commander went out and announced that the lady suddenly took ill and could not continue, but they had found another to take her place. There was a hooting and hollering, and just then Ivan walked out and proceeded with his strip tease; that miraculously broke the tension, and by the time he got to the old lady's corset, they were rolling in the aisles.

They found the political skits Ivan did, especially the one with Castro, even more funny. The end of the story was that they wouldn't let Dee and his partner off the stage for a full two hours, calling for "More! More!" After the show we were smuggled out of camp just to find that several fist fights had already started. Between the military camp shows, we did one night stands, often traveling overnight between countries in Europe to get to the next gig. It was very tiring but rewarding.

One night coming from Belgium on our way back to Frankfurt, Dee told me to look out for somewhere where we could eat and rest before he fell asleep behind the wheel. We passed a few places, but they were all shrouded in darkness. But just round a bend I spotted a place that looked like an all-night restaurant. It was brightly lit and I saw people walking in and out. Through the big picture windows I saw people sitting behind tables. I told Dee to pull up and I would go in and inquire about prices and possible accommodation for the night.

Dee said he would wait in the car; he did not speak any language besides English, and hated to negotiate anything.

I thought the lady greeting me at the door with a broad smile was a little too overdressed, and the ladies at the tables were a little too under-dressed, and saw very few men around. In my best French I addressed her.

"Madam, nous voulons cushee,(should have said dormier) et mange quelque chose." She looked at me and started telling me it would be extra for clean sheets, and if we wanted food in the room it would be extra, what would I like to eat, and then told me how much it would be for extra people in the room, and how much it would be per hour. I was just explaining that we don't mind what we have because it was around three in the morning when Dee walked in.

She took one look at Dee, and said, "My girls don't do deviant sex. It would be better that you take your business elsewhere." Up to that moment I still thought that it was an all night restaurant, but it suddenly dawned on me that by the looks of it may be a bordello.

"Are you a Madam then?" I asked.

She threw her shoulders back replying, "Yes and I'm proud that my girls don't practice deviant sex." Somehow she had a preconceived idea that dwarfs only did kinky sex. Dee, still in the dark about the delay, asked "What's up?"

So I turned to him and said, "Darling they don't do deviant sex here. We will have to take our business somewhere else." I quickly explained to him in English, and we were still laughing when we got to the car.

"So are you in the mood for a bit of deviant sex?"

"I'll settle for anything if it includes something to eat and a bed to sleep on. Let's press on to Frankfurt! I rested enough while you were inside."

64
Delayed Honeymoon — Bullfight

We had nearly been a year on the Army circuit entertaining, and had not had time for a honeymoon when Dee proposed that we go to Madrid to see a bullfight for our honeymoon. I had no objection. I had seen a bullfight in Portuguese, East Africa. There the men pole vaulted over the bull, and when the bull fight was over the bulls went back to pasture to await the next fight. I had also seen movies with bullfights, but they seldom showed the blood and gore, only the "Oles" and the excitement of the crowd that glorified the toreador.

They usually panned away from the animals suffering. So I thought nothing of it, even looked forward to it.

In a bar at the International we met the killer of bulls himself. He was extremely handsome, taller than the usual bullfighter, with raven black hair and eyes. His curly hair was slicked back and tied into a small braid. A raised silver scar ran across his cheek up to his chin. I found it strangely attractive. He saw my eyes follow the line of the scar, and smiled a disarming smile, which certainly would have made me swoon if I did not think, *Watch it, girl, you're on your honeymoon.* I lowered my eyes. He laughed. "He nearly had me that time."

A bunch of men wearing the same kind of braid egged him on to tell them the story again. They hung onto his every word as he recounted the story for the hundredth time. He was proud of it, like a living trophy.

"The horn cut across my chest." He opened his shirt and there across his chest lay the greater scar. "As the bull then lifted me into the air the tip of the horn pierced my cheek. I was angry that he had the better of me, and determined even though I was bleeding profusely not to let him disgrace me in front of the crowd. I somehow got to my feet, let him make a final pass, and gave him the coup de gras. The sword went straight to his heart. A perfect kill! We looked at one another. He dropped in his tracks. They told me later the crowd went wild. I had redeemed myself. That day they carried me out with the bull."

There was a moment of silent admiration. Bravo, the men acclaimed his bravery. Dee went up to him and shook his hand. He responded to Dee by giving us tickets to all three fights as his honored guests, winking at me as we walked out. It would look good for him to have a tall blonde and a dwarf sitting in the honored place. Dee was thrilled.

Blood in the Sand

The bullring was circular in shape with seats all around, reminded me of the Coliseum in Rome, only this was smaller and did not sacrifice Christians to the lions. It sacrificed bulls for five pesos to satisfy the blood-hunger of the peasants. We sat in the honored seat right in front. A magnificent gilded red rose cape hung over the wall in front of us.

The sun baked down hot on the eager crowd, intensifying the smell of human sweat that mingled with the exotic musk smell of Tabu perfume in which the ladies had bathed. They were dressed in their finest Spanish frills, tight enough to choke them, with richly embroidered mantillas and lace scarves draped over their heads.

I became aware of a faint smell of animal excrement that wafted up from the holding pens below our seats. Every now and then our seats trembled as one of the bulls butted the wall. Perhaps they were aware they were about to die, by sensing the presence and excitement of so many people collectively anticipating the kill. Impatiently the ladies with perfect olive complections fanned themselves with beautifully hand-painted fans, or slyly peeped through the lace at the eligible men, occasionally losing their cool by smacking a pesky fly that settled on their oil-slicked black hair. Some of them wore flowers in their hair over the left ear to indicate their unmarried status, pinned down with a variety of tortoise shell hair combs, or richly carved ivory ones. I too had pinned a flower in my hair, but it definitely looked out of place with my pale face and sun-bleached blonde hair. They looked at me with contempt and at Dee with blatant curiosity, but envied us both for sitting in the toreador's honored seat. Wondering who we were to receive that honor and wondering why WE were chosen for that privilege and not them!

A cacophonous bussing of voices filled the air as the people excitedly discussed the crowd, the food, the bullfighters and their chances of surviving. Who was favored and who was not. They were both fearful of seeing a goring, yet secretly wished for it. It was a national tradition someone said. But it was also a blood sport, otherwise they would not be there. Only the innocents abroad did not know what to expect.

The crowd finally settled down. A strange silence fell over everyone. An expectancy of death hung in the air. A loud bellow of a bull confined to a small space and now being prodded to enter the ring acted as an announcement that the games were about to begin. I looked at the beauty of the intricate embroidery of red roses on the cape that belied the cruelty that I was about to witness. A double gate on the far side opened slowly, The "Jinete Hombre a Caballo" entered. The horses, heavily padded, walked almost sideways, skittish at the lightest sound. They had carried their masters many times before, and somehow were aware of their own peril. Behind them came a marching band, sounding the fanfare as the toreadors and matadors walked in in single file, allowing one another enough space to be acknowledged. Resplendent in their magnificent suits of light, they slowly paraded the full circle of the arena. "Bravo! Bravo!" the crowd applauded, chanting the name
of their favorite, who acknowledged the acolytes with deep bows waving and lifting their astrachan pillboxes to favored people in the stands.

Antonio Brava was the last to enter; the crowd went wild. He was dressed in pristine white, his *chaleco* fitted snugly over his chest, with gold epaulettes on the shoulders; it was gloriously embroidered in gold and red roses that matched the cloak in front of us. His skintight pants showed his bulges off to advantage. Tiny mirrors sewn into the side seams flashed into the crowds as the sun reflected in them. His white socks, which came up to his knees, slipped into his pant legs held there by garters with gold tassels. As he passed us he threw one single red rose up to me. Instinctively I caught it.

The crowd wondered who the blonde was that he was targeting. He was known throughout Spain for his womanizing. Dee did not move a muscle; sat in silence. Fuming inside with jealousy. This was, after all, our honeymoon.

Several clowns now made their appearance from behind the escape wall, one clown with a cape taunting the other clown, brandishing a set of horns. They made a few fumbling passes. The crowd laughed, breaking the deadly silence. The clowns disappeared one by one, leaving one only in the ring. Again the door opened on the far side. For a moment the bull was blinded by the bright sun, then he spotted the clown with the cape. He charged, his magnificent body glistening with vitality, muscles rippling under the sleek black skin. Well fed and vibrantly alive. What an incredible sight of pure strength. The clown turned his back on him, but making a clever pass tumbled over the wall.

A small cloud of dust blew into the air as the bull's feet dug two furrows in the sand, trying not to impact the wall. During the distraction of the clowns, the Jinette, better known as Hombre a Caballo entered for the second time, his horse now blindfolded at his command. He sat bolt upright. Banderillas, festooned with gay ribbons, were ready, the target was the bull's hump. The bull turned and charged the heavily padded horse repeatedly on his rump, trying to dig his horns in under the drapes to get to the belly of the horse. That move was to the advantage of the man on the horse. With the next charge when the bull lowered his head, the Jinette lunged forward, and the four-inch blade of the lance found its mark. It dug in up to the hilt, the gay ribbons concealing the blood. He planted all four. With every successful placement of the banderillas, the crowd shouted.

" BRAVO! BRAVO!"

With the last one's placement, something went wrong—it entered between the shoulder bones, and stuck deep enough to pierce a vital organ. Yet the crowd still shouted.

"BRAVO! BRAVO!"

The rider now pulled the blindfold off the horse's face and rode off triumphantly. He had done his gruesome job of incapacitating the bull well. A shudder of disgust ran through my body.

The toreador now entered. The crowd became silent. He walked to the center of the arena and took in a position gently waving the red cloak. The bull looked around, bewildered with pain that tore through his back. A thin stream of blood trickled out of the lance holes, hidden by the red blue and green ribbons. He tried to shake the banderillas out of his back, but they were too deep in and with every shake just dug deeper in. The pain was starting to turn into anger; he pawed in the sand now splattered with blood and kicked up his hind legs. The crowd sat on the edge of their seats, waiting for the bull to charge the man. Brava had done this many times before, his heart pounded but he was confident that with his intelligence, reasoning, and strategy that he could outwit the bull. He had the upper hand, so he waited calmly for the bull to make the first move.

The bull on the other hand acted purely on instinct and used brute strength. Now his eye caught the flutter of the red cape, and he charged. The toreador made a deft turn in his own footsteps, flipping the cape over the head of the bull. The bull missed him within inches, turned, and charged again. The toreador made another good pass. The crowd was thrilled, screaming in unison, "OLE! OLE!"

Sweet tasting blood bubbled pink out of the bull's mouth, as time after time he pursued the cape. One time he almost got the man, but Antonio Brava deftly turned the cape away, passing it over the eyes of the bull, then over his back. One banderilla became dislodged and dropped to the ground. Fresh blood poured across his back in a shiny red waterfall. In fury, he defecated his last meal mixed with blood. It indicated internal bleeding. I couldn't stand it any longer. I could see the pain in his eyes. I jumped and up in my seat and shouted, "KILL HIM, BULL ! Kill him, bull!" The people around me thought I said, "Kill the bull!"

I hated the blood and gore, hated the peoples "Oles." Hated the toreador's upper hand over the defenseless bull, even hated Dee's enthusiasm and his joining in the "Oles and Bravos!"

The bull was slowing down, the loss of blood and internal bleeding had weakened him. His breathing was labored, his tongue protruding out of his mouth was dry from exhaustion. Pink foam bubbled out of the corner of his mouth, an indication that his lungs were damaged. He was suffering, and I was suffering with him. His legs buckled under him as he stumbled forward. There was red everywhere, even in his eyes, dancing with the cape, in the embroidery of the calico. Blood running out of his nose. The matador entered. In his hand concealed in a short cape was the short sword. Antonio usually did his own killing, so he handed him the sword. The bull saw only another cape. His last energy was poured into the final pass. At last he and the man saw eye-to-eye.

He charged and stopped short of the toreador as if waiting for the death blow, he lowered his head. The "coup de gras" was compassionate and went straight to his heart, but he did not fall. Slowly he sank into a kneeling position with his front legs. The crowd scarcely took a breath. It seemed he stood forever, almost like praying; *"Father, forgive them for they know not what they are doing."*

The matador then came forward with a thin, short stiletto, stuck it in the back of the bull's neck, and twisted it. When he at last fell and tumbled, the crowd went wild, shouting, "BRAVO! BRAVO! BRAVO!"

Showers of flowers rained down on the toreador and matador as they took their strut around the arena. When Antonio passed us he removed his black pillbox and bowed. We stood up and acknowledged him. But in my heart I felt like a traitor.

A wheeled flatbed appeared out of the far gate. Without fanfare or applause for the bravery of the bull it was dragged onto it. The matador went over and cut the ear off the bull and handed it on the stiletto to the toreador as a sign of his bravery, and his compassion with a clean kill. My mind screamed out in protest. *Where was the compassion? The Carcass was covered in blood, slime, feces. He was totally degraded and defeated.*

Now they dragged him through the same gate through which he had made his entrance. Unscarred and glorious. That was how I would remember this creature of God that died so needlessly, in such agony, to give an hour's pleasure to the blood-thirsty throng that had no other thought in their minds but to go and fill their bellies with beer and food before the next fight started.

I told Dee I was leaving. I felt ashamed that I even stayed for one. He couldn't understand why I didn't want to see the other three.

He said he was staying. I was seemingly alone in my grief for the bull, because there was excitement and exhilaration all around me as I left the place of death and went back to the hotel with "OLE!" still ringing in my ears!

Dee went to the victory party alone.

65

Sweet Revenge — Payback for the Bull

Dee said after the bullfight, that I was far too sensitive about the bull's fate. "He was born and raised for the fight"

"But the bull had no choice and was treated very cruelly. Besides, the deck was stacked against him, the bull fighter went into the arena for the money, and the bull's fate was already decided before he went in."

"That's not so; he is treated very well before the fights, gets the best pasture, and can have all the cows he wants, and during the bull fight he gives pleasure to at least a thousand."

"But does he ever leave the arena alive? If he manages to outwit the toreador? No! How would you like to be in that no win situation where you are? Helpless about what was to happen with you?"

"I am intelligent enough to prevent situations that would put me in a similar situation," Dee replied, convinced that it could never happen to him.

"But what if the situation was thrust upon you in an unguarded moment?"

"I still say it wouldn't happen to me without my knowledge." To Dee, that was the end of the conversation. But to me it was not over. A few days later, I MADE HIM EAT HIS WORDS!

We were staying in a grand old hotel in Madrid. Our honeymoon suite had a large canopied bed, and on a raised platform right in the middle of the room was a sunken bathtub the size of a small swimming pool.

We had been out sightseeing the whole day. Dee said he was too tired to even take a bath, and was going to take a nap before we went out that night. Soon he was asleep spread eagled on the bed. That's when our conversation of a few days ago popped into my head. As I looked at him, I thought, *How vulnerable, I could do anything to him.* He usually slept through everything.

I whispered, "So nothing could happen to you without your knowledge, well let's see?"

I took out two pairs of my stockings tied one to each of the four posters, then tied his hands and feet still in the spread-eagled position so that he couldn't move. Some time later he woke up. What was his surprise when he discovered he was tied up! "What's going on? Did you do this? It's NOT FUNNY, untie me!" Then he tried humor. "I didn't know you were into S&M." Then he tried pleading. "Please untie me, pet, it's really not funny."

"SO?" I gloated, "How does it feel being helpless and in a situation you could not prevent?"

"You're not still on that bull thing? Okay you've proved your point, now untie me."

"I've not yet proved my point, but then I haven't decided yet what I am going to do with you. Now that you are the helpless bull, you're in my power. But don't worry, I will treat you well! I'll feed you, but about all the *cows* you could handle, I definitely put a stop to that luxury. I will have to be the whole show, but first I'm going to have a leisurely bath to think about it. Then I'm going to eat." His face lit up. That was his last resort.

"They are going to cancel our dinner reservation. Please untie me so that I can get ready."

"Don't worry. I've cancelled it and ordered room service—only the best pasture for you," I said sweetly.

Dee was a person easily stimulated visually, so I took my time undressing and wandering around. The striptease was enough to wake the dead, but I banked on the slow suggestive tantalizing in the bath to arouse his interest, rubbing the soap slowly over my breasts and thighs and caressing my body sensuously with gentle gyrations. "Come in with me." He struggled against his bonds, but I could see I had achieved what I had hoped for. "OLE! OLE!" I shouted. He was my bull and his horn stood ready and erect for the games to begin. I wanted him to feel the helplessness the bull felt. My naked body became the toreador's cape. I played a stop and go game I was in it for sweet revenge.

One snip of my nail scissors on either side of the brief bikini under pants that he slept in, released the proud erection. I knelt over him barely touching and rubbed my breasts across him, teasing and pulling away till he was bursting with excitement, then got down from off the bed. When the doorbell rang, I stopped to answer the door. He thought I would release him then, but I put on a frilly dressing gown, peeped shyly round the door as it becomes a new bride, and asked the waiter to please leave the food cart out side the door. "WE are busy."

I gave the waiter a generous tip. He understood. It was the honeymoon suite and we wanted privacy. I pulled the cart right next to the bed and put a chair at both ends. But I didn't release him. On the cart was everything he loved. However, on his side there was a big bowl of lettuce symbolic of the grass the bull would eat before his execution. Seeing that, his passion deflated. But I was by far not finished taunting him. I proceeded to eat all his favorite food, not touching the lettuce. When I got to the strawberry mousse, his favorite, I scooped it out by the handfuls and slowly but sensuously spread it all over him, then began to lick it off him, from head to toe and back to the head again lingering longer at certain areas till I felt the hardness of the sword in my mouth without bringing him to a climax. I had just pulled the red cloak over him. "OLE! OLE!" I shouted.

I dragged the seduction out. I squatted over him, not touching him, with only our private areas touching, making sure there was no penetration. He arched up to receive me. At that crucial moment I got off him. Swung my body (symbolic of the cape) out of his reach. He lay there still erect, but unsatisfied, shocked at my actions!

"OLE! OLE!" I shouted. The seduction was over. He felt the frustration the bull must have felt. I walked away and sat some distance away, watching the proud erection die. Only when his ardor had subsided, I finally cut him loose. I had delivered the "coup de gras" and got my point across.

"That was extremely cruel," he cried.

66

India — Horrifically Fascinating

I had looked forward to India for so long, always associating it with the romance of the tiger hunts. Fairytale temples and ancient buildings. Women in billowing saris. And of course Rudyard Kipling's dripping jungles out of *Jungle Book*.

All of that vanished when I stepped off the plane in Calcutta. All I noticed in the beginning were the contrasts. The horrifying poverty and extreme riches were at the top of the list. Next came the "untouchable's barrier" that segregated the millions. But the worst of all was the maiming! Horrors of self-inflicted or family-inflicted deformity, to aide them financially. On the side of the road ran chocolate-colored water canals used for public toilets and bathing. Domestic water buffalo were also kept in there. They made their presence known every time they stuck their noses up out of the water and blew brown bubbles in the air. My conscious thought was, *But this is only Calcutta, there are many cities and places that I'm sure would still nurture my fantasies of the dream India.*

Our cab wound its way, honking as we went to disperse the throngs of people. Millions of them poured out into the streets—everywhere there were people. Some sitting on windowsills tied up with cloth ropes, or bits of string. (Later I found out that's where they slept to get off the streets and out of the sudden down pouring of rain and out of reach from the hungry rats who escaped the cooking fires.) The pavements were already covered with

491

horizontal bodies like the carnage after war. While others were still trying to find a spot to lay down their mats and prepare for the night. Not an inch of space was wasted. Between two buildings an ingenious person had constructed shelves. Eight layers deep, stacked one on top of the other. The shelves were wide enough for people to crawl in with their possessions, which consisted of what they could carry. This makeshift shelter was on a "first come understanding," and entire families were squeezed in, *living books with their own sad stories.*

"WHAT happened?" I asked the cab driver.

He looked at me strangely. "What do you mean what happened?" He did not know anything other than what he saw daily, and in his estimation nothing was different. Nothing and everything happened. He ignored me for being so ignorant and replied simply "They are sleeping!"

He kept winding his way through the horde of people. Like Moses parting the Red Sea. In our wake, desperately thin men pulled flea-infested rickshaws, loaded with people on their way back to homes and hovels. I was looking at a hell-hole of squalor, yet at the same time it was horrifically intriguing, with its own vitality!

The extremely rich also lived among the poor, sheltered behind twenty-foot-high walls to hide their affluence. The had simply learned to ignore all around them. Tapping inspiration for their art and poetry from the same filthy streets.

The Marwaris were by far the richest, most hailing from Rajasthan and other areas. They were the first entrepreneurs who took advantage of British enterprise, after they left India. And then cleaned up after everyone else who came along. They owned their own private rickshaws, beautifully decorated. They were distinguishable by their magnificent gold filigreed, gossamer Saris blowing in the breeze. Their pullers were well fed and smiling. Their children went to private schools, usually accompanied by nannies, or had home tutors. They were *the* untouched by the *untouchables.* They lived in incredible affluence in old stately mansions the British left behind.

The ultra rich, a confluence of many cultural streams, lacked nothing. They had a full social life in their private clubs. They gathered at the Horse races, concert halls, the opera. Their private lives bubbled with intellectual pursuits. They entertained the visiting opera stars and entertainers, with social teas and poetry readings. Or showed the latest movies on their private screens.

Yet not wanting to appear as totally segregated, these Marwaris could also be seen in public places, chewing betel nuts like the commoners, but prepared by their own lackeys. Their tongues and teeth were stained red with the juice. Or they stood around in the parks and streets talking shop with the collection of Australian and British foreigners who made a good living for themselves. Sometimes they frequented the more sophisticated tea rooms to sip strong brewed tea, or 11-Up, their own version of the American Coca Cola.

A group of ladies stopped their gossiping for a moment and stepped aside to let a funeral procession pass. I noticed the different dots of dye between their eyes indicating their different castes. Only one had a fine gold line outlining her dot to match her aqua and gold sari.

Our cab, too, pulled aside momentarily to let another funeral procession pass. The emaciated corpse of an old man swayed precariously on a makeshift bier of bamboo, carried aloft on the shoulders of equally skeletal relatives dressed in soil dyed loin cloths. His long gray hair, always kept in a turban and never cut, now released, showed its glory for the first time to the world. Some of it lay draped across his thin body, while the rest cascaded over the bier touching the ground. Wilted flowers, retrieved from the rich trash cans, were stuck in around the corpse, under the armpits, around the face, into the hair, and even between the toes. A motley procession followed. They were on the way to the Hoogly burning altars to burn their beloved father and teacher and place his ashes on a small raft, which they would send off down the Holy Hoogly so that his spirit would receive peace. The bearers jogged lightly beneath their burden to get to their destination before dark.

Everywhere little makeshift cooking fires had sprung up, sending thin spirals of smoke into the air. The ones who were lucky that day to earn a few Annas, were happily stirring the unknown contents in a fire-blackened pot.

Some children chased *their* supper with sticks; the same rats that would bite raw wounds in unprotected bodies that night now cooked on a spit would nourish their bodies. While their younger siblings dressed only in amulets round their hips played in seepage water and drank from deep potholes in the street.

A young man aged beyond his eighteen years, sat slumped beside his bundle of wares he had carried the whole day with a strap across his head on his back like some kind of pack animal. This was not yet his destination, but he could not make it any farther. He sat hugging his weary knees, pillowing his aching head and shoulders in a semi-unconscious state, too tired to search for food. He had swallowed a small parcel of sprouting beans wrapped in a leaf. It would sprout in the warmth of his stomach and expand to fill the empty space. It would stop the cramping, but would not nourish him. Tomorrow he would have better luck!

In an hour, I saw life pass before my eyes. There were millions of people and each individual had a different tragic story. A man was setting his *board* up for the night. The board was usually chained against a fence. It was a two-foot-wide, six-foot-long plank with a cross-beam foot piece on either side. It would keep him off the concrete that got very cold in the night. And in the day it turned into his shop, where he consulted his clients on their astrology charts. When the rainy season started it was a roof over his head. He was not burdened with worldly possessions, and what he had hung on a string around his waist. A spoon, a shallow cup that doubled as drinking cup and when there was no money, became his begging cup. His astrology charts he carried in his hand. He lifted the board down and hoped that the sun baking against the wall had seeped its warmth into it to provide a little warmth for the night. This was his corner of the world. This was his story! His neighbor, a woman, unwrapped her sari that long ago lost its identity. The years of wear, the body grease, soil and other grime, gave it insulation. She lovingly tucked the cloth, around her three children lying on a folded cardboard box. This was their 'home' the only home they had ever known. She leaned up against the warm wall folding her arms across her naked upper torso, not out of modesty, but to provide some warmth. She had hoped that that night she wouldn't have to put them to sleep hungry. The tourists had not bought the simple flower leis she had made. The smell of other cooking pots made her mouth water, but she knew there was not enough for sharing. Next to her was a pile of black and white ashes. Instinctively she moistened her fingers and dipped it into the ashes, rubbed it in patterns across the faces of her sleeping children. *At least she would give them that protection, making them unattractive to the demons of the night.* This was her story! I asked the cabby to stop so that I could go and give her some money.

"NO!" he shouted. "It would be too dangerous!"

"Why?" I wanted to know.

"A few months ago a friend of mine, a baker, decided to give away some of the bread that wasn't picked up on order. He took the boxes of bread into the courtyard of the shop to distribute it to the street dwellers. Then he opened the gates. Within seconds the few grew to a multitude. That swarmed in to take the bread. When the stampede was over, their benefactor lay dead! The hungry mass had trampled him to death. If you want to do something for them you have to do it very stealthily or else you would be mobbed."

How our cab got through the horizontal mass, avoiding cows and children, I don't know. He apologized to the sleepers as he moved them. Finally we arrived at an upperclass section with elegant old homes behind high walls. The street was lined with giant banyan trees that formed a bower over the road. At the end of the lane he pulled up in front of an enormous decorative wrought-iron gate. A ten-foot brick wall enclosed a three-story house. There was a narrow gatehouse with guard on either side of the gate. In front of the gate a woman sat relieving herself. I closed my eyes not to see. The driver honked to make her move. She finished her business and then stepped aside.

A tall Indian man stepped out of the gatehouse, holding onto the collar of a Doberman guard dog. With one hand he unlocked the gate and swung it open.

After he secured the dog in a holding cage and closed the gates, he escorted us on a long path with green lawns to the three-story Victorian house. In the bright light of the moon I saw beautiful flowerbeds trimmed with low neatly clipped hedges a foot high. The house was owned by a very rich man. Mr. K. owned half of Calcutta, as well as the housekeeper and the fourteen servants that awaited us patiently inside the entrance hall. A thin man (but then, I had yet to see a fat man) awaited us at the heavy mahogany carved front door. With hands clasped in a prayerful gesture, he stepped forward, bowing to us. He was dressed in an immaculate white long robe, with sharply ironed in pleats, a broad wine-red cumber band at his waist. An elaborately knotted turban in the same color was on his head. The golden crest on the front of the turban was that of our host-employer who booked our show. Walking backward he escorted us into the hallway polished to a mirror finish.

With a sign from him the rest of the staff stood to attention. He introduced himself as Hamir. He spoke English fluently with a British accent, but addressed his staff in Hindi.

"I am here to please you, and will assign your servants for different needs. I will now have them take your luggage to your rooms that are located on the second floor, and then if you wish to have a bath after your journey you will have servants to assist you."

I thanked him, and said that would be nice. A servant busied himself with our luggage, and by the time we got upstairs, he had placed the luggage in three rooms, and another was unpacking it into the dressers and wardrobes. Another servant had run a bath for me and was standing to attention inside the bathroom with towels draped over his arm. I took the towels from him and said, "Thank you, you may go now." He stood his ground. "Thank you, that is all," I tried again. Just then Hamir made his rounds to see that everything

went smoothly. I explained to him that the man would not leave the bathroom. He looked puzzled. "He would not leave madam unless I tell him to, because I assigned him to bathe you, you do not wish to be bathed?"

"Yes, I do want to bathe, but I'm a big girl now, and I can do it myself, thank you." Hamir clapped his hands in a certain way and the man left and stood to attention outside the bathroom door.

A little while later, hearing the dinner bell, we descended to the dining room. Ivan, my husband's partner, was smiling from ear to ear.

"You look like the cat that swallowed the canary."

"This is the life. I was just bathed from head to toe, by a beautiful woman, and she even washed my hair for me. I could get used to it."

"Aren't you ashamed of yourself?" I scolded.

"The service comes with the house, Hamir told me, so why not accept?"

The banisters of black ebony shone like onyx, so did the brass rods gleam holding the Persian carpet on the spiral staircase. Large five-foot Chinese-tableau vases decorated each landing between floors.

Hamir met us at the foot of the stairs and escorted us into the dining room. He pulled out my chair and unfolded my serviette. The table had a full setting for a simple but elegant meal of chicken curry and vegetables that the cook had prepared for us. He explained that evening meals would in future be served at the hotel where we would be performing, and breakfast and light lunches and teas would be at the main house.

After we had eaten, he explained the servant situation.

"They belong to Mr. K., the richest man in India; altogether there are fourteen servants. Those who are assigned in the house stay in the house at their posts. They work in groups of two in the kitchen, for bath duty, for personal duties such as hair brushing, washing and ironing, for men's valet duty and helping to dress and cleaning shoes. The ones who work outdoors stay in the compound at the back of the house. There are two for gardening, and two at the gate on two shifts so that the gates are guarded night and day. And two more care for the chickens and the guard dogs. They receive their own rations and do their own cooking in the compound. The ones in the house sleep on mats at their stations in case you may need them in the night. I am the overseer and have my own quarters also in the compound. Complaints will be accepted, but is not tolerated and will result in immediate dismissal."

I just couldn't get used to literally falling over bodies in the night.

One night I went to the kitchen to get a drink of milk and then to the bathroom. A string of servants jumped up to attention, soon all the servants were awake and up just in case. That made up my mind, this arrangement should end. I called Hamir in the morning and told him that it was no need for the servants to be on duty in the night.

"But that WAS their duty!" he started to object.

After that we arranged that the staff sleep on the lower floors and not on the floor that we lived on. I took a thermos into the room with hot milk, not to upset the show of their loyalty to Hamir. Hamir was all too happy to put the names of his staff onto my tape recorder. He was absolutely hooked on his own voice and holding the mike. So was the staff at hearing their names on the tape. They laughed at my mispronouncing their names. They accepted the changes.

A few days later I tried to sneak out of the house and through the gates to see the sights. That was a definite no no! Hamir hailed me a rickshaw and made sure that the driver took me wherever I wanted to go. He asked him to stay with me at all times, and not let me out of his sight. His voice became very excited. I took it that he warned the little man that if anything happened to me, he would be responsible. The poor little man looked terrified as he started pulling me.

I felt sorry for him, almost ashamed that I was a burden to him. I could count every rib and vertebra as his skinny little legs pounded the concrete. He knew English, proud that he had learned his English "very good," then through huffs and puffs he started singing the little songs he learned mixed with a few old Methodist hymns. He enjoyed this rendition, and at times his feet lifted off the ground, but it never interrupted our journey.

"I want to see everything. But first I would like to go to the marketplace I heard so much about. Then home."

Slowly we entered the mainstream of bustling people. The putrid smells of human feces and urine floated up from the already overflowing sewers, blocked with everything from a decaying dog carcass to the contents of a little brick shed with two earthenware buckets substituting for a public toilet. The municipality fought a losing battle to have the buckets emptied, but no one showed up so it simply overflowed into the sewers. When the monsoons came it sloshed into the streets, which under normal circumstances were used as public toilets anyway. This in turn flowed into the canals from which the poor people drank causing, a multitude of diseases.

At night the streets of Calcutta, where two thirds of the population of over a million lived rent free, over flowed. The streets were used for bedroom, living room, and toilet, not forgetting cattle coral for the holy cattle. Because the majority had no form of income, they earned from 8 Niapas (an American penny) to a small note, the equivalent of a quarter a day. Everywhere I looked there was deformity and leprosy. I was horrified and near tears. The wallah stayed silent; perhaps he felt guilty for the terrible atrocities families performed on one another in the name of poverty and survival. In a family of many, one child was selected to be sacrificed for the others. An arm or leg was chopped off, or faces burned to create pity. Or they were blinded with hot coals and led around by another child with a begging bowl. The tourists are very generous if not put off. But that was not all. Later I learned that there were actually syndicates of men, *if you can call them men, and not monsters,* who maimed for profit! I saw some of their *creations!* Babies born on the street are often abandoned to be raised by other children like living dolls. These babies are taken by these monsters who break their backs, leaving them paralyzed. They are placed on a board with wheels and dragged around by another child to beg, handing over what money they make to the monsters who drive around in big cars. Some of the maiming was ingenious; it required nothing but a small iron cage in which the child was locked, and as it grew the body intertwined like some weird plant. Or if they're lucky they were let out of the cage and walked on all fours. They were called the dog people. A beautiful girl child approached us when we stopped at a corner, her beauty comparable to a fine china doll. She had perfect features with big black eyes made even larger by long curling lashes. Long black hair tumbled over her shoulders and hung luxuriantly down her back. She was absolute perfection. The wallah warned me that the children of the affluent often do the begging thing like a game. He waved the girl away but she didn't go because she was being watched by an older child. She rubbed her hand in a circular motion over her stomach and forcing tears from her eyes she murmured the sing song all children do.

"No mommy, no daddy, no mommy, no daddy, no food, hungry."

The wallah shoved her to one side and said, "Go away," in Hindi. She picked up her little dress up to her chin. I gasped in horror. From her waist to above her knees, she was horribly burned, as if someone had taken a metal object and burned away all her private parts; deep scarring lay across her stomach and thighs.

"My God! My God!" was all I could say. I folded some notes up into a little ball and shoved it in her palms. Within seconds a swarm of children were round her to take away the money. "She was their beggar!"

To take my mind off the subject, my wallah told me that some people preferred the streets to subdividing rooms into 10 to 20 spaces to avoid the sweltering heat of the day and the morning freezes. He said he was lucky; his family built a hut in the jungle outside Calcutta. He had two children he sent to school, and they in turn taught the other children all they learned. He himself could read and knew enough about sums to give his customers change. To support his family and send money back to the village, he stayed in Calcutta for six months at a time. To earn more he worked for private individuals like Mr. Kapur. At first he shared a small room with 14 other men, but they robbed him blind, and he was afraid the rickshaw would be stolen, so he moved what worldly possessions into the rickshaw and slept there.

"What if the monsoons come?" I wanted to know.

"I welcome the rains, it doubles my earnings; most people don't want to walk knee deep in the polluted water. It is amazing that there is so much water in India, but very little of it is drinkable because of the pollution. Dysentery is the curse of Calcutta because people are unable to find clean water." At a small faucet by a gas station I saw a long lineup of people, just to take a drink. They did their bathing and laundry in the Hoogly and the canals that ran through the city. The Hoogly was the main waterway for international shipping trade. Freight ships anchored there. It has a very fast current with waves, but not fast enough to carry off the pollution that entered into it. It was also the cradle for the dead. Bodies were openly dumped into it.

We passed the same man I had seen days before struggling with yet another refrigerator box on his back. The only assistance he had in carrying his load was with a broad leather strap across his head, crossing it over and under the box. The look on his face was that of a beast of burden, the humble donkey who was often subjected to these mind boggling loads.

As he walked, he was oblivious to his surroundings; he was a one-man truck, and everyone simply moved out of his way.

The throng of human beings thickened as we entered the business section. The ones who had some kind of paper job stood out like bright stars in their pristine white pajamas. At a construction site, some women were carrying bricks in a basket on their heads up a bamboo ladder, precariously balanced against the wall. By the culvert a group of men were sawing with hand saws through a thick sewage pipe. Life was an orgy for the eyes. Farther up in a courtyard a swarm of bodies milled round some cows to receive their share of milk. The cows belonged to the city and it was an ingenious way of getting fresh milk without refrigeration. Everyone brought their own container along. In exchange for food the cows provided milk on the spot. But some cows were owned by people who demanded rupees for the milk. But to the street children they showed compassion by milking directly into their mouths. On the farm we did the same thing, but it was the cats that lined up and caught the stream of milk in their mouths. After their unusual breakfast, the children ran laughing to look at a man who had set up a rat circus. He had taught them simple things like pushing a ball, tightrope walking to receive a morsel of food on the end of the rope, and climbing a small bamboo ladder to retrieve another morsel. Near him in an isolated corner a handsome man squatted. His hair and beard rolled into a coil and looped around his chin was tucked into a white turban. His white loincloth wrapped around him was pulled up between his legs and tucked in at the waist. *ASTROLOGER* written on a piece of cardboard was stuck into a nail on the wall above his head. He was telling fortunes. Everywhere something was happening.

An organ grinder caught my eye He was hand cranking the organ while two monkeys dressed in satin pants and gay little waistcoats and pill box hats performed tricks like somersaults and stuck out their little palms to the people watching. Coyly refusing coins, they only accepted paper money which they promptly shoved into their little caps.

The offices had not yet opened, but thousands of rural people were pouring into the city. Those who could not get into the busses were hanging in clusters onto the outside.

"They do that with the trains going out of the city, too. When the inside was stuffed to capacity, they stand on the window sills and hang on, others hang onto them in turn, some have hooks they hook onto anything that would support it. Often it is so overloaded that it has tragic results. They fall off round bends, or get knocked off going through tunnels. Would you believe it a conductor tries to get the fare from those hanging on the outside by climbing around them?"

The streets filled up with bicycles, bicycles with side cars delivering mail, flowers, paper goods. Men were pulling and pushing carts, rickshaws were taking children to school, and other destinations. Horse-drawn covered buggies galloped down the street. Everywhere people were carrying small and large bundles on their backs with straps across their heads. I became aware of a gentle tinkling of bells. When we stopped for a moment a colorfully dressed man carrying a fantastic piece of brass artwork, covered with spigots, inlays, bells and tassels approached us.

"What's he selling?"

"Wonderful, pure, cool water!" the wallah replied as if he was describing the best vintage of French wines.

"Call him back," I ordered as the man walked away. "But, memsaab, he wants a lot of money." He hailed the man. I bought water for me and my wallah and filled up all his water bottles. I also bought water for people deriving pleasure at watching us drink. They were in awe at my generosity, and when I calculated it didn't come to $3. I realized that some of the people who received my gift of water did not get that sum in a month. Opportunity seldom knocks, so while I was handing out water, a man carrying a flat basket on his head filled with a pyramid of sweet cakes coated with caster sugar that sifted through the basket onto his face and shoulders like snow. I bought his whole load and passed it out to anyone who wanted one, making sure I kept enough for my wallah and Hamir. It looked like a street party.

Four men passed us walking in formation with doughnut cloths on their heads, on which they supported a gilded mirror that flashed streaks across the men working on quilting on the roof above us. Not an inch of space was lost in a city that supported a million people. We were somewhere near Chitpore Road, the cotton producers' area. A slight breeze rained down soft flecks of cotton fluffing down from the looms above us. I was glad I did not eat one of the sweet cakes, as I would have ended up with a mouth full of cotton for sure.

The sleeping crates of the previous night had turned into open front mini shops. The customers melted into the picture. The roofs and alleys turned into factories. Bamboo rods hung from window to window, draped with cloth. Large vats of multi color dyes stood in the alley filled with skeins of wool and yards of silk or newly spun cotton, and were being stirred by men with wooden paddles, arm deep in color that spilled over into a modern painting onto the earth canvas.

When the desired color was reached, they hung it onto the overhead bamboo where it dripped dry. Pedestrians dodged the rainbow drops that rained down, laughing heartily when it left its mark on their threadbare wraps.

I stopped the rickshaw to look at the wares in the mini mall set up in the alley. Took a walk among the incredible array of saris hung from steel rods imbedded into the walls. Magnificent hand-woven silks obtained from the common silk worm. The man selling the incredible selection of colors enhanced with gold and silver threads took off his ring and demonstrated how fine it was by pulling a whole yard of material through it. On boards on the wall there hung gold and silver filigree necklaces, earrings, and bracelets that were all handmade. In a shady corner a man was chiseling a dining table out of a solid block of hardwood into a grape arbor; it was divided into a sandwich with three dimensional bunches of grapes, leaves, and vines carved out in between. Looking from the side I could see through to the other side. Yet the top was so smooth that he stood a glass on it.

Loving wood carving myself, I was amazed at the primitive homemade tools and common hammer he used to achieve this magnificent piece of art. The whole table took ten years to make and he would ask a mere three hundred dollars for it.

Next to him another craftsman was working in silver. His masterpiece was a set of teacups in the form of a water lily on a saucer of a lily pad. He had already finished five and was lining the cups with dainty blue glass. He shaped the sixth one over a block-form made of wood. Pounding the silver with a regular hammer, he put it aside to switch to the next project. He had very little to work with. His whole body became a tool. It was incredible to watch. He used his toes and knees and fingers to add the finishing touches to a dainty condiment set. With a common nail and an upholstery hammer, he sculpted delicate rural scenes of tropical jungle and working elephants into the silver.

I immediately fell in love with it. Bought it right there and then to take with me, but ordered a cocktail shaker and glasses for Dee to be delivered at the Kapur address. Immediately we were swamped by other merchants wanting to sell us something.

The wallah warned me not to pay up front but let him deliver it, and wanted to take me home. So he dismissed the merchants, and we continued with our trip. To avoid more confrontations we turned up a narrow street. Here there were all kinds of businesses conducted out of upturned crates.

At the first one there was a sign that said *THE BEST TEA IN INDIA.* Here several men sat on small wooden stools, while others simply squatted around. The owner of this enterprise sat behind a Primus stove in lotus position, setting glasses of tea covered with a saucer to brew out on a makeshift table made from bricks and a plank he had covered with a white cloth. Behind him on a shelf stood several mugs with writing on them, which I presumed were names of regular customers. Strange enough tea drinking wasn't a throw back from the British, but had been around for as long as can be remembered. The tea was brought down from the foot hills of the Himalayas three to four hundred miles away. Carried on the backs of men, through the Bay of Bengal to the thirsty world. In that crate it was brewed by a master. "One gram of tea to 50CCs of rapidly boiling water, never overboil the water!" He gave a running commentary.

After a crucial brewing, then and only then the bright red, strong tea, laced with sugar, was passed to the customer. Stop I ordered the wallah, "Please go and order two cups"

"Two cups?" he questioned. He didn't quite understand why I wanted two cups.

"For you and me," I explained. "And also some funnel cakes." With no possibility of it being covered in quilting fluff this time, I was dying to taste it. We pulled up to one side to enjoy our tea.

While the wallah washed our cups in a copper urn I watched the goings on in the crate next to the tea man. This man was deftly preparing a betel-nut chew for one of his customers. Then he sold some herbs to a person addressing him as doctori. He was an all around non-certified healer; what he couldn't heal with herbs he healed with incantations. Next I watched him pull teeth, using hypnosis and an ordinary pliers that he rinsed in a mug between customers. He waited until a big enough crowd assembled to watch him pull the teeth. Took advantage of the opportunity to sell his medicine. Of all things he sold potency pills. "Just one anna a pill" he shouted. I looked around at the over population and silently thought, *It would be more appropriate if he sold condoms!*

The next crate was a miniature butcher shop with dishes of God alone knew what meat! I had noticed the streets were strangely empty of dogs and cats. The only recognizable meat to me was a bony chicken and a goat's head sawed in half. The dead eyes were looking in both directions. With a protein starved nation, this butcher sold out before the flies had time to settle down. As for the bony chicken, two people were playing tug of war when we left. With the wisdom of Solomon the temporary butcher quickly solved the problem by cutting it in half as neither would let go of it.

A little way away from the crates stood a miasmic child with the undeniable symptoms of grayish skin color and bulging eyes. He was scooping the last morsels of sago porridge out of his eating bowl with his fingers. His desperately poor mother, unable to provide him with a more nourishing meal, had given him the cheapest possible to still his hunger. Occasionally she would give him a substitute of ground up yellow powder made from ground up lentils and chick peas mixed with rice, which contained about 25% protein value. This was sold in one ounce parcels bound in a banana leaf. Most street people bought the *chuttah*, pounded it into a flat cake and ate it, leaf and all, calling it a square meal, but hardly satisfying. The ones who were lucky in earning some money that day bought some of the by-products the other food sellers offered. Mango chutney rice, fried banana, boiled meat, peanuts, and pickles. Most people coming from Bengal looked down on those who ate *chuttah* as inferior, so they cooked the sago starch and very little else. This protein starvation caused miasma, the socio-cultural Bengali disease.

The mangy dogs (those who were not already eaten) hung around the food vendors in the hopes that something would fall or someone would take pity and give them leftovers. The children of the streets also hung around for the same reason. Several children too weak to try sat against the wall, suffering from another starvation disease, kwashiorkor. One little one cried. Not a healthy cry, but a hoarse cry of desperation. I bought food and handed it out; begging hands shot out. I bought some more, and still some more came. But my contribution was only a drop in a bucket. *God,* I thought. *This is only today; there are still a thousand other tomorrows!* One of the children had caught a young cow, her udder was almost empty from an earlier milking, but he knelt down in the hope that there would be enough left for him and sucked the teat. The stimulation helped, he smiled and sucked some more. It was like the Biblical story of the widow's urn that never emptied. After he was done, others followed to fill their tummies. They would not go to sleep that night hungry. The little cow stood placidly chewing on a discarded banana leaf; she alone seemed to understand. After she moved on I saw some people picking up the dung for their evening fires—nothing was wasted. I had seen enough. In my heart I sent a prayer of grace for providing that meal.

"Come, let us go to the market."

The market was indoors, surrounded by a high wrought iron fence and gate. I was let in by the gates because of the rickshaw. The gates promptly closed down behind us. I entered the shed-like building while arrangements were made where the rickshaw could park. The contrast from the street markets was overwhelming.

Inside the market was enough fruit, vegetables and food to feed thousands. Yet only a select few servants of the upper class were shopping. Baskets were loaded with fresh greens and carrots that would turn into creamy carrot pudding revered by the rich.

I felt guilty as I loaded a box full of red-cheeked mangoes, bunches of bananas, and strange looking fruit pale green and lumpy. I had never seen one before. The vendor saw my perplexed look and promptly opened one by breaking it in half. Inside was a waxy, lumpy flesh, I didn't know what to expect, but the taste was heavenly, inside the lump there was a small black seed. I couldn't wait to share it back home, so I bought several. Then filled a basket with staples for the wallah. Once more he couldn't understand my generosity, but I was grateful that he graciously accepted it.

On the way to the Rickshaw, a swarm of well-nourished, half naked children surrounded us shouting "Me carry! Me carry!" I told the wallah to hand the packages to the children to carry. He looked at me strangely, as if to say, *I am quite capable, besides it's only a few paces away.* But he could see in my eyes what I meant. He handed the packages over to them but in the tone of his voice I knew he was warning them not to run off with the stuff.

"Memsaab, you are taking a chance—they will most likely steal everything." I just knew they wouldn't and when they handed the packages over to him to load into the rickshaw I gave each one a rupee. They hollered and hooped. It was the most they had ever received. People usually rewarded them with just an anna, the equivalent of an eighth of an American penny. One of the older children told me with pride it was his "pack." Their families abandoned them. He was grateful that they were abandoned inside the marketplace. They slept indoors under the tables, and had plenty to eat. They helped with the cleaning up of the sheds and the stalls.

He was glad his little *pack* did not fall in the hands of the monsters that preyed on abandoned children for slave labor. He said that the little girls ended up in the cages as young as five years of age as prostitutes, and disappeared by the time they reached fifteen. He was told that they were chained together and dropped in the ocean. I could not believe my ears. But then he smiled. "I have a dream of one day owning my own vegetable stall."

It was already dark. All over the little shops, using oil-burning lamps, were trying to do some business.

Two wrestlers and a fire eater were giving a free show to the crowd around them. It made everyone forget their hunger. The "Picture man" with the help of a flashlight told stories, projecting cardboard cutouts of two sword-yielding warriors against the wall. It made the children watching forget their own little war on hunger. The small portion they received was not enough, they were still hungry. But watching the cardboard soldiers battling, made them laugh and it lightened their existence for a while. I felt guilty with all the food I had in the rickshaw!

The wallah told me that the house we passed was a refuge for the dying run by an Albanian-born woman named Teresa, who took the dying off the streets and out of the gutters. She cleaned them up, gave them a last meal, and gave them a clean place to die in dignity. I remembered the place because a few days before I saw the house surrounded by children and old people left there by families who couldn't care for them and hoped that someone would. So it not only was the house of dying, but also the house of hope. I remember telling the wallah that some day they would declare her a saint.

The large gates swung open to let me into another world. The world of luxury and plenty. I was richly blessed, but my heart ached for those less fortunate as I shared the wealth of my fruit with my staff. Strange that I pitied them before, but now I realized they were the fortunate ones, even though they received a pittance in salary. They at least were assured of a roof over their heads, food, clean water and protection, while the ones on the outside starved.

One morning looking out of the window I realized how lucky we were to be in show business. We were living in a three story house, with servants to jump to every whim you may have. Earning in one week what someone outside our gates earned for a year. That thought hurt me. But I put it out of my mind. It was an incredibly beautiful day. The garden was in full bloom, color bursting out in wild profusion in every corner. Two men were squatting on the perfectly manicured lawn cutting stray blades of grass with a hand scissors. A small boy sat on a ledge watching over a leopard cub, playing with the chain around his neck. The little boy reminded me of another boy called Sabu in a film about India I once saw. Perhaps it was the mode of dress. This one had a loin cloth and turban too, but had the Kapur crest on the turban. He was one of the lawn cutter's children.

In an adjoining lot pockmarked with deep holes, the Kapur water buffaloes were kept. They were tended by the children of the servants. Each one sat on the back of a buffalo wetting down the hides and scrubbing them down with a handful of grass. They were having a wonderful time splashing one another in the process, laughing and carefree in their task, which was their insurance against starvation.

The only thing that disturbed my peace was the scraping of the chains of the Dobermans at the gate. Their triangular, short-cropped ears were tightly drawn together in line with the yellow spots above their eyes. Bodies ever tensed waiting for that command to attack so that they could earn their food. They had been chained up the whole night and were anxious to have a run around the garden.

As soon as the gardeners and the little boy had gone, the gate keeper made sure that no one was in the garden. Then he led them into the garden and loosened the chains. They shot across the garden, sniffing at everything in their path, lifted their legs against the hedge and relieving themselves before continuing on their discovery tour.

They stopped short at one of the topiary bushes. The keeper shouted to them to come to him, but they ignored him. They had found something and they were not going to give it up. They were pawing at the bush and snarling drool dripping from their mouths. They must have found a bunny or something. But then I saw the object of their excitement and my heart nearly stopped. It was a small kitten, it's tiny claw reaching up, trying to defend itself from his pending attackers.

I screamed out of the window. "PUT THE CHAINS ON! For God's sake, put the chains on!"

While they were preoccupied he snapped their chains on and tried to drag them away. He had them in a strangle hold. I ran down as fast as I could, determined to snatch the kitten up before they got to it. Hamir saw me from the kitchen and threw everything down to intercept me and prevent me from going into the garden.

The dog's keeper was still desperately trying to drag the drooling killing machines away from the kitten. But to my horror they were dragging him toward their goal foaming at the mouth. In a second the lead dog charged forward his mouth closed over the head of the defenseless creature, shaking it from side to side, and within seconds the two dogs were playing tug-of-war, ripping the tiny little body to shreds.

The keeper in his embarrassment at not being able to control them, grabbed a thick stick and started beating the dogs unmercifully as if his brutality would compensate for their behavior. I told Hamir, who in the meantime had placed himself between me and the dogs, "Please tell the man it was not his fault and his job is not in jeopardy. It was just an accident, they were taught to kill, and their instinct took over."

For days my heart ached for the kitten, and for those around me who were being torn to shreds in the same way but by poverty and disease. But the show must go on.

The theater where we performed could only be reached by going through the kitchen of the hotel. Being a five star hotel the food was incredibly presented like a culinary advertisement. There were pheasants, mussels, escargot, and steaming vegetables. The giant lobsters they were pulling out of the pot had a healthy red glow. "I could go for one of those right now" Dee whispered. He detested doing a show while people dined. As we arrived a waiter passed us with squab on a flaming sword. Another man followed with a dish of mashed potatoes done up in a very artistic swirl. Everyone's attention was focused on that. But Dee was the professional attention grabber, and signaled for the band to start and did a few of his somersaults up to the mike. Nothing could top that. We had their attention and kept it for the rest of the show. The comedy routines brought riotous laughter; our Indian audience understood English humor, and they were sensitive to the sad songs that brought tears, which pleased our employer.

After the show he did one of his famous hand claps, and two lobster thermadors were delivered to our table. "It looks like your wish came true."

I admired the twirl in the mash, complimenting the waiter. I was hungry so I didn't waste a minute and lifted my fork up. The tines sunk deep into the succulent white flesh dripping with garlic butter. But as I lifted it out of the shell, my eye saw a big fat roach cooked quite mushy with parts missing. The host waited for that exclamation of delight as I take the first bite. But I replaced it quickly.

"Excuse me, Dee I suddenly don't feel well, forgive me. I'm going up to lay down."

"Aren't you going to finish the lobster?"

I dare not answer him without making a spectacle right there in the dining room.

I ran out through the kitchen. At the work table a cook was using his fingers with a deft scoop he was making the curl.

When Dee got back home, I couldn't wait to tell him what happened. But before I could he interrupted. "You missed out on a fantastic treat. I ate mine and then I polished yours off that you didn't touch. I ate every morsel." The vision of that roach popped into my mind, I promptly ran to the bathroom and threw up. Green around the gills, I went back into the room. "What brought that on?" he asked.

I told him. I must have been a little too descriptive, because it had the same results; he made it as far as the door.

The following day we missed breakfast, Hamir was quite worried that it had something to do with his staff. That night when they offered us a free meal at the hotel, I was afraid that the previous night could repeat itself. I said

I wasn't hungry. So he offered me a strawberry milkshake instead. I accepted. *What could possibly go wrong with ice cream?* It had pretty little umbrellas and a strawberry cut into a flower on the side of the glass. We happily slurped on our thick milkshakes; it was hard to suck it through the thin straw. Then I got a piece of strawberry stuck on the end of the straw. I sucked and sucked, but when I removed the straw from the glass, there on the end of the straw sat the cousin of the roach that was in the lobster, only this one went into me! My first reaction was not to tell, but I calmly picked up the glass and asked the manager if there was some place we could talk. I told him about the lobster and that we both were sick, and now there was another one stuck in the straw. He tried to talk it away; "Must be a raisin or a piece of stem or something." I took the straw and shook it right onto his desk. With a plop it fell out minus a head and two legs. We poured the rest out into the dust bin. But to my disgust the other parts were not there. But even though he was still denying it, he took my advice.

That night after the show, walking through the kitchen, the whole staff was there, pants rolled up. Big pots were boiling on the stove but not for some culinary creation. This was an outright war on roaches. The owner of the restaurant in galoshes and apron was directing the attack.

"All cupboards and drawers open! Bring the boiling water! POUR!"

The boiling water sloshed into every corner, nook, and cranny till the floor was covered in bodies that would never find their way into lobsters or milkshakes again. The owner thanked us for our honesty and discretion. He promised that henceforth they would do it weekly. But I still made a point to inspect every morsel of food that was sent to the house; sometimes I just handed it over to the staff. Hamir thought it strange that I had an obsession with feeding everyone.

None of the other performers ever bothered.

One day I told Hamir that I was going to entertain at least twenty people and that I wanted the large table set with the finest linen, china, and silver for tea, with the finest cakes and finger foods. When he asked me who the guests would be, I told him it would be a surprise. The table looked beautiful. I knew my special guests would find it the experience of a lifetime. Most of the people in the city were born and raised on the streets, without once in their lives stepping inside a house.

Imagine a commoner who never set foot inside a castle. I went outside our gates and rounded up all the street people that I usually fed and invited them in.

Hamir was in shock. For the special guests it was the first time. They admired everything in the house with the same reverence that a commoner would admire the possessions of the King. I watched the wonder on their faces. The children had never seen so much food in their life. Hamir in turn watched their every move; he tried to hoard them together so that he could account for their movements. He was determined that while he was alive, nothing would accidentally or on purpose leave the house. He was accountable for everything in the house. When called to the table, they did not fight or grab. There was an over abundance. And they were used to sharing even the smallest of portion of food outside in their world. The older children poured the tea out into a saucer for the little ones who lapped it up with their tongues like kittens. After the tea party I took them on a tour of the house, allowing them as much freedom as I could muster with Hamir hovering over me like some dragon. The more bold ones climbed onto the beds and lay there with their hands clasped to their sides. The little ones jumped on it. While the others giggled into their hands awaiting their turn, so that they could tell someone they had felt a real bed. But the thing that fascinated them the most was the toilet. A strange thing that with the mere press of the handle produced bowls and bowls full of clean water. To them the toilet water in comparison to the water puddles in the streets and the Hoogly was pristine. They played with their hands in the water, drank it trickling through their fingers. Hamir tried to stop them, telling them the function of the toilet. They argued with him that you do those things outside or in the bushes. Then they flushed it over and over just to see so much water disappear. I opened the faucets in the bath. Several of them waded in the water, and when the plug was pulled, little black footprints stayed on the bottom. When it came time for my guests to leave, the food was evenly divided among them. As soon as they were out of the gates, Hamir made a inventory of everything. He found nothing missing. I told him I knew nothing would be missing, because good repays with good.

We were there for six months, but I could never get used to the terrible contrasts that existed. The poor and the maimed were everywhere. They lay dying of hunger outside the gates of the ultra rich, who stuffed themselves with food for a week that the outsiders didn't see in a life time. They simply closed their eyes to what went on in the streets because it was beneath their understanding how *some people* could live like that. When I brought the subject up, they dismissed it and said; "We felt like you in the beginning. You will get used to it!"

But I never did because they were everywhere. Nowhere one could escape the soul destroying poverty. Groups of beggars swarmed around us like waking nightmares, thrusting deformities at us. Gruesome self mutilations that provoked sympathy.

They crawled and limped up to us at cocktail parties in the parks or at the horse races, at the theaters. Alone or in the company of royalty. In every corner sat a poor soul wrapped in rags that concealed worse deformities caused by the dreaded master of deformity leprosy. The streets were full of children who belonged to no one, trying to make a living for themselves. I bought food and gave money but it wasn't enough, would NEVER be enough!

One day while walking along in the street with Dee, I felt tiny hands grabbing at my ankle. I looked down thinking it could be the street entertainer with his trained monkey. But it was a naked little baby who had just learned to crawl.

The street people are very protective of their children, I thought, so I looked around to see if there was a mother or other sibling near, but saw no one! I gently loosened his little hands from my leg picked him up and put him in a safe place away from the street. *Dear Lord, send someone to get him,* I prayed. But I had just taken a few steps when he crawled into the street into the path of an oncoming vehicle. Both Dee and I made a dive for him and put him down on the pavement. But still no one came. So I told Dee, "I'm taking him back to the house."

"Then what? We are leaving in a week for Bombay, it's not like picking up a kitten. He must belong to someone."

"I don't care, Hamir will look after him." By now I was crying. "He'll be killed if we leave him, he'll crawl back into the street."

Dee pulled a note from his pocket. "I bet this will work." He put the note in the baby's hand. Within seconds a raggedy pack of children ran up to the baby, scooped him up, and took him into the alley. The baby belonged to them. He was their means to survival. The money we put in the baby's hand was enough to keep them in food for weeks.

By now I thought I had seen everything, but in conversation with Hamir I asked, "I have seen so many funeral processions and dying in the streets, but have not seen any grave yards. Where do they go?"

"To the banks of the Hoogly, to be cremated."

"Can anyone go and see a funeral?"

"If you're part of the family I suppose." He looked surprised that I asked something like that.

The following day I asked for the use of the rickshaw, When the wallah asked me where to, I said, "I want to see a cremation." No one had ever asked him to go to the burning place. So after a few minutes of reflection he agreed on one condition that I stayed in the rickshaw, didn't take photographs, and covered my face.

On the way there he explained to me that not too long ago when an influential man died, his wife threw herself onto the bier, to keep the corpse down into the flames.

But that no longer was the case. A body was already on the pyre. The family and friends were piling firewood on it and around and under the corpse. I withdrew deep into the corner of the rickshaw, and put a see-through scarf over my face.

I felt like a voyeur invading their privacy as they chanted prayers and then lit the fire. Very soon the flames crept round the body and there was the strong smell of cloth burning. Then the pungent smell of flesh. What horror to watch the flames dance over a human cadaver. But greater horror still when suddenly the corpse sat bolt upright. Out of my lips escaped a muffled cry, "My God, he's still alive!"

The wallah looked around to see if anyone heard or saw us. But they calmly proceeded with the ceremony. A family member grabbed a log out of the fire and beat the corpse over the head; steam and gray matter exploded over the fire and the corpse lay down.

"It's the muscles that contract making the corpse sit up. Breaking the skull releases the steam," he said matter-of-factly. We went away at this stage, and coming back several hours later, the family was sweeping the ashes into a basket. They had made a small floating wooden raft bedecked with flowers and candles. On this they placed the ashes of their beloved, lit the candles, waded into the water, and set the little raft afloat. It sailed slowly into the faster flowing current where it bobbed up and down for a while, and then slowly sank into its watery grave. There was always the ugly, but there was an abundance of beauty, too.

It was dark already, the moon was rising, and so the wallah took the long way round, following a branch of the Hoogly. There was a magic silver glow that reflected the moon's shape and every stone in the water so I asked the Wallah to stop for a minute. I caught a glimpse of something moving. Then I saw *him*. As an artist it was a never to be forgotten moment. He stood naked beneath a small waterfall on a flat rock. He was young and beautiful! Splashing the water innocently over him, unaware that a woman's eyes were sharing that very personal thing with him at that very moment. His naked skin shone like molten gold in the light of the moon. Something black was draped across his arm. He was rubbing soap into it, then he dropped it down into the water, rinsed it and when he shook the water from it. An indescribable thrill ran through my body. It was his hair, his glorious jet black hair that hung nearly to his feet. As he shook the water out it splashed and formed multiple little circles that melted into each other and grew bigger and bigger till they disappeared into the trees on the embankment. I motioned to the wallah to go closer. He flatly refused this time. He didn't mind taking me to a funeral, it was a different thing. But this was just the opposite, this man was still alive, and this was his sacred-secret moment. That he shared with no one. "I do understand," I said.

"One day I will paint this unforgettable picture, and believe me, I am richly blessed to have been able to watch and drink in his beauty, even though it was a moment stolen from time.

Bombay, Roman Coins for Greek Island

The move to Bombay was like going to Heaven after having a taste of Hell.

It looked almost empty of people, even though it had 8.2 million living there. Everything and everyone seemed to have a space so the influx of people wasn't so evident. Because of the rag trade and various other businesses that thrived, it was considered the commercial capital of India.

Bombay had retained some of the characteristics of the British. The most charming being the red double-decker busses, and the other delightful habit, the four o'clock tea ceremony. The first thing that I noticed was the lack of lepers in the streets.

"We still have them, but that was one good thing the British did for us, they established a leper colony outside of the city limits." I still came across some beggars in the streets, but there were none who were maimed like in Calcutta.

There was a puzzling assortment of people, living in harmony together. Each fitting like a puzzle into the overall picture.

The Marathi, Muslims ,and Jews worked in the clothing factories and banks. The Christians handled the meat products, and the vegetarian Hindi looked after the markets and produce. Everyone had his own little niche. The history of India was as diverse as any country. The Kolis were the first inhabitants, and then followed the Parsis, who still maintained special set-aside land. Their beliefs came with them from Persia. They hallowed earth, water, and fire. Therefore they did not believe in disposal of their dead by internment into the soil, nor by burning, or sending the ashes into the water.

"But what was left over after the main three elements were considered and rejected?" I wanted to know.

"They are taken to the Garden of Silence."

I was taken to Malabar Hill where several circular towers rose above the trees. I also saw one of these towers near the railway station. "Do they all belong to the Parsis?" I wanted to know.

"No, that one belonged to the Hindi who had burning Gnats within its walls, and ashes are still set adrift onto the water, but not by the Parsis."

"Doesn't it affect the people living near the towers?"

"Only the people living in the high-rises on Malabar Hill complain that they can see into the towers, and they describe the gruesome scenes. Within the walls there were several tiers, on which the cadavers of the Parsis were placed. Below the tiers lived some untouchables who devoted their lives to tending to the dead, in the belief that that would elevate them to a better life in their next incarnation. Their job was to dismember the corpses for the vultures that always circled overhead. When the cadaver bones were picked clean, and nature had taken its course, they were then stacked in vaults under the tiers.

"What if the spaces for stacking became full?"

"Another tower would be built."

"And what if the vultures died out or left?"

"I suppose they would have to turn to burning then, because there is no space for internment when we don't have enough space for the living. There are some terrible accounts of body parts falling from the sky; one in particular had its own gruesome humor. Some high-up dignitary was giving a garden party. The food was beautifully set up, when a vulture flew overhead and dropped an arm right in the middle of the punch." It was horrible, but I couldn't help laughing, picturing the consternation that would have caused among the guests.

"So you see, the people living there have a lot to complain about." Joe said. I told him about going to see a funeral burning in Calcutta, undercover of course. "Why on earth would you do that? Of course all this primitive disrespect of body disposal and living among the body temples makes me terrified of my own mortality, especially thinking that my body parts would land on one of the tiers, and the vultures pecking at my eyes—they say they always go for the eyes first."

"You wouldn't know anything if you're dead, so why worry about it now while you're alive?"

"But I do, so to put my mind at rest I have hired a man to stay in my room and wake me every now and then to assure I don't die in my sleep." Dee exploded with laughter.

"And what if you die between the waking up process?"

He was very serious when he answered. "You know I never thought of that, and then I'll be dead without ever knowing, wouldn't I?" He burst out laughing, and soon we were all rolling on the floor with laughter.

There was a big commotion out in the street. It was getting close to the autumn festival when the large paper effigies of all the favorite gods were paraded through the streets. A giant elephant *Ganesh,* lord of prosperity, passed the window, and the street suddenly took on an air of festivity. The effigy was beautifully made in paper over a wooden frame mounted on a push cart, festooned with flowers. He was painted bright pink, richly embellished with gold and gay decorations of other minor gods. Joe the Australian told us all about the festival and invited us all to go with him to Chowpatty Beach to partake in the festivities.

Dee and Ivan bowed out, convinced that they would become the side show. But I was all for it. Joe had some friends living in a high rise on the beach, where we would have a wonderful view of everything, but explained that mingling was part of the fun. So we dropped the car after crossing the bridge and walked the rest of the way. Thousands upon thousands thronged the beach. They assured a sitting space by camping out days before. Small sections were roped off for the performers who were given priority. The monkey acts paraded their monkeys among the spectators. "Hold onto your valuables," we were warned, because the monkeys were also trained as pickpockets, and were experts at that. But anywhere there was a crowd, theft always had the possibility, so I played it safe and left all valuables back at the hotel, except for money that was pinned into my bra.

All the roped off areas were already occupied. We watched a trapeze act on a flimsy contraption that looked more like a washing line performing with amazing skill. Saw a fire eater blowing two-foot long flames, making everyone scatter in all directions. In another circle I saw a man stand on his head, usually that would not be anything extraordinary, but this was. His head was buried in the sand. I expected him to pop up out of the sand any minute, but one hour later he was still there in the same position. Next to him was a small circle of marigolds that in the meantime had filled up with coins.

"Why don't the people steal the coins?" I asked. If there were pickpockets about, that would be the easiest take. "And how does he breathe?

"The people don't steal the coins because he is a holy man, and that would be a big debt to repay in the next reincarnation. As for the second question, He has devised ways and means that allow him to breathe, and uses mind over matter to maintain that pose, perhaps he is even fast asleep like that. They do amazing things." On a box next to him a handsome young man was reciting poetry, and a group of young women were hanging on his every word and gesture, ignoring the holy man completely.

Some vendors approached Joe, who asked for a *bhel puri*. He stuffed it in his mouth and asked for another. "You must try this!" The man gave him some stuff that looked like burned rice on a leaf.

"What is it?"

With mouth full he explained, "Puffed rice, diced potato, onion with chutney sauce."

One of the other vendors handed me a small pink and white coconut bar; it looked like the candy bars my mom used to make. So I paid him and bought a dozen more, handing them out to people around me. But suddenly the crowd's excitement rose to a fever pitch. Across the sand came a procession of men in evil looking costumes. Behind them came giant effigies of all the feared bad demons on platforms with wheels borrowed from bicycles. Children cried and hid behind their mothers' saris. The whole procession headed for a designated spot. Their evil was short lived because the men in costumes had lit some torches, and one by one the paper giants went up in flames, despite the magnificent art work that took days to make, with expensive gold overlays and paper flowers. Cheers went up out of the spectators as the flames shot up into the air, much to the delight of everyone. Children came out from their hiding places and received candy and sweet cakes. People brought out picnic baskets and shared with everyone, danced, and made merry.

As in Calcutta, there was Extreme wealth and extreme poverty. The poor, however, had something that lacked in Calcutta—they had optimism. The people lived in grossly subdivided tenements, sometimes two families in two small rooms with rotting walls and ill fitting doors, with no electricity or running water. Yet they resented the tourists, calling their accommodations *SLUMS*. Looking into them, each sleeping area was divided by a drape and neatly organized and clean. They took advantage of the monsoons to hang all their washing out, bedding and all, to be laundered by nature. Collected buckets full to drink and be used for other purposes. Our driver explained that they considered the temporary shacks built at the edge of the jungles to be slums, because the people inside houses paid rent. My jaw dropped, I was amazed that anybody had the audacity to charge for such accommodations. "How much do they charge for the two rooms?"

"Twenty rupees." A quick calculation put their rent at $2 and some cents.

That was a large amount considering that some people only made pennies a day for their work. Businessmen made considerably more and could afford sharing a hotel room, which had the luxury of light and water and toilet facilities. We on the other hand were the luckiest of all, and had a suite thrown in on our performing contract in a five star hotel. We had room service delivered to our suite, but still remembering the *roach infestation* in Calcutta, I was particular of what we ate. So I carefully inspected everything that they brought. There was an over abundance of everything. I had noticed a family living in a lean-to behind a gas station, so I went out and bought a picnic basket and filled the containers every night with food. Even the leftovers off our plates. I took the basket to the woman. She was so grateful she knelt down and kissed my feet. I was so humbled that I took her in my arms and hugged her. Minutes later she stood on the corner of the street, stuck her fingers in her mouth and whistled with such force that it astounded me. The people came from everywhere. She motioned them to sit in a circle. She then took a small portion between three fingers of her hand and starting at the first mouth, like a mother bird fed each one in the circle till nothing was left. I stood watching this amazing thing, thinking of the story when Jesus fed the multitude with bread and fish. The hotel must have thought of us as gluttons, because after that I ordered everything that was on the menu to feed my *fledglings*.

The rains came at regular intervals; it was shower and wash day. But to those still living on the street, it was a problem. I saw an entire family sleeping under a huge black umbrella, their bodies and legs sticking like spikes of a wheel out in the rain while their heads and upper bodies were under the umbrella.

Outside of our hotel there was a policeman with a big rainbow umbrella helping tourists out of the cabs and walking them to the entrance. Right behind him stood a small boy sheltering from the rain. To the Tourists this was amusing but the policeman didn't think so. He became quite agitated and took a swipe at the boy every now and then, but then seconds later the little boy was behind him again. I saw this little comedy take place. But when the policeman gave him a cuff that sent him flying, I went out and gave him a piece of my mind. Then I took the child to the fledgling family at the garage. That night I added another portion to their food because I somehow knew that this was a child on his own, fending for himself.

We had the best of everything, and hobnobbed with the prince of Nepal, who didn't think about wealth, and wanted only to be a pig farmer. We were sought after for Dinner guests and parties.

After the show one night we met a ship's captain. In conversation I told him about my coin collection I acquired at Baalbeck in the Middle East. "If you ever think of a trade, I have something very valuable I would trade. When you come over later for drinks on board, bring the coins and we can talk trading." I was not aware that Dee had accepted his invitation. His ship was anchored in the Arabian Sea so we were to accompany him on a small boat to the ship which loomed big and black a mile or so in the water. It was a muggy night and I felt uncomfortable with high heels and wearing a long evening dress of lace. There was a spooky mist over the river as we sailed out of the Harbor to the open sea. When we reached the ship there was a strong wake that slammed our little boat up against the gang plank. To transfer from the small boat, I pulled my tight fitting dress to above my knees and took my shoes off, to the delight of the ship's crew, but just as I was transferring, a big wave washed over us and I got thoroughly drenched. On board a sailor brought me a towel and everyone started drying me off. The gold dots on my evening dress started coming off; I discovered they were only glued on. It became a running joke for the rest of the night. Everywhere I sat or leaned, I would leave a few dots. The captain was very serious about the swap, even though he had not seen the coins; he went purely on my description of them.

"Follow me to my cabin. I have something I want to show you." He led us down a long passage. When he opened the door of his cabin, on top of an old-fashioned four-poster bed anchored to the floor lay a beautiful Indian girl, about eleven years old, and quite naked, covered only in her long black hair.

"That wasn't exactly what I expected," I said in a shocked voice.

"Don't mind her, she is like the furniture, she is sleeping. I find her every night waiting on my bed. Her mother gave her to me as a present so that she can see the world. She thinks she owes me her body, but she is far too young!" I thought, *How tragic. When would he think she is not too young?* He was in his early fifties, unshaven, and unbathed from the body odor that leaped out of his clothes. He had a pot belly from drinking, and her life was still before her.

"No, the thing I want to show you is under the bed." I knelt down and looked. Under the bed there lay a giant bone. By the looks of it, it belonged to a dinosaur.

"Where did you get that?" I wanted to know, because that was quite a large object to lug around without being detected.

"It doesn't matter, at some kind of digging, just like yours. Do you like it? You could make a fortune selling it."

"I'm sorry but it's too big to hang around my neck, I wouldn't know where to put it, and I feel uncomfortable where it came from."

"I told you. I got it from a digging like yours," he repeated sarcastically.

"Yes, but I paid for mine and I can carry it in my pocketbook."

"If you don't like this deal, I have another one for you. I hold a 99-year deed to a small island near San Torini in Greece, called Aspronisi. It has a shack and a water tank, but the water has to come from the main island, because rain is few and far between. I no longer use it. It's available. I got my supplies from San Torini." He brought out a map and some postcards that he showed me. I showed him my coins, but again had to decline. It all sounded too good to be true. Besides, a good salesman could sell the Brooklyn Bridge to someone. I kept my coins.

The Death Wish

The last week in India I did a lot of thinking. After the contract arrived for Johannesburg, South Africa, I took long walks and thought about what I would do when we arrived in South Africa. I read the contract and it did not stipulate a time limit, so it would be inevitable that I ran into Peter. How would I react? Right from the beginning I had doubts about my marriage to Dee. People warned me rebound marriages never worked, but I was infatuated with him and didn't listen to their advice. Now I was certain that we were never meant to be together. The biggest irritation was Dee's drinking. He was an alcoholic in denial. He described his drinking as "social drinking, because my fans want to drink with me." But I was repulsed by his drinking.

I put aside my unhappiness for a while, and headed for the beautiful little bridge I saw not far from where we lived. I was admiring the giant banyan trees and the flowers growing on the bank of a canal running through under the bridge. I was about to cross the bridge when I heard an earth shattering scream emanating from hell itself. It came from under the bridge. At first I thought that someone had fallen into the water and could not swim. I heard no splash. But it was obvious that someone was in pain and needed help. I scrambled down the embankment. Just then the tortured scream came again. I froze in my tracks. There under the bridge sat the last remnants of a human being. There were no distinguishable features that determined gender. The face was eaten away by leprosy; where the nose had been there were two gaping holes out of which crawled the unspeakable. Maggots! The lips were raw, cracked, and bleeding! The hands were wrapped in dirty brown, blood-stained rags. As I watched in horror more maggots crawled out! The eyes alone were alive and begged me for release from Purgatory. And I was helpless. Through my mind I visualized Jesus simply laying his hands on the lepers, and they were instantly cured. I did not have his power, so I stood there paralyzed in my weak faith, and all I could do was pray for her deliverance. The death wish was clear. If I had a gun I would have fired the fatal shot, to end the pain. Instead I fled from the scene. Running back home I thought of Joe, who had nothing wrong with him and didn't want to die, and here sat a person starving and tortured with pain, begging to die, and I perfectly fed and healthy had to go on living with that knowledge that I did nothing and ran away. I told the hotel owner to ask the leper colony to come and pick her up. He promised to do that. *I still wonder sometimes if he did?* I also told him that I had provided food to the family behind the garage and I would leave the picnic basket so that he could fill it with leftovers and give it to them. He promised that he would do that too. Then I went shopping. Material for saris, blankets, ribbons, and children's clothes, and gave it to my mother bird woman who fed everybody.

When we left India, the last thing I saw was a group of people at a distance near the tarmac waving at us. The children were wearing the clothes, and the mother held up the baby for me to see; it was our fledgling group. None of our so-called fans were there to see us off, but this little bunch that must have walked more than 40 miles to see us leave did come! I cried!

"What's going to happen to them now with you gone?" Dee asked as we took off.

"I asked the hotel owner to continue feeding them."

"You think he is going to bother?"

"He promised! If he doesn't, I think Joe will continue to feed them, I think We rubbed off on him."

67
Contract in South Africa

On the way to South Africa, our plane developed problems and the captain announced that we had to make an unscheduled emergency stop in Cairo. We would be in North Africa for four days.

"Four days, that will be wonderful. I always wanted to go and see the Pyramids, and take a camel ride," I told Dee.

Egypt

At the airport we ran into a snag, though. We were not allowed to take our luggage off. We were told we could only take an overnight bag and personal cosmetics, that's all. I had packed everything in the checked luggage and it left us with just the clothes we were wearing. I looked forward to going sight-seeing. But both of us were inappropriately dressed. I wore a three-piece Dior silk suit and Dee wore a custom-made $400 handwoven Indian-silk suit. There was nothing suitable to change into in our overnight bags. The airline put us up in one of Cairo's finest hotels, with hallways almost as wide as freeways, and a ceiling at least thirty feet high. It had no air conditioning but an over-sized ceiling fan that made loud whirring noises but had very little air circling. We pulled the beds into the middle of the floor directly under the fan and stripped naked. Still it was unbelievably hot. Taking a cold shower helped a bit, but we had to lay on top of the bedding to benefit from the fan. Unable to sleep, we tossed and turned, relieving our discomfort with more showers. Before going to bed we booked a tour to the Pyramids for the following morning.

In the morning when we got downstairs. The concierge said the camels were waiting in the courtyard out back. Neither one of us had ever been on a camel so it was a total surprise when we found them indeed waiting.

The guide who brought our camels took one look at our clothes and said that would not do. I explained that our luggage was still on the airport. He went to his own camel and came back with a sheet. "Put this on," he motioned. I did not hesitate, wrapped the sheet around me and managed to take my tight fitting skirt off under it. He commanded the camels to get down, and showed us how to mount a camel and warned us that once on we had to hold on tight and lean back, because the camel had a strange way of first straightening his back legs to get back up, tipping his passenger over his neck. The five-mile ride was wonderful. I expected a rough ride, and was pleasantly surprised, they have a soothing gait and galloping on tip-toes. It felt as if they had pillows tied to their feet, swaying gently from side to side. Mine, however, would give a warning squawk sound and then turn his head around and try and bite me with nasty looking yellow teeth. I had to dodge with every warning. We spent the rest of the day exploring the Pyramids. With a guide's help I climbed the Pyramid on a steep path between house-sized blocks. The Sphinx, still being excavated, was off limits and we settled for the surrounding areas, returning in time to the hotel to go out and see a movie, hoping that it would be air-conditioned.

When we enquired where it was, the desk clerk said, "A few blocks away, you can easily walk there." It seemed easy enough so we set off on foot. Dee was carrying around two thousand dollars on him rolled up in the secret pocket I had sewn into the front of his pants. He did not want to leave it behind in the hotel.

But he was still paranoid because he kept saying someone was following us. To put his mind at rest and assure him I turned around, and all I could see was two people heading in the same direction as us. We kept on going. It wasn't unusual for people to follow us. A tall shapely blonde and her dwarf companion would always be a spectacle worth investigation. Wherever we had gone in the past we were followed and would be in the future. Somehow I did not expect it in Cairo.

But now I heard more voices laughing and giggling, and when I looked around there were about seven behind us pointing and whispering. That too was a common occurrence. I was used to it by now.

So I simply ignored them. Two blocks farther on the few had multiplied to a crowd.

Now I felt uncomfortable and apprehension crawled up my spine. But to put Dee's mind at rest I said. "There must be something going on, perhaps the circus?" I was immediately sorry saying that. Because if there was one thing Dee detested most was the circus. Because everyone always took it for granted that he was working in a circus.

"Yes, we ARE the circus!" he replied, getting more and more agitated.

I was afraid he would turn around and lash out at the people who were behind us, and to the side of us; they were breathing down our necks by then. I was afraid if he did that, they would attack us. A street cop must have thought that something big like the circus was happening too, and someone omitted telling him, because he stopped the cars to let the mass of people surrounding us, cross the street. In this crossing over, a jostle started and we were pushed off the sidewalk and pinned against a car. Somewhere in their past the people had been told that if you rubbed a Dwarf's stomach or his head, you will have good fortune. They did not waste another minute but started rubbing Dee's stomach and head. I knew just how it irritated him, because even some of his normal-sized friends often did that in a friendly playful way, or tousled his hair, which he was very proud of.

He had a beautiful head of black hair. I on the other hand worried that they would discover the money roll. His hand shot down to the roll and he started shouting.

"GET THE HELL AWAY FROM US!" I begged him to calm down, because if he angered someone, the whole thing could explode into a bloody riot.

In a café opposite the car, against which we were pinned a man was drinking coffee and wondering what the crowd was all about. All he could see was a tall blonde pinned against a car. HIS car! He jumped up, dashed through the milling crowd, yelling as he went. "Get away from my car!" He was afraid they would turn his car over when a riot started. He reached me, and then saw Dee.

He unlocked the car and said, "Quick, get in!" We didn't hesitate, we fell into the car.

He started the car honking his way out and took off.

"What happened?" he asked.

"I don't know, we wanted to see a movie, and they started following us, it turned into a crowd." We were shaken and unhurt and I still wanted to see the movie. The man dropped us off at the theater; we were only a few blocks away.

By the time the show was over, there wasn't a cab in sight, so we waited in the foyer till most of the people left. The only one that was there was a small boy selling little leather camels.

"Wannah buy?" He must have seen what happened to us earlier on, because he pointed to the street. "People's gone, I show better way home if you buy a camel, yes?"

"Yes, but no tricks or I will put the evil eye on you," Dee warned him.

"Okey dokey! Come."

Dee whispered to me that we most likely will be mugged, and our throats slashed, but he didn't want to experience another mobbing. So we followed the little boy.

The little boy led us out the back exit and down a dark deserted alley.

Our bodies tensed with fear of the unknown. We kept looking to the side and over our shoulder, but to our amazement we were safely through the alley in a minute. He led us around corners and through back yards, with not a person in sight. Within minutes we found ourselves at the back door of our hotel.

The boy was smiling from ear to ear. "You're hotel, yes?" He walked us to the front entrance. "Now you buy my camel?"

"Now I buy ALL your camels, how much?" After some haggling over a price, Dee gave him the money. The boy was overwhelmed and thanked him.

But then as we started to go inside Dee turned around and handed the boy back all the camels, only keeping one. To the boy it meant pure profit, and to us, it meant much more—we got safely home. Two days later when we left Cairo there was one person to see us off. Coincidence or not. The camel boy was there. I remembered the "fledgling" family. I just knew that the camel boy would make it in the harsh world. He had enterprise, took notice of everything that went on around him. He was helpful and compassionate to strangers.

I secretly handed enough money to him to last for some time and start up his own camel selling business, and not settle for mere pennies in commission.

When we went to reclaim our luggage, we discovered that one of our trunks had been stolen, with all our publicity, and some stage costumes and most of Dee's clothes. The simple reason why they didn't want to release our luggage. We thought the joke was on the ones that stole the trunk; most of Dee's custom made clothes were in the trunk, and he was a four-foot-tall dwarf, and his clothes wouldn't fit anybody except of course another dwarf.

We had a two day layover in Kenya before going to Johannesburg. This gave us the opportunity to go on a mini safari. But it would never equal second safari.

We landed in Johannesburg with a lot of advanced publicity. When we stepped off the Plane, the cameras were flashing everywhere. Our manager had sent some of the news clippings from Argentina, and Europe, so they repeated the headlines; *THE ROMANCE OF THE CENTURY, RAMONA, RUBY OF THE MOULIN ROUGE, Romeo and Juliet Arrive in Johannesburg Fresh From Their World Tour.* The papers were full of stories exaggerating our stature. They made me six feet, and Dee two-foot-six. They said no one wanted me or Dee, so we found one another in the Moulin Rouge. They followed us in the streets, and into the hotel, photographing us eating out and shopping. We were on the news in the movie houses. It was unusual seeing two dwarfs and their wives, headlining a show.

Till then my family had seen photos of Dee, but not met him in the flesh. The true test came when my family met Dee for the first time. People were simply people in our family, so they took him in their stride. Dee was dwarfed by my 6-foot, 3-inch father. They accepted him from the start, because I had married him and he was a charmer, but suddenly my sister wondered why I had not stayed with Peter. And had I considered what would happen if I had a child? I had to explain that genetically Dee was considered a plastoid-dwarf, and would produce normal-sized children. My nephews accepted him as Snow White's eighth dwarf, and said, "Wouldn't it be wonderful when they have children and they turned out to be fairies?" They wanted to know why he was so little. So I said that he didn't eat his food so that he could grow as big as his Daddy. The smallest suddenly pushed his food away and said then he was going to stop eating so that he could stay as small as Uncle Dee and become the ninth dwarf.

We invited all the adults to see our show, and even though their religion did not permit them to enter a night club they accepted much to my surprise, because they were always against my being in show business, and had never seen me perform on stage.

The show was sold out every night. Dee was convinced that the people were paid to applaud—it was thunderous, they were so enthusiastic. We had several curtain calls. And Dee went on to do several encores. The joy was having my family see our success.

Dee knew that Peter was in Johannesburg; so did I and wondered how Peter would take all the publicity that stated I had never loved anyone before meeting Dee. Dee had asked me before we left India if I was going to see him. So one night it came out directly when he saw Peter in the audience. "Are you going to see him?" I did not answer, I was simply speechless.

The *HE* of course was Peter. I had thought of it and actually phoned a few times just to hear his voice, but couldn't get myself to talk to him. The only thing that hurt was how much of the media hype he believed? Just to put Dee's mind at ease, I said, "Did I marry you or him and have I not pleased you?" He seemed satisfied with my answer and I'm sure he was relieved when a week later we left for Cape Town to do a show; we would be away from Peter. I on the other hand was apprehensive because I knew that somewhere in Cape Town I would run into Ingrid, Peter's estranged wife and his daughter, Simone. It happened sooner than I thought. We were going to do a publicity shoot, and like a moth drawn to a candle, I was drawn to Fourth Beach where I met Peter in my cove that I named Shangri-la. I suggested we do the shoot there.

Our manager spotted a little girl playing with a ball on the beach, and he thought it would make a beautiful contrast. He told me to go over to her and play with her so that it didn't look posed. When I approached her and asked if I could play with her, she withdrew shyly. There was something very familiar about her little face. Peter had sent me some pictures of her soon after her mother had abducted her and left him to go to her lover in Cape Town. It was a shot in the dark. I spoke to her in Afrikaans.

"Jou naam is Simone?"(Your name is Simone?)

"How do you know my name?" she asked back in Afrikaans.

"You're Peters little girl, you have his eyes and his mouth." She looked at me strangely. I don't know how much her mother had told her about her father because she was only eighteen months when Ingrid left. Or the way Ingrid felt about him. She may never have said anything or perhaps that he was dead. I guessed she was about five or six. I touched her gently on the head. In seeing her and touching her, I had again touched him, because she was his flesh and blood.

A blonde woman sitting on a beach towel must have seen me touch her and called out, "Simone, what have I told you about speaking to strangers? Come here at once!" I heard her scold the child. It was Ingrid!

As Simone gathered up her ball and walked back to the woman, I wanted to shout out, *I'm no stranger, I will be eternally linked to you because I love your father,* but I whispered instead to myself. But she will never know, because who knew what the future held?

"Who was the little girl you spoke too? It looked like you knew her."

"Just a child playing on the beach; her mother doesn't want her to speak to strangers."

On that trip I never spoke to Peter, but saw him on several occasions in the audience, while we performed in Johannesburg. I wondered how the publicity was affecting him, with headlines like "The Romance of the Century" and "Never a Love Like This."

68
House in England — Promises?

The offers from England kept pouring in while we were in South Africa, Dee hadn't seen his family since our wedding two years before, and so we headed home. At least it was home to him. I still felt I had just left my home, after all the traveling; I was still living out of a suitcase. He was happy to be back in his own country. England, after his big success in Europe and India and South Africa, welcomed him with open arms. We played the whole circuit of Army camps, and then on to Steel Piers and night clubs. But I was tired of one night stands and the bar scenes and decided to quit. Dee said he too was tired of traveling and wanted to open his own night club; he thought that after Blackpool would be the ideal time for him to quit and settle down. Blackpool was every performer's dream including Dee's. That was were everyone who was someone in the entertainment field performed. Somebody offered us their house for the summer. I yearned for a place where I could settle down and perhaps raise a family. I was 32 years old and time was running out to start one. So for a while I was happy. I played house, even cooked Dee his favorite English dishes like steak and kidney pie and corn beef and cabbage; we even had an herb garden. His family visited on weekends. We hid our differences from them, and his father thought we were the ideal married couple. Every time his mother saw me, she wanted to know when she could expect a grandchild. I felt embarrassed when she said, "Now that you aren't on stage anymore, are you even trying?"

Well it wasn't as if I wasn't trying I told her, but it takes two to tango. I attributed it to the hectic schedule we just finished. Also Dee was seldom at home now, and all he wanted to do was rest when he came home, sometimes at three and four in the morning. I felt like telling her the real truth that sometimes he was so drunk that he could hardly make it to the bed after partying with the audience after the show. I would have liked to add that perhaps she could expect a grandchild from another source, but she was a kind gentle woman, who thought the world of her only son.

Dee's father too must have asked him when he was going to settle down and have a family, because a few weeks later he told Dee that there was a house for sale on Langdale Road with enough rooms to raise a family of ten. He was right!

We went to see the house. It was in an exclusive gated park area with four bedrooms downstairs and four more up. A beautiful wide spiral stairway lead to the upper level, it also had an attic and a basement with four rooms that could be altered into a game room or separate apartment. Within a few weeks the house was ours. I couldn't have been more happy! I now had a home of my own, no more hotels and motels.

"I have plenty of time on my hands, and I want to do the interior renovations and furnish it myself," I told Dee, "and when your contract is up at Blackpool you can start to concentrate on establishing your own night club that you dreamed of, and maybe then we can also concentrate on the grandchild your parents want."

The house really was a monster with large almost walk-in fireplaces in every room. I tore them down and free sculpted the fireplaces with chicken mesh and concrete into soft flowing lines. And I removed all the years of wallpaper, and painted the walls instead. It kept me busy till all hours of the night. Dee was sometimes away till dawn. I took it for granted that he was trying to make contacts to establish his own business. I had gotten used to his irregular hours but one night his partner informed me, "It isn't the show that keeps him away so often, but the ladies. He is getting r*eacquainted* with some of his old girlfriends. I hate to tell you this, but one in particular he is seeing in a 'Biblical way,' if you get what I mean?" I didn't want to believe it, till he showed me a film that he had taken in the sly of Dee in the buff chasing a naked woman around in his apartment.

Suddenly home didn't feel like home anymore. I somehow knew that something was going on; he always flirted outrageously with girls that took his fancy in the audience I allowed him that. But this was adultery! I did not tell Dee of the film but asked him where he was till the early hours of the morning. He got quite mad at me and answered. "Being loyal to my fans— what else do you think I am doing?" I had felt insecure in my marriage all along. But now I had proof.

My insecurity increased when he came home one morning and said that he was offered a contract in Las Vegas, America.

"But I had just completed fixing up the house," I moaned, "and now I would have to pack up again."

"I didn't say you were included. I thought buying you the house would keep you happy. The contract is for three months. If they prolong it. I will let you know and you can go over till the contract ends."

I tried to make sense of this new development. "But you promised to settle down and quit show bus—"

He interrupted, "Just because you quit performing, don't think I'm ready to quit!" He looked at me as if I was insane. "What gave you that idea? I didn't mean right now, this is my career that's at stake, and I'm not going to lose the opportunity to go to America. I'm not ready to have children and settle down yet." That to me meant the last nail into the coffin of our marriage.

The last few months before leaving for America, he was drinking a little less and paying a little more attention to my needs, but I lost my respect for him and knew the marriage was in trouble. People warned me that a rebound marriage had more downs than ups, but this I had categorized as a down period. He on the other hand thought that everything was going well! So no matter how I felt about his infidelity and reneged promises, when the time arrived he was leaving for America,
he couldn't understand why I didn't show more emotion about his going, but I knew somehow that the marriage was on its last legs.

After his leaving, I dreaded the nights alone in the old house that had a spooky feel about it, no matter how many modern convenience we had installed. I still made big glowing fires in most of the living areas' fireplaces, to give the place a "lived in" look. At the same time going down into the vast unoccupied area into the basement to get the coal for the fires gave me the creeps. In each of the dank rooms there hung a single light bulb. One of the rooms had been converted to a coal receptacle room. The coal was poured down a wide aluminum chute directly from the street covered only by an iron lid that could not be locked.

The chute was wide enough for anyone to slide down into the basement. So every time I went down there to fill the coal shuttles, I imagined every shadow to be an attacker. The basement steps led straight up into the kitchen. I installed a hook at the door but every sound outside sounded like someone kicking the door open. Every night I dragged a big old kitchen cupboard in front of the door. One night in exploring the downstairs basement, I discovered an old bicycle that still functioned. On one of the shelves I also found a slaughterhouse pistol. It looked like an old fashioned cowboy long-barrel pistol. The only difference was it didn't fire bullets. It had an inner rod inside the outer barrel with four bladed prongs at the front, that shot out when the trigger was pulled. The gun was meant to cut the brain stems of cattle before they were butchered. This now I carried around with me for protection. The only thing now deterring my happiness was I was lonely.

My in-laws lived about a mile away, so now I peddled the bike through fog and rain there and back every night to seek company. I felt safe taking the gun with me in my pocket, but before entering the house I would release the safety. That meant I expected the intruder to already be in the house waiting for me, and I would have to be a foot away from him to let the gun be of any use. I knew just where I would be aiming, especially if the intruder was a rapist.

About three months after Dee left for America, I received the first letter from Dee saying:

The contract is being prolonged for Las Vegas, and other contract offers are coming in. It looks like I am here for at least a year. Put an ad in the papers and rent the house out, and when I can I will sell it. If you want to come. I'll send you a ticket.

He had not asked my opinion or even told me in advance that he meant to sell the house. But I suddenly didn't care anymore. I had come to hate the cold of England and the eternal fog so thick that when I opened the windows in the morning the fog drifted in thick enough to slice with a knife. I enclosed the stairs with an ornamental gate that could be locked and divided the house into two separate apartments with the main entrance in the front lobby. One up and one down. Each with their own bathrooms, which were the main attraction, because many of the older houses still lacked an indoor bathroom and people had to go to public bath houses. When I put the ad in, they came in droves, and after careful screening I found the right tenants. I had them sign an honor lease in which they deposited the rent directly into a bank account. The bank then would send us the statements to America.

69
When Planets Align

I had taken a bath and put my old silk Moulin Rouge dressing gown on and planned on having an early night with a good book.

Earlier on I had reluctantly taken the red leather suitcases down so that I could start packing; the prospect of America was exciting. But would anything change between Dee and me? My mother- in-law didn't know that Dee had been unfaithful and was happy that I was going to see Dee in America, now we could start on the grandchild she wanted. She insisted that I go on the rhythm method to conceive, thinking a baby was all we needed to make our marriage more perfect, and so to make her happy I had been taking my temperature just to see if it really would work. I had taken it that very morning and it shot up to 99, which was supposed to indicate my most fertile time. But I didn't feel in the least that it could produce a baby the way our marriage was going. I was still wondering when the front door bell rang.

"Damn," I cursed as I ran down the steps two at a time. *More people to see the house? I already have prospective tenants. I don't feel like confronting anybody. I was planning to have a relaxing night to myself. I will just tell them that both the apartments are rented and that will be that.*

Arriving breathless at the front door, I jerked it open. There on the doorstep stood Peter. I stared at him in unbelieving silence; we did not speak for what seemed like an eternity, but it was only seconds.

"Is it okay if I come in?" I was dumbstruck and simply nodded. He stepped inside, and as the door closed behind him I melted into his arms. I had no shame, no reservation, or hesitation but that terrible hunger for his love. Through the passionate kisses, we mumbled the missing years as if there had been no ice age intermission. Like a frozen mountain stream that knew its well-known river bed suddenly comes to life after the sudden thaw and tumbled down its course, we tore feverishly at clothes that barred the way to our union and flowed into each other with no thought of "them" or "they" or consequences of our actions. There were no yesterdays, no questions, or tomorrows empty promises. There was just the moments of now; that in itself was timeless. He wasn't in the written line of letters or in the secret fantasy of dreams. He was REAL and nothing else mattered. Hours later reality dawned; we were in one of the bedrooms downstairs and the fire had gone out in the fireplace, but not in our desire. Tenderly we loved just one more time. I kissed his fingertips and pressed my face into his silver hair, drinking in his smell. I was drunk with the smell of our bodies' union that hung like the rarest of perfumes around us as we held one another, almost brutally afraid to let go lest one of us disappeared again. Above our head the grandfather clock ticked off the seconds toward our parting. He had dozed off in my arms, and suddenly awoke with a start.

"My flight leaves at midnight, my love. I must leave you now."

I looked at the clock; it was a few minutes to eleven—only four hours since he stepped into the front door. And he had to leave! The guillotine had dropped. My head lay in a basket drained of its life blood, with his taste still on my lips, his smell bathing my breasts and loins, and his touch still alive in my five senses. His life belonged to him. His wife had finally succeeded in committing suicide. Tragically, he was now free but I belonged to another.

Lovingly I dressed him, like a mother dresses the child of her womb, as a last gesture of my love for him, and then dressed myself in black as if I was on my way to a funeral, my own funeral.

Reality only dawned on us that we were once more parting as we ran clinging to one another to the bus stop of the last bus to the airport, which would tear him away to South Africa. I held on to his out-stretched hand for just a moment more till his fingers slipped away from mine, then as the bus picked up speed, he was gone!

I dared not think of Dee and America. That was unreal! The few hours with Peter were more real than the three years with Dee. I too had committed adultery but felt no guilt. I could not go upstairs to the bed that Dee and I shared. I stayed downstairs in the bed of my exaltation and also my sorrow, and cried myself asleep.

70
America the Beautiful

Arriving in America after a long and tiring flight, I felt disappointed, but not surprised. Dee wasn't at the airport to meet me. He had sent his manager instead to take me to our hotel. In our room there was a bouquet of roses with a card from him that read: *Make yourself comfortable I'll see you after rehearsal.*

We had a few warm moments in our marriage, but this reception left me cold. The roses didn't mean a thing. We had been separated for three months, and he couldn't even ask time off from rehearsal to at least come and welcome me?

Lew, his American manager kept me company for a short while and said that he had made a reservation for Dee and Me for dinner at the Aku-Aku.

"You will love the turtle steaks. Dee said he would meet us there. You must be tired from the long flight, rest a while and I will pick you up in an hour."

When we arrived at the restaurant there was a telephone message that said, *I'm sorry pet, I just couldn't make it.* I half expected it. Dee was back to his old tricks of promising but then reneging on his promises. His manager and I ate in silence except for the information that after Las Vegas Dee was booked in San Diego. I told his manager that I thought that after Las Vegas Dee would be returning with me to the house in Manchester to open the club.

"That, my dear, is a fantasy that Dee has had for a long time, and if that ever becomes a reality I would be very surprised, so don't even think about that."

After the dinner we went to the Thunderbird where Dee was appearing with Eddy Fisher on the billing. He was his usual magnificent self on stage. But I thought, *Who's that Stranger? The future father of my child? If that's the only way we would be able to settle down, I must get pregnant! Soon!*

Daily while Dee was rehearsing, I just sat around at the pool reading and sunbathing. The old routines had become the normal again. Sex was the "forgive me" pill that was supposed to heal all.

Out of boredom I started taking my temperature again, it stayed the same, and then one week after my arrival it suddenly shot up to 99 again. This is it! It makes a sudden drop soon after. So it was imperative that I make love within the hour to literally *make a baby*. Dee was at the Thunderbird again rehearsing with his band. He had told me not to call him unless it was an emergency. *Surely, making a baby could count as an emergency.* So I called him.

He hated anybody interrupting his rehearsal. His voice was quite blunt when they said it was his wife calling.

"What do you want?" he asked sharply. I felt like throwing the phone down in his face.

"I want you to make a baby with me," I replied, equally blunt. There was a shocked silence on the other end of the line. He couldn't figure it out. I must have said it loud enough for the band to hear.

I heard them laugh, and he must have made faces because one of the musicians said, "I'll go if you don't want to!" It must have suddenly dawned on Dee about the temperature thing.

He laughed and his voice softened as he replied, "Darling, you know I'm in rehearsal, it will have to be a quickie."

Again there was laughter, and whispering coming from the band.

"I'll be waiting!" I cooed. I didn't take a shower, afraid that it would change the temperature, stripped and got into the sexy nighty he had bought for me, put a drop of perfume on strategic places, got on the bed in my most provocative pose, and waited. After a while I started cramping, and half dozed off.

Two hours later I heard the front door open; there wasn't a sound. I felt ridiculous in my get-up. *What if it was the manager, or the maid?* Then I heard footsteps approach the bedroom. I quickly got into my provocative pose again.

There stood Dee in the bedroom doorframe, stark-naked, with only his shoes and socks on, a rose between teeth, with a mighty erection!

Still clenching the rose between his teeth, he mumbled; "I hope this is the right address, I got a call from this lady who said, 'Come make a baby with me.'" I couldn't help laughing when he did his stage somersault across the room, landing right on top of me. He tore the nighty off me and with no foreplay or sweet talk, we had our quickie. "Here's your baby, lady," he said hoarsely when he came. With no lingering kiss, he jumped up and ran out of the bedroom. I lay back stunned, thinking he would return. But then I heard the front door slam shut. This WAS just a quickie! I always thought the Earth would move when I conceived, like it did just two weeks before. Perhaps THAT was the real thing? And this quickie did not count? Two weeks later I was late menstruating. I thought it was too fast, and couldn't believe that the quickie could have worked, so I contributed the lateness to the long flight and the country change. To everything else except that I could be pregnant. I would wait another week and then have a rabbit test. But within the week, the first appearance of a morning sickness was the first indication. The American tour started, and by the time we got to San Diego, the rabbit test proved I was at least two months pregnant.

Dee was as surprised as I was, but announced to everyone that I was indeed barefoot and pregnant. As if he had just won the world marathon or something. I thought he would immediately start pampering me, but nothing changed. If anything my daily throwing up sickened him, he started chain smoking. This only made it worse. So I begged him to stop smoking. He just got mad at me, but the following day I found his cigarettes on the table. "I'm quitting" he said. "Now I hope the throwing up stops!"So much for compassion, but the good thing was he never touched a cigarette again. At least the baby would be protected from second-hand smoke. Unfortunately for him the morning sickness remained.

On one of our overnight flights I had a scare, almost sure I could lose the baby. When we reached Miami Beach, our next destination, I was taken off the plane on a stretcher and taken directly to the hospital for a week of observation and rest so as not to lose the baby. The biggest hurdle would be if I passed the first trimester they said.

So when Dee was called on tour, I begged off and asked him to get me an apartment so that I could await the baby. I was already starting to show; at least it was visible to me. When Dee left to go on tour, I started working on my baby trousseau. Everything I knitted was pink. My mother on her death bed predicted I would have a daughter and a remarkable one, who would carry her name. And here she was finally firmly attached to the umbilical vine right beneath my heart. Dee was away for most of the time till it came near to delivery. Then I read in the *Sun* that he had arranged to do all his shows in the Miami Beach area to await the birth of "his" baby, and to take care of "his" wife. Only if "taking care" was his intention, I never felt it. Oh yes, he brought me a apple pie one time, and ate most of it himself. He was out doing the shows till late, then came back to the apartment to eat and sleep. Usually he slept till midday, ate, and went fishing, then came back and started drinking with his buddies. And I was left alone with "my pregnancy," without the little things that would make me feel that I was really "his" wife, carrying "his " baby.

I called her my Pipit from the first day that I felt her move like a butterfly caught in one's hand flutters softly to escape the hands that enfold it. I talked to her, and when she refused to let me sleep with her kicking, I would put my small pocket radio on my little lump and it soothed her so that we both could sleep.

The last day before deliverance, I found myself on a public bus coming from the doctor's examination. It was all bad news. Some for me. He was going in for surgery and he wanted me to change the hospital to the one he would be in so that he would be able to help when needed. The bad news for me was, "Because the baby is very big and is lying in a breech position, and if it doesn't turn in the next eight hours the baby will be in trouble, and so will you."

It just wasn't my day, the bus was full. I struggled on. Every seat was taken. A group of very unsympathetic faces stared back at me. I steadied my self against one pole and grabbed the leather strap with my free hand above my head and hung on for dear life.

Then it HAPPENED! My baby decided to turn! She flipped from the breech position into a normal delivery one. And that in front of a busload of people staring. It was a strange sensation! I looked down to see my entire mid section move to the left side and then stay there; it was empty on the right, nothing else moved, as if the little being in the inside in the dark was taking a break to rest before making the final move in the confined space. Not only was I aware of the strange thing taking place inside of me, but all the indifferent eyes were riveted on my stomach, or rather on the twisting and turning that looked like I had a puppy concealed under my dress that was trying to get out. Young people, who were never taught to respect older people and pregnant women, stared in awed fascination at this visibly moving stomach, but did not move a muscle to get up and give me a seat. A woman in her sixties got up.

"My God, the baby is turning! She's going to have her baby, have you all forgotten your manners?" She addressed no one in particular, but everyone who refused me the comfort of their seats seemed as if they had suddenly remembered, and her reminder awakened their decency. There was a scramble among them to give me their seats. I took the first one offered me and fell into it, thanked them profusely, and tried to hide the turning that was still happening again in all earnest. They now also tried to avert their eyes, only sneaking a peak now and then, not to miss anything, just in case the baby did come.

Yet I sensed a great relief in all when I finally reached my stop. They wouldn't be forced to see me have my baby. I had several hands helping me off the bus. The nausea that had been welling up in me now washed over me like a tidal wave. But standing again on solid ground gave me the courage to resist. I was only a block away from the apartment. *Hold on, girl, you'll soon be home and then Dee would help you,* I told myself. But then the nausea overtook me again and the bushes were the nearest.

I made it into the apartment with no further incidents, but contrary to my belief that I would be helped, no one came to my aid. Dee and his friends had been drinking the whole afternoon, playing cards. The stale beer smell that hung in the air was all I could stand. I ran into the bathroom and shamelessly barfed up the rest of my pent up emotions, glad at least that I didn't have to do it in the bushes again. I cleaned up and went to tell Dee what the doctor had said about changing hospitals.

"The baby turned in the bus coming home; the doctor said I could deliver tonight," I told Dee. But concentrating on the game, he took no notice; nobody even looked up.

I went into the bedroom and lay down. Immediately I felt a strange but stabbing pain in my lower back that radiated into my thighs. I attributed it to my baby's turning in the bus. But shortly after that I felt small and nagging cramps similar to my period and instinct told me I was in labor. *I'm in labor,* I told the walls. When the next one came a few minutes later, I must have let out a yell, because Dee came in and looked at his watch. *Perhaps he heard me and thought he was timing whatever was happening to me,* but he had a glazed look on his face. "Its past six already—aren't you going to make dinner for us?" There were no words of sympathy. He was concerned only about his own stomach and his friends' needs, even though I was prostrate in pain, with the beginnings of labor. My words weren't very kind.

"Damn your friends! Didn't you hear what I said? Can't you see I'm in labor? The doctor said not to eat anything just in case they have to do surgery. Go and get a pizza for all I care!" He went back to his friends. They were laughing about who was sober enough to drive and get a pizza. Dee came into the bedroom.

"What now?"

"Please bring me the kitchen clock and a pencil and paper, the contractions are coming in regularly now. I'll have to time them myself—I don't think you are capable right now." At the mention of "contractions" the truth of the situation suddenly sunk in; it was a sobering shock.

"You sure?" Dee asked. "Then I'll ask one of the boys to stay so that they can drive you to the hospital."

"Yes, I'm sure I will trust them," I said sarcastically. " No, I'd rather you get a cab when the time is right. They can't even stand up to go and get a pizza, and you will trust them with our baby?"

It was now seven o'clock, the contractions were coming at intervals, but nothing was happening.

"The boys" left around 11 p.m., and I gave a sigh of relief. Dee got into bed next to me and in a minute he was fast asleep. With the night light on, I wrote down the next contraction It was four hours since it started, and nothing was happening. I wrote down the next and the next and tried to relax, hoping to fall asleep, but I was too excited, and too worried, because between contractions, I could not feel Pipit moving as if she too was resting up for her great debut. The luminous letters of the kitchen clock showed two o'clock in the morning when I had a calling of nature, but just when I pulled myself up to go, my water broke. Too late, I lay down again, now in the wet. I thought it was time to get to the hospital. The pains were now coming fast and furious. We had meant to put in a phone, but they did not come to put it in yet. I tried to wake Dee, but he was dead to the world. When he finally opened his eyes, he was confused.

"What happened?"

"Get dressed, it's time to go to the hospital. There's a phone cubical on the corner two blocks up—go call the doctor and then call a cab." He was up in a flash, and I heard the front door slam shut. A few moments later he was back. "After throwing the money in, I couldn't reach the dials. They don't make the phones for dwarfs like me; now I'm out of change also."

"There's change in the vase in the kitchen and there are two large cans of fruit juice in the fridge you can stand on."

One can under each arm he rushed out, to return within minutes.

"Good news is I got a cab, bad news is your doctor had a heart attack and they have taken him to Mt. Sinai Hospital, where his associate told me to take you, as he will be doing the delivery." While he was gone I hurriedly got dressed, and when the cab honked, we went out, Dee carrying the suitcase.

Just as I reached the cab I doubled over with a contraction and leaned up against the cab to steady myself. The cabby took one look at me with hippopotamus proportions and a grimace on my face, and refused to take me.

"Hey, she's not going to have a baby in my cab, I just cleaned it!" He had about as much compassion as an icicle in Antarctica, because the next moment he simply drove off, nearly knocking me over. We stared in shocked silence after him.

Dee didn't hesitate; he grabbed some more change out of the vase and with the cans under his arms he was off to get another cab. Luckily another cab passed him on the way to the phone, and he hailed it. He got in without telling the man what his purpose was, and stopped and picked me up; there was no way the cab driver could refuse this time. At the hospital in order to help me out, Dee planted both feet on the step and pulled, but couldn't budge me. The driver just laughed and helped me out. It was now about three o'clock. The nurse at the desk did not look up, so I stumbled to the desk. I said who I was. Then Dee said, his head hidden below the high counter, "Dr. J. said to bring her here." She looked up but did not see my lips move.

"Are you a ventriloquist or something? I heard you, but I did not see your mouth move?" she addressed me.

"Because it's me, her husband, who spoke!" He pulled a chair up to the desk and got on it. "We are having a baby!" The nurse apologized and sent for a wheelchair. The girl who took me to the delivery room said her name was Susie, and that this was her first day, and would I call the baby Susie if it's a girl? She was obviously very nervous. So now I had a doctor I did not know, and a nurse called Susie who was to assist him, and wanted my first child to be named after her.

To compensate for her "first day," she explained everything as she went along.

"First we are getting into a gown, then we are going to have blood drawn, then I'm going to shave you and prep you." I was glad she switched from the plural to the singular, because seeing her get into a gown and taking her own blood would have really distressed me. The other thing she was very good at doing was apologizing.

"I'm sorry my hands are so cold."

"I'm sorry the razor isn't sharp."

"I'm sorry the Gentian Violet stings."

"I'm sorry I'm so nervous."

Then when I refused any painkiller or muscle relaxant or drug because I wanted a "normal birth."

"I'm sorry you won't take my pill."

By then I was in excruciating pain, and being a very demonstrative person, I was screaming every time the pain came. Poor little Susie demonstrated the third thing she was very good at. She felt personally responsible because I refused medication, and every time a pain came she dropped what she was doing to hold my hand.

"I'm so sorry," she sobbed in sympathy, begging me to accept the medication that "would make me feel better!"

I was beginning to feel sorry for the agony she was going through, and tried to assure her why I didn't want to be put to sleep, or have a caudal injection or pain killer to forget my own pain.

"My dear Susie, I don't want it because I don't want to wake up with a baby I don't even know, because I had nothing to do with the delivery." I told her to pull herself together and go and find out if I could have a mirror to watch my child come into the world.

By ten a.m. the substitute doctor arrived and introduced himself. He lacked the bedside manners of Dr. J. He was professional and abrupt. After fifteen hours of labor I was already exhausted when they wheeled me into the main delivery room. I noticed the mirror I requested was there, so that too was something Susie was good at, following my orders. When my feet hit the stirrups, the sheet covering me, obscured my view, so I started pulling the sheet away. The doctor playfully slapped my hand and had someone restrain me. It made me furious. I can't remember anyone telling me to push, but I needed no telling—that urge was overwhelming. Between screams, I pushed and Susie cried and said she was sorry. She also had other talents I discovered. When I first looked into the mirror. She was definitely artistic. She had transformed the backs of my thighs, my buttocks, and belly into a flower equal to a Picasso masterpiece with only one color, the bright yellow of Gentian Violet. That particular flower only became evident when my baby's head crowned. Her hair was wet, and showed up black. I looked up into the mirror.

"It's a sunflower!" I managed to gasp.

"No, I'm sure it's going to be a baby as soon as we can get her out. I will have to use forceps and you must give me the best you have."

"Untie my hands first," I ordered. I held onto the top of the bed, and pushed. One shoulder appeared. I could hear a slight panic in the doctor's voice. "I am making another cut; the baby has very brood shoulders." He ordered Susie to give me some gas that I could regulate. I took a big sniff, almost knocking myself out, and minutes later he laid her on my chest. "It's not a sunflower after all. It's a beautiful, healthy, big girl." He tied up the life line and handed me the scissors to cut it, something husbands usually do. "Give her her freedom." I cut the umbilical because Dee was nowhere to be found. Then Susie took her to clean her up, tears running down her cheeks. She entered the world quietly, without a sound at 11:25. I didn't want her slapped, so she only uttered a faint mewing sound when they suctioned her.

"When do they serve lunch?" I asked the nurse who was tending to my needs after the birth. She looked at me in disbelief.

"How can you eat after what you have just gone through?"

"I'm starving, that's how! I haven't eaten since breakfast yesterday morning, and do you think you can get me something to eat? Anything will do, but I really could go for a big steak right now. But first I want to see my baby."

"They are cleaning her up, but I'll tell them to stop at the nursery on the way to your room."

"And can you find out what happened to my husband? I know he brought me in." At the nursery I stared in disbelief. God had given me the gift of a beautiful daughter. Tina Mara was perfect! And at that moment I felt my mother's presence. They moved me to my room. A few minutes later the nurse came in.

"How's this for service?" She handed me a tray with a big steak and salad. "Your husband is in the lounge talking to the news media. The TV stations 4, 7, and 10 are also here waiting to interview you. I didn't know we were delivering a VIP. I told them to wait. Have your lunch first, and as soon as you're done, I will come to fix your hair and put on some makeup for the interview."

When Dee came in, I was sitting up heartily chomping on my steak, he said as a joke,"What happened? Haven't we had our baby yet?" He handed me a present of a blue dressing gown and a blue baby blanket. "I bought it in the gift shop, just in case the SHE you were expecting turned out a HE, I'm sorry it's a little late because I've just seen her, and she is beautiful, and I'm sorry about the interview, but that's something I couldn't stop."

He left for the nursery, and half an hour later, he walked in wearing a doctor's gown dragging on the floor and operating cap and mask, with the TV crew and reporters in tow, also wearing caps and masks. A nurse carried Tina Mara in and laid her in my arms. She became an instant celebrity because her mother was an ex showgirl Can-Can dancer who was nearly six feet and her father was four-foot-three with his shoes on and was starring in the world famous Fountain Blue. Dee was a proud father after all, announcing it that night on his show.

He stayed in Miami Beach playing the new daddy, but left the care completely over to me with the excuse that I was breast feeding. But right after the christening when Tina was four months old, he announced that he was going on tour again. I had three options. I could go back to England to raise her in the big old house that we owned. Stay in Florida, where he could visit as often as his schedule dictated, or come on the road with him. I had very little time to decide, so I chose to stay put in Florida till she was at least walking. For the year following her birth I remained in Florida while he went on tour. At first he tried to come home as often as possible, but with tight schedules the visits dwindled to sometimes months in between. The marriage became very strained, on the times he did come, T. would look on him as a stranger and cry.

When she turned nine months and was already walking and talking I decided to go on tour with him so that she could get to know her daddy. She adjusted well to the hectic schedule, and for the first three years things went well. She was Daddy's little girl, but my poor baby got motion sick every time we were in a train, a bus, or a plane, which was almost daily. She was shuttled around from state to state, where Dee did one night stands. I would carry her onto the plane, when she was asleep and she would wake up in another 5-star hotel, or a no-star Motel in another state. This was our life and I felt sorry for her. But she had her own way of rating the change. She would flit around like a little butterfly touching everything in the room, stroking the bed and furniture, then come to me with her deliberation declare, "This is a pretty housie," or "This is a stinky housie." I was glad that she was able to be with her daddy, but the more we traveled together the more there was friction between us, because he had not stopped his drinking and womanizing. When I confronted him about his infidelities and adultery when he was away from me, there were terrible verbal fights, and he would bring up the fact that I had a vivid imagination and he was innocent of my accusations. He finally confessed that he was seeing someone, and he would grant me a separation that would give us both a time to reflect. He handed me a two-way ticket to go and see my family in South Africa. I accepted his offer and went because I hadn't seen my father, who was now in his eighties, for a very long time, and he had not yet seen my daughter, and it would give me time to think.

My daughter and I were in a different world, surrounded by my family with love to spare. I thought of Peter, but wanted to just enjoy my family. My dad made such a fuss over his granddaughter, and she in turn blossomed with the love and attention that she got surrounded by all the nieces and nephews—the most children she had ever seen in her young life. On tour I had to almost kidnap a child to celebrate her birthdays. And here they were planning a fourth birthday with plenty of children.

It was also inevitable that I eventually would meet Peter. Because I was separated pending a divorce and legally could see anyone I wished.

My sister and his sister, Nonnie, were friends and he heard that I was visiting my father. I always wanted my father to meet him when they were so against him before I left for London. So one day while my daughter was playing in the garden, I went out to get her to come and feed the little ducklings my stepmother was raising. When she said, " Mom, see the little blue car, it's the fourth time it has already come past the house." She was very proud of her counting ability and was simply showing off. But then I saw the silver hair and pointed beard, and there was no mistaking—it was my Peter. When he came around again for the fifth time, I dashed out to the street and waved him down. He was almost apologetic when he said; "I was gathering up courage to come and knock on the door."

He picked Tina up. "So this is Tina?" He had become acquainted with her through my letters; we never stopped writing in all the years of separation.

She took to him immediately. Just then my dad came out to the gate.

"Daddy, I want you to meet someone." Finally I had the opportunity to introduce the two men who meant the most to me in my life.

"Pleased to meet you, we're just about to have tea, do come in." Having never met him, he didn't have a clue who he was. Or what role he played in our lives. They headed for the sitting room. My stepmother, curious to see who it was, peeped out of the kitchen, but moments later came in with hair combed and Sunday apron on and charmingly served the tea. They obviously did not remember that they were so terribly against this very man before I went to England, and how dramatically it changed my life. For the next few hours, there they sat, the best of friends. They had everything in common, lived parallel lives. My dad was a game warden on safari. Peter was in African safaris. They talked about their experiences, Dad told about his experience with the leopard and camp life, and Peter told about our safari experiences, and they talked about their love for books, and everything that they still had in common. My stepmother told him about her ducklings; forgetting that he was speaking in English to Daddy, she spoke to him in Dutch. And he, being a linguist, naturally spoke to her in the language he was addressed in. She even brought some ducklings in her apron to show him when she went out to show them to Tina.

Before he left, he asked my dad if it was okay if he took me and Tina to the ice cream parlor and would they like some too? Not only was Tina in love with this new uncle who treated her to the ice cream parlor, but he also bought her a coloring book and crayons, and some lucky packets that had candies in and all kinds of little animals. That night when Peter left to return to Johannesburg, Dad and my stepmom pulled me aside and asked me whatever made me marry Dee, when that was the man I should have married. I did not answer.

I didn't want to remind them that they were the ones who fought to separate Peter and me, because I did not want them to feel bad, and left it at that.

Peter visited me regularly while I was visiting my father. He told me he was in the audience when our show opened in Johannesburg, not just once but several times, and sat where I was not able to see him. He also read the stories of Dee and my "Romance of the Century" in the news and it hurt him so badly; it was shortly after his wife's suicide. He was so depressed about my marriage to Dee that he plunged into another disastrous marriage because he needed a mother for his daughter. They too were separated from bed and table, but still in the same house because he also had a daughter with her.

The next week I went to stay with my sister in Pretoria for a month. She knew I had seen Peter at my dad's, and one day we saw this little sport car cruise down the mountain and enter her driveway.

"I wonder who it can be?"

"It's Peter," I blurted out.

"Oh," she pretended to be surprised. But she was anything but surprised because Peter's sister had told her about Peter's rebound marriage when he thought he had lost me forever to Dee, but that he had told her that I was his soul mate and that he still loved me He and his current wife were not in good terms but were staying together because of the daughter he had with her.

By now she realized that he was my true love. First of all my dad could not stop talking about him, and she closed her eyes for the next few weeks when he met me secretly again under the same giant old tree next to the house.

She also knew that Peter and my anniversary of our meeting was coming up on my birthday.

So she said: "For your birthday, my present to you will be I am going to look after Tina for a weekend so that you and Peter can have some time together. I know I'm most likely committing some awful sin, but I owe you this."

On the day he came to collect me, she had packed a basket for our "travel." He brought the same tent we used during our second safari and we headed for our favorite camping spot next to a lake. Here we relived the wonder of our love, in the one hundred and twenty heavenly hours granted to us by my beloved sister, Ethel. To forget about "Them" and "They," aware of only "Us." That was the last time I ever saw Peter again.

Dee kept calling and writing that he would grant me my divorce in Miami Beach, if I came back to him so that he could see his daughter again, and even gave me a ticket again to get back to my family if things don't work out. He suggested that I bring her to Hollywood, California, where he was appearing for Christmas, so that he could spend Christmas with her. Then we would go and see a lawyer in Florida and arrange everything.

My sister said, "He sounds sincere. If you really want the divorce, go to him, seeing he promised you he would help you get back to us."

But when I got to California, Dee denied everything he said, and continued as if we had just gone on vacation, and were now back in his life. I tried to play along for Tina's sake, and when we got back to Miami Beach, he asked me for the divorce because he had fallen in love with someone else for the three months I was in South Africa.

I expected a compatible divorce, so that I could return to South Africa and marry Peter. But he did it in a sly way, giving three different dates, so that I could not contest the divorce. When he claimed a extreme cruelty clause, the judge ordered a restraint on my movements. I could not leave the State of Florida with my daughter. Should I remove her, I would be incarcerated for kidnaping. This assured Dee that I would not go back to Peter. Now I was really trapped.

Peter was convinced that Dee would drop this cruel clause when he got married to the woman that he was in love with who was expecting his child. But he didn't! My daughter wanted to go with me to my family and Peter. Dee stuck to his clause and would not give in, even though he dropped out of my daughter's life. This battle dragged on and on. Dee got divorced and remarried again after the second wife. And Peter and I lived our loveless lives, while we longed to be together. There was no solution. The only solace we had was through 300 love letters that filled a cedar box. Tina turned eighteen. She was on her own; the clause no longer was valid.

The years went by, and then the telegram came. *"This is the final Exodus; I am free and finally you are free. Pack up and come to me so that we can grow old together."* He was selling his house and had his eye on another house with no memories, just for us. I was walking on clouds—finally we would be able to be together till death do us part! I had only to wait until the sale of his house was through so that I could start shipping my crates over. His letters came almost daily and then I received a telegram from his best friend and also publisher. "Peter in intensive care, said to contact you, don't worry." I was indeed worried, I didn't even know that he was sick. Two weeks later a letter arrived from Peter. *"I was very ill but had a bone marrow transplant and am in remission. I'm doing well even worked on my poetry and the new house. I painted the rainbow in Tina's room per her request if she wants to come. Exodus is still on."* There was nothing in his handwriting or a hint of what was wrong in that letter or the other letters that followed.

Then his letters suddenly stopped, and mine started coming back. *RETURN TO SENDER.* I started phoning his home, but there was no answer. I called my sister to find out if she knew what was going on, but she only said he was in the hospital, and his family was looking after him was the last she heard, because she also could not get answers there.

One night the phone rang as usual when I called his house, and I expected a no answer.

A woman answered. "Hello, hello!"

My heart beat explosively. I stammered, "Can I please speak to Peter?"

"No you can't," a voice answered gruffly. I couldn't understand—had he met someone else and was now afraid to tell me, and that accounted for his silence and my returned letters?

"I must speak to him."

" I now own this house."

"I don't care who you are, but I must find out what is going on! I was coming over to marry Peter and his letters suddenly started coming back to me. What is happening?"

"Yes, I sent them back."

"Why?" There was a moment of silence on the other side.

"Don't you know?

I waited for the guillotine to drop, expecting her to say that she was now with him, but she continued.

" I'm sorry, I bought the house." *A deadly silence followed.* "Peter died three months ago from adult leukemia."

THE GUILLOTINE DROPPED FOR THE LAST TIME.

I saw my head roll across the African veld, through the jungles, over the mountains of the moon, through Europe and the Far East—and fall into the black hole of NEVER, and then I fainted.

Glossary

Afrikaans: Pioneer colony language of first settlers in South Africa, derived from Dutch.

Baobab Fruit: Size and shape of large avocado. Pale green, fuzzy, extremely hard shell. Inside is a white powdery substance around a black seed. It tastes like sherbet when sucked off the seed.

Biskuit: Afrikaans for rusk or hardtack.

Boggom: South African; sound a baboon makes, also the name of my baboon.

Bloomers: Over-sized panties reaching from waist down to knees.

Bootsan: French name for paste-on two little shields for nipple covers used by show girls.

Crombi: First name of the safari camp cook.

Dwarrels: Afrikaans for thin spiral of dust.

Frou-Frou: French for frilly.

"Gammat":   Bastardized language made up from Afrikaans and English.

Indoena: Tribal warrior.

Kruitfontein: First safari camp.

Kondoweh: First name of Chief's first son from first wife.

Lalela: Tribal name for crocodile.

Loogas: A soap bush, which acts as soap and foams like soap when rubbed.

Luv: British endearment for love.

Mabalel: Chief Charlie's daughter by 25th wife.

Maboekie Grass:4-foot-tall savannah grass, favored by lion stalking.

Makulu: Big man, big animal, tree, etc.

Malala: Beer.Tapped from a palm, tastes fruity the first day. When fermented in the sun, it becomes a potent alcoholic drink.

Mapani: Worms. High protein. Harvested from tree by that name. 2 inches long. Cooked in greens or dried in the sun for a tasty nutty snack, or ground up and sprinkled on porridge.

Maroella: An apricot-sized, pale green, wild fruit with a moist, waxlike interior over brown seed. Fallen fruit fermented by the sun becomes alcoholic. Loved by elephants and monkeys for that reason.

Marog: A weed. Top tender leaves are harvested to substitute for spinach.

Mavenda: South African tribe. Our neighbor tribe in Northern Transvaal.

Mielie Pap: Corn, stone ground turned into cooked mush.

Muti: Medicine. Also, "The witch doctor's magic is strong medicine."

Niet: Russian for "No."

Oom: Afrikaans for uncle.

Ousus: Older sister in Afrikaans, abbreviated to "sis" in English.

Poppie: Afrikaans for "little doll."

Pop-lappie: Pet name meaning "doll material."

Pogotklo: Corn meal porridge, cooked in little water with Arabic couscous consistency.

Potgieter: One of the strange Afrikaans surnames.

Shesheba: Side dish to the main meal of corn meal mush. Anything cooked into a stew for dunking the mush, squeezed into a ball in the palm of the hand.

Telly: British for television.

Tokkelosie: Small evil spirit (shape changer) who sees all, hears all, knows all. Used by witch doctor, and parents to invoke fear, and keep people in tow. "Boogeyman" is his American cousin.

Verdomde: Afrikaans word for "damned"or "blasted."

Witch Doctor: A medicine man or shaman among primitive peoples. He believes that good and evil spirits pervade the world, uses incantations, herbs and psychiatry, psychology, and plain magic arts and a great deal of coincidence to achieve his goals.

Printed in the United States
65261LVS00005B/1-48

9 781413 730210